THE
OXFORD BOOK OF
ENGLISH LOVE
STORIES

John Sutherland is Lord Northcliffe Professor of Modern English Literature at University College London. Among his publications are biographies of *Mrs Humphry Ward* (1990) and *The Life of Walter Scott: A Critical Biography* (1995); *The Longman Companion to Victorian Fiction* (1990), and editions of novels by Anthony Trollope, W. M. Thackeray and others for the World's Classics series.

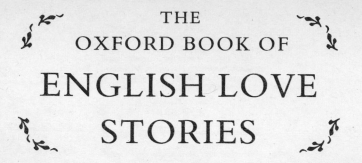

THE
OXFORD BOOK OF
ENGLISH LOVE
STORIES

Edited by

John Sutherland

Oxford · New York
OXFORD UNIVERSITY PRESS
1997

Oxford University Press, Great Clarendon Street, Oxford OX2 6DP

Oxford New York

Athens Auckland Bangkok Bogota Bombay
Buenos Aires Calcutta Cape Town Dar es Salaam
Delhi Florence Hong Kong Istanbul Karachi
Kuala Lumpur Madras Madrid Melbourne
Mexico City Nairobi Paris Singapore
Taipei Tokyo Toronto

and associated companies in
Berlin Ibadan

Oxford is a trade mark of Oxford University Press

Additional copyright information appears on pp. 451–2

© Oxford is a trade mark of Oxford University Press
Introduction, selection, and biographical notes © John Sutherland 1996

First published by Oxford University Press 1996
First issued as an Oxford University Press paperback 1997

British Library Cataloguing in Publication Data
Data available

Library of Congress Cataloging in Publication Data
The Oxford book of English love stories / edited by John Sutherland.
p. cm.
1. Love stories, English. I. Sutherland, John, 1938– .
PR1309.L68094 1997 823'.08508—dc20 96–38252
ISBN 0–19–283268–9

1 3 5 7 9 10 8 6 4 2

Printed in Great Britain by
Mackays Ltd
Chatham, Kent

CONTENTS

INTRODUCTION

THE novel ('new thing') as a literary genre and romantic love are both of recent historical origin, finding their essential modern forms in the seventeenth and eighteenth centuries. 'Prose Romance' as it has evolved over the last 300 years has enjoyed a privileged relationship with romance. Traditionally, fiction tells us what modern love is and how *à la mode* lovers should conduct themselves. Sometimes the instruction has tragic results. Goethe's *The Sorrows of Young Werther* inspired hundreds of lovelorn young men to imitative suicide. The less melodramatically inclined merely affected the hero's blue waistcoat and yellow breeches. Erich Segal's *Love Story*, if it did not trigger an epidemic of picturesque death by leukemia, certainly encouraged a short-lived vogue for pale make-up on the campuses of America.

Nancy Mitford memorably entitled her 1949 study of English amatory practices, *Love in a Cold Climate*. Mitford implied (and nicely demonstrated in the novel's comedy) that English love is as different from Latin love, American love, or, presumably, Eskimo love (to go to the coldest climate of all) as is the English weather from that of other countries. *The Oxford Book of English Love Stories* is not merely a collection of stories in English about love, chronologically arranged. It aims to trace the lineaments of 'English love', as they have varied over the last four centuries. The majority of the contributors (twenty-three out of twenty-eight) are English by birth or upbringing, or both. Joyce Cary was born in Londonderry which is still, at the time of writing, in the United Kingdom. Elizabeth Bowen was born in Dublin, but the story reprinted here dates from her 'English period', following her marriage to Alan Cameron. Katherine Mansfield was born in New Zealand, but came to England at the age of 20 and married an Englishman, John Middleton Murry. So, too, the American Sylvia Plath came to Britain as a graduate student, married an Englishman, and spent most of her subsequent (tragically short) life in England. Paul Theroux is an American who has travelled widely and written successfully about his travels. He has lived for many years in London, and made England the subject of much of his fiction—as he does in the piece reprinted here. One could make a plea for the eligibility of these writers as 'technically

English'. But there is a better reason for including them. Their half-in, half-out relationship enables them to bring a sharper perspective to the mysteries of the English in love.

From the social historian's point of view, one of the more informative pieces in this collection is Sylvia Plath's *Stone Boy with Dolphin*, a story which captures the intricate rituals of courtship, as they were practised at Cambridge University in the mid-1950s. (According to Anne Stevenson's biography of Plath, *Bitter Fame*, the story records, under fictional disguise, the author's first encounter with her future husband, Ted Hughes.) The Cambridge of *Stone Boy with Dolphin* is a world dominated by barriers—most uncomfortably, the spiked college wall over which the heroine Dody must clamber before she can enjoy (if that is the word) her furtive act of love. With the arrival of the 1960s, Plath's Cambridge was suddenly as bygone as Pompeii and just as fascinating to later generations in its perfectly preserved antique detail.

The codes of romantic love have rarely been regulated by English law, nor has love typically been part of the Anglo-Saxon educational curriculum (even today 'sex education' is an explosive issue in British and American schools). It was Anthony Trollope who observed, in the 1870s, that the principal duty of the British novel was to educate British maidens in how they should conduct themselves in the most important matter of their lives—how they should deal with the lovers who might, or might not, become their husbands and the fathers of their children. Trollope, of course, overstated things and overrated the kind of fiction he himself preferred to write. But there is an element of truth in what he said. Fiction is a great popular educator in the trickier areas of human relations. This role in the 1990s is most usefully present in the stories of overtly gay love, with which the chronological coverage of this collection ends. Homosexual acts between consenting adults were made legal in Britain as recently as 1967 (before then, even writing about them in a non-censorious way constituted a criminal act). Most straight readers, I suspect, have gained a sympathetic insight into the mores and crises of gay love not from Hollywood or television (both of which have been very skittish on the subject) but from recent prose fiction. And because the gay love story is a relatively new genre a writer like Adam Mars-Jones—whose appeal extends well beyond the closed circuit of the gay/lesbian community—can write with an unembarrassed directness (see, for instance, the moving last paragraphs of *A Small Spade*). Unlike his straight counterparts Mars-Jones is not inhibited by the self-consciousness of centuries of literary tradition.

Anyone wishing to understand what Jean Renoir in his 1930 film calls the '*règles du jeu*' should consult love stories of the day. But love is a game unlike cricket or tennis in that its rules tend to change with every new set of players and with each generation. In D. H. Lawrence's *Samson and Delilah*, the game is as violent and fraught with physical injury as American football. In Katherine Mansfield's *Something Childish but very Natural*, it is more reminiscent of blindfold chess. In Joyce Cary's *The Tunnel*, it seems that the lovers cannot, tantalizingly, even get themselves on to the same playing field. Sometimes the changes in the ground rules of the game are so seismic that even that part of the publishing industry which lives by merchandising love stories is taken by surprise. In September 1994 it was announced that Argus Publications had abruptly suspended its magazines *True Romance* and *Love Story*, pending what was called 'a raunchy relaunch'. It was, as the *Independent on Sunday* (25 Sept.) observed, 'farewell, lovelorn secretaries and saturnine bosses, inching decorously towards each other around the filing cabinets; from now on it's sex on the desk in stilettos'.

True Romance, it seems, is a very unfixed thing. How, one wonders, would a Trollopian maiden (or a Trollopian trollop, for that matter) like Patience Woolsworthy, handle herself if conducted by time machine to the spiky 1980s lesbian community described in Sara Maitland's *The Loveliness of the Long-Distance Runner*. Would she, like a fish out of water, expire? Or would she turn to, and join in? One of the pleasures in following a line of love stories over two hundred years is the fluctuating value put on a quality like feminine modesty. 'I am a bitch . . . I am a slut' Plath's heroine hears herself exclaim ('with no conviction'). In the world of Aphra Behn's *The Black Lady*—with its Hogarthian backdrop of sexual predators and victims—Dody Ventura (the name has overtones of 'adventuress') would be neither slut nor bitch, merely a woman of spirit. She would be, of course, a foul thing among Trollope's, or Anne Ritchie's, or even Thomas Hardy's demure maidens, and the necessary stones would be thrown. By the standards of her own transient little world of privileged *jeunesse*, judgement is harder to reach. Dody, one guesses, would qualify as a bit of a bitch, but probably not quite a slut, 1956-style. With the class of Germaine Greer and 'liberation' just six years away, she is merely somewhat ahead of her time.

Love is a word which our society keeps deliberately unclear, so that an infinite number of meanings can be packed into its four letters: eros, agape, caritas, adulterous love, marital love, virginal love, religious devotion, lust. All you need is love, the song tells us, but what kind, exactly? Within the foggy semantic territory marked by the word, fiction is a useful instrument for anatomizing the infinite varieties of love and its shifting rules. There is, however, a distinction to be made between the story about love, and 'love story' in its conventional and anti-conventional form. In the following collection, all the stories take love as their subject—in that sense, they are love stories. More importantly, they all have an intimate relationship to the 'love story' as a genre product, or the predefined category of fiction to be found ranked by the thousand on the 'romance' shelves in any high street bookshop, or mall bookstore.

According to Denis de Rougemont in *Passion and Society* (1946), 'Happy love has no history. Romance only comes into existence where love is fatal, frowned upon, and doomed by life itself.' The idea is familiar from another, more epigrammatic statement, to be found as the first sentence of Tolstoy's *Anna Karenina* ('the greatest love story of all time', as my American paperback version proclaims): 'All happy families resemble each other, each unhappy family is unhappy in its own way.' But, *pace* de Rougemont, 'happy love' does have a history. And that history is found reiterated some 200 million times a year (by the latest count) in the products of Harlequin and Mills & Boon romances. The rules governing the construction of these stories are firmly laid down as guidelines to prospective authors. Transgression means instant irrevocable rejection. The principal law of the Mills & Boon/Harlequin universe is that love shall have a happy ending. There are no such mass-produced 'happy-love' stories reproduced here (although they are by no means as dismissible as Q. D. Leavis once told us they were). None the less, the generic product is everywhere invoked in the following pages. The stories gathered in this collection congregate on the uneasy fringe where the formulaic love story meets literature, prompting it to emulation and contradiction. Nearest to a conventional romance—

although it is overhung by a cosmopolitan, self-consciously brittle narrative tone—is Arnold Bennett's *Claribel*, a story which one could easily imagine stripped of its literariness and rewritten for the mass market by Annie S. Swan. C. C. K. Gonner's deceptively serene *Olive's Lover*, Anne Ritchie's *To Esther* (written by Thackeray's daughter, at a time when she anticipated old-maidhood as her destiny in life), and Trollope's ultra-Trollopian *The Parson's Daughter of Oxney Colne*, come very close to the lineaments of the happy-love story, only to veer away at the last moment, leaving a bitter-sweet aftertaste of the ending that almost was. Other pieces represented here, like Kipling's *The Wish House* (with its ghastly equation of lover's malady and cancer) and Hardy's resolutely anti-*Enoch Arden* effort, *Enter a Dragoon*, invoke the happy-love formula, only to kick it down with a vindictive energy. Both stories have bitter stings in their tails. Most bitter of all, is Maugham's *Episode*, a story which makes the reader wonder (to paraphrase Gosse on Hardy) what Venus has done to Mr Maugham that he should so rage against love. Still other stories, such as Graham Greene's *The Blue Film* and V. S. Pritchett's *Blind Love*, twist the platitudes of the generic love story (that first love is invariably pure, that love is blind) into startling ironic patterns.

The romantic love story traditionally avoids comedy (there is probably a Mills & Boon guideline on the subject). Two notable exceptions here are H. G. Wells's *Miss Winchelsea's Heart* which ponders the great question whether love can flourish where the (otherwise eminently eligible) man is discovered to be called 'Snooks' and Paul Theroux's sardonic study of American innocence exploited by a *femme fatale* with the depraved morals of the British estate agent, *An English Unofficial Rose*.

Putting together an anthology is an interesting exercise for what it tells one about oneself. In this collection, I have primarily aimed to lay down a strong chronological line and a variety of literary perspectives on love, ranging from the black (blackest of all is Thackeray's savage *Dennis Haggarty's Wife*) to the rose-tinted. All the writers represented here are, within the technical limitations of their time, superior artists. As they practise their art over successive literary periods, the reader will trace the gradual increments of narrative sophistication, particularly after 1900 and the full absorption of Chekhov and James into the mainstream of British fiction. By the time of

Aldous Huxley the short story is a literary machine which has progressed as far beyond its nineteenth-century origins as the motor car is beyond the hansom cab. This does not, of course, make Mrs Gaskell's robust offering, *The Heart of John Middleton*, with its blend of love story and Christian tract, any less enjoyable. In making a selection of this kind there is a temptation to round up the usual anthologized pieces, for the good reason that they can be enjoyed over and again (I was strongly inclined to include Elizabeth Bowen's much reprinted *The Demon Lover*, before eventually deciding on the less well-known *A Love Story*, an intricately wrought study of late 1930s decadence). There are a few familiar pieces here, and a larger number of unfamiliar pieces by familiar names. There are also some surprising instances of writers writing out of their best-known character (John Galsworthy's delicately nuanced *A Long-Ago Affair* may surprise readers who know him only through his clumping saga). I have, on principle, included only whole works, except for the extract from Hazlitt's fragmented *Liber Amoris* (a work given recent currency by its protracted evocation in Melvyn Bragg's bestselling modern love story, *A Time to Dance*) and the Plath piece which was, apparently, intended to form part of a longer, unwritten narrative.

In the late twentieth century one art form, above all others, has taken love as its subject matter—popular music. Pop's main consumers are young; English literature's main consumers tend to be mature verging on ancient (the point can be readily grasped by comparing the clientele of the Virgin Records store in London's Oxford Street with that of the bookshop Hatchard's, just round the corner in Piccadilly). The principal contention of popular music— reiterated billions of times a day in the English-speaking world on radio, MTV, juke-box and private CD-player—is that love is pre-eminently a possession of the young. Young love (the only real love) is, moreover, banally stereotyped in its dialect and expression. The English love story makes a quite different assertion. Love, it contends, can flourish at all seasons of life, and can take the most unexpected of forms. Love stories, like love itself, are full of surprises.

APHRA BEHN

The *Adventure* of the Black Lady

ABOUT the Beginning of last *June* (as near as I can remember)
Bellamora came to Town from *Hampshire*, and was obliged to lodge
the first Night at the same Inn where the Stage-Coach set up. The
next Day she took Coach for *Covent-Garden*, where she thought to
find Madam *Brightly*, a Relation of hers, with whom she design'd
to continue for about half a Year undiscover'd, if possible, by her
Friends in the Country: and order'd therefore her Trunk, with her
Clothes, and most of her Money and Jewels, to be brought after
her to Madame *Brightly's* by a strange Porter, whom she spoke to
in the Street as she was taking Coach; being utterly unacquainted
with the neat Practices of this fine City. When she came to *Bridges-
Street*, where indeed her Cousin had lodged near three or four Years
since, she was strangely surprized that she could not learn anything
of her; no, nor so much as meet with anyone that had ever heard
of her Cousin's Name: Till, at last, describing Madam *Brightly* to
one of the House-keepers in that Place, he told her, that there was
such a kind of Lady, whom he had sometimes seen there about a
Year and a half ago; but that he believed she was married and
remov'd towards *Soho*. In this Perplexity she quite forgot her Trunk
and Money, &c, and wander'd in her Hackney-Coach all over St
Anne's Parish; inquiring for Madam *Brightly*, still describing her
Person, but in vain; for no Soul could give her any Tale or Tidings
of such a Lady. After she had thus fruitlessly rambled, till she, the
Coachman, and the very Horses were even tired, by good Fortune
for her, she happen'd on a private House, where lived a good, discreet, ancient Gentlewoman, who was fallen to Decay, and forc'd
to let Lodgings for the best Part of her Livelihood: From whom
she understood, that there was such a kind of Lady, who had lain
there somewhat more than a Twelvemonth, being near three Months
after she was married; but that she was now gone abroad with the

Gentleman her Husband, either to the Play, or to take the fresh Air; and she believ'd would not return till Night. This Discourse of the Good Gentlewoman's so elevated *Bellamora's* drooping Spirits, that after she had beg'd the liberty of staying there till they came home, she discharg'd the Coachman in all haste, still forgetting her Trunk, and the more valuable Furniture of it.

When they were alone, *Bellamora* desired she might be permitted the Freedom to send for a Pint of Sack; which, with some little Difficulty, was at last allow'd her. They began then to chat for a matter of half an Hour of things indifferent: and at length the ancient Gentlewoman ask'd the fair Innocent (I must not say foolish) one, of what Country, and what her Name was: to both which she answer'd directly and truly, tho' it might have prov'd not discreetly. She then enquir'd of *Bellamora* if her Parents were living, and the Occasion of her coming to Town. The fair unthinking Creature reply'd, that her Father and Mother were both dead; and that she had escap'd from her Uncle, under the pretence of making a Visit to a young Lady, her Cousin, who was lately married, and liv'd above twenty Miles from her Uncle's, in the Road to *London*, and that the Cause of her quitting the Country, was to avoid the hated Importunities of a Gentleman, whose pretended Love to her she fear'd had been her eternal Ruin. At which she wept and sigh'd most extravagantly. The discreet Gentlewoman endeavour'd to comfort her by all the softest and most powerful Arguments in her Capacity; promising her all the friendly Assistance that she could expect from her, during *Bellamora's* stay in Town: which she did with so much Earnestness, and visible Integrity, that the pretty innocent Creature was going to make her a full and real Discovery of her imaginary insupportable Misfortunes; and (doubtless) had done it, had she not been prevented by the Return of the Lady, whom she hop'd to have found her Cousin *Brightly*. The Gentleman, her Husband just saw her within Doors, and orderd the Coach to drive to some of his Bottle-Companions; which gave the Women the better Opportunity of entertaining one another, which happen'd to be with some Surprize on all Sides. As the Lady was going up into her Apartment, the Gentlewoman of the House told her there was a young Lady in the Parlour, who came out of the Country that very Day on purpose to visit her: The Lady stept immediately to see who it was, and *Bellamora* approaching to receive her hop'd-for Cousin, stop'd on the sudden just as she came to her; and sigh'd out aloud, Ah, Madam! I am lost—It is not your Ladyship I seek. No, Madam (return'd the other) I am apt to think you did not intend me this Honour. But you are as welcome to me, as you could be to the dearest of your Acquaintance: Have you forgot me, Madame *Bellamora*? (continued she.) That Name startled the other: However, it was with a kind of Joy. Alas! Madam, (replied the young one) I now remember that I have been so happy to have seen you; but where and when, my Memory can't tell me. 'Tis indeed some Years since, (return'd the Lady) But of that another time.—Mean while, if you are unprovided of a Lodging, I dare undertake, you shall be welcome to this Gentlewoman. The Unfortunate returned her Thanks; and whilst a Chamber was preparing for her, the Lady entertain'd her in her own. About Ten o'Clock they parted, *Bellamora* being conducted to her Lodging by the Mistress of the House, who then left her to take what Rest she could amidst her so many Misfortunes; returning to the other Lady, who desir'd her to search into the Cause of *Bellamora's* Retreat to Town.

The next Morning the good Gentlewoman of the House coming up to her, found *Bellamora* almost drown'd in Tears, which by many kind and sweet Words she at last stopp'd; and asking whence so great Signs of Sorrow should proceed, vow'd a most profound Secrecy if she would discover to her their Occasion; which, after some little Reluctancy, she did, in this manner.

I was courted (said she) above three Years ago, when my Mother was yet living, by one Mr *Fondlove*, a Gentleman of good Estate, and true Worth; and one who, I dare believe, did then really love me: He continu'd his Passion for me, with all the earnest and honest Solicitations imaginable, till some Months before my Mother's Death; who, at that time, was most desirous to see me disposed of in Marriage to another Gentleman, of much better Estate than Mr *Fondlove*; but one whose Person and Humour did by no means hit with my Inclinations: And this gave *Fondlove* the unhappy Advantage over me. For, finding me one Day all alone in my Chamber, and lying on my Bed, in as mournful and wretched a Condition to my then foolish Apprehension, as now I am, he urged his Passion with such Violence, and accursed Success for me, with reiterated Promises of Marriage, whensoever I pleas'd to challenge 'em, which he bound with the most sacred Oaths, and most dreadful Execrations: that partly with my Aversion to the other, and partly with my Inclinations to pity him, I ruin'd my self.—Here she relaps'd into a greater Extravagance of Grief than before; which was so extreme that it did not continue long. When therefore she was pretty well come to herself, the ancient Gentlewoman ask'd her, why she imagin'd herself ruin'd: To which she answer'd, I am great with Child by him, Madam, and wonder you did not perceive it last Night. Alas! I have not a Month to go: I am asham'd, ruin'd, and damn'd, I fear, for ever lost. Oh! fie, Madam, think not so, (said the other) for the Gentleman may yet prove true, and marry you. Ay, Madam (replied *Bellamora*) I doubt not that he would marry me; for soon after my Mother's Death, when I came to be at my own Disposal, which happen'd about two Months after, he offer'd, nay most earnestly solicited me to it, which still he perseveres to do. This is strange! (return'd the other) and it appears to me to be your own Fault, that you are yet miserable. Why did you not, or why will you not consent to your own Happiness? Alas! (cry'd *Bellamora*) 'tis the only Thing I dread in this World: For, I am certain, he can never love me after. Besides, ever since I have abhorr'd the Sight of him: and this is the only Cause that obliges me to forsake my Uncle, and all my Friends and Relations in the Country, hoping in this populous and publick Place to be most private, especially, Madam, in your House, and in your Fidelity and Discretion. Of the last you may assure yourself, Madam, (said the other:) but what Provision have you made for the Reception of the young Stranger that you carry about you? Ah, Madam! (cry'd *Bellamora*) you have brought to my Mind another Misfortune: Then she acquainted her with the suppos'd loss of her Money and Jewels, telling her withal, that she had but three Guineas and some Silver left, and the Rings she wore, in her present possession. The good Gentlewoman of the House told her, she would send to enquire at the Inn where she lay the first Night she came to Town; for, haply, they might give some Account of the Porter to whom she had entrusted her Trunk; and withal repeated her Promise of all the Help in her Power, and for that time left her much more compos'd than she found her. The good Gentlewoman went directly to the other Lady, her Lodger, to whom she recounted *Bellamora's* mournful Confession; at which the Lady appear'd mightily concern'd: and at last she told her Landlady, that she would take Care that *Bellamora* should lie in according to her Quality: For, added she, the Child, it seems, is my own Brother's.

As soon as she had din'd, she went to the *Exchange*, and bought Child-bed Linen; but desired that *Bellamora* might not have the least Notice of it: And at her return dispatch'd a Letter to her Brother *Fondlove* in *Hampshire*, with an Account of every Particular; which soon brought him up to Town, without satisfying any of his or her Friends with the Reason of his sudden Departure. Mean while, the good Gentlewoman of the House had sent to the *Star Inn* on *Fish-street-Hill*, to demand the Trunk, which she rightly suppos'd to have been carried back thither: For by good Luck, it was a Fellow that ply'd thereabouts, who brought it to *Bellamora's* Lodgings that very Night, but unknown to her. *Fondlove* no sooner got to *London*, but he posts to his Sister's Lodgings, where he was advis'd not to be seen of *Bellamora* till they had work'd farther upon her, which the Landlady began in this manner; she told her that her Things were miscarried, and she fear'd, lost; that she had but a little Money her self, and if the Overseers of the Poor (justly so call'd from their over-looking 'em) should have the least Suspicion of a strange and unmarried Person, who was entertain'd in her House big with Child, and so near her Time as *Bellamora* was, she should be troubled, if they could not give Security to the Parish of twenty or thirty Pounds, that they should not suffer by her, which she could not; or otherwise she must be sent to the House of Correction, and her Child to a Parish-Nurse. This Discourse, one may imagine, was very dreadful to a Person of her Youth, Beauty, Education, Family and Estate: However, she resolutely protested, that she had rather undergo all this, than be expos'd to the Scorn of her Friends and Relations in the Country. The other told her then, that she must write down to her Uncle a Farewell-Letter, as if she were just going aboard the Pacquet-Boat for *Holland*, that he might not send to enquire for her in Town, when he should understand she was not at her new-married Cousin's in the Country; which accordingly she did, keeping her self close Prisoner to her Chamber; where she was daily visited by *Fondlove's* Sister and the Landlady, but by no Soul else, the first dissembling the Knowledge she had of her Misfortunes. Thus she continued for above three Weeks, not a Servant being suffer'd to enter her Chamber, so much as to make her Bed, lest they should take Notice of her great Belly: but for all this Caution, the Secret had taken Wind, by the means of an Attendant of the other Lady below, who had over-heard her speaking of it to her Husband. This soon got out of Doors, and spread abroad, till it reach'd the long Ears of the Wolves of the Parish, who next Day design'd to pay her a Visit: But *Fondlove*, by good Providence, prevented it; who, the Night before, was usher'd into *Bellamora's* Chamber by his Sister, his Brother-in-Law, and the Landlady. At the Sight of him she had like to have swoon'd away: but he taking her in his Arms, began again, as he was wont to do, with Tears in his Eyes, to beg that she would marry him ere she was deliver'd; if not for his, nor her own, yet for the Child's Sake, which she hourly expected; that it might not be born out of Wedlock, and so be made uncapable of inheriting either of their Estates; with a great many more pressing Arguments on all Sides: To which at last she consented; and an honest officious Gentleman, whom they had before provided, was call'd up, who made an End of the Dispute: So to Bed they went together that Night; next Day to the *Exchange*, for several pretty Businesses that Ladies in her Condition want. Whilst they were abroad, came the Vermin of the Parish, (I mean, the Overseers of the Poor, who eat the Bread from 'em) to search for a young Blackhair'd Lady (for so was *Bellamora*) who was either brought to Bed, or just ready to lie down. The Landlady shew'd 'em all the Rooms in her House, but no such Lady could be found. At last she bethought her self, and led 'em into her Parlour, where she open'd a little Closet-door, and shew'd 'em a black Cat that had just kitten'd: assuring 'em, that she should never trouble the Parish as long as she had Rats or Mice in the House; and so dismiss'd 'em like Loggerheads as they came.

WILLIAM HAZLITT

The Picture

H. Oh! is it you? I had something to shew you—I have got a picture here. Do you know any one it's like?

S. No, Sir.

H. Don't you think it like yourself?

S. No: it's much handsomer than I can pretend to be.

H. That's because you don't see yourself with the same eyes that others do. *I* don't think it handsomer, and the expression is hardly so fine as your's sometimes is.

S. Now you flatter me. Besides, the complexion is fair, and mine is dark.

H. Thine is pale and beautiful, my love, not dark! But if your colour were a little heightened, and you wore the same dress, and your hair were let down over your shoulders, as it is here, it might be taken for a picture of you. Look here, only see how like it is. The forehead is like, with that little obstinate protrusion in the middle; the eyebrows are like, and the eyes are just like yours, when you look up and say—'No—never!'

S. What then, do I always say 'No—never!' when I look up?

H. I don't know about that—I never heard you say so but once: but that was once too often for my peace. It was when you told me, 'you could never be mine'. Ah! if you are never to be mine, I shall not long be myself. I cannot go on as I am. My faculties leave me: I think of nothing, I have no feeling about any thing but thee: thy sweet image has taken possession of me, haunts me, and will drive me to distraction. Yet I could almost wish to go mad for thy sake: for then I might fancy that I had thy love in return, which I cannot live without!

S. Do not, I beg, talk in that manner, but tell me what this is a picture of.

H. I hardly know; but it is a very small and delicate copy (painted

in oil on a gold ground) of some fine old Italian picture, Guido's
or Raphael's, but I think Raphael's. Some say it is a Madonna; others
call it a Magdalen, and say you may distinguish the tear upon the
cheek, though no tear is there. But it seems to me more like
Raphael's St Cecilia, 'with looks commercing with the skies', than
anything else.—See, Sarah, how beautiful it is! Ah! dear girl, these
are the ideas I have cherished in my heart, and in my brain; and I
never found any thing to realize them on earth till I met with thee,
my love! While thou didst seem sensible of my kindness, I was but
too happy: but now thou hast cruelly cast me off.

S. You have no reason to say so: you are the same to me as ever.

H. That is, nothing. You are to me every thing, and I am nothing to you. Is it not too true?

S. No.

H. Then kiss me, my sweetest. Oh! could you see your face
now—your mouth full of suppressed sensibility, your downcast eyes,
the soft blush upon that cheek, you would not say the picture is
not like because it is too handsome, or because you want complexion. Thou art heavenly-fair, my love—like her from whom the
picture was taken—the idol of the painter's heart, as thou art of
mine! Shall I make a drawing of it, altering the dress a little, to
shew you how like it is?

S. As you please.—

The Trial of Love

HAVING obtained leave from the Signora Priora to go out for a few hours, Angeline, who was a boarder at the convent of Sant' Anna, in the little town of Este, in Lombardy, set out on her visit. She was dressed with simplicity and taste; her faziola covered her head and shoulders; and from beneath, gleamed her large black eyes, which were singularly beautiful. And yet she was not, perhaps, strictly handsome; but, she had a brow smooth, open, and noble; a profusion of dark silken hair, and a clear, delicate, though brunette complexion. She had, too, an intelligent and thoughtful expression of countenance; her mind appeared often to commune with itself; and there was every token that she was deeply interested in, and often pleased with, the thoughts that filled it. She was of humble birth: her father had been steward to Count Moncenigo, a Venetian nobleman; her mother had been foster-mother to his only daughter. Both her parents were dead; they had left her comparatively rich; and she was a prize sought by all the young men of the class under nobility; but Angeline lived retired in her convent, and encouraged none of them.

She had not been outside its walls for many months; and she felt almost frightened as she found herself among the lanes that led beyond the town, and up the Euganean hills, to Villa Moncenigo, whither she was bending her steps. Every portion of the way was familiar to her. The Countess Moncenigo had died in childbirth of her second child, and from that time, Angeline's mother had lived at the villa. The family consisted of the Count, who was always, except during a few weeks in the autumn, at Venice, and the two children. Ludovico, the son, was early settled at Padua, for the sake of his education, and then Faustina only remained, who was five years younger than Angeline.

Faustina was the loveliest little thing in the world: unlike an

Italian, she had laughing blue eyes, a brilliant complexion, and auburne hair; she had a sylph-like form, slender, round, and springy; she was very pretty, and vivacious, and self-willed, with a thousand winning ways, that rendered it delightful to yield to her. Angeline was like an elder sister: she waited on Faustina; she yielded to her in every thing; a word or smile of hers, was all-powerful. 'I love her too much,' she would sometimes say; 'but I would endure any misery rather than see a tear in her eye.' It was Angeline's character to concentrate her feelings, and to nurse them till they became passions; while excellent principles, and the sincerest piety, prevented her from being led astray by them.

Three years before, Angeline had, by the death of her mother, been left quite an orphan, and she and Faustina went to live at the convent of Sant' Anna, in the town of Este; but a year after, Faustina, then fifteen, was sent to complete her education at a very celebrated convent in Venice, whose aristocratic doors were closed against her ignoble companion. Now, at the age of seventeen, having finished her education, she returned home, and came to Villa Moncenigo with her father, to pass the months of September and October. They arrived this very night, and Angeline was on her way from her convent, to see and embrace her dearest companion.

There was something maternal in Angeline's feelings—five years makes a considerable difference at the ages of ten to fifteen, and much, at seventeen and two-and-twenty. 'The dear child,' thought Angeline, as she walked along, 'she must be grown taller, and, I dare say, more beautiful than ever. How I long to see her, with her sweet arch smile! I wonder if she found any one at her Venetian convent to humour and spoil her, as I did here—to take the blame of her faults, and indulge her in her caprices. Ah! those days are gone!—she will be thinking now of becoming a sposa. I wonder if she has felt any thing of love.' Angeline sighed. 'I shall hear all about it soon—she will tell me every thing, I am sure.—And I wish I might tell her—secrecy and mystery are so very hateful; but I must keep my vow, and in a month it will be all over—in a month I shall know my fate. In a month!—shall I see him then?—shall I ever see him again! But I will not think of that, I will only think of Faustina—sweet, beloved Faustina!'

And now Angeline was toiling up the hill side; she heard her name called; and on the terrace that overlooked the road, leaning over the balustrade, was the dear object of her thoughts—the pretty Faustina, the little fairy girl, blooming in youth, and smiling with happiness. Angeline's heart warmed to her with redoubled fondness.

Soon they were in each other's arms; and Faustina laughed, and her eyes sparkled, and she began to relate all the events of her two years' life, and showed herself as self-willed, childish, and yet as engaging and caressing as ever. Angeline listened with delight, gazed on her dimpled cheeks, sparkling eyes, and graceful gestures, in a perfect, though silent, transport of admiration. She would have had no time to tell her own story, had she been so inclined, Faustina talked so fast.

'Do you know, Angelinetta mia,' said she, 'I am to become a sposa this winter?'

'And who is the Signor Sposino?'

'I don't know yet; but during next carnival he is to be found. He must be very rich and very noble, papa says; and *I* say he must be very young and very good-tempered, and give me my own way, as you have always done, Angelina carina.'

At length Angeline rose to take leave. Faustina did not like her going—she wanted her to stay all night—she would send to the convent to get the Priora's leave; but Angeline knowing that this was not to be obtained, was resolved to go, and at last, persuaded her friend to consent to her departure. The next day, Faustina would come herself to the convent to pay her old friends a visit, and Angeline could return with her in the evening, if the Priora would allow it. When this plan had been discussed and arranged, with one more embrace, they separated; and, tripping down the road, Angeline looked up, and Faustina looked down from the terrace, and waved her hand to her and smiled. Angeline was delighted with her kindness, her loveliness, the animation and sprightliness of her manner and conversation. She thought of her, at first, to the exclusion of every other idea, till, at a turn in the road, some circumstance recalled her thoughts to herself. 'O, how too happy I shall be,' she thought, 'if he prove true!—with Faustina and Ippolito, life will be Paradise!' And then she traced back in her faithful memory, all that had occurred during the last two years. In the briefest possible way, we must do the same.

Faustina had gone to Venice, and Angeline was left alone in her convent. Though she did not much attach herself to any one, she became intimate with Camilla della Toretta, a young lady from Bologna. Camilla's brother came to see her, and Angeline accompanied her in the parlour to receive his visit. Ippolito fell desperately in love, and Angeline was won to return his affection. All her feelings were earnest and passionate; and yet, she could regulate their effects, and her conduct was irreproachable. Ippolito, on the contrary, was fiery and impetuous: he loved ardently, and could brook no opposition to the fulfilment of his wishes. He resolved on marriage, but being noble, feared his father's disapprobation: still it was necessary to seek his consent; and the old aristocrat, full of alarm and indignation, came to Este, resolved to use every measure to separate the lovers for ever. The gentleness and goodness of Angeline softened his anger, and his son's despair moved his compassion. He disapproved of the marriage, yet he could not wonder that Ippolito desired to unite himself to so much beauty and sweetness: and then, again, he reflected, that his son was very young, and might change his mind, and reproach him for his too easy acquiescence. He therefore made a compromise; he would give his consent in one year from that time, provided the young pair would engage themselves, by the most solemn oath, not to hold any communication by speech or letter during that interval. It was understood that this was to be a year of trial; that no engagement was to be considered to subsist until its expiration; when, if they continued faithful, their constancy would meet its reward. No doubt the father supposed, and even hoped, that, during their absence, Ippolito would change his sentiments, and form a more suitable attachment.

Kneeling before the cross, the lovers engaged themselves to one year of silence and separation; Angeline, with her eyes lighted up by gratitude and hope; Ippolito, full of rage and despair at this interruption to his felicity, to which he never would have assented, had not Angeline used every persuasion, every command, to instigate him to compliance; declaring, that unless he obeyed his father, she would seclude herself in her cell, and spontaneously become a prisoner, until the termination of the prescribed period. Ippolito took the vow, therefore, and immediately after set out for Paris.

One month only was now wanting before the year should have expired; and it cannot be wondered that Angeline's thoughts wandered from her sweet Faustina, to dwell on her own fate. Joined to the vow of absence, had been a promise to keep their attachment, and all concerning it, a profound secret from every human being, during the same term. Angeline consented readily (for her friend was away) not to come back till the stipulated period; but the latter had returned, and now, the concealment weighed on Angeline's conscience: there was no help—she must keep her word.

With all these thoughts occupying her, she had reached the foot of the hill, and was ascending again the one on which the town of Este stands, when she heard a rustling in the vineyard that bordered one side of the road—footsteps—and a well-known voice speaking her name.

'Santa Vergine! Ippolito!' she exclaimed, 'is this your promise?'

'And is this your reception of me?' he replied, reproachfully. 'Unkind one! because I am not cold enough to stay away—because this last month was an intolerable eternity, you turn from me—you wish me gone. It is true, then, what I have heard—you love another! Ah! my journey will not be fruitless—I shall learn who he is, and revenge your falsehood.'

Angeline darted a glance full of wonder and reproach; but she was silent, and continued her way. It was in her heart not to break her vow, and so to draw down the curse of heaven on their attachment. She resolved not to be induced to say another word; and, by her steady adherence to her oath, to obtain forgiveness for his infringement. She walked very quickly, feeling happy and miserable at the same time—and yet not so—happiness was the genuine, engrossing sentiment; but she feared, partly her lover's anger, and more, the dreadful consequences that might ensue from his breach of his solemn vow. Her eyes were radiant with love and joy, but her lips seemed glued together; and resolved not to speak, she drew her faziola close round her face, that he might not even see it, as she walked speedily on, her eyes fixed on the ground. Burning with rage, pouring forth torrents of reproaches, Ippolito kept close to her side—now reproaching her for infidelity—now swearing revenge —now describing and lauding his own constancy and immutable love. It was a pleasant, though a dangerous theme. Angeline was tempted a thousand times to reward him by declaring her own unaltered feelings; but she overcame the desire, and, taking her rosary in her hand, began to tell her beads. They drew near the town, and finding that she was not to be persuaded, Ippolito at length left her, with protestations that he would discover his rival, and take vengeance on him for her cruelty and indifference. Angeline entered her convent, hurried into her cell—threw herself on her knees—prayed God to forgive her lover for breaking his vow; and then, overcome with joy at the proof he had given of his constancy, and of the near prospect of their perfect happiness, her head sank on her arms, and she continued absorbed in a reverie which bore the very hues of heaven. It had been a bitter struggle to withstand his entreaties, but her doubts were dissipated, he was true, and at the appointed hour would claim her; and she who had loved through the long year with such fervent, though silent, devotion, would be rewarded! She felt secure—thankful to heaven—happy.—Poor Angeline!

The next day, Faustina came to the convent: the nuns all crowded round her. '*Quanto è bellina,*' cried one. '*E tanta carina!*' cried another. '*S' è fatta la sposina?*'—'Are you betrothed yet?' asked a third. Faustina answered with smiles and caresses, and innocent jokes and laughter. The nuns idolized her; and Angeline stood by, admiring her lovely friend, and enjoying the praises lavished on her. At length, Faustina must return; and Angeline, as anticipated, was permitted to accompany her.

'She might go to the villa with her,' the Priora said, 'but not stay all night—it was against the rules.'

Faustina entreated, scolded, coaxed, and at length succeeded in persuading the superior to allow her friend's absence for a single night. They then commenced their return together, attended by a maid servant—a sort of old duenna. As they walked along, a cavalier passed them on horseback.

'How handsome he is!' cried Faustina: 'who can he be?'

Angeline blushed deeply, for she saw that it was Ippolito. He passed on swiftly, and was soon out of sight. They were now ascending the hill, the villa almost in sight, when they were alarmed by a bellowing, a hallooing, a shrieking, and a bawling, as if a den of wild beasts, or a madhouse, or rather both together, had broken loose. Faustina turned pale; and soon her companion was equally frightened, for a buffalo, escaped from the yoke, was seen tearing down the hill, filling the air with roarings, and a whole troop of *contadini* after him, screaming and shrieking—he was exactly in the path of the friends. The old duenna cried out, '*O, Gesu Maria!*' and fell flat on the earth. Faustina uttered a piercing shriek, and caught Angeline round the waist; who threw herself before the terrified girl, resolved to suffer the danger herself, rather than it should meet her friend—the animal was close upon them. At that moment, the cavalier rode down the hill, passing the buffalo, and then, wheeling round, intrepidly confronted the wild animal. With a ferocious bellow he swerved aside, and turned down a lane that opened to the left; but the horse, frightened, reared, threw his rider, and then galloped down the hill. The cavalier lay motionless, stretched on the earth.

It was now Angeline's turn to scream; and she and Faustina both anxiously ran to their preserver. While the latter fanned him with her large green fan, which Italian ladies carry to make use of as a parasol, Angeline hurried to fetch some water. In a minute or two, colour revisited his cheeks, and he opened his eyes; he saw the beautiful Faustina, and tried to rise. Angeline at this moment arrived, and presenting the water in a bit of gourd, put it to his lips—he pressed her hand—she drew it away. By this time, old Caterina, finding all quiet, began to look about her, and seeing only the two girls hovering over a fallen man, rose and drew near.

'You are dying!' cried Faustina: 'you have saved my life, and are killed yourself.'

Ippolito tried to smile. 'I am not dying,' he said, 'but I am hurt.'

'Where? how?' cried Angeline. 'Dear Faustina, let us send for a carriage for him, and take him to the villa.'

'O! yes,' said Faustina: 'go, Caterina—run—tell papa what has happened—that a young cavalier has killed himself in saving my life.'

'Not killed myself,' interrupted Ippolito; 'only broken my arm, and, I almost fear, my leg.'

Angeline grew deadly pale, and sank on the ground.

'And you will die before we get help,' said Faustina; 'that stupid Caterina crawls like a snail.'

'I will go to the villa,' cried Angeline, 'Caterina shall stay with you and Ip——*Buon dio!* what am I saying?'

She rushed away, and left Faustina fanning her lover, who again grew very faint. The villa was soon alarmed, the Signor Conte sent off for a surgeon, and caused a mattress to be slung, with four men to carry it, and came to the assistance of Ippolito. Angeline remained in the house; she yielded at last to her agitation, and wept bitterly, from the effects of fright and grief. 'O that he should break his vow thus to be punished—would that the atonement had fallen upon me!' Soon she roused herself, however, prepared the bed, sought what bandages she thought might be necessary, and by that time he had been brought in. Soon after the surgeon came; he found that the left arm was certainly broken, but the leg was only bruised: he then set the limb, bled him, and giving him a composing draught, ordered that he should be kept very quiet. Angeline watched by him all night, but he slept soundly, and was not aware of her presence. Never had she loved so much. His misfortune, which was accidental, she took as a tribute of his affection, and gazed on his handsome countenance, composed in sleep, thinking, 'Heaven preserve the truest lover that ever blessed a maiden's vows!'

The next morning Ippolito woke without fever and in good spirits. The contusion on his leg was almost nothing; he wanted to rise: the surgeon visited him, and implored him to remain quiet only a day or two to prevent fever, and promised a speedy cure if he would implicitly obey his mandates. Angeline spent the day at the villa, but would not see him again. Faustina talked incessantly of his courage, his gallantry, his engaging manners. She was the heroine of the story. It was for her that the cavalier had risked his life; her he had saved. Angeline smiled a little at her egotism. 'It would mortify her if I told her the truth,' she thought: so she remained silent. In the evening it was necessary to return to the convent; should she go in and say adieu to Ippolito? Was it right? Was it not breaking her vow? Still how could she resist? She entered and approached him softly; he heard her step, and looked up eagerly, and then seemed a little disappointed.

'Adieu! Ippolito,' said Angeline, 'I must go back to my convent. If you should become worse, which heaven forbid, I will return to wait on you, nurse you, die with you; if you get well, as with God's blessing there seems every hope, in one short month, I will thank you as you deserve. Adieu! dear Ippolito.'

'Adieu! dear Angeline; you mean all that is right, and your conscience approves you: do not fear for me. I feel health and strength in my frame, and I bless the inconvenience and pain I suffer since you and your sweet friend are safe. Adieu! Yet, Angeline, one word:— my father, I hear, took Camilla back to Bologna with him last year— perhaps you correspond?'

'You mistake; by the Marchese's desire, no letters have passed.'

'And you have obeyed in friendship as in love—you are very good. Now I ask a promise also—will you keep one to me as well as to my father?'

'If it be nothing against our vow.'

'Our vow! you little nun—are our vows so mighty?—No, nothing against our vow; only that you will not write to Camilla nor my father, nor let this accident be known to them; it would occasion anxiety to no purpose:—will you promise?'

'I will promise not to write without your permission.'

'And I rely on your keeping your word as you have your vow. Adieu, Angeline. What! go without one kiss?'

She ran out of the room, not to be tempted, for compliance with this request would have been a worse infringement of her engagement than any she had yet perpetrated.

She returned to Este, anxious, yet happy; secure in her lover's faith, and praying fervently that he might speedily recover. For several days after, she regularly went to Villa Moncenigo to ask after him, and heard that he was getting progressively well, and at last she was informed that he was permitted to leave his room. Faustina told her this, her eyes sparkling with delight. She talked a great deal of her cavalier, as she called him, and her gratitude and admiration. Each day, accompanied by her father, she had visited him, and she had always some new tale to repeat of his wit, his elegance, and his agreeable compliments. Now he was able to join them in the saloon, she was doubly happy. Angeline, after receiving this information, abstained from her daily visit, since it could no longer be paid without subjecting her to the risk of encountering her lover. She sent each day, and heard of his recovery; and each day she received messages from her friend, inviting her to come. But she was firm—she felt that she was doing right; and though she feared that he was angry, she knew that in less than a fortnight, to such had the month decreased since she first saw him, she could display her real sentiments, and as he loved her, he would readily forgive. Her heart was light, or full only of gratitude and happiness.

Each day, Faustina entreated her to come, and her entreaties became more urgent, while still Angeline excused herself. One morning her young friend rushed into her cell to reproach, and question, and wonder at her absence. Angeline was obliged to promise to go; and then she asked about the cavalier, to discover how she

might so time her visit, as to avoid seeing him. Faustina blushed—
a charming confusion overspread her face as she cried,

'O, Angeline! it is for his sake I wish you to come.'

Angeline blushed now in her turn, fearing that her secret was
betrayed, and asked hastily,

'What has he said?'

'Nothing,' replied her vivacious friend; 'and that is why I need
you. O, Angeline, yesterday, papa asked me how I liked him, and
added that if his father consented, he saw no reason why we should
not marry—Nor do I—and yet, does he love me? O, if he does
not love me, I would not have a word said, nor his father asked—
I would not marry him for the world!' and tears sprung into the
sensitive girl's eyes, and she threw herself into Angeline's arms.

'Poor Faustina,' thought Angeline, 'are you to suffer through me?'
and she caressed and kissed her with soothing fondness. Faustina
continued. She felt sure, she said, that Ippolito did love her. The
name fell startlingly on Angeline's ear, thus pronounced by another;
and she turned pale and trembled, while she struggled not to betray
herself. The tokens of love he gave were not much, yet he looked
so happy when she came in, and pressed her so often to remain—
and then his eyes—

'Does he ever ask anything about me?' said Angeline.

'No—why should he?' replied Faustina.

'He saved my life,' the other answered, blushing.

'Did he—when?—O, I remember; I only thought of mine; to
be sure, your danger was as great—nay, greater, for you threw yourself before me. My own dearest friend, I am not ungrateful, though
Ippolito renders me forgetful.'

All this surprised, nay, stunned Angeline. She did not doubt her
lover's fidelity, but she feared for her friend's happiness, and every
idea gave way to that—She promised to pay her visit, that very
evening.

And now, see her again walking slowly up the hill, with a heavy
heart on Faustina's account, and hoping that her love, sudden and
unreturned, would not involve her future happiness. At the turn of
the road near the villa, her name was called, and she looked up,
and again bending from the balustrade, she saw the smiling face of
her pretty friend; and Ippolito beside her. He started and drew back
as he met her eyes. Angeline had come with a resolve to put him

on his guard, and was reflecting how she could speak so as not to compromise her friend. It was labour lost; Ippolito was gone when she entered the saloon, and did not appear again. 'He would keep his vow,' thought Angeline; but she was cruelly disturbed on her friend's account, and she knew not what to do. Faustina could only talk of her cavalier. Angeline felt conscience-stricken; and totally at loss how to act. Should she reveal her situation to her friend? That, perhaps, were best, and yet she felt it most difficult of all; besides, sometimes she almost suspected that Ippolito had become unfaithful. The thought came with a spasm of agony, and went again; still it unhinged her, and she was unable to command her voice. She returned to her convent, more unquiet, more distressed than ever.

Twice she visited the villa, and still Ippolito avoided her, and Faustina's account of his behaviour to her, grew more inexplicable. Again and again, the fear that she had lost him, made her sick at heart; and again she reassured herself that his avoidance and silence towards her resulted from his vow, and that his mysterious conduct towards Faustina existed only in the lively girl's imagination. She meditated continually on the part she ought to take, while appetite and sleep failed her; at length she grew too ill to visit the villa, and for two days, was confined to her bed. During the feverish hours that now passed, unable to move, and miserable at the thought of Faustina's fate, she came to a resolve to write to Ippolito. He would not see her, so she had no other means of communication. Her vow forbade the act; but that was already broken in so many ways; and now she acted without a thought of self; for her dear friend's sake only. But, then, if her letter should get into the hands of others; if Ippolito meant to desert her for Faustina?—then her secret should be buried for ever in her own heart. She therefore resolved to write so that her letter would not betray her to a third person. It was a task of difficulty. At last it was accomplished.

'The signor cavaliere would excuse her, she hoped. She was—she had ever been as a mother to the Signorina Faustina—she loved her more than her life. The signor cavaliere was acting, perhaps, a thoughtless part.—Did he understand?—and though he meant nothing, the world would conjecture. All she asked was, for his permission to write to his father, that this state of mystery and uncertainty might end as speedily as possible.'

She tore ten notes—was dissatisfied with this, yet sealed it, and crawling out of her bed, immediately despatched it by the post.

This decisive act calmed her mind, and her health felt the benefit. The next day, she was so well that she resolved to go up to the villa, to discover what effect her letter had created. With a beating heart she ascended the lane, and at the accustomed turn looked up. No Faustina was watching. That was not strange, since she was not expected; and yet, she knew not why, she felt miserable: tears started into her eyes. 'If I could only see Ippolito for one minute—obtain the slightest explanation, all would be well!'

Thinking thus, she arrived at the villa, and entered the saloon. She heard quick steps, as of some one retreating as she came in. Faustina was seated at a table reading a letter—her cheeks flushed, her bosom heaving with agitation. Ippolito's hat and cloak were near her, and betrayed that he had just left the room in haste. She turned—she saw Angeline—her eyes flashed fire—she threw the letter she had been reading at her friend's feet; Angeline saw that it was her own.

'Take it!' said Faustina: 'it is yours. Why you wrote it—what it means—I do not ask: it was at least indelicate, and, I assure you, useless—I am not one to give my heart unasked, nor to be refused when proposed by my father. Take up your letter, Angeline. O, I could not believe that you would have acted thus by me!'

Angeline stood as if listening, but she heard not a word; she was motionless—her hands clasped, her eyes swimming with tears, fixed on her letter.

'Take it up, I say,' said Faustina, impatiently stamping with her little foot; 'it came too late, whatever your meaning was. Ippolito has written to his father for his consent to marry me; my father has written also.'

Angeline now started and gazed wildly on her friend.

'It is true! Do you doubt—shall I call Ippolito to confirm my words?'

Faustina spoke exultingly. Angeline struck—terrified—hastily took up the letter, and without a word turned away, left the saloon—the house, descended the hill, and returned to her convent. Her heart bursting, on fire, she felt as if her frame was possessed of a spirit not her own: she shed no tears, but her eyes were starting from her head—convulsive spasms shook her limbs; she rushed into her cell—

threw herself on the floor, and then she could weep—and after torrents of tears, she could pray, and then—think again her dream of happiness was ended for ever, and wish for death.

The next morning, she opened her unwilling eyes to the light, and rose. It was day; and all must rise to live through the day, and she among the rest, though the sun shone not for her as before, and misery converted life into torture. Soon she was startled by the intelligence that a cavalier was in the parlour desirous of seeing her. She shrunk gloomily within herself, and refused to go down. The portress returned a quarter of an hour after. He was gone, but had written to her; and she delivered the letter. It lay on the table before Angeline—she cared not to open it all was over, and needed not this confirmation. At length, slowly, and with an effort, she broke the seal. The date was the anniversary of the expiration of the year. Her tears burst forth; and then a cruel hope was born in her heart that all was a dream, and that now, the Trial of Love being at an end, he had written to claim her. Instigated by this deceitful suggestion, she wiped her eyes, and read these words:

'I am come to excuse myself from an act of baseness. You refuse to see me, and I write; for, unworthy as I must ever be in your eyes, I would not appear worse than I am. I received your letter in Faustina's presence—she recognized your handwriting. You know her wilfulness, her impetuosity; she took it from me, and I could not prevent her. I will say no more. You must hate me; yet rather afford me your pity, for I am miserable. My honour is now engaged; it was all done almost before I knew the danger—but there is no help—I shall know no peace till you forgive me, and yet I deserve your curse. Faustina is ignorant of our secret. Farewell.'

The paper dropped from Angeline's hand.

It were vain to describe the variety of grief that the poor girl endured. Her piety, her resignation, her noble, generous nature came to her assistance, and supported her when she felt that without them, she must have died. Faustina wrote to say that she would have seen her, but that Ippolito was averse from her doing so. The answer had come from the Marchese della Toretta—a glad consent; but he was ill, and they were all going to Bologna: on their return they would meet.

This departure was some comfort to the unfortunate girl. And soon another came in the shape of a letter from Ippolito's father, full of praises for her conduct. His son had confessed all to him, he said; she was an angel—heaven would reward her, and still greater would be her recompence, if she would deign to forgive her faithless lover. Angeline found relief in answering this letter, and pouring forth a part of the weight of grief and thought that burthened her. She forgave him freely, and prayed that he and his lovely bride might enjoy every blessing.

Ippolito and Faustina were married, and spent two or three years in Paris and the south of Italy. She had been ecstatically happy at first; but soon the rough world, and her husband's light, inconstant nature inflicted a thousand wounds in her young bosom. She longed for the friendship, the kind sympathy of Angeline; to repose her head on her soft heart, and to be comforted. She proposed a visit to Venice—Ippolito consented—and they visited Este in their way. Angeline had taken the veil in the convent of Sant' Anna. She was cheerful, if not happy; she listened in astonishment to Faustina's sorrows, and strove to console. her. Ippolito, also, she saw with calm and altered feelings; he was not the being her soul had loved; and if she had married him, with her deep feelings, and exalted ideas of honour, she felt that she should have been even more dissatisfied than Faustina.

The couple lived the usual life of Italian husband and wife. He was gay, inconstant, careless; she consoled herself with a cavaliere servente. Angeline, dedicated to heaven, wondered at all these things; and how any could so easily make transfer of affections, which with her, were sacred and immutable.

The Heart of John Middleton

I WAS born at Sawley, where the shadow of Pendle Hill falls at sunrise. I suppose Sawley sprang up into a village in the time of the monks, who had an abbey there. Many of the cottages are strange old places; others, again, are built of the abbey stones, mixed up with the shale from the neighbouring quarries; and you may see many a quaint bit of carving worked into the walls, or forming the lintels of the doors. There is a row of houses, built still more recently, where one Mr Peel came to live for the sake of the water-power, and gave the place a fillip into something like life—though a different kind of life, as I take it, from the grand, slow ways folks had when the monks were about.

Now it was—six o'clock, ring the bell, throng to the factory; sharp home at twelve; and even at night, when work was done, we hardly knew how to walk slowly, we had been so bustled all day long. I can't recollect the time when I did not go to the factory. My father used to drag me there when I was quite a little fellow, in order to wind reels for him. I never remember my mother. I should have been a better man than I have been, if I had only had a notion of the sound of her voice, or the look on her face.

My father and I lodged in the house of a man who also worked in the factory. We were sadly thronged in Sawley, so many people came from different parts of the country to earn a livelihood at the new work; and it was some time before the row of cottages I have spoken of could be built. While they were building, my father was turned out of his lodgings for drinking and being disorderly, and he and I slept in the brick-kiln; that is to say, when we did sleep o' nights; but, often and often, we went poaching; and many a hare and pheasant have I rolled up in clay, and roasted in the embers of the kiln. Then, as followed to reason, I was drowsy next day over my work; but father had no mercy on me for sleeping, for all he knew the cause of it, but kicked me where I lay, a heavy lump on the factory floor, and cursed and swore at me till I got up for very fear, and to my winding again. But, when his back was turned, I paid him off with heavier curses than he had given me, and longed to be a man, that I might be revenged on him. The words I then spoke I would not now dare to repeat; and, worse than hating words, a hating heart went with them. I forget the time when I did not know how to hate. When I first came to read, and learnt about Ishmael, I thought I must be of his doomed race, for my hand was against every man, and every man's against me. But I was seventeen or more before I cared for my book enough to learn to read.

After the row of cottages was finished, father took one, and set up for himself, in letting lodgings. I can't say much for the furnishing; but there was plenty of straw, and we kept up good fires; and there is a set of people who value warmth above everything. The worst lot about the place lodged with us. We used to have a supper in the middle of the night; there was game enough, or, if there was not game, there was poultry to be had for the stealing. By day, we all made a show of working in the factory. By night, we feasted and drank.

Now this web of my life was black enough, and coarse enough; but by-and-by, a little golden, filmy thread began to be woven in— the dawn of God's mercy was at hand.

One blowy October morning, as I sauntered lazily along to the mill, I came to the little wooden bridge over a brook that falls into the Bribble. On the plank there stood a child, balancing the pitcher on her head, with which she had been to fetch water. She was so light on her feet that, had it not been for the weight of the pitcher, I almost believe the wind would have taken her up, and wafted her away as it carries off a blow-ball in seed-time; her blue cotton dress was blown before her, as if she were spreading her wings for a flight; she turned her face round, as if to ask me for something, but when she saw who it was, she hesitated, for I had a bad name in the village, and I doubt not she had been warned against me. But her heart was too innocent to be distrustful; so she said to me, timidly—

'Please, John Middleton, will you carry me this heavy jug just over the bridge?'

It was the very first time I had ever been spoken to gently. I was ordered here and there by my father and his rough companions; I was abused and cursed by them if I failed in doing what they wished; if I succeeded, there came no expression of thanks or gratitude. I was informed of facts necessary for me to know. But the gentle words of request or entreaty were aforetime unknown to me, and now their tones fell on my ear soft and sweet as a distant peal of bells. I wished that I knew how to speak properly in reply; but though we were of the same standing as regarded worldly circumstances, there was some mighty difference between us, which made me unable to speak in her language of soft words and modest entreaty. There was nothing for me but to take up the pitcher in a kind of gruff, shy silence, and carry it over the bridge, as she had asked me. When I gave it her back again, she thanked me and tripped away, leaving me, wordless, gazing after her like an awkward lout as I was. I knew well enough who she was. She was grandchild to Eleanor Hadfield, an aged woman, who was reputed as a witch by my father and his set, for no other reason, that I can make out, than her scorn, dignity, and fearlessness of rancour. It was true we often met her in the grey dawn of the morning, when we returned from poaching, and my father used to curse her, under his breath, for a witch, such as were burnt long ago on Pendle Hill top; but I had heard that Eleanor was a skilful sick nurse, and ever ready to give her services to those who were ill; and I believe that she had been sitting up through the night (the night that we had been spending under the wild heavens, in deeds as wild) with those who were appointed to die. Nelly was her orphan granddaughter—her little handmaiden, her treasure, her one ewe lamb. Many and many a day have I watched by the brook-side, hoping that some happy gust of wind, coming with opportune bluster down the hollow of the dale, might make me necessary once more to her. I longed to hear her speak to me again. I said the words she had used to myself, trying to catch her tone; but the chance never came again. I do not know that she ever knew how I watched for her there. I found out that she went to school, and nothing would serve me but that I must go too. My father scoffed at me; I did not care. I knew nought of what reading was, nor that it was likely that I should be laughed at: I, a great hulking lad of seventeen or upwards, for going to learn my A, B, C, in the midst of a crowd of little ones. I stood just this way in my mind. Nelly was at school; it was the best place for seeing her, and hearing her voice again. Therefore I would go too. My father talked, and swore, and threatened, but I stood to it. He said I should leave school, weary of it in a month. I swore a deeper oath than I like to remember, that I would stay a year, and come out a reader and a writer. My father hated the notion of folks learning to read, and said it took all the spirit out of them; besides, he thought he had a right to every penny of my wages, and though, when he was in good humour, he might have given me many a jug of ale, he grudged my twopence a week for schooling. However, to school I went. It was a different place to what I had thought it before I went inside. The girls sat on one side, and the boys on the other; so I was not near Nelly. She, too, was in the first class; I was put with the little toddling things that could hardly run alone. The master sat in the middle, and kept pretty strict watch over us. But I could see Nelly, and hear her read her chapter; and even when it was one with a long list of hard names, such as the master was very fond of giving her, to show how well she could hit them off without spelling, I thought I had never heard a prettier music. Now and then she read other things. I did not know what they were, true or false; but I listened because she read; and, by-and-by, I began to wonder. I remember the first word I ever spoke to her was to ask her (as we were coming out of school) who was the Father of whom she had been reading, for when she said the words 'Our Father', her voice dropped into a soft, holy kind of low sound, which struck me more than any loud reading, it seemed so loving and tender. When I asked her this, she looked at me with her great blue wondering eyes, at first shocked; and then, as it were, melted down into pity and sorrow, she said in the same way, below her breath, in which she read the words, 'Our Father',—

'Don't you know? It is God.'

'God?'

'Yes; the God that grandmother tells me about.'

'Tell me what she says, will you?' So we sat down on the hedge-bank, she a little above me, while I looked up into her face, and she told me all the holy texts her grandmother had taught her, as explaining all that could be explained of the Almighty. I listened in silence, for indeed I was overwhelmed with astonishment. Her knowledge was principally rote-knowledge; she was too young for much more; but we, in Lancashire, speak a rough kind of Bible language, and the texts seemed very clear to me. I rose up, dazed and over-powered. I was going away in silence, when I bethought me of my manners, and turned back, and said 'Thank you,' for the first time I ever remember saying it in my life. That was a great day for me, in more ways than one.

I was always one who could keep very steady to an object when once I had set it before me. My object was to know Nelly. I was conscious of nothing more. But it made me regardless of all other things. The master might scold, the little ones might laugh; I bore it all without giving it a second thought. I kept to my year, and came out a reader and writer; more, however, to stand well in Nelly's good opinion, than because of my oath. About this time, my father committed some bad, cruel deed, and had to fly the country. I was glad he went; for I had never loved or cared for him, and wanted to shake myself clear of his set. But it was no easy matter. Honest folk stood aloof; only bad men held out their arms to me with a welcome. Even Nelly seemed to have a mixture of fear now with her kind ways towards me. I was the son of John Middleton, who, if he were caught, would be hung at Lancaster Castle. I thought she looked at me sometimes with a sort of sorrowful horror. Others were not forbearing enough to keep their expression of feeling confined to looks. The son of the overlooker at the mill never ceased twitting me with my father's crime; he now brought up his poaching against him, though I knew very well how many a good supper he himself had made on game which had been given him to make him and his father wink at late hours in the morning. And how were such as my father to come honestly by game?

This lad, Dick Jackson, was the bane of my life. He was a year or two older than I was, and had much power over the men who worked at the mill, as he could report to his father what he chose. I could not always hold my peace when he 'threaped' me with my father's sins, but gave it him back sometimes in a storm of passion. It did me no good; only threw me farther from the company of better men, who looked aghast and shocked at the oaths I poured out—blasphemous words learnt in my childhood, which I could not forget now that I would fain have purified myself of them; while all the time Dick Jackson stood by, with a mocking smile of intelligence; and when I had ended, breathless and weary with spent passion, he would turn to those whose respect I longed to earn, and ask if I were not a worthy son of my father, and likely to tread in his steps. But this smiling indifference of his to my miserable vehemence was not all, though it was the worst part of his conduct, for it made the rankling hatred grow up in my heart, and overshadow it like the great gourd-tree of the prophet Jonah. But his was a merciful shade, keeping out the burning sun; mine blighted what it fell upon.

What Dick Jackson did besides, was this. His father was a skilful overlooker, and a good man. Mr Peel valued him so much, that he was kept on, although his health was failing; and when he was unable, through illness, to come to the mill, he deputed his son to watch over, and report the men. It was too much power for one so young—I speak it calmly now. Whatever Dick Jackson became, he had strong temptations when he was young, which will be allowed for hereafter. But at the time of which I am telling, my hate raged like a fire. I believed that he was the one sole obstacle to my being received as fit to mix with good and honest men. I was sick of crime and disorder, and would fain have come over to a different kind of life and have been industrious, sober, honest, and right spoken (I had no idea of higher virtue then), and at every turn Dick Jackson met me with his sneers. I have walked the night through, in the old abbey field, planning how I could outwit him, and win men's respect in spite of him. The first time I ever prayed was underneath the silent stars, kneeling by the old abbey walls, throwing up my arms, and asking God for the power of revenge upon him.

I had heard that if I prayed earnestly, God would give me what I asked for, and I looked upon it as a kind of chance for the fulfilment of my wishes. If earnestness would have won the boon for me, never were wicked words so earnestly spoken. And oh, later on, my prayer was heard, and my wish granted! All this time I saw little of Nelly. Her grandmother was failing, and she had much to do indoors. Besides, I believed I had read her looks aright, when I took them to speak of aversion; and I planned to hide myself from her sight, as it were, until I could stand upright before men, with fearless eyes, dreading no face of accusation. It was possible to acquire a good character; I would do it—I did it: but no one brought up among respectable untempted people can tell the unspeakable hardness of the task. In the evenings I would not go forth among the village throng; for the acquaintances that claimed me were my father's old associates, who would have been glad enough to enlist a strong young man like me in their projects; and the men who would have shunned me, and kept aloof, were the steady and orderly. So I stayed indoors, and practised myself in reading. You will say I should have found it easier to earn a good character away from Sawley, at some place where neither I nor my father was known. So I should; but it would not have been the same thing to my mind. Besides, representing all good men, all goodness to me, in Sawley Nelly lived. In her sight I would work out my life, and fight my way upwards to men's respect. Two years passed on. Every day I strove fiercely; every day my struggles were made fruitless by the son of the overlooker; and I seemed but where I was—but where I must ever be esteemed by all who knew me—but as the son of the criminal—wild, reckless, ripe for crime myself. Where was the use of my reading and writing? These acquirements were disregarded and scouted by those among whom I was thrust back to take my portion. I could have read any chapter in the Bible now; and Nelly seemed as though she would never know it. I was driven in upon my books; and few enough of them I had. The pedlars brought them round in their packs, and I bought what I could. I had the 'Seven Champions', and the 'Pilgrim's Progress'; and both seemed to me equally wonderful, and equally founded on fact. I got Byron's 'Narrative', and Milton's 'Paradise Lost'; but I lacked the knowledge which would give a clue to all. Still they afforded me pleasure, because they took me out of myself, and made me forget my miserable position, and made me unconscious (for the time at least) of my one great passion of hatred against Dick Jackson.

When Nelly was about seventeen her grandmother died. I stood aloof in the churchyard, behind the great yew-tree, and watched the funeral. It was the first religious service that ever I heard; and to my shame, as I thought, it affected me to tears. The words seemed so peaceful and holy that I longed to go to church, but I durst not, because I had never been. The parish church was at Bolton, far enough away to serve as an excuse for all who did not care to go. I heard Nelly's sobs, filling up every pause in the clergyman's voice; and every sob of hers went to my heart. She passed me on her way out of the churchyard; she was so near I might have touched her; but her head was hanging down, and I durst not speak to her. Then the question arose, what was to become of her? She must earn her living; was it to be as a farm-servant or by working at the mill? I knew enough of both kinds of life to make me tremble for her. My wages were such as to enable me to marry, if I chose; and I never thought of woman, for my wife, but Nelly. Still, I would not have married her now, if I could; for, as yet, I had not risen up to the character which I determined it was fit that Nelly's husband should have. When I was rich in good report, I would come forward and take my chance, but until then I would hold my peace. I had faith in the power of my long-continued dogged breasting of opinion. Sooner or later it must, it should, yield, and I be received among the ranks of good men. But, meanwhile, what was to become of Nelly? I reckoned up my wages; I went to inquire what the board of a girl would be who should help her in her household work, and live with her as a daughter, at the house of one of the most decent women of the place; she looked at me suspiciously. I kept down my temper, and told her I would never come near the place; that I would keep away from that end of the village, and that the girl for whom I made the inquiry should never know but what the parish paid for her keep. It would not do; she suspected me; but I know I had power over myself to have kept my word; and besides, I would not for worlds have had Nelly put under any obligation to me, which should speck the purity of her love, or dim it by a mixture of gratitude—the love that I craved to earn, not for my money, not for my kindness, but for myself. I heard that Nelly had met with a place in Bolland; and I could see no reason why I might not speak to her once before she left our neighbourhood. I meant it to be a quiet friendly telling her of my sympathy in her sorrow. I felt I could command myself. So, on the Sunday before she was to leave Sawley, I waited near the wood-path by which I knew that she would return from afternoon church. The birds made such a melodious warble, such a busy sound among the leaves, that I did not hear approaching footsteps till they were close at hand, and then there were sounds of two persons' voices. The wood was near that part of Sawley where Nelly was staying with friends; the path through it led to their house, and theirs only, so I knew it must be she, for I had watched her setting out to church alone.

But who was the other?

The blood went to my heart and head, as if I were shot, when

I saw that it was Dick Jackson. Was this the end of it all? In the steps of sin which my father had trod, I would rush to my death and my doom. Even where I stood I longed for a weapon to slay him. How dared he come near my Nelly? She too—I thought her faithless, and forgot how little I had ever been to her in out-ward action; how few words, and those how uncouth, I had ever spoken to her; and I hated her for a traitress. There feelings passed through me before I could see, my eyes and head were so dizzy and blind. When I looked I saw Dick Jackson holding her hand, and speaking quick and low and thick, as a man speaks in great vehemence. She seemed white and dismayed; but all at once, at some word of his (and what it was she never would tell me), she looked as though she defied a fiend, and wrenched herself out of his grasp. He caught hold of her again, and began once more the thick whisper that I loathed. I could bear it no longer, nor did I see why I should. I stepped out from behind the tree where I had been lying. When she saw me, she lost her look of one strung up to desperation, and came and clung to me; and I felt like a giant in strength and might. I held her with one arm, but I did not take my eyes off him; I felt as if they blazed down into his soul and scorched him up. He never spoke, but tried to look as though he defied me. At last, his eyes fell before mine; I dared not speak, for the old horrid oaths thronged up to my mouth, and I dreaded giv-ing them way, and terrifying my poor, trembling Nelly.

At last, he made to go past me: I drew her out of the pathway. By instinct she wrapped her garments round her, as if to avoid his accidental touch; and he was stung by this, I suppose—I believe— to the mad, miserable revenge he took. As my back was turned to him, in an endeavour to speak some words to Nelly that might soothe her into calmness, she, who was looking after him, like one fascinated with terror, saw him take a sharp, shaley stone, and aim it at me. Poor darling! she clung round me as a shield, making her sweet body into a defence for mine. It hit her, and she spoke no word, kept back her cry of pain, but fell at my feet in a swoon. He—the coward! ran off as soon as he saw what he had done. I was with Nelly alone in the green gloom of the wood. The quiver-ing and leaf-tinted light made her look as if she were dead. I carried her, not knowing if I bore a corpse or not, to her friend's house. I did not stay to explain, but ran madly for the doctor.

Well! I cannot bear to recur to that time again. Five weeks I lived in the agony of suspense; from which my only relief was in laying savage plans for revenge. If I hated him before, what think ye I did now? It seemed as if earth could not hold us twain, but that one of us must go down to Gehenna. I could have killed him; and would have done it without a scruple, but that seemed too poor and bold a revenge. At length—oh, the weary waiting!—oh, the sickening of my heart!—Nelly grew better; as well as she was ever to grow. The bright colour had left her cheek; the mouth quivered with repressed pain; the eyes were dim with tears that agony had forced into them; and I loved her a thousand times better and more than when she was bright and blooming! What was best of all, I began to perceive that she cared for me. I know her grandmother's friends warned her against me, and told her I came of a bad stock; but she had passed the point where remonstrance from bystanders can take effect—she loved me as I was, a strange mixture of bad and good, all unworthy of her. We spoke together now, as those do whose lives are bound up in each other. I told her I would marry her as soon as she had recovered her health. Her friends shook their heads; but they saw that she would be unfit for farm-service or heavy work, and they perhaps thought, as many a one does, that a bad husband was better than none at all. Anyhow, we were married; and I learnt to bless God for my happiness so far beyond my deserts. I kept her like a lady. I was a skilful workman, and earned good wages; and every want she had I tried to gratify. Her wishes were few and simple enough, poor Nelly! If they had been ever so fanciful, I should have had my reward in the new feeling of the holiness of home. She could lead me as a little child with the charm of her gentle voice, and her ever-kind words. She would plead for all when I was full of anger and passion; only Dick Jackson's name passed never between our lips during all that time. In the evening she lay back in her beehive chair, and read to me. I think I see her now, pale and weak, with her sweet young face lighted by her holy, earnest eyes, telling me of the Saviour's life and death, till they were filled with tears. I longed to have been there, to have avenged Him on the wicked Jews. I liked Peter the best of all the disciples. But I got the Bible myself, and read the mighty act of God's vengeance, in the old Testament, with a kind of triumphant faith that, sooner or later, He would take my cause in hand, and revenge me on mine enemy.

In a year or so, Nelly had a baby—a little girl with eyes just like hers, that looked, with grave openness, right into yours. Nelly recovered but slowly. It was just before winter, the cotton-crop had failed, and master had to turn off many hands. I thought I was sure of being kept on, for I had earned a steady character, and did my work well; but once again it was permitted that Dick Jackson should do me wrong. He induced his father to dismiss me among the first in my branch of the business; and there was I, just before winter set in, with a wife and new-born child, and a small enough store of money to keep body and soul together till I could get to work again. All my savings had gone by Christmas Eve, and we sat in the house foodless for the morrow's festival. Nelly looked pinched and worn; the baby cried for a larger supply of milk than its poor starving mother could give it. My right hand had not forgot its cunning, and I went out once more to my poaching. I knew where the gang met; and I knew what a welcome back I should have— a far warmer and more hearty welcome than good men had given me when I tried to enter their ranks. On the road to the meeting-place I fell in with an old man, one who had been a companion to my father in his early days.

'What, lad!' said he, 'art thou turning back to the old trade? It's the better business, now that cotton has failed.'

'Ay,' said I, 'cotton is starving us outright. A man may bear a deal himself, but he'll do aught bad and sinful to save his wife and child.'

'Nay, lad,' said he, 'poaching is not sinful; it goes against man's laws, but not against God's.'

I was too weak to argue or talk much. I had not tasted food for two days. But I murmured, 'At any rate, I trusted to have been clear of it for the rest of my days. It led my father wrong at first. I have tried and I have striven. Now I give all up. Right or wrong shall be the same to me. Some are fore-doomed; and so am I.' And, as I spoke, some notion of the futurity that would separate Nelly, the pure and holy, from me, the reckless and desperate one, came over me with an irrepressible burst of anguish. Just then the bells of Bolton-in-Bolland struck up a glad peal, which came over the woods, in the solemn midnight air, like the sons of the morning shouting for joy—they seemed so clear and jubilant. It was Christmas Day: and I felt like an outcast from the gladness and the salvation. Old Jonah spoke out:

'Yon's the Christmas bells. I say, Johnny, my lad, I've no notion of taking such a spiritless chap as thou into the thick of it, with thy rights and thy wrongs. We don't trouble ourselves with such fine lawyer's stuff, and we bring down the "varmint" all the better. Now, I'll not have thee in our gang, for thou art not up to the fun, and thou'd hang fire when the time came to be doing. But I've a shrewd guess that plaguey wife and child of thine are at the bottom of thy half-and-half joining. Now, I was thy father's friend afore he took to them helter-skelter ways, and I've five shillings and a neck of mutton at thy service. I'll not list a fasting man; but if thou'lt come to us with a full stomach, and say, "I like your life, my lads, and I'll make one of you with pleasure, the first shiny night," why, we'll give you a welcome and a half; but, tonight, make no more ado, but turn back with me for the mutton and the money.'

I was not proud: nay, I was most thankful. I took the meat, and boiled some broth for my poor Nelly. She was in a sleep, or in a faint, I know not which; but I roused her, and held her up in bed, and fed her with a teaspoon, and the light came back to her eyes, and the faint moonlight smile to her lips; and when she had ended, she said her innocent grace, and fell asleep, with her baby on her breast. I sat over the fire, and listened to the bells, as they swept past my cottage on the gusts of the wind. I longed and yearned for the second coming of Christ, of which Nelly had told me. The world seemed cruel, and hard, and strong—too strong for me; and I prayed to cling to the hem of His garment, and be borne over the rough places when I fainted and bled, and found no man to pity or help me but poor old Jonah, the publican and sinner. All this time my own woes and my own self were uppermost in my mind, as they are in the minds of most who have been hardly used. As I thought of my wrongs, and my sufferings, my heart burned against Dick Jackson; and as the bells rose and fell, so my hopes waxed and waned, that in those mysterious days, of which they were both the remembrance and the prophecy, he would be purged from off the earth. I took Nelly's Bible, and turned, not to the gracious story of the Saviour's birth, but to the records of the former days, when the Jews took such wild revenge upon all their opponents. I was a Jew—a leader among the people. Dick Jackson was as Pharaoh, as the King Agag, who walked delicately, thinking the bitterness of death was past—in short, he was the conquered enemy, over whom I gloated, with my Bible in my hand—that Bible which contained our Saviour's words on the Cross. As yet, those words seemed faint and meaningless to me, like a tract of country seen in the starlight haze; while the histories of the Old Testament were grand and distinct in the blood-red colour of sunset. By-and-by that night passed into day, and little piping voices came round carol-singing. They wakened Nelly. I went to her as soon as I heard her stirring.

'Nelly,' said I, 'there's money and food in the house; I will be off to Padiham seeking work, while thou hast something to go upon.'

'Not today,' said she; 'stay today with me. If thou wouldst only go to church with me this once'—for you see I had never been inside a church but when we were married, and she was often pray-ing me to go; and now she looked at me, with a sigh just creep-ing forth from her lips, as she expected a refusal. But I did not refuse. I had been kept away from church before because I dared not go; and now I was desperate, and dared do anything. If I did look like a heathen in the face of all men, why, I was a heathen in my heart, for I was falling back into all my evil ways. I had resolved, if my search of work at Padiham should fail, I would fol-low my father's footsteps, and take with my own right hand and by my strength of arm what it was denied me to obtain honestly. I had resolved to leave Sawley, where a curse seemed to hang over me: so what did it matter if I went to church, all unbeknowing what strange ceremonies were there performed? I walked thither as a sinful man—sinful in my heart. Nelly hung on my arm, but even she could not get me to speak. I went in; she found my places, and pointed to the words, and looked up into my eyes with hers, so full of faith and joy. But I saw nothing but Richard Jackson—I heard nothing but his loud nasal voice, making response, and desec-rating all the holy words. He was in broadcloth of the best—I in my fustian jacket. He was prosperous and glad—I was starving and desperate. Nelly grew pale, as she saw the expression in my eyes; and she prayed ever and ever more fervently as the thought of me tempted by the Devil even at that very moment came more fully before her.

By-and-by she forgot even me, and laid her soul bare before God, in a long, silent, weeping prayer, before we left the church. Nearly all had gone; and I stood by her, unwilling to disturb her, unable to join her. At last she rose up, heavenly calm. She took my arm, and we went home through the woods, where all the birds seemed tame and familiar. Nelly said she thought all living creatures knew it was Christmas Day, and rejoiced, and were loving together. I believe it was the frost that had tamed them; and I felt the hatred that was in me, and knew that, whatever else was loving, I was full of malice and uncharitableness; nor did I wish to be otherwise. That afternoon I bade Nelly and our child farewell, and tramped to Padiham. I got work—how I hardly know; for stronger and stronger came the force of the temptation to lead a wild, free life of sin; legions seemed whispering evil thoughts to me, and only my gentle, pleading Nelly to pull me back from the great gulf. However, as I said before, I got work, and set off homewards to move my wife and child to that neighbourhood. I hated Sawley, and yet I was fiercely indignant to leave it, with my purposes unaccomplished. I was still an outcast from the more respectable, who stood afar off from such as I; and mine enemy lived and flourished in their regard. Padiham, however, was not so far away for me to despair—to relinquish my fixed determination. It was on the eastern side of the great Pendle Hill, ten miles away, maybe. Hate will overleap a greater obstacle. I took a cottage on the Fell, high up on the side of the hill. We saw a long black moorland slope before us, and then the grey stone houses of Padiham, over which a black cloud hung, different from the blue wood or turf smoke about Sawley. The wild winds came down and whistled round our house many a day when all was still below. But I was happy then. I rose in men's esteem. I had work in plenty. Our child lived and throve. But I forgot not our country proverb—'Keep a stone in thy pocket for seven years; turn it, and keep it seven years more; but have it ever ready to cast to thine enemy when the time comes.'

One day a fellow-workman asked me to go to a hill-side preaching. Now, I never cared to go to church; but there was something newer and freer in the notion of praying to God right under His great dome; and the open air had had a charm to me ever since my wild boyhood. Besides, they said, these ranters had strange ways with them, and I thought it would be fun to see their way of setting about it; and this ranter of all others had made himself a name in our parts. Accordingly we went; it was a fine summer's evening, after work was done. When we got to the place we saw such a crowd as I never saw before—men, women, and children; all ages were gathered together, and sat on the hill-side. They were care-worn, diseased, sorrowful, criminal; all that was told on their faces, which were hard and strongly marked. In the midst, standing in a cart, was the ranter. When I first saw him, I said to my companion, 'Lord! what a little man to make all this pother! I could trip him up with one of my fingers'; and then I sat down, and looked about me a bit. All eyes were fixed on the preacher; and I turned mine upon him too. He began to speak; it was in no fine-drawn language, but in words such as we heard every day of our lives, and about things we did every day of our lives. He did not call our shortcomings pride or worldliness, or pleasure-seeking, which would have given us no clear notion of what he meant; but he just told us outright what we did, and then he gave it a name, and said that it was accursed, and that we were lost if we went on so doing.

By this time the tears and sweat were running down his face; he was wrestling for our souls. We wondered how he knew our inner-most lives as he did, for each one of us saw his sin set before him in plain-spoken words. Then he cried out to us to repent; and spoke first to us, and then to God, in a way that would have shocked many but it did not shock me. I liked strong things, and I liked the bare, full truth; and I felt brought nearer to God in that hour—the summer darkness creeping over us, and one after one the stars coming out above us, like the eyes of the angels watching us—than I had ever done in my life before. When he had brought us to our tears and sighs, he stopped his loud voice of upbraiding, and there was a hush, only broken by sobs and quivering moans, in which I heard through the gloom the voices of strong men in anguish and supplication, as well as the shriller tones of women. Suddenly he was heard again; by this time we could not see him; but his voice was now tender as the voice of an angel, and he told us of Christ, and implored us to come to Him. I never heard such passionate entreaty. He spoke as if he saw Satan hovering near us in the dark, dense night, and as if our only safety lay in a very present coming to the Cross; I believe he did see Satan: we know he haunts the desolate old hills, awaiting his time, and now or never it was with many a soul. At length there was a sudden silence; and, by the cries of those nearest to the preacher, we heard that he had fainted. We had all crowded round him, as if he were our safety and our guide; and he was overcome by the heat and the fatigue, for we were the fifth set of people whom he had addressed that day. I left the crowd who were leading him down, and took a lonely path myself.

Here was the earnestness I needed. To this weak and weary fainting man, religion was a life and a passion. I look back now, and wonder at my blindness as to what was the root of all my Nelly's patience and long-suffering; for I thought now I had found out what religion was, and that hitherto it had been all an unknown thing to me.

Henceforward, my life was changed. I was zealous and fanatical. Beyond the set to whom I had affiliated myself, I had no sympathy. I would have persecuted all who differed from me, if I had only had the power. I became an ascetic in all bodily enjoyments. And, strange and inexplicable mystery, I had some thoughts that by every act of self-denial I was attaining to my unholy end, and that, when I had fasted and prayed long enough, God would place my vengeance in my hands. I have knelt by Nelly's bedside, and vowed to live a self-denying life, as regarded all outward things, if so that God would grant my prayer. I left it in His hands. I felt sure He would trace out the token and the word; and Nelly would listen to my passionate words, and lie awake sorrowful and heart-sore through the night; and I would get up and make her tea, and rearrange her pillows, with a strange and wilful blindness that my bitter words and blasphemous prayers had cost her miserable, sleepless nights. My Nelly was suffering yet from that blow. How or where the stone had hurt her, I never understood; but in consequence of that one moment's action, her limbs became numb and dead, and, by slow degrees, she took to her bed, from whence she was never carried alive. There she lay, propped up by pillows, her meek face ever bright, and smiling forth a greeting; her white, pale hands ever busy with some kind of work; and our little Grace was as the power of motion to her. Fierce as I was away from her, I never could speak to her but in my gentlest tones. She seemed to me as if she had never wrestled for salvation as I had; and, when away from her, I resolved many a time and oft, that I would rouse her up to her state of danger when I returned home that evening—even if strong reproach were required I would rouse her up to her soul's need. But I came in and heard her voice singing some holy word of patience, some psalm which, maybe, had comforted the martyrs; and when I saw her face like the face of an angel, full of patience and happy faith, I put off my awakening speeches till another time.

One night, long ago, when I was yet young and strong, although my years were past forty, I sat alone in my house-place. Nelly was always in bed, as I have told you, and Grace lay in a cot by her side. I believed them to be both asleep; though how they could sleep I could not conceive, so wild and terrible was the night. The wind came sweeping down from the hill-top in great beats, like the pulses of heaven; and, during the pauses, while I listened for the coming roar, I felt the earth shiver beneath me. The rain beat against windows and doors, and sobbed for entrance. I thought the Prince of the Air was abroad; and I heard, or fancied I heard, shrieks come on the blast, like the cries of sinful souls given over to his power.

The sounds came nearer and nearer. I got up and saw to the fast-enings of the door, for, though I cared not for mortal man, I did care for what I believed was surrounding the house, in evil might and power. But the door shook as though it, too, were in deadly terror, and I thought the fastenings would give way. I stood facing the entrance, lashing my heart up to defy the spiritual enemy that I looked to see, every instant, in bodily presence; and the door did burst open, and before me stood—what was it? man or demon? a grey-haired man, with poor, worn clothes all wringing wet, and he himself battered and piteous to look upon, from the storm he had passed through.

'Let me in!' he said. 'Give me shelter. I am poor, or I would reward you. And I am friendless, too,' he said, looking up in my face, like one seeking what he cannot find. In that look, strangely changed, I knew that God had heard me; for it was the old cow-ardly look of my life's enemy. Had he been a stranger, I might not have welcomed him; but as he was mine enemy. I gave him wel-come in a lordly dish. I sat opposite to him. 'Whence do you come?' said I. 'It is a strange night to be out on the fells.'

He looked up at me sharp; but in general he held his head down like a beast or hound.

'You won't betray me. I'll not trouble you long. As soon as the storm abates, I'll go.'

'Friend,' said I, 'what have I to betray?' and I trembled lest he should keep himself out of my power and not tell me. 'You come for shelter, and I give you of my best. Why do you suspect me?'

'Because', said he, in his abject bitterness, 'all the world is against me. I never met with goodness or kindness; and now I am hunted like a wild beast. I'll tell you—I'm a convict returned before my time. I was a Sawley man', (as if I, of all men, did not know it!) 'and I went back, like a fool, to the old place. They've hunted me out where I would fain have lived rightly and quietly, and they'll send me back to that hell upon earth, if they catch me. I did not know it would be such a night. Only let me rest and get warm once more, and I'll go away. Good, kind man, have pity upon me!' I smiled all his doubts away; I promised him a bed on the floor, and I thought of Jael and Sisera. My heart leaped up like a war-horse at the sound of the trumpet, and said, 'Ha, ha, the Lord hath heard my prayer and supplication; I shall have vengeance at last!'

He did not dream who I was. He was changed; so that I, who had learned his features with all the diligence of hatred, did not, at first, recognize him; and he thought not of me, only of his own woe and affright. He looked into the fire with the dreamy gaze of one whose strength of character, if he had any, is beaten out of him, and cannot return at any emergency whatsoever. He sighed and pitied himself, yet could not decide on what to do. I went softly about my business, which was to make him up a bed on the floor, and, when he was lulled to sleep and security, to make the best of my way to Padiham, and summon the constable, into whose hands I would give him up, to be taken back to his 'hell upon earth'. I went into Nelly's room. She was awake and anxious. I saw she had been listening to the voices.

'Who is there?' said she. 'John, tell me; it sounded like a voice I knew. For God's sake, speak!'

I smiled a quiet smile. 'It is a poor man, who has lost his way. Go to sleep, my dear—I shall make him up on the floor. I may not come for some time. Go to sleep'; and I kissed her. I thought she was soothed, but not fully satisfied. However, I hastened away before there was any further time for questioning. I made up the bed, and Richard Jackson, tired out, lay down and fell asleep. My contempt for him almost equalled my hate. If I were avoiding return to a place which I thought to be a hell upon earth, think you I would have taken a quiet sleep under any man's roof till, somehow or another, I was secure. Now comes this man, and, with incontinence of tongue, blabs out the very thing he most should conceal, and then lies down to a good, quiet, snoring sleep. I looked again. His face was old, and worn, and miserable. So should mine enemy look. And yet it was sad to gaze upon him, poor, hunted creature! I would gaze no more, lest I grew weak and pitiful. Thus I took my hat, and softly opened the door. The wind blew in, but did not disturb him, he was so utterly weary. I was out in the open air of night. The storm was ceasing, and, instead of the black sky of doom that I had seen when I last looked forth, the moon was come out, wan and pale, as if wearied with the fight in the heavens, and her white light fell ghostly and calm on many a well-known object. Now and then, a dark, torn cloud was blown across her home in the sky; but they grew fewer and fewer, and at last she shone out steady and clear. I could see Padiham down before me. I heard the noise of the watercourses down the hill-side. My mind was full of one thought, and strained upon that one thought, and yet my senses were most acute and observant. When I came to the brook, it was swollen to a rapid, tossing river; and the little bridge, with its handrail, was utterly swept away. It was like the bridge at Sawley, where I had first seen Nelly; and I remembered that day even then in the midst of my vexation at having to go round. I turned away from the brook, and there stood a little figure facing me. No spirit from the dead could have affrighted me as it did; for I saw it was Grace, whom I had left in bed by her mother's side.

She came to me, and took my hand. Her bare feet glittered white in the moonshine, and sprinkled the light upwards, as they plashed through the pool.

'Father,' said she, 'mother bade me say this.' Then, pausing to gather breath and memory, she repeated these words like a lesson of which she feared to forget a syllable—

'Mother says, "There is a God in heaven; and in His house are many mansions. If you hope to meet her there, you will come back and speak to her; if you are to be separate for ever and ever, you will go on, and may God have mercy on her and on you!" Father, I have said it right—every word.'

I was silent. At last, I said—

'What made mother say this? How came she to send you out?'

'I was asleep, father, and I heard her cry. I wakened up, and I think you had but just left the house, and that she was calling for you. Then she prayed, with the tears rolling down her cheeks, and kept saying—"Oh, that I could walk!—oh, that for one hour I could run and walk!" So I said, "Mother, I can run and walk. Where must I go?" And she clutched at my arm, and bade God bless me, and told me not to fear, for that He would compass me about, and taught me my message: and now, father, dear father, you will meet mother in heaven, won't you, and not be separate for ever and ever?' She clung to my knees, and pleaded once more in her mother's words. I took her up in my arms, and turned homewards.

'Is yon man there, on the kitchen floor?' asked I.

'Yes!' she answered. At any rate, my vengeance was not out of my power yet.

When we got home I passed him, dead asleep.

In our room, to which my child guided me, was Nelly. She sat up in bed, a most unusual attitude for her, and one of which I thought she had been incapable of attaining to without help. She had her hands clasped, and her face rapt, as if in prayer; and when she saw me, she lay back with a sweet ineffable smile. She could not speak at first; but when I came near, she took my hand and kissed it; and then she called Grace to her, and made her take off her cloak and her wet things, and dressed her in her short scanty night-gown; she slipped in to her mother's warm side; and all this time my Nelly never told me why she summoned me: it seemed enough that she should hold my hand, and feel that I was there. I believe she had read my heart; and yet I durst not speak to ask her. At last, she looked up. 'My husband,' said she, 'God has saved you and me from a great sorrow this night.' I would not understand, and I felt her look die away into disappointment.

'That poor wanderer in the house-place is Richard Jackson, is it not?'

I made no answer. Her face grew white and wan.

'Oh,' said she, 'this is hard to bear. Speak what is in your mind, I beg of you. I will not thwart you harshly; dearest John, only speak to me.'

'Why need I speak? You seem to know all.'

'I do know that his is a voice I can never forget; and I do know the awful prayers you have prayed; and I know how I have lain awake, to pray that your words might never be heard; and I am a powerless cripple. I put my cause in God's hands. You shall not do the man any harm. What you have it in your thoughts to do, I cannot tell. But I know that you cannot do it. My eyes are dim with a strange mist; but some voice tells me that you will forgive even Richard Jackson. Dear husband—dearest John, it is so dark, I cannot see you; but speak once to me.'

I moved the candle; but when I saw her face, I saw what was drawing the mist over those loving eyes—how strange and woeful that she could die! Her little girl lying by her side looked in my face, and then at her; and the wild knowledge of death shot through her young heart, and she screamed aloud.

Nelly opened her eyes once more. They fell upon the gaunt, sorrow-worn man who was the cause of all. He roused him from his sleep, at that child's piercing cry, and stood at the doorway, looking in. He knew Nelly, and understood where the storm had driven him to shelter. He came towards her—

'Oh, woman—dying woman—you have haunted me in the loneliness of the Bush far away—you have been in my dreams for ever—the hunting of men has not been so terrible as the hunting of your spirit—that stone—that stone!' He fell down by her bedside in an agony; above which her saint-like face looked on us all, for the last time, glorious with the coming light of heaven. She spoke once again—

'It was a moment of passion; I never bore you malice for it. I forgive you; and so does John, I trust.'

Could I keep my purpose there? It faded into nothing. But, above my choking tears, I strove to speak clear and distinct, for her dying ear to hear, and her sinking heart to be gladdened.

'I forgive you, Richard! I will befriend you in your trouble.'

She could not see; but, instead of the dim shadow of death stealing over her face, a quiet light came over it, which we knew was the look of a soul at rest.

That night I listened to his tale for her sake; and I learned that it is better to be sinned against than to sin. In the storm of the night mine enemy came to me; in the calm of the grey morning I led him forth, and bade him 'God speed'. And a woe had come upon me, but the burning burden of a sinful, angry heart was taken off. I am old now, and my daughter is married. I try to go about preaching and teaching in my rough, rude way; and what I teach is, how Christ lived and died, and what was Nelly's faith of love.

W. M. THACKERAY

Dennis Haggarty's Wife

THERE was an odious Irishwoman who with her daughter used to frequent the 'Royal Hotel' at Leamington some years ago, and who went by the name of Mrs Major Gam. Gam had been a distinguished officer in His Majesty's service, whom nothing but death and his own amiable wife could overcome. The widow mourned her husband in the most becoming bombazeen she could muster, and had at least half an inch of lampblack round the immense visiting tickets which she left at the houses of the nobility and gentry her friends.

Some of us, I am sorry to say, used to call her Mrs Major Gammon; for if the worthy widow had a propensity, it was to talk largely of herself and family (of her own family, for she held her husband's very cheap), and of the wonders of her paternal mansion, Molloyville, county of Mayo. She was of the Molloys of that county; and though I never heard of the family before, I have little doubt, from what Mrs Major Gam stated, that they were the most ancient and illustrious family of that part of Ireland. I remember there came down to see his aunt a young fellow with huge red whiskers and tight nankeens, a green coat, and an awful breastpin, who, after two days' stay at the Spa, proposed marriage to Miss S——, or, in default, a duel with her father; and who drove a flash curricle with a bay and a grey, and who was presented with much pride by Mrs Gam as Castlereagh Molloy of Molloyville. We all agreed that he was the most insufferable snob of the whole season, and were delighted when a bailiff came down in search of him.

Well, this is all I know personally of the Molloyville family; but at the house if you met the widow Gam, and talked on any subject in life, you were sure to hear of it. If you asked her to have peas at dinner, she would say, 'Oh, sir, after the peas at Molloyville, I really don't care for any others,—do I, dearest Jemima? We always had a dish in the month of June, when my father gave his head gardener a guinea (we had three at Molloyville), and sent him with his compliments and a quart of peas to our neighbour, dear Lord Marrowfat. What a sweet place Marrowfat Park is! isn't it, Jemima?' If a carriage passed by the window, Mrs Major Gammon would be sure to tell you that there were three carriages at Molloyville, 'the barouche, the chawiot, and the covered cyar'. In the same manner she would favour you with the number and names of the footmen of the establishment; and on a visit to Warwick Castle (for this bustling woman made one in every party of pleasure that was formed from the hotel), she gave us to understand that the great walk by the river was altogether inferior to the principal avenue of Molloyville Park. I should not have been able to tell so much about Mrs Gam and her daughter, but that, between ourselves, I was particularly sweet upon a young lady at the time, whose papa lived at the 'Royal', and was under the care of Doctor Jephson.

The Jemima appealed to by Mrs Gam in the above sentence was, of course, her daughter, apostrophized by her mother, 'Jemima, my soul's darling!' or, 'Jemima, my blessed child!' or, 'Jemima, my own love!' The sacrifices that Mrs Gam had made for that daughter were, she said, astonishing. The money she had spent in masters upon her, the illnesses through which she had nursed her, the ineffable love the mother bore her, were only known to Heaven, Mrs Gam said. They used to come into the room with their arms round each other's waists: at dinner between the courses the mother would sit with one hand locked in her daughter's; and if only two or three young men were present at the time, would be pretty sure to kiss her Jemima more than once during the time whilst the bohea was poured out.

As for Miss Gam, if she was not handsome, candour forbids me to say she was ugly. She was neither one nor t'other. She was a person who wore ringlets and a band round her forehead; she knew four songs, which became rather tedious at the end of a couple of months' acquaintance; she had excessively bare shoulders; she inclined to wear numbers of cheap ornaments, rings, brooches, *ferronnières*, smelling-bottles, and was always, we thought, very smartly dressed: though old Mrs Lynx hinted that her gowns and her mother's were turned over and over again, and that her eyes were almost put out by darning stockings.

These eyes Miss Gam had very large, though rather red and weak, and used to roll them about at every eligible unmarried man in the place. But though the widow subscribed to all the balls, though she hired a fly to go to the meet of the hounds, though she was constant at church, and Jemima sang louder than any person there except the clerk, and though, probably, any person who made her a happy husband would be invited down to enjoy the three footmen, gardeners, and carriages at Molloyville, yet no English gentleman was found sufficiently audacious to propose. Old Lynx used to say that the pair had been at Tunbridge, Harrogate, Brighton, Ramsgate, Cheltenham, for this eight years past; where they had met, it seemed, with no better fortune. Indeed, the widow looked rather high for her blessed child: and as she looked with the contempt which no small number of Irish people feel upon all persons who get their bread by labour or commerce; and as she was a person whose energetic manners, costume, and brogue were not much to the taste of quiet English country gentlemen, Jemima—sweet, spotless flower—still remained on her hands, a thought withered, perhaps, and seedy.

Now, at this time, the 120th Regiment was quartered at Weedon Barracks, and with the corps was a certain Assistant-Surgeon Haggarty, a large, lean, tough, raw-boned man, with big hands, knock-knees, and carroty whiskers, and, withal, as honest a creature as ever handled a lancet. Haggarty, as his name imports, was of the very same nation as Mrs Gam, and, what is more, the honest fellow had some of the peculiarities which belonged to the widow, and bragged about his family almost as much as she did. I do not know of what particular part of Ireland they were kings; but monarchs they must have been, as have been the ancestors of so many thousand Hibernian families; but they had been men of no small consideration in Dublin, 'where my father', Haggarty said, 'is as well known as King William's statue, and where he "rowls his carriage, too", let me tell ye'.

Hence, Haggarty was called by the wags 'Rowl the carriage', and several of them made inquiries of Mrs Gam regarding him: 'Mrs Gam, when you used to go up from Molloyville to the Lord Lieutenant's balls, and had your town-house in Fitzwilliam Square, used you to meet the famous Doctor Haggarty in society?'

'Is it Surgeon Haggarty of Gloucester Street ye mean? The black Papist! D'ye suppose that the Molloys would sit down to table with a creature of that sort?'

'Why, isn't he the most famous physician in Dublin, and doesn't he rowl his carriage there?'

'The horrid wretch! He keeps a shop, I tell ye, and sends his sons out with the medicine. He's got four of them off into the army, Ulick and Phil, and Terence and Denny, and now it's Charles that takes out the physic. But how should I know about these odious creatures? Their mother was a Burke, of Burke's Town, county Cavan, and brought Surgeon Haggarty two thousand pounds. She was a Protestant; and I am surprised how she could have taken up with a horrid odious Popish apothecary!'

From the extent of the widow's information, I am led to suppose that the inhabitants of Dublin are not less anxious about their neighbours than are the natives of English cities; and I think it is very probable that Mrs Gam's account of the young Haggartys who carried out the medicine is perfectly correct, for a lad in the 120th made a caricature of Haggarty coming out of a chemist's shop with an oilcloth basket under his arm, which set the worthy surgeon in such a fury that there would have been a duel between him and the ensign, could the fiery doctor have had his way.

Now, Dionysius Haggarty was of an exceedingly inflammable temperament, and it chanced that of all the invalids, the visitors, the young squires of Warwickshire, the young manufacturers from Birmingham, the young officers from the barracks—it chanced, unluckily for Miss Gam and himself, that he was the only individual who was in the least smitten by her personal charms. He was very tender and modest about his love, however, for it must be owned that he respected Mrs Gam hugely, and fully admitted, like a good simple fellow as he was, the superiority of that lady's birth and breeding to his own. How could he hope that he, a humble assistant-surgeon, with a thousand pounds his Aunt Kitty left him for all his fortune—how could he hope that one of the race of Molloyville would ever condescend to marry him?

Inflamed, however, by love, and inspired by wine, one day at a picnic at Kenilworth, Haggarty, whose love and raptures were the talk of the whole regiment, was induced by his waggish comrades to make a proposal in form.

'Are you aware, Mr Haggarty, that you are speaking to a Molloy?' was all the reply majestic Mrs Gam made when, according to the usual formula, the fluttering Jemima referred her suitor to 'Mamma'.

She left him with a look which was meant to crush the poor fellow to earth; she gathered up her cloak and bonnet, and precipitately called for her fly. She took care to tell every single soul in Leamington that the son of the odious Papist apothecary had had the audacity to propose for her daughter (indeed a proposal, coming from whatever quarter it may, does no harm), and left Haggarty in a state of extreme depression and despair.

His down-heartedness, indeed, surprised most of his acquaintances in and out of the regiment, for the young lady was no beauty, and a doubtful fortune, and Dennis was a man outwardly of an unromantic turn, who seemed to have a great deal more liking for beefsteak and whisky-punch than for women, however fascinating.

But there is no doubt this shy uncouth rough fellow had a warmer and more faithful heart hid within him than many a dandy who is as handsome as Apollo. I, for my part, never can understand why a man falls in love, and heartily give him credit for so doing, never mind with what or whom. *That* I take to be a point quite as much beyond an individual's own control as the catching of the small-pox or the colour of his hair. To the surprise of all, Assistant-Surgeon Dionysius Haggarty was deeply and seriously in love; and I am told that one day he very nearly killed the before-mentioned young ensign with a carving-knife, for venturing to make a second caricature, representing Lady Gammon and Jemima in a fantastical park, surrounded by three gardeners, three carriages, three footmen, and the covered cyar. He would have no joking concerning them. He became moody and quarrelsome of habit. He was for some time much more in the surgery and hospital than in the mess. He gave up the eating, for the most part, of those vast quantities of beef and pudding, for which his stomach used to afford such ample and swift accommodation; and when the cloth was drawn, instead of taking twelve tumblers, and singing Irish melodies, as he used to do, in a horrible cracked yelling voice, he would retire to his own apartment, or gloomily pace the barrack-yard, or madly whip and spur a grey mare he had on the road to Leamington, where his Jemima (although invisible for him) still dwelt.

The season at Leamington coming to a conclusion by the withdrawal of the young fellows who frequented that watering-place, the widow Gam retired to her usual quarters for the other months of the year. Where these quarters were, I think we have no right to ask, for I believe she had quarrelled with her brother at Molloyville, and besides, was a great deal too proud to be a burden on anybody.

Not only did the widow quit Leamington, but very soon after-wards the 120th received its marching orders, and left Weedon and Warwickshire. Haggarty's appetite was by this time partially restored, but his love was not altered, and his humour was still morose and gloomy. I am informed that at this period of his life he wrote some poems relative to his unhappy passion; a wild set of verses of several lengths, and in his handwriting, being discovered upon a sheet of paper in which a pitch-plaster was wrapped up, which Lieutenant and Adjutant Wheezer was compelled to put on for a cold.

Fancy then, three years afterwards, the surprise of all Haggarty's acquaintances on reading in the public papers the following announcement:—

Married, at Monkstown on the 12th instant, Dionysius Haggarty, Esq., of HM 120th Foot, to Jemima Amelia Wilhelmina Molloy, daughter of the late Major Lancelot Gam, RM, and granddaughter of the late, and niece of the present Burke Bodkin Blake Molloy, Esq., Molloyville, county Mayo.

'Has the course of true love at last begun to run smooth?' thought I, as I laid down the paper; and the old times, and the old leering bragging widow, and the high shoulders of her daughter, and the jolly days with the 120th, and Doctor Jephson's one-horse chaise, and the Warwickshire hunt, and—and Louisa S——, but never mind *her*,—came back to my mind. Has that good-natured simple fellow at last met with his reward? Well, if he has not to marry the mother-in-law too, he may get on well enough.

Another year announced the retirement of Assistant-Surgeon Haggarty from the 120th, where he was replaced by Assistant-Surgeon Angus Rothsay Leech, a Scotchman, probably; with whom I have not the least acquaintance, and who has nothing whatever to do with this little history.

Still more years passed on, during which time I will not say that I kept a constant watch upon the fortunes of Mr Haggarty and his lady; for, perhaps, if the truth were known, I never thought for a moment about them; until one day, being at Kingstown, near Dublin, dawdling on the beach, and staring at the Hill of Howth, as most people at that watering-place do, I saw coming towards me a tall gaunt man, with a pair of bushy red whiskers, of which I thought I had seen the like in former years, and a face which could be no other than Haggarty's. It was Haggarty, ten years older than when we last met, and greatly more grim and thin. He had on one shoulder a young gentleman in a dirty tartan costume, and a face exceedingly like his own peeping from under a battered plume of black feathers, while with his other hand he was dragging a light green go-cart, in which reposed a female infant of some two years old. Both were roaring with great power of lungs.

As soon as Dennis saw me, his face lost the dull puzzled expression which had seemed to characterize it; he dropped the pole of the go-cart from one hand, and his son from the other, and came jumping forward to greet me with all his might, leaving his progeny roaring in the road.

'Bless my sowl,' says he, 'sure it's Fitz-Boodle? Fitz, don't you remember me? Dennis Haggarty of the 120th? Leamington, you know? Molloy, my boy, hould your tongue, and stop your screeching, and Jemima's too; d'ye hear? Well, it does good to sore eyes to see an old face. How fat you're grown, Fitz; and were ye ever in Ireland before? and a'n't ye delighted with it? Confess, now, isn't it beautiful?'

This question regarding the merits of their country, which I have remarked is put by most Irish persons, being answered in a satisfactory manner, and the shouts of the infants appeased from an apple-stall hard by, Dennis and I talked of old times; I congratulated him on his marriage with the lovely girl whom we all admired, and hoped he had a fortune with her, and so forth. His appearance, however, did not bespeak a great fortune: he had an old grey hat, short old trousers, an old waistcoat with regimental buttons, and patched Blucher boots, such as are not usually sported by persons in easy life.

'Ah!' says he, with a sigh, in reply to my queries, 'times are changed since them days, Fitz-Boodle. My wife's not what she was— the beautiful creature you knew her. Molloy, my boy, run off in a hurry to your mamma, and tell her an English gentleman is coming home to dine; for you'll dine with me, Fitz, in course?' And I agreed to partake of that meal; though Master Molloy altogether declined to obey his papa's orders with respect to announcing the stranger.

'Well, I must announce you myself,' said Haggarty, with a smile. 'Come, it's just dinner-time, and my little cottage is not a hundred yards off.' Accordingly, we all marched in procession to Dennis's little cottage, which was one of a row and a half of one-storied houses, with little courtyards before them, and mostly with very fine names on the door-posts of each. 'Surgeon Haggarty' was emblazoned on Dennis's gate, on a stained green copper-plate; and, not content with this, on the door-post above the bell was an oval with the inscription of 'New Molloyville'. The bell was broken, of course; the court, or garden-path, was mouldy, weedy, seedy; there were some dirty rocks, by way of ornament, round a faded glass-plat in the centre, some clothes and rags hanging out of most part of the windows of New Molloyville, the immediate entrance to which was by a battered scraper, under a broken trellis-work, up which a withered creeper declined any longer to climb.

'Small, but snug,' says Haggarty: 'I'll lead the way, Fitz; put your hat on the flower-pot there, and turn to the left into the drawing-room.' A fog of onions and turf-smoke filled the whole of the house, and gave signs that dinner was not far off. Far off? You could hear it frizzling in the kitchen, where the maid was also endeavouring to hush the crying of a third refractory child. But as we entered, all three of Haggarty's darlings were in full roar.

'Is it you, Dennis?' cried a sharp raw voice, from a dark corner in the drawing-room to which we were introduced, and in which a dirty tablecloth was laid for dinner, some bottles of porter and a cold mutton-bone being laid out on a rickety grand piano hard by. 'Ye're always late, Mr Haggarty. Have you brought the whisky from Nowlan's? I'll go bail ye've not, now.'

'My dear, I've brought an old friend of yours and mine to take pot-luck with us today,' said Dennis.

'When is he to come?' said the lady. At which speech I was rather surprised, for I stood before her.

'Here he is, Jemima my love,' answered Dennis, looking at me. 'Mr Fitz-Boodle: don't you remember him in Warwickshire, darling?'

'Mr Fitz-Boodle! I am very glad to see him,' said the lady, rising and curtseying with much cordiality.

Mrs Haggarty was blind.

Mrs Haggarty was not only blind, but it was evident that small-pox had been the cause of her loss of vision. Her eyes were bound with a bandage, her features were entirely swollen, scarred and distorted by the horrible effects of the malady. She had been knitting in a corner when we entered, and was wrapped in a very dirty bedgown. Her voice to me was quite different to that in which she addressed her husband. She spoke to Haggarty in broad Irish: she addressed me in that most odious of all languages—Irish-English, endeavouring to the utmost to disguise her brogue, and to speak with the true dawdling *distingué* English air.

'Are you long in I-a-land?' said the poor creature in this accent. 'You must faind it a sad ba'ba'ous place, Mr Fitz-Boodle, I'm shuah! It was vary kaind of you to come upon us *en famille*, and accept a dinner *sans cérémonie*. Mr Haggarty, I hope you'll put the waine into aice, Mr Fitz-Boodle must be melted with this hot weathah.'

For some time she conducted the conversation in this polite strain, and I was obliged to say, in reply to a query of hers, that I did not find her the least altered, though I should never have recognized her but for this rencontre. She told Haggarty with a significant air to get the wine from the cellah, and whispered to me that he was his own butlah; and the poor fellow, taking the hint, scudded away into the town for a pound of beefsteak and a couple of bottles of wine from the tavern.

'Will the childhren get their potatoes and butther here?' said a barefoot girl, with long black hair flowing over her face, which she thrust in at the door.

'Let them sup in the nursery, Elizabeth, and send—ah! Edwards to me.'

'Is it cook you mane, ma'am?' said the girl.

'Send her at once!' shrieked the unfortunate woman; and the noise of frying presently ceasing, a hot woman made her appearance, wiping her brows with her apron, and asking, with an accent decidedly Hibernian, what the misthress wanted.

'Lead me up to my dressing-room, Edwards: I really am not fit to be seen in this dishabille by Mr Fitz-Boodle.'

'Fait' I can't!' says Edwards; 'sure the masther's out at the butcher's, and can't look to the kitchen-fire!'

'Nonsense, I must go!' cried Mrs Haggarty; and so Edwards, putting on a resigned air, and giving her arm and face a further rub with her apron, held out her arm to Mrs Dennis, and the pair went upstairs.

She left me to indulge my reflections for half-an-hour, at the end of which period she came downstairs dressed in an old yellow satin, with the poor shoulders exposed just as much as ever. She had mounted a tawdry cap, which Haggarty himself must have selected for her. She had all sorts of necklaces, bracelets, and earrings in gold, in garnets, in mother-of-pearl, in ormolu. She brought in a furious savour of musk, which drove the odours of onions and turf-smoke before it; and she waved across her wretched angular mean scarred features an old cambric handkerchief with a yellow lace-border.

'And so you would have known me anywhere, Mr Fitz-Boodle?' said she, with a grin that was meant to be most fascinating. 'I was sure you would; for though my dreadful illness deprived me of my sight, it is a mercy that it did not change my features or complexion at all!'

This mortification had been spared the unhappy woman; but I don't know whether, with all her vanity, her infernal pride, folly, and selfishness, it was charitable to leave her in her error.

Yet why correct her? There is a quality in certain people which is above all advice, exposure, or correction. Only let a man or woman have DULNESS sufficient, and they need bow to no extant authority A dullard recognizes no betters; a dullard can't see that he is in the wrong; a dullard has no scruples of conscience, no doubts of pleasing, or succeeding, or doing right; no qualms for other people's feelings, no respect but for the fool himself. How can you make a fool perceive he is a fool? Such a personage can no more see his own folly than he can see his own ears. And the great quality of Dulness is to be unalterably contented with itself. What myriads of souls are there of this admirable sort,—selfish, stingy, ignorant, passionate, brutal; bad sons, mothers, fathers, never known to do kind actions!

To pause, however, in this disquisition, which was carrying us far off Kingstown, New Molloyville, Ireland—nay, into the wide world wherever Dulness inhabits—let it be stated that Mrs Haggarty, from my brief acquaintance with her and her mother, was of the order of persons just mentioned. There was an air of conscious merit about her, very hard to swallow along with the infamous dinner poor Dennis managed, after much delay, to get on the table. She did not fail to invite me to Molloyville, where she said her cousin would be charmed to see me; and she told me almost as many anecdotes about that place as her mother used to impart in former days. I observed, moreover, that Dennis cut her the favourite pieces of the beefsteak, that she ate thereof with great gusto, and that she drank with similar eagerness of the various strong liquors at table. 'We Irish ladies are all fond of a leetle glass of punch,' she said, with a playful air, and Dennis mixed her a powerful tumbler of such violent grog as I myself could swallow only with some difficulty. She talked of her suffering a great deal, of her sacrifices, of the luxuries to which she had been accustomed before marriage,—in a word, of a hundred of those themes on which some ladies are in the custom of enlarging when they wish to plague some husbands.

But honest Dennis, far from being angry at this perpetual, wearisome, impudent recurrence to her own superiority, rather encouraged the conversation than otherwise. It pleased him to hear his wife discourse about her merits and family splendours. He was so thoroughly beaten down and henpecked, that he, as it were, gloried in his servitude, and fancied that his wife's magnificence reflected credit on himself. He looked towards me, who was half sick of the woman and her egotism, as if expecting me to exhibit the deepest sympathy, and flung me glances across the table as much as to say, 'What a gifted creature my Jemima is, and what a fine fellow I am to be in possession of her!' When the children came down she scolded them, of course, and dismissed them abruptly (for which circumstance, perhaps, the writer of these pages was not in his heart very sorry), and, after having sat a preposterously long time, left us, asking whether we would have coffee there or in her boudoir.

'Oh! here, of course,' said Dennis, with rather a troubled air, and in about ten minutes the lovely creature was led back to us again by 'Edwards', and the coffee made its appearance. After coffee her husband begged her to let Mr Fitz-Boodle hear her voice: 'He longs for some of his old favourites.'

'No! do you?' said she; and was led in triumph to the jingling old piano, and with a screechy wiry voice, sang those very abominable old ditties which I had heard her sing at Leamington ten years back.

Haggarty, as she sang, flung himself back in the chair delighted. Husbands always are, and with the same song, one that they have heard when they were nineteen years old, probably; most Englishmen's tunes have that date, and it is rather affecting, I think, to hear an old gentleman of sixty or seventy quavering the old ditty that was fresh when *he* was fresh and in his prime. If he has a musical wife, depend on it he thinks her old songs of 1788 are better than any he has heard since: in fact he has heard *none* since. When the old couple are in high good-humour the old gentleman will take the old lady round the waist, and say, 'My dear, do sing me one of your own songs,' and she sits down and sings with her old voice, and, as she sings, the roses of her youth bloom again for a moment. Ranelagh resuscitates, and she is dancing a minuet in powder and a train.

This is another digression. It was occasioned by looking at poor Dennis's face while his wife was screeching (and, believe me, the former was the more pleasant occupation). Bottom tickled by the fairies could not have been in greater ecstasies. He thought the music was divine; and had further reason for exulting in it, which was, that his wife was always in a good humour after singing, and never would sing but in that happy frame of mind. Dennis had hinted so much in our little colloquy during the ten minutes of his lady's absence in the 'boudoir'; so, at the conclusion of each piece, we shouted 'Bravo!' and clapped our hands like mad.

Such was my insight into the life of Surgeon Dionysius Haggarty and his wife; and I must have come upon him at a favourable moment too, for poor Dennis has spoken, subsequently, of our delightful evening at Kingstown, and evidently thinks to this day that his friend was fascinated by the entertainment there. His inward economy was as follows: he had his half-pay, a thousand pounds, about a hundred a year that his father left, and his wife had sixty pounds a year from the mother; which the mother, of course, never paid. He had no practice, for he was absorbed in attention to his Jemima and the children, whom he used to wash, to dress, to carry out, to walk, or to ride, as we have seen, and who could not have a servant, as their dear blind mother could never be left alone. Mrs Haggarty, a great invalid, used to lie in bed till one, and have breakfast and hot luncheon there. A fifth part of his income was spent in having her wheeled about in a chair, by which it was his duty to walk daily for an allotted number of hours. Dinner would ensue, and the amateur clergy, who abound in Ireland, and of whom Mrs Haggarty was a great admirer, lauded her everywhere as a model of resignation and virtue, and praised beyond measure the admirable piety with which she bore her sufferings.

Well, every man to his taste. It did not certainly appear to me that *she* was the martyr of the family.

'The circumstances of my marriage with Jemima', Dennis said to me, in some after conversations we had on this interesting subject, 'were the most romantic and touching you can conceive. You saw what an impression the dear girl had made upon me when we were at Weedon; for from the first day I set eyes on her, and heard her sing her delightful song of "Dark-eyed Maiden of Araby", I felt, and said to Turniquet of ours, that very night, that *she* was the dark-eyed maid of Araby for *me*—not that she was, you know, for she was born in Shropshire. But I felt that I had seen the woman who was to make me happy or miserable for life. You know how I proposed for her at Kenilworth, and how I was rejected, and how I almost shot myself in consequence—no, you don't know that, for I said nothing about it to anyone, but I can tell you it was a very near thing; and a very lucky thing for me I didn't do it: for,—would you believe it?—the dear girl was in love with me all the time.'

'Was she really?' said I, who recollected that Miss Gam's love of those days showed itself in a very singular manner; but the fact is, when women are most in love they most disguise it.

'Over head and ears in love with poor Dennis,' resumed that worthy fellow, 'who'd ever have thought it? But I have it from the best authority, from her own mother, with whom I'm not over and above good friends now; but of this fact she assured me, and I'll tell you when and how.

'We were quartered at Cork three years after we were at Weedon, and it was our last year at home; and a great mercy that my dear girl spoke in time, or where should we have been *now*? Well, one day, marching home from parade, I saw a lady seated at an open window, by another who seemed an invalid, and the lady at the window, who was dressed in the profoundest mourning, cried out, with a scream, "Gracious heavens! it's Mr Haggarty of the 120th."

'"Sure I know that voice," says I to Whiskerton.

'"It's a great mercy you don't know it a deal too well," says he: "it's Lady Gammon. She's on some husband-hunting scheme, depend on it, for that daughter of hers. She was at Bath last year on the same errand, and at Cheltenham the year before, where, Heaven bless you! she's as well known as the 'Hen and Chickens.'"

'"I'll thank you not to speak disrespectfully of Miss Jemima Gam," said I to Whiskerton; "she's of one of the first families in Ireland, and whoever says a word against a woman I once proposed for, insults me,—do you understand?"

'"Well, marry her, if you like," says Whiskerton, quite peevish: "marry her, and be hanged!"

'Marry her! the very idea of it set my brain a-whirling, and made me a thousand times more mad than I am by nature.

'You may be sure I walked up the hill to the parade-ground that afternoon, and with a beating heart too. I came to the widow's house. It was called "New Molloyville", as this is. Wherever she takes a house for six months she calls it "New Molloyville"; and has had one in Mallow, in Bandon, in Sligo, in Castlebar, in Fermoy, in Drogheda, and the deuce knows where besides: but the blinds were down, and though I thought I saw somebody behind 'em, no notice was taken of poor Denny Haggarty, and I paced up and down all mess-time in hopes of catching a glimpse of Jemima, but in vain. The next day I was on the ground again; I was just as much in love as ever, that's the fact. I'd never been in that way before, look you; and when once caught, I knew it was for life.

'There's no use in telling you how long I beat about the bush, but when I *did* get admittance to the house (it was through the means of young Castlereagh Molloy, whom you may remember at Leamington, and who was at Cork for the regatta, and used to dine at our mess, and had taken a mighty fancy to me)—when I *did* get into the house, I say, I rushed *in medias res* at once; I couldn't keep myself quiet, my heart was too full.

'Oh, Fitz! I shall never forget the day,—the moment I was inthrojuiced into the dthrawing-room' (as he began to be agitated, Dennis's brogue broke out with greater richness than ever; but though a stranger may catch, and repeat from memory, a few words, it is next to impossible for him to *keep up a conversation* in Irish, so that we had best give up all attempts to imitate Dennis). 'When I saw old mother Gam,' said he, 'my feelings overcame me all at once. I rowled down on the ground, sir, as if I'd been hit by a musket-ball. "Dearest madam," says I, "I'll die if you don't give me Jemima."

'"Heavens, Mr Haggarty!" says she, "how you seize me with

surprise! Castlereagh, my dear nephew, had you not better leave us?". and away he went, lighting a cigar, and leaving me still on the floor.

'"Rise, Mr Haggarty," continued the widow. "I will not attempt to deny that this constancy towards my daughter is extremely affecting, however sudden your present appeal may be. I will not attempt to deny that, perhaps, Jemima may have a similar feeling; but, as I said, I never could give my daughter to a Catholic."

'"I'm as good a Protestant as yourself, ma'am," says I; "my mother was an heiress, and we were all brought up her way."

'"That makes the matter very different," says she, turning up the whites of her eyes. "How could I ever have reconciled it to my conscience to see my blessed child married to a Papist? How could I ever have taken him to Molloyville? Well, this obstacle being removed, *I* must put myself no longer in the way between two young people. *I* must sacrifice myself; as I always have when my darling girl was in question. You shall see her, the poor dear lovely gentle sufferer, and learn your fate from her own lips."

'"The sufferer, ma'am," says I; "has Miss Gam been ill?"

'": What! haven't you heard?" cried the widow. "Haven't you heard of the dreadful illness which so nearly carried her from me? For nine weeks, Mr Haggarty, I watched her day and night, without taking a wink of sleep,—for nine weeks she lay trembling between death and life; and I paid the doctor eighty-three guineas. She is restored now; but she is the wreck of the beautiful creature she was. Suffering, and, perhaps, *another disappointment*—but we won't mention that *now*—have so pulled her down. But I will leave you, and prepare my sweet girl for this strange, this entirely unexpected visit."

'I won't tell you what took place between me and Jemima, to whom I was introduced as she sat in the darkened room, poor sufferer! nor describe to you with what a thrill of joy I seized (after groping about for it) her poor emaciated hand. She did not withdraw it; I came out of that room an engaged man, sir; and *now* I was enabled to show her that I had always loved her sincerely, for there was my will, made three years back, in her favour: that night she refused me, as I told ye. I would have shot myself, but they'd have brought me in *non compos*; and my brother Mick would have contested the will, and so I determined to live, in order that she might benefit by my dying. I had but a thousand pounds then: since that my father has left me two more. I willed every shilling to her, as you may fancy, and settled it upon her when we married, as we did soon after. It was not for some time that I was allowed to see the poor girl's face, or, indeed, was aware of the horrid loss she had sustained. Fancy my agony, my dear fellow, when I saw that beautiful wreck!'

There was something not a little affecting to think, in the conduct of this brave fellow, that he never once, as he told his story, seemed to allude to the possibility of his declining to marry a woman who was not the same as the woman he loved; but that he was quite as faithful to her now, as he had been when captivated by the poor tawdry charms of the silly Miss of Leamington. It was hard that such a noble heart as this should be flung away upon yonder foul mass of greedy vanity. Was it hard, or not, that he should remain deceived in his obstinate humility, and continue to admire the selfish silly being whom he had chosen to worship?

'I should have been appointed surgeon of the regiment', continued Dennis, 'soon after, when it was ordered abroad to Jamaica, where it now is. But my wife would not hear of going, and said she would break her heart if she left her mother. So I retired on half-pay, and took this cottage; and in case any practice should fall in my way—why, there is my name on the brass plate, and I'm ready for anything that comes. But the only case that ever *did* come was one day when I was driving my wife in the chaise; and another, one night, of a beggar with a broken head. My wife makes me a present of a baby every year, and we've no debts; and between you and me and the post, as long as my mother-in-law is out of the house, I'm as happy as I need be.'

'What! you and the old lady don't get on well?' said I.

'I can't say we do; it's not in nature, you know,' said Dennis, with a faint grin. 'She comes into the house, and turns it topsy-turvy. When she's here I'm obliged to sleep in the scullery. She's never paid her daughter's income since the first year, though she brags about her sacrifices as if she had ruined herself for Jemima; and besides, when she's here, there's a whole clan of the Molloys, horse, foot, and dragoons, that are quartered upon us, and eat me out of house and home.'

'And is Molloyville such a fine place as the widow described it?' asked I, laughing, and not a little curious.

'Oh, a mighty fine place entirely!' said Dennis. 'There's the oak park of two hundred acres, the finest land ye ever saw, only they've cut all the wood down. The garden in the old Molloys' time, they say, was the finest ever seen in the West of Ireland; but they've taken all the glass to mend the house windows: and small blame to them either. There's a clear rent-roll of thirty-five hundred a year, only it's in the hand of receivers; besides other debts, for which there is no land security.'

'Your cousin-in-law, Castlereagh Molloy, won't come into a large fortune?'

'Oh, he'll do very well,' said Dennis. 'As long as he can get credit, he's not the fellow to stint himself. Faith, I was fool enough to put my name to a bit of paper for him, and as they could not catch him in Mayo, they laid hold of me at Kingstown here. And there was a pretty to do. Didn't Mrs Gam say I was ruining her family, that's all? I paid it by instalments (for all my money is settled on Jemima); and Castlereagh, who's an honourable fellow, offered me any satisfaction in life. Anyhow, he couldn't do more than *that*.'

'Of course not: and now you're friends?'

'Yes, and he and his aunt have had a tiff, too; and he abuses her properly, I warrant ye. He says that she carried about Jemima from place to place, and flung her at the head of every unmarried man in England a'most—my poor Jemima, and she all the while dying in love with me! As soon as she got over the small-pox—she took it at Fermoy—God bless her, I wish I'd been by to be her nurse-tender—as soon as she was rid of it, the old lady said to Castlereagh, "Castlereagh, go to the bar'cks, and find out in the Army List where the 120th is." Off she came to Cork hot foot. It appears that while she was ill, Jemima's love for me showed itself in such a violent way that her mother was overcome, and promised that, should the dear child recover, she would try and bring us together. Castlereagh says she would have gone after us to Jamaica.'

'I have no doubt she would,' said I.

'Could you have a stronger proof of love than that?' cried Dennis. 'My dear girl's illness and frightful blindness have, of course, injured her health and her temper. She cannot in her position look to the children, you know, and so they come under my charge for the most part; and her temper is unequal, certainly. But you see what a sensitive, refined, elegant creature she is, and may fancy that she's often put out by a rough fellow like me.'

Here Dennis left me, saying it was time to go and walk out the children; and I think his story has matter of some wholesome reflection in it for bachelors who are about to change their condition, or may console some who are mourning their celibacy. Marry, gentlemen, if you like; leave your comfortable dinner at the club for cold-mutton and curl-papers at your home; give up your books or pleasures, and take to yourselves wives and children; but think well on what you do first, as I have no doubt you will after this advice and example. Advice is always useful in matters of love; men always take it; they always follow other people's opinions, not their own: they always profit by example. When they see a pretty woman, and feel the delicious madness of love coming over them, they always stop to calculate her temper, her money, their own money, or suitableness for the married life. . . . Ha, ha, ha! Let us fool in this way no more. I have been in love forty-three times with all ranks and conditions of women, and would have married every time if they would have let me. How many wives had King Solomon, the wisest of men? And is not that story a warning to us that Love is master of the wisest? It is only fools who defy him.

I must come, however, to the last, and perhaps the saddest, part of poor Denny Haggarty's history. I met him once more, and in such a condition as made me determine to write this history.

In the month of June last I happened to be at Richmond, a delightful little place of retreat; and there, sunning himself upon the terrace, was my old friend of the 120th: he looked older, thinner, poorer, and more wretched than I had ever seen him. 'What! you have given up Kingstown?' said I, shaking him by the hand.

'Yes,' says he.

'And is my lady and your family here at Richmond?'

'No,' says he, with a sad shake of the head; and the poor fellow's hollow eyes filled with tears.

'Good heavens, Denny! what's the matter?' said I. He was squeezing my hand like a vice as I spoke.

'They've LEFT me!' he burst out with a dreadful shout of passionate grief—a horrible scream which seemed to be wrenched out of his heart. 'Left me!' said he, sinking down on a seat, and clenching his great fists, and shaking his lean arms wildly. 'I'm a wise man now, Mr Fitz-Boodle. Jemima has gone away from me, and yet you know how I loved her, and how happy we were! I've got nobody now; but I'll die soon, that's one comfort: and to think it's she that'll kill me after all!'

The story, which he told with a wild and furious lamentation such as is not known among men of our cooler country, and such as I don't like now to recall, was a very simple one. The mother-in-law had taken possession of the house, and had driven him from it. His property at his marriage was settled on his wife. She had never loved him, and told him this secret at last, and drove him out of doors with her selfish scorn and ill-temper. The boy had died; the girls were better, he said, brought up among the Molloys than they could be with him; and so he was quite alone in the world, and was living, or rather dying, on forty pounds a year.

His troubles are very likely over by this time. The two fools who caused his misery will never read this history of him; *they* never read godless stories in magazines: and I wish, honest reader, that you and I went to church as much as they do. These people are not wicked *because* of their religious observances, but *in spite* of them. They are too dull to understand humility, too blind to see a tender and simple heart under a rough ungainly bosom. They are sure that all their conduct towards my poor friend here has been perfectly righteous, and that they have given proofs of the most Christian virtue. Haggarty's wife is considered by her friends as a martyr to a savage husband, and her mother is the angel that has come to rescue her. All they did was to cheat him and desert him. And safe in that wonderful self-complacency with which the fools of this earth are endowed, they have not a single pang of conscience for their villany towards him, and consider their heartlessness as a proof and consequence of their spotless piety and virtue.

ANTHONY TROLLOPE

The Parson's Daughter of Oxney Colne

THE prettiest scenery in all England—and if I am contradicted in that assertion, I will say in all Europe—is in Devonshire, on the southern and south-eastern skirts of Dartmoor, where the rivers Dart, and Avon, and Teign form themselves, and where the broken moor is half cultivated, and the wild-looking upland fields are half moor. In making this assertion I am often met with much doubt, but it is by persons who do not really know the locality. Men and women talk to me on the matter, who have travelled down the line of railway from Exeter to Plymouth, who have spent a fortnight at Torquay, and perhaps made an excursion from Tavistock to the convict prison on Dartmoor. But who knows the glories of Chagford? Who has walked through the parish of Manaton? Who is conversant with Lustleigh Cleeves and Withycombe in the moor? Who has explored Holne Chase? Gentle reader, believe me that you will be rash in contradicting me, unless you have done these things.

There or thereabouts—I will not say by the waters of which little river it is washed—is the parish of Oxney Colne. And for those who would wish to see all the beauties of this lovely country, a sojourn in Oxney Colne would be most desirable, seeing that the sojourner would then be brought nearer to all that he would wish to visit, than at any other spot in the country. But there is an objection to any such arrangement. There are only two decent houses in the whole parish, and these are—or were when I knew the locality—small and fully occupied by their possessors. The larger and better is the parsonage, in which lived the parson and his daughter; and the smaller is the freehold residence of a certain Miss Le Smyrger, who owned a farm of a hundred acres, which was rented by one Farmer Cloysey, and who also possessed some thirty acres round her own house, which she managed herself, regarding herself to be quite as great in cream as Mr Cloysey, and altogether superior to him in the article of cider. 'But yeu has to pay no rent, Miss,' Farmer Cloysey would say, when Miss Le Smyrger expressed this opinion of her art in a manner too defiant. 'Yeu pays no rent, or yeu couldn't do it.' Miss Le Smyrger was an old maid, with a pedigree and blood of her own, a hundred and thirty acres of fee-simple land on the borders of Dartmoor, fifty years of age, a constitution of iron, and an opinion of her own on every subject under the sun.

And now for the parson and his daughter. The parson's name was Woolsworthy—or Woolathy as it was pronounced by all those who lived around him—the Revd Saul Woolsworthy; and his daughter was Patience Woolsworthy, or Miss Patty, as she was known to the Devonshire world of those parts. That name of Patience had not been well chosen for her, for she was a hot-tempered damsel, warm in her convictions, and inclined to express them freely. She had but two closely intimate friends in the world, and by both of them this freedom of expression had now been fully permitted to her since she was a child. Miss Le Smyrger and her father were well accustomed to her ways, and on the whole well satisfied with them. The former was equally free and equally warm-tempered as herself, and as Mr Woolsworthy was allowed by his daughter to be quite paramount on his own subject—for he had a subject—he did not object to his daughter being paramount on all others. A pretty girl was Patience Woolsworthy at the time of which I am writing, and one who possessed much that was worthy of remark and admiration, had she lived where beauty meets with admiration, or where force of character is remarked. But at Oxney Colne, on the borders of Dartmoor, there were few to appreciate her, and it seemed as though she herself had but little idea of carrying her talent further afield, so that it might not remain for ever wrapped in a blanket.

She was a pretty girl, tall and slender, with dark eyes and black hair. Her eyes were perhaps too round for regular beauty, and her hair was perhaps too crisp; her mouth was large and expressive; her nose was finely formed, though a critic in female form might have declared it to be somewhat broad. But her countenance altogether was wonderfully attractive—if only it might be seen without that resolution for dominion which occasionally marred it, though sometimes it even added to her attractions.

It must be confessed on behalf of Patience Woolsworthy, that the circumstances of her life had peremptorily called upon her to exercise dominion. She had lost her mother when she was sixteen, and had had neither brother nor sister. She had no neighbours near her fit either from education or rank to interfere in the conduct of her life, excepting always Miss Le Smyrger. Miss Le Smyrger would have done anything for her, including the whole management of her morals and of the parsonage household, had Patience been content with such an arrangement. But much as Patience had ever loved Miss Le Smyrger, she was not content with this, and therefore she had been called on to put forth a strong hand of her own. She had put forth this strong hand early, and hence had come the character which I am attempting to describe. But I must say on behalf of this girl, that it was not only over others that she thus exercised dominion. In acquiring that power she had also acquired the much greater power of exercising rule over herself.

But why should her father have been ignored in these family arrangements? Perhaps it may almost suffice to say, that of all living men her father was the man best conversant with the antiquities of the county in which he lived. He was the Jonathan Oldbuck of Devonshire, and especially of Dartmoor, without that decision of character which enabled Oldbuck to keep his womenkind in some kind of subjection, and probably enabled him also to see that his weekly bills did not pass their proper limits. Our Mr Oldbuck, of Oxney Colne, was sadly deficient in these. As a parish pastor with but a small cure, he did his duty with sufficient energy to keep him, at any rate, from reproach. He was kind and charitable to the poor, punctual in his services, forbearing with the farmers around him, mild with his brother clergymen, and indifferent to aught that bishop or archdeacon might think or say of him. I do not name this latter attribute as a virtue, but as a fact. But all these points were as nothing in the known character of Mr Woolsworthy, of Oxney Colne. He was the antiquarian of Dartmoor. That was his line of life. It was in that capacity that he was known to the Devonshire world; it was as such that he journeyed about with his humble carpet-bag, staying away from his parsonage a night or two at a time; it was in that character that he received now and again stray visitors in the single spare bedroom—not friends asked to see him and his girl because of their friendship—but men who knew something as to this buried stone, or that old land-mark. In all these things his daughter let him have his own way, assisting and encouraging him. That was his line of life, and therefore she respected it. But in all other matters she chose to be paramount at the parsonage.

Mr Woolsworthy was a little man, who always wore, except on Sundays, grey clothes—clothes of so light a grey that they would hardly have been regarded as clerical in a district less remote. He had now reached a goodly age, being full seventy years old; but still he was wiry and active, and shewed but few symptoms of decay. His head was bald, and the few remaining locks that surrounded it were nearly white. But there was a look of energy about his mouth, and a humour in his light grey eye, which forbade those who knew him to regard him altogether as an old man. As it was, he could walk from Oxney Colne to Priestown, fifteen long Devonshire miles across the moor; and he who could do that could hardly be regarded as too old for work.

But our present story will have more to do with his daughter than with him. A pretty girl, I have said, was Patience Woolsworthy; and one, too, in many ways remarkable. She had taken her outlook into life, weighing the things which she had and those which she had not, in a manner very unusual, and, as a rule, not always desirable for a young lady. The things which she had not were very many. She had not society; she had not a fortune; she had not any assurance of future means of livelihood; she had not high hope of procuring for herself a position in life by marriage; she had not that excitement and pleasure in life which she read of in such books as found their way down to Oxney Colne Parsonage. It would be easy to add to the list of the things which she had not; and this list against herself she made out with the utmost vigour. The things which she had, or those rather which she assured herself of having, were much more easily counted. She had the birth and education of a lady, the strength of a healthy woman, and a will of her own. Such was the list as she made it out for herself, and I protest that I assert no more than the truth in saying that she never added to it either beauty, wit, or talent.

I began these descriptions by saying that Oxney Colne would, of all places, be the best spot from which a tourist could visit those parts of Devonshire, but for the fact that he could obtain there none of the accommodation which tourists require. A brother antiquarian might, perhaps, in those days have done so, seeing that there was, as I have said, a spare bedroom at the parsonage. Any intimate friend of Miss Le Smyrger's might be as fortunate, for she was equally well provided at Oxney Combe, by which name her house was known. But Miss Le Smyrger was not given to extensive hospitality, and it was only to those who were bound to her, either by ties of blood or of very old friendship, that she delighted to open her doors. As her old friends were very few in number, as those few lived at a distance, and as her nearest relations were higher in the world than she was, and were said by herself to look down upon her, the visits made to Oxney Combe were few and far between.

But now, at the period of which I am writing, such a visit was about to be made. Miss Le Smyrger had a younger sister, who had inherited a property in the parish of Oxney Colne equal to that of the lady who now lived there; but this the younger sister had inherited beauty also, and she therefore, in early life, had found sundry lovers, one of whom became her husband. She had married a man even then well to do in the world, but now rich and almost mighty; a Member of Parliament, a Lord of this and that board, a man who had a house in Eaton-square, and a park in the north of England; and in this way her course of life had been very much divided from that of our Miss Le Smyrger. But the Lord of the Government Board had been blessed with various children; and perhaps it was now thought expedient to look after Aunt Penelope's Devonshire acres. Aunt Penelope was empowered to leave them to whom she pleased; and though it was thought in Eaton-square that she must, as a matter of course, leave them to one of the family, nevertheless a little cousinly intercourse might make the thing more certain. I will not say that this was the sole cause for such a visit, but in these days a visit was to be made by Captain Broughton to his aunt. Now Captain John Broughton was the second son of Alfonso Broughton, of Clapham Park and Eaton-square, Member of Parliament, and Lord of the aforesaid Government Board.

'And what do you mean to do with him?' Patience Woolsworthy asked of Miss Le Smyrger when that lady walked over from the Combe to say that her nephew John was to arrive on the following morning.

'Do with him? Why, I shall bring him over here to talk to your father.'

'He'll be too fashionable for that, and papa won't trouble his head about him if he finds that he doesn't care for Dartmoor.'

'Then he may fall in love with you, my dear.'

'Well, yes; there's that resource at any rate, and for your sake I dare say I should be more civil to him than papa. But he'll soon get tired of making love, and what you'll do then I cannot imagine.'

That Miss Woolsworthy felt no interest in the coming of the Captain I will not pretend to say. The advent to any stranger with whom she would be called on to associate must be matter of interest to her in that secluded place; and she was not so absolutely unlike other young ladies that the arrival of an unmarried young man would be the same to her as the advent of some patriarchal paterfamilias. In taking that outlook into life of which I have spoken she had never said to herself that she despised those things from which other girls received the excitement, the joys, and the disappointment of their lives. She had simply given herself to understand that very little of such things would come her way, and that it behoved her to live—to live happily if such might be possible—without experiencing the need of them. She had heard, when there was no thought of any such visit to Oxney Colne, that John Broughton was a handsome, clever man—one who thought much of himself, and was thought much of by others—that there had been some talk of his marrying a great heiress, which marriage, however, had not taken place through unwillingness on his part, and that he was on the whole a man of more mark in the world than the ordinary captain of ordinary regiments.

Captain Broughton came to Oxney Combe, stayed there a fortnight,—the intended period for his projected visit having been fixed at three or four days—and then went his way. He went his way back to his London haunts, the time of the year then being the close of the Easter holydays; but as he did so he told his aunt that he should assuredly return to her in the autumn.

'And assuredly I shall be happy to see you, John—if you come with a certain purpose. If you have no such purpose, you had better remain away.'

'I shall assuredly come,' the Captain had replied, and then he had gone on his journey.

The summer passed rapidly by, and very little was said between Miss Le Smyrger and Miss Woolsworthy about Captain Broughton.

In many respects—nay, I may say, as to all ordinary matters, no two women could well be more intimate with each other than they were,—and more than that, they had the courage each to talk to the other with absolute truth as to things concerning themselves— a courage in which dear friends often fail. But, nevertheless, very little was said between them about Captain John Broughton. All that was said may be here repeated.

'John says that he shall return here in August,' Miss Le Smyrger said, as Patience was sitting with her in the parlour at Oxney Combe, on the morning after that gentleman's departure.

'He told me so himself,' said Patience; and as she spoke her round dark eyes assumed a look of more than ordinary self-will. If Miss Le Smyrger had intended to carry the conversation any further, she changed her mind as she looked at her companion. Then, as I said, the summer ran by, and towards the close of the warm days of July, Miss Le Smyrger, sitting in the same chair in the same room, again took up the conversation.

'I got a letter from John this morning. He says that he shall be here on the third.'

'Does he?'

'He is very punctual to the time he named.'

'Yes; I fancy that he is a punctual man,' said Patience.

'I hope that you will be glad to see him,' said Miss Le Smyrger.

'Very glad to see him,' said Patience, with a bold clear voice; and then the conversation was again dropped, and nothing further was said till after Captain Broughton's second arrival in the parish.

Four months had then passed since his departure, and during that time Miss Woolsworthy had performed all her usual daily duties in their accustomed course. No one could discover that she had been less careful in her household matters than had been her wont, less willing to go among her poor neighbours, or less assiduous in her attentions to her father. But not the less was there a feeling in the minds of those around her that some great change had come upon her. She would sit during the long summer evenings on a certain spot outside the parsonage orchard, at the top of a small sloping field in which their solitary cow was always pastured, with a book on her knees before her, but rarely reading. There she would sit, with the beautiful view down to the winding river below her, watching the setting sun, and thinking, thinking, thinking—thinking of something of which she had never spoken. Often would Miss Le Smyrger come upon her there, and sometimes would pass by her even without a word; but never—never once did she dare to ask her of the matter of her thoughts. But she knew the matter well enough. No confession was necessary to inform her that Patience Woolsworthy was in love with John Broughton—ay, in love, to the full and entire loss of her whole heart.

On one evening she was so sitting till the July sun had fallen and hidden himself for the night, when her father came upon her as he returned from one of his rambles on the moor. 'Patty,' he said, 'you are always sitting there now. Is it not late? Will you not be cold?'

'No, papa,' she said, 'I shall not be cold.'

'But won't you come to the house? I miss you when you come in so late that there's no time to say a word before we go to bed.'

She got up and followed him into the parsonage, and when they were in the sitting-room together, and the door was closed, she came up to him and kissed him. 'Papa,' she said, 'would it make you very unhappy if I were to leave you?'

'Leave me!' he said, startled by the serious and almost solemn tone of her voice. 'Do you mean for always?'

'If I were to marry, papa?'

'Oh, marry! No; that would not make me unhappy. It would make me very happy, Patty, to see you married to a man you would love—very, very happy; though my days would be desolate without you.'

'That is it, papa. What would you do if I went from you?'

'What would it matter, Patty? I should be free, at any rate, from a load which often presses heavy on me now. What will you do when I shall leave you? A few more years and all will be over with me. But who is it, love? Has anybody said anything to you?'

'It was only an idea, papa. I don't often think of such a thing; but I did think of it then.' And so the subject was allowed to pass by. This had happened before the day of the second arrival had been absolutely fixed and made known to Miss Woolsworthy.

And then that second arrival took place. The reader may have understood from the words with which Miss Le Smyrger authorized her nephew to make his second visit to Oxney Combe that Miss Woolsworthy's passion was not altogether unauthorized. Captain

Broughton had been told that he was not to come unless he came with a certain purpose; and having been so told, he still persisted in coming. There can be no doubt but that he well understood the purport to which his aunt alluded. 'I shall assuredly come,' he had said. And true to his word, he was now there.

Patience knew exactly the hour at which he must arrive at the station at Newton Abbot, and the time also which it would take to travel over those twelve uphill miles from the station to Oxney. It need hardly be said that she paid no visit to Miss Le Smyrger's house on that afternoon; but she might have known something of Captain Broughton's approach without going thither. His road to the Combe passed by the parsonage-gate, and had Patience sat even at her bedroom window she must have seen him. But on such a morning she would not sit at her bedroom window—she would do nothing which would force her to accuse herself of a restless longing for her lover's coming. It was for him to seek her. If he chose to do so, he knew the way to the parsonage.

Miss Le Smyrger—good, dear, honest, hearty Miss Le Smyrger, was in a fever of anxiety on behalf of her friend. It was not that she wished her nephew to marry Patience—or rather that she had entertained any such wish when he first came among them. She was not given to match-making, and moreover thought, or had thought within herself, that they of Oxney Colne could do very well without any admixture from Eaton-square. Her plan of life had been that, when old Mr Woolsworthy was taken away from Dartmoor, Patience should live with her; and that when she also shuffled off her coil, then Patience Woolsworthy should be the maiden mistress of Oxney Combe—of Oxney Combe and Mr Cloysey's farm—to the utter detriment of all the Broughtons. Such had been her plan before nephew John had come among them—a plan not to be spoken of till the coming of that dark day which should make Patience an orphan. But now her nephew had been there, and all was to be altered. Miss Le Smyrger's plan would have provided a companion for her old age; but that had not been her chief object. She had thought more of Patience than of herself, and now it seemed that a prospect of a higher happiness was opening for her friend.

'John,' she said, as soon as the first greetings were over, 'do you remember the last words that I said to you before you went away?'

Now, for myself, I much admire Miss Le Smyrger's heartiness, but I do not think much of her discretion. It would have been better, perhaps, had she allowed things to take their course.

'I can't say that I do,' said the Captain. At the same time the Captain did remember very well what those last words had been.

'I am so glad to see you, so delighted to see you, if—if—if—,' and then she paused, for with all her courage she hardly dared to ask her nephew whether he had come there with the express purpose of asking Miss Woolsworthy to marry him.

To tell the truth—for there is no room for mystery within the limits of this short story,—to tell, I say, at a word the plain and simple truth, Captain Broughton had already asked that question. On the day before he left Oxney Colne, he had in set terms proposed to the parson's daughter, and indeed the words, the hot and frequent words, which previously to that had fallen like sweetest honey into the ears of Patience Woolsworthy, had made it imperative on him to do so. When a man in such a place as that has talked to a girl of love day after day, must not he talk of it to some definite purpose on the day on which he leaves her? Or if he do not, must he not submit to be regarded as false, selfish, and almost fraudulent? Captain Broughton, however, had asked the question honestly and truly. He had done so honestly and truly, but in words, or, perhaps, simply with a tone, that had hardly sufficed to satisfy the proud spirit of the girl he loved. She by that time had confessed to herself that she loved him with all her heart; but she had made no such confession to him. To him she had spoken no word, granted no favour, that any lover might rightfully regard as a token of love returned. She had listened to him as he spoke, and bade him keep such sayings for the drawing-rooms of his 'fashionable friends'. Then he had spoken out and had asked for that hand,—not, perhaps, as a suitor tremulous with hope,—but as a rich man who knows that he can command that which he desires to purchase.

'You should think more of this,' she had said to him at last. 'If you would really have me for your wife, it will not be much to you to return here again when time for thinking of it shall have passed by.' With these words she had dismissed him, and now he had again come back to Oxney Colne. But still she would not place herself at the window to look for him, nor dress herself in other than her simple morning country dress, nor omit one item of her daily work. If he wished to take her at all, he should wish to take her as she really was, in her plain country life, but he should take her also with full observance of all those privileges which maidens are allowed to claim from their lovers. He should contract no ceremonious observance because she was the daughter of a poor country parson who would come to him without a shilling, whereas he stood high in the world's books. He had asked her to give him all that she had, and that all she was ready to give, without stint. But the gift must be valued before it could be given or received. He also was to give her as much, and she would accept it as being beyond all price. But she would not allow that that which was offered to her was in any degree the more precious because of his outward worldly standing.

She would not pretend to herself that she thought he would come to her that day, and therefore she busied herself in the kitchen and about the house, giving directions to her two maids as though the afternoon would pass as all other days did pass in that household. They usually dined at four, and she rarely, in these summer months, went far from the house before that hour. At four precisely she sat down with her father, and then said that she was going up as far as Helpholme after dinner. Helpholme was a solitary farmhouse in another parish, on the border of the moor, and Mr Woolsworthy asked her whether he should accompany her.

'Do, papa,' she said, 'if you are not too tired.' And yet she had thought how probable it might be that she should meet John Broughton on her walk. And so it was arranged; but, just as dinner was over, Mr Woolsworthy remembered himself.

'Gracious me,' he said, 'how my memory is going. Gribbles, from Ivybridge, and old John Poulter, from Bovey, are coming to meet here by appointment. You can't put Helpholme off till tomorrow?'

Patience, however, never put off anything, and therefore at six o'clock, when her father had finished his slender modicum of toddy, she tied on her hat and went on her walk. She started forth with a quick step, and left no word to say by which route she would go. As she passed up along the little lane which led towards Oxney Combe, she would not even look to see if he was coming towards her; and when she left the road, passing over a stone stile into a little path which ran first through the upland fields, and then across the moor ground towards Helpholme, she did not look back once, or listen for his coming step.

She paid her visit, remaining upwards of an hour with the old bedridden mother of the tenant of Helpholme. 'God bless you, my darling!' said the old woman as she left her; 'and send you some one to make your own path bright and happy through the world.' These words were still ringing in her ears with all their significance as she saw John Broughton waiting for her at the first stile which she had to pass after leaving the farmer's haggard.

'Patty,' he said, as he took her hand, and held it close within both his own, 'what a chase I have had after you!'

'And who asked you, Captain Broughton?' she answered, smiling. 'If the journey was too much for your poor London strength, could you not have waited till tomorrow morning, when you would have found me at the parsonage?' But she did not draw her hand away from him, or in any way pretend that he had not a right to accost her as a lover.

'No, I could not wait. I am more eager to see those I love than you seem to be.'

'How do you know whom I love, or how eager I might be to see them? There is an old woman there whom I love, and I have thought nothing of this walk with the object of seeing her.' And now, slowly drawing her hand away from him, she pointed to the farmhouse which she had left.

'Patty,' he said, after a minute's pause, during which she had looked full into his face with all the force of her bright eyes; 'I have come from London today, straight down here to Oxney, and from my aunt's house close upon your footsteps after you, to ask you that one question. Do you love me?'

'What a Hercules!' she said, again laughing. 'Do you really mean that you left London only this morning? Why, you must have been five hours in a railway carriage and two in a postchaise, not to talk of the walk afterwards. You ought to take more care of yourself, Captain Broughton!'

He would have been angry with her—for he did not like to be quizzed—had she not put her hand on his arm as she spoke, and the softness of her touch had redeemed the offence of her words.

'All that have I done,' said he, 'that I may hear one word from you.'

'That any word of mine should have such potency! But let us walk on, or my father will take us for some of the standing stones of the moor. How have you found your aunt? If you only knew the cares that have sat on her dear shoulders for the last week past, in order that your high mightiness might have a sufficiency to eat and drink in these desolate half-starved regions.'

'She might have saved herself such anxiety. No one can care less for such things than I do.'

'And yet I think I have heard you boast of the cook of your club.' And then again there was silence for a minute or two.

'Patty,' said he, stopping again in the path; 'answer my question. I have a right to demand an answer. Do you love me?'

'And what if I do? What if I have been so silly as to allow your perfections to be too many for my weak heart? What then, Captain Broughton?'

'It cannot be that you love me, or you would not joke now.'

'Perhaps not, indeed,' she said. It seemed as though she were resolved not to yield an inch in her own humour. And then again they walked on.

'Patty,' he said once more, 'I shall get an answer from you tonight,— this evening; now, during this walk, or I shall return tomorrow, and never revisit this spot again.'

'Oh, Captain Broughton, how should we ever manage to live without you?'

'Very well,' he said; 'up to the end of this walk I can bear it all;—and one word spoken then will mend it all.'

During the whole of this time she felt that she was ill-using him. She knew that she loved him with all her heart; that it would nearly kill her to part with him; that she had heard his renewed offer with an ecstacy of joy. She acknowledged to herself that he was giving proof of his devotion as strong as any which a girl could receive from her lover. And yet she could hardly bring herself to say the word he longed to hear. That word once said, and then she knew that she must succumb to her love for ever! That word once said, and there would be nothing for her but to spoil him with her idolatry! That word once said, and she must continue to repeat it into his ears, till perhaps he might be tired of hearing it! And now he had threatened her, and how could she speak it after that? She certainly would not speak it unless he asked her again without such threat. And so they walked on again in silence.

'Patty,' he said at last. 'By the heavens above us you shall answer me. Do you love me?'

She now stood still, and almost trembled as she looked up into his face. She stood opposite to him for a moment, and then placing her two hands on his shoulders, she answered him. 'I do, I do, I do,' she said, 'with all my heart; with all my heart—with all my heart and strength.' And then her head fell upon his breast.

Captain Broughton was almost as much surprised as delighted by the warmth of the acknowledgment made by the eager-hearted passionate girl whom he now held within his arms. She had said it now; the words had been spoken; and there was nothing for her but to swear to him over and over again with her sweetest oaths, that those words were true—true as her soul. And very sweet was the walk down from thence to the parsonage gate. He spoke no more of the distance of the ground, or the length of his day's journey. But he stopped her at every turn that he might press her arm the closer to his own, that he might look into the brightness of her eyes, and prolong his hour of delight. There were no more gibes now on her tongue, no raillery at his London finery, no laughing comments on his coming and going. With downright honesty she told him everything: how she had loved him before her heart was warranted in such a passion; how, with much thinking, she had resolved that it would be unwise to take him at his first word, and had thought it better that he should return to London, and then think over it; how she had almost repented of her courage when she had feared, during those long summer days, that he would forget her; and how her heart had leapt for joy when her old friend had told her that he was coming.

'And yet,' said he, 'you were not glad to see me!'

'Oh, was I not glad? You cannot understand the feelings of a girl who has lived secluded as I have done. Glad is no word for the joy I felt. But it was not seeing you that I cared for so much. It was the knowledge that you were near me once again. I almost wish now that I had not seen you till tomorrow.' But as she spoke she pressed his arm, and this caress gave the lie to her last words.

'No, do not come in tonight,' she said, when she reached the little wicket that led up to the parsonage. 'Indeed, you shall not. I could not behave myself properly if you did.'

'But I don't want you to behave properly.'

'Oh! I am to keep that for London, am I? But, nevertheless, Captain Broughton, I will not invite you either to tea or to supper tonight.'

'Surely I may shake hands with your father.'

'Not tonight—not till—. John, I may tell him, may I not? I must tell him at once.'

'Certainly,' said he.

'And then you shall see him tomorrow. Let me see—at what hour shall I bid you come?'

'To breakfast.'

'No, indeed. What on earth would your aunt do with her broiled turkey and the cold pie? I have got no cold pie for you.'

'I hate cold pie.'

'What a pity! But, John, I should be forced to have you directly after breakfast. Come down—come down at two, or three; and then I will go back with you to Aunt Penelope. I must see her tomorrow;' and so at last the matter was settled, and the happy Captain, as he left her, was hardly resisted in his attempt to press her lips to his own.

When she entered the parlour in which her father was sitting, there still were Gribbles and Poulter discussing some knotty point of Devon lore. So Patience took off her hat, and sat herself down, waiting till they should go. For full an hour she had to wait, and then Gribbles and Poulter did go. But it was not in such matters as this that Patience Woolsworthy was impatient. She could wait, and wait, and wait, curbing herself for weeks and months, while the thing waited for was in her eyes good; but she could not curb her hot thoughts or her hot words when things came to be discussed which she did not think to be good.

'Papa,' she said, when Gribbles' long-drawn last word had been spoken at the door. 'Do you remember how I asked you the other day what you would say if I were to leave you?'

'Yes, surely,' he replied, looking up at her in astonishment.

'I am going to leave you now,' she said. 'Dear, dearest father, how am I to go from you?'

'Going to leave me,' said he, thinking of her visit to Helpholme, and thinking of nothing else.

Now, there had been a story about Helpholme. That bedridden old lady there had a stalwart son, who was now the owner of the Helpholme pastures. But though owner in fee of all those wild acres, and of the cattle which they supported, he was not much above the farmers around him, either in manners or education. He had his merits, however; for he was honest, well-to-do in the world, and modest withal. How strong love had grown up, springing from neighbourly kindness, between our Patience and his mother, it needs not here to tell; but rising from it had come another love—or an ambition which might have grown to love. The young man, after much thought, had not dared to speak to Miss Woolsworthy, but he had sent a message by Miss Le Smyrger. If there could be any hope for him, he would present himself as a suitor—on trial. He did not owe a shilling in the world, and had money by him—saved. He wouldn't ask the parson for a shilling of fortune. Such had been the tenor of his message, and Miss Le Smyrger had belivered it faithfully. 'He does not mean it,' Patience had said with her stern voice. 'Indeed he does, my dear. You may be sure he is in earnest,' Miss Le Smyrger had replied; 'and there is not an honester man in these parts.'

'Tell him,' said Patience, not attending to the latter portion of her friend's last speech, 'that it cannot be—make him understand, you know—and tell him also that the matter shall be thought of no more.' The matter had, at any rate, been spoken of no more, but the young farmer still remained a bachelor, and Helpholme still wanted a mistress. But all this came back upon the parson's mind when his daughter told him that she was about to leave him.

'Yes, dearest,' she said; and as she spoke she now knelt at his knees. 'I have been asked in marriage, and I have given myself away.'

'Well, my love, if you will be happy——'

'I hope I shall; I think I shall. But you, papa?'

'You will not be far from us.'

'Oh, yes; in London.'

'In London?'

'Captain Broughton lives in London generally.'

'And has Captain Broughton asked you to marry him?'

'Yes, papa—who else? Is he not good? Will you not love him? Oh, papa, do not say that I am wrong to love him?'

He never told her his mistake, or explained to her that he had not thought it possible that the high-placed son of the London great man should have fallen in love with his undowered daughter; but he embraced her, and told her, with all his enthusiasm, that he rejoiced in her joy, and would be happy in her happiness. 'My own Patty,' he said, 'I have ever known that you were too good for this life of ours here.' And then the evening wore away into the night, with many tears, but still with much happiness.

Captain Broughton, as he walked back to Oxney Combe, made up his mind that he would say nothing on the matter to his aunt till the next morning. He wanted to think over it all, and to think it over, if possible, by himself. He had taken a step in life, the most important that a man is ever called on to take, and he had to reflect whether or no he had taken it with wisdom.

'Have you seen her?' said Miss Le Smyrger, very anxiously, when he came into the drawing-room.

'Miss Woolsworthy you mean,' said he. 'Yes, I've seen her. As I found her out, I took a long walk, and happened to meet her. Do you know, aunt, I think I'll go to bed; I was up at five this morning, and have been on the move ever since.'

Miss Le Smyrger perceived that she was to hear nothing that evening, so she handed him his candlestick and allowed him to go to his room.

But Captain Broughton did not immediately retire to bed, nor when he did so was he able to sleep at once. Had this step that he had taken been a wise one? He was not a man who, in worldly matters, had allowed things to arrange themselves for him, as is the case with so many men. He had formed views for himself, and had a theory of life. Money for money's sake he had declared to himself to be bad. Money, as a concomitant to things which were in themselves good, he had declared to himself to be good also. That concomitant in this affair of his marriage, he had now missed. Well; he had made up his mind to that, and would put up with the loss. He had means of living of his own, the means not so extensive as might have been desirable. That it would be well for him to become a married man, looking merely to that state of life as opposed to his present state, he had fully resolved. On that point, therefore, there was nothing to repent. That Patty Woolsworthy was good, affectionate, clever, and beautiful he was sufficiently satisfied. It would be odd indeed if he were not so satisfied now, seeing that for the last four months he had so declared to himself daily with many inward asseverations. And yet though, he repeated, now again that he was satisfied, I do not think that he was so fully satisfied of it as he had been throughout the whole of those four months. It is sad to say so, but I fear—I fear that such was the case. When you have your plaything, how much of the anticipated pleasure vanishes, especially if it be won easily.

He had told none of his family what were his intentions in this second visit to Devonshire, and now he had to bethink himself whether they would be satisfied. What would his sister say, she who had married the Honourable Augustus Gumbleton, gold-stick-in-waiting to Her Majesty's Privy Council? Would she receive Patience with open arms, and make much of her about London? And then how far would London suit Patience, or would Patience suit London? There would be much for him to do in teaching her, and it would be well for him to set about the lesson without loss of time. So far he got that night, but when the morning came he went a step further, and began mentally to criticize her manner to himself. It had been very sweet, that warm, that full, that ready declaration of love. Yes; it had been very sweet; but—but—; when, after her little jokes, she did confess her love, had she not been a little too free for feminine excellence? A man likes to be told that he is loved, but he hardly wishes that the girl he is to marry should fling herself at his head!

Ah me! yes; it was thus he argued to himself as on that morning he went through the arrangements of his toilet. 'Then he was a brute,' you say, my pretty reader. I have never said that he was not a brute. But this I remark, that many such brutes are to be met with in the beaten paths of the world's high highway. When Patience Woolsworthy had answered him coldly, bidding him go back to London and think over his love; while it seemed from her manner that at any rate as yet she did not care for him; while he was absent from her, and, therefore, longing for her, the possession of her charms, her talent and bright honesty of purpose had seemed to him a thing most desirable. Now they were his own. They had, in fact, been his own from the first. The heart of this country-bred girl had fallen at the first word from his mouth. Had she not so confessed to him? She was very nice—very nice indeed. He loved her dearly. But had he not sold himself too cheaply?

I by no means say that he was not a brute. But whether brute or no he was an honest man, and had no remotest dream, either then, on that morning, or during the following days on which such thoughts pressed more thickly on his mind—of breaking away from his pledged word. At breakfast on that morning he told all to Miss Le Smyrger, and that lady, with warm and gracious intentions, confided to him her purpose regarding her property. 'I have always regarded Patience as my heir,' she said, 'and shall do so still.'

'Oh, indeed,' said Captain Broughton.

'But it is a great, great pleasure to me to think that she will give back the little property to my sister's child. You will have your mother's, and thus it will all come together again.'

'Ah!' said Captain Broughton. He had his own ideas about property, and did not, even under existing circumstances, like to hear that his aunt considered herself at liberty to leave the acres away to one who was by blood quite a stranger to the family.

'Does Patience know of this?' he asked.

'Not a word,' said Miss Le Smyrger. And then nothing more was said upon the subject.

On that afternoon he went down and received the parson's benediction and congratulations with a good grace. Patience said very little on the occasion, and indeed was absent during the greater part of the interview. The two lovers then walked up to Oxney Combe, and there were more benedictions and more congratulations. 'All went merry as a marriage bell,' at any rate as far as Patience was concerned. Not a word had yet fallen from that dear mouth, not a look had yet come over that handsome face, which tended in any way to mar her bliss. Her first day of acknowledged love was a day altogether happy, and when she prayed for him as she knelt beside her bed there was no feeling in her mind that any fear need disturb her joy.

I will pass over the next three or four days very quickly, merely saying that Patience did not find them so pleasant as that first day after her engagement. There was something in her lover's manner—something which at first she could not define—which by degrees seemed to grate against her feelings. He was sufficiently affectionate, that being a matter on which she did not require much demonstration; but joined to his affection there seemed to be——; she hardly liked to suggest to herself a harsh word, but could it be possible that he was beginning to think that she was not good enough for him? And then she asked herself the question—was she good enough for him? If there were doubt about that, the match should be broken off, though she tore her own heart out in the struggle. The truth, however, was this—that he had begun that teaching which he had already found to be so necessary. Now, had any one essayed to teach Patience German or mathematics, with that young lady's free consent, I believe that she would have been found a meek scholar. But it was not probable that she would be meek when she found a self-appointed tutor teaching her manners and conduct without her consent.

So matters went on for four or five days, and on the evening of the fifth day, Captain Broughton and his aunt drank tea at the parsonage. Nothing very especial occurred; but as the parson and Miss Le Smyrger insisted on playing backgammon with devoted perseverance during the whole evening, Broughton had a good opportunity of saying a word or two about those changes in his lady-love which a life in London would require—and some word he said also—some single slight word as to the higher station in life to which he would exalt his bride. Patience bore it—for her father and Miss Le Smyrger were in the room—she bore it well, speaking no syllable of anger, and enduring, for the moment, the implied scorn of the old parsonage. Then the evening broke up, and Captain Broughton walked back to Oxney Combe with his aunt. 'Patty,' her father said to her before they went to bed, 'he seems to me to be a most excellent young man.' 'Dear papa,' she answered, kissing him. 'And terribly deep in love,' said Mr Woolsworthy. 'Oh, I don't know about that,' she answered, as she left him with her sweetest smile. But though she could thus smile at her father's joke, she had already made up her mind that there was still something to be learned as to her promised husband before she could place herself altogether in his hands. She would ask him whether he thought himself liable to injury from this proposed marriage; and though he should deny any such thought, she would know from the manner of his denial what his true feelings were.

And he, too, on that night, during his silent walk with Miss Le Smyrger, had entertained some similar thoughts. 'I fear she is obstinate,' he had said to himself, and then he had half accused her of being sullen also. 'If that be her temper, what a life of misery I have before me!'

'Have you fixed a day yet?' his aunt asked him as they came near to her house.

'No, not yet: I don't know whether it will suit me to fix it before I leave.'

'Why, it was but the other day you were in such a hurry.'

'Ah—yes—I have thought more about it since then.'

'I should have imagined that this would depend on what Patty thinks,' said Miss Le Smyrger, standing up for the privileges of her sex. 'It is presumed that the gentleman is always ready as soon the lady will consent.'

'Yes, in ordinary cases it is so; but when a girl is taken out of her own sphere—'

'Her own sphere! Let me caution you, Master John, not to talk to Patty about her own sphere.'

'Aunt Penelope, as Patience is to be my wife and not yours, I must claim permission to speak to her on such subjects as may seem suitable to me.' And then they parted—not in the best humour with each other.

On the following day Captain Broughton and Miss Woolsworthy did not meet till the evening. She had said, before those few ill-omened words had passed her lover's lips, that she would probably be at Miss Le Smyrger's house on the following morning. Those ill-omened words did pass her lover's lips, and then she remained at home. This did not come from sullenness, nor even from anger, but from a conviction that it would be well that she should think much before she met him again. Nor was he anxious to hurry a meeting. His thought—his base thought—was this; that she would be sure to come up to the Combe after him; but she did not come, and therefore in the evening he went down to her, and asked her to walk with him.

They went away by the path that led to Helpholme, and little was said between them till they had walked some miles together. Patience, as she went along the path, remembered almost to the letter the sweet words which had greeted her ears as she came down that way with him on the night of his arrival; but he remembered nothing of that sweetness then. Had he not made an ass of himself during these last six months? That was the thought which very much had possession of his mind.

'Patience,' he said at last, having hitherto spoken only an indifferent word now and again since they had left the parsonage, 'Patience,

I hope you realize the importance of the step which you and I are about to take?'

'Of course I do,' she answered: 'what an odd question that is for you to ask!'

'Because,' said he, 'sometimes I almost doubt it. It seems to me as though you thought you could remove yourself from here to your new home with no more trouble than when you go from home up to the Combe.'

'Is that meant for a reproach, John?'

'No, not for a reproach, but for advice. Certainly not for a reproach.'

'I am glad of that.'

'But I should wish to make you think how great is the leap in the world which you are about to take.' Then again they walked on for many steps before she answered him.

'Tell me then, John,' she said, when she had sufficiently considered what words she would speak; and as she spoke a bright colour suffused her face, and her eyes flashed almost with anger. 'What leap do you mean? Do you mean a leap upwards?'

'Well, yes; I hope it will be so.'

'In one sense, certainly, it would be a leap upwards. To be the wife of the man I loved; to have the privilege of holding his happiness in my hand; to know that I was his own—the companion whom he had chosen out of all the world—that would, indeed, be a leap upwards; a leap almost to heaven, if all that were so. But if you mean upwards in any other sense——'

'I was thinking of the social scale.'

'Then, Captain Broughton, your thoughts were doing me dishonour.'

'Doing you dishonour!'

'Yes, doing me dishonour. That your father is, in the world's esteem, a greater man than mine is doubtless true enough. That you, as a man, are richer than I am as a woman, is doubtless also true. But you dishonour me, and yourself also, if these things can weigh with you now.'

'Patience,—I think you can hardly know what words you are saying to me.'

'Pardon me, but I think I do. Nothing that you can give me— no gifts of that description—can weigh aught against that which I am giving you. If you had all the wealth and rank of the greatest lord in the land, it would count as nothing in such a scale. If—as I have not doubted—if in return for my heart you have given me yours, then—then—then you have paid me fully. But when gifts such as those are going, nothing else can count even as a makeweight.'

'I do not quite understand you,' he answered, after a pause. 'I fear you are a little high-flown.' And then, while the evening was still early, they walked back to the parsonage almost without another word.

Captain Broughton at this time had only one full day more to remain at Oxney Colne. On the afternoon following that he was to go as far as Exeter, and thence return to London. Of course, it was to be expected that the wedding day would be fixed before he went, and much had been said about it during the first day or two of his engagement. Then he had pressed for an early time, and Patience, with a girl's usual diffidence, had asked for some little delay. But now nothing was said on the subject; and how was it probable that such a matter could be settled after such a conversation as that which I have related? That evening, Miss Le Smyrger asked whether the day had been fixed. 'No,' said Captain Broughton harshly; 'nothing has been fixed.' 'But it will be arranged before you go.' 'Probably not,' he said; and then the subject was dropped for the time.

'John,' she said, just before she went to bed, 'if there be anything wrong between you and Patience, I conjure you to tell me.'

'You had better ask her,' he replied. 'I can tell you nothing.'

On the following morning he was much surprised by seeing Patience on the gravel path before Miss Le Smyrger's gate immediately after breakfast. He went to the door to open it for her, and she, as she gave him her hand, told him that she came up to speak to him. There was no hesitation in her manner, nor any look of anger in her face. But there was in her gait and form, in her voice and countenance, a fixedness of purpose which he had never seen before, or at any rate had never acknowledged.

'Certainly,' said he. 'Shall I come out with you, or will you come up stairs?'

'We can sit down in the summer-house,' she said; and thither they both went.

'Captain Broughton,' she said—and she began her task the moment that they were both seated—'You and I have engaged ourselves as man and wife, but perhaps we have been over rash.'

'How so?' said he.

'It may be—and indeed I will say more—it is the case that we have made this engagement without knowing enough of each other's character.'

'I have not thought so.'

'The time will perhaps come when you will so think, but for the sake of all that we most value, let it come before it is too late. What would be our fate—how terrible would be our misery—if such a thought should come to either of us after we have linked our lots together.'

There was a solemnity about her as she thus spoke which almost repressed him,—which for a time did prevent him from taking that tone of authority which on such a subject he would choose to adopt. But he recovered himself. 'I hardly think that this comes well from you,' he said.

'From whom else should it come? Who else can fight my battle for me; and, John, who else can fight that same battle on your behalf? I tell you this, that with your mind standing towards me as it does stand at present, you could not give me your hand at the altar with true words and a happy conscience. Am I not true? You have half repented of your bargain already. Is it not so?'

He did not answer her; but getting up from his seat walked to the front of the summer-house, and stood there with his back turned upon her. It was not that he meant to be ungracious, but in truth he did not know how to answer her. He had half repented of his bargain.

'John,' she said, getting up and following him, so that she could put her hand upon his arm, 'I have been very angry with you.'

'Angry with me!' he said, turning sharp upon her.

'Yes, angry with you. You would have treated me like a child. But that feeling has gone now. I am not angry now. There is my hand;—the hand of a friend. Let the words that have been spoken between us be as though they had not been spoken. Let us both be free.'

'Do you mean it?' he asked.

'Certainly I mean it.' As she spoke these words her eyes were filled with tears, in spite of all the efforts she could make; but he was not looking at her, and her efforts had sufficed to prevent any sob from being audible.

'With all my heart,' he said; and it was manifest from his tone that he had no thought of her happiness as he spoke. It was true that she had been angry with him—angry, as she had herself declared; but nevertheless, in what she had said and what she had done, she had thought more of his happiness than of her own. Now she was angry once again.

'With all your heart, Captain Broughton! Well, so be it. If with all your heart, then is the necessity so much the greater. You go tomorrow. Shall we say farewell now?'

'Patience, I am not going to be lectured.'

'Certainly not by me. Shall we say farewell now?'

'Yes, if you are determined.'

'I am determined. Farewell, Captain Broughton. You have all my wishes for your happiness.' And she held out her hand to him.

'Patience!' he said. And he looked at her with a dark frown, as though he would strive to frighten her into submission. If so, he might have saved himself any such attempt.

'Farewell, Captain Broughton. Give me your hand, for I cannot stay.' He gave her his hand, hardly knowing why he did so. She lifted it to her lips and kissed it, and then, leaving him, passed from the summer-house down through the wicket-gate, and straight home to the parsonage.

During the whole of that day she said no word to anyone of what had occurred. When she was once more at home she went about her household affairs as she had done on that day of his arrival. When she sat down to dinner with her father he observed nothing to make him think that she was unhappy; nor during the evening was there any expression in her face, or any tone in her voice, which excited his attention. On the following morning Captain Broughton called at the parsonage, and the servant-girl brought word to her mistress that he was in the parlour. But she would not see him. 'Laws, miss, you ain't a quarrelled with your beau?' the poor girl said. 'No, not quarrelled,' she said; 'but give him that.' It was a scrap of paper, containing a word or two in pencil. 'It is better that we should not meet again. God bless you.' And from that day to this, now more than ten years, they never have met.

'Papa,' she said to her father that afternoon, 'dear papa, do not be angry with me. It is all over between me and John Broughton. Dearest, you and I will not be separated.'

It would be useless here to tell how great was the old man's surprise and how true his sorrow. As the tale was told to him no cause was given for anger with anyone. Not a word was spoken against the suitor who had on that day returned to London with a full conviction that now at least he was relieved from his engagement. 'Patty, my darling child,' he said, 'may God grant that it be for the best!'

'It is for the best,' she answered stoutly. 'For this place I am fit; and I much doubt whether I am fit for any other.'

On that day she did not see Miss Le Smyrger, but on the following morning, knowing that Captain Broughton had gone off, having heard the wheels of the carriage as they passed by the parsonage gate on his way to the station,—she walked up to the Combe.

'He has told you, I suppose?' said she.

'Yes,' said Miss Le Smyrger. 'And I will never see him again unless he asks your pardon on his knees. I have told him so. I would not even give him my hand as he went.'

'But why so, thou kindest one? The fault was mine more than his.'

'I understand. I have eyes in my head,' said the old maid. 'I have watched him for the last four or five days. If you could have kept the truth to yourself and bade him keep off from you, he would have been at your feet now, licking the dust from your shoes.'

'But, dear friend, I do not want a man to lick dust from my shoes.'

'Ah, you are a fool. You do not know the value of your own wealth.'

'True; I have been a fool. I was a fool to think that one coming from such a life as he has led could be happy with such as I am. I know the truth now. I have bought the lesson dearly,—but perhaps not too dearly, seeing that it will never be forgotten.'

There was but little more said about the matter between our three friends at Oxney Colne. What, indeed, could be said? Miss Le Smyrger for a year or two still expected that her nephew would return and claim his bride; but he has never done so, nor has there been any correspondence between them. Patience Woolsworthy had learned her lesson dearly. She had given her whole heart to the man; and, though she so bore herself that no one was aware of the violence of the struggle, nevertheless the struggle within her bosom was very violent. She never told herself that she had done wrong; she never regretted her loss; but yet—yet!—the loss was very hard to bear. He also had loved her, but he was not capable of a love which could much injure his daily peace. Her daily peace was gone for many a day to come.

Her father is still living; but there is a curate now in the parish. In conjunction with him and with Miss Le Smyrger she spends her time in the concerns of the parish. In her own eyes she is a confirmed old maid; and such is my opinion also. The romance of her life was played out in that summer. She never sits now lonely on the hill-side thinking how much she might do for one whom she really loved. But with a large heart she loves many, and, with no romance, she works hard to lighten the burdens of those she loves.

As for Captain Broughton, all the world knows that he did marry that great heiress with whom his name was once before connected, and that he is now a useful member of Parliament, working on committees three or four days a week with a zeal that is indefatigable. Sometimes, not often, as he thinks of Patience Woolsworthy, a gratified smile comes across his face.

ANNE RITCHIE

To Esther

THE first time that I ever knew you, was at Rome one winter's evening. I had walked through the silent streets—I see them now—dark with black shadows, lighted by the blazing stars overhead and by the lamps dimly flickering before the shrines at street corners. After crossing the Spanish-place I remember turning into a narrow alley and coming presently to a great black archway, which led to a glimmering court. A figure of the Virgin stood with outstretched arms above the door of your house, and the light burning at her feet dimly played upon the stone, worn and stained, of which the walls were built. Through the archway came a glimpse of the night sky above the court-yard, shining wonderfully with splendid stars; and I also caught the plashing sound of a fountain flowing in the darkness. I groped my way up the broad stone staircase, only lighted by the friendly star-shine, stumbling and knocking my shins against those ancient steps, up which two centuries of men and women had clambered; and at last, ringing at a curtained door, I found myself in a hall, and presently ushered through a dining-room, where the cloth was laid, and announced at the drawing-room door as Smith.

It was a long room with many windows, and cabinets and tables along the wall, with a tall carved mantel-piece, at which you were standing, and a Pompeian lamp burning on a table near you. Would you care to hear what manner of woman I saw; what impression I got from you as we met for the first time together? In after days, light, mood, circumstance, may modify this first image more or less, but the germ of life is in it—the identical presence—and I fancy it is rarely improved by keeping, by painting up, with love, or dislike, or long use, or weariness, as the case may be. Be this as it may, I think I knew you as well after the first five minutes' acquaintance as I do now. I saw an ugly woman, whose looks I liked somehow;

thick brows, sallow face, a tall and straight-made figure, honest eyes that had no particular merit besides, dark hair, and a pleasant, cordial smile. And somehow, as I looked at you and heard you talk, I seemed to be aware of a frank spirit, uncertain, blind, wayward, tender, under this somewhat stern exterior; and so, I repeat, I liked you, and, making a bow, I said I was afraid I was before my time.

'I'm afraid it is my father who is after his,' you said. 'Mr Halbert is coming, and he, too, is often late'; and so we went on talking for about ten minutes.

Yours is a kindly manner, a sad-toned voice; I know not if your life has been a happy one; you are well disposed towards every soul you come across; you love to be loved, and try with a sweet artless art to win and charm over each man or woman that you meet. I saw that you liked me, that you felt at your ease with me, that you held me not quite your equal, and might perhaps laugh at, as well as with me. But I did not care. My aim in life, heaven knows, has not been to domineer, to lay down the law, and triumph over others, least of all over those I like.

The colonel arrived presently, with his white hair trimly brushed and his white neckcloth neatly tied. He greeted me with great friendliness and cordiality. You have got his charm of manner; but with you, my dear, it is not manner only, for there is loyalty and heartiness shining in your face, and sincerity ringing in every tone of your voice. All this you must have inherited from your mother, if such things are an inheritance. As for the colonel, your father, if I mistake not, he is a little shrivelled-up old gentleman, with a machine inside to keep him going, and outside a well-cut coat and a well-bred air and knowledge of the world, to get on through life with. Not a very large capital to go upon. However this is not the way to speak to a young lady about her father; and besides it is you, and not he, in whom I take the interest which prompts these maudlin pages.

Mr Halbert and little Latham, the artist, were the only other guests. You did not look round when Halbert was announced, but went on speaking to Latham, with a strange flush in your face; until Halbert had, with great *empressement*, made his way through the chairs and tables, and had greeted, rather than been greeted by, you, as I and Latham were.

So thinks I to myself, concerning certain vague notions I had already begun to entertain, I am rather late in the field, and the city is taken and has already hoisted the conqueror's colours. Perhaps those red flags might have been mine had I come a little sooner; who knows? *'De tout laurier un poison est l'essence,'* says the Frenchman; and my brows may be as well unwreathed.

'I came upstairs with the dinner,' Mr Halbert was saying. 'It reassured me as to my punctuality. I rather pique myself on my punctuality, colonel.'

'And I'm afraid I have been accusing you of being always late,' you said, as if it were a confession.

'Have you thought so, Miss Olliver?' cried Halbert.

'Dinner, sir,' said Baker, opening the door.

All dinner-time Halbert, who has very high spirits, talked and laughed without ceasing. You, too, laughed, listened, looked very happy, and got up with a smile at last, leaving us to drink our wine. The colonel presently proposed cigars.

'In that case I shall go and talk to your daughter in the drawing-room,' Halbert said. 'I'm promised to Lady Parker's tonight; it would never do to go there smelling all over of smoke. I must be off in half-an-hour,' he added, looking at his watch.

I, too, had been asked, and was rather surprised that he should be in such a desperate hurry to get there. Talking to Miss Olliver in the next room, I could very well understand; but leaving her to rush off to Lady Parker's immediately, did not accord with the little theories I had been laying down. Could I have been mistaken? In this case it seemed to me this would be the very woman to suit me —(you see I am speaking without any reserve, and simply describing the abrupt little events as they occurred)—and I thought, who knows that there may not be a chance for me yet? But, by the time my cigar had crumbled into smoke and ashes, it struck me that my little castle had also wreathed away and vanished. Going into the drawing-room, where the lamps were swinging in the dimness, and the night without streaming in through the uncurtained windows, we found you in your white dress, sitting alone at one of them. Mr Halbert was gone, you said; he went out by the other door. And then you were silent again, staring out at the stars with dreamy eyes. The colonel rang for tea, and chirped away very pleasantly to Latham by the fire. I looked at you now and then, and could not help surprising your thoughts somehow, and knowing that I had not been mistaken after all. There you sat, making simple schemes of future happiness; you could not, would not, look beyond the present. You were very calm, happy, full of peaceful reliance. Your world was alight with shining stars, great big shining meteors, all flaring up as they usually do before going out with a splutter at the end of the entertainment. People who are in love I have always found very much alike; and now, having settled that you belonged to that crack-brained community, it was not difficult to guess at what was going on in your mind.

I, too, as I have said, had been favoured with a card for Lady Parker's rout; and as you were so absent and ill-inclined to talk, and the colonel was anxious to go off and play whist at his club, I thought I might as well follow in Halbert's traces, and gratify any little curiosity I might feel as to his behaviour and way of going on in your absence. I found that Latham was also going to her lady-ship's. As we went downstairs together Latham said, 'It was too bad of Halbert to break up the party and go off at that absurd hour. I didn't say I was going, because I thought his rudeness might strike them.'

'But surely,' said I, 'Mr Halbert seems at home there, and may come and go as he likes.' Latham shrugged his shoulders. 'I like the girl; I hope she is not taken in by him. He has been very thick all the winter in other quarters. Lady Parker's niece, Lady Fanny Fareham, was going to marry him, they said; but I know very little of him. He is much too great a swell to be on intimate terms with a dis-reputable little painter like myself. What a night it is!' As he spoke we came out into the street again, our shadows falling on the stones; the Virgin overhead still watching, the lamp burning faithfully, the solemn night waning on. Lady Parker had lodgings in the Corso. I felt almost ashamed of stepping from the great entertainment with-out into the close racketing little tea-party that was clattering on within. We came in, in the middle of a jangling tune, the com-pany spinning round and round. Halbert, twirling like a Dervish, was almost the first person I saw; he was flushed, and looked exceed-ingly handsome, and his tall shoulders overtopped most of the other heads. As I watched him I thought with great complacency that if any woman cared for me, it would not be for my looks. No! no! what are mere good looks compared to those mental qualities which, etc., etc. Presently, not feeling quite easy in my mind about these said mental qualities, I again observed that it was still better to be liked for one's self than for one's mental qualities; by which time I turned my attention once more to Mr Halbert. The youth was devoting himself most assiduously to a very beautiful, oldish young lady, in a green gauzy dress; and I now, with a mixture of satisfaction and vexation, recognized the very same looks and tones which had misled me at dinner.

I left him still at it and walked home, wondering at the great law of natural equality which seems to level all mankind to one standard, notwithstanding all those artificial ones which we ourselves have raised. Here was a successful youth, with good looks and good wits and position and fortune; and here was I, certainly no wonder, insignificant, and plain, and poor, and of commonplace intelligence, and as well satisfied with my own possessions, such as they were, as he, Halbert, could be with the treasures a prodigal fortune had showered upon him. Here was I, judging him, and taking his measure as accurately as he could take mine, were it worth his while to do so. Here was I, walking home under the stars, while he was flirting and whispering with Lady Fanny, and both our nights sped on. Constellations sinking slowly, the day approaching through the awful realms of space, hours waning, life going by for us both alike: both of us men waiting together amidst these awful surroundings.

You and I met often after this first meeting—in churches where tapers were lighting and heavy censers swinging—on the Pincio, in the narrow, deep-coloured streets: it was not always chance only which brought me so constantly into your presence. You yourself were the chance, at least, and I the blind follower of fortune.

All round about Rome there are ancient gardens lying basking in the sun. Gardens and villas built long since by dead cardinals and popes; terraces, with glinting shadows, with honeysuckle clambering in desolate luxuriance; roses flowering and fading and falling in showers on the pathways; and terraces and marble steps yellow with age. Lonely fountains plash in their basins, statues of fawns and slender nymphs stand out against the solemn horizon of blue hills and crimson-streaked sky; of cypress-trees and cedars, with the sunset showing through their stems. At home, I lead a very busy, anxious life: the beauty and peace of these Italian villas fill me with inexpressible satisfaction and gratitude towards those mouldering

pontiffs, whose magnificent liberality has secured such placid resting-
places for generations of weary men. Taking a long walk out of
Rome one day, I came to the gates of one of these gardens. I
remember seeing a carriage waiting in the shade of some cedar-
trees; hard by, horses with drooping heads, and servants smoking as
they waited. This was no uncommon sight; the English are for ever
on their rounds; but somehow, on this occasion, I thought I recognized one of the men, and instead of passing by, as had been my
intention, I turned in at the half-opened gate, which the angels
with the flaming swords had left unguarded and unlocked for once,
and, after a few minutes' walk, I came upon the Eve I looked for.

You were sitting on some time-worn steps; you wore a green silk
dress, and your brown hair, with the red tints in it, was all ablaze
with the light. You looked very unhappy, I thought: got up with an
effort, and smiled a pitiful smile.

'Are you come here for a little quiet?' I asked. 'I am not going
to disturb you.'

'I came here for pleasure, not quiet,' you said, 'with papa and
some friends. I was tired, so they walked on and left me.'

'That is the way with one's friends,' said I. 'Who are the culprits,
Miss Olliver?'

'I am the only culprit,' you said, grimly. 'Lady Fanny and Mr
Halbert came with us today. Look, there they are at the end of that
alley.'

And as you spoke, you raised one hand and pointed, and I made
up my mind. It was a very long alley. The figures in the distance
were advancing very slowly. When they reach that little temple,
thought I, I will tell her what I think.

This was by no means so sudden a determination as it may appear
to you, reading over these pages. It seems a singular reason to give;
but I really think it was your hopeless fancy for that rosy youth
which touched me and interested me so. I know I used to carry
home sad words, spoken not to me, and glances that thrilled me
with love, pity, and sympathy. What I said was, as you know, very
simple and to the purpose. I knew quite well your fancy was elsewhere; mine was with you, perhaps as hopelessly placed. I didn't
exactly see what good this confession was to do either of us, only,
there I was, ready to spend my life at your service.

When I had spoken there was a silent moment, and then you

glowed up—your eyes melted, your mouth quivered. 'Oh, what can I say? Oh, I am so lonely. Oh, I have not one friend in the world; and now, suddenly, a helping hand is held out, and I can't—I *can't* push it away. Oh, don't despise. Oh, forgive me.'

Despise! scorn! . . . Poor child! I only liked you the more for your plaintive appeal; though I wondered at it.

'Take your time,' I said; 'I can wait, and I shall not fly away. Call me when you want me; send me away when I weary you. Here is your father; shall I speak to him? But no. Remember there is no single link between us, except what you yourself hold in your own hands.'

Here your father and Halbert and Lady Fanny came up. 'Well, Esther, are you rested,' says the colonel cheerfully. 'Why, how do you do (*to me*)? What have you been talking about so busily?'

You did not answer, but fixed your eyes on your father's face. I said something; I forget what. Halbert, looking interested, turned from one to the other. Lady Fanny, who held a fragrant heap of roses, shook a few petals to the ground, where they lay glowing after we had all walked away.

If you remember, I did not go near you for a day or two after this. But I wrote you a letter, in which I repeated that you were entirely free to use me as you liked: marry me—make a friend of me—I was in your hands. One day, at last, I called; and I shall never forget the sweetness and friendly gratefulness with which you received me. A solitary man, dying of lonely thirst, you meet me smiling with a cup of sparkling water: a weary watcher through the night— suddenly I see the dawn streaking the bright horizon. Those were very pleasant times. I remember now, one afternoon in early spring, open windows, sounds coming in from the city, the drone of the *pifferari* buzzing drowsily in the sultry streets. You sat at your window in some light-coloured dress, laughing now and then, and talking your tender little talk. The colonel, from behind *The Times*, joined in now and again: the pleasant half-hours slid by. We were still basking there, when Halbert was announced, and came in, looking very tall and handsome. The bagpipes droned on, the flies sailed in and out on the sunshine: you still sat tranquilly at the open casement; but somehow the golden atmosphere of the hour was gone. Your smiles were gone; your words were silenced; and that happy little hour was over for ever.

When I got up to come away Halbert rose too: he came down-stairs with me, and suddenly looking me full in the face said, 'When is it to be?'

'You know much more about it than I do,' I answered.

'You don't mean to say that you are not very much smitten with Miss Esther?' said he.

'Certainly I am,' said I; 'I should be ready enough to marry her, if that is what you mean. I daresay I shan't get her. She is to me the most sympathetic woman I have ever known. You are too young, Mr Halbert, to understand and feel her worth. Don't be offended,' I added, seeing him flush up. 'You young fellows can't be expected to see with the same eyes as we old ones. You will think as I do in another ten years.'

'How do you mean,' he asked.

'Isn't it the way with all of us,' said I; 'we begin by liking uni-versally; as we go on we pick and choose, and weary of things which had only the charm of novelty to recommend them; only as our life narrows we cling more and more to the good things which remain, and feel their value ten times more keenly? And surely a sweet, honest-hearted young woman like Esther Olliver is a good thing.'

'She is very nice,' Halbert said. 'She has such good manners. I have had more experience than you give me credit for, and I am very much of your way of thinking. They say that old courtly colonel is dreadfully harsh to her—wants to marry her, and get her off his hands. I assure you you have a very good chance.'

'I mistrust that old colonel,' said I, dictatorially; 'as I trust his daughter. Somehow she and I chime in tune together'; and, as I spoke, I began to understand why you once said woefully, that you had not one friend in the world; and my thoughts wandered away to the garden where I had found you waiting on the steps of the terrace.

'What do you say to the "Elisíre d'Amore" Lady Fanny and I have been performing lately?' Halbert was saying, meanwhile, very confidentially. 'Sometimes I cannot help fancying that the colonel wants to take a part in the performance, and a cracked old tenor part, too. In that case I shall cry off, and give up my engagements.' And then, nodding good-bye, he left me.

I met him again in the Babuino a day or two after. He came

straight up to me, saying, 'Going to the Ollivers', eh? Will you take a message for me, and tell the colonel I mean to look in there this evening. That old fox the colonel—you have heard that he *is* actually going to marry Lady Fanny. She told me so herself, yesterday.'

'I think her choice is a prudent one,' I answered, somewhat surprised. 'I suppose Colonel Olliver is three times as rich as yourself? You must expect a woman of thirty to be prudent. I am not fond of that virtue in very young people, but it is not unbecoming with years.'

Halbert flushed up. 'I suppose from that you mean she was very near marrying me. I'm not sorry she has taken up with the colonel after all. You see, my mother was always writing, and my sisters at home; and they used to tell me . . . and I myself thought she——, you know what I mean. But, of course, they have been reassured on that point.'

'Do you mean to say,' I asked, in a great panic, 'that you would marry any woman who happened to fall in love with you?'

'I don't know what I might have done a year ago,' said he, laughing; 'but just now, you see, I have had a warning, and besides it is my turn to make the advances.'

I was immensely relieved at this, for I didn't know what I was not going to say.

Here, as we turned a street corner, we came upon a black-robed monk, standing, veiled and motionless, with a skull in one bony hand. This cheerful object changed the current of our talk, and we parted presently at a fountain. Women with black twists of hair were standing round about, waiting in grand, careless attitudes, while the limpid water flowed.

When I reached your door, I found the carriage waiting, and you and your father under the archway. 'Come with us,' said he, and I gladly accepted. And so we drove out at one of the gates of the city, out into the Campagna, over which melting waves of colour were rolling. Here and there we passed ancient ruins crumbling in the sun; the roadsides streamed with colour and fragrance from violets and anemones and sweet-smelling flowers. After some time we came suddenly to some green hills, and leaving the carriage climbed up the sides. Then we found ourselves looking down into a green glowing valley, with an intense heaven above all melting into light. You, with a little transient gasp of happiness, fell down kneeling in the grass. I shall always see the picture I had before me then—the light figure against the bright green, the black hat, and long falling feather; the eager face looking out at the world. May it be for ever green and pleasant to you as it was then, O eager face!

As we were parting in the twilight, I suddenly remembered to give Halbert's message. It did not greatly affect your father; but how was it? Was it because I knew you so well that I instinctively guessed you were moved by it? When I shook hands with you and said goodnight, your hand trembled in mine.

'Won't you look in too?' said the colonel.

But I shook my head. 'Not tonight—no, thank you.' And so we parted.

My lodgings were in the Gregoriana; the windows looked out over gardens and cupolas; from one of them I could see the Pincio. From that one, next morning, as I sat drinking my coffee, I suddenly saw you, walking slowly along by the parapet, with your dog running by your side. You went to one of those outlying terraces which flank the road, and leaning over the stone-work looked out at the great panorama lying at your feet:—Rome, with her purple mantle of mist, regally spreading, her towers, her domes, and great St Peter's rising over the house-tops, her seven hills changing and deepening with noblest colour, her golden crown of sunlight stream ing and melting with the mist. Somehow I, too, saw all this presently when I reached the place where you were still standing.

And now I have almost come to the end of my story, that is, of those few days of my life of which you, Esther, were the story. You stood there waiting, and I hastened towards you, and fate (I fancied you were my Fate) went on its course quite unmoved by my hopes or your fears. I thought that you looked almost handsome for once. You certainly seemed more happy. Your face flushed and faded, your eyes brightened and darkened. As you turned and saw me, a radiant quiver, a piteous smile came to greet me somewhat strangely. You seemed trying to speak, but the words died away on your lips—to keep silence, at least, but the faltering accents broke forth.

'What is it, my dear?' said I at last, with a queer sinking of the heart, and I held out my hand.

You caught it softly between both yours. 'Oh!' you said, with sparkling eyes, 'I am a mean, wretched girl—oh! don't think too ill of me. He, Mr Halbert, came to see me last night, and—and, he says . . . Oh! I don't deserve it. Oh! forgive me, for I am so happy;' and you burst into tears. 'You have been so good to me,' you whispered on. 'I hardly know how good. He says he only thought of me when you spoke of me to him, when—when he saw you did not dislike me. I am behaving shamefully—yes, shamefully, but it is because I know you are too kind not to forgive—not to forgive. What can I do? You know how it has always been. You don't know what it would be to marry one person, caring for another. Ah! you don't know what it would be to have it otherwise than as it is' (this clasping your hands). 'But you don't ask it. Ah! forgive me, and say you don't ask it.' Then standing straight and looking down with a certain sweet dignity, you went on—'Heaven has sent me a great and unexpected happiness, but there is, indeed, a bitter, bitter cup to drink as well. Though I throw you over, though I behave so selfishly, don't think that I am utterly conscienceless, that I do not suffer a cruel pang indeed; when I think how you must look at me, when I remember what return I am making for all your forbearance and generosity. When I think of myself, I am ashamed and humiliated; when I think of him——' Here you suddenly broke off, and turned away your face.

Ah me! turned away your face for ever from me. The morning mists faded away; the mid-day sun streamed over hills and towers and valley. The bell of the Trinità hard by began to toll.

I said, 'Good-bye, and Heaven keep you, my dear. I would not have had you do otherwise.' And so I went back to my lodging.

THOMAS HARDY

Enter a Dragoon

I LATELY had a melancholy experience (said the gentleman who is answerable for the truth of this story). It was that of going over a doomed house with whose outside aspect I had long been familiar—a house, that is, which by reason of age and dilapidation was to be pulled down during the following week. Some of the thatch, brown and rotten as the gills of old mushrooms, had, indeed, been removed before I walked over the building. Seeing that it was only a very small house—which is usually called a 'cottage-residence'—situated in a remote hamlet, and that it was not more than a hundred years old, if so much, I was led to think in my progress through the hollow rooms, with their cracked walls and sloping floors, what an exceptional number of abrupt family incidents had taken place therein—to reckon only those which had come to my own knowledge. And no doubt there were many more of which I had never heard.

It stood at the top of a garden stretching down to the lane or street that ran through a hermit-group of dwellings in Mellstock parish. From a green gate at the lower entrance, over which the thorn hedge had been shaped to an arch by constant clippings, a gravel path ascended between the box edges of once trim raspberry, strawberry, and vegetable plots, towards the front door. This was in colour an ancient and bleached green that could be rubbed off with the finger, and it bore a small long-featured brass knocker covered with verdigris in its crevices. For some years before this eve of demolition the homestead had degenerated, and been divided into two tenements to serve as cottages for farm labourers; but in its prime it had indisputable claim to be considered neat, pretty, and genteel.

The variety of incidents above alluded to was mainly owing to the nature of the tenure, whereby the place had been occupied by families not quite of the kind customary in such spots—people whose circumstances, position, or antecedents were more or less of a critical happy-go-lucky cast. And of these residents the family whose term comprised the story I wish to relate was that of Mr Jacob Paddock the market-gardener, who dwelt there for some years with his wife and grown-up daughter.

I

An evident commotion was agitating the premises, which jerked busy sounds across the front plot, resembling those of a disturbed hive. If a member of the household appeared at the door it was with a countenance of abstraction and concern.

Evening began to bend over the scene; and the other inhabitants of the hamlet came out to draw water, their common well being in the public road opposite the garden and house of the Paddocks. Having wound up their bucketsfull respectively they lingered, and spoke significantly together. From their words any casual listener might have gathered information of what had occurred.

The woodman who lived nearest the site of the story told most of the tale. Selina, the daughter of the Paddocks opposite, had been surprised that afternoon by receiving a letter from her once intended husband, then a corporal, but now a sergeant-major of dragoons, whom she had hitherto supposed to be one of the slain in the Battle of the Alma two or three years before.

'She picked up wi'en against her father's wish, as we know, and before he got his stripes,' their informant continued. 'Not but that the man was as hearty a feller as you'd meet this side o' London. But Jacob, you see, wished her to do better, and one can understand it. However, she was determined to stick to him at that time; and for what happened she was not much to blame, so near as they were to matrimony when the war broke out and spoiled all.'

'Even the very pig had been killed for the wedding,' said a woman, 'and the barrel o' beer ordered in. O, the man meant honourable enough. But to be off in two days to fight in a foreign country— 'twas natural of her father to say they should wait till he got back.'

'And he never came,' murmured one in the shade.

'The war ended but her man never turned up again. She was not sure he was killed, but was too proud, or too timid, to go and hunt for him.'

'One reason why her father forgave her when he found out how matters stood was, as he said plain at the time, that he liked the man, and could see that he meant to act straight. So the old folks made the best of what they couldn't mend, and kept her there with 'em, when some wouldn't. Time has proved seemingly that he did mean to act straight, now that he has writ to her that he's coming. She'd have stuck to him all through the time, 'tis my belief, if t'other hadn't come along.'

'At the time of the courtship,' resumed the woodman, 'the regiment was quartered in Casterbridge Barracks, and he and she got acquainted by his calling to buy a penn'orth of rathe-ripes off that tree yonder in her father's orchard—though 'twas said he seed *her* over hedge as well as the apples. He declared 'twas a kind of apple he much fancied; and he called for a penn'orth every day till the tree was cleared. It ended in his calling for her.'

''Twas a thousand pities they didn't jine up at once and ha' done wi' it.'

'Well; better late than never, if so be he'll have her now. But, Lord, she'd that faith in 'en that she'd no more belief that he was alive, when a' didn't come, than that the undermost man in our churchyard was alive. She'd never have thought of another but for that—O no!'

''Tis awkward, altogether, for her now.'

'Still she hadn't married wi' the new man. Though to be sure she would have committed it next week, even the licence being got, they say, for she'd have no banns this time, the first being so unfortunate.'

'Perhaps the sergeant-major will think he's released, and go as he came.'

'O, not as I reckon. Soldiers bain't particular, and she's a tidy piece o' furniture still. What will happen is that she'll have her soldier, and break off with the master-wheelwright, licence or no— daze me if she won't.'

In the progress of these desultory conjectures the form of another neighbour arose in the gloom. She nodded to the people at the well, who replied 'G'd night, Mrs Stone,' as she passed through Mr Paddock's gate towards his door. She was an intimate friend of the latter's household, and the group followed her with their eyes up the path and past the windows, which were now lighted up by candles inside.

II

Mrs Stone paused at the door, knocked, and was admitted by Selina's mother, who took her visitor at once into the parlour on the left hand, where a table was partly spread for supper. On the 'beaufet' against the wall stood probably the only object which would have attracted the eye of a local stranger in an otherwise ordinarily furnished room, a great plum-cake guarded as if it were a curiosity by a glass shade of the kind seen in museums—square, with a wooden back like those enclosing stuffed specimens of rare feather or fur. This was the mummy of the cake intended in earlier days for the wedding-feast of Selina and the soldier, which had been religiously and lovingly preserved by the former as a testimony to her intentional respectability in spite of an untoward subsequent circumstance, which will be mentioned. This relic was now as dry as a brick, and seemed to belong to a pre-existent civilization. Till quite recently, Selina had been in the habit of pausing before it daily, and recalling the accident whose consequences had thrown a shadow over her life ever since—that of which the water-drawers had spoken—the sudden news one morning that the Route had come for the —th Dragoons, two days only being the interval before departure; the hurried consultation as to what should be done, the second time of asking being past but not the third; and the decision that it would be unwise to solemnize matrimony in such haphazard circumstances, even if it were possible, which was doubtful.

Before the fire the young woman in question was now seated on a low stool, in the stillness of reverie, and a toddling boy played about the floor around her.

'Ah, Mrs Stone!' said Selina, rising slowly. 'How kind of you to come in. You'll bide to supper? Mother has told you the strange news, of course?'

'No. But I heard it outside, that is, that you'd had a letter from Mr Clark—Sergeant-Major Clark, as they say he is now—and that he's coming to make it up with 'ee.'

'Yes; coming tonight—all the way from the north of England where he's quartered. I don't know whether I'm happy or—frightened at it. Of course I always believed that if he was alive he'd come and keep his solemn vow to me. But when it is printed that a man is killed—what can you think?'

'It *was* printed?'

'Why, yes. After the Battle of the Alma the book of the names of the killed and wounded was nailed up against Casterbridge Town Hall door. 'Twas on a Saturday, and I walked there o' purpose to read and see for myself, for I'd heard that his name was down. There was a crowd of people round the book, looking for the names of relations; and I can mind that when they saw me they made way for me—knowing that we'd been just going to be married—and that, as you may say, I belonged to him. Well, I reached up my arm, and turned over the farrels of the book, and under the "killed" I read his surname, but instead of "John" they'd printed "James", and I thought 'twas a mistake, and that it must be he. Who could have guessed there were two nearly of one name in one regiment.'

'Well—he's coming to finish the wedding of 'ee as may be said; so never mind, my dear. All's well that ends well.'

'That's what he seems to say. But then he has not heard yet about Mr Miller; and that's what rather terrifies me. Luckily my marriage with him next week was to have been by licence, and not banns, as in John's case; and it was not so well known on that account. Still, I don't know what to think.'

'Everything seems to come just 'twixt cup and lip with 'ee, don't it now, Miss Paddock. Two weddings broke off—'tis odd! How came you to accept Mr Miller, my dear?'

'He's been so good and faithful! Not minding about the child at all; for he knew the rights of the story. He's dearly fond o' Johnny, you know—just as if 'twere his own—isn't he, my duck? Do Mr Miller love you or don't he?'

'Iss! An' I love Mr Miller,' said the toddler.

'Well, you see, Mrs Stone, he said he'd make me a comfortable home; and thinking 'twould be a good thing for Johnny, Mr Miller being so much better off than me, I agreed at last, just as a widow might—which is what I have always felt myself, ever since I saw what I thought was John's name printed there. I hope John will forgive me!'

'So he will forgive 'ee, since 'twas no manner of wrong to him. He ought to have sent 'ee a line, saying 'twas another man.'

Selina's mother entered. 'We've not known of this an hour, Mrs Stone,' she said. 'The letter was brought up from Lower Mellstock post-office by one of the school children, only this afternoon. Mr Miller was coming here this very night to settle about the wedding doings. Hark! Is that your father? Or is it Mr Miller already come?'

The footsteps entered the porch; there was a brushing on the mat, and the door of the room sprung back to disclose a rubicund man about thirty years of age, of thriving master-mechanic appearance and obviously comfortable temper. On seeing the child, and before taking any notice whatever of the elders, the comer made a noise like the crowing of a cock and flapped his arms as if they were wings, a method of entry which had the unqualified admiration of Johnny.

'Yes—it is he,' said Selina constrainedly advancing.

'What—were you all talking about me, my dear?' said the genial young man when he had finished his crowing and resumed human manners. 'Why what's the matter,' he went on. 'You look struck all of a heap.' Mr Miller spread an aspect of concern over his own face, and drew a chair up to the fire.

'O mother, would you tell Mr Miller, if he don't know?'

'*Mister* Miller! and going to be married in six days!' he interposed.

'Ah—he don't know it yet!' murmured Mrs Paddock.

'Know what?'

'Well—John Clark—now Sergeant-Major Clark—wasn't shot at Alma after all. 'Twas another of almost the same name.'

'Now that's interesting! There were several cases like that.'

'And he's home again; and he's coming here tonight to see her.'

'Whatever shall I say, that he may not be offended with what I've done?' interposed Selina.

'But why should it matter if he be?'

'O! I must agree to be his wife if he forgives me—of course I must.'

'Must! But why not say nay, Selina, even if he do forgive 'ee?'

'O no! How can I without being wicked? You were very very kind, Mr Miller, to ask me to have you; no other man would have done it after what had happened; and I agreed, even though I did not feel half so warm as I ought. Yet it was entirely owing to my believing him in the grave, as I knew that if he were not he would carry out his promise; and this shows that I was right in trusting him.'

'Yes. . . . He must be a goodish sort of fellow,' said Mr Miller, for a moment so impressed with the excellently faithful conduct of the sergeant-major of dragoons that he disregarded its effect upon his own position. He sighed slowly and added, 'Well, Selina, 'tis for you to say. I love you, and I love the boy; and there's my chimney-corner and sticks o' furniture ready for 'ee both.'

'Yes, I know! But I mustn't hear it any more now,' murmured Selina quickly. 'John will be here soon. I hope he'll see how it all was when I tell him. If so be I could have written it to him it would have been better.'

'You think he doesn't know a single word about our having been on the brink o't. But perhaps it's the other way—he's heard of it and that may have brought him.'

'Ah—perhaps he has!' she said brightening. 'And already forgives me.'

'If not, speak out straight and fair, and tell him exactly how it fell out. If he's a man he'll see it.'

'O he's a man true enough. But I really do think I shan't have to tell him at all, since you've put it to me that way!'

As it was now Johnny's bedtime he was carried upstairs, and when Selina came down again her mother observed with some anxiety, 'I fancy Mr Clark must be here soon if he's coming; and that being so, perhaps Mr Miller wouldn't mind—wishing us good-night! since you are so determined to stick to your sergeant-major.' A little bitterness bubbled amid the closing words. 'It would be less awkward, Mr Miller not being here—if he will allow me to say it.'

'To be sure; to be sure,' the master-wheelwright exclaimed with instant conviction, rising alertly from his chair. 'Lord bless my soul,' he said, taking up his hat and stick, 'and we to have been married in six days! But Selina—you're right. You do belong to the child's father since he's alive. I'll try to make the best of it.'

Before the generous Miller had got further there came a knock to the door accompanied by the noise of wheels.

'I thought I heard something driving up!' said Mrs Paddock.

They heard Mr Paddock, who had been smoking in the room opposite, rise and go to the door, and in a moment a voice familiar enough to Selina was audibly saying, 'At last I am here again—not without many interruptions! How is it with 'ee, Mr Paddock? And how is she? Thought never to see me again, I suppose?' A step with a clink of spurs in it struck upon the entry floor.

'Danged if I bain't catched!' murmured Mr Miller, forgetting company-speech. 'Never mind—I may as well meet him here as elsewhere; and I should like to see the chap, and make friends with en, as he seems one o' the right sort.' He returned to the fireplace just as the sergeant-major was ushered in.

III

He was a good specimen of the long-service soldier of those days; a not unhandsome man, with a certain undemonstrative dignity, which some might have said to be partly owing to the stiffness of his uniform about his neck, the high stock being still worn. He was much stouter than when Selina had parted from him. Although she had not meant to be demonstrative she ran across to him directly she saw him, and he held her in his arms and kissed her.

Then in much agitation she whispered something to him, at which he seemed to be much surprised.

'He's just put to bed,' she continued. 'You can go up and see him. I knew you'd come if you were alive! But I had quite gi'd you up for dead. You've been home in England ever since the war ended?'

'Yes, dear.'

'Why didn't you come sooner?'

'That's just what I ask myself! Why was I such a sappy as not to hurry here the first day I set foot on shore! Well, who'd have thought it—you are as pretty as ever!'

He relinquished her to peep upstairs a little way, where, by look-ing through the ballusters, he could see Johnny's cot just within an open door. On his stepping down again Mr Miller was preparing to depart.

'Now, what's this? I am sorry to see anybody going the moment I've come,' expostulated the sergeant-major. 'I thought we might make an evening of it. There's a nine gallon cask o' "Phoenix" beer outside in the trap, and a ham, and half a rawmil' cheese; for I thought you might be short o' forage in a lonely place like this; and it struck me we might like to ask in a neighbour or two. But perhaps it would be taking a liberty?'

'O no, not at all,' said Mr Paddock, who was now in the room, in a judicial measured manner. 'Very thoughtful of 'ee, only 'twas not necessary, for we had just laid in an extry stock of eatables and drinkables in preparation for the coming event.'

''Twas very kind, upon my heart,' said the soldier, 'to think me worth such a jocund preparation, since you could only have got my letter this morning.'

Selina gazed at her father to stop him, and exchanged embarrassed glances with Miller. Contrary to her hopes Sergeant-Major Clark plainly did not know that the preparations referred to were for something quite other than his own visit.

The movement of the horse outside, and the impatient tapping of a whip-handle upon the vehicle reminded them that Clark's driver was still in waiting. The provisions were brought into the house, and the cart dismissed. Miller, with very little pressure indeed, accepted an invitation to supper, and a few neighbours were induced to come in to make up a cheerful party.

During the laying of the meal, and throughout its continuance, Selina, who sat beside her first intended husband, tried frequently to break the news to him of her engagement to the other—now terminated so suddenly, and so happily for her heart, and her sense of womanly virtue. But the talk ran entirely upon the late war; and though fortified by half a horn of the strong ale brought by the sergeant-major she decided that she might have a better opportunity when supper was over of revealing the situation to him in private.

Having supped, Clark leaned back at ease in his chair and looked around. 'We used sometimes to have a dance in that other room after supper, Selina dear, I recollect. We used to clear out all the furniture into this room before beginning. Have you kept up such goings on?'

'No, not at all!' said his sweetheart, sadly.

'We were not unlikely to revive it in a few days,' said Mr Paddock. 'But, howsomever, there's seemingly many a slip, as the saying is.'

'Yes, I'll tell John all about that by and by!' interposed Selina; at which, perceiving that the secret which he did not like keeping was to be kept even yet, her father held his tongue with some show of testiness.

The subject of a dance having been broached, to put the thought in practice was the feeling of all. Soon after the tables and chairs were borne from the opposite room to this by zealous hands, and two of the villagers sent home for a fiddle and tambourine, when the majority began to tread a measure well known in that secluded vale. Selina naturally danced with the sergeant-major, not altogether to her father's satisfaction, and to the real uneasiness of her mother, both of whom would have preferred a postponement of festivities till the rashly anticipated relationship between their daughter and Clark in the past had been made fact by the church's ordinances. They did not, however, express a positive objection, Mr Paddock remembering, with self-reproach, that it was owing to his original strongly expressed disapproval of Selina's being a soldier's wife that the wedding had been delayed, and finally hindered—with worse consequences than were expected; and ever since the misadventure brought about by his government he had allowed events to steer their own courses.

'My tails will surely catch in your spurs, John!' murmured the daughter of the house, as she whirled around upon his arm with the rapt soul and look of a somnambulist. 'I didn't know we should dance, or I would have put on my other frock.'

'I'll take care, my love. We've danced here before. Do you think your father objects to me now? I've risen in rank. I fancy he's still a little against me.'

'He has repented, times enough.'

'And so have I! If I had married you then 'twould have saved many a misfortune. I have sometimes thought it might have been possible to rush the ceremony through somehow before I left; though we were only in the second asking, were we? And even if I had come back straight here when we returned from the Crimea, and married you then, how much happier I should have been!'

'Dear John, to say that! Why didn't you?'

'O—dilatoriness and want of thought, and a fear of facing your father after so long. I was in hospital a great while, you know. But how familiar the place seems again! What's that I saw on the beaufet in the other room? It never used to be there. A sort of withered corpse of a cake—not an old bride-cake surely?'

'Yes, John, ours. 'Tis the very one that was made for our wedding three years ago.'

'Sakes alive! Why, time shuts up together, and all between then and now seems not to have been! What became of that wedding-gown that they were making in this room, I remember—a bluish, whitish, frothy thing?'

'I have that too.'

'Really! . . . Why, Selina——'

'Yes!'

'Why not put it on now?'

'Wouldn't it seem——. And yet, O how I should like to! It would remind them all, if we told them what it was, how we really meant to be married on that bygone day!' Her eyes were again laden with wet.

'Yes. . . . The pity that we didn't—the pity!' Moody mournfulness seemed to hold silent awhile one not naturally taciturn. 'Well—will you?' he said.

'I will—the next dance, if mother don't mind.'

Accordingly, just before the next figure was formed, Selina disappeared, and speedily came downstairs in a creased and box-worn, but still airy and pretty, muslin gown, which was indeed the very one that had been meant to grace her as a bride three years before.

'It is dreadfully old-fashioned,' she apologized.

'Not at all. What a grand thought of mine! Now, let's to't again.'

She explained to some of them, as he led her to the second dance, what the frock had been meant for, and that she had put it on at his request. And again athwart and around the room they went.

'You seem the bride!' he said.

'But I couldn't wear this gown to be married in now!' she replied, ecstatically, 'or I shouldn't have put it on and made it dusty. It is really too old-fashioned, and so folded and fretted out, you can't think. That was with my taking it out so many times to look at. I have never put it on—never—till now!'

'Selina, I am thinking of giving up the army. Will you emigrate with me to New Zealand? I've an uncle out there doing well, and he'd soon help me to making a larger income. The English army is glorious, but it ain't altogether enriching.'

'Of course, anywhere that you decide upon. Is it healthy there for Johnny?'

'A lovely climate. And I shall never be happy in England. . . . Aha!' he concluded again, with a bitterness of unexpected strength, 'would to Heaven I had come straight back here!'

As the dance brought round one neighbour after another the reunited pair were thrown into juxtaposition with Bob Heartall among the rest who had been called in; one whose chronic expression was that he carried inside him a joke on the point of bursting with its own vastness. He took occasion now to let out a little of its quality, shaking his head at Selina as he addressed her in an undertone—

'This is a bit of a topper to the bridegroom, ho! ho! 'Twill teach en the liberty you'll expect when you've married en!'

'What does he mean by a "topper",' the sergeant-major asked, who, not being of local extraction, despised the venerable local language, and also seemed to suppose 'bridegroom' to be an anticipatory name for himself. 'I only hope I shall never be worse treated than you've treated me to-night!'

Selina looked frightened. 'He didn't mean you, dear,' she said as they moved on. 'We thought perhaps you knew what had happened, owing to your coming just at this time. Had you—heard anything about—what I intended?'

'Not a breath—how should I—away up in Yorkshire? It was by the merest accident that I came just at this date to make peace with you for my delay.'

'I was engaged to be married to Mr Bartholomew Miller. That's what it is! I would have let 'ee know by letter, but there was no time, only hearing from 'ee this afternoon. . . . You won't desert me for it, will you, John? Because, as you know, I quite supposed you dead, and—and—' Her eyes were full of tears of trepidation, and he might have felt a sob heaving within her.

IV

The soldier was silent during two or three double bars of the tune. 'When were you to have been married to the said Mr Bartholomew Miller?' he inquired.

'Quite soon.'

'How soon?'

'Next week—O yes—just the same as it was with you and me. There's a strange fate of interruption hanging over me, I sometimes think! He had bought the licence, which I preferred so that it mightn't be like—ours. But it made no difference to the fate of it.'

'Had bought the licence! The devil!'

'Don't be angry, dear John. I didn't know!'

'No, no, I'm not angry.'

'It was so kind of him, considering!'

'Yes. . . . I see, of course, how natural your action was—never thinking of seeing me any more! Is it the Mr Miller who is in this dance?'

'Yes.'

Clark glanced round upon Bartholomew and was silent again for some little while, and she stole a look at him, to find that he seemed changed. 'John, you look ill!' she almost sobbed. ''Tisn't me, is it?'

'O dear, no. Though I hadn't, somehow, expected it. I can't find fault with you for a moment—and I don't. . . . This is a deuce of a long dance, don't you think? We've been at it twenty minutes if a second, and the figure doesn't allow one much rest. I'm quite out of breath.'

'They like them so dreadfully long here. Shall we drop out? Or I'll stop the fiddler.'

'O no, no, I think I can finish. But although I look healthy enough I have never been so strong as I formerly was, since that long illness I had in the hospital at Scutari.'

'And I knew nothing about it!'

'You couldn't, dear, as I didn't write. What a fool I have been altogether!' He gave a twitch, as of one in pain. 'I won't dance again when this one is over. The fact is I have travelled a long way today, and it seems to have knocked me up a bit.'

There could be no doubt that the sergeant-major was unwell, and Selina made herself miserable by still believing that her story was the cause of his ailment. Suddenly he said in a changed voice, and she perceived that he was paler than ever:

'I must sit down.'

Letting go her waist he went quickly to the other room. She followed, and found him in the nearest chair, his face bent down upon his hands and arms, which were resting on the table.

'What's the matter?' said her father, who sat there dozing by the fire.

'John isn't well. . . . We are going to New Zealand when we are married, father. A lovely country! . . . John, would you like something to drink?'

'A drop o' that Schiedam of old Owlett's, that's under stairs, perhaps,' suggested her father. 'Not that nowadays 'tis much better than licensed liquor.'

'John,' she said, putting her face close to his and pressing his arm. 'Will you have a drop of spirits or something?'

He did not reply, and Selina observed that his ear and the side of his face were quite white. Convinced that his illness was serious, a growing dismay seized hold of her. The dance ended; her mother came in, and learning what had happened, looked narrowly at the sergeant-major.

'We must not let him lie like that, lift him up,' she said. 'Let him rest in the window-bench on some cushions.'

They unfolded his arms and hands as they lay clasped upon the table, and on lifting his head found his features to bear the very impress of death itself. Bartholomew Miller, who had now come in, assisted Mr Paddock to make a comfortable couch in the window-seat, where they stretched out Clark upon his back.

Still he seemed unconscious. 'We must get a doctor,' said Selina. 'O, my dear John, how is it you be taken like this?'

'My impression is that he's dead!' murmured Mr Paddock. 'He don't breathe enough to move a tomtit's feather.'

There were plenty to volunteer to go for a doctor, but as it would be at least an hour before he could get there the case seemed somewhat hopeless. The dancing-party ended as unceremoniously as it had begun; but the guests lingerèd round the premises till the doctor should arrive. When he did come the sergeant-major's extremities were already cold, and there was no doubt that death had overtaken him almost at the moment that he had sat down.

The medical practitioner quite refused to accept the unhappy Selina's theory that her revelation had in any way induced Clark's sudden collapse. Both he and the coroner afterwards, who found the immediate cause to be heart-failure, held that such a supposition was unwarranted by facts. They asserted that a long day's journey, a hurried drive, and then an exhausting dance, were sufficient for such a result upon a heart enfeebled by fatty degeneration after the privations of a Crimean winter and other trying experiences, the coincidence of the sad event with any disclosure of hers being a pure accident.

This conclusion, however, did not dislodge Selina's opinion that the shock of her statement had been the immediate stroke which had felled a constitution so undermined.

V

At this date the Casterbridge Barracks were cavalry quarters, their adaptation to artillery having been effected some years later. It had been owing to the fact that the —th Dragoons, in which John Clark had served, happened to be lying there that Selina made his acquaintance. At the time of his death the barracks were occupied by the Scots Greys, but when the pathetic circumstances of the sergeant-major's end became known in the town the officers of the Greys offered the services of their fine reed and brass band, that he might have a funeral marked by due military honours. His body was accordingly removed to the barracks, and carried thence to the churchyard in the Durnover quarter on the following afternoon, one of the Greys' most ancient and docile chargers being blacked up to represent Clark's horse on the occasion.

Everybody pitied Selina, whose story was well known. She followed the corpse as the only mourner, Clark having been without relations in this part of the country, and a communication with his regiment having brought none from a distance. She sat in a little shabby brown-black mourning carriage, squeezing herself up in a corner to be as much as possible out of sight during the slow and dramatic march through the town to the tune from *Saul*. When the interment had taken place, the volleys been fired, and the return journey begun, it was with something like a shock that she found the military escort to be moving at a quick march to the lively strains of 'Off she goes!' as if all care for the sergeant-major was expected to be ended with the late discharge of the carbines. It was, by chance, the very tune to which they had been footing when he died, and unable to bear its notes, she hastily told her driver to drop behind. The band and military party diminished up the High Street, and Selina turned over Swan bridge and homeward to Mellstock.

Then recommenced for her a life whose incidents were precisely of a suit with those which had preceded the soldier's return; but how different in her appreciation of them! Her narrow miss of the recovered respectability they had hoped for from that tardy event worked upon her parents as an irritant, and after the first week or two of her mourning her life with them grew almost insupportable. She had impulsively taken to herself the weeds of a widow, for such she seemed to herself to be, and clothed little Johnny in sables likewise. This assumption of a moral relationship to the deceased, which she asserted to be only not a legal one by two most unexpected accidents, led the old people to indulge in sarcasm at her expense whenever they beheld her attire, though all the while it cost them more pain to utter than it gave her to hear it.

Having become accustomed by her residence at home to the business carried on by her father, she surprised them one day by going off with the child to Chalk-Newton, in the direction of the town of Ivell, and opening a miniature fruit and vegetable shop, attending Ivell market with her produce. Her business grew somewhat larger, and it was soon sufficient to enable her to support herself and the boy in comfort. She called herself 'Mrs John Clark' from the day of leaving home, and painted the name on her signboard—no man forbidding her.

By degrees the pain of her state was forgotten in her new circumstances, and getting to be generally accepted as the widow of a sergeant-major of dragoons—an assumption which her modest and mournful demeanour seemed to substantiate—her life became a placid one, her mind being nourished by the melancholy luxury of dreaming what might have been her future in New Zealand with John, if he had only lived to take her there. Her only travels now were a journey to Ivell on market-days, and once a fortnight to the churchyard in which Clark lay, there to tend, with Johnny's assistance, as widows are wont to do, the flowers she had planted upon his grave.

On a day about eighteen months after his unexpected decease, Selina was surprised in her lodging over her little shop by a visit from Bartholomew Miller. He had called on her once or twice before, on which occasions he had used without a word of comment the name by which she was known.

'I've come this time,' he said, 'less because I was in this direction than to ask you, Mrs Clark, what you mid well guess. I've come o' purpose, in short.'

She smiled.

"Tis to ask me again to marry you?'

'Yes, of course. You see, his coming back for 'ee proved what I always believed of 'ee, though others didn't. There's nobody but would be glad to welcome you to our parish again, now you've showed your independence and acted up to your trust in his promise. Well, my dear, will you come?'

'I'd rather bide as Mrs Clark, I think,' she answered. 'I am not ashamed of my position at all; for I am John's widow in the eyes of Heaven.'

'I quite agree—that's why I've come. Still, you won't like to be always straining at this shop-keeping and market-standing; and 'twould be better for Johnny if you had nothing to do but tend him.'

He here touched the only weak spot in Selina's resistance to his proposal—the good of the boy. To promote that there were other men she might have married offhand without loving them if they had asked her to; but though she had known the worthy speaker from her youth, she could not for the moment fancy herself happy as Mrs Miller.

He paused awhile. 'I ought to tell 'ee, Mrs Clark,' he said by and by, 'that marrying is getting to be a pressing question with me. Not on my own account at all. The truth is, that mother is growing old, and I am away from home a good deal, so that it is almost necessary there should be another person in the house with her besides me. That's the practical consideration which forces me to think of taking a wife, apart from my wish to take you; and you know there's nobody in the world I care for so much.'

She said something about there being far better women than she, and other natural commonplaces; but assured him she was most grateful to him for feeling what he felt, as indeed she sincerely was. However, Selina would not consent to be the useful third person in his comfortable home—at any rate just then. He went away, after taking tea with her, without discerning much hope for him in her good-bye.

VI

After that evening she saw and heard nothing of him for a great while. Her fortnightly journeys to the sergeant-major's grave were continued, whenever weather did not hinder them; and Mr Miller must have known, she thought, of this custom of hers. But though the churchyard was not nearly so far from his homestead as was her shop at Chalk-Newton, he never appeared in the accidental way that lovers use.

An explanation was forthcoming in the shape of a letter from her mother, who casually mentioned that Mr Bartholomew Miller had gone away to the other side of Shottsford-Forum to be married to a thriving dairyman's daughter that he knew there. His chief motive, it was reported, had been less one of love than a wish to provide a companion for his aged mother.

Selina was practical enough to know that she had lost a good and possibly the only opportunity of settling in life after what had happened, and for a moment she regretted her independence. But she became calm on reflection, and to fortify herself in her course started that afternoon to tend the sergeant-major's grave, in which she took the same sober pleasure as at first.

On reaching the churchyard and turning the corner towards the spot as usual, she was surprised to perceive another woman, also apparently a respectable widow, and with a tiny boy by her side, bending over Clark's turf, and spudding up with the point of her umbrella some ivy-roots that Selina had reverently planted there to form an evergreen mantle over the mound.

'What are you digging up my ivy for!' cried Selina, rushing forward so excitedly that Johnny tumbled over a grave with the force of the tug she gave his hand in her sudden start.

'Your ivy?' said the respectable woman.

'Why yes! I planted it there—on my husband's grave.'

'*Your* husband's!'

'Yes. The late Sergeant-Major Clark. Anyhow, as good as my husband, for he was just going to be.'

'Indeed. But who may be my husband, if not he? I am the only Mrs John Clark, widow of the late Sergeant-Major of Dragoons, and this is his only son and heir.'

'How can that be?' faltered Selina, her throat seeming to stick together as she just began to perceive its possibility. 'He had been—going to marry me twice—and we were going to New Zealand.'

'Ah!—I remember about you,' returned the legitimate widow calmly and not unkindly. 'You must be Selina; he spoke of you now and then, and said that his relations with you would always be a weight on his conscience. Well; the history of my life with him is soon told. When he came back from the Crimea he became acquainted with me at my home in the north, and we were married within a month of first knowing each other. Unfortunately, after living together a few months, we could not agree; and after a particularly sharp quarrel, in which, perhaps, I was most in the wrong—as I don't mind owning here by his graveside—he went away from me, declaring he would buy his discharge and emigrate to New Zealand, and never come back to me any more. The next thing I heard was that he had died suddenly at Mellstock at some low carouse; and as he had left me in such anger to live no more with me, I wouldn't come down to his funeral, or do anything in relation to him. 'Twas temper, I know, but that was the fact. Even if we had parted friends it would have been a serious expense to travel three hundred miles to get there, for one who wasn't left so very well off. . . . I am sorry I pulled up your ivy-roots; but that common sort of ivy is considered a weed in my part of the country.'

C. C. K. GONNER

Olive's Lover

THERE is a short story told by Goldsmith of a man who lived a double life, adding to his more material existence a second, and so far as he was concerned equally real, existence in dreamland. Unlike the visions of others, his dreams followed one another in well-continued series, till he only woke to eat, drink, and loiter away a few harsh hours on earth before plunging once again into the scenes of his ideal life. He loved, wooed, and that successfully, the fair lady of his dreams. They lived together in happiness till an untoward fate snatched her from him, and he remained alone and widowed. Under such circumstances as these, his lot became too hard to bear. When awake he was unmarried and lonely; when asleep, desolate and a widower. Gradually his strength failed him; and though he still continued to alternate between one life and the other, the melancholy which filled his sleeping hours pressed upon him with such a heaviness that one morning when they came to waken him he was found dead. One mystery, of course, history cannot solve. Did he die in his dream, or did he cease dreaming? But without waiting for an answer to such a question, we may lay the moral to heart, and remember not to lie on our backs when we go to bed. Thus much by prelude.

It was in the suburbs of one of our large northern towns that the family lived which provides the heroine of this story. Wandering up from the noisy highway there ran a quiet lane, shaded to gloom with high trees, which hid the houses from the passers-by. One of these houses was the residence of a doctor with a large family, and still better, with a large practice. Many as the children were in number, the real centre of the household was fixed in the person of the second daughter, Olive. Her sisters, indeed, were good enough and pretty enough to serve as attraction for many a lawn-tennis party, but she seemed to stand apart from them rather by a certain indefinable charm of manner and power of social sympathy than by reason of any peculiar gift of beauty. To such she could scarcely lay claim, and though not deficient in intelligence, she gained no reputation as a wit, while she failed in most of the little practical enterprises which she undertook. Yet despite, and, perhaps, almost in consequence of, these deficiencies, she continued to rule her sisters and parents, and so to madden the hearts of all the youth of the suburb that they went in their multitudes to all the places where she played tennis, and expended their hard-earned money in bouquets when the neighbourhood ventured on its somewhat miniature balls. Yet, notwithstanding all this, she, at least, remained heart-whole and free. So often had she to exercise her prerogative of rejection that it seemed hardly possible that she would ever be able to fly in the face of habit by answering a suitor in the affirmative.

For some time before the beginning of our story there had been little of note in the annals of the family. One sister had been married and another become engaged, but Olive lived on, contented and happy, oftenest, indeed, quietly at home, but sometimes making short rounds of visits among friends.

On her return from one of these short tours of courtesy her manner seemed as though it had undergone a change. The old quiet was superseded by a fitful restlessness; and though she still was lively at times, she loved best to seek out quaint paths in the surrounding country, where she might wander unobserved and unhurried. She would come in from her rambles flushed and bright, and then would join gaily in the outbursts of mirth so common in a large family. But the cause of the change was soon revealed. One morning she had wandered into the lane before breakfast, and when she came back she had brought the usual budget of letters, which she had taken from the postman at the gate. There was one which she had hidden in her pocket, only to rest there for a time, since no sooner was the meal over than she darted off to read it in private, but shortly afterwards returned to her mother with her version of the old, old story.

It ran in this wise:—While staying at Swansea with some friends she had met a young man, a barrister. They had fallen in love, but he, as he had no means of his own, had striven, apparently with success, to conceal his feelings; and so they had parted without any understanding, and indeed, according to her, without any knowledge

of their mutual attachment. But now a change had come in his fortunes. A distant relative had died in New Zealand, leaving him heir
to his sheep farm, which report had exalted to a most fabulous
value; yet even after every method of discount had been exhausted,
there still remained enough to make him a very wealthy man. No
sooner did he receive the news than he wrote a hasty letter to Olive,
in which he besought her to be his wife. He would, indeed, have
come down to the north himself, but the condition in which the
estate was left made it necessary for him to take a short trip out,
while the necessity of settling his affairs and making a few preparations rendered the few hours still remaining before the departure of
the overland mail far too short to allow of his absence. It was a
fine, manly letter, and the few words that accompanied it addressed
to the parents made them hesitate in their resolve to refuse, or postpone, their consent till he could ask it in person. Thus it was that
on the eve of his departure he received a letter which gave him the
answer he wished.

Thenceforth he was swept on in his preparations by a hurricane
of joy, and yet, being prudent and a barrister, unburdened by too
many briefs, he cultivated an acquaintance with a solicitor and made
his will. This, at least, he told her, and the reason which he assigned
was hardly such as to ease a fond heart, for he wrote that he wished
to leave her everything he had, in case an accident of some kind
should overtake him. But love was not much damped by such forebodings, and Olive seemed content with the written vows of ardent
love, though the ocean widened between her and her receding
lover.

But now her very life was transformed. She would sit for hours
reading over the few letters she had had time to receive, or talking
with her friends of the days when she knew him, but did not know
that he loved her, while oftenest of all she loved to calculate when
he would return and where he might be. Indeed, the one great
question which exercised the whole family was, when could Henry
be back? It is not necessary to add that she was ever on the look-
out for the postman, and her father laughed again and again at the
new-born punctuality of her habits, and at the sanctity which attached
to letters, which she always received with her own hands. Her devotion in this respect was almost ludicrous, and fortunately it was well
rewarded, while she herself was encouraged in her new habit of

early rising by the coincidence that on the one or two occasions when she was late, no letters came by the mail.

Time flew by and her lover's approach was expected. She had received news of the vessel by which he intended to return, and as this letter was posted only just in advance, his arrival was reasonably expected in a few days. But the vessel which was to have brought him, only brought a letter in which he explained the cause of his unfortunate detention. The agent whom he had confirmed in the management of the property, owing to the failure of a company in which he was concerned, had been obliged to quit the country, and Henry Brinton (such was his name) overtaken by the news at Sydney, had been forced to quit the vessel and return once more to New Zealand. But shortly afterwards another letter announced that he was once more on his way home, and this time he asked that, as he had been so delayed, the marriage might take place the week after his return. Of course there were many objections, but, equally of course, these objections were overruled, and the day of the ceremony was fixed on the Wednesday after the arrival of the traveller.

Unfortunately the chapter of accidents was only at its beginning. As they speedily found, the marriage was not to take place when arranged, for another letter told Olive how Mr Brinton had been attacked by fever in the Red Sea, and of the desperate extremity to which he was brought. At the bottom of this letter, written in a strange hand, there was a faint pencil scrawl in which the lover himself had tried to send his own brief message of affection, despite the weakness which scarcely allowed his fingers to guide a pencil.

A terrible time of anxiety spread itself out before those at home. Olive seemed to fail in health and to shun all exertion, while all her interest centred in the visits of the postman, for whose arrival she would watch wistfully, and too often in vain. It was only at his approach that she shook off the lassitude which had become habitual; on such occasions she would run to the gate, and even walk down the lane to meet him and to see whether he had a letter for her. Sometimes she returned brighter than she went, for then she had a letter and knew at least that he still lived. They followed his course closely. It was at first but a poor consolation to hear that he had been put ashore at Malta, but after that letters came more frequently, and each one seemed to give further accounts of improvement, till at length it was announced that he was coming over to the mainland to make the best of his way home. There was something of comfort in the thought that the distance which lay between them could be bridged in days, and anxiety grew less and hope more hardy as mail after mail brought the news of increasing strength.

Once clear of the hot south his health seemed to return with a sudden bound, and when a letter came from Paris, there seemed no longer room for doubt as to his speedy return. In the train to Boulogne, however, he showed signs of fresh feebleness, once indeed fainting away, to the alarm of an old friend who had come over to France to meet him. When he revived his first remark, as his friend wrote to Olive's mother, was a true evidence of the strength of his attachment, for with a faint smile he said, 'Ah! I've quite falsified my little Olive's pet theory.' She, it seems, with girlish petulance, had oftentimes maintained that nobody need faint if only their mind was made up to resist the impulse. At Boulogne he was taken into the hotel and put to bed. To his friend's mingled horror and amusement he showed symptoms of having caught the measles, a matter soon put beyond a doubt by the opinion of an English doctor staying in the house. Fortunately the attack was but slight, and the lapse of three weeks saw him restored to a state of health more satisfactory than that which he had enjoyed since his first illness.

Now, indeed, we must return to Olive. At last her hopes were nearing their fulfilment. She grew more cheerful, brighter, and every morning she came downstairs humming a light song of gladness, while her eyes glistened softly with the feelings of love rendered more potent by the trials it had undergone. She and her father were to go up to London to greet him on his arrival; but at the last minute their departure was postponed by a letter from the friends with whom they were to stay. They were in great trouble, indeed wholly unable to take them in. But this matter seemed of slight account, as the next day they heard that Henry had reached town, and proposed, after a delay of two days, to come straight on to the north.

Their surmise was all too hasty, for a few days proved that it had been better for them to go up to town despite all inconvenience. The measles had left a weakness of the eyesight, and after seeing his doctor, Henry Brinton found it necessary to remain for a week longer to consult an oculist. It was not without feelings of trepidation that they awaited the account of the interview; but when it came they were once more to experience the feeling, so often repeated in their case, of relief. He wrote that there was little the matter with his eyes, and that he could come down the day they would receive his note. They met the train he had chosen, but he was not in it, a fact easily accounted for in the evening, when they got a hurried scrawl to say that he had been forced to attend at a police court to give evidence in a trumpery case of assault, of which he had been a witness the day before. This over, there was nothing to delay him, and he would leave by the newspaper train on the following morning. The day came, and with it the appearance of breakfast. Still, to anyone who can view the conditions of the case without prejudice, it must appear consolatory that none of their appetites were keen, since they were bound to be unsatisfied through the necessity of hurrying down to the station some half-hour before it was necessary.

Olive, with her sister and father, paced up and down the long platform in an excitement hardly unnatural under all the circumstances. They all felt irritated; first with the train, because it did not come before its time; then with themselves, because they had hurried. Olive herself was the calmest of the trio, though her eager eyes showed how she felt, and her tightly interlaced fingers were an evidence of the constraint which she was putting on her emotions. At last the bell rang, and slowly the train swept into the station. They had hurried forward to welcome him—Olive to meet her lover, the others to greet a stranger. But where was he? At first they had waited for him to step out on the platform; then not seeing him they went hurriedly along the train peering into carriage after carriage, but the most diligent search could convince them of but one thing, his absence. There was no passenger by the train, hunt though they might. The train moved out, and they remained perplexed and bewildered. As the last hope seemed to vanish, a low cry from Olive reached her father, and he turned just in time to catch her before she fell to the ground. He called a cab and put her in, thinking as he did so that the strain was now going to tell upon her, and that a sharp illness would be the probable result. Yet by the time home was reached she seemed better, and, despite all their efforts, she refused to go to bed. She insisted on staying up and waiting—for what? They would have telegraphed, but remembered just in time that Henry, in his last letter, had said that he was leaving the hotel at which he had been stopping in order to sleep at one nearer the station, so that they had no address to which they could send a message. It was a terrible day, for the hours crept by and yet no news came, till some time after midday Olive, looking anxiously from the window, spied out the postman in the distance and hurriedly ran to meet him. There was a letter to her in a strange writing; but all the news it contained was in a few lines, which said how Mr Brinton had met with an accident at the station which prevented his travelling that day. With this they had to remain content as best they could. The others went about their duties with heavy hearts; but Olive sat drearily gazing down the lane, watching for the lover who did not come, while her lips seemed to form the refrain of the old childish sport, 'he cometh, he cometh not'.

So the day wore away; but just as dark seemed to close in and preclude all further hope of news, the whole household was startled by a loud shriek. They rushed down to find Olive lying motionless on the hall floor, her hand clenched over a letter just opened. The last post had been delayed, and once more she had been the one to receive the letters. One glance at the note revealed all. It was from a stranger, who stated that Mr Brinton had met with a severe accident, from which concussion of the brain of so fatal a character had ensued that he had died some five hours after the fall. All this was told in the most hurried of scrawls, so brief and hasty that the writer had forgotten to add his address, or to give any details as to arrangements which might be made.

Of course, the first care with the doctor was to see to his daughter; but when she had been put to bed, he sat up to consider the whole matter. He would, of course, have hurried up to town himself but for the impossibility of leaving his patients at a moment's notice; while, in addition, it seemed scarcely wise to go till Olive woke out of the unconsciousness into which she had fallen. Next morning, indeed, she was better; though her white drawn face and listless manner betrayed the full extent of the shock. Even then she was hardly able to do more than lie languidly back in a chair, letting others do all that was necessary in getting mourning. Her chief employment seemed to be that of reading over and over again the announcement of death which had appeared in the morning papers. It must be owned that the punctual appearance of this had allayed much of the uneasiness in the worthy doctor's mind, though he wished most fervently that, in addition to stating that death was due to an accident, it had contained some information as to the place where the ill-fated Henry Brinton had died. Still he rested content in the knowledge that the solicitors to the deceased would communicate with him when they came to examine into the will.

A few days had worn away when Olive received a letter stating that the funeral had taken place at the Highgate Cemetery. This news turned her thoughts in a fresh direction, and she followed her father into his study with the request that he would take her up to see the grave as soon as he could. The only thing which delayed his consent a minute was a doubt whether the condition of her health did not prohibit such a scheme as unwise; but when he noticed the plaintive—even piteous—endurance with which she pressed her request, he gave way, thinking as he did so that it would be just as well for him to go up himself and see after matters. The opportunity was a welcome one on that account, for as he received no communication a fear came over him lest the silver (nay, the golden) lining to their cloud should prove illusory.

They went to London the next morning, but as she obviously shrank from meeting anyone, whether stranger or friend, he decided to drive off to the cemetery at once, and then to try and discover some place where she would be willing to go and rest for an hour or two. All throughout the drive her nervous excitement increased, till he feared that he had made a mistake in allowing her to encounter so severe a trial. The burial-ground reached, she asked her father to let her stroll on while he went in to inquire the locality of the grave. He watched her as she went slowly into a bye-path, feeling all a father's sadness for the heavy sorrow that had come and bowed the slight figure that looked so fragile in its deep mourning; then he turned and asked the attendant to tell him where the grave of Mr Brinton was. As he awaited the answer, which was a little delayed, he could not avoid commenting to himself on the denseness of a memory so clogged that its machinery was long in bringing out the required note. His thoughts were broken in on by the voice of the man.

'I don't think there has been a burial in that name, sir.'

'Oh, yes,' he replied, 'it was on Tuesday last.'

'Tuesday,' echoed the attendant, and once again he seemed to

wind up his memory to its necessary work. But with all the winding he could not recall the name. At last he said he would go and
look in the register: but the register contained no entry of the name
of Brinton. Not content with looking through the list of funerals
on Tuesday, they glanced at all that had occurred since, and then
went so far back as to make sure that he had not been buried on
the day previous to his decease. It was all to no purpose; and when
the doctor ceased his search, he stood in the porch of the lodge,
the perspiration standing on his brow, while his important bearing
and evident indignation only heightened the mockery of the scene.
At first he had given way to a little outburst of wrath, bidding the
official find the grave, look for it, and not stand gaping there. It
was a last straw to lose the grave after losing a future son-in-law.
Then the folly of his anger dawned on him, and he had come to
the open door, and now stood looking down the path at the bereaved
girl, who passed slowly on, scanning each new-turned mound with
an unconcealed apprehension. He had to tell the news to her.
Thanking the officials, who, at first irritated, were now half sympathetic in their manner, he went quickly along the path till he
overtook Olive. She turned to meet him with an inquiring glance
which took no heed of the signs of perplexity on his countenance.

'Olive,' he said, trying to assume the light tone in which he would
utter some mere commonplace; 'Olive, I'm afraid there's been some
mistake.'

'Yes, father, what?' but the tone in which the question was uttered
showed a lack of interest; there was but one subject about which
she felt anxiety.

'Why,' and in trying to break the news he put it as bluntly as
possible, 'it seems that Henry was not buried here.'

For the time she thought he merely referred to the part of the
cemetery where they were; her lips were just parting to reveal her
thoughts when he went on: 'He was not buried in this cemetery
at all; in fact, my dear, we've come to the wrong place.'

'Where was it then?' and this time the dreaminess of tone seemed
gone.

'Oh,' he said, 'I don't quite know; indeed, there has been an
entire mistake, and we must try and find out.'

What more he might have said was stayed when he saw the
look of despair that spread over the young girl's countenance. He

hurried her away, called for a cab, and drove off once more to the station. Now his only wish was to get her home in safety. His anxiety was not without ground, for even before they reached the north she sank into a half-unconscious condition, and when they got her to her room it was only too evident that the excitement of the past days had induced a severe attack of brain fever. Of course she could not be left, so the doctor, determined to get the mystery solved as soon as possible, went to his brother, who lived in the same town, and asked him to go up to London and make inquiries in his stead.

The next few days were chiefly marked by the increase of anxiety and the absence of news. Only one letter had been received, and that letter intimated that nothing had yet been discovered of the smallest importance. Meantime everything betokened severity in the illness that had overtaken Olive. There was little hope of her recovery, thought the doctor, as he stood by her bedside that very evening after the receipt of this note: yet even he did not know how near to her was an end of the weary series of disappointments and trials that had been crowded into so brief a time. As he turned to quit the room he heard her murmur the name 'Henry', and when he glanced round in haste he spied the new stillness that had come over her face. She had died with the name of her lover on her lips.

By his plate, on the morrow, he found a fresh despatch from his brother. As he opened the envelope to take out the letter, an enclosed slip of paper fluttered to his feet. He did not stay to pick it up, but began reading at once:

The Clarence, Wednesday.

My dear Douglas,—Please read this letter when you are by yourself, as the news which it contains is, I am sorry to say, anything but pleasing. When I wrote to you this morning I had not made up my mind as to the course of action for the day, but the letter was hardly posted when I determined to go to the newspaper office and see if I could get any clue as to the place from which the advertisement of Mr Brinton's death had been sent. Accordingly I went in. They were very polite when I told them the reason of my errand, and the manager of the department came to me at once. He sent for the *original* of the advertisement, which came through their country agent. Now I must ask you to take heed to yourself, for here comes the terrible revelation: *The announcement of death was written in Olive's handwriting.* Of this I have no doubt whatever. On further inquiry we found that it had been paid for by a postal order drawn at your own post office—a fact impressed on the mind of the clerk who opened the note because he had lived not far from there when a child. I fear the whole thing was an illusion.

Enclosed is the original of the announcement.

Your affectionate brother,

E. A. CAMPBELL.

He read the letter twice over, for he scarcely caught its purport in the first perusal. Then stooped and read through the paper that had fallen to the ground. The news was only too true. For a moment he sat quiet; then, and not till then, did it strike him that Olive, and Olive only, had taken in the foreign letters from the postman.

RUDYARD KIPLING

The Wish House

THE new Church Visitor had just left after a twenty minutes' call. During that time, Mrs Ashcroft had used such English as an elderly, experienced, and pensioned cook should, who had seen life in London. She was the readier, therefore, to slip back into easy, ancient Sussex ('t's softening to 'd's as one warmed) when the 'bus brought Mrs Fettley from thirty miles away for a visit, that pleasant March Saturday. The two had been friends since childhood; but, of late, destiny had separated their meetings by long intervals.

Much was to be said, and many ends, loose since last time, to be ravelled up on both sides, before Mrs Fettley, with her bag of quilt-patches, took the couch beneath the window commanding the garden, and the football-ground in the valley below.

'Most folk got out at Bush Tye for the match there,' she explained, 'so there weren't no one for me to cushion agin, the last five mile. An' she *do* just-about bounce ye.'

'You've took no hurt,' said her hostess. 'You don't brittle by agein', Liz.'

Mrs Fettley chuckled and made to match a couple of patches to her liking. 'No, or I'd ha' broke twenty year back. You can't ever mind when I was so's to be called round, can ye?'

Mrs Ashcroft shook her head slowly—she never hurried—and went on stitching a sack-cloth lining into a list-bound rush tool-basket. Mrs Fettley laid out more patches in the Spring light through the geraniums on the window-sill, and they were silent awhile.

'What like's this new Visitor o' yourn?' Mrs Fettley inquired with a nod towards the door. Being very short-sighted, she had, on her entrance, almost bumped into the lady.

Mrs Ashcroft suspended the big packing-needle judicially on high, ere she stabbed home. 'Settin' aside she don't bring much news with her yet, I dunno as I've anythin' special agin her.'

'Ourn, at Keyneslade,' said Mrs Fettley, 'she's full o' words an' pity, but she don't stay for answers. Ye can get on with your thoughts while she clacks.'

'This 'un don't clack. She's aimin' to be one o' those High Church nuns, like.'

'Ourn's married, but, by what they say, she've made no great gains of it . . .' Mrs Fettley threw up her sharp chin. 'Lord! How they dam' cherubim do shake the very bones o' the place!'

The tile-sided cottage trembled at the passage of two specially chartered forty-seat charabancs on their way to the Bush Tye match; a regular Saturday 'shopping' 'bus, for the county's capital, fumed behind them; while, from one of the crowded inns, a fourth car backed out to join the procession, and held up the stream of through pleasure-traffic.

'You're as free-tongued as ever, Liz,' Mrs Ashcroft observed.

'Only when I'm with you. Otherwhiles, I'm Granny—three times over. I lay that basket's for one o' your gran'chiller—ain't it?'

''Tis for Arthur—my Jane's eldest.'

'But he ain't workin' nowheres, is he?'

'No. 'Tis a picnic-basket.'

'You're let off light. My Willie, he's allus at me for money for them aireated wash-poles folk puts up in their gardens to draw the music from Lunnon, like. An' I give it 'im—pore fool me!'

'An' he forgets to give you the promise-kiss after, don't he?' Mrs Ashcroft's heavy smile seemed to strike inwards.

'He do. 'No odds 'twixt boys now an' forty year back. 'Take all an' give naught—an' we to put up with it! Pore fool we! Three shillin' at a time Willie'll ask me for!'

'They don't make nothin' o' money these days,' Mrs Ashcroft said.

'An' on'y last week,' the other went on, 'me daughter, she ordered a quarter pound suet at the butchers's; an' she sent it back to 'um to be chopped. She said she couldn't bother with choppin' it.'

'I lay he charged her, then.'

'I lay he did. She told me there was a whisk-drive that afternoon at the Institute, an' she couldn't bother to do the choppin'.'

'Tck!'

Mrs Ashcroft put the last firm touches to the basket-lining. She had scarcely finished when her sixteen-year-old grandson, a maiden of the moment in attendance, hurried up the garden-path shouting to know if the thing were ready, snatched it, and made off without acknowledgment. Mrs Fettley peered at him closely.

'They're goin' picnickin' somewheres,' Mrs Ashcroft explained.

'Ah,' said the other, with narrowed eyes. 'I lay *he* won't show much mercy to any he comes across, either. Now 'oo the dooce do he remind me of, all of a sudden?'

'They must look arter theirselves—'same as we did.' Mrs Ashcroft began to set out the tea.

'No denyin' *you* could, Gracie,' said Mrs Fettley.

'What's in your head now?'

'Dunno . . . But it come over me, sudden-like—about dat woman from Rye—I've slipped the name—Barnsley, wadn't it?'

'Batten—Polly Batten, you're thinkin' of.'

'That's it—Polly Batten. That day she had it in for you with a hay-fork—'time we was all hayin' at Smalldene—for stealin' her man.'

'But you heered me tell her she had my leave to keep him?' Mrs Ashcroft's voice and smile were smoother than ever.

'I did—an' we was all looking that she'd prod the fork spang through your breastes when you said it.'

'No-oo. She'd never go beyond bounds—Polly. She shruck too much for reel doin's.'

'Allus seem to *me*,' Mrs Fettley said after a pause, 'that a man 'twixt two fightin' women is the foolishest thing on earth. 'Like a dog bein' called two ways.'

'Mebbe. But what set ye off on those times, Liz?'

'That boy's fashion o' carryin' his head an' arms. I haven't rightly looked at him since he's growed. Your Jane never showed it, but— *him*! Why, 'tis Jim Batten and his tricks come to life again! . . . Eh?'

'Mebbe. There's some that would ha' made it out so—bein' barren-like, themselves.'

'Oho! Ah well! Dearie, dearie me, now! . . . An' Jim Batten's been dead this——'

'Seven and twenty years,' Mrs Ashcroft answered briefly. 'Won't ye draw up, Liz?'

Mrs Fettley drew up to buttered toast, currant bread, stewed tea, bitter as leather, some home-preserved pears, and a cold boiled pig's tail to help down the muffins. She paid all the proper compliments.

'Yes. I dunno as I've ever owed me belly much,' said Mrs Ashcroft thoughtfully. 'We only go through this world once.'

'But don't it lay heavy on ye, sometimes?' her guest suggested.

'Nurse says I'm a sight liker to die o' me indigestion than me leg.' For Mrs Ashcroft had a long-standing ulcer on her shin, which needed regular care from the Village Nurse, who boasted (or others did, for her) that she had dressed it one hundred and three times already during her term of office.

'An' you that *was* so able, too! It's all come on ye before your full time, like. *I*'ve watched ye goin'.' Mrs Fettley spoke with real affection.

'Somethin's bound to find ye sometime. I've me 'eart left me still,' Mrs Ashcroft returned.

'You was always big-hearted enough for three. That's somethin' to look back on at the day's eend.'

'I reckon you've *your* back-lookin's, too,' was Mrs Ashcroft's answer.

'You know it. But I don't think much regardin' such matters except' when I'm along with you, Gra'. 'Takes two sticks to make a fire.'

Mrs Fettley stared, with jaw half-dropped, at the grocer's bright calendar on the wall. The cottage shook again to the roar of the motor-traffic, and the crowded football-ground below the garden roared almost as loudly; for the village was well set to its Saturday leisure.

Mrs Fettley had spoken very precisely for some time without interruption, before she wiped her eyes. 'And,' she concluded, 'they read 'is death-notice to me, out o' the paper last month. O' course it wadn't any o' *my* becomin' concerns—let be I 'adn't set eyes on him for so long. O' course *I* couldn't say nor show nothin'. Nor I've no rightful call to go to Eastbourne to see 'is grave, either. I've been schemin' to slip over there by the 'bus some day; but they'd ask questions at 'ome past endurance. So I 'aven't even *that* to stay me.'

'But you've 'ad your satisfaction?'

'Godd! Yess! Those four years 'e was workin' on the rail near us. An' the other drivers they gave him a brave funeral, too.'

'Then you've naught to cast-up about. 'Nother cup o' tea?'

The light and air had changed a little with the sun's descent, and the two elderly ladies closed the kitchen-door against chill. A couple of jays squealed and skirmished through the undraped apple-trees in the garden. This time, the word was with Mrs Ashcroft, her elbows on the tea-table, and her sick leg propped on a stool. . . .

'Well I never! But what did your 'usband say to that?' Mrs Fettley asked, when the deep-toned recital halted.

"E said I might go where I pleased for all of 'im. But seein' 'e was bedrid, I said I'd 'tend 'im out. 'E knowed I wouldn't take no advantage of 'im in that state. 'E lasted eight or nine weeks. Then he was took with a seizure-like; an' laid stone-still for days. Then 'e propped 'imself up abed an' says: "You pray no man'll ever deal with you like you've dealed with some." "An' you?" I says, for *you* know, Liz, what a rover 'e was. "It cuts both ways," says 'e, "but *I*'m death-wise, an' I can see what's comin' to you." He died a-Sunday an' was buried a-Thursday . . . An' yet I'd set a heap by him—one time or—did I ever?'

'You never told me that before,' Mrs Fettley ventured.

'I'm payin' ye for what ye told me just now. Him bein' dead, I wrote up, sayin' I was free for good, to that Mrs Marshall in Lunnon—which gave me my first place as kitchen-maid—Lord, how long ago! She was well pleased, for they two was both gettin' on, an' I knowed their ways. You remember, Liz, I used to go to 'em in service between whiles, for years—when we wanted money, or— or my 'usband was away—on occasion.'

"E *did* get that six months at Chichester, didn't 'e?' Mrs Fettley whispered. 'We never rightly won to the bottom of it.'

"E'd ha' got more, but the man didn't die.'

"None o' your doin's, was it, Gra'?'

'No! 'Twas the woman's husband this time. An' so, my man bein' dead, I went back to them Marshalls, as cook, to get me legs under a gentleman's table again, and be called with a handle to me name. That was the year you shifted to Portsmouth.'

'Cosham,' Mrs Fettley corrected. 'There was a middlin' lot o' new buildin' bein' done there. My man went first, an' got the room, an' I follered.'

'Well, then, I was a year-abouts in Lunnon, all at a breath, like, four meals a day an' livin' easy. Then, 'long towards autumn, they two went travellin', like, to France; keepin' me on, for they couldn't do without me. I put the house to rights for the caretaker, an' then I slipped down 'ere to me sister Bessie—me wages in me pockets, an' all 'ands glad to be 'old of me.'

'That would be when I was at Cosham,' said Mrs Fettley.

'*You* know, Liz, there wasn't no cheap-dog pride to folk, those days, no more than there was cinemas nor whisk-drives. Man or woman 'ud lay hold o' any job that promised a shillin' to the backside of it, didn't they? I was all peaked up after Lunnon, an' I thought the fresh airs 'ud serve me. So I took on at Smalldene, obligin' with a hand at the early potato-liftin', stubbin' hens, an' such-like. They'd ha' mocked me sore in my kitchen in Lunnon, to see me in men's boots, an' me petticoats all shorted.'

'Did it bring ye any good?' Mrs Fettley asked.

''Twadn't for that I went. You know, 's'well's me, that na'un happens to ye till it '*as* 'appened. Your mind don't warn ye before'and of the road ye've took, till you're at the far eend of it. We've only a backwent view of our proceedin's.'

''Oo was it?'

''Arry Mockler.' Mrs Ashcroft's face puckered to the pain of her sick leg.

Mrs Fettley gasped. ''Arry? Bert Mockler's son! An' *I* never guessed!'

Mrs Ashcroft nodded. 'An' I told myself—*an*' I beleft it—that I wanted field-work.'

'What did ye get out of it?'

'The usuals. Everythin' at first—worse than naught after. I had signs an' warnings a-plenty, but I took no heed of 'em. For we was burnin' rubbish one day, just when we'd come to know how 'twas with—with both of us. 'Twas early in the year for burnin', an' I said so. "No!" says he. "The sooner dat old stuff's off an' done with", 'e says, "the better." 'Is face was harder'n rocks when he spoke. Then it come over me that I'd found me master, which I 'adn't ever before. I'd allus owned 'em, like.'

'Yes! Yes! They're yourn or you're theirn,' the other sighed. 'I like the right way best.'

'I didn't. But 'Arry did . . . 'Long then, it come time for me to go back to Lunnon. I couldn't. I clean couldn't! So, I took an' tipped a dollop o' scaldin' water out o' the copper one Monday mornin' over me left 'and and arm. Dat stayed me where I was for another fortnight.'

'Was it worth it?' said Mrs Fettley, looking at the silvery scar on the wrinkled fore-arm.

Mrs Ashcroft nodded. 'An' after that, we two made it up 'twixt us so's 'e could come to Lunnon for a job in a liv'ry-stable not far from me. 'E got it. *I* 'tended to that. There wadn't no talk nowhere. His own mother never suspicioned how 'twas. He just slipped up to Lunnon, an' there we abode that winter, not 'alf a mile 'tother from each.'

'Ye paid 'is fare an' all, though'; Mrs Fettley spoke convincedly.

Again Mrs Ashcroft nodded. 'Dere wadn't much I didn't do for him. 'E was me master, an'—O God, help us!—we'd laugh over it walkin' together after dark in them paved streets, an' me corns fair wrenchin' in me boots! I'd never been like that before. Ner he! Ner he!'

Mrs Fettley clucked sympathetically.

'An' when did ye come to the eend?' she asked.

'When 'e paid it all back again, every penny. Then I knowed, but I wouldn't *suffer* meself to know. "You've been mortal kind to me," he says. "Kind!" I said. '"Twixt *us?*" But 'e kep' all on tellin' me 'ow kind I'd been an' 'e'd never forget it all his days. I held it from off o' me for three evenin's, because I would *not* believe. Then 'e talked about not bein' satisfied with 'is job in the stables, an' the men there puttin' tricks on 'im, an' all they lies which a man tells when 'e's leavin' ye. I heard 'im out, neither 'elpin' nor 'inderin'. At the last, I took off a liddle brooch which he'd give me an' I says: "Dat'll do. *I* ain't askin' na'un." An' I turned me round an' walked off to me own sufferin's. 'E didn't make 'em worse. 'E didn't come nor write after that. 'E slipped off 'ere back 'ome to 'is mother again.'

'An' 'ow often did ye look for 'en to come back?' Mrs Fettley demanded mercilessly.

'More'n once—more'n once! Goin' over the streets we'd used, I throught de very pave-stones 'ud shruck out under me feet.'

'Yes,' said Mrs Fettley. 'I dunno but dat don't 'urt as much as aught else. An' dat was all ye got?'

'No. 'Twadn't. That's the curious part, if you'll believe it, Liz.'

'I do. I lay you're further off lyin' now than in all your life, Gra'.'

'I am . . . An' I suffered, like I'd not wish my most arrantest enemies to. God's Own Name! I went through the hoop that spring! One part of it was headaches which I'd never known all me days before. Think o' *me* with an 'eddick! But I come to be grateful for 'em. They kep' me from thinkin' . . .'

"Tis like a tooth,' Mrs Fettley commented. 'It must rage an' rugg till it tortures itself quiet on ye; an' then—then there's na'un left.'

'*I* got enough lef' to last me all *my* days on earth. It come about through our charwoman's liddle girl—Sophy Ellis was 'er name— all eyes an' elbers an' hunger. I used to give 'er vittles. Otherwhiles, I took no special notice of 'er, an' a sight less, o' course, when me trouble about 'Arry was on me. But—you know how liddle maids first feel it sometimes—she come to be crazy-fond o' me, pawin' an' cuddlin' all whiles; an' I 'adn't the 'eart to beat 'er off . . . One afternoon, early in spring 'twas, 'er mother 'ad sent 'er round to scutchel up what vittles she could off of us. I was settin' by the fire, me apern over me head, half-mad with the 'eddick, when she slips in. I reckon I was middlin' short with 'er. "Lor'!" she says. "Is *that* all? I'll take it off you in two-twos!" I told her not to lay a finger on me, for I throught she'd want to stroke my forehead; an'— I ain't that make. "*I* won't tech ye," she says, an' slips out again. She 'adn't been gone ten minutes 'fore me old 'eddick took off quick as bein' kicked. So I went about my work. Prasin'ly, Sophy comes back, an' creeps into my chair quiet as a mouse. 'Er eyes was deep in 'er 'ead an' 'er face all drawed. I asked 'er what 'ad 'appened. "Nothin'," she says. "On'y *I*'ve got it now." "Got what?" I says. "Your 'eddick," she says, all hoarse an' sticky-lipped. "I've took it on me." "Nonsense," I says, "it went of itself when you was out. Lay still an' I'll make ye a cup o' tea." "'Twon't do no good," she says, "'til your time's up. 'Ow long do *your* 'eddicks last?" "Don't talk silly," I says, "or I'll send for the Doctor." It looked to me like she might be hatchin' de measles. "Oh, Mrs Ashcroft," she says, stretchin' out 'er liddle thin arms. "I *do* love ye." There wasn't any holdin' agin that. I took 'er into me lap an' made much of 'er. "Is it truly gone?" she says. "Yes", I says, "an' if 'twas you took it away, I'm truly grateful." "'Twas me," she says, layin' 'er cheek to mine. "No one but me knows how." An' then she said she'd changed me 'eddick for me at a Wish 'Ouse.'

'Whatt?' Mrs Fettley spoke sharply.

'A Wish House. No! *I* 'adn't 'eard o' such things, either. I couldn't get it straight at first, but, puttin' all together, I made out that a Wish 'Ouse 'ad to be a house which 'ad stood unlet an' empty long enough for Some One, like, to come an' in'abit there. She said, a liddle girl that she'd played with in the livery-stables where

'Arry worked 'ad told 'er so. She said the girl 'ad belonged in a caravan that laid up, o' winters, in Lunnon. Gipsy, I judge.'

'Ooh! There's no sayin' what Gippos know, but I've never 'eard of a Wish 'Ouse, an' I know—some things,' said Mrs Fettley.

'Sophy said there was a Wish 'Ouse in Wadloes Road—just a few streets off, on the way to our greengrocer's. All you 'ad to do, she said, was to ring the bell an' wish your wish through the slit o' the letter-box. I asked 'er if the fairies give it 'er? "Don't ye know," she says, "there's no fairies in a Wish 'Ouse? There's only a Token."'

'Goo' Lord A'mighty! Where did she come by *that* word?' cried Mrs Fettley; for a Token is a wraith of the dead or, worse still, of the living.

'The caravan-girl 'ad told 'er, she said. Well, Liz, it troubled me to 'ear 'er, an' lyin' in me arms she must ha' felt it. "That's very kind o' you," I says, holdin' 'er tight, "to wish me 'eddick away. But why didn't ye ask somethin' nice for yourself?" "You can't do that," she says. "All you'll get at a Wish 'Ouse is leave to take some one else's trouble. I've took Ma's 'eadaches, when she's been kind to me; but this is the first time I've been able to do aught for you. Oh, Mrs Ashcroft, I *do* just-about love you." An' she goes on all like that. Liz, I tell you my 'air e'en a'most stood on end to 'ear 'er. I asked 'er what like a Token was. "I dunno," she says, "but after you've ringed the bell, you'll 'ear it run up from the base-ment, to the front door. Then say your wish," she says, "an' go away." "The Token don't open de door to ye, then?" I says. "Oh, no," she says. "You on'y 'ear gigglin', like, be'ind the front door. Then you say you'll take the trouble off of 'oo ever 'tis you've chose for your love; an' ye'll get it," she says. I didn't ask no more—she was too 'ot an' fevered. I made much of 'er till it come time to light de gas, an' a liddle after that, 'er 'eddick—mine, I suppose—took off, an' she got down an' played with the cat.'

'Well, I never!' said Mrs Fettley. 'Did—did ye foller it up, any-ways?'

'She askt me to, but I wouldn't 'ave no such dealin's with a child.'

'What *did* ye do, then?'

''Sat in me own room 'stid o' the kitchen when me 'eddicks come on. But it lay at de back o' me mind.'

''Twould. Did she tell ye more, ever?'

'No. Besides what the Gippo girl 'ad told 'er, she knew naught, 'cept that the charm worked. An', next after that—in May 'twas—I suffered the summer out in Lunnon. 'Twas hot an' windy for weeks, an' the streets stinkin' o' dried 'orse-dung blowin' from side to side an' lyin' level with the kerb. We don't get that nowadays. I 'ad my 'ol'day just before hoppin',* an' come down 'ere to stay with Bessie again. She noticed I'd lost flesh, an' was all poochy under the eyes.'

'Did ye see 'Arry?'

Mrs Ashcroft nodded. 'The fourth—no, the fifth day. Wednesday 'twas. I knowed 'e was workin' at Smalldene again. I asked 'is mother in the street, bold as brass. She 'adn't room to say much, for Bessie—you know 'er tongue—was talkin' full-clack. But that Wednesday, I was walkin' with one o' Bessie's chillern hangin' on me skirts, at de back o' Chanter's Tot. Prasin'ly, I felt 'e was be'ind me on the footpath, an' I knowed by 'is tread 'e'd changed 'is nature. I slowed, an' I heard 'im slow. Then I fussed a piece with the child, to force him past me, like. So 'e *'ad* to come past. 'E just says "Good-evenin'," and goes on, tryin' to pull 'isself together.'

'Drunk, was he?' Mrs Fettley asked.

'Never! S'runk an' wizen; 'is clothes 'angin' on 'im like bags, an' the back of 'is neck whiter'n chalk. 'Twas all I could do not to oppen my arms an' cry after him. But I swallered me spittle till I was back 'ome again an' the chillern abed. Then I says to Bessie, after supper, "What in de world's come to 'Arry Mockler?" Bessie told me 'e'd been a-Hospital for two months, 'long o' cuttin' 'is foot wid a spade, muckin' out the old pond at Smalldene. There was poison in de dirt, an' it rooshed up 'is leg, like, an' come out all over him. 'E 'and't been back to 'is job—carterin' at Smalldene— more'n a fortnight. She told me the Doctor said he'd go off, likely, with the November frostes; an' 'is mother 'ad told 'er that 'e didn't rightly eat nor sleep, an' sweated 'imself into pools, no odds 'ow chill 'e lay. An' spit terrible o' mornin's. "Dearie me," I says. "But, mebbe hoppin' 'll set 'im right again," an' I licked me thread-point an' I fetched me needle's eye up to it an' I threads me needle under de lamp, steady as rocks. An' dat night (me bed was in de wash-house) I cried an' I cried. An' *you* know, Liz—for you've been with me in my throes—it takes summat to make me cry.'

---

* Hop-picking

'Yes; but chile-bearin' is on'y just pain,' said Mrs Fettley.

'I come round by cock-crow, an' dabbed cold tea on me eyes to take away the signs. Long towards nex' evenin'—I was settin' out to lay some flowers on me 'usband's grave, for the look o' the thing—I met 'Arry over against where the War Memorial is now. 'E was comin' back from 'is 'orses, so 'e couldn't *not* see me. I looked 'im all over, an' "'Arry," I says twix' me teeth, "come back an' rest-up in Lunnon." "I won't take it," he says, "for I can give ye naught." "I don't ask it," I says. "By God's Own Name, I don't ask na'un! On'y come up an' see a Lunnon doctor." 'E lifts 'is two 'eavy eyes at me: "'Tis past that, Gra'," 'e says. "I've but a few months left." "'Arry!" I says. "*My* man!" I says. I couldn't say no more. 'Twas all up in me throat. "Thank ye kindly, Gra'," 'e says (but 'e never says "my woman"), an' 'e went on up-street an' 'is mother—Oh, damn 'er!—she was watchin' for 'im, an' she shut de door be'ind 'im.'

Mrs Fettley stretched an arm across the table, and made to finger Mrs Ashcroft's sleeve at the wrist, but the other moved it out of reach.

'So I went on to the churchyard with my flowers, an' I remembered my 'usband's warnin' that night he spoke. 'E *was* death-wise, an' it '*ad* 'appened as 'e said. But as I was settin' down de jam-pot on the grave-mound, it come over me there was one thing I *could* do for 'Arry. Doctor or no Doctor, I thought I'd make a trial of it. So I did. Nex' mornin', a bill came down from our Lunnon greengrocer. Mrs Marshall, she'd lef' me petty cash for suchlike—o' course—but I tole Bess 'twas for me to come an' open the 'ouse. So I went up, afternoon train.'

'An'—but I know you 'adn't—'adn't you no fear?'

'What for? There was nothin' front o' me but my own shame an' God's croolty. I couldn't ever get 'Arry—'ow *could* I? I knowed it must go on burnin' till it burned me out.'

'Aie!' said Mrs Fettley, reaching for the wrist again, and this time Mrs Ashcroft permitted it.

'Yit 'twas a comfort to know I could try *this* for 'im. So I went an' I paid the greengrocer's bill, an' put 'is receipt in me hand-bag, an' then I stepped round to Mrs Ellis—our char—an' got the 'ouse-keys an' opened the 'ouse. First, I made me bed to come back to (God's Own Name! Me bed to lie upon!). Nex' I made me a cup o' tea an' sat down in the kitchen thinkin', till 'long towards dusk.

Terrible close, 'twas. Then I dressed me an' went out with the receipt in me 'and-bag, feignin' to study it for an address, like. Fourteen, Wadloes Road, was the place—a liddle basement-kitchen 'ouse, in a row of twenty-thirty such, an' tiddy strips o' walled garden in front—the paint off the front doors, an' na'un done to na'un since ever so long. There wasn't 'ardly no one in the streets 'cept the cats. '*Twas* 'ot, too! I turned into the gate bold as brass; up de steps I went an' I ringed the front-door bell. She pealed loud, like it do in an empty house. When she'd all ceased, I 'eard a cheer, like, pushed back on de floor o' the kitchen. Then I 'eard feet on de kitchen-stairs, like it might ha' been a heavy woman in slippers. They come up to de stairhead, acrost the hall—I 'eard the bare boards creak under 'em—an' at de front door dey stopped. I stooped me to the letter-box slit, an' I says: "Let me take everythin' bad that's in store for my man, 'Arry Mockler, for love's sake." Then, whatever it was t'other side de door let its breath out, like, as if it 'ad been holdin' it for to 'ear better.'

'Nothin' was *said* to ye?' Mrs Fettley demaded.

'Na'un. She just breathed out—a sort of *A-ah*, like. Then the steps went back an' down-stairs to the kitchen—all draggy—an' I heard the cheer drawed up again.'

'An' you abode on de doorstep, throughout all, Gra'?'

Mrs Ashcroft nodded.

'Then I went away, an' a man passin' says to me: "Didn't you know that house was empty?" "No," I says. "I must ha' been give the wrong number." An' I went back to our 'ouse, an' I went to bed; for I was fair flogged out. 'Twas too 'ot to sleep more'n snatches, so I walked me about, lyin' down betweens, till crack o' dawn. Then I went to the kitchen to make me a cup o' tea, an' I hitted meself just above the ankle on an old roastin'-jack o' mine that Mrs Ellis had moved out from the corner, her last cleanin'. An' so—nex' after that—I waited till the Marshalls come back o' their holiday.'

'Alone there? I'd ha' thought you'd 'ad enough of empty houses,' said Mrs Fettley, horrified.

'Oh, Mrs Ellis an' Sophy was runnin' in an' out soon's I was back, an' 'twixt us we cleaned de house again top-to-bottom. There's allus a hand's turn more to do in every house. An' that's 'ow 'twas with me that autumn an' winter, in Lunnon.'

'Then na'un hap—overtook ye for your doin's?'

Mrs Ashcroft smiled. 'No. Not then. 'Long in November I sent Bessie ten shillin's.'

'You was allus free-'anded,' Mrs Fettley interrupted.

'An' I got what I paid for, with the rest o' the news. She said the hoppin' 'ad set 'im up wonderful. 'E'd 'ad six weeks of it, and now 'e was back again carterin' at Smalldene. No odds to me *'ow* it 'ad 'appened—'slong's it *'ad*. But I dunno as my ten shillin's eased me much. 'Arry bein' *dead*, like, 'e'd ha' been mine, till Judgment. 'Arry bein' alive, 'e'd like as not pick up with some woman middlin' quick. I raged over that. Come spring, I 'ad somethin' else to rage for. I'd growed a nasty little weepin' boil, like, on me shin, just above the boot-top, that wouldn't heal no shape. It made me sick to look at it, for I'm clean-fleshed by nature. Chop me all over with a spade, an' I'd heal like turf. Then Mrs Marshall she set 'er own doctor at me. 'E said I ought to ha' come to him at first go-off, 'stead o' drawin' all manner o' dyed stockin's over it for months. 'E said I'd stood up too much to me work, for it was settin' very close atop of a big swelled vein, like, behither the small o' me ankle. "Slow come, slow go," 'e says. "Lay your leg up on high an' rest it," he says, "an' 'twill ease off. Don't let it close up too soon. You've got a very fine leg, Mrs Ashcroft," 'e says. An' he put wet dressin's on it.'

"'E done right.' Mrs Fettley spoke firmly. 'Wet dressin's to wet wounds. They draw de humours, same's a lamp-wick draws de oil.'

'That's true. An' Mrs Marshall was allus at me to make me set down more, an' dat nigh healed it up. An' then after a while they packed me off down to Bessie's to finish the cure; for I ain't the sort to sit down when I ought to stand up. You was back in the village then, Liz.'

'I was. I was, but—never did I guess!'

'I didn't desire ye to.' Mrs Ashcroft smiled. 'I saw 'Arry once or twice in de street, wonnerful fleshed up an' restored back. Then, one day I didn't see 'im, an' 'is mother told me one of 'is 'orses 'ad lashed out an' caught 'im on the 'ip. So 'e was abed an' middlin' painful. An' Bessie, she says to his mother, 'twas a pity 'Arry 'adn't a woman of 'is own to take the nursin' off 'er. And the old lady *was* mad! She told us that 'Arry 'ad never looked after any woman in 'is born days, an' as long as she was atop the mowlds, she'd contrive for 'im till 'er two 'ands dropped off. So I knowed she'd do watch-dog for me, 'thout askin' for bones.'

Mrs Fettley rocked with small laughter.

'That day,' Mrs Ashcroft went on, 'I'd stood on me feet nigh all the time, watchin' the doctor go in an' out; for they thought it might be 'is ribs, too. That made my boil break again, issuin' an' weepin'. But it turned out 'twadn't ribs at all, an' 'Arry 'ad a good night. When I heard that, nex' mornin', I says to meself, "I won't lay two an' two together *yit*. I'll keep me leg down a week, an' see what comes of it." It didn't hurt me that day, to speak of—'seemed more to draw the strength out o' me like—an' 'Arry 'ad another good night. That made me persevere; but I didn't dare lay two an' two together till the weekend, an' then, 'Arry come forth e'en a'most 'imself again—na'un hurt outside ner in of him. I nigh fell on me knees in de wash-house when Bessie was up-street. "I've got ye now, my man," I says, "You'll take your good from me 'thout knowin' it till my life's end. O God send me long to live for 'Arry's sake!" I says. An' I dunno that didn't still me ragin's.'

'For good?' Mrs Fettley asked.

'They come back, plenty times, but, let be how 'twould, I knowed I was doin' for 'im. I *knowed* it. I took an' worked me pains on an' off, like regulatin' my own range, till I learned to 'ave 'em at my commandments. An' that was funny, too. There was times, Liz, when my trouble 'ud all s'rink an' dry up, like. First, I used to try an' fetch it on again; bein' fearful to leave 'Arry alone too long for anythin' to lay 'old of. Prasin'ly I come to see that was a sign he'd do all right awhile, an' so I saved myself.'

''Ow long for?' Mrs Fettley asked, with deepest interest.

'I've gone de better part of a year onct or twice with na'un more to show than the liddle weepin' core of it, like, *All* s'rinked up an' dried off. Then he'd inflame up—for a warnin'—an' I'd suffer it. When I couldn't no more—an' I *'ad* to keep on goin' with my Lunnon work—I'd lay me leg high on a cheer till it eased. Not too quick. I knowed by the feel of it, those times, dat 'Arry was in need. Then I'd send another five shillin's to Bess, or somethin' for the chillern, to find out if, mebbe, 'e'd took any hurt through my neglects. 'Twas *so*! Year in, year out, I worked it dat way, Liz, an' 'e got 'is good from me 'thout knowin'—for years and years.'

'But what did *you* get out of it, Gra'?' Mrs Fettley almost wailed. 'Did ye see 'im reg'lar?'

'Times—when I was 'ere on me 'ol'days. An' more, now that I'm 'ere for good. But 'e's never looked at me, ner any other woman 'cept 'is mother. 'Ow I used to watch an' listen! So did she.'

'Years an' years!' Mrs Fettley repeated. 'An' where's 'e workin' at now?'

'Oh, 'e's give up carterin' quite a while. He's workin' for one o' them big tractorisin' firms—ploughin' sometimes, an' sometimes off with lorries—fur as Wales, I've 'eard. He comes 'ome to 'is mother 'tween whiles; but I don't set eyes on him now, fer weeks on end. No odds! 'Is job keeps 'im from continuin' in one stay anywheres.'

'But—just for de sake o' sayin' somethin'—s'pose 'Arry *did* get married?' said Mrs Fettley.

Mrs Ashcroft drew her breath sharply between her still even and natural teeth. '*Dat* ain't been required of me,' she answered. 'I reckon my pains 'ull be counted agin that. Don't *you*, Liz?'

'It ought to be, dearie. It ought to be.'

'It *do* 'urt sometimes. You shall see it when Nurse comes. She thinks I don't know it's turned.'

Mrs Fettley understood. Human nature seldom walks up to the word 'cancer'.

'Be ye certain sure, Gra'?' she asked.

'I was sure of it when old Mr Marshall 'ad me up to 'is study an' spoke a long piece about my faithful service. I've obliged 'em on an' off for a goodish time, but not enough for a pension. But they give me a weekly 'lowance for life. I knew what *that* sinnified— as long as three years ago.'

'Dat don't *prove* it, Gra'.'

'To give fifteen bob a week to a woman 'oo'd live twenty year in the course o' nature? It *do*!'

'You're mistook! You're mistook!' Mrs Fettley insisted.

'Liz, there's *no* mistakin' when the edges are all heaped up, like— same as a collar. You'll see it. An' I laid out Dora Wickwood, too. *She* 'ad it under the arm-pit, like.'

Mrs Fettley considered awhile, and bowed her head in finality.

''Ow long d'you reckon 'twill allow ye, countin' from now, dearie?'

'Slow come, slow go. But if I don't set eyes on ye 'fore next hoppin', this'll be good-bye, Liz.'

'Dunno as I'll be able to manage by then—not 'thout I have a liddle dog to lead me. For de chillern, dey won't be troubled, an'— O Gra'!—I'm blindin' up—I'm blindin' up!'

'Oh, *dat* was why you didn't more'n finger with your quilt-patches all this while! I was wonderin' . . . But the pain *do* count, don't ye think, Liz? The pain *do* count to keep 'Arry—where I want 'im. Say it can't be wasted, like.'

'I'm sure of it—sure of it, dearie. You'll 'ave your reward.'

'I don't want no more'n this—*if* de pain is taken into de reckonin'.'

"Twill be—'twill be, Gra'.'

There was a knock on the door.

'That's Nurse. She's before 'er time,' said Mrs Ashcroft. 'Open to 'er.'

The young lady entered briskly, all the bottles in her bag clicking. 'Evenin', Mrs Ashcroft,' she began. 'I've come raound a little earlier than usual because of the Institute dance to-na-ite. You won't ma-ind, will you?'

'Oh, no. Me dancin' days are over.' Mrs Ashcroft was the self-contained domestic at once. 'My old friend, Mrs Fettley 'ere, has been settin' talkin' with me a while.'

'I hope she 'asn't been fatiguing you?' said the Nurse a little frostily.

'Quite the contrary. It 'as been a pleasure. Only—only—just at the end I felt a bit—a bit flogged out, like.'

'Yes, yes.' The Nurse was on her knees already, with the washes to hand. 'When old ladies get together they talk a deal too much, I've noticed.'

'Mebbe we do,' said Mrs Fettley, rising. 'So, now, I'll make myself scarce.'

'Look at it first, though,' said Mrs Ashcroft feebly. 'I'd like ye to look at it.'

Mrs Fettley looked, and shivered. Then she leaned over, and kissed Mrs Ashcroft once on the waxy yellow forehead, and again on the faded grey eyes.

'It *do* count, don't it—de pain?' The lips that still kept trace of their original moulding hardly more than breathed the words.

Mrs Fettley kissed them and moved towards the door.

H. G. WELLS

Miss Winchelsea's Heart

MISS WINCHELSEA was going to Rome. The matter had filled her mind for a month or more, and had overflowed so abundantly into her conversation that quite a number of people who were not going to Rome, and who were not likely to go to Rome, had made it a personal grievance against her. Some indeed had attempted quite unavailingly to convince her that Rome was not nearly such a desirable place as it was reported to be, and others had gone so far as to suggest behind her back that she was dreadfully 'stuck up' about 'that Rome of hers'. And little Lily Hardhurst had told her friend Mr Binns that so far as she was concerned Miss Winchelsea might 'go to her old Rome and stop there; *she* (Miss Lily Hardhurst) wouldn't grieve'. And the way in which Miss Winchelsea put herself upon terms of personal tenderness with Horace and Benvenuto Cellini and Raphael and Shelley and Keats—if she had been Shelley's widow she could not have professed a keener interest in his grave— was a matter of universal astonishment. Her dress was a triumph of tactful discretion, sensible but not too 'touristy'—Miss Winchelsea had a great dread of being 'touristy'—and her Baedeker was carried in a cover of grey to hide its glaring red. She made a prim and pleasant little figure on the Charing Cross platform, in spite of her swelling pride, when at last the great day dawned and she could start for Rome. The day was bright, the Channel passage would be pleasant, and all the omens promised well. There was the gayest scene of adventure in this unprecedented departure.

She was going with two friends who had been fellow-students with her at the training college, nice honest girls both, though not so good at history and literature as Miss Winchelsea. They both looked up to her immensely, though physically they had to look down, and she anticipated some pleasant times to be spent in 'stirring them up' to her own pitch of aesthetic and historical enthusiasm. They had secured seats already, and welcomed her effusively at the carriage door. In the instant criticism of the encounter she noted that Fanny had a slightly 'touristy' leather strap, and that Helen had succumbed to a serge jacket with side pockets, into which her hands were thrust. But they were much too happy with themselves and the expedition for their friend to attempt any hint at the moment about these things. As soon as the first ecstasies were over—Fanny's enthusiasm was a little noisy and crude, and consisted mainly in emphatic repetitions of 'Just *fancy*! we're going to Rome, my dear!—Rome!'—they gave their attention to their fellow-travellers. Helen was anxious to secure a compartment to themselves, and, in order to discourage intruders, got out and planted herself firmly on the step. Miss Winchelsea peeped out over her shoulder, and made sly little remarks about the accumulating people on the platform, at which Fanny laughed gleefully.

They were travelling with one of Mr Thomas Gunn's parties—fourteen days in Rome for fourteen pounds. They did not belong to the personally conducted party of course—Miss Winchelsea had seen to that—but they travelled with it because of the convenience of that arrangement. The people were the oddest mixture, and wonderfully amusing. There was a vociferous red-faced polyglot personal conductor in a pepper and salt suit, very long in the arms and legs and very active. He shouted proclamations. When he wanted to speak to people he stretched out an arm and held them until his purpose was accomplished. One hand was full of papers, tickets, counterfoils of tourists. The people of the personally conducted party were, it seemed, of two sorts; people the conductor wanted and could not find, and people he did not want and who followed him in a steadily growing tail up and down the platform. These people seemed, indeed, to think that their one chance of reaching Rome lay in keeping close to him. Three little old ladies were particularly energetic in his pursuit, and at last maddened him to the pitch of clapping them into a carriage and daring them to emerge again. For the rest of the time, one, two, or three of their heads protruded from the window wailing enquiries about 'a little wickerwork box' whenever he drew near. There was a very stout man with a very stout wife in shiny black; there was a little old man like an aged ostler.

'What *can* such people want in Rome?' asked Miss Winchelsea.

'What can it mean to them?' There was a tall curate in a very small straw hat, and a short curate encumbered by a long camera stand. The contrast amused Fanny very much. Once they heard someone calling for 'Snooks'. 'I always thought that name was invented by novelists,' said Miss Winchelsea. 'Fancy! Snooks. I wonder which *is* Mr Snooks.' Finally they picked out a stout and resolute little man in a large check suit. 'If he isn't Snooks, he ought to be,' said Miss Winchelsea.

Presently the conductor discovered Helen's attempt at a corner in carriages. 'Room for five,' he bawled with a parallel translation on his fingers. A party of four together—mother, father, and two daughters—blundered in, all greatly excited. 'It's all right, Ma— you let *me*,' said one of the daughters, hitting her mother's bonnet with a handbag she struggled to put in the rack. Miss Winchelsea detested people who banged about and called their mother 'Ma'. A young man travelling alone followed. He was not at all 'touristy' in his costume, Miss Winchelsea observed; his Gladstone bag was of good pleasant leather with labels reminiscent of Luxembourg and Ostend, and his boots, though brown, were not vulgar. He carried an overcoat on his arm. Before these people had properly settled in their places, came an inspection of tickets and a slamming of doors, and behold! they were gliding out of Charing Cross station on their way to Rome.

'Fancy!' cried Fanny, 'we are going to Rome, my dear! Rome! I don't seem to believe it, even now.'

Miss Winchelsea suppressed Fanny's emotions with a little smile, and the lady who was called 'Ma' explained to people in general why they had 'cut it so close' at the station. The two daughters called her 'Ma' several times, toned her down in a tactless effective way, and drove her at last to the muttered inventory of a basket of travelling requisites. Presently she looked up. 'Lor!' she said, 'I didn't bring *them*!' Both the daughters said 'Oh, Ma!' but what 'them' was did not appear. Presently Fanny produced Hare's *Walks in Rome*, a sort of mitigated guide-book very popular among Roman visitors; and the father of the two daughters began to examine his books of tickets minutely, apparently in a search after English words. When he had looked at the tickets for a long time right way up, he turned them upside down. Then he produced a fountain pen and dated them with considerable care. The young man having completed an unostentatious survey of his fellow travellers produced a book and fell to reading. When Helen and Fanny were looking out of the window at Chislehurst—the place interested Fanny because the poor dear Empress of the French used to live there—Miss Winchelsea took the opportunity to observe the book the young man held. It was not a guide-book but a thin volume of poetry—*bound*. She glanced at his face—it seemed a refined pleasant face to her hasty glance. He wore a gilt *pince-nez*. 'Do you think she lives there now?' said Fanny, and Miss Winchelsea's inspection came to an end.

For the rest of the journey Miss Winchelsea talked little, and what she said was as pleasant and as stamped with refinement as she could make it. Her voice was always low and clear and pleasant, and she took care that on this occasion it was particularly low and clear and pleasant. As they came under the white cliffs the young man put his book of poetry away, and when at last the train stopped beside the boat, he displayed a graceful alacrity with the impedimenta of Miss Winchelsea and her friends. Miss Winchelsea 'hated nonsense', but she was pleased to see the young man perceived at once that they were ladies, and helped them without any violent geniality; and how nicely he showed that his civilities were to be no excuse for further intrusions. None of her party had been out of England before, and they were all excited and nervous at the Channel passage. They stood in a little group in a good place near the middle of the boat—the young man had taken Miss Winchelsea's hold-all there and had told her it was a good place—and they watched the white shores of Albion recede and quoted Shakespeare and made quiet fun of their fellow travellers in the English way.

They were particularly amused at the precautions the bigger-sized people had taken against the waves—cut lemons and flasks prevailed, one lady lay full length in a deck chair with a handkerchief over her face, and a very broad resolute man in a bright brown 'touristy' suit walked all the way from England to France along the deck, with his legs as widely apart as Providence permitted. These were all excellent precautions, and nobody was ill. The personally conducted party pursued the conductor about the deck with enquiries, in a manner that suggested to Helen's mind the rather vulgar image of hens with a piece of bacon peel, until at last he went into hiding below. And the young man with the thin volume of poetry stood in the stern watching England receding, looking, to Miss Winchelsea's eye, rather lonely and sad.

And then came Calais and tumultuous novelties, and the young man had not forgotten Miss Winchelsea's hold-all and the other little things. All three girls, though they had passed government examinations in French to any extent, were stricken with a dumb shame of their accents, and the young man was very useful. And he did not intrude. He put them in a comfortable carriage and raised his hat and went away. Miss Winchelsea thanked him in her best manner—a pleasing cultivated manner—and Fanny said he was 'nice' almost before he was out of earshot. 'I wonder what he can be,' said Helen. 'He's going to Italy, because I noticed green tickets in his book.' Miss Winchelsea almost told them of the poetry, and decided not to do so. And presently the carriage windows seized hold upon them and the young man was forgotten. It made them feel that they were doing an educated sort of thing to travel through a country whose commonest advertisements were in idiomatic French, and Miss Winchelsea made unpatriotic comparisons because there were weedy little sign-board advertisements by the rail side instead of the broad hoardings that deface the landscape in our land. But the north of France is really uninteresting country, and after a time Fanny reverted to Hare's *Walks* and Helen initiated lunch. Miss Winchelsea awoke out of a happy reverie; she had been trying to realize, she said, that she was actually going to Rome, but she perceived at Helen's suggestion that she was hungry, and they lunched out of their baskets very cheerfully. In the afternoon they were tired and silent until Helen made tea. Miss Winchelsea might have dozed, only she knew Fanny slept with her mouth open; and as their fellow passengers were two rather nice critical-looking ladies of uncertain age—who knew French well enough to talk it—she employed herself in keeping Fanny awake. The rhythm of the train became insistent, and the streaming landscape outside at last quite painful to the eye. Before their night's stoppage came they were already dreadfully tired of travelling.

The stoppage for the night was brightened by the appearance of the young man, and his manners were all that could be desired and his French quite serviceable. His coupons availed for the same hotel as theirs, and by chance as it seemed he sat next Miss Winchelsea at the *table d'hôte*. In spite of her enthusiasm for Rome, she had thought out some such possibility very thoroughly, and when he ventured to make a remark upon the tediousness of travelling—he let the soup and fish go by before he did this—she did not simply assent to his proposition, but responded with another. They were soon comparing their journeys, and Helen and Fanny were cruelly overlooked in the conversation. It was to be the same journey, they found; one day for the galleries at Florence—'from what I hear,' said the young man, 'it is barely enough,'—and the rest at Rome. He talked of Rome very pleasantly; he was evidently quite well read, and he quoted Horace about Soracte. Miss Winchelsea had 'done' that book of Horace for her matriculation, and was delighted to cap his quotation. It gave a sort of tone to things, this incident—a touch of refinement to mere chatting. Fanny expressed a few emotions, and Helen interpolated a few sensible remarks, but the bulk of the talk on the girls' side naturally fell to Miss Winchelsea.

Before they reached Rome this young man was tacitly of their party. They did not know his name nor what he was, but it seemed he taught, and Miss Winchelsea had a shrewd idea he was an extension lecturer. At any rate he was something of that sort, something gentlemanly and refined without being opulent and impossible. She tried once or twice to ascertain whether he came from Oxford or Cambridge, but he missed her timid opportunities. She tried to get him to make remarks about those places to see if he would say 'go up' to them instead of 'go down'—she knew that was how you told a 'Varsity man. He used the word "Varsity'—not university— in quite the proper way.

They saw as much of Mr Ruskin's Florence as their brief time permitted; the young man met them in the Pitti Gallery and went round with them, chatting brightly, and evidently very grateful for their recognition. He knew a great deal about art, and all four enjoyed the morning immensely. It was fine to go round recognizing old favourites and finding new beauties, especially while so many people fumbled helplessly with Baedeker. Nor was he a bit of a prig, Miss Winchelsea said, and indeed she detested prigs. He had a distinct undertow of humour, and was funny, for example, without being vulgar, at the expense of the quaint work of Beato Angelico. He had a grave seriousness beneath it all, and was quick to seize the moral lessons of the pictures. Fanny went softly among these masterpieces; she admitted 'she knew so little about them', and she confessed that to her they were 'all beautiful'. Fanny's 'beautiful' inclined to be a little monotonous, Miss Winchelsea thought. She had been quite glad when the last sunny Alp had vanished, because of the staccato of Fanny's admiration. Helen said little, but Miss Winchelsea had found her a little wanting on the aesthetic side in the old days and was not surprised; sometimes she laughed at the young man's hesitating delicate little jests and sometimes she didn't, and sometimes she seemed quite lost to the art about them in the contemplation of the dresses of the other visitors.

At Rome the young man was with them intermittently. A rather 'touristy' friend of his took him away at times. He complained comically to Miss Winchelsea. 'I have only two short weeks in Rome,' he said, 'and my friend Leonard wants to spend a whole day at Tivoli looking at a waterfall.'

'What is your friend Leonard?' asked Miss Winchelsea abruptly.

'He's the most enthusiastic pedestrian I ever met,' the young man replied—amusingly, but a little unsatisfactorily, Miss Winchelsea thought.

They had some glorious times, and Fanny could not think what they would have done without him. Miss Winchelsea's interest and Fanny's enormous capacity for admiration were insatiable. They never flagged—through pictures and sculpture galleries, immense crowded churches, ruins and museums, Judas trees and prickly pears, wine carts and palaces, they admired their way unflinchingly. They never saw a stone pine nor a eucalyptus but they named and admired it; they never glimpsed Soracte but they exclaimed. Their common ways were made wonderful by imaginative play. 'Here Cæsar may have walked,' they would say. 'Raphael may have seen Soracte from this very point.' They happened on the tomb of Bibulus. 'Old Bibulus', said the young man. 'The oldest monument of Republican Rome!' said Miss Winchelsea.

'I'm dreadfully stupid,' said Fanny, 'but who *was* Bibulus?'

There was a curious little pause.

'Wasn't he the person who built the wall?' said Helen.

The young man glanced quickly at her and laughed. 'That was Balbus,' he said. Helen reddened, but neither he nor Miss Winchelsea threw any light upon Fanny's ignorance about Bibulus.

Helen was more taciturn than the other three, but then she was always taciturn; and usually she took care of the tram tickets and things like that, or kept her eye on them if the young man took them, and told him where they were when he wanted them. Glorious times they had, these young people, in that pale brown cleanly city of memories that was once the world. Their only sorrow was the shortness of the time. They said indeed that the electric trams and the '70 buildings, and that criminal advertisement that glares upon the Forum, outraged their aesthetic feelings unspeakably; but that was only part of the fun. And indeed Rome is such a wonderful place that at times it made Miss Winchelsea forget some of her most carefully prepared enthusiasms, and Helen, taken unawares, would suddenly admit the beauty of unexpected things. Yet Fanny and Helen would have liked a shop window or so in the English quarter if Miss Winchelsea's uncompromising hostility to all other English visitors had not rendered that district impossible.

The intellectual and aesthetic fellowship of Miss Winchelsea and the scholarly young man passed insensibly towards a deeper feeling. The exuberant Fanny did her best to keep pace with their recondite admiration by playing her 'beautiful' with vigour, and saying 'Oh! *let's* go,' with enormous appetite whenever a new place of interest was mentioned. But Helen towards the end developed a certain want of sympathy, that disappointed Miss Winchelsea a little. She refused to 'see anything' in the face of Beatrice Cenci— Shelley's Beatrice Cenci!—in the Barberini gallery; and one day, when they were deploring the electric trams, she said rather snappishly that 'people must get about somehow, and it's better than torturing horses up these horrid little hills'. She spoke of the Seven Hills of Rome as 'horrid little hills!'

And the day they went on the Palatine—though Miss Winchelsea did not know of this—she remarked suddenly to Fanny, 'Don't hurry like that, my dear; *they* don't want us to overtake them. And we don't say the right things for them when we *do* get near.'

'I wasn't trying to overtake them,' said Fanny, slackening her excessive pace; 'I wasn't indeed.' And for a minute she was short of breath.

But Miss Winchelsea had come upon happiness. It was only when she came to look back across an intervening tragedy that she quite realized how happy she had been, pacing among the cypress-shadowed ruins, and exchanging the very highest class of information the human mind can possess, the most refined impressions it is possible to convey. Insensibly emotion crept into their intercourse, sunning itself openly and pleasantly at last when Helen's modernity was not too near. Insensibly their interest drifted from the wonderful associations about them to their more intimate and personal feelings. In a tentative way information was supplied; she spoke allusively of her school, of her examination successes, of her gladness that the days of 'Cram' were over. He made it quite clear that he also was a teacher. They spoke of the greatness of their calling, of the necessity of sympathy to face its irksome details, of a certain loneliness they sometimes felt.

That was in the Colosseum, and it was as far as they got that day, because Helen returned with Fanny—she had taken her into the upper galleries. Yet the private dreams of Miss Winchelsea, already vivid and concrete enough, became now realistic in the highest degree. She figured that pleasant young man, lecturing in the most edifying way to his students, herself modestly prominent as his intellectual mate and helper; she figured a refined little home, with two bureaus, with white shelves of high-class books, and autotypes of the pictures of Rossetti and Burne-Jones, with Morris's wall papers and flowers in pots of beaten copper. Indeed she figured many things. On the Pincio the two had a few precious moments together, while Helen marched Fanny off to see the *muro Torto*, and he spoke at once plainly. He said he hoped their friendship was only beginning, that he already found her company very precious to him, that indeed it was more than that.

He became nervous, thrusting at his glasses with trembling fingers as though he fancied his emotions made them unstable. 'I should of course,' he said, 'tell you things about myself. I know it is rather unusual my speaking to you like this. Only our meeting has been so accidental—or providential—and I am snatching at things. I came to Rome expecting a lonely tour . . . and I have been so very happy, so very happy. Quite recently I have found myself in a position— I have dared to think—— And——'

He glanced over his shoulder and stopped. He said 'Damn!' quite distinctly—and she did not condemn him for that manly lapse into profanity. She looked and saw his friend Leonard advancing. He drew nearer; he raised his hat to Miss Winchelsea, and his smile was almost a grin. 'I've been looking for you everywhere, Snooks,' he said. 'You promised to be on the Piazza steps half an hour ago.'

Snooks! The name struck Miss Winchelsea like a blow in the face. She did not hear his reply. She thought afterwards that Leonard must have considered her the vaguest-minded person. To this day she is not sure whether she was introduced to Leonard or not, nor what she said to him. A sort of mental paralysis was upon her. Of all offensive surnames—Snooks!

Helen and Fanny were returning, there were civilities and the young men were receding. By a great effort she controlled herself to face the inquiring eyes of her friends. All that afternoon she lived the life of a heroine under the indescribable outrage of that name, chatting, observing, with 'Snooks' gnawing at her heart. From the moment that it first rang upon her ears, the dream of her happiness was prostrate in the dust. All the refinement she had figured was ruined and defaced by that cognomen's inexorable vulgarity.

What was that refined little home to her now, spite of autotypes, Morris papers, and bureaus? Athwart it in letters of fire ran an incredible inscription: 'Mrs Snooks'. That may seem a small thing to the reader, but consider the delicate refinement of Miss Winchelsea's mind. Be as refined as you can and then think of writing yourself down: 'Snooks'. She conceived herself being addressed as Mrs Snooks by all the people she liked least, conceived the patronymic touched with a vague quality of insult. She figured a card of grey and silver bearing 'Winchelsea' triumphantly effaced by an arrow, Cupid's arrow, in favour of 'Snooks'. Degrading confession of feminine weakness! She imagined the terrible rejoicings of certain girl friends, of certain grocer cousins from whom her growing refinement had long since estranged her. How they would make it sprawl across the envelope that would bring their sarcastic congratulations. Would even his pleasant company compensate her for that? 'It is impossible,' she muttered; 'impossible! Snooks!'

She was sorry for him, but not so sorry as she was for herself. For him she had a touch of indignation. To be so nice, so refined, while all the time he was 'Snooks', to hide under a pretentious gentility of demeanour the badge sinister of his surname seemed a sort of treachery. To put it in the language of sentimental science she felt he had 'led her on'.

There were of course moments of terrible vacillation, a period even when something almost like passion bid her throw refinement to the winds. And there was something in her, an unexpurgated vestige of vulgarity that made a strenuous attempt at proving that Snooks was not so very bad a name after all. Any hovering hesitation flew before Fanny's manner, when Fanny came with an air of catastrophe to tell that she also knew the horror. Fanny's voice fell to a whisper when she said *Snooks*. Miss Winchelsea would not give him any answer when at last, in the Borghese, she could have a minute with him; but she promised him a note.

She handed him that note in the little book of poetry he had lent her, the little book that had first drawn them together. Her refusal was ambiguous, allusive. She could no more tell him why she rejected him than she could have told a cripple of his hump. He too must feel something of the unspeakable quality of his name. Indeed he had avoided a dozen chances of telling it, she now perceived. So she spoke of 'obstacles she could not reveal'—'reasons why the thing he spoke of was impossible'. She addressed the note with a shiver, 'E. K. Snooks'.

Things were worse than she had dreaded; he asked her to explain. How *could* she explain? Those last two days in Rome were dreadful. She was haunted by his air of astonished perplexity. She knew she had given him intimate hopes, she had not the courage to examine her mind thoroughly for the extent of her encouragement. She knew he must think her the most changeable of beings. Now that she was in full retreat, she would not even perceive his hints of a possible correspondence. But in that matter he did a thing that seemed to her at once delicate and romantic. He made a go-between of Fanny. Fanny could not keep the secret, and came and told her that night under a transparent pretext of needed advice. 'Mr Snooks', said Fanny, 'wants to write to me. Fancy! I had no idea. But should I let him?' They talked it over long and earnestly, and Miss Winchelsea was careful to keep the veil over her heart. She was already repenting his disregarded hints. Why should she not hear of him sometimes—painful though his name must be to her? Miss Winchelsea decided it might be permitted, and Fanny kissed her good-night with unusual emotion. After she had gone Miss Winchelsea sat for a long time at the window of her little room. It was moonlight, and down the street a man sang 'Santa Lucia' with almost heart-dissolving tenderness. . . . She sat very still.

She breathed a word very softly to herself. The word was '*Snooks*'. Then she got up with a profound sigh, and went to bed. The next morning he said to her meaningly, 'I shall hear of you through your friend.'

Mr Snooks saw them off from Rome with that pathetic interrogative perplexity still on his face, and if it had not been for Helen he would have retained Miss Winchelsea's hold-all in his hand as a sort of encyclopaedic keepsake. On their way back to England Miss Winchelsea on six separate occasions made Fanny promise to write to her the longest of long letters. Fanny, it seemed, would be quite near Mr Snooks. Her new school—she was always going to new schools—would be only five miles from Steely Bank, and it was in the Steely Bank Polytechnic, and one or two first-class schools, that Mr Snooks did his teaching. He might even see her at times. They could not talk much of him—she and Fanny always spoke of 'him', never of Mr Snooks—because Helen was apt to say unsympathetic things about him. Her nature had coarsened very much, Miss Winchelsea perceived, since the old Training College days; she had become hard and cynical. She thought he had a weak face, mistaking refinement for weakness as people of her stamp are apt to do, and when she heard his name was Snooks, she said she had expected something of the sort. Miss Winchelsea was careful to spare her own feelings after that, but Fanny was less circumspect.

The girls parted in London, and Miss Winchelsea returned with a new interest in life, to the Girls' High School in which she had been an increasingly valuable assistant for the last three years. Her new interest in life was Fanny as a correspondent, and to give her a lead she wrote her a lengthy descriptive letter within a fortnight of her return. Fanny answered very disappointingly. Fanny indeed had no literary gift, but it was new to Miss Winchelsea to find herself deploring the want of gifts in a friend. That letter was even criticized aloud in the safe solitude of Miss Winchelsea's study, and her criticism, spoken with great bitterness, was 'Twaddle!' It was full of just the things Miss Winchelsea's letter had been full of, particulars of the school. And of Mr Snooks, only this much: 'I have had a letter from Mr Snooks, and he has been over to see me on two Saturday afternoons running. He talked about Rome and you; we both talked about you. Your ears must have burnt, my dear. . . .'

Miss Winchelsea repressed a desire to demand more explicit information, and wrote the sweetest long letter again. 'Tell me all about yourself, dear. That journey has quite refreshed our ancient

friendship, and I do so want to keep in touch with you.' About Mr
Snooks she simply wrote on the fifth page that she was glad Fanny
had seen him, and that if he *should* ask after her, she was to be
remembered to him *very kindly* (underlined). And Fanny replied most
obtusely in the key of that 'ancient friendship', reminding Miss
Winchelsea of a dozen foolish things of those old schoolgirl days at
the training college, and saying not a word about Mr Snooks!

For nearly a week Miss Winchelsea was so angry at the failure
of Fanny as a go-between that she could not write to her. And
then she wrote less effusively, and in her letter she asked point blank,
'Have you seen Mr Snooks?' Fanny's letter was unexpectedly satisfactory. 'I *have* seen Mr Snooks,' she wrote, and having once named
him she kept on about him; it was all Snooks—Snooks this and
Snooks that. He was to give a public lecture, said Fanny, among
other things. Yet Miss Winchelsea, after the first glow of gratification,
still found this letter a little unsatisfactory. Fanny did not report Mr
Snooks as saying anything about Miss Winchelsea, nor as looking
white and worn, as he ought to have been doing. And behold!
before she had replied, came a second letter from Fanny on the
same theme, quite a gushing letter, and covering six sheets with her
loose feminine hand.

And about this second letter was a rather odd little thing that
Miss Winchelsea only noticed as she reread it the third time. Fanny's
natural femininity had prevailed even against the round and clear
traditions of the training college; she was one of those she-creatures
born to make all her *m*'s and *n*'s and *u*'s and *r*'s and *e*'s alike, and
to leave her *o*'s and *a*'s open and her *i*'s undotted. So that it was
only after an elaborate comparison of word with word that Miss
Winchelsea felt assured Mr Snooks was not really 'Mr Snooks' at
all! In Fanny's first letter of gush he was Mr 'Snooks', in her second the spelling was changed to Mr 'Senoks'. Miss Winchelsea's
hand positively trembled as she turned the sheet over—it meant so
much to her. For it had already begun to seem to her that even
the name of Mrs Snooks might be avoided at too great a price, and
suddenly—this possibility! She turned over the six sheets, all
dappled with that critical name, and everywhere the first letter
had the form of an *e*! For a time she walked the room with a hand
pressed upon her heart.

She spent a whole day pondering this change, weighing a letter of inquiry that should be at once discreet and effectual, weighing too what action she should take after the answer came. She was resolved that if this altered spelling was anything more than a quaint fancy of Fanny's, she would write forthwith to Mr Snooks. She had now reached a stage when the minor refinements of behaviour disappear. Her excuse remained uninvented but she had the subject of her letter clear in her mind, even to the hint that 'circumstances in my life have changed very greatly since we talked together'. But she never gave that hint. There came a third letter from that fitful correspondent Fanny. The first line proclaimed her 'the happiest girl alive'.

Miss Winchelsea crushed the letter in her hand—the rest unread—and sat with her face suddenly very still. She had received it just before morning school, and had opened it when the junior mathematicians were well under way. Presently she resumed reading with an appearance of great calm. But after the first sheet she went on reading the third without discovering the error: 'told him frankly I did not like his name,' the third sheet began. 'He told me he did not like it himself—you know that sort of sudden frank way he has—Miss Winchelsea did know. 'So I said, "Couldn't you change it?" He didn't see it at first. Well, you know, dear, he had told me what it really meant; it means Sevenoaks, only it has got down to Snooks—both Snooks and Noaks, dreadfully vulgar surnames though they be, are really worn forms of Sevenoaks. So I said—even I have my bright ideas at times—"if it got down from Sevenoaks to Snooks, why not get it back from Snooks to Sevenoaks?" And the long and the short of it is, dear, he couldn't refuse me, and he changed his spelling there and then to Senoks for the bills of the new lecture. And afterwards, when we are married, we shall put in the apostrophe and make it Se'noks. Wasn't it kind of him to mind that fancy of mine, when many men would have taken offence? But it is just like him all over; he is as kind as he is clever. Because he knew as well as I did that I would have had him in spite of it, had he been ten times Snooks. But he did it all the same.'

The class was startled by the sound of paper being viciously torn, and looked up to see Miss Winchelsea white in the face, and with some very small pieces of paper clenched in one hand. For a few seconds they stared at her stare, and then her expression changed back to a more familiar one. 'Has anyone finished number three?'

she asked in an even tone. She remained calm after that. But impositions ruled high that day. And she spent two laborious evenings writing letters of various sorts to Fanny, before she found a decent congratulatory vein. Her reason struggled hopelessly against the persuasion that Fanny had behaved in an exceedingly treacherous manner.

One may be extremely refined and still capable of a very sore heart. Certainly Miss Winchelsea's heart was very sore. She had moods of sexual hostility, in which she generalized uncharitably about mankind. 'He forgot himself with me,' she said. 'But Fanny is pink and pretty and soft and a fool—a very excellent match for a Man.' And by way of a wedding present she sent Fanny a gracefully bound volume of poetry by George Meredith, and Fanny wrote back a grossly happy letter to say that it was '*all* beautiful'. Miss Winchelsea hoped that some day Mr Senoks might take up that slim book and think for a moment of the donor. Fanny wrote several times before and about her marriage, pursuing that fond legend of their 'ancient friendship', and giving her happiness in the fullest detail. And Miss Winchelsea wrote to Helen for the first time after the Roman journey, saying nothing about the marriage, but expressing very cordial feelings.

They had been in Rome at Easter, and Fanny was married in the August vacation. She wrote a garrulous letter to Miss Winchelsea, describing her home-coming, and the astonishing arrangements of their 'teeny weeny' little house. Mr Se'noks was now beginning to assume a refinement in Miss Winchelsea's memory out of all proportion to the facts of the case, and she tried in vain to imagine his cultured greatness in a 'teeny weeny' little house. 'Am busy enamelling a cosy corner,' said Fanny, sprawling to the end of her third sheet, 'so excuse more.' Miss Winchelsea answered in her best style, gently poking fun at Fanny's arrangements, and hoping intensely that Mr Se'noks might see the letter. Only this hope enabled her to write at all, answering not only that letter but one in November and one at Christmas.

The two latter communications contained urgent invitations for her to come to Steely Bank on a visit during the Christmas holidays. She tried to think that *he* had told her to ask that, but it was too much like Fanny's opulent good-nature. She could not but believe that he must be sick of his blunder by this time; and she had more than a hope that he would presently write her a letter beginning 'Dear Friend'. Something subtly tragic in the separation was a great support to her, a sad misunderstanding. To have been jilted would have been intolerable. But he never wrote that letter beginning 'Dear Friend'.

For two years Miss Winchelsea could not go to Steely Bank, in spite of the reiterated invitations of Mrs Sevenoaks—it became full Sevenoaks in the second year. Then one day near the Easter rest she felt lonely and without a soul to understand her in the world, and her mind ran once more on what is called Platonic friendship. Fanny was clearly happy and busy in her new sphere of domesticity, but no doubt *he* had his lonely hours. Did he ever think of those days in Rome—gone now beyond recalling. No one had understood her as he had done; no one in all the world. It would be a sort of melancholy pleasure to talk to him again, and what harm could it do? Why should she deny herself? That night she wrote a sonnet, all but the last two lines of the octave—which would not come, and the next day she composed a graceful little note to tell Fanny she was coming down.

And so she saw him again.

Even at the first encounter it was evident he had changed; he seemed stouter and less nervous, and it speedily appeared that his conversation had already lost much of its old delicacy. There even seemed a justification for Helen's discovery of weakness in his face— in certain lights it *was* weak. He seemed busy and preoccupied about his affairs, and almost under the impression that Miss Winchelsea had come for the sake of Fanny. He discussed his dinner with Fanny in an intelligent way. They only had one good long talk together, and that came to nothing. He did not refer to Rome, and spent some time abusing a man who had stolen an idea he had had for a text-book. It did not seem a very wonderful idea to Miss Winchelsea. She discovered he had forgotten the names of more than half the painters whose work they had rejoiced over in Florence.

It was a sadly disappointing week, and Miss Winchelsea was glad when it came to an end. Under various excuses she avoided visiting them again. After a time the visitor's room was occupied by their two little boys, and Fanny's invitations ceased. The intimacy of her letters had long since faded away.

JOHN GALSWORTHY

A Long-Ago Affair

HUBERT MARSLAND, the landscape painter, returning from a day's sketching on the river in the summer of 1921, had occasion to stay the progress of his two-seater about ten miles from London for a minor repair, and while his car was being seen to, strolled away from the garage to have a look at a house where he had often spent his holidays as a boy. Walking through a gateway and passing a large gravel-pit on his left, he was soon opposite the house, which stood back a little in its grounds. Very much changed! More pretentious, not so homely as when his Uncle and Aunt lived there, and he used to play cricket on this warren opposite, where the cricket ground, it seemed, had been turned into a golf course. It was late—the dinner-hour, nobody playing, and passing on to the links he stood digesting the geography. Here must have been where the old pavilion was. And there—still turfed—where he had made that particularly nice stroke to leg, when he went in last and carried his bat for thirteen. Thirty-nine years ago—his sixteenth birthday. How vividly he remembered his new pads! A. P. Lucas had played against them and only made thirty-two—one founded one's style on A. P. Lucas in those days—feet in front of the bat, and pointed a little forward, elegant; you never saw it now, and a good thing too—one could sacrifice too much to style! Still, the tendency was all the other way; style was too much 'off', perhaps!

He stepped back into the sun and sat down on the grass. Peaceful—very still! The haze of the distant downs was visible between his Uncle's old house and the next; and there was the clump of elms on the far side behind which the sun would be going down just as it used to then. He pressed the palms of his hands to the turf. A glorious summer—something like that summer of long ago. And warmth from the turf, or perhaps from the past, crept into his heart and made it ache a little. Just here he must have sat, after his innings, at Mrs Monteith's feet peeping out of a flounced dress. Lord! The fools boys were! How headlong and uncalculating their devotions! A softness in voice and eyes, a smile, a touch or two—and they were slaves! Young fools, but good young fools. And, standing behind her chair—he could see him now—that other idol Captain MacKay, with his face of browned ivory—just the colour of that elephant's tusk his Uncle had, which had gone so yellow—and his perfect black moustache, his white tie, check suit, carnation, spats, Malacca cane—all so fascinating! Mrs Monteith, 'the grass widow' they had called her! He remembered the look in people's eyes, the tone in their voices. Such a pretty woman! He had 'fallen for her' at first sight, as the Yanks put it—her special scent, her daintiness, her voice! And that day on the river, when she made much of him, and Captain MacKay attended Evelyn Curtiss so assiduously that he was expected to propose. Quaint period! They used the word courting then, wore full skirts, high stays; and himself a blue elastic belt round his white-flannelled waist. And in the evening afterwards, his Aunt had said with an arch smile: 'Good-night, *silly* boy!' Silly boy indeed, with a flower the grass widow had dropped pressed by his cheek into his pillow! What folly! And that next Sunday—looking forward to Church—passionately brushing his top hat; all through the service spying at her creamy profile, two pews in front on the left, between goat-bearded old Hallgrave her Uncle, and her pink, broad, white-haired Aunt; scheming to get near her when she came out, lingering, lurking, getting just a smile and the rustle of her flounces. Ah, ha! A little went a long way then! And the last day of his holidays and its night with the first introduction to reality. Who said the Victorian Age was innocent?

Marsland put his palm up to his cheek. No! the dew was not yet falling! And his mind lightly turned and tossed his memories of women, as a man turns and tosses hay to air it; but nothing remembered gave him quite the feeling of that first experience.

His Aunt's dance! His first white waistcoat, bought *ad hoc*, from the local tailor, his tie laboriously imitating the hero—Captain MacKay's. All came back with such freshness in the quiet of the warren—the expectancy, the humble shy excitement, the breathless asking for a dance, the writing 'Mrs Monteith' twice on his little gilt-edged programme with its tiny tasselled white pencil; her slow-moving fan, her smile. And the first dance when it came; what infinite care not to tread on her white satin toes; what a thrill when her arm pressed his in the crush—such holy rapture, about all the first part of that evening, with yet another dance to come! If only he could have twirled her and 'reversed' like his pattern, Captain MacKay! Then delirium growing as the second dance came near, making him cut his partner—the cool grass-scented air out on the dark terrace, with the chafers booming by, and in the starshine the poplars wondrously tall; the careful adjustment of his tie and waistcoat, the careful polishing of his hot face! A long breath then, and into the house to find her! Ballroom, supper-room, stairs, library, billiard-room, all drawn blank—'Estudiantina' going on and on, and he a wandering, white-waistcoated young ghost. Ah! The conservatory—and the hurrying there! And then the moment which had always been, was even now, such a blurred confused impression. Smothered voices from between a clump of flowers: 'I saw her.' 'Who was the man?' A glimpse, gone past in a flash, of an ivory face, a black moustache! And then her voice: 'Hubert'; and her hot hand clasping his, drawing him to her; her scent, her face smiling, very set! A rustling behind the flowers, those people spying; and suddenly her lips on his cheek, the kiss sounding in his ears, her voice saying, very softly: 'Hubert, dear boy!' The rustle receded, ceased. What a long silent minute, then, among the ferns and blossoms in the dusk with her face close to his, pale, perturbed, before she led him out into the light, while he was slowly realizing that she had made use of him to shelter her. A boy—not old enough to be her lover, but old enough to save her name and that of Captain MacKay! Her kiss—the last of many—but not upon *his* lips, *his* cheeks! Hard work realizing that! A boy—of no account—a boy, who in a day would be at school again, kissed that *he* and *she* might renew their intrigue unsuspected!

How had he behaved the rest of that evening of romance bedrabbled? He hardly knew. Betrayed with a kiss! Two idols in the dust! And did they care what he was feeling? Not they! All they cared for was to cover up their tracks with him! But somehow—somehow—he had never shown her that he knew. Only, when their dance was over, and someone came and took her for the next, he escaped up to his little room, tore off his gloves, his waistcoat; lay on his bed, thought bitter thoughts. A boy! There he had stayed, with the thrum of the music in his ears, till at last it died away for good and the carriages were gone, and the night was quiet.

Squatting on the warren grass, still warm and dewless, Marsland rubbed his knees. Nothing like boys for generosity! And, with a little smile, he thought of his Aunt next morning, half-arch and half-concerned: 'It isn't nice, dear, to sit out in dark corners, and—well, perhaps, it wasn't your fault, but still, it isn't nice—not—quite ——' and of how suddenly she had stopped, looking in his face, where his lips were curling in his first ironic laugh. She had never forgiven him that laugh—thinking him a cynical young Lothario? And Marsland thought: 'Live and learn! Wonder what became of those two? Victorian Age! Hatches were battened down in those days! But, innocent—my hat!'

Ah! The sun was off, dew falling! He got up, rubbing his knees to take the stiffness out of them. Pigeons in the wood beyond were calling. A window in his Uncle's old home blazed like a jewel in the sun's last rays between the poplar trees. Heh! dear—a little long-ago affair!

ARNOLD BENNETT

Claribel

I

CLARIBEL FROSSACK, after attending a rather late teaparty at the
flat of her only friend in Paris, an American widow named
Sonnenschein, was returning home on foot along the Boulevard du
Montparnasse on an evening in October. A tall, well-made, nice-
looking blonde girl, tremendously English, with big bones and a
good stride to her gait, she officially gave her age as thirty, and her
face was a fair confirmation of the statement. The expression on
her features was sometimes bright and sometimes overcast, according to her varying attitude towards the phenomena which she encountered; but a sanguine cheerfulness predominated. Her hat and coat
were splashed with vivid crimson—the innocent, unconscious signal
of the maiden to whomever it might concern.

Rain began to fall, and, in falling, to shape her destiny. She was
rather beautifully dressed, with all the skill and sense which she had
industriously acquired in six months of Paris. Some years earlier she
would have enjoyed and scorned the rain, but she had replaced the
physical ideals of her athletic, sporting youth by quite other ideals;
she took scrupulous care of her clothes, and even of her complexion, with an anxiety which would have earned merely the contempt of her old self. The sky had given everybody in Paris good
notice of a change, but Claribel had ignored it, from a certain vagueness of mind; and she had no umbrella. There was no taxi in sight.
Trams and motor-buses there were; Claribel, however, had not the
courage and decision to try to halt them in their implacable progress,
nor did she know where they were going. Moreover, they were all
suddenly full.

Putting her trust in the reputation of the Parisian climate, she
hoped that the rain would soon cease, unaware that in Paris the
rain is capable of raining for three days and three nights without a

168 · *Arnold Bennett*

moment's mercy. And she was optimistic about a taxi, unaware that a sharp shower will miraculously empty every street in Paris of plying taxis. Opposite the Montparnasse station an empty taxi passed her. She timidly hailed it. The driver, with an odious grin, sneered at her simplicity and held his rapid course.

The rain was now pouring down. A serious crisis was at hand in the history of Claribel's attire and complexion. The famous and vast Café de Versailles was in front of her, with its covered *terrasse* full of occupied chairs and tables, and its white-flowing waiters. She hesitated. She certainly could not sit out on the *terrasse*; such a proceeding was in her opinion utterly impossible for an unaccompanied girl. But might she not go inside? She had never been in a *café* alone. There is probably not a more decorous public resort on earth than the old-established Café de Versailles. Yet Claribel feared lest terrible things might happen to her if she entered it. She was a solitary creature, wistful, undecided—she felt as though all Paris was leagued against her friendless, unsupported self. Then, between the rain on one side and the glances of the quizzing people of the *terrasse* on the other, she nerved herself to a frightful, perilous resolve, and strode with beating heart and the most absurd bounce into the crowded interior. Inside she took a long breath.

The first thing she clearly saw was a young man standing up and smiling and bowing to her—with much deference. She blushed a little, just as though she had been caught in a questionable act.

'Just my luck!' she thought, scared. Like everybody else, when anything untoward happened to her, she imagined that her luck was as a rule worse than other people's. However, he was a very nice young man, whose ingenuous face and dark, lustrous, wistful eyes she well remembered.

'I came to one of your At Homes,' he explained himself. 'A friend of mine brought me—François Polin. We'd been shopping together. My name's Arroll.'

One of her At Homes! Well, she had had two, and the guests had been almost exclusively her various professors, who taught her French, Italian, music, painting. François Polin was her piano-instructor. She was ashamed of her two miserable fiascos of At Homes.

'Yes,' said she. 'James Arroll, and he introduced you as "Jimmie".'

'It's awfully nice of you to remember me,' said Jimmie, obviously pleased that this tall, opulent powerful, rather imposing lady did remember his timid little self.

The *café* was very full. Claribel looked about vaguely for a free table, and saw none.

'Will you sit here—if you don't mind sharing a table?'

'If you're sure *you* don't mind.'

'I should simply love it,' said Jimmie, eagerly.

She sat down by him, feeling adventurous, imperilled, and exalted in spirit. She suddenly loved life; her face shone. Then of course she had to account for her entrance into the *café*. Naturally a fib came first into her mind. She had to meet a friend—a girl, oh, a girl! The friend wouldn't arrive, and the explanation of her absence would be the downpour. Somewhat clumsy. The truth was simpler, and she told the truth, brushing drops of rain off her shoulders as it were in corroboration of her story.

'I came,' said Jimmie, 'because it was too dark even to draw— bad gas, you know. I usually draw a bit when my painting's done. But I get lonely, and then I have to go out. Paris is fearfully lonely.'

'Oh, it *is*!' she agreed with strong sympathetic emotion. She had always assumed that men were never lonely. They were free, with a free code, and they picked up acquaintances easily; they understood and trusted one another; they were all freemasons together. She thought of her desolating loneliness in Paris and liked Jimmie tremendously for being lonely. His admission gave her ease.

A waiter stood in front of her.

'May I——?' Jimmie began.

She cut him short by ordering tea. Jimmie was having a bock. All around people were drinking coloured and exciting liquids out of various shapes of glasses. She would have loved to drink something dangerous out of a glass, but her upbringing compelled her to keep within a traditional respectability; besides, she would not have known what to order.

She was now sufficiently composed to examine the *café*. She adored its foreignness, its stuffy smell, the click of billiard balls far, far up the great room, the flowing gestures of the waiter as he deposed the shiny tea-things on the marble, the murmur of strange tongues, the perpendicular rain through the glass walls, the constant swishing of the revolving doors, the ring of checks on the cashier's counter, the occasional sharp cry of some impatient little bearded customer, the newspapers furled on sticks, the dominoes, the chess, the writing of letters on vile blotting-pads. Enchantment!

'Quite a number of Germans here now,' observed Jimmie.

'Yes,' she said, cautiously hostile.

'I think it's rather a good thing,' Jimmie continued. 'Of course, it's unpleasant in a way, and you wonder how they have the nerve; but it gets people used to what they've got to get used to sooner or later. They can't go on hating and sulking for ever. Of course I don't know, but that's how it seems to me.' He gave a little nervous laugh.

This piece of political wisdom greatly astonished Claribel, for two reasons. First, because it had issued from the almost babyish mouth of one whom she had supposed to be interested solely in the arts—and here he was taking notice of the great world and thinking for himself internationally; he had ideas! And secondly, his ideas were so at variance with those with which she was familiar. Germans had not many years since killed her only brother, and killed her brother-in-law—both professional soldiers. The people whom she knew in England never discussed Germans, save in regard to their brilliant military qualities. Germans had to exist, but they must be ignored as human beings; they were outside the pale. Certainly it was like their unspeakable nerve to force themselves on Paris; but they were Germans, and there was nothing to be said—though much to be suffered in silence. And Jimmie was accepting them with calm, unprejudiced, far-seeing satisfaction. It was a feat on his part.

'Oh, I quite agree,' she said, warmly.

The curious thing was that she did agree. And she was aware in herself of an accession of wisdom and broadmindedness.

Further, she admired the baby James. He was assuredly not of her class, which had owned land and hunted and shot and stuck animals and men for centuries; he did not wear a club-necktie, though he wore a necktie which reminded her of the sacred scarf of the Eton Wanderers; he had obviously never been to a public school. But his manners were nevertheless perfect; and he was not dull, as she and hers were; and his mind was free and easy and alert and not afraid of new notions; and his accent was faultless. She admitted that his clothes might have shocked her males; his hair, too, not to mention his dark, lustrous eyes.

'It was so beautiful it made me cry,' he was saying, the conversation having shifted from politics to river landscapes.

Not a man of hers but would have killed himself rather than

confess to such a weakness! Then there was an interruption. Customers were looking with hope into the street. A few departed; a few more departed. The rain had ceased; Claribel must go. She would have liked to stay; she hated to go. But she must go. She simply could not be free. She had sheltered from the rain; the rain was over; there was no reason for staying. True, neither was there any reason for going, for she had no appointment and naught to do. Still, she must go. She paid—no silly attempt on Jimmie's part to settle for her tea—and she went. Jimmie also paid and went; and he put her into a taxi. No suggestion about meeting again. He said not a word. And she could not.

Fate, however, had Claribel's affairs in hand. Its method of action was violent but effective. Another taxi, turning the corner, as Paris taxis will, on the wrong side of the road out of the Rue de Rennes, caught the bonnet of Claribel's taxi before the latter had moved a dozen yards, and, in addition to putting it out of action, gave Claribel a shaking in body and mind. A small crowd, a policeman, an alter-cation between two vituperative chauffeurs, a trunk in the roadway, note-taking by the policeman! The rain then sharply resumed its baptismal work and did something to tranquillize the fever of men.

'Excuse me. Hadn't you better come back inside again?'

It was Jimmie, who had apparently witnessed the accident from afar and returned.

'Oh, no. I'm perfectly all right,' said Claribel, in a voice rendered loud by excitement.

'You look rather pale. I think——'

'Very well, I will,' she agreed. She did feel a little unsteady. The policeman detained her a moment; Jimmie talked to him; and then they re-entered the *café*.

'I'm awfully sorry,' said Jimmie.

They sat down.

'I think you'd better have some brandy,' said Jimmie.

She yielded to his caprice. She did not need the brandy, but she found pleasure in obeying his suggestion. As soon as he had ordered the cognac she suspected that perhaps she did need it, and after drinking it she had an idea that she might have fainted without it. They discussed the accident, and the naughtiness of French taxi-drivers, at great length.

The *café* was now becoming a restaurant. Waiters covered table after marble table with white linen, and the white linen with cruets and cutlery. Odours multiplied; warmth increased; the place grew even cosier, homelier, more congenial; it proved itself the resort of a race that understood the art of living.

'I think I shall stick here for dinner,' said Claribel, with a sudden audacity that rather frightened her.

'I wish *I* could,' said Jimmie. 'But it's too dear for me. I eat at a pension-restaurant. If I wasn't so frightfully poor I should have ventured to ask you to dine with me.' He spoke quite simply, neither ashamed nor defiant, and he gave her the sweetest smile.

'But you can't leave me,' said she, with a flash of the imperiousness of the governing class. 'You must dine with *me*, of course.'

'Well,' said he, 'I won't be silly about it. It's awfully nice of you to ask me.'

His tone was faultless. Claribel thought he was out of sight the most sensible young man she had ever met. She imagined how any young man of her own set in England would have bridled and jibbed and blushed and protested under such an invitation—and ended by accepting it!

They dined—slowly, savouringly, and towards the close of the meal lusciously. Years seemed to have passed since Claribel first entered the adorable Café de Versailles. And it had been raining for years. Existence was transformed for Claribel. The pall of loneliness had been lifted from her. She formed part of humanity; she had a contact. Not ordinarily a facile talker, especially with mere acquaintances, she was now talking with marked ease. Jimmie talked without any effort. He was a natural talker, and he talked naturally. He seemed to say whatever came into his mind, but his mind was an interesting mind and a nice mind—no necessity to filter or censor its contents before letting them forth!

At intervals, in pauses of argument, Jimmie would point out celebrities or notorieties among the customers. Possibly not notables of the world, but notables of the Montparnasse quarter, which honestly considered itself the centre of the world.

The ornate clock over the cashier's counter behaved in an extraordinary manner; its fingers raced round the dial. Claribel tried to will them into deliberateness, but they would not be restrained. They showed twenty-five minutes to twelve when the other clock, in

Claribel's head, said that the hour could not be later than twenty-five minutes to ten. An evening unlike any other evening that ever was in Paris or in paradise!

Just as Claribel was beginning to make a successful fight against the mysterious magnetic force which held her to her chair and absolutely prevented her from rising to depart—the bill had long ago, through Jimmie's agency, been paid and the change handed over and the tip given—Psichari came up, on his way out of the *café*. Psichari was one of the celebrities already indicated to Claribel by Jimmie. Claribel had felt an artistic thrill at being even in the same *café* with Psichari. You could tell how great a painter Psichari was in Paris by the fact that Jimmie blushed when he most surprisingly stopped at the table, and rose with much deferential ceremony to greet him.

'Present me,' murmured the handsome, bearded hero of the studios in an undertone. And he was duly presented to Claribel. Thereupon he sat down at the table, and talked in French.

'You will pardon me, mademoiselle, but I have not been able to prevent myself from regarding you all the evening. You are so exquisitely an English type. It is so romantic to me. No women exist save the English. There are none save the English.'

Still, in a more general vein, he talked admirably—better than Jimmie. Claribel, however, was now restless—pleased, but confused and apprehensive. She said that she must leave. And she did leave, escorted to the pavement by the two men. The rain continued with infinite strong perseverance to descend in generous cascades. Claribel got into a taxi, and, while Jimmie was giving the address to the driver, Psichari also got into the taxi. He was not intoxicated—or at least he was not suffering from anything more deleterious than the romantical quality of Claribel's blonde English appearance; but he was uplifted. He stated in an uplifted voice that it would not be safe for Miss Frossack to travel home unaccompanied. Claribel glanced with a certain appeal at Jimmie. Jimmie seized the great painter first by one arm and then by two, and pulled him out of the cab. The two men, Psichari taller than Jimmie and ten years older, faced each other on the pavement.

'*Fiche-nous la paix!*' Jimmie exhorted the celebrity.

And as Psichari would not listen to the exhortation to leave them in peace, Jimmie hit him on the chest, and the idol of Montparnasse subsided on to the pavement. Jimmie nipped into the taxi, which drove off.

Little was said, but the cave-woman in Claribel could not sleep that night because she had been fought for by two artists on the Parisian pavement; and the English girl in Claribel could not sleep because the delicious Jimmie had asked her to sit for him and she had consented to do so.

The next really thrilling thing that happened to her was the arrival, one evening, of an express letter, which ran: 'May I call tonight about nine? I want very much to see you about a matter which is important to me.—Your devoted Jimmie.'

Claribel blushed and shook. She blushed and shook all by herself in her own drawing-room.

II

On the morning of the day on which Claribel received the express note from Jimmie in the late afternoon, she had been sitting to him in his studio in the Rue Léopold Robert, a street south of Montparnasse and plenteously inhabited by Anglo-Saxon youths of both sexes of a status similar to that of James Arroll. It was the final sitting for the portrait, and nearly three months had passed since the great scenes inside and outside the Café de Versailles. Claribel had just gone, and Jimmie was still watching her as she primly and brightly descended the four double flights of stairs that separated his lair from the solid earth, when he heard footsteps above him. A figure was coming down from the heights of the fifth storey—a young man dressed in golden brown, very baggy corduroys, heavy boots, a black wide-awake hat with a circumference of about one yard, and a muffler that seemed like a slice off a blanket. The ferocity of the black moustache argued, perhaps falsely, that the hip-pocket held a revolver to match it. Of course, an English painter; French and other painters no longer wore the classic uniform of art.

'Josh!' called Jimmie, shivering in the icy January draughts of the staircase. 'Come in and have a look at this blessed thing I've just finished.'

'Thy wildest caprice is an order. Let her loose,' replied Josh, entering with a swagger the large, naked, and dirty studio of his friend. He examined Claribel's portrait with a lofty and judicial air for an extraordinarily long time. Then, in silence, he went and poked the stove, and then he examined the portrait again.

'Look here, brother,' said he, at last. 'What in the name of the late esteemed Lord Leighton have you been trying to get at?'

'Don't you like it?'

'Rotten!' said the critic. 'Rotten! It's all over the place. It isn't like anything on earth.'

'I feared it,' murmured Jimmie, with submission.

'You don't mean to tell me you have the nerve to like it yourself?'

'Frankly, I don't. But she does.'

'Oh, she does, does she? Well, that settles it. They never like anything but the completely putrid.'

'But really she isn't quite the——'

'Silence, sir!' the bandit stopped him. 'If you're thinking of inform- ing me that she's subtly different from all other girls, think better of it and don't. Because I doubt if our friendship would stand it. No girl is different from all other girls. And when she says she likes this portrait, she simply and unaffectedly means that she likes *you*. Have I lived, or was I born this morning?'

'That's where you're wrong, Josh. She may be a bad critic, but there's no nonsense about her of that sort. She's even cold. You can talk to her just as if she was a man.'

'And you do?'

'I do.'

'Laddie, you must introduce me to her. It will be the day of my life. I bid you good morning.'

'I say,' said Jimmie, timidly, to Josh in the doorway. 'You might let me doss in your studio tomorrow night.'

'Not on your life!' said Josh. 'I have other arrangements in view. Why?'

'The landlord was here at eight-fifteen today. I owe him two quarters and I can't pay. He's given me till tomorrow.'

'The dirty dog!' exclaimed Josh, with feeling, the basis of his philosophy of existence being the axiom that all persons not painters ought to be willing and proud to be owed money by all painters.

'I haven't had my supplies from London, and I shan't have just yet, and it's six months since I sold a thing,' Jimmie explained, gloomily.

'Serious, eh?'

'Yes.'

'Then sell a thing at once. Sell her this portrait. From the look of her raiment, wealth is not what she's short of.'

'Oh, she's rich all right,' said Jimmie, 'but I couldn't possibly ask her to buy this.'

'Why not?'

'Because it's not good enough.'

'What an ass of a reason! Unload the bad, my excellent fool. Unload, I say. If *I* do anything decent I always want to keep it. Besides, there are "passages" as we critics say, in this that aren't positively criminal. I don't mind stating that the hair is the best bit of pure painting you ever did. But the rest—oh, Mohammed and Buddha!'

Jimmie shook his head.

'No. I won't do it.'

'Then touch her for a thousand francs. Tell her she's helping the sacred cause. She'd love to lend it to you.'

Jimmie coloured slightly.

'I was wondering whether I might ask her. But she's so jolly decent I don't really care to take advantage——' He gave a nervous laugh.

'Well I beg leave to say no more. She has the stuff. You want it. Which is the same as saying she has your future and you want it. Ask her to lend you a thousand francs, and report to me tonight or tomorrow morning, if you please. And have a care!'

Josh stalkingly departed.

After some hours of mental travail, Jimmie brought himself to the point of telephoning to Claribel about money, from a *café*. She was not at home. Then he dispatched the express note, to which he received an answer at seven o'clock: 'Delighted to see you. Nine o'clock.—C.F.'

III

Claribel put the little blue note from Jimmie away, with several other specimens of his handwriting, at the back of a drawer in her dressing-table. Then she pulled it out and read it again and replaced it in the drawer. And all this in the middle of her dressing! And, further, she was dressing after dinner, not before it. She was dressing all over afresh, in the light of her beautiful bedroom lamps and of the note, which had arrived after her first evening dressing.

She was far gone in love with Jimmie. Jimmie was unlike any other man she had ever known, and especially unlike the men of her own tribe. She admired these men, in a fashion, but how dull and narrow and rigid and incurious they were in their subconscious self-satisfaction and their dependable honesty! Jimmie had dependable honesty, too, but what a different, what a superior and finer mind! Of course, he was five years younger than herself, but did that matter? Besides, she had frankly told him her age—after he had guessed twenty-seven; and he did not seem to mind in the least. She knew him now, at the end of twenty-five or thirty sittings; she knew him through and through; and he was sound through and through. And she had decided that he was, or would be, a great painter—no doubt the greatest painter of the age. He had taught her an immense amount about life and art and Paris and the European outlook and such things. Indeed he was a Titan. Yet not on these counts did she adore him. She adored him because he had fought for her on the pavement in front of the Café de Versailles, and because he had such dark, lustrous, wistful eyes, and such an appealing voice and such gentle gestures, and because he was a baby. Strange that he could be at once a Titan and a baby. But so it was. He had no more notion of looking after himself than a baby.

And if he had taught her, she had taught him. She had softened some crudities and she had shown him what a woman thinks, and how and why. And he had learnt eagerly and thankfully.

Her maid (French) now came in.

'Monsieur Arroll.'

'A little moment,' said Claribel. 'Arrange me this tulle, Louise.'

She was agitated—and for an excellent reason. She was convinced in her heart that Jimmie had come to ask her to marry him, and she very well knew that she would not refuse him. She had noticed the frequent tendernesses in his voice, the admiration in his eyes, the shy hesitations in his adoring demeanour. At least once, she judged, he had been on the very edge of a proposal in his studio, but timidity had held him back. She could not be mistaken. In half an hour, in an hour, she would be an engaged girl, with vistas of thrilling happiness stretching before her.

Fortunately she was under no obligation to consult anybody. She had no ties; she had full control of her own plenteous money.

Imagine having to obtain consent to marry a painter from one of those queer, good, misguided persons who had given her the ridiculous name of Claribel—after some ridiculous poem of Tennyson's! Awful!

She passed shaking into the drawing-room, Louise following her as far as the bedroom door with pats and smoothings of her skirt. She stood hesitant, frightened and blissful in the doorway, showing herself for admiration, at her very best; not offering herself, but expecting to be demanded. She smiled exquisitely, and her lower lip trembled. Nothing of the outdoor athletic girl in her now! She was the indoor, the boudoir girl, richly attired—moulded and prepared for love. She made a splendid vision in the luxurious, luminous drawing-room.

And there stood Jimmie, somewhat threadbare in his neat lounge-suit. Might he not be disconcerted, impeded, by her luxury, by the economic difference between them? Not he! He had a mind above such accidents of fortune. He had genius, outweighing any quantity of money; and moreover, like all artists, he had a taste for luxury—could not resist it.

They sat down. She noticed that he was just as nervous as she was, and this lessened her own nervousness and gave her confidence.

'I'm so glad you've come,' she said, brightly, 'because I wanted to ask you something.'

'Yes?'

'I want you to let me buy that portrait. I should have mentioned it this morning, but I felt a bit awkward about it.'

'I'm glad you didn't,' said Jimmie. 'And I'm sorry you mentioned it now. Because I don't want to part with it.'

'Why not?' She asked the question, but she knew the answer. He wished not to part with it because he felt the absolute necessity of having her reminding portrait in his studio. Still she repeated: 'Why not?'

'It's not good enough,' said Jimmie. 'I don't like it well enough to let it go.'

'But, Jimmie, I've set my heart on having it. I think it's simply beautiful.'

Jimmie shook his head. 'No, I must be firm about that.' His voice sounded hard to her. He added: 'May I tell you right out what I've come for? I want——'

The fatal words were on the very edge of his lips when he stopped and jumped up. Claribel was crying; she was sobbing. His attitude concerning the portrait, acting on her extremely excited nerves, had overset her. She was perhaps quite as startled by the tears as himself. But there they were! And Jimmie was gravely disturbed. He was absurdly disturbed. For it is a remarkable fact that, though a woman's tears mean vastly less than a man's, her—shall we call it?—effervescing point being much lower than a man's, a young man will treat those tears just as seriously as if he had shed them himself.

Jimmie thought it was his duty somehow to stanch them; but he could not devise any method of doing so. And he was aware of remorse. Also he saw the utter impossibility of asking her for a loan. Indeed, the situation was excessively delicate and demanded for its handling all the experienced, wise, diplomatic ingenuity of a man of the world. And Jimmie knew too well that he was by no means a man of the world.

He merely hovered around the fount of tears in a state of rather silly indecision, suffering acutely from the shock which always accompanies an increase of knowledge of the baffling psychology of women. At the same time his emotions were not wholly unpleasant. He actually enjoyed the spectacle of her woe. The tears softened her. They gave her a touch of 'nonsense' which hitherto, according to Jimmie's observation, she had lacked. They indicated to him that never in the future could he talk to her as to another man. Formerly he liked her because she could be treated as a male comrade. Now he liked her rather more because she had suddenly ceased to be a male comrade. Her tears melted her, and they melted him too.

As for Claribel, what she chiefly felt was resentment and disillusion. And she also enjoyed her tears. Then she remembered her Spartan youth, and with a heroical effort resumed command of herself. And then she opened her bag and began to rebuild her damaged complexion. Never in the old days would she have put powder to her face in the presence of a man. But things were changed. Neither of them spoke a word. It was most ridiculous. Jimmie sat down again.

At length he said:

'I'm awfully sorry. You shall have the portrait.'

She looked at the radiator, there being no fire.

'But, of course,' he added, 'I shall give it to you. I really couldn't take anything for it.'

Whereat she sobbed once more.

'Can't you see I can't accept presents from you?' she mumbled, inarticulately.

'I beg pardon,' said he, comprehending nothing.

She made a new attempt.

'I say it's fearfully nice of you, but I can't accept presents from you.'

'Then I'll sell it to you at any price you like,' he yielded, beaten. But she continued to weep and to mumble.

'I know what a genius you are, and I wanted to be able to say I'd bought a picture from you when you were unknown.' And more loudly and distinctly: 'However, it doesn't matter!'

Jimmie stood up again. He wanted to cry himself; for she had become to him the most touching and heavenly sight ever seen in the world. She had become exquisite, fragile, defenceless, and desirable. Simultaneously it occurred to him that in certain circumstances there is only one right method of stanching a woman's tears. He used that method.

The mayor of the sixth arrondissement, with the French flag tied round his rich waist, united them in marriage. Claribel never knew that, had she begun to weep five seconds later than she did, the direction of her whole life would have been changed, for her sentiments would never have survived the blow of being asked for money when she was expecting to be asked for love. And Jimmie's heart would stop beating at the mere awful recollection of the moment when her tears in the nick of time saved him from stepping over a precipice into—into what?

W. SOMERSET MAUGHAM

Episode

It was quite a small party, because our hostess liked general conversation; we never sat down to dinner more than eight, and generally only six, and after dinner when we went up to the drawing-room the chairs were so arranged that it was impossible for two persons to go into a huddle in a corner and so break things up. I was glad on arriving to find that I knew everyone. There were two nice clever women besides our hostess and two men besides myself. One was my friend Ned Preston. Our hostess made it a point never to ask wives with their husbands, because she said each cramped the other's style and if they didn't like to come separately they needn't come at all. But since her food and her wine were good and the talk almost always entertaining they generally came. People sometimes accused her of asking husbands more often than wives, but she defended herself by saying that she couldn't possibly help it because more men were husbands than women were wives.

Ned Preston was a Scot, a good-humoured, merry soul, with a gift for telling a story, sometimes too lengthily, for he was uncommonly loquacious, but with dramatic intensity. He was a bachelor with a small income which sufficed for his modest needs, and in this he was lucky since he suffered from that form of chronic tuberculosis which may last for years without killing you, but which prevents you from working for your living. Now and then he would be ill enough to stay in bed for two or three weeks, but then he would get better and be as gay, cheerful, and talkative as ever. I doubt whether he had enough money to live in an expensive sanatorium and he certainly hadn't the temperament to suit himself to its life. He was worldly. When he was well he liked to go out, out to lunch, out to dinner, and he liked to sit up late into the night smoking his pipe and drinking a good deal of whisky. If he had been content to live the life of an invalid he might have been alive now, but he wasn't; and who can blame him? He died at the age of fifty-five of a haemorrhage which he had one night after coming home from some house where, he may well have flattered himself, he was the success of the party.

He had that febrile vitality that some consumptives have, and was always looking for an occupation to satisfy his desire for activity. I don't know how he heard that at Wormwood Scrubs they were in want of prison visitors, but the idea took his fancy so he went to the Home Office and saw the official in charge of prisons to offer his services. The job is unpaid, and though a number of persons are willing to undertake it, either from compassion or curiosity, they are apt to grow tired of it, or find it takes up too much time, and the prisoners whose problems, interests, and future they have been concerned with are left somewhat in the lurch. The Home Office people consequently are wary of taking on anyone who does not look as if he would persevere, and they make careful inquiries into the applicant's antecedents, character, and general suitability. Then he is given a trial, is discreetly watched, and if the impression is unfavourable is politely thanked and told that his services are no longer required. But Ned Preston satisfied the dour and shrewd official who interviewed him that he was in every way reliable, and from the beginning he got on well with the governor, the warders, and the prisoners. He was entirely lacking in class-consciousness, so prisoners, whatever their station in life, felt at ease with him. He neither preached nor moralized. He had never done a criminal, or even a mean, thing in his life, but he treated the crime of the prisoners he had to deal with as though it were an illness like his own tuberculosis which was a nuisance you had to put up with, but which it did no good to talk about.

Wormwood Scrubs is a first offenders' prison and it is a building, grim and cold, of forbidding appearance. Ned took me over it once and I had goose-flesh as the gates were unlocked for us and we went in. We passed through the halls in which the men were working.

'If you see any pals of yours take no notice of them,' Ned said to me. 'They don't like it.'

'Am I likely to see any pals of mine?' I asked dryly.

'You never can tell. I shouldn't be surprised if you had had friends who'd passed bad cheques once too often or were caught in a compromising situation in one of the parks. You'd be surprised how often I run across chaps I've met out at dinner.'

One of Ned's duties was to see prisoners through the first difficult days of their confinement. They were often badly shaken by their trial and sentence; and when, after the preliminary proceedings they had to go through on entering the gaol, the stripping, the bath, the medical examination and the questioning, the getting into prison clothes, they were led into a cell and locked up, they were apt to break down. Sometimes they cried hysterically; sometimes they could neither eat nor sleep. Ned's business then was to cheer them, and his breezy manner, his natural kindliness, often worked wonders. If they were anxious about their wives and children he would go to see them and if they were destitute provide them with money. He brought them news so that they might get over the awful feeling that they were shut away from the common interests of their fellow men. He read the sporting papers to be able to tell them what horse had won an important race or whether the champion had won his fight. He would advise them about their future, and when the time approached for their release see what jobs they were fitted for and then persuade employers to give them a chance to make good.

Since everyone is interested in crime it was inevitable that sooner or later, with Ned there, the conversation should turn upon it. It was after dinner and we were sitting comfortably in the drawing-room with drinks in our hands.

'Had any interesting cases at the Scrubs lately, Ned?' I asked him. 'No, nothing much.'

He had a high, rasping voice and his laugh was a raucous cackle. He broke into it now.

'I went to see an old girl today who was a packet of fun. Her husband's a burglar. The police have known about him for years, but they've never been able to get him till just now. Before he did a job he and his wife concocted an alibi, and though he's been arrested three or four times and sent up for trial, the police have never been able to break it and he's always got off. Well, he was arrested again a little while ago, but he wasn't upset, the alibi he and his wife had made up was perfect and he expected to be acquitted as he'd been before. His wife went into the witness-box and to his utter amazement she didn't give the alibi and he was convicted.

I went to see him. He wasn't so much worried at being in gaol as puzzled by his wife not having spoken up, and he asked me to go and see her and ask what the game was. Well I went, and d'you know what she said to me? She said: "Well, sir, it's like this; it was such a beautiful alibi I just couldn't bear to waste it.'"

Of course we all laughed. The story-teller likes an appreciative audience, and Ned Preston was never disinclined to hold the floor. He narrated two or three more anecdotes. They tended to prove a point he was fond of making, that in what till we all got democratic in England were called the lower orders there was more passion, more romance, more disregard of consequences than could ever be found in the well-to-do and presumably educated classes, whom prudence has made timid and convention inhibited.

'Because the working man doesn't read much,' he said, 'because he has no great gift for expressing himself, you think he has no imagination. You're wrong. He's extravagantly imaginative. Because he's a great husky brute you think he has no nerves. You're wrong again. He's a bundle of nerves.'

Then he told us a story which I shall tell as best I can in my own words.

Fred Manson was a good-looking fellow, tall, well-made, with blue eyes, good features, and a friendly, agreeable smile, but what made him remarkable so that people turned round in the streets to stare at him was that he had a thick head of hair, with a great wave in it, of a deep rich red. It was really a great beauty. Perhaps it was this that gave him so sensual a look. His maleness was like a heady perfume. His eyebrows were thick, only a little lighter than his hair, and he was lucky enough not to have the ugly skin that so often disfigures red-heads. His was a smooth olive. His eyes were bold, and when he smiled or laughed, which in the healthy vitality of his youth he did constantly, his expression was wonderfully alluring. He was twenty-two and he gave you the rather pleasant impression of just loving to be alive. It was inevitable that with such looks and above all with that troubling sexuality he should have success with women. He was charming, tender, and passionate, but immensely promiscuous. He was not exactly callous or brazen, he had a kindly nature, but somehow or other he made it quite clear to the objects of his passing fancy that all he wanted was a little bit of fun and that it was impossible for him to remain faithful to anyone.

Fred was a postman. He worked in Brixton. It is a densely pop-
ulated part of London, and has the curious reputation of harbour-
ing more criminals than any other suburb because trams run to it
from across the river all night long, so that when a man has done
a job of housebreaking in the West End he can be sure of getting
home without difficulty. Fred liked his job. Brixton is a district of
innumerable streets lined with little houses inhabited by the people
who work in the neighbourhood and also by clerks, shop-assistants,
skilled workers of one sort or another whose jobs take them every
day across the river. He was strong and healthy and it was a pleasure to him to walk from street to street delivering the letters.
Sometimes there would be a postal packet to hand in or a regis-
tered letter that had to be signed for, and then he would have
the opportunity of seeing people. He was a sociable creature. It
was never long before he was well known on whatever round he was
assigned to. After a time his job was changed. His duty then was
to go to the red pillar-boxes into which the letters were put, empty
them, and take the contents to the main post-office of the district.
His bag would be pretty heavy sometimes by the time he was
through, but he was proud of his strength and the weight only made
him laugh.

One day he was emptying a box in one of the better streets, a
street of semi-detached houses, and had just closed his bag when a
girl came running along.

'Postman,' she cried, 'take this letter, will you. I want it to go
by this post most particularly.'

He gave her his good-natured smile.

'I never mind obliging a lady,' he said, putting down his bag and
opening it.

'I wouldn't trouble you, only it's urgent,' she said as she handed
him the letter she had in her hand.

'Who is it to—a feller?' he grinned.

'None of your business.'

'All right, be haughty. But I tell you this, he's no good. Don't
you trust him.'

'You've got a nerve,' she said.

'So they tell me.'

He took off his cap and ran his hand through his mop of curling red hair. The sight of it made her gasp.

'Where d'you get your perm?' she asked with a giggle.

'I'll show you one of these days if you like.'

He was looking down at her with his amused eyes, and there was something about him that gave her a funny little feeling in the pit of her stomach.

'Well, I must be on my way,' he said. 'If I don't get on with the job pretty damn quick I don't know what'll happen to the country.'

'I'm not detaining you,' she said coolly.

'That's where you make a mistake,' he answered.

He gave her a look that made her heart beat nineteen to the dozen and she felt herself blushing all over. She turned away and ran back to the house. Fred noticed it was four doors away from the pillar-box. He had to pass it and as he did so he looked up. He saw the net curtains twitch and knew she was watching. He felt pleased with himself. During the next few days he looked at the house whenever he passed it, but never caught a glimpse of the girl. One afternoon he ran across her by chance just as he was entering the street in which she lived.

'Hulloa,' he said, stopping.

'Hulloa.'

She blushed scarlet.

'Haven't seen you about lately.'

'You haven't missed much.'

'That's what you think.'

She was prettier than he remembered, dark-haired, dark-eyed, rather tall, slight, with a good figure, a pale skin and very white teeth.

'What about coming to the pictures with me one evening?'

'Taking a lot for granted, aren't you?'

'It pays,' he said with his impudent, charming grin.

She couldn't help laughing.

'Not with me, it doesn't.'

'Oh, come on. One's only young once.'

There was something so attractive in him that she couldn't bring herself to give him a saucy answer.

'I couldn't really. My people wouldn't like me going out with a fellow I don't know. You see, I'm the only one they have and they think a rare lot of me. Why, I don't even know your name.'

'Well, I can tell you, can't I? Fred. Fred Manson. Can't you say you're going to the pictures with a girl friend?'

She had never felt before what she was feeling then. She didn't know if it was pain or pleasure. She was strangely breathless.

'I suppose I could do that.'

They fixed the night, the time, and the place. Fred was waiting for her and they went in, but when the picture started and he put his arm round her waist, without a word, her eyes fixed on the screen, she quietly took it away. He took hold of her hand, but she withdrew it. He was surprised. That wasn't the way girls usually behaved. He didn't know what one went to the pictures for if it wasn't to have a bit of a cuddle. He walked home with her after the show. She told him her name. Grace Carter. Her father had a shop of his own in the Brixton Road, he was a draper and he had four assistants.

'He must be doing well,' said Fred.

'He doesn't complain.'

Gracie was a student at London University. When she got her degree she was going to be a school teacher.

'What d'you want to do that for when there's a good business waiting for you?'

'Pa doesn't want me to have anything to do with the shop—not after the education he's given me. He wants me to better myself, if you know what I mean.'

Her father had started life as an errand boy, then become a draper's assistant and because he was hard-working, honest, and intelligent was now owner of a prosperous little business. Success had given him grand ideas for his only child. He didn't want her to have anything to do with trade. He hoped she'd marry a professional man perhaps, or at least someone in the City. Then he'd sell the business and retire, and Gracie would be quite the lady.

When they reached the corner of her street Gracie held out her hand.

'You'd better not come to the door,' she said.

'Aren't you going to kiss me good-night?'

'I am not.'

'Why?'

'Because I don't want to.'

'You'll come to the pictures again, won't you?'

'I think I'd better not.'

'Oh, come on.'

There was such a warm urgency in his voice that she felt as though her knees would give way.

'Will you behave if I do?' He nodded. 'Promise?'

'Swop me bob.'

He scratched his head when he left her. Funny girl. He'd never met anyone quite like her. Superior, there was no doubt about that. There was something in her voice that got you. It was warm and soft. He tried to think what it was like. It was like as if the words kissed you. Sounded silly, that did, but that's just what it was like.

From then on they went to the pictures once or twice a week. After a while she allowed him to put his arm round her waist and to hold her hand, but she never let him go farther than that.

'Have you ever been kissed by a fellow?' he asked her once.

'No, I haven't,' she said simply. 'My ma's funny, she says you've got to keep a man's respect.'

'I'd give anything in the world just to kiss you, Gracie.'

'Don't be so silly.'

'Won't you let me just once?' She shook her head. 'Why not?'

'Because I like you too much,' she said hoarsely, and then walked quickly away from him.

It gave him quite a turn. He wanted her as he'd never wanted a woman before. What she'd said finished him. He'd been thinking of her a lot, and he'd looked forward to the evenings they spent together as he'd never looked forward to anything in his life. For the first time he was uncertain of himself. She was above him in every way, what with her father making money hand over fist and her education and everything, and him only a postman. They had made a date for the following Friday night and he was in a fever of anxiety lest she shouldn't come. He repeated to himself over and over again what she'd said: perhaps it meant that she'd made up her mind to drop him. When at last he saw her walking along the street he almost sobbed with relief. That evening he neither put his arm round her nor took her hand and when he walked her home he never said a word.

'You're very quiet tonight, Fred,' she said at last. 'What's the matter with you?'

He walked a few steps before he answered.

'I don't like to tell you.'

She stopped suddenly and looked up at him. There was terror on her face.

'Tell me whatever it is,' she said unsteadily.

'I'm gone, I can't help myself, I'm so stuck on you I can't see straight. I didn't know what it was to love like I love you.'

'Oh, is that all? You gave me such a fright. I thought you were going to say you were going to be married.'

'Me? Who d'you take me for? It's you I want to marry.'

'Well, what's to prevent you, silly?'

'Gracie! D'you mean it?'

He flung his arms round her and kissed her full on the mouth. She didn't resist. She returned his kiss and he felt in her a passion as eager as his own.

They arranged that Gracie should tell her parents that she was engaged to him and that on the Sunday he should come and be introduced to them. Since the shop stayed open late on Saturday and by the time Mr Carter got home he was tired out, it was not till after dinner on Sunday that Gracie broke her news. George Carter was a brisk, not very tall man, but sturdy, with a high colour, who with increasing prosperity had put on weight. He was more than rather bald and he had a bristle of grey moustache. Like many another employer who has risen from the working class he was a slave-driver and he got as much work out of his assistants for as little money as was possible. He had an eye for everything and he wouldn't put up with any nonsense, but he was reasonable and even kindly, so that they did not dislike him. Mrs Carter was a quiet, nice woman, with a pleasant face and the remains of good looks. They were both in the early fifties, for they had married late after 'walking out' for nearly ten years.

They were very much surprised when Gracie told them what she had to tell, but not displeased.

'You are a sly one,' said her father. 'Why, I never suspected for a minute you'd taken up with anyone. Well, I suppose it had to come sooner or later. What's his name?'

'Fred Manson.'

'A fellow you met at college?'

'No. You must have seen him about. He clears our pillar-box. He's a postman.'

'Oh, Gracie,' cried Mrs Carter, 'you can't mean it. You can't marry a common postman, not after all the education we've given you.'

For an instant Mr Carter was speechless. He got redder in the face than ever.

'Your ma's right, my girl,' he burst out now. 'You can't throw yourself away like that. Why, it's ridiculous.'

'I'm not throwing myself away. You wait till you see him.'

Mrs Carter began to cry.

'It's such a come-down. It's such a humiliation. I shall never be able to hold up my head again.'

'Oh, Ma, don't talk like that. He's a nice fellow and he's got a good job.'

'You don't understand,' she moaned.

'How d'you get to know him?' Mr Carter interrupted. 'What sort of a family's he got?'

'His pa drives one of the post-office vans,' Gracie answered defiantly.

'Working-class people.'

'Well, what of it? His pa's worked twenty-four years for the post-office and they think a lot of him.'

Mrs Carter was biting the corner of her handkerchief.

'Gracie, I want to tell you something. Before your pa and me got married I was in domestic service. He wouldn't ever let me tell you because he didn't want you to be ashamed of me. That's why we was engaged all those years. The lady I was with said she'd leave me something in her will if I stayed with her till she passed away.'

'It was that money that gave me my start,' Mr Carter broke in. 'Except for that I'd never have been where I am today. And I don't mind telling you your ma's the best wife a man ever had.'

'I never had a proper education,' Mrs Carter went on, 'but I always was ambitious. The proudest moment of my life was when your pa said we could afford a girl to help me and he said then: "The time'll come when you have a cook *and* a housemaid," and he's been as good as his word, and now you're going back to what I come from. I'd set my heart on your marrying a gentleman.'

She began crying again. Gracie loved her parents and couldn't bear to see them so distressed.

'I'm sorry, Ma, I knew it would be a disappointment to you, but I can't help it, I can't really. I love him so, I love him so terribly. I'm sure you'll like him when you see him. We're going for a walk on the Common this afternoon. Can't I bring him back to supper?'

Mrs Carter gave her husband a harassed look. He sighed.

'I don't like it and it's no good pretending I do, but I suppose we'd better have a look at him.'

Supper passed off better than might have been expected. Fred wasn't shy, and he talked to Gracie's parents as though he had known them all his life. If to be waited on by a maid, if to sup in a dining-room furnished in solid mahogany and afterwards to sit in a drawing-room that had a grand piano in it was new to him, he showed no embarrassment. After he had gone and they were alone in their bedroom Mr and Mrs Carter talked him over.

'He is handsome, you can't deny that,' she said.

'Handsome is as handsome does. D'you think he's after her money?'

'Well, he must know that you've got a tidy little bit tucked away somewhere, but he's in love with her all right.'

'Oh, what makes you think that?'

'Why, you've only got to see the way he looks at her.'

'Well, that's something at all events.'

In the end the Carters withdrew their opposition on the condition that the young things shouldn't marry until Gracie had taken her degree. That would give them a year, and at the back of their minds was the hope that by then she would have changed her mind. They saw a good deal of Fred after that. He spent every Sunday with them. Little by little they began quite to like him. He was so easy, so gay, so full of high spirits, and above all so obviously head over ears in love with Gracie, that Mrs Carter soon succumbed to his charm, and after a while even Mr Carter was prepared to admit that he didn't seem a bad fellow. Fred and Gracie were happy. She went to London every day to attend lectures and worked hard. They spent blissful evenings together. He gave her a very nice engage-ment ring and often took her out to dinner in the West End and to a play. On fine Sundays he drove her out into the country in a car that he said a friend had lent him. When she asked him if he could afford all the money he spent on her he laughed, and said a chap had given him a tip on an outsider and he'd made a packet. They talked interminably of the little flat they would have when they were married and the fun it would be to furnish it. They were more in love with one another than ever.

Then the blow fell. Fred was arrested for stealing money from the letters he collected. Many people, to save themselves the trouble of buying postal orders, put notes in their envelopes, and it wasn't difficult to tell that they were there. Fred went up for trial, pleaded guilty, and was sentenced to two years' hard labour. Gracie went to the trial. Up to the last moment she had hoped that he would be able to prove his innocence. It was a dreadful shock to her when he pleaded guilty. She was not allowed to see him. He went straight from the dock to the prison van. She went home and, locking herself up in her bedroom, threw herself on the bed and wept. When Mr Carter came back from the shop Gracie's mother went up to her room.

'Gracie, you're to come downstairs,' she said. 'Your father wants to speak to you.'

Gracie got up and went down. She did not trouble to dry her eyes.

'Seen the paper?' he said, holding out to her the *Evening News*. She didn't answer.

'Well, that's the end of that young man,' he went on harshly.

They too, Gracie's parents, had been shocked when Fred was arrested, but she was so distressed, she was so convinced that everything could be explained, that they hadn't had the heart to tell her that she must have nothing more to do with him. But now they felt it time to have things out with her.

'So that's where the money came from for those dinners and theatres. And the car. I thought it funny he should have a friend who'd lend him a car on Sundays when he'd be wanting it himself. He hired it, didn't he?'

'I suppose so,' she answered miserably. 'I just believed what he told me.'

'You've had a lucky escape, my girl, that's all I can say.'

'He only did it because he wanted to give me a good time. He didn't want me to think I couldn't have everything as nice when I was with him as what I've been used to at home.'

'You're not going to make excuses for him, I hope. He's a thief, that's what he is.'

'I don't care,' she said sullenly.

'You don't care? What d'you mean by that?'

'Exactly what I say. I'm going to wait for him and the moment he comes out I'm going to marry him.'

Mrs Carter gave a gasp of horror.

'Gracie, you can't do a thing like that,' she cried. 'Think of the disgrace. And what about us? We've always held our heads high. He's a thief, and once a thief always a thief.'

'Don't go on calling him a thief,' Gracie shrieked, stamping her foot with rage. 'What he did he did just because he loved me. I don't care if he is a thief. I love him more than ever I loved him. You don't know what love is. You waited ten years to marry Pa just so as an old woman should leave you some money. D'you call that love?'

'You leave your ma out of this,' Mr Carter shouted. Then an idea occurred to him and he gave her a piercing glance. 'Have you *got* to marry the feller?'

Gracie blushed furiously.

'No. There's never been anything of that sort. And not through any fault of mine either. He loved me too much. He didn't want to do anything perhaps he'd regret afterwards.'

Often on summer evenings in the country when they'd been lying in a field in one another's arms, mouth to mouth, her desire had been as intense as his. She knew how much he wanted her and she was ready to give him what he asked. But when things got too desperate he'd suddenly jump up and say:

'Come on, let's walk.'

He'd drag her to her feet. She knew what was in his mind. He wanted to wait till they were married. His love had given him a delicacy of sentiment that he'd never known before. He couldn't make it out himself, but he had a funny sort of feeling about her, he felt that if he had her before marriage it would spoil things. Because she guessed what was in his heart she loved him all the more.

'I don't know what's come over you,' moaned Mrs Carter. 'You was always such a good girl. You've never given us a day's uneasiness.'

'Stop it, Ma,' said Mr Carter violently. 'We've got to get this straight once and for all. You've got to give up this man, see? I've got me own position to think of and if you think I'm going to have a gaolbird for a son-in-law you'd better think again. I've had enough of this nonsense. You've got to promise me that you'll have nothing more to do with the feller ever.'

'D'you think I'm going to give him up now? How often d'you want me to tell you I'm going to marry him the moment he gets out?'

'All right, then you can get out of my house and get out pretty damn quick. And stay out.'

'Pa!' cried Mrs Carter.

'Shut up.'

'I'll be glad to go,' said Gracie.

'Oh, will you? And how d'you think you're going to live?'

'I can work, can't I? I can get a job at Payne & Perkins. They'll be glad to have me.'

'Oh, Gracie, you couldn't go and work in a shop. You can't demean yourself like that,' said Mrs Carter.

'Will you shut up, Ma,' shouted Mr Carter, beside himself now with rage. 'Work, will you? You that's never done a stroke of work in your life except that tomfoolery at the college. Bright idea it was of your ma's to give you an education. Fat lot of good it'll be to you when you've got to stand on your feet for hours and got to be civil and pleasant to a lot of old trouts who just try and give you all the trouble they can just to show how superior they are. I bet you'll like it when you're bawled out by the manageress because you're not bright and snappy. All right, marry your gaolbird. I suppose you know you'll have to keep him too. You don't think anyone's going to give him a job, do you, not with his record. Get out, get out, get out.'

He had worked himself up to such a pitch of fury that he sank panting into a chair. Mrs Carter, frightened, poured out a glass of water and gave him some to drink. Gracie slipped out of the room.

Next day, when her father had gone to work and her mother was out shopping, she left the house with such effects as she could get into a suitcase. Payne & Perkins was a large department store in the Brixton Road, and with her good appearance and pleasant manner she found no difficulty in getting taken on. She was put in the ladies' lingerie. For a few days she stayed at the YWCA and then arranged to share a room with one of the girls who worked with her.

Ned Preston saw Fred in the evening of the day he went to gaol. He found him shattered, but only because of Gracie. He took his thieving very lightly.

'I had to do the right thing by her, didn't I? Her people, they didn't think I was good enough for her; I wanted to show them I was just as good as they were. When we went up to the West End I couldn't give her a sandwich and half of bitter in a pub, why, she's never been in a pub in her life, I *had* to take her to a restaurant. If people are such fools as to put money in letters, well, they're just asking for it.'

But he was frightened. He wasn't sure that Gracie would see it like that.

'I've got to know what she's going to do. If she chucks me now— well, it's the end of everything for me, see? I'll find some way of doing meself in, I swear to God I will.'

He told Ned the whole story of his love for Gracie.

'I could have had her over and over again if I'd wanted to. And I did want to and so did she. I knew that. But I respected her, see? She's not like other girls. She's one in a thousand, I tell you.'

He talked and talked. He stormed, he wept. From that confused torrent of words emerged one thing very clearly. A passionate, a frenzied love. Ned promised that he would see the girl.

'Tell her I love her, tell her that what I did I just did because I wanted her to have the best of everything, and tell her I just can't live without her.'

As soon as he could find time Ned Preston went to the Carters' house, but when he asked for Gracie the maid who opened the door told him that she didn't live there any more. Then he asked to see her mother.

'I'll go and see if she's in.'

He gave the maid his card, thinking the name of his club engraved in the corner would impress Mrs Carter enough to make her willing to see him. The maid left him at the door, but in a minute or two asked him to come in. He was shown into the stiff and little-used sitting-room. Mrs Carter kept him waiting for some time and when she came in, holding his card in the tips of her fingers, he guessed it was because she had thought fit to change her dress. The black silk she wore was evidently a dress for occasions. He told her his connection with Wormwood Scrubs and said that he had to do with a man named Frederick Manson. The moment he mentioned the name Mrs Carter assumed a hostile attitude.

'Don't speak to me of that man,' she cried. 'A thief, that's what he is. The trouble he's caused us. They ought to have given him five years, they ought.'

'I'm sorry he's caused you trouble,' said Ned mildly. 'Perhaps if you'd give me a few facts I might help to straighten things out.'

Ned Preston certainly had a way with him. Perhaps Mrs Carter was impressed because he was a gentleman. 'Class he is,' she probably said to herself. Anyhow it was not long before she was telling him the whole story. She grew upset as she told it and began to cry.

'And now she's gone and left us. Run away. I don't know how she could bring herself to do a thing like that. God knows, we love her. She's all we've got and we done everything in the world for her. Her pa never meant it when he told her to get out of the house. Only she was so obstinate. He got in a temper, he always was a quick-tempered man, he was just as upset as I was when we found she'd gone. And d'you know what's she's been and gone and done? Got herself a job at Payne & Perkins. Mr Carter can't abide them. Cutting prices all the time they are. Unfair competition, he calls it. And to think of our Gracie working with a lot of shop-girls—oh, it's so humiliating.'

Ned made a mental note of the store's name. He hadn't been at all sure of getting Gracie's address out of Mrs Carter.

'Have you seen her since she left you?' he asked.

'Of course I have. I knew they'd jump at her at Payne & Perkins, a superior girl like that, and I went there, and there she was, sure enough—in the ladies' lingerie. I waited outside till closing time and then I spoke to her. I asked her to come home. I said her pa was willing to let bygones be bygones. And d'you know what she said? She said she'd come home if we never said a word against Fred and if we was prepared to have her marry him as soon as ever he got out. Of course I had to tell her pa. I never saw him in such a state, I thought he was going to have a fit, he said he'd rather see her dead at his feet than married to that gaolbird.'

Mrs Carter again burst into tears and as soon as he could Ned Preston left her. He went to the department store, up to the ladies' lingerie, and asked for Grace Carter. She was pointed out to him and he went up to her.

'Can I speak to you for a minute? I've come from Fred Manson.'

She went deathly white. For a moment it seemed that she could not utter a word.

'Follow me, please.'

She took him into a passage smelling of disinfectants which seemed to lead to the lavatories. They were alone. She stared at him anxiously.

'He sends you his love. He's worried about you. He's afraid you're awfully unhappy. What he wants to know really is if you're going to chuck him.'

'Me?' Her eyes filled with tears, but on her face was a look of ecstasy. 'Tell him that nothing matters to me as long as he loves me. Tell him I'd wait twenty years for him if I had to. Tell him I'm counting the days till he gets out so as we can get married.'

For fear of the manageress she couldn't stay away from her work for more than a minute or two. She gave Ned all the loving messages she could get into the time to give Fred Manson. Ned didn't get to the Scrubs till nearly six. The prisoners are allowed to put down their tools at five-thirty and Fred had just put his down. When Ned entered the cell he turned pale and sank on to the bed as though his anxiety was such that he didn't trust his legs. But when Ned told him his news he gave a gasp of relief. For a while he couldn't trust himself to speak.

'I knew you'd seen her the moment you came in. I smelt her.'

He sniffed as though the smell of her body were strong in his nostrils, and his face was as if it were a mask of desire. His features on a sudden seemed strangely blurred.

'You know, it made me feel quite uncomfortable so that I had to look the other way,' said Ned Preston when he told us this, with a cackle of his shrill laughter. 'It was sex in its nakedness all right.'

Fred was an exemplary prisoner. He worked well, he gave no trouble. Ned suggested books for him to read and he took them out of the library, but that was about as far as he got.

'I can't get on well with them somehow,' he said. 'I start reading and then I begin thinking of Gracie. You know, when she kisses you ordinary-like—oh, it's so sweet, but when she kisses you really, my God, it's lovely.'

Fred was allowed to see Gracie once a month, but their meetings, with a glass screen between, under the eyes of a warder, were so painful that after several visits they agreed it would be better if she didn't come any more. A year passed. Owing to his good behaviour he could count on a remittance of his sentence and so would be free in another six months. Gracie had saved every penny she could out of her wages and now as the time approached for Fred's release she set about getting a home ready for him. She took two rooms in a house and furnished them on the hire purchase system. One room of course was to be their bedroom and the other the living-room and kitchen. There was an old-fashioned range in it and this she had taken out and replaced by a gas-stove. She wanted everything to be nice and new and clean and comfortable. She took pains to make the two little rooms bright and pretty. To do all this she had to go without all but the barest necessities of existence and she grew thin and pale. Ned suspected that she was starving herself and when he went to see her took a box of chocolates or a cake so that she should have at least something to eat. He brought the prisoner news of what Gracie was doing and she made him promise to give him accurate accounts of every article she bought. He took fond, more than fond, passionate messages from one to the other. He was convinced that Fred would go straight in future and he got him a job as commissionaire from a firm that had a chain of restaurants in London. The wages were good and by calling taxis or fetching cars he would be able to make money on the side. He was to start work as soon as he came out of gaol. Gracie took the necessary steps so that they could get married at once. The eighteen months of Fred's imprisonment were drawing to an end. Gracie was in a fever of excitement.

It happened then that Ned Preston had one of his periodical bouts of illness and was unable to go to the prison for three weeks. It bothered him, for he didn't like to abandon his prisoners, so as soon as he could get out of bed he went to the Scrubs. The chief warder told him that Manson had been asking for him.

'I think you'd better go and see him. I don't know what's the matter with him. He's been acting rather funny since you've been away.'

It was just a fortnight before Fred was due to be released. Ned Preston went to his cell.

'Well, Fred, how are you?' he asked. 'Sorry I haven't been able to come and see you. I've been ill, and I haven't been able to see Gracie either. She must be all of a dither by now.'

'Well, I want you to go and see her.'

His manner was so surly that Ned was taken aback. It was unlike him to be anything but pleasant and civil.

'Of course I will.'

'I want you to tell her that I'm not going to marry her.'

Ned was so astounded that for a minute he could only stare blankly at Fred Manson.

'What on earth d'you mean?'

'Exactly what I say.'

'You can't let her down now. Her people have thrown her out. She's been working all this time to get a home ready for you. She's got the licence and everything.'

'I don't care. I'm not going to marry her.'

'But why, why, why?'

Ned was flabbergasted. Fred Manson was silent for a bit. His face was dark and sullen.

'I'll tell you. I've thought about her night and day for eighteen months and now I'm sick to death of her.'

When Ned Preston reached this point of his story our hostess and our fellow guests broke into loud laughter. He was plainly taken aback. There was some little talk after that and the party broke up. Ned and I, having to go in the same direction, walked along Piccadilly together. For a time we walked in silence.

'I noticed you didn't laugh with the others,' he said abruptly.

'I didn't think it funny.'

'What d'you make of it?'

'Well, I can see his point, you know. Imagination's an odd thing, it dries up; I suppose, thinking of her incessantly all that time he'd exhausted every emotion she could give him, and I think it was quite literally true, he'd just got sick to death of her. He'd squeezed the lemon dry and there was nothing to do but throw away the rind.'

'I didn't think it funny either. That's why I didn't tell them the rest of the story. I wouldn't accept it at first. I thought it was just hysteria or something. I went to see him two or three days running. I argued with him. I really did my damnedest. I thought if he'd only see her it would be all right, but he wouldn't even do that. He said he hated the sight of her. I couldn't move him. At last I had to go and tell her.'

We walked on a little longer in silence.

'I saw her in that beastly, stinking corridor. She saw at once there was something the matter and she went awfully white. She wasn't a girl to show much emotion. There was something gracious and rather noble about her face. Tranquil. Her lips quivered a bit when I told her and she didn't say anything for a minute. When she spoke it was quite calmly, as though—well, as though she'd just missed a bus and would have to wait for another. As though it was a nuisance, you know, but nothing to make a song and dance about. "There's nothing for me to do now but put my head in the gasoven," she said.

'And she did.'

A. E. COPPARD

Fifty Pounds

AFTER tea Philip Repton and Eulalia Burnes discussed their gloomy circumstances. Repton was the precarious sort of London journalist, a dark deliberating man, lean and drooping, full of genteel unprosperity, who wrote articles about *Single Tax, Diet and Reason, The Futility of this, that and the other*, or *The Significance of the other, that and this*; all done with a bleak care and signed P. Stick Repton. Eulalia was brown-haired and hardy, undeliberating and intuitive; she had been milliner, clerk, domestic help, and something in a canteen; and P. Stick Repton had, as one commonly says, picked her up at a time when she was drifting about London without a penny in her purse, without even a purse, and he had not yet put her down.

'I can't understand! It's sickening, monstrous!' Lally was fumbling with a match in front of the gas fire, for when it was evening, in September, it always got chilly on a floor so high up. Their flat was a fourth-floor one and there were—Oh, fifteen thousand stairs! Out of the window and beyond the chimneys you could see the long glare from lights in High Holborn, and hear the hums and hoots of buses. And that was a comfort.

'Lower! Turn it lower!' yelled Philip. The gas had ignited with an astounding thump; the kneeling Lally had thrown up her hands and dropped the matchbox, saying 'Damn' in the same tone as one might say good morning to a milkman.

'You shouldn't do it, you know,' grumbled Repton. 'You'll blow us to the deuce.' And that was just like Lally, that was Lally all over, always: the gas, the knobs of sugar in his tea, the way she . . . and the, the . . . O dear, dear! In their early life together, begun so abruptly and illicitly six months before, her simple hidden beauties had delighted him by their surprises; they had peered and shone brighter, had waned and recurred; she was less the one star in his universe than a faint galaxy.

This room of theirs was a dingy room, very small but very high. A lanky gas tube swooped from the middle of the ceiling towards the middle of the table-cloth as if burning to discover whether that was pink or saffron or fawn—and it *was* hard to tell—but on perceiving that the cloth, whatever its tint, was disturbingly spangled with dozens of cupstains and several large envelopes, the gas tube in the violence of its disappointment contorted itself abruptly, assumed a lateral bend, and put out its tongue of flame at an oleograph of Mona Lisa which hung above the fireplace.

Those envelopes were the torment to Lally; they were the sickening, monstrous manifestations which she could not understand. There were always some of them lying there, or about the room, bulging with manuscripts that no editors—they *couldn't* have perused them—wanted; and so it had come to the desperate point when, as Lally was saying, something had to be done about things. Repton had done all *he* could; he wrote unceasingly, all day, all night, but all his projects insolvently withered, and morning, noon, and evening brought his manuscripts back as unwanted as snow in summer. He was depressed and baffled and weary. And there was simply nothing else he could do, nothing in the world. Apart from his own wonderful gift he was useless, Lally knew, and he was being steadily and stupidly murdered by those editors. It was weeks since they had eaten a proper meal. Whenever they obtained any real nice food now, they sat down to it silently, intently, and destructively. As far as Lally could tell there seemed to be no prospect of any such meals again in life or time, and the worst of it all was Philip's pride—he was actually too proud to ask anyone for assistance! Not that he would be too proud to accept help if it were offered to him: O no, if it came he would rejoice at it! But still, he had that nervous shrinking pride that coiled upon itself, and he would not *ask*; he was like a wounded animal that hid its woe far away from the rest of the world. Lally alone knew his need, but why could not other people see it—those villainous editors! His own wants were so modest and he had a generous mind.

'Phil,' Lally said, seating herself at the table. Repton was lolling in a wicker armchair beside the gas fire. 'I'm not going on waiting and waiting any longer, I must go and get a job. Yes, I must. We get poorer and poorer. We can't go on like this any longer, it's no use, and I can't bear it.'

'No, no, I can't have that, my dear. . . .'

'But I will!' she cried. 'Oh, why are you so proud?'

'Proud! Proud!' He stared into the gas fire, his tired arms hanging limp over the arms of the chair. 'You don't understand. There
are things the flesh has to endure, and things the spirit too must
endure. . . .' Lally loved to hear him talk like that; and it was just
as well, for Repton was much given to such discoursing. Deep in
her mind was the conviction that he had simple access to profound,
almost unimaginable, wisdom. 'It isn't pride, it is just that there is
a certain order in life, in my life, that it would not do for. I could
not bear it, I could never rest: I can't explain that, but just believe
it, Lally.' His head was empty but unbowed; he spoke quickly and
finished almost angrily. 'If only I had money! It's not for myself. I
can stand all this, any amount of it. I've done so before, and I shall
do again and again I've no doubt. But I have to think of you.'

That was fiercely annoying. Lally got up and went and stood over
him.

'Why are you so stupid? I can think for myself and fend for
myself. I'm not married to you. You have your pride, but I can't
starve for it. And I've a pride, too, I'm a burden to you. If you
won't let me work now while we're together, then I must leave you
and work for myself.'

'Leave! Leave me now? When things are so bad?' His white face
gleamed his perturbation up at her. 'O well, go, go.' But then,
mournfully moved, he took her hands and fondled them. 'Don't be
a fool, Lally; it's only a passing depression, this; I've known worse
before, and it never lasts long, something turns up, always does.
There's good and bad in it all, but there's more goodness than anything else. You see.'

'I don't want to wait for ever, even for goodness. I don't believe
in it, I never see it, never feel it, it is no use to me. I could go
and steal, or walk the streets, or do any dirty thing—easily. What's
the good of goodness if it isn't any use?'

'But, but,' Repton stammered, 'what's the use of bad, if it isn't
any better?'

'I mean . . .' began Lally.

'You don't mean anything, my dear girl.'

'I mean, when you haven't any choice it's no use talking moral,
or having pride, it's stupid. Oh, my darling,' she slid down to him

and lay against his breast, 'it's not you, you are everything to me; that's why it angers me so, this treatment of you, all hard blows and no comfort. It will never be any different, I feel it will never be different now, and it terrifies me.'

'Pooh!' Repton kissed her and comforted her: she was his beloved. 'When things are wrong with us our fancies take their tone from our misfortunes, badness, evil. I sometimes have a queer stray feeling that one day I shall be hanged. Yes, I don't know what for, what *could* I be hanged for? And, do you know, at other times I've had a kind of intuition that one day I shall be—what do you think?— Prime Minister of the country! Yes, well you can't reason against such things. I know what I should do, I've my plans, I've even made a list of the men for my cabinet. Yes, well, there you are!'

But Lally had made up her mind to leave him; she would leave him for a while and earn her own living. When things took a turn for the better she would join him again. She told him this. She had friends who were going to get her some work.

'But what are you going to do, Lally, I . . .'

'I'm going away to Glasgow,' said she.

'Glasgow?' He had heard things about Glasgow! Good heavens!

'I've some friends there,' the girl went on steadily. She had got up and was sitting on the arm of his chair. 'I wrote to them last week. They can get me a job almost anywhen, and I can stay with them. They want me to go—they've sent the money for my fare. I think I shall have to go.'

'You don't love me then!' said the man.

Lally kissed him.

'But *do* you? Tell me!'

'Yes, my dear,' said Lally, 'of course.'

An uneasiness possessed him; he released her moodily. Where was their wild passion flown to? She was staring at him intently, then she tenderly said: 'My love, don't you be melancholy, don't take it to heart so. I'd cross the world to find you a pin.'

'No, no, you mustn't do that,' he exclaimed idiotically. At her indulgent smile he grimly laughed too, and then sank back in his chair. The girl stood up and went about the room doing vague things, until he spoke again.

'So you are tired of me?'

Lally went to him steadily and knelt down by his chair. 'If I was tired of you, Phil, I'd kill myself.'

Moodily he ignored her. 'I suppose it had to end like this. But I've loved you desperately.' Lally was now weeping on his shoulder, and he began to twirl a lock of her rich brown hair absently with his fingers as if it were a seal on a watch chain. 'I'd been thinking we might as well get married, as soon as things had turned round.'

'I'll come back, Phil,' she clasped him so tenderly, 'as soon as you want me.'

'But you are not really going?'

'Yes,' said Lally.

'You're not to go!'

'I wouldn't go if . . . if anything . . . if you had any luck. But as we are now I must go away, to give you a chance. You see that, darling Phil?'

'You're not to go; I object. I just love you, Lally, that's all, and of course I want to keep you here.'

'Then what are we to do?'

'I . . . don't . . . know. Things drop out of the sky. But we must be together. You're not to go.'

Lally sighed: he was stupid. And Repton began to turn over in his mind the dismal knowledge that she had taken this step in secret, she had not told him while she was trying to get to Glasgow. Now here she was with the fare, and as good as gone! Yes, it was all over.

'When do you propose to go?'

'Not for a few days, nearly a fortnight.'

'Good God,' he moaned. Yes, it was all over then. He had never dreamed that this would be the end, that she would be the first to break away. He had always envisaged a tender scene in which he could tell her, with dignity and gentle humour, that . . . Well, he never had quite hit upon the words he would use, but that was the kind of setting. And now, here she was with her fare to Glasgow, her heart turned towards Glasgow, and she as good as gone to Glasgow! No dignity, no gentle humour—in fact he was enraged, sullen but enraged; he boiled furtively. But he said with mournful calm:

'I've so many misfortunes, I suppose I can bear this, too.' Gloomy and tragic he was.

'Dear, darling Phil, it's for your own sake I'm going.'

Repton sniffed derisively. 'We are always mistaken in the reasons for our commonest actions; Nature derides us all. You are sick of me; I can't blame you.'

Eulalia was so moved that she could only weep again. Nevertheless she wrote to her friends in Glasgow promising to be with them by a stated date.

Towards the evening of the following day, at a time when she was alone, a letter arrived addressed to herself. It was from a firm of solicitors in Cornhill inviting her to call upon them. A flame leaped up in Lally's heart: it might mean the offer of some work which would keep her in London after all! If only it were so she would accept it on the spot, and Philip would have to be made to see the reasonability of it. But at the office in Cornhill a more astonishing outcome awaited her. There she showed her letter to a little office boy with scarcely any fingernails and very little nose, and he took it to an elderly man who had a superabundance of both. Smiling affably the long-nosed man led her upstairs into the sombre den of a gentleman who had some white hair and a lumpy yellow complexion. Having put to her a number of questions relating to her family history, and appearing to be satisfied and not at all surprised by her answers, this gentleman revealed to Lally the overpowering tidings that she was entitled to a legacy of eighty pounds by the will of a forgotten and recently deceased aunt. Subject to certain formalities, proofs of identity and so forth, he promised Lally the possession of the money within about a week.

Lally's descent to the street, her emergence into the clamouring atmosphere, her walk along to Holborn, were accomplished in a state of blessedness and trance, a trance in which life became a thousand times aerially enlarged, movement was a delight, and thought a rapture. She would give all the money to Philip, and if he very much wanted it she would even marry him now. Perhaps, though, she would save ten pounds of it for herself. The other seventy would keep them for . . . it was impossible to say how long it would keep them. They could have a little holiday somewhere in the country together, he was so worn and weary. Perhaps she had better not tell Philip anything at all about it until her lovely money was really in her hand. Nothing in life, at least nothing about money, was ever certain; something horrible might happen at the crucial moment and the money be snatched from her very fingers. Oh, she would go mad then! So for some days she kept her wonderful secret.

Their imminent separation had given Repton a tender sadness

that was very moving. 'Eulalia', he would say; for he had suddenly adopted the formal version of her name: 'Eulalia, we've had a great time together, a wonderful time, there will never be anything like it again.' She often shed tears, but she kept the grand secret still locked in her heart. Indeed, it occurred to her very forcibly that even now his stupid pride might cause him to reject her money altogether. Silly, silly Philip! Of course it would have been different if they had married; he would naturally have taken it then, and really, it would have *been* his. She would have to think out some dodge to overcome his scruples. Scruples were *such* a nuisance, but then it was very noble of him: there were not many men who wouldn't take money from a girl they were living with.

Well, a week later she was summoned again to the office in Cornhill and received from the white-haired gentleman a cheque for eighty pounds drawn on the Bank of England to the order of Eulalia Burnes. Miss Burnes desired to cash the cheque straightway, so the large-nosed elderly clerk was deputed to accompany her to the Bank of England close by and assist in procuring the money.

'A very nice errand!' exclaimed that gentleman as they crossed to Threadneedle Street past the Royal Exchange. Miss Burnes smiled her acknowledgment, and he began to tell her of other windfalls that had been disbursed in his time—but vast sums, very great persons—until she began to infer that Blackbean, Carp, and Ransome were universal dispensers of heavenly largesse.

'Yes, but,' said the clerk, hawking a good deal from an affliction of catarrh, 'I never got any myself, and never will. If I did, do you know what I would do with it?' But at that moment they entered the portals of the bank, and in the excitement of the business, Miss Burnes forgot to ask the clerk how he would use a legacy, and thus she possibly lost a most valuable slice of knowledge. With one fifty-pound note and six five-pound notes clasped in her handbag she bade good-bye to the long-nosed clerk, who shook her fervently by the hand and assured her that Blackbean, Carp, and Ransome would be delighted at all times to undertake any commissions on her behalf. Then she fled along the pavement, blithe as a bird, until she was breathless with her flight. Presently she came opposite the window of a typewriting agency. Tripping airily into its office she laid a scrap of paper before a lovely Hebe who was typing there.

'I want this typed, if you please,' said Lally.

The beautiful typist read the words on the scrap of paper and stared at the heiress.

'I don't want any address to appear,' said Lally; 'just a plain sheet, please.'

A few moments later she received a neatly typed page folded in an envelope, and after paying the charge she hurried off to a District Messenger office. Here she addressed the envelope in a disguised hand to *P. Stick Repton, Esq.*, at their address in Holborn. She read the typed letter through again:

DEAR SIR,

In common with many others I entertain the greatest admiration for your literary abilities, and I therefore beg you to accept this tangible expression of that admiration from a constant reader of your articles who, for purely private reasons, desires to remain anonymous.

> Your very sincere
> WELLWISHER.

Placing the fifty-pound note upon the letter Lally carefully folded them together and put them both into the envelope. The attendant then gave it to a uniformed lad, who sauntered off whistling very casually, somewhat to Lally's alarm—he looked so small and careless to be entrusted with fifty pounds. Then Lally went out, changed one of her five-pound notes and had a lunch—half-a-crown, but it was worth it. Oh, how enchanting and exciting London was! In two days more she would have been gone: now she would have to write off at once to her Glasgow friends and tell them she had changed her mind, that she was now settled in London. Oh, how enchanting and delightful! And tonight he would take her out to dine in some fine restaurant, and they would do a theatre. She did not really want to marry Phil, they had got on so well without it, but if he wanted that too she did not mind—much. They would go away into the country for a whole week. What money would do! Marvellous! And looking round the restaurant she felt sure that no other woman there, no matter how well-dressed, had as much as thirty pounds in her handbag.

Returning home in the afternoon she became conscious of her own betraying radiance; very demure and subdued and usual she would have to be, or he might guess the cause of it. Though she danced up the long flights of stairs she entered their room quietly, but the sight of Repton staring out of the window, forlorn as a drowsy horse, overcame her and she rushed to embrace him cry-ing 'Darling!'

'Hullo, hullo!' he smiled.

'I'm so fond of you, Phil dear.'

'But . . . but you're deserting me!'

'O no,' she cried archly; 'I'm not—not deserting you.'

'All right.' Repton shrugged his shoulders, but he seemed hap-pier. He did not mention the fifty pounds then: perhaps it had not come yet—or perhaps he was thinking to surprise her.

'Let's go for a walk, it's a screaming lovely day,' said Lally.

'Oh, I dunno.' He yawned and stretched. 'Nearly tea-time, isn't it?'

'Well, we . . .' Lally was about to suggest having tea out some-where, but she bethought herself in time. 'I suppose it is. Yes, it is.'

So they stayed in for tea. No sooner was tea over than Repton remarked that he had an engagement somewhere. Off he went, leav-ing Lally disturbed and anxious. Why had he not mentioned the fifty pounds? Surely it had not gone to the wrong address? This suspicion once formed, Lally soon became certain, tragically sure, that she had misaddressed the envelope herself. A conviction that she had put No. 17 instead of No. 71 was almost overpowering, and she fancied that she hadn't even put London on the envelope—but Glasgow. That was impossible, though, but—Oh, the horror!—somebody else was enjoying their fifty pounds. The girl's fears were not allayed by the running visit she paid to the messenger office that evening, for the rash imp who had been entrusted with her letter had gone home and therefore could not be interrogated until the morrow. By now she was sure that he had blundered; he had been so casual with an important letter like that! Lally never did, and never would again, trust any little boys who wore their hats so much on one side, were so glossy with hair-oil, and went about whistling just to madden you. She burned to ask where the boy lived, but in spite of her desperate desire she could not do so. She dared not, it would expose her to . . . to something or other she could only feel, not name; you had to keep cool, to let nothing, not even curiosity, master you.

Hurrying home again, though hurrying was not her custom, and there was no occasion for it, she wrote the letter to her Glasgow friends. Then it crossed her mind that it would be wiser not to post the letter that night; better wait until the morning, after she had discovered what the horrible little messenger had done with her letter. Bed was a poor refuge from her thoughts, but she accepted it, and when Phil came home she was not sleeping. While he undressed he told her of the lecture he had been to, something about Agrarian Depopulation it was, but even after he had stretched himself beside her, he did not speak about the fifty pounds. Nothing, not even curiosity, should master her, and so she calmed herself, and in time fitfully slept.

At breakfast next morning he asked her what she was going to do that day.

'Oh,' replied Lally offhandedly, 'I've a lot of things to see to, you know; I must go out. I'm sorry the porridge is so awful this morning, Phil, but . . .'

'Awful?' he broke in. 'But it's nicer than usual! Where are you going? I thought—our last day, you know—we might go out somewhere together.'

'Dear Phil!' Lovingly she stretched out a hand to be caressed across the table. 'But I've several things to do. I'll come back early, eh?' She got up and hurried round to embrace him.

'All right,' he said. 'Don't be long.'

Off went Lally to the messenger office, at first as happy as a bird, but on approaching the building the old tremors assailed her. Inside the room was the cocky little boy who bade her 'Good morning' with laconic assurance. Lally at once questioned him, and when he triumphantly produced a delivery book she grew limp with her suppressed fear, one fear above all others. For a moment she did not want to look at it: Truth hung by a hair, and as long as it so hung she might swear it was a lie. But there it was, written right across the page, an entry of a letter delivered, signed for in the well-known hand, *P. Stick Repton*. There was no more doubt, only a sharp indignant agony as if she had been stabbed with a dagger of ice.

'O yes, thank you,' said Lally calmly. 'Did you hand it to him yourself?'

'Yes'm,' replied the boy, and he described Philip.

'Did he open the letter?'

'Yes'm.'

'There was no answer?'

'No'm.'

'All right.' Fumbling in her bag, she added: 'I think I've got a sixpence for you.'

Out in the street again she tremblingly chuckled to herself. 'So that is what he is like, after all. Cruel and mean!' He was going to let her go and keep the money in secret to himself! How despicable! Cruel and mean, cruel and mean. She hummed it to herself: 'Cruel and mean, cruel and mean!' It eased her tortured bosom. 'Cruel and mean!' And he was waiting at home for her, waiting with a smile for their last day together. It would *have* to be their last day. She tore up the letter to her Glasgow friends, for now she *must* go to them. So cruel and mean! Let him wait! A bus stopped beside her and she stepped on to it, climbing to the top and sitting there while the air chilled her burning features. The bus made a long journey to Plaistow. She knew nothing of Plaistow, she wanted to know nothing of Plaistow, but she did not care where the bus took her; she only wanted to keep moving, and moving away, as far away as possible from Holborn and from him, and not once let those hovering tears down fall.

From Plaistow she turned and walked back as far as the Mile End Road. Thereabouts, wherever she went she met clergymen, dozens of them. There must be a conference, about charity or something, Lally thought. With a vague desire to confide her trouble to some one, she observed them; it would relieve the strain. But there was none she could tell her sorrow to, and failing that, when she came to a neat restaurant she entered it and consumed a fish. Just beyond her three sleek parsons were lunching, sleek and pink; bald, affable, consoling men, all very much alike.

'I saw Carter yesterday,' she heard one say. Lally liked listening to the conversation of strangers, and she had often wondered what clergymen talked about among themselves.

'What, Carter! Indeed. Nice fellow Carter. How was he?'

'Carter loves preaching, you know!' cried the third.

'O yes, he loves preaching!'

'Ha ha ha, yes.'

'Ha ha ha, oom.'

'Awf'ly good preacher, though.'

'Yes, awf'ly good.'

'And he's awf'ly good at comic songs, too.'

'Yes?'

'Yes!'

Three glasses of water, a crumbling of bread, a silence suggestive of prayer.

'How long has he been married?'

'Twelve years,' returned the cleric who had met Carter.

'Oh, twelve years!'

'I've only been married twelve years myself,' said the oldest of them.

'Indeed!'

'Yes, I tarried very long.'

'Ha ha ha, yes.'

'Ha ha ha, oom.'

'Er . . . have you any family?'

'No.'

Very delicate and dainty in handling their food they were; very delicate and dainty.

'My rectory is a magnificent old house,' continued the recently married one. 'Built originally in 1700. Burnt down. Rebuilt 1784.'

'Indeed!'

'Humph!'

'Seventeen bedrooms and two delightful tennis courts.'

'Oh, well done!' the others cried, and then they all fell with genteel gusto upon a pale blancmange.

From the restaurant the girl sauntered about for a while, and then there was a cinema wherein, seated warm and comfortable in the twitching darkness, she partially stilled her misery. Some nervous fancy kept her roaming in that district for most of the evening. She knew that if she left it she would go home, and she did not want to go home. The naphtha lamps of the booths at Mile End were bright and distracting, and the hum of the evening business was good despite the smell. A man was weaving sweetstuffs from a pliant roll of warm toffee that he wrestled with as the athlete wrestles with the python. There were stalls with things of iron, with fruit or fish, pots and pans, leather, string, nails. Watches for use—or for ornament—what d'ye lack? A sailor told naughty stories while selling bunches of green grapes out of barrels of cork dust which he swore he had stolen from the Queen of Honolulu. People clamoured for them both. You could buy back numbers of the comic papers at four a penny, rolls of linoleum for very little more—and use either for the other's purpose.

'At thrippence per foot, mesdames,' cried the sweating cheapjack, lashing himself into ecstatic furies, 'that's a piece of fabric weft and woven with triple-strength Andalusian jute, double-hot-pressed with rubber from the island of Pagama, and stencilled by an artist as poisoned his grandfather's cook. That's a piece of fabric, mesdames, as the king of heaven himself wouldn't mind to put down in his parlour—if he had the chance. Do I ask thrippence a foot for that piece of fabric? Mesdames, I was never a daring chap.'

Lally watched it all, she looked and listened; then looked and did not see, listened and did not hear. Her misery was not the mere disappointment of love, not that kind of misery alone; it was the crushing of an ideal in which love had had its home, a treachery cruel and mean. The sky of night, so smooth, so bestarred, looked wrinkled through her screen of unshed tears; her sorrow was a wild cloud that troubled the moon with darkness.

In miserable desultory wandering she had spent her day, their last day, and now, returning to Holborn in the late evening, she suddenly began to hurry, for a new possibility had come to lighten her dejection. Perhaps, after all, so whimsical he was, he was keeping his 'revelation' until the last day, or even the last hour, when (nothing being known to her, as he imagined) all hopes being gone and they had come to the last kiss, he would take her in his arms and laughingly kill all grief, waving the succour of a flimsy banknote like a flag of triumph. Perhaps even, in fact surely, that was why he wanted to take her out today! Oh, what a blind wicked stupid girl she was, and in a perfect frenzy of bubbling faith she panted homewards for his revealing sign.

From the pavement below she could see that their room was lit. Weakly she climbed the stairs and opened the door. Phil was standing up, staring so strangely at her. Helplessly and half-guilty she began to smile. Without a word said he came quickly to her and crushed her in his arms, her burning silent man, loving and exciting her. Lying against his breast in that constraining embrace, their passionate disaster was gone, her doubts were flown; all perception of the feud was torn from her and deeply drowned in a gulf of bliss. She was aware only of the consoling delight of their reunion, of his amorous kisses, of his tongue tingling the soft down on her upper lip that she disliked and he admired. All the soft wanton endearments that she so loved to hear him speak were singing in her ears, and then he suddenly swung and lifted her up, snapped out the gaslight, and carried her off to bed.

Life that is born of love feeds on love; if the wherewithal be hidden, how shall we stay our hunger? The galaxy may grow dim, or the stars drop in a wandering void; you can neither keep them in your hands nor crumble them in your mind.

What was it Phil had once called her? Numskull! After all it was his own fifty pounds, she had given it to him freely, it was his to do as he liked with. A gift was a gift, it was poor spirit to send money with the covetous expectation that it would return to you. She would surely go tomorrow.

The next morning he awoke her early, and kissed her.

'What time does your train go?' said he.

'Train!' Lally scrambled from his arms and out of bed.

A fine day, a glowing day. O bright, sharp air! Quickly she dressed, and went into the other room to prepare their breakfast. Soon he followed, and they ate silently together, although whenever they were near each other he caressed her tenderly. Afterwards she went into the bedroom and packed her bag; there was nothing more to be done, he was beyond hope. No woman wants to be sacrificed, least of all those who sacrifice themselves with courage and a quiet mind. When she was ready to go she took her portmanteau into the sitting-room; he, too, made to put on his hat and coat.

'No,' murmured Lally, 'you're not to come with me.'

'Pooh, my dear!' he protested; 'nonsense.'

'I won't have you come,' cried Lally with an asperity that impressed him.

'But you can't carry that bag to the station by yourself!'

'I shall take a taxi.' She buttoned her gloves.

'My dear!' His humourous deprecation annoyed her.

'O bosh!' Putting her gloved hands around his neck she kissed him coolly. 'Good-bye. Write to me often. Let me know how you thrive, won't you, Phil? And'—a little waveringly—'love me always.' She stared queerly at the two dimples in his cheeks; each dimple was a nest of hair that could never be shaved.

'Lally darling, beloved girl! I never loved you more than now, this moment. You are more precious than ever to me.'

At that, she knew her moment of sardonic revelation had come—
but she dared not use it, she let it go. She could not so deeply
humiliate him by revealing her knowledge of his perfidy. A com-
passionate divinity smiles at our puny sins. She knew his perfidy,
but to triumph in it would defeat her own pride. Let him keep his
gracious, mournful airs to the last, false though they were. It was
better to part so, better from such a figure than from an abject
scarecrow, even though both were the same inside. And something
capriciously reminded her, for a flying moment, of elephants she
had seen swaying with the grand movement of tidal water—and
groping for monkey-nuts.

Lally tripped down the stairs alone. At the end of the street she
turned for a last glance. There he was, high up in the window,
waving good-byes. And she waved back to him.

VIRGINIA WOOLF

The Legacy

'FOR Sissy Miller.' Gilbert Clandon, taking up the pearl brooch that lay among a litter of rings and brooches on a little table in his wife's drawing-room, read the inscription: 'For Sissy Miller, with my love.'

It was like Angela to have remembered even Sissy Miller, her secretary. Yet how strange it was, Gilbert Clandon thought once more, that she had left everything in such order—a little gift of some sort for every one of her friends. It was as if she had foreseen her death. Yet she had been in perfect health when she left the house that morning, six weeks ago; when she stepped off the kerb in Piccadilly and the car had killed her.

He was waiting for Sissy Miller. He had asked her to come; he owed her, he felt, after all the years she had been with them, this token of consideration. Yes, he went on, as he sat there waiting, it was strange that Angela had left everything in such order. Every friend had been left some little token of her affection. Every ring, every necklace, every little Chinese box—she had a passion for little boxes—had a name on it. And each had some memory for him. This he had given her; this—the enamel dolphin with the ruby eyes—she had pounced upon one day in a back street in Venice. He could remember her little cry of delight. To him, of course, she had left nothing in particular, unless it were her diary. Fifteen little volumes, bound in green leather, stood behind him on her writing table. Ever since they were married, she had kept a diary. Some of their very few—he could not call them quarrels, say tiffs—had been about that diary. When he came in and found her writing, she always shut it or put her hand over it. 'No, no, no,' he could hear her say, 'After I'm dead—perhaps.' So she had left it him, as her legacy. It was the only thing they had not shared when she was alive. But he had always taken it for granted that she would out-live him. If only she had stopped one moment, and had thought what she was doing, she would be alive now. But she had stepped straight off the kerb, the driver of the car had said at the inquest. She had given him no chance to pull up. . . . Here the sound of voices in the hall interrupted him.

'Miss Miller, Sir,' said the maid.

She came in. He had never seen her alone in his life, nor, of course, in tears. She was terribly distressed, and no wonder. Angela had been much more to her than an employer. She had been a friend. To himself, he thought, as he pushed a chair for her and asked her to sit down, she was scarcely distinguishable from any other woman of her kind. There were thousands of Sissy Millers— drab little women in black carrying attaché cases. But Angela, with her genius for sympathy, had discovered all sorts of qualities in Sissy Miller. She was the soul of discretion, so silent; so trustworthy, one could tell her anything, and so on.

Miss Miller could not speak at first. She sat there dabbing her eyes with her pocket handkerchief. Then she made an effort.

'Pardon me, Mr Clandon,' she said.

He murmured. Of course he understood. It was only natural. He could guess what his wife had meant to her.

'I've been so happy here,' she said, looking round. Her eyes rested on the writing table behind him. It was here they had worked— she and Angela. For Angela had her share of the duties that fall to the lot of the wife of a prominent politician. She had been the greatest help to him in his career. He had often seen her and Sissy sitting at that table—Sissy at the typewriter, taking down letters from her dictation. No doubt Miss Miller was thinking of that, too. Now all he had to do was to give her the brooch his wife had left her. A rather incongruous gift it seemed. It might have been bet- ter to have left her a sum of money, or even the typewriter. But there it was—'For Sissy Miller, with my love.' And, taking the brooch, he gave it her with the little speech that he had prepared. He knew, he said, that she would value it. His wife had often worn it. . . . And she replied, as she took it, almost as if she too had pre- pared a speech, that it would always be a treasured possession. . . . She had, he supposed, other clothes upon which a pearl brooch would not look quite so incongruous. She was wearing the little black coat and skirt that seemed the uniform of her profession. Then he remem- bered—she was in mourning, of course. She too had had her tragedy—a brother, to whom she was devoted, had died only a week or two before Angela. In some accident was it? He could remember only Angela telling him; Angela, with her genius for sympathy, had been terribly upset. Meanwhile Sissy Miller had risen. She was putting on her gloves. Evidently she felt that she ought not to intrude. But he could not let her go without saying something about her future. What were her plans? Was there any way in which he could help her?

She was gazing at the table, where she had sat at her typewriter, where the diary lay. And, lost in her memories of Angela, she did not at once answer his suggestion that he should help her. She seemed for a moment not to understand. So he repeated:

'What are your plans, Miss Miller?'

'My plans? Oh, that's all right, Mr Clandon,' she exclaimed. 'Please don't bother yourself about me.'

He took her to mean that she was in no need of financial assistance. It would be better, he realized, to make any suggestion of that kind in a letter. All he could do now was to say as he pressed her hand. 'Remember, Miss Miller, if there's any way in which I can help you, it will be a pleasure. . . .' Then he opened the door. For a moment, on the threshold, as if a sudden thought had struck her, she stopped.

'Mr Clandon,' she said, looking straight at him for the first time, and for the first time he was struck by the expression, sympathetic yet searching, in her eyes. 'If at any time,' [she] was saying, 'there's anything I can do to help you, remember, I shall feel it, for your wife's sake, a pleasure. . . .'

With that she was gone. Her words and the look that went with them were unexpected. It was almost as if she believed, or hoped, that he would have need of her. A curious, perhaps a fantastic idea occurred to him as he returned to his chair. Could it be, that during all those years when he had scarcely noticed her, she, as the novelists say, had entertained a passion for him? He caught his own reflection in the glass as he passed. He was over fifty; but he could not help admitting that he was still, as the looking-glass showed him, a very distinguished-looking man.

'Poor Sissy Miller!' he said, half laughing. How he would have liked to share that joke with his wife! He turned instinctively to her diary. 'Gilbert,' he read, opening it at random, 'looked so wonderful . . . .' It was as if she had answered his question. Of course, she seemed to say, you're very attractive to women. Of course Sissy Miller felt that too. He read on. 'How proud I am to be his wife!' And he had always been very proud to be her husband. How often when they dined out somewhere he had looked at her across the table and said to himself, She is the loveliest woman here! He read on. That first year he had been standing for Parliament. They had toured his constituency. 'When Gilbert sat down the applause was terrific. The whole audience rose and sang: "For he's a jolly good fellow." I was quite overcome.' He remembered that, too. She had been sitting on the platform beside him. He could still see the glance she cast at him, and how she had tears in her eyes. And then? He turned the pages. They had gone to Venice. He recalled that happy holiday after the election. 'We had ices at Florians.' He smiled— she was still such a child, she loved ices. 'Gilbert gave me a most interesting account of the history of Venice. He told me that the Doges . . .' she had written it all out in her schoolgirl hand. One of the delights of travelling with Angela had been that she was so eager to learn. She was so terribly ignorant, she used to say, as if that were not one of her charms. And then—he opened the next volume—they had come back to London. 'I was so anxious to make a good impression. I wore my wedding dress.' He could see her now sitting next old Sir Edward; and making a conquest of that formidable old man, his chief. He read on rapidly, filling in scene after scene from her scrappy fragments. 'Dined at the House of Commons. . . . To an evening party at the Lovegroves. Did I realize my responsibility, Lady L. asked me, as Gilbert's wife?' Then as the years passed—he took another volume from the writing table— he had become more and more absorbed in his work. And she, of course, was more often alone. It had been a great grief to her, apparently, that they had had no children. 'How I wish,' one entry read, 'that Gilbert had a son!' Oddly enough he had never much regretted that himself. Life had been so full, so rich as it was. That year he had been given a minor post in the government. A minor post only, but her comment was: 'I am quite certain now that he will be Prime Minister!' Well, if things had gone differently, it might have been so. He paused here to speculate upon what might have been. Politics was a gamble, he reflected; but the game wasn't over yet. Not at fifty. He cast his eyes rapidly over more pages, full of the little trifles, the insignificant, happy, daily trifles that had made up her life.

He took up another volume and opened it at random. 'What a coward I am! I let the chance slip again. But it seemed selfish to bother him about my own affairs, when he has so much to think about. And we so seldom have an evening alone.' What was the meaning of that? Oh here was the explanation—it referred to her work in the East End. 'I plucked up courage and talked to Gilbert at last. He was so kind, so good. He made no objection.' He remembered that conversation. She had told him that she felt so idle, so useless. She wished to have some work of her own. She wanted to do something—she had blushed so prettily, he remembered, as she said it sitting in that very chair—to help others. He had bantered her a little. Hadn't she enough to do looking after him, after her home? Still if it amused her of course he had no objection. What was it? Some district? Some committee? Only she must promise not to make herself ill. So it seemed that every Wednesday she went to Whitechapel. He remembered how he hated the clothes she wore on those occasions. But she had taken it very seriously it seemed. The diary was full of references like this: 'Saw Mrs Jones. . . . She has ten children. . . . Husband lost his arm in an accident. . . . Did my best to find a job for Lily.' He skipped on. His own name occurred less frequently. His interest slackened. Some of the entries conveyed nothing to him. For example: 'Had a heated argument about socialism with B.M.' Who was B.M.? He could not fill in the initials; some woman, he supposed, that she had met on one of her committees. 'B.M. made a violent attack upon the upper classes. . . . I walked back after the meeting with B.M. and tried to convince him. But he is so narrow-minded.' So B.M. was a man— no doubt one of those 'intellectuals' as they call themselves, who are so violent, as Angela said, and so narrow-minded. She had invited him to come and see her apparently. 'B.M. came to dinner. He shook hands with Minnie!' That note of exclamation gave another twist to his mental picture. B.M. it seemed wasn't used to parlour-maids; he had shaken hands with Minnie. Presumably he was one of those tame working men who air their views in ladies' drawing-rooms. Gilbert knew the type, and had no liking for this particular specimen, whoever B.M. might be. Here he was again. 'Went with B.M. to the Tower of London. . . . He said revolution is bound to come. . . . He said we live in a Fool's Paradise.' That was just the kind of thing B.M. would say—Gilbert could hear him. He could also see him quite distinctly—a stubby little man, with a rough beard, red tie, dressed as they always did in tweeds, who had never done an honest day's work in his life. Surely Angela had the sense to see through him? He read on. 'B.M. said some very disagreeable things about . . .' The name was carefully scratched out. 'I told him I would not listen to any more abuse of . . .' Again the name was obliterated. Could it have been his own name? Was that why Angela covered the page so quickly when he came in? The thought added to his growing dislike of B.M. He had had the impertinence to discuss him in this very room. Why had Angela never told him? It was very unlike her to conceal anything; she had been the soul of candour. He turned the pages, picking out every reference to B.M. 'B.M. told me the story of his childhood. His mother went out charring. . . . When I think of it, I can hardly bear to go on living in such luxury. . . . Three guineas for one hat!' If only she had discussed the matter with him, instead of puzzling her poor little head about questions that were much too difficult for her to understand! He had lent her books. Karl Marx. 'The Coming Revolution.' The initials B.M., B.M., B.M., recurred repeatedly. But why never the full name? There was an informality, an intimacy in the use of initials that was very unlike Angela. Had she called him B.M. to his face? He read on. 'B.M. came unexpectedly after dinner. Luckily, I was alone.' That was only a year ago. 'Luckily'—why luckily?—'I was alone.' Where had he been that night? He checked the date in his engagement book. It had been the night of the Mansion House dinner. And B.M. and Angela had spent the evening alone! He tried to recall that evening. Was she waiting up for him when he came back? Had the room looked just as usual? Were there glasses on the table? Were the chairs drawn close together? He could remember nothing—nothing whatever, nothing except his own speech at the Mansion House dinner. It became more and more inexplicable to him—the whole situation: his wife receiving an unknown man alone. Perhaps the next volume would explain. Hastily he reached for the last of the diaries—the one she had left unfinished when she died. There on the very first page was that cursed fellow again. 'Dined alone with B.M. . . . He became very agitated. He said it was time we understood each other. . . . I tried to make him listen. But he would not. He threatened that if I did not . . .' the rest of the page was scored over. She had written 'Egypt. Egypt. Egypt.' over the whole page. He could not make out a single word; but there could be only one interpretation: the scoundrel had asked her to become his mistress. Alone in his room! The blood rushed to Gilbert Clandon's face. He turned the pages rapidly. What had been her answer? Initials had ceased. It was simply 'he' now. 'He came again. I told him I could not come to any decision. . . . I implored him to leave me.' He had forced himself upon her in this very house? But why hadn't she told him? How could she have hesitated for an instant? Then: 'I wrote him a letter.' Then pages were left blank. Then there was this: 'No answer to my letter.' Then more blank pages; and then this. 'He has done what he threatened.' After that—what came after that? He turned page after page. All were blank. But there, on the very day before her death, was this entry: 'Have I the courage to do it too?' That was the end.

Gilbert Clandon let the book slide to the floor. He could see her in front of him. She was standing on the kerb in Piccadilly. Her eyes stared; her fists were clenched. Here came the car. . . .

He could not bear it. He must know the truth. He strode to the telephone.

'Miss Miller!' There was silence. Then he heard someone moving in the room.

'Sissy Miller speaking'—her voice at last answered him.

'Who,' he thundered, 'is B.M.?'

He could hear the cheap clock ticking on her mantelpiece; then a long drawn sigh. Then at last she said:

'He was my brother.'

He *was* her brother; her brother who had killed himself.

'Is there,' he heard Sissy Miller asking, 'anything that I can explain?'

'Nothing!' he cried. 'Nothing!'

He had received his legacy. She had told him the truth. She had stepped off the kerb to rejoin her lover. She had stepped off the kerb to escape from him.

D. H. LAWRENCE

Samson and Delilah

A MAN got down from the motor-omnibus that runs from Penzance to St Just-in-Penwith, and turned northwards, uphill towards the Polestar. It was only half-past six, but already the stars were out, a cold little wind was blowing from the sea, and the crystalline, three-pulse flash of the lighthouse below the cliffs beat rhythmically in the first darkness.

The man was alone. He went his way unhesitating, but looked from side to side with cautious curiosity. Tall, ruined power-houses of tin-mines loomed in the darkness from time to time, like remnants of some by-gone civilization. The lights of many miners' cottages scattered on the hilly darkness twinkled desolate in their disorder, yet twinkled with the lonely homeliness of the Celtic night.

He tramped steadily on, always watchful with curiosity. He was a tall, well-built man, apparently in the prime of life. His shoulders were square and rather stiff, he leaned forwards a little as he went, from the hips, like a man who must stoop to lower his height. But he did not stoop his shoulders: he bent his straight back from the hips.

Now and again short, stump, thick-legged figures of Cornish miners passed him, and he invariably gave them good-night, as if to insist that he was on his own ground. He spoke with the west-Cornish intonation. And as he went along the dreary road, looking now at the lights of the dwellings on land, now at the lights away to sea, vessels veering round in sight of the Longships Lighthouse, the whole of the Atlantic Ocean in darkness and space between him and America, he seemed a little excited and pleased with himself, watchful, thrilled, veering along in a sense of mastery and of power in conflict.

The houses began to close on the road, he was entering the straggling, formless, desolate mining village, that he knew of old. On the left was a little space set back from the road, and cosy lights of

an inn. There it was. He peered up at the sign: 'The Tinners' Rest.'
But he could not make out the name of the proprietor. He listened. There was excited talking and laughing, a woman's voice
laughing shrilly among the men's.

Stooping a little, he entered the warmly-lit bar. The lamp was
burning, a buxom woman rose from the white-scrubbed deal table
where the black and white and red cards were scattered, and several men, miners, lifted their faces from the game.

The stranger went to the counter, averting his face. His cap was
pulled down over his brow.

'Good-evening!' said the landlady, in her rather ingratiating voice.

'Good-evening. A glass of ale.'

'A glass of ale,' repeated the landlady suavely. 'Cold night—but
bright.'

'Yes,' the man assented, laconically. Then he added, when nobody
expected him to say any more: 'Seasonable weather.'

'Quite seasonable, quite,' said the landlady. 'Thank you.'

The man lifted his glass straight to his lips, and emptied it. He
put it down again on the zinc counter with a click.

'Let's have another,' he said.

The woman drew the beer, and the man went away with his glass
to the second table, near the fire. The woman, after a moment's
hesitation, took her seat again at the table with the card-players.
She had noticed the man: a big fine fellow, well dressed, a stranger.

But he spoke with that Cornish-Yankee accent she accepted as
the natural twang among the miners.

The stranger put his foot on the fender and looked into the fire.
He was handsome, well coloured, with well-drawn Cornish eyebrows and the usual dark, bright, mindless Cornish eyes. He seemed
abstracted in thought. Then he watched the card-party.

The woman was buxom and healthy, with dark hair and small,
quick brown eyes. She was bursting with life and vigour, the energy
she threw into the game of cards excited all the men, they shouted,
and laughed, and the woman held her breast, shrieking with laughter.

'Oh, my, it'll be the death o' me,' she panted. 'Now come on,
Mr Trevorrow, play fair. Play fair, I say, or I s'll put the cards down.'

'Play fair! Why who's played unfair?' ejaculated Mr Trevorrow.
'Do you mean t'accuse me, as I haven't played fair, Mrs Nankervis?'

'I do. I say it, and I mean it. Haven't you got the queen of spades? Now come on, no dodging round me. *I* know you've got that queen, as well as I know my name's Alice.'

'Well—if your name's Alice, you'll have to have it——'

'Ay now—what did I say? Did ever you see such a man? My word, but your missus must be easy took in, by the looks of things.'

And off she went into peals of laughter. She was interrupted by the entrance of four men in khaki, a short, stumpy sergeant of middle age, a young corporal, and two young privates. The woman leaned back in her chair.

'Oh my!' she cried. 'If there isn't the boys back: looking perished, I believe——'

'Perished, Ma!' exclaimed the sergeant. 'Not yet.'

'Near enough,' said a young private, uncouthly.

The woman got up.

'I'm sure you are, my dears. You'll be wanting your suppers, I'll be bound.'

'We could do with 'em.'

'Let's have a wet first,' said the sergeant.

The woman bustled about getting the drinks. The soldiers moved to the fire, spreading out their hands.

'Have your suppers in here, will you?' she said. 'Or in the kitchen?'

'Let's have it here,' said the sergeant. 'More cosier—*if* you don't mind.'

'You shall have it where you like, boys, where you like.'

She disappeared. In a minute a girl of about sixteen came in. She was tall and fresh, with dark, young, expressionless eyes, and well-drawn brows, and the immature softness and mindlessness of the sensuous Celtic type.

'Ho, Maryann! Evenin' Maryann! How's Maryann, now?' came the multiple greeting.

She replied to everybody in a soft voice, a strange, soft *aplomb* that was very attractive. And she moved round with rather mechanical, attractive movements, as if her thoughts were elsewhere. But she had always this dim far-awayness in her bearing: a sort of modesty. The strange man by the fire watched her curiously. There was an alert, inquisitive, mindless curiosity on his well-coloured face.

'I'll have a bit of supper with you, if I might,' he said.

She looked at him, with her clear, unreasoning eyes, just like the eyes of some non-human creature.

'I'll ask mother,' she said. Her voice was soft-breathing, gently singsong.

When she came in again:

'Yes,' she said, almost whispering. 'What will you have?'

'What have you got?' he said, looking up into her face.

'There's cold meat——'

'That's for me, then.'

The stranger sat at the end of the table, and ate with the tired, quiet soldiers. Now, the landlady was interested in him. Her brow was knit rather tense, there was a look of panic in her large, healthy face, but her small brown eyes were fixed most dangerously. She was a big woman, but her eyes were small and tense. She drew near the stranger. She wore a rather loud-patterned flannelette blouse, and a dark skirt.

'What will you have to drink with your supper?' she asked, and there was a new, dangerous note in her voice.

He moved uneasily.

'Oh, I'll go on with ale.'

She drew him another glass. Then she sat down on the bench at the table with him and the soldiers, and fixed him with her attention.

'You've come from St Just, have you?' she said.

He looked at her with those clear, dark, inscrutable Cornish eyes, and answered at length:

'No, from Penzance.'

'Penzance!—but you're not thinking of going back there tonight?'

'No—no.'

He still looked at her with those wide, clear eyes that seemed like very bright agate. Her anger began to rise. It was seen on her brow. Yet her voice was still suave and deprecating.

'I *thought* not—but you're not living in these parts, are you?'

'No—no, I'm not living here.' He was always slow in answering, as if something intervened between him and any outside question.

'Oh, I see,' she said. 'You've got relations down here.'

Again he looked straight into her eyes, as if looking her into silence.

'Yes,' he said.

He did not say any more. She rose with a flounce. The anger was tight on her brow. There was no more laughing and card-playing that evening, though she kept up her motherly, suave, good-humoured way with the men. But they knew her, they were all afraid of her.

The supper was finished, the table cleared, the stranger did not go. Two of the young soldiers went off to bed, with their cheery: 'Good-night, Ma. Good-night, Maryann.'

The stranger talked a little to the sergeant about the war, which was in its first year, about the new army, a fragment of which was quartered in this district, about America.

The landlady darted looks at him from her small eyes, minute by minute the electric storm welled in her bosom, as still he did not go. She was quivering with suppressed, violent passion, something frightening and abnormal. She could not sit still for a moment. Her heavy form seemed to flash with sudden, involuntary movements as the minutes passed by, and still he sat there, and the tension on her heart grew unbearable. She watched the hands of the clock move on. Three of the soldiers had gone to bed, only the crop-headed, terrier-like old sergeant remained.

The landlady sat behind the bar fidgeting spasmodically with the newspaper. She looked again at the clock. At last it was five minutes to ten.

'Gentlemen—the enemy!' she said, in her diminished, furious voice. 'Time, please. Time, my dears. And good-night all!'

The men began to drop out, with a brief good-night. It was a minute to ten. The landlady rose.

'Come,' she said. 'I'm shutting the door.'

The last of the miners passed out. She stood, stout and menacing, holding the door. Still the stranger sat on by the fire, his black overcoat opened, smoking.

'We're closed now, Sir,' came the perilous, narrowed voice of the landlady.

The little, dog-like, hard-headed sergeant touched the arm of the stranger.

'Closing time,' he said.

The stranger turned round in his seat, and his quick-moving, dark, jewel-like eyes went from the sergeant to the landlady.

'I'm stopping here tonight,' he said, in his laconic Cornish-Yankee accent.

The landlady seemed to tower. Her eyes lifted strangely, frightening.

'Oh, indeed!' she cried. 'Oh, indeed! And whose orders are those, may I ask?'

He looked at her again.

'My orders,' he said.

Involuntarily she shut the door, and advanced like a great, dangerous bird. Her voice rose, there was a touch of hoarseness in it.

'And what might *your* orders be, if you please?' she cried. 'Who might *you* be, to give orders, in the house?'

He sat still, watching her.

'You know who I am,' he said. 'At least, I know who you are.'

'Oh, do you? Oh, do you? And who am *I* then, if you'll be so good as to tell me?'

He stared at her with his bright, dark eyes.

'You're my Missis, you are,' he said. 'And you know it, as well as I do.'

She started as if something had exploded in her.

Her eyes lifted and flared madly.

'*Do* I know it, indeed!' she cried. 'I know no such thing! I know no such thing! Do you think a man's going to walk into this bar, and tell me off-hand I'm his Missis, and I'm going to believe him?— I say to you, whoever you may be, you're mistaken. I know myself for no Missis of yours, and I'll thank you to go out of this house, this minute, before I get those that will put you out.'

The man rose to his feet, stretching his head towards her a little. He was a handsomely built Cornishman in the prime of life.

'What you say, eh? You don't know me?' he said, in his singsong voice, emotionless, but rather smothered and pressing: it reminded one of the girl's. 'I should know you anywhere, you see. I should! I shouldn't have to look twice to know you, you see. You see, now, don't you?'

The woman was baffled.

'So you may say,' she replied, staccato. 'So you may say. That's easy enough. My name's known, and respected, by most people for ten miles round. But I don't know *you*.'

Her voice ran to sarcasm. 'I can't say I know *you*. You're a *perfect* stranger to me, and I don't believe I've ever set eyes on you before tonight.'

Her voice was very flexible and sarcastic.

'Yes, you have,' replied the man, in his reasonable way. 'Yes, you have. Your name's my name, and that girl Maryann is my girl; she's my daughter. You're my Missis right enough. As sure as I'm Willie Nankervis.'

He spoke as if it were an accepted fact. His face was handsome, with a strange, watchful alertness and a fundamental fixity of intention that maddened her.

'You villain!' she cried. 'You villain, to come to this house and dare to speak to me. You villain, you downright rascal!'

He looked at her.

'Ay,' he said, unmoved. 'All that.' He was uneasy before her. Only he was not afraid of her. There was something impenetrable about him, like his eyes, which were as bright as agate.

She towered, and drew near to him menacingly.

'You're going out of this house, aren't you?'—She stamped her foot in sudden madness. '*This minute!*'

He watched her. He knew she wanted to strike him.

'No,' he said, with suppressed emphasis. 'I've told you, I'm stopping here.'

He was afraid of her personality, but it did not alter him. She wavered. Her small, tawny-brown eyes concentrated in a point of vivid, sightless fury, like a tiger's. The man was wincing, but he stood his ground. Then she bethought herself. She would gather her forces.

'We'll see whether you're stopping here,' she said. And she turned, with a curious, frightening lifting of her eyes, and surged out of the room. The man, listening, heard her go upstairs, heard her tapping at a bedroom door, heard her saying: 'Do you mind coming down a minute, boys? I want you. I'm in trouble.'

The man in the bar took off his cap and his black overcoat, and threw them on the seat behind him. His black hair was short and touched with grey at the temples. He wore a well-cut, well-fitting suit of dark grey, American in style, and a turn-down collar. He looked well-to-do, a fine, solid figure of a man. The rather rigid look of the shoulders came from his having had his collar-bone twice broken in the mines.

The little terrier of a sergeant, in dirty khaki, looked at him furtively.

'She's your Missis?' he asked, jerking his head in the direction of the departed woman.

'Yes, she is,' barked the man. 'She's that, sure enough.'

'Not seen her for a long time, haven't ye?'

'Sixteen years come March month.'

'Hm!'

And the sergeant laconically resumed his smoking.

The landlady was coming back, followed by the three young soldiers, who entered rather sheepishly, in trousers and shirt and stocking-feet. The woman stood histrionically at the end of the bar, and exclaimed:

'That man refuses to leave the house, claims he's stopping the night here. You know very well I have no bed, don't you? And this house doesn't accommodate travellers. Yet he's going to stop in spite of all! But not while I've a drop of blood in my body, that I declare with my dying breath. And not if you men are worth the name of men, and will help a woman as has no one to help her.'

Her eyes sparkled, her face was flushed pink. She was drawn up like an Amazon.

The young soldiers did not quite know what to do. They looked at the man, they looked at the sergeant, one of them looked down and fastened his braces on the second button.

'What say, sergeant?' asked one whose face twinkled for a little devilment.

'Man says he's husband to Mrs Nankervis,' said the sergeant.

'He's no husband of mine. I declare I never set eyes on him before this night. It's a dirty trick, nothing else, it's a dirty trick.'

'Why you're a liar, saying you never set eyes on me before,' barked the man near the hearth. 'You're married to me, and that girl Maryann you had by me—well enough you know it.'

The young soldier looked on in delight, the sergeant smoked imperturbed.

'Yes,' sang the landlady, slowly shaking her head in supreme sarcasm, 'it sounds very pretty, doesn't it? But you see we don't believe a word of it, and *how* are you going to prove it?' She smiled nastily.

The man watched in silence for a moment, then he said:

'It wants no proof.'

'Oh, yes, but it does! Oh, yes, but it does, sir, it wants a lot of proving!' sang the lady's sarcasm. 'We're not such gulls as all that, to swallow your words whole.'

But he stood unmoved near the fire. She stood with one hand

resting on the zinc-covered bar, the sergeant sat with legs crossed, smoking, on the seat halfway between them, the three young soldiers in their shirts and braces stood wavering in the gloom behind the bar. There was silence.

'Do you know anything of the whereabouts of your husband, Mrs Nankervis? Is he still living?' asked the sergeant, in his judicious fashion.

Suddenly the landlady began to cry, great scalding tears, that left the young men aghast.

'I know nothing of him,' she sobbed, feeling for her pocket handkerchief. 'He left me when Maryann was a baby, went mining to America, and after about six months never wrote a line nor sent me a penny bit. I can't say whether he's alive or dead, the villain. All I've heard of him's to the bad—and I've heard nothing for years an' all, now.' She sobbed violently.

The golden-skinned, handsome man near the fire watched her as she wept. He was frightened, he was troubled, he was bewildered, but none of his emotions altered him underneath.

There was no sound in the room but the violent sobbing of the landlady. The men, one and all, were overcome.

'Don't you think as you'd better go, for tonight?' said the sergeant to the man, with sweet reasonableness. 'You'd better leave it a bit, and arrange something between you. You can't have much claim on a woman, I should imagine, if it's how she says. And you've come down on her a bit too sudden-like.'

The landlady sobbed heart-brokenly. The man watched her large breasts shaken. They seemed to cast a spell over his mind.

'How I've treated her, that's no matter,' he replied. 'I've come back, and I'm going to stop in my own home,—for a bit, anyhow. There you've got it.'

'A dirty action,' said the sergeant, his face flushing dark. 'A dirty action, to come, after deserting a woman for that number of years, and want to force yourself on her! A dirty action—as isn't allowed by the law.'

The landlady wiped her eyes.

'Never you mind about law nor nothing,' cried the man, in a strange, strong voice. 'I'm not moving out of this public tonight.'

The woman turned to the soldiers behind her, and said in a wheedling, sarcastic tone:

'Are we going to stand it, boys?—Are we going to be done like this, Sergeant Thomas, by a scoundrel and a bully as has led a life beyond *mention*, in those American mining-camps, and then wants to come back and make havoc of a poor woman's life and savings, after having left her with a baby in arms to struggle as best she might? It's a crying shame if nobody will stand up for me—a crying shame——!'

The soldiers and the little sergeant were bristling. The woman stooped and rummaged under the counter for a minute. Then, unseen to the man away near the fire, she threw out a plaited grass rope, such as is used for binding bales, and left it lying near the feet of the young soldiers, in the gloom at the back of the bar.

Then she rose and fronted the situation.

'Come now,' she said to the man, in a reasonable, coldly-coaxing tone, 'put your coat on and leave us alone. Be a man, and not worse than a brute of a German. You can get a bed easy enough in St Just, and if you've nothing to pay for it sergeant would lend you a couple of shillings, I'm sure he would.'

All eyes were fixed on the man. He was looking down at the woman like a creature spell-bound or possessed by some devil's own intention.

'I've got money of my own,' he said. 'Don't you be frightened for your money, I've plenty of that, for the time.'

'Well, then,' she coaxed, in a cold, almost sneering propitiation, 'put your coat on and go where you're wanted—be a *man*, not a brute of a German.'

She had drawn quite near to him, in her challenging coaxing intentness. He looked down at her with his bewitched face.

'No, I shan't,' he said. 'I shan't do no such thing. *You'll* put me up for tonight.'

'Shall I?' she cried. And suddenly she flung her arms round him, hung on to him with all her powerful weight, calling to the soldiers: 'Get the rope, boys, and fasten him up. Alfred—John, quick now——'

The man reared, looked round with maddened eyes, and heaved his powerful body. But the woman was powerful also, and very heavy, and was clenched with the determination of death. Her face, with its exulting, horribly vindictive look, was turned up to him from his own breast; he reached back his head frantically, to get away from it. Meanwhile the young soldiers, after having watched this frightful Laocoon swaying for a moment, stirred, and the malicious one darted swiftly with the rope. It was tangled a little.

'Give me the end here,' cried the sergeant.

Meanwhile the big man heaved and struggled, swung the woman round against the seat and the table, in his convulsive effort to get free. But she pinned down his arms like a cuttlefish wreathed heavily upon him. And he heaved and swayed, and they crashed about the room, the soldiers hopping, the furniture bumping.

The young soldier had got the rope once round, the brisk sergeant helping him. The woman sank heavily lower, they got the rope round several times. In the struggle the victim fell over against the table. The ropes tightened till they cut his arms. The woman clung to his knees. Another soldier ran in a flash of genius, and fastened the strange man's feet with the pair of braces. Seats had crashed over, the table was thrown against the wall, but the man was bound, his arms pinned against his sides, his feet tied. He lay half fallen, sunk against the table, still for a moment.

The woman rose, and sank, faint, on to the seat against the wall. Her breast heaved, she could not speak, she thought she was going to die. The bound man lay against the overturned table, his coat all twisted and pulled up beneath the ropes, leaving the loins exposed. The soldiers stood around, a little dazed, but excited with the row.

The man began to struggle again, heaving instinctively against the ropes, taking great, deep breaths. His face, with its golden skin, flushed dark and surcharged, he heaved again. The great veins in his neck stood out. But it was no good, he went relaxed. Then again, suddenly, he jerked his feet.

'Another pair of braces, William,' cried the excited soldier. He threw himself on the legs of the bound man, and managed to fasten the knees. Then again there was stillness. They could hear the clock tick.

The woman looked at the prostrate figure, the strong, straight limbs, the strong back bound in subjection, the wide-eyed face that reminded her of a calf tied in a sack in a cart, only its head stretched dumbly backwards. And she triumphed.

The bound-up body began to struggle again. She watched fascinated the muscles working, the shoulders, the hips, the large, clean thighs. Even now he might break the ropes. She was afraid. But the lively young soldier sat on the shoulders of the bound man, and after a few perilous moments, there was stillness again.

'Now,' said the judicious sergeant to the bound man, 'if we untie you, will you promise to go off and make no more trouble.'

'You'll not untie him in here,' cried the woman. 'I wouldn't trust him as far as I could blow him.'

There was silence.

'We might carry him outside, and undo him there,' said the soldier. 'Then we could get the policeman, if he made any more bother.'

'Yes,' said the sergeant. 'We could do that.' Then again, in an altered, almost severe tone, to the prisoner. 'If we undo you outside, will you take your coat and go without creating any more disturbance?'

But the prisoner would not answer, he only lay with wide, dark, bright eyes, like a bound animal. There was a space of perplexed silence.

'Well then, do as you say,' said the woman irritably. 'Carry him out amongst you, and let us shut up the house.'

They did so. Picking up the bound man, the four soldiers staggered clumsily into the silent square in front of the inn, the woman following with the cap and the overcoat. The young soldiers quickly unfastened the braces from the prisoner's legs, and they hopped indoors. They were in their stocking-feet, and outside the stars flashed cold. They stood in the doorway watching. The man lay quite still on the cold ground.

'Now,' said the sergeant, in a subdued voice, 'I'll loosen the knot, and he can work himself free, if you go in, Missis.'

She gave a last look at the dishevelled, bound man, as he sat on the ground. Then she went indoors, followed quickly by the sergeant. Then they were heard locking and barring the door.

The man seated on the ground outside worked and strained at the rope. But it was not so easy to undo himself even now. So, with hands bound, making an effort, he got on his feet and went and worked the cord against the rough edge of an old wall. The rope, being of a kind of plaited grass, soon frayed and broke, and he freed himself. He had various contusions. His arms were hurt and bruised from the bonds. He rubbed them slowly. Then he pulled his clothes straight, stooped, put on his cap, struggled into his overcoat, and walked away.

The stars were very brilliant. Clear as crystal, the beam from the lighthouse under the cliffs struck rhythmically on the night. Dazed, the man walked along the road past the churchyard. Then he stood leaning up against a wall, for a long time.

He was roused because his feet were so cold. So he pulled himself together, and turned again in the silent night, back towards the inn.

The bar was in darkness. But there was a light in the kitchen. He hesitated. Then very quietly he tried the door.

He was surprised to find it open. He entered, and quietly closed it behind him. Then he went down the step past the bar-counter, and through to the lighted doorway of the kitchen. There sat his wife, planted in front of the range, where a furze fire was burning. She sat in a chair full in front of the range, her knees wide apart on the fender. She looked over her shoulder at him as he entered, but she did not speak. Then she stared in the fire again.

It was a small, narrow kitchen. He dropped his cap on the table that was covered with yellowish American cloth, and took a seat with his back to the wall, near the oven. His wife still sat with her knees apart, her feet on the steel fender and stared into the fire, motionless. Her skin was smooth and rosy in the firelight. Everything in the house was very clean and bright. The man sat silent, too, his head dropped. And thus they remained.

It was a question who would speak first. The woman leaned forward and poked the ends of the sticks in between the bars of the range. He lifted his head and looked at her.

'Others gone to bed, have they?' he asked.

But she remained closed in silence.

''S a cold night, out,' he said, as if to himself.

And he laid his large, yet well-shapen workman's hand on the top of the stove, that was polished black and smooth as velvet. She would not look at him, yet she glanced out of the corners of her eyes.

His eyes were fixed brightly on her, the pupils large and electric like those of a cat.

'I should have picked you out among thousands,' he said. 'Though you're bigger than I'd have believed. Fine flesh you've made.'

She was silent for some time. Then she turned in her chair upon him.

'What do you think of yourself,' she said, 'coming back on me like *this* after over fifteen year? You don't think I've not heard of you, neither, in Butte City and elsewhere?'

He was watching her with his clear, translucent, unchallenged eyes.

'Yes,' he said. 'Chaps comes an' goes—I've heard tell of you from time to time.'

She drew herself up.

'And what lies have you heard about *me*?' she demanded superbly.

'I dunno as I've heard any lies at all—'cept as you was getting on very well, like.'

His voice ran warily and detached. Her anger stirred again in her, violently. But she subdued it, because of the danger there was in him, and more, perhaps, because of the beauty of his head and his level-drawn brows, which she could not bear to forfeit.

'That's more than I can say of *you*,' she said. 'I've heard more harm than good about *you*.'

'Ay, I dessay,' he said, looking in the fire. It was a long time since he had seen the furze burning, he said to himself. There was a silence, during which she watched his face.

'Do you call yourself a *man*?' she said, more in contemptuous reproach than in anger. 'Leave a woman as you've left me, you don't care to what!—and then to turn up in *this* fashion, without a word to say for yourself.'

He stirred in his chair, planted his feet apart, and resting his arms on his knees, looked steadily into the fire, without answering. So near to her was his head, and the close black hair, she could scarcely refrain from starting away, as if it would bite her.

'Do you call that the action of a *man*?' she repeated.

'No,' he said, reaching and poking the bits of wood into the fire with his fingers. 'I didn't call it anything, as I know of. It's no good calling things by any names whatsoever, as I know of.'

She watched him in his actions. There was a longer and longer pause between each speech, though neither knew it.

'I *wonder* what you think of yourself!' she exclaimed, with vexed emphasis. 'I *wonder* what sort of a fellow you take yourself to be!' She was really perplexed as well as angry.

'Well,' he said, lifting his head to look at her. 'I guess I'll answer for my own faults, if everybody else'll answer for theirs.'

Her heart beat fiery hot as he lifted his face to her. She breathed heavily, averting her face, almost losing her self-control.

'And what do you take *me* to be?' she cried, in real helplessness.

His face was lifted watching her, watching her soft, averted face, and the softly heaving mass of her breasts.

'I take you,' he said, with that laconic truthfulness which exercised such power over her, 'to be the deuce of a fine woman— darn me if you're not as fine a built woman as I've seen, handsome with it as well. I shouldn't have expected you to put on such handsome flesh: 'struth I shouldn't.'

Her heart beat fiery hot, as he watched her with those bright agate eyes, fixedly.

'Been very handsome to *you*, for fifteen years, my sakes!' she replied.

He made no answer to this, but sat with his bright, quick eyes upon her.

Then he rose. She started involuntarily. But he only said, in his laconic, measured way:

'It's warm in here now.'

And he pulled off his overcoat, throwing it on the table. She sat as if slightly cowed, whilst he did so.

'Them ropes has given my arms something, by Ga-ard,' he drawled, feeling his arms with his hands.

Still she sat in her chair before him, slightly cowed.

'You was sharp, wasn't you, to catch me like that, eh?' he smiled slowly. 'By Ga-ard, you had me fixed proper, proper you had. Darn me, you fixed me up proper—proper, you did.'

He leaned forwards in his chair towards her.

'I don't think no worse of you for it, no, darned if I do. Fine pluck in a woman's what I admire. That I do, indeed.'

She only gazed into the fire.

'We fet from the start, we did. And my word, you begin again quick the minute you see me, you did. Darn me, you was too sharp for me. A darn fine woman, puts up a darn good fight. Darn me if I could find a woman in all the darn States as could get me down like that. Wonderful fine woman you be, truth to say, at this minute.'

She only sat glowering into the fire.

'As grand a pluck as a man could wish to find in a woman, true as I'm here,' he said, reaching forward his hand and tentatively touching her between her full, warm breasts, quietly.

She started, and seemed to shudder. But his hand insinuated itself between her breasts, as she continued to gaze in the fire.

'And don't you think I've come back here a–begging,' he said. 'I've more than *one* thousand pounds to my name, I have. And a bit of a fight for a how–de–do pleases me, that it do. But that doesn't mean as you're going to deny as you're my Missis . . .'

JOYCE CARY

The Tunnel

For instance, you're going out to supper with Alice, you've written that you'd love to come; but you'd much rather have stayed at
home. It's raining frosty fog, and you're tired out. How will you
face those awful stairs? Alice lives at the top of a decayed family
mansion in West Kensington, with peeling stucco pillars and a long
flight of cracked steps. It has the special squalor of imitation
magnificence in its old age, like rabbit-mink going bald, and rolled
gold showing the nickel. The stairway inside reminds you of the
old pictures of the bad man's road from luxury to hell. The first
flight has a pile carpet; the next two are cord carpets; the fourth,
a worn oilcloth; and the last is quite bare. What's more, it's stained
all over with mysterious chemicals, jaundice yellow, gas green, and
a kind of mouldy blue; they look like poisons, and on the top landing there is a great dark red splash, like blood. Alice's door, too, is
more sinister than that of any jail; low, black, and crooked. It squints
as if it hated you, as if it had murders to hide.

If Alice hadn't sent that note, one of her last-minute notes which
give you no time to invent an excuse, you'd be at home in front
of a nice fire, eating a chop from your excellent landlady. She knows
how to cook—Alice can't, but you couldn't tell her so. Even though
you've been engaged for a fortnight; that is, re-engaged since that
last breaking off about—what was it about? But what's it matter.
Now we're fixed; we're sensible, we don't expect too much, and all
the surprises are out. Yes, of course, a tender soul, but how cross
when she has a conscience, and what terrible colds. The rain is
getting heavier and colder—that right shoe is leaking again through
the hole, and your corn is beginning to shoot, like toothache. The
pavements are jammed with people looking at the Christmas shops;
and how? They see nothing, they say nothing, they don't know
what they want, they only get in your way and their own. They

drift along in the wet like rubbish down a drain—their faces are like yesterday's newspapers. What do you care? Not a damn for a damn thing. You always go this way to supper with Alice, you don't need to think or feel. You just flow along in the drain—and all at once she's there, out of nothing. The presence of Alice. She's breathing about you, she's blowing her nose within you—you discover suddenly that Alice is special. Even with her most exasperating cold, even with a red nose. Especially then. You adore her. In fact, for the first time in your life, you know what it is to be in—how can you say it. No word can describe this sensation, this extraordinary— For instance, if you had a gun and could fire it off, all six shots, not for her—Alice wouldn't understand it, she'd be terrified for you in case you hurt yourself, or got into trouble with the police—but for yourself. Or better, you think, as you dodge the umbrellas in a rather dirty Burberry and your wet weather hat—suppose you could just spread out your arms and float over the people, and while they gazed upwards in absolute amazement, you explained, 'This is because of Alice.' But of course, these lumps, these cabbage stalks wouldn't notice you at all—they'd simply go on brooding at the shops, or if they did look up they'd only say, 'What nonsense—I suppose it's some advertisement,' and they'd be disgusted, not only with you, but with everything. That would be the last straw.

To hell with them; to hell with everybody. And you dash along the road at the risk of your life, and when you arrive you leap up the stairs like spring-heeled Jack. And now the stairway is like the soul's ascent to heaven, at every turn it throws off another temptation of the devil, another materialist illusion and gets nearer to that noble austerity which belongs to the lives of the saints. And in fact, Alice is a saint. She's poor enough, God knows, her usual lunch is a bun, but what's the betting she's spent half a week's pay on this supper. Nothing is too good for you, and what have you done for her? What has anyone done for Alice? She's had to fight every yard from birth, but now things are going to be different—a new era begins. At last you can make her realize that she's appreciated at something like her real worth. You shout, knock, ring. You hear a step, and your heart pauses; you think, now you're going to see her, Alice, your Alice. The door opens, and a young woman is standing there, a stranger—for twenty seconds at least you don't know her. You don't realize it's Alice. This isn't only because the landing is dark, and the light behind her is dazzling in your eyes, but because she has a different face, a new smile, and wears an enormous apron you've never seen before, an incredible apron from her chin to her feet. Your lips mutter at last, 'Am I too early?' And she answers with the same extraordinary smile, 'No, of course not; do come in,' but you know already that something is wrong, fearfully, catastrophically wrong. What can it be? You walk into the room, the only room, in a kind of daze as if you had been sandbagged. Alice has disappeared into the cupboard where she cooks. Her frock is hanging on a chair, her make-up things are on the chest of drawers. She hasn't yet done her face or dressed. You look at your watch and discover that, in fact, you *are* early—by twenty minutes. So that's the trouble. And you're shocked. How can the girl be so silly, don't she know how plain she is? Of course she does. She's often remarked that hats are her big problem because of her queer face, so why be upset at being caught with a shiny nose? What does she think you come here for? To gaze at her ridiculous nose and admire last year's frock, that doesn't suit her anyhow? Don't she realize that the only reason anyone could ever love her would be for her character, her gaiety, her intelligence, her self, her soul? That is to say, if and when he did love her, really and truly, without romanticizing the thing.

You'd like to go away and come back at the proper time, but of course that's impossible just because of that smile, that apron, of this whole ridiculous situation.

Alice reappears with a proud indifferent look like a princess challenged by a cockroach, snatches the dress from the chair and vanishes again into the cupboard—you hear sounds as of a wrestling match and a bottle falls down. But you don't hear Alice say, 'Bother the thing,' as usual, and the tension increases. She brings in supper and only then does her face, with deliberate and brazen elaboration; but when at last she comes to the table you see her mouth is crooked and her nose is as white as chalk, a frost-bitten nose.

The silence is now unbearable, and you cast about wildly for a remark. But, as all the interesting subjects, that is, anything about furniture, flats, gas versus electric stoves, crockery or bedding, are impossible, you find yourself talking about the news—as neither of you takes the least interest in the news, the conversation at once reaches a very high level.

By the time you reach the customary veal Alice is growing animated about the atomic bomb, the terrible times we live in, and you are saying that civilization is done for. The sort of thing you read in all the best modern authors, not because they believe it, but because they said it years ago when it was the right thing and they can't say anything else now, or perhaps because they want to frighten people, or simply because they're annoyed about the income tax.

Both of you know that all this is nonsense, that you don't believe a word of it. What if some bomb did kill you tomorrow, you wouldn't know anything about it. It might be a good deal better to die that way than in the way you will die. It's not just cowardly to fear wars and bombs, it's simply stupid, and perhaps bogus too. You look at Alice and think, 'I don't ask that she should throw herself into my arms; I don't expect anything exceptional; Alice is not a genius at self-expression. Far from it; she couldn't bring off the grand gesture if she tried; I should have been quite satisfied if she'd been glad to see me.'

You reflect, 'And why couldn't she welcome me? After coming down that horrible road in the horrible rain. Do I really know Alice? Aren't I deceiving myself about this very ordinary girl. I think her so modest, so affectionate, a shy and innocent creature who simply doesn't know how to hide her most trifling reactions. But isn't this the very disguise that cunning girls take to catch a man. I don't suggest even that she does it deliberately; to say that every woman, yes, from the age of one year, is a born actress is to repeat something so trite that it isn't worth saying. That's why I was forgetting it.

'And if Alice isn't an actress then what did that horrid grin mean, that haughty step? What does she mean now by talking about Egypt and Russia and Chinese Imperialism—stuff only fit for suspicious-looking strangers chance-met in a bus queue. It can only mean she wants to insult me. I don't want to be unfair to the girl. Naturally she is touchy about her looks—with such looks. But it is perfectly clear that if she is not at least slightly deceitful—then she has certain flaws, deep flaws, in character and temper, that will have to be set off against her charm, if that's the right word for whatever it was that got me into this embarrassing relationship.'

Meanwhile you are remarking with the air of a Prime Minister,

'Of course the United Nations is a step in the right direction, or perhaps you don't agree.' And Alice makes a solemn face (but her face as well as her voice, her whole attitude, with a flat back, and her neck bent on one side, is completely false, and also, as it were, tense with the knowledge that the evening is becoming more and more disastrous) and says, 'But if Russia really has all these complexes, then you can hardly see how——'

'Oh yes, Russia is terrified, there's bound to be a war.'

'On the other hand if she isn't terrified——'

'Oh, if she's not afraid of war, we're absolutely done for, I agree.'

'Though we weren't done for last time there was a war.'

'No, but this time——'

And then we're back at the hopeless dilemma of the modern world, and the impossibility of enjoying life, especially for the young, like us. But both of us know perfectly well that life is not merely enjoyable, it is moments of such bliss that——

But it is impossible to describe that bliss; that compound of devotion and gratitude, and amusement (because you want to laugh at yourself for being in such an exalted state) and the sense that all this is understood, is shared, that you aren't alone (of course, nothing is really understood, but at this level you get away from words, you enter on the intimate, the real, the divine), that you are, in short, blissful—and not only blissful but happy.

For that is there too, happiness; a quite different thing from bliss, a kind of—what would you say—if bliss is slightly drunk, champagne drunk, happiness is just the opposite, it's a feather bed, a vast tranquillity, enormous contentment, entire confidence. Small babies have it when they sit on their mother's laps, you can see it in their eyes, but they don't know it, they don't know anything and you know too much; yet you can recognize happiness at once, you feel it and greet it. And such moments are not so rare either; they may crop up once, even twice a week; they can be got at even by art, when both parties are gifted with some talent for the thing, when they can laugh, for instance, at the same bad joke.

'So, in fact, you don't think life is worth living,' Alice says. And her voice is an accusation. What she means is, 'You don't love me.'

And the correct answer, of course, is to agree, to be, if possible, a little more pessimistic, a little more grand in despair. But for a moment you hesitate, you rebel, you ask yourself if it's really necessary for you to make this answer. Have you not control of your tongue, and your imagination? You resolve to break out of this tunnel down which you are being conducted by invisible forces, and you open your mouth to say, 'What awful nonsense you're talking,' but what you hear yourself say, quite lost in despairing astonishment at your own words, is, 'Logically speaking, and if one isn't afraid to face the facts, I don't see why any sensible person doesn't cut his throat pronto.'

Ten minutes later you are in the street; you are full of misery and rage. That good-night kiss, cold as bacon, how did she dare? What hypocrisy, what spite; and you say to yourself, 'This is the end, I'll never see her again, what an escape. She is a block, a lump, an automatic machine; no, she is worse, she knew that I was longing to be nice to her, but she wouldn't allow it. She was determined to spite me because I caught her with a shiny nose; what pettiness. What a small, mean creeping creature, what a scorpion, a bug, a vampire!'

You wake up next morning with a stomach-ache, cramp in the right leg, black spots in front of the eyes, and feeling as if you had been but half resuscitated from a deep and muddy grave. Your mouth tastes of dirt. You are full of despair and self-satisfaction; at least you've escaped from ruining your life. How crazy you were to think you ever liked that girl, that pug-nosed, green-eyed, pigeon-toed, tittuping lop-lolly, that butter-fingered, small town, high school throw-out. Her mouth is bigger than her mind is small. Oh, how she drops things, cups, pens, ear-rings, saucepans, hairpins, and handkerchiefs. Oh, how she leaves her gloves in churches and her handbag in the ladies'. How she lets the kettle boil over and cries, 'What a fool I am,' and then does it all over again. Oh, how she gazes at you with intense interest while you tell her a new story from the office and interrupts in the middle with the question, 'Did you remember to get your shoes mended?' How she apologizes for each new cold and won't take anything to stop her colds, and don't care either. Oh, how she says, 'You know what I mean,' when she hasn't the faintest idea what she means and is too lazy to find out.

You sit down at once to write, to make your getaway. 'Are we absolutely sure we're really suited to each other?' That's the tone; you'll post it on your way to the office.

You'll be late for the office but you don't care; if they sack you,

you can always go to Australia, get right away from Alice—twelve thousand miles is not too much. A note in the letter-box. Alice's writing—to break it off? So she saw it coming. Just like last time. And just like her to rush in first. No date, as usual, and no beginning—she won't even write, 'Dear Dick.' But what's this—'I can't go to bed without writing, I feel so wretched. I can't even honestly say I had a headache or the blight. It was a kind of a horrible thing that got hold of me; I can't describe it—it was a sort of devilish thing—and you were such an angel. My darling, I don't suppose you will ever want to speak to me again. I couldn't blame you, and I've no excuse. But if it is for the last time I do want to tell you what a great and exciting thing it has been to know that you have sometimes wanted to be with me—the greatest thing in my life.'

And you don't go any further, you don't wait even to look at the second page. What do the words matter? The point is that if you are to see Alice before she goes to her office, you must fly. You'll be scandalously late at your own office but you don't care a damn, you don't care if they do sack you, though you can't go to Australia, though you can't get another job anywhere. You must make Alice understand that nothing, nothing, nothing, was her fault, that you were deliberately torturing her.

Look at that old colonel, or perhaps a banker. Certainly an important person, old and important, poor old chap, old, important, and ridiculous. He's absolutely furious with you for running your eye into his umbrella. What a liberty! And it *was* a liberty—you didn't even notice him. You wish you could stop and explain, for instance, that you're blind on that side, or that your foot slipped. It wouldn't be any good telling him the truth and why you have to be in Kensington by half-past eight. He'd be still more furious. He'd think you were laughing at him. Nobody, nobody, could understand what's happened to you. You don't understand it yourself—it never happened to you before; no, never before have you even begun to understand what Alice is to you—the miracle of her goodness, of that true soul which forgives everything because it only knows how to love. My darling, at last I can make you understand what I feel— what I mean when I say that at last I am really and truly in—but how flat that would be—how stupid, how absolutely nothing.

KATHERINE MANSFIELD

Something Childish but very Natural

WHETHER he had forgotten what it felt like, or his head had really grown bigger since the summer before, Henry could not decide. But his straw hat hurt him: it pinched his forehead and started a dull ache in the two bones just over the temples. So he chose a corner seat in a third-class 'smoker', took off his hat and put it in the rack with his large black cardboard portfolio and his Aunt B's Christmas-present gloves. The carriage smelt horribly of wet india-rubber and soot. There were ten minutes to spare before the train went, so Henry decided to go and have a look at the bookstall. Sunlight darted through the glass roof of the station in long beams of blue and gold; a little boy ran up and down carrying a tray of primroses; there was something about the people—about the women especially—something idle and yet eager. The most thrilling day of the year, the first real day of Spring had unclosed its warm delicious beauty even to London eyes. It had put a spangle in every colour and a new tone in every voice, and city folks walked as though they carried real live bodies under their clothes with real live hearts pumping the stiff blood through.

Henry was a great fellow for books. He did not read many nor did he possess above half-a-dozen. He looked at all in the Charing Cross Road during lunch-time and at any odd time in London; the quantity with which he was on nodding terms was amazing. By his clean neat handling of them and by his nice choice of phrase when discussing them with one or another bookseller you would have thought that he had taken his pap with a tome propped before his nurse's bosom. But you would have been quite wrong. That was only Henry's way with everything he touched or said. That afternoon it was an anthology of English poetry, and he turned over the pages until a title struck his eye—*Something Childish but very Natural*!

Had I but two little wings,
And were a little feathery bird,
To you I'd fly, my dear,
But thoughts like these are idle things,
And I stay here.

But in my sleep to you I fly,
I'm always with you in my sleep,
The world is all one's own,
But then one wakes and where am I?
All, all alone.

Sleep stays not though a monarch bids,
So I love to wake at break of day,
For though my sleep be gone,
Yet while 'tis dark one shuts one's lids,
And so, dreams on.

He could not have done with the little poem. It was not the words so much as the whole air of it that charmed him! He might have written it lying in bed, very early in the morning, and watching the sun dance on the ceiling. 'It is *still*, like that,' thought Henry. 'I am sure he wrote it when he was half-awake some time, for it's got a smile of a dream on it.' He stared at the poem and then looked away and repeated it by heart, missed a word in the third verse and looked again, and again until he became conscious of shouting and shuffling, and he looked up to see the train moving slowly.

'God's thunder!' Henry dashed forward. A man with a flag and a whistle had his hand on a door. He clutched Henry somehow . . . Henry was inside with the door slammed, in a carriage that wasn't a 'smoker', that had not a trace of his straw hat or the black portfolio or his Aunt B's Christmas-present gloves. Instead, in the opposite corner, close against the wall, there sat a girl. Henry did not dare to look at her, but he felt certain she was staring at him. 'She must think I'm mad,' he thought, 'dashing into a train without even a hat, and in the evening, too.' He felt so funny. He didn't know how to sit or sprawl. He put his hands in his pockets and tried to appear quite indifferent and frown at a large photograph of Bolton Abbey. But feeling her eyes on him he gave her just the tiniest glance. Quick she looked away out of the window, and then Henry, careful of her slightest movement, went on looking. She sat pressed against the window, her cheek and shoulder half hidden by a long wave of marigold-coloured hair. One little hand in a grey cotton glove held a leather case on her lap with the initials E.M. on it. The other hand she had slipped through the window-strap, and Henry noticed a silver bangle on the wrist with a Swiss cowbell and a silver shoe and a fish. She wore a green coat and a hat with a wreath round it. All this Henry saw while the title of the new poem persisted in his brain—*Something Childish but very Natural.* 'I suppose she goes to some school in London,' thought Henry. 'She might be in an office. Oh, no, she is too young. Besides she'd have her hair up if she was. It isn't even down her back.' He could not keep his eyes off that beautiful waving hair. '"My eyes are like two drunken bees. . . ." Now, I wonder if I read that or made it up?'

That moment the girl turned round and, catching his glance, she blushed. She bent her head to hide the red colour that flew in her cheeks, and Henry, terribly embarrassed, blushed too. 'I shall have to speak—have to—have to!' He started putting up his hand to raise the hat that wasn't there. He thought that funny; it gave him confidence.

'I'm—I'm most awfully sorry,' he said, smiling at the girl's hat. 'But I can't go on sitting in the same carriage with you and not explaining why I dashed in like that, without my hat even. I'm sure I gave you a fright, and just now I was staring at you—but that's only an awful fault of mine; I'm a terrible starer! If you'd like me to explain—how I got in here—not about the staring, of course,'— he gave a little laugh—'I will.'

For a minute she said nothing, then in a low, shy voice—'It doesn't matter.'

The train had flung behind the roofs and chimneys. They were swinging into the country, past little black woods and fading fields and pools of water shining under an apricot evening sky. Henry's heart began to thump and beat to the beat of the train. He couldn't leave it like that. She sat so quiet, hidden in her fallen hair. He felt that it was absolutely necessary that she should look up and understand him—understand him at least. He leant forward and clasped his hands round his knees.

'You see I'd just put all my things—a portfolio—into a third-class "smoker" and was having a look at the bookstall,' he explained.

As he told the story she raised her head. He saw her grey eyes under the shadow of her hat and her eyebrows like two gold feathers. Her lips were faintly parted. Almost unconsciously he seemed to absorb the fact that she was wearing a bunch of primroses and that her throat was white—the shape of her face wonderfully delicate against all that burning hair. 'How beautiful she is! How simply beautiful she is!' sang Henry's heart, and swelled with the words, bigger and bigger and trembling like a marvellous bubble—so that he was afraid to breathe for fear of breaking it.

'I hope there was nothing valuable in the portfolio,' said she, very grave.

'Oh, only some silly drawings that I was taking back from the office,' answered Henry, airily. 'And—I was rather glad to lose my hat. It had been hurting me all day.'

'Yes,' she said, 'it's left a mark,' and she nearly smiled.

Why on earth should those words have made Henry feel so free suddenly and so happy and so madly excited? What was happening between them? They said nothing, but to Henry their silence was alive and warm. It covered him from his head to his feet in a trembling wave. Her marvellous words, 'It's made a mark,' had in some mysterious fashion established a bond between them. They could not be utter strangers to each other if she spoke so simply and so naturally. And now she was really smiling. The smile danced in her eyes, crept over her cheeks to her lips and stayed there. He leant back. The words flew from him.—'Isn't life wonderful!'

At that moment the train dashed into a tunnel. He heard her voice raised against the noise. She leant forward.

'I don't think so. But then I've been a fatalist for a long time now'—a pause—'months.'

They were shattering through the dark. 'Why?' called Henry. 'Oh. . . .'

Then she shrugged, and smiled and shook her head, meaning she could not speak against the noise. He nodded and leant back. They came out of the tunnel into a sprinkle of lights and houses. He waited for her to explain. But she got up and buttoned her coat and put her hands to her hat, swaying a little. 'I get out here,' she said. That seemed quite impossible to Henry.

The train slowed down and the lights outside grew brighter. She moved towards his end of the carriage.

'Look here!' he stammered. 'Shan't I see you again?' He got up,

too, and leant against the rack with one hand. 'I *must* see you again.'
The train was stopping.

She said breathlessly, 'I come down from London every evening.'
'You—you—you do—really?' His eagerness frightened her. He
was quick to curb it. Shall we or shall we not shake hands? raced
through his brain. One hand was on the door-handle, the other
held the little bag. The train stopped. Without another word or
glance she was gone.

Then came Saturday—a half day at the office—and Sunday between.
By Monday evening Henry was quite exhausted. He was at the
station far too early, with a pack of silly thoughts at his heels as it
were driving him up and down. 'She didn't say she came by this
train!' 'And supposing I go up and she cuts me.' 'There may be
somebody with her.' 'Why do you suppose she's ever thought of
you again?' 'What are you going to say if you do see her?' He even
prayed, 'Lord if it be Thy will, let us meet.'

But nothing helped. White smoke floated against the roof of the
station—dissolved and came again in swaying wreaths. Of a sudden,
as he watched it, so delicate and so silent, moving with such mysterious grace above the crowd and the scuffle, he grew calm. He
felt very tired—he only wanted to sit down and shut his eyes—she
was not coming—a forlorn relief breathed in the words. And then
he saw her quite near to him walking towards the train with the
same little leather case in her hand. Henry waited. He knew, somehow, that she had seen him, but he did not move until she came
close to him and said in her low, shy voice—'Did you get them
again?'

'Oh, yes, thank you, I got them again,' and with a funny half
gesture he showed her the portfolio and the gloves. They walked
side by side to the train and into an empty carriage. They sat down
opposite to each other, smiling timidly but not speaking, while the
train moved slowly, and slowly gathered speed and smoothness.
Henry spoke first.

'It's so silly,' he said, 'not knowing your name.' She put back a
big piece of hair that had fallen on her shoulder, and he saw how her
hand in the grey glove was shaking. Then he noticed that she was
sitting very stiffly with her knees pressed together—and he was, too
—both of them trying not to tremble so. She said 'My name is Edna.'

'And mine is Henry.'

In the pause they took possession of each other's names and turned them over and put them away, a shade less frightened after that.

'I want to ask you something else now,' said Henry. He looked at Edna, his head a little on one side. 'How old are you?'

'Over sixteen,' she said, 'and you?'

'I'm nearly eighteen. . . .'

'Isn't it hot?' she said suddenly, and pulled off her grey gloves and put her hands to her cheeks and kept them there. Their eyes were not frightened—they looked at each other with a sort of desperate calmness. If only their bodies would not tremble so stupidly! Still half hidden by her hair, Edna said:

'Have you ever been in love before?'

'No, never! Have you?'

'Oh, never in all my life.' She shook her head. 'I never even thought it possible.'

His next words came in a rush. 'Whatever have you been doing since last Friday evening? Whatever did you do all Saturday and all Sunday and today?'

But she did not answer—only shook her head and smiled and said, 'No, you tell *me*.'

'I?' cried Henry—and then he found he couldn't tell her either. He couldn't climb back to those mountains of days, and he had to shake his head, too.

'But it's been agony,' he said, smiling brilliantly—'agony.' At that she took away her hands and started laughing, and Henry joined her. They laughed until they were tired.

'It's so—so extraordinary,' she said. 'So suddenly, you know, and I feel as if I'd known you for years.'

'So do I . . .' said Henry. 'I believe it must be the Spring. I believe I've swallowed a butterfly—and it's fanning its wings just here.' He put his hand on his heart.

'And the really extraordinary thing is,' said Edna, 'that I had made up my mind that I didn't care for—men at all. I mean all the girls at College——'

'Were you at College?'

She nodded. 'A training college, learning to be a secretary.' She sounded scornful.

'I'm in an office,' said Henry. 'An architect's office—such a funny little place up one hundred and thirty stairs. We ought to be build-ing nests instead of houses, I always think.'

'Do you like it?'

'No, of course I don't. I don't want to do anything, do you?'

'No, I hate it. . . . And,' she said, 'my mother is a Hungarian—I believe that makes me hate it even more.'

That seemed to Henry quite natural. 'It would,' he said.

'Mother and I are exactly alike. I haven't a thing in common with my father; he's just . . . a little man in the City—but mother has got wild blood in her and she's given it to me. She hates our life just as much as I do.' She paused and frowned. 'All the same, we don't get on a bit together—that's funny—isn't it? But I'm abso-lutely alone at home.'

Henry was listening—in a way he was listening, but there was something else he wanted to ask her. He said, very shyly, 'Would you—would you take off your hat?'

She looked startled. 'Take off my hat?'

'Yes—it's your hair. I'd give anything to see your hair properly.'

She protested. 'It isn't really . . .'

'Oh, it *is*,' cried Henry, and then, as she took off the hat and gave her head a little toss, 'Oh, Edna! it's the loveliest thing in the world.'

'Do you like it?' she said, smiling and very pleased. She pulled it round her shoulders like a cape of gold. 'People generally laugh at it. It's such an absurd colour.' But Henry would not believe that. She leaned her elbows on her knees and cupped her chin in her hands. 'That's how I often sit when I'm angry and then I feel it burning me up. . . . Silly?'

'No, no, not a bit,' said Henry. 'I knew you did. It's your sort of weapon against all the dull horrid things.'

'However did you know that? Yes, that's just it. But however did you know?'

'Just knew,' smiled Henry. 'My God!' he cried, 'what fools people are! All the little pollies that you know and that I know. Just look at you and me. Here we are—that's all there is to be said. I know about you and you know about me—we've just found each other—quite simply—just by being natural. That's all life is—some-thing childish and very natural. Isn't it?'

'Yes—yes,' she said eagerly. 'That's what I've always thought.'

'It's people that make things so—silly. As long as you can keep away from them you're safe and you're happy.'

'Oh, I've thought that for a long time.'

'Then you're just like me,' said Henry. The wonder of that was so great that he almost wanted to cry. Instead he said very solemnly: 'I believe we're the only two people alive who think as we do. In fact, I'm sure of it. Nobody understands me. I feel as though I were living in a world of strange beings—do you?'

'Always.'

'We'll be in that loathsome tunnel again in a minute,' said Henry. 'Edna! can I—just touch your hair?'

She drew back quickly. 'Oh, no, please don't,' and as they were going into the dark she moved a little away from him.

'Edna! I've bought the tickets. The man at the concert hall didn't seem at all surprised that I had the money. Meet me outside the gallery doors at three, and wear that cream blouse and the corals— will you? I love you. I don't like sending these letters to the shop. I always feel those people with "Letters received" in their window keep a kettle in their back parlour that would steam open an elephant's ear of an envelope. But it really doesn't matter, does it, darling? Can you get away on Sunday? Pretend you are going to spend the day with one of the girls from the office, and let's meet at some little place and walk or find a field where we can watch the daisies uncurling. I do love you, Edna. But Sundays without you are simply impossible. Don't get run over before Saturday, and don't eat anything out of a tin or drink anything from a public fountain. That's all, darling.'

'My dearest, yes, I'll be there on Saturday—and I've arranged about Sunday, too. That is one great blessing. I'm quite free at home. I have just come in from the garden. It's such a lovely evening. Oh, Henry, I could sit and cry, I love you so tonight. Silly—isn't it? I either feel so happy I can hardly stop laughing or else so sad I can hardly stop crying and both for the same reason. But we are so young to have found each other, aren't we? I am sending you a violet. It is quite warm. I wish you were here now, just for a minute even. Good-night, darling. I am Edna.'

*

'Safe,' said Edna, 'safe! And excellent places, aren't they, Henry?'

She stood up to take off her coat and Henry made a movement to help her. 'No—no—it's off.' She tucked it under the seat. She sat down beside him. 'Oh, Henry, what have you got there? Flowers?'

'Only two tiny little roses.' He laid them in her lap.

'Did you get my letter all right?' asked Edna, unpinning the paper.

'Yes,' he said, 'and the violet is growing beautifully. You should see my room. I planted a little piece of it in every corner and one on my pillow and one in the pocket of my pyjama jacket.'

She shook her hair at him. 'Henry, give me the programme.'

'Here it is—you can read it with me. I'll hold it for you.'

'No, let me have it.'

'Well, then, I'll read it for you.'

'No, you can have it after.'

'Edna,' he whispered.

'Oh, please don't,' she pleaded. 'Not here—the people.'

Why did he want to touch her so much and why did she mind? Whenever he was with her he wanted to hold her hand or take her arm when they walked together, or lean against her—not hard—just lean lightly so that his shoulder should touch her shoulder—and she wouldn't even have that. All the time that he was away from her he was hungry, he craved the nearness of her. There seemed to be comfort and warmth breathing from Edna that he needed to keep him calm. Yes, that was it. He couldn't get calm with her because she wouldn't let him touch her. But she loved him. He knew that. Why did she feel so curiously about it? Every time he tried to or even asked for her hand she shrank back and looked at him with pleading frightened eyes as though he wanted to hurt her. They could say anything to each other. And there wasn't any question of their belonging to each other. And yet he couldn't touch her. Why, he couldn't even help her off with her coat. Her voice dropped into his thoughts.

'Henry!' He leaned to listen, setting his lips. 'I want to explain something to you. I will—I will—I promise—after the concert.'

'All right.' He was still hurt.

'You're not sad, are you?' she said.

He shook his head.

'Yes, you are, Henry.'

'No, really not.' He looked at the roses lying in her hands.

'Well, are you happy?'

'Yes. Here comes the orchestra.'

It was twilight when they came out of the hall. A blue net of light hung over the streets and houses, and pink clouds floated in a pale sky. As they walked away from the hall Henry felt they were very little and alone. For the first time since he had known Edna his heart was heavy.

'Henry!' She stopped suddenly and stared at him. 'Henry, I'm not coming to the station with you. Don't—don't wait for me. Please, please leave me.'

'My God!' cried Henry, and started, 'what's the matter—Edna—darling—Edna, what have I done?'

'Oh, nothing—go away,' and she turned and ran across the street into a square and leaned up against the square railings—and hid her face in her hands.

'Edna—Edna—my little love—you're crying. Edna, my baby girl!' She leaned her arms along the railings and sobbed distractedly.

'Edna—stop—it's all my fault. I'm a fool—I'm a thundering idiot. I've spoiled your afternoon. I've tortured you with my idiotic mad bloody clumsiness. That's it. Isn't it, Edna? For God's sake.'

'Oh,' she sobbed, 'I do hate hurting you so. Every time you ask me to let—let you hold my hand or—or kiss me I could kill myself for not doing it—for not letting you. I don't know why I don't even.' She said wildly, 'It's not that I'm frightened of you—it's not that—it's only a feeling, Henry, that I can't understand myself even. Give me your handkerchief, darling.' He pulled it from his pocket. 'All through the concert I've been haunted by this, and every time we meet I know it's bound to come up. Somehow I feel if once we did that—you know—held each other's hands and kissed it would be all changed—and I feel we wouldn't be free like we are—we'd be doing something secret. We wouldn't be children any more . . . silly, isn't it? I'd feel awkward with you, Henry, and I'd feel shy, and I do so feel that just because you and I are you and I, we don't need that sort of thing.' She turned and looked at him, pressing her hands to her cheeks in the way he knew so well, and behind her as in a dream he saw the sky and half a white moon and the trees of the square with their unbroken buds. He kept twisting, twisting up in his hands the concert programme. 'Henry! You do understand me—don't you?'

'Yes, I think I do. But you're not going to be frightened any more, are you?' He tried to smile. 'We'll forget, Edna. I'll never mention it again. We'll bury the bogy in this square—now—you and I—won't we?'

'But,' she said, searching his face—'will it make you love me less?'

'Oh, no,' he said. 'Nothing could—nothing on earth could do that.'

London became their playground. On Saturday afternoons they explored. They found their own shops where they bought cigarettes and sweets for Edna—and their own tea-shop with their own table—their own streets—and one night when Edna was supposed to be at a lecture at the Polytechnic they found their own village. It was the name that made them go there. 'There's white geese in that name,' said Henry, telling it to Edna. 'And a river and little low houses with old men sitting outside them—old sea captains with wooden legs winding up their watches, and there are little shops with lamps in the windows.'

It was too late for them to see the geese or the old men, but the river was there and the houses and even the shops with lamps. In one a woman sat working a sewing-machine on the counter. They heard the whirring hum and they saw her big shadow filling the shop. 'Too full for a single customer,' said Henry. 'It is a perfect place.'

The houses were small and covered with creepers and ivy. Some of them had worn wooden steps leading up to the doors. You had to go down a little flight of steps to enter some of the others; and just across the road—to be seen from every window—was the river, with a walk beside it and some high poplar trees.

'This is the place for us to live in,' said Henry. 'There's a house to let, too. I wonder if it would wait if we asked it. I'm sure it would.'

'Yes, I would like to live there,' said Edna. They crossed the road and she leaned against the trunk of a tree and looked up at the empty house, with a dreamy smile.

'There is a little garden at the back, dear,' said Henry, 'a lawn with one tree on it and some daisy bushes round the wall. At night the stars shine in the tree like tiny candles. And inside there are two rooms downstairs and a big room with folding doors upstairs and above that an attic. And there are eight stairs to the kitchen—

very dark, Edna. You are rather frightened of them, you know. "Henry, dear, would you mind bringing the lamp? I just want to make sure that Euphemia has raked out the fire before we go to bed."'

'Yes,' said Edna. 'Our bedroom is at the very top—that room with the two square windows. When it is quiet we can hear the river flowing and the sound of the poplar trees far, far away, rustling and flowing in our dreams, darling.'

'You're not cold—are you?' he said, suddenly.

'No—no, only happy.'

'The room with the folding doors is yours.' Henry laughed. 'It's a mixture—it isn't a room at all. It's full of your toys and there's a big blue chair in it where you sit curled up in front of the fire with the flames in your curls—because though we're married you refuse to put your hair up and only tuck it inside your coat for the church service. And there's a rug on the floor for me to lie on, because I'm so lazy. Euphemia—that's our servant—only comes in the day. After she's gone we go down to the kitchen and sit on the table and eat an apple, or perhaps we make some tea, just for the sake of hearing the kettle sing. That's not joking. If you listen to a kettle right through it's like an early morning in Spring.'

'Yes, I know,' she said. 'All the different kinds of birds.'

A little cat came through the railings of the empty house and into the road. Edna called it and bent down and held out her hands—'Kitty! Kitty!' The little cat ran to her and rubbed against her knees.

'If we're going for a walk just take the cat and put it inside the front door,' said Henry, still pretending. 'I've got the key.'

They walked across the road and Edna stood stroking the cat in her arms while Henry went up the steps and pretended to open the door.

He came down again quickly. 'Let's go away at once. It's going to turn into a dream.'

The night was dark and warm. They did not want to go home. 'What I feel so certain of is,' said Henry, 'that we ought to be living there, now. We oughtn't to wait for things. What's age? You're as old as you'll ever be and so am I. You know,' he said, 'I have a feeling often and often that it's dangerous to wait for things—that if you wait for things they only go further and further away.'

'But, Henry,—money! You see we haven't any money.'

'Oh, well,—perhaps if I disguised myself as an old man we could get a job as caretakers in some large house—that would be rather fun. I'd make up a terrific history of the house if anyone came to look over it and you could dress up and be the ghost moaning and wringing your hands in the deserted picture gallery, to frighten them off. Don't you ever feel that money is more or less accidental—that if one really wants things it's either there or it doesn't matter?'

She did not answer that—she looked up at the sky and said, 'Oh dear, I don't want to go home.'

'Exactly—that's the whole trouble—and we oughtn't to go home. We ought to be going back to the house and find an odd saucer to give the cat the dregs of the milk-jug in. I'm not really laughing—I'm not even happy. I'm lonely for you, Edna—I would give anything to lie down and cry' . . . and he added limply, 'with my head in your lap and your darling cheek in my hair.'

'But, Henry,' she said, coming closer, 'you have faith, haven't you? I mean you are absolutely certain that we shall have a house like that and everything we want—aren't you?'

'Not enough—that's not enough. I want to be sitting on those very stairs and taking off these very boots this very minute. Don't you? Is faith enough for you?'

'If only we weren't so young . . .' she said miserably. 'And yet,' she sighed, 'I'm sure I don't feel very young—I feel twenty at least.'

Henry lay on his back in the little wood. When he moved the dead leaves rustled beneath him, and above his head the new leaves quivered like fountains of green water steeped in sunlight. Somewhere out of sight Edna was gathering primroses. He had been so full of dreams that morning that he could not keep pace with her delight in the flowers. 'Yes, love, you go and come back for me. I'm too lazy.' She had thrown off her hat and knelt down beside him, and by and by her voice and her footsteps had grown fainter. Now the wood was silent except for the leaves, but he knew that she was not far away and he moved so that the tips of his fingers touched her pink jacket. Ever since waking he had felt so strangely that he was not really awake at all, but just dreaming. The time before, Edna was a dream and now he and she were dreaming together and somewhere in some dark place another dream waited for him. 'No, that can't be true because I can't ever imagine the world without us. I feel that we two together mean something that's got to be there just as naturally as trees or birds or clouds.' He tried to remember what it had felt like without Edna, but he could not get back to those days. They were hidden by her; Edna, with the marigold hair and strange, dreamy smile filled him up to the brim. He breathed her; he ate and drank her. He walked about with a shining ring of Edna keeping the world away or touching whatever it lighted on with its own beauty. 'Long after you have stopped laughing,' he told her, 'I can hear your laugh running up and down my veins—and yet—are we a dream?' And suddenly he saw himself and Edna as two very small children walking through the streets, looking through windows, buying things and playing with them, talking to each other, smiling—he saw even their gestures and the way they stood, so often, quite still, face to face—and then he rolled over and pressed his face in the leaves—faint with longing. He wanted to kiss Edna, and to put his arms round her and press her to him and feel her cheek hot against his kiss and kiss her until he'd no breath left and so stifle the dream.

'No, I can't go on being hungry like this,' said Henry, and jumped up and began to run in the direction she had gone. She had wandered a long way. Down in a green hollow he saw her kneeling, and when she saw him she waved and said—'Oh, Henry—such beauties! I've never seen such beauties. Come and look.' By the time he had reached her he would have cut off his hand rather than spoil her happiness. How strange Edna was that day! All the time she talked to Henry her eyes laughed; they were sweet and mocking. Two little spots of colour like strawberries glowed on her cheeks and 'I wish I could feel tired,' she kept saying. 'I want to walk over the whole world until I die. Henry—come along. Walk faster—Henry! If I start flying suddenly, you'll promise to catch hold of my feet, won't you? Otherwise I'll never come down.' And 'Oh,' she cried, 'I am so happy. I'm so frightfully happy!' They came to a weird place, covered with heather. It was early afternoon and the sun streamed down upon the purple.

'Let's rest here a little,' said Edna, and she waded into the heather and lay down. 'Oh, Henry, it's so lovely. I can't see anything except the little bells and the sky.'

Henry knelt down by her and took some primroses out of her

basket and made a long chain to go round her throat. 'I could almost fall asleep,' said Edna. She crept over to his knees and lay hidden in her hair just beside him. 'It's like being under the sea, isn't it, dearest, so sweet and so still?'

'Yes,' said Henry, in a strange husky voice. 'Now I'll make you one of violets.' But Edna sat up. 'Let's go in,' she said.

They came back to the road and walked a long way. Edna said, 'No, I couldn't walk over the world—I'm tired now.' She trailed on the grass edge of the road. 'You and I are tired, Henry! How much further is it?'

'I don't know—not very far,' said Henry, peering into the distance. Then they walked in silence.

'Oh,' she said at last, 'it really is too far, Henry, I'm tired and I'm hungry. Carry my silly basket of primroses.' He took them without looking at her.

At last they came to a village and a cottage with a notice 'Teas Provided'.

'This is the place,' said Henry. 'I've often been here. You sit on the little bench and I'll go and order the tea.' She sat down on the bench, in the pretty garden all white and yellow with spring flowers. A woman came to the door and leaned against it watching them eat. Henry was very nice to her, but Edna did not say a word. 'You haven't been here for a long spell,' said the woman.

'No—the garden's looking wonderful.'

'Fair,' said she. 'Is the young lady your sister?' Henry nodded Yes, and took some jam.

'There's a likeness,' said the woman. She came down into the garden and picked a head of white jonquils and handed it to Edna. 'I suppose you don't happen to know anyone who wants a cottage,' said she. 'My sister's taken ill and she left me hers. I want to let it.'

'For a long time?' asked Henry, politely.

'Oh,' said the woman vaguely, 'that depends.'

Said Henry, 'Well—I might know of somebody—could we go and look at it?'

'Yes, it's just a step down the road, the little one with the apple trees in front—I'll fetch you the key.'

While she was away Henry turned to Edna and said, 'Will you come?' She nodded.

They walked down the road and in through the gate and up the

grassy path between the pink and white trees. It was a tiny place—
two rooms downstairs and two rooms upstairs. Edna leaned out of
the top window, and Henry stood at the doorway. 'Do you like it?'
he asked.

'Yes,' she called, and then made a place for him at the window.
'Come and look. It's so sweet.'

He came and leant out of the window. Below them were the
apple trees tossing in a faint wind that blew a long piece of Edna's
hair across his eyes. They did not move. It was evening—the pale
green sky was sprinkled with stars. 'Look!' she said—'stars, Henry.'
'There will be a moon in two T's,' said Henry.

She did not seem to move and yet she was leaning against Henry's
shoulder; he put his arm round her—'Are all those trees down
there—apple?' she asked in a shaky voice.

'No, darling,' said Henry. 'Some of them are full of angels and
some of them are full of sugar almonds—but evening light is awfully
deceptive.' She sighed. 'Henry—we mustn't stay here any longer.'

He let her go and she stood up in the dusky room and touched
her hair. 'What has been the matter with you all day?' she said—
and then did not wait for an answer but ran to him and put her
arms round his neck, and pressed his head into the hollow of her
shoulder. 'Oh,' she breathed, 'I do love you. Hold me, Henry.' He
put his arms round her, and she leaned against him and looked into
his eyes. 'Hasn't it been terrible, all today?' said Edna. 'I knew what
was the matter and I've tried every way I could to tell you that I
wanted you to kiss me—that I'd quite got over the feeling.'

'You're perfect, perfect, perfect,' said Henry.

'The thing is,' said Henry, 'how am I going to wait until evening?'
He took his watch out of his pocket, went into the cottage and
popped it into a china jar on the mantelpiece. He'd looked at it
seven times in one hour, and now he couldn't remember what time
it was. Well, he'd look once again. Half-past four. Her train arrived
at seven. He'd have to start for the station at half-past six. Two
hours more to wait. He went through the cottage again—downstairs and upstairs. 'It looks lovely,' he said. He went into the garden and picked a round bunch of white pinks and put them in a
vase on the little table by Edna's bed. 'I don't believe this,' thought
Henry. 'I don't believe this for a minute. It's too much. She'll be

here in two hours and we'll walk home, and then I'll take that white jug off the kitchen table and go across to Mrs Biddie's and get the milk, and then come back, and when I come back she'll have lighted the lamp in the kitchen and I'll look through the window and see her moving about in the pool of lamplight. And then we shall have supper, and after supper (Bags I washing up!) I shall put some wood on the fire and we'll sit on the hearth-rug and watch it burning. There won't be a sound except the wood and perhaps the wind will creep round the house once. . . . And then we shall change our candles and she will go up first with her shadow on the wall beside her, and she will call out, Good-night, Henry—and I shall answer—Good-night, Edna. And then I shall dash upstairs and jump into bed and watch the tiny bar of light from her room brush my door, and the moment it disappears will shut my eyes and sleep until morning. Then we'll have all tomorrow and tomorrow and tomorrow night. Is she thinking all this, too? Edna, come quickly!

> Had I two little wings,
> And were a little feathery bird,
> To you I'd fly, my dear—

No, no, dearest. . . . Because the waiting is a sort of Heaven, too, darling. If you can understand that. Did you ever know a cottage could stand on tip-toe. This one is doing it now.'

He was downstairs and sat on the doorstep with his hands clasped round his knees. That night when they found the village—and Edna said, 'Haven't you faith, Henry?' 'I hadn't then. Now I have,' he said, 'I feel just like God.'

He leaned his head against the lintel. He could hardly keep his eyes open, not that he was sleepy, but . . . for some reason . . . and a long time passed.

Henry thought he saw a big white moth flying down the road. It perched on the gate. No, it wasn't a moth. It was a little girl in a pinafore. What a nice little girl, and he smiled in his sleep, and she smiled, too, and turned in her toes as she walked. 'But she can't be living here,' thought Henry. 'Because this is ours. Here she comes.'

When she was quite close to him she took her hand from under her pinafore and gave him a telegram and smiled and went away. There's a funny present! thought Henry, staring at it. 'Perhaps it's only a make-believe one, and it's got one of those snakes inside it that fly up at you.' He laughed gently in the dream and opened it very carefully. 'It's just a folded paper.' He took it out and spread it open.

The garden became full of shadows—they span a web of darkness over the cottage and the trees and Henry and the telegram. But Henry did not move.

PHYLLIS BENTLEY

Love and Money

I

WHEN Lavinia Crabtree married Walter Egmont just after the first
World War, Walter was a large, handsome easy-going young man
in his late twenties, who had just ceased to be a captain in one of
the West Riding regiments, and wore a decoration said to be well-
deserved. He was rich, and well-born as Annotsfield understood the
term, for he belonged to one of those textile families which had
made cloth on the banks of the river Ire for goodness knew how
long and had enjoyed wealth since the coming of the Industrial
Revolution. His people lived in a large mid-Victorian mansion in
the Ire Valley known as Mount Hall, there was a baronetcy somewhere among his cousins, the fact that his ancestors had probably
been Flemish weavers was long forgotten, and the Egmonts mixed
with 'county' society. In short, Walter was quite the best match in
Annotsfield at that time.

Accordingly a good deal of irritation and scepticism was expressed
when Lavinia Crabtree, who did not come out of the same social
drawer at all and it was no use pretending otherwise, got hold of
Walter. Her father was in textiles too, of course—who in Annotsfield
wasn't?—but the difference between Messrs Crabtree and Crabtree's
small backstreet premises and the huge Egmont mills was as vast as
that in those days between the Annotsfield secondary school which
had sharpened Lavinia's wits, and the famous public school which
Walter had attended. How ever had Lavinia met Walter in the first
place? At the Annotsfield Choral Society, replied rumour. A famous
tenor who came to sing in the *Messiah* was staying with the Egmonts,
who were always musically inclined, so naturally Walter and his
mother (a widow at this time) went behind the scenes in the interval to drink coffee with the conductor and artists. Lavinia, whose
clear, penetrating, and accurate if small soprano had won her a place

in the choir, was helping to serve the coffee—just like her, said rumour unkindly; always fussing about and managing everything—and some incident concerning a dropped cup or missing sugar had placed the Egmonts under a small obligation to her.

In fact, while Lavinia fussed at Mrs Egmont's elbow with the sugar bowl, that large lady, turning aside impatiently, spilt her coffee over Lavinia's *de rigueur* white choral frock. Accordingly when Walter saw Lavinia at the Annotsfield Mayor's Ball he felt obliged to ask her to dance with him—just like Walter, said rumour, shaking its head; the kindest, the nicest, the most chivalrous and truly *gentlemanly* man, was Walter Egmont—and of course after that he had no *chance*. Lavinia was shrewd, and pretty enough in a way though a poky little thing, said rumour (reluctantly signing a cheque for a wedding present suitable to the Egmont status); she couldn't be shaken off once she got her claws into him. It was said that Mrs Egmont senior disliked the match and opposed it bitterly, and certainly she withdrew from Mount Hall and went to live in Bournemouth, where she soon conveniently died. Councillor Crabtree, on the other hand, determined to show that his daughter was as good as any Egmont, settled a row of small houses, called Irebridge Terrace, on her by way of marriage portion. One must admit, concluded rumour grudgingly, that Lavinia adored Walter—but so she should considering all he offered her; it was easy to adore such a husband as Walter Egmont in 1919.

Rumour was correct in several of its external facts, as rumour often is. But the details of the incident at the Mayor's Ball which bound Walter to Lavinia were known only to Walter, Lavinia, and Mrs Egmont senior. If Mrs Egmont senior could have been omitted from that list, perhaps everything would have turned out differently.

Probably only those who belonged to that first war generation will remember what a craze for dancing seized upon the young men and women returning from the war. They danced morning, noon, and night; they drove about the country in search of dancing; some of them thronged to dancing classes to learn the latest variants of the art. Lavinia, whose ambitious parents wished to give her every possible social advantage, had had the very best dancing tuition available in Annotsfield, and her mind, clear and sharp like her voice, had picked up accurately every turn and twist imposed by local fashion. She was small and neat and performed these (sometimes rather ridiculous) turns with an earnest precision rather lacking in grace. Walter, on the other hand, tall and big and careless, had certainly not thought that attendance at dancing classes was the sort of thing Walter Egmont should do. Accordingly he lumbered along through the tango he and Lavinia were supposed to be dancing, in a cheerful waltzing style, rather amused than otherwise by the antics about him, protecting Lavinia skilfully with his large person from clashing couples, humming the tune below his breath, occasionally smiling kindly down at the thin little girl quivering anxiously in his arms, but not in the least attempting the proper steps. Lavinia tripped over his feet.

'Sorry,' apologized Walter cheerfully, holding her up firmly in his massive arms.

'Sorry,' he said a moment later, as she tripped again.

Her third stumble produced more serious results, for Lavinia, quite off balance, positively butted his white shirt-front with her head. She blushed crimson with mortification, for several passing couples had seen the *contretemps* and smiled, no doubt thinking it all her fault.

'I'm afraid I'm not very good at this dance, what?' said Walter in his deep pleasant tones. 'Let's give up, shall we?'

He tucked her skinny little arm beneath his and led her from the ballroom. Just outside the door there was a foyer, quite empty, surrounded by settees and palms. The empty space of the foyer was Lavinia's undoing.

'The steps are quite easy, really,' ventured Lavinia.

'I daresay,' agreed Walter, steering her towards the least languishing settee.

'They go like this, you see,' said Lavinia. She detached her arm from Walter's and began to tango alone up and down the foyer, counting and explaining the steps.

'You just go on doing the same series of steps over and over again,' she said. 'You see, it's quite easy. If you'd just try, I'm sure you'd find it easy,' she pleaded, stretching a hand out as if to take one of Walter's. 'It's easiest at first to do it side by side.'

'Well,' said Walter, colouring with embarrassment: 'Perhaps some other time. . . .'

'Why not now?' said Lavinia brightly. She picked up his hand where it lay limply down his trouser-seam and gave him a little pull towards her. 'Like this—*one* and *two* and——'

It was at this moment that Mrs Egmont senior, escorted by a 'regular' colonel in full-dress scarlet, swept across the foyer. Her look of horror as she perceived her son—*her son*—playing tricks of some kind in a public room with a common little girl in a rather sharp shade of pink, was for a moment uncontrollable and Lavinia received its full blast. Then Mrs Egmont with an effort composed her features.

'Are you coming up soon to the buffet, Walter?' she drawled in a cold commanding tone.

'In a moment, mother,' returned Walter, courteous and easy as always.

A trifle reassured—her son quite lacked the confusion of guilt— Mrs Egmont swept on towards the staircase.

Walter and Lavinia sat down on a settee side by side. There was a pause.

'I'm terribly sorry,' gulped Lavinia at length.

'For what? It was very kind of you to try to teach me—I'm very grateful,' said the chivalrous Walter. 'Only I'm no good at that kind of thing, I'm afraid.'

'It's very good of you to take it like that, Captain Egmont,' said Lavinia in a trembling tone.

'Not a captain now,' said Walter mildly.

For the first time since the débacle he looked at her, and saw to his horror that tears were standing in her eyes. All his protective instinct rushed up to the summons of a woman's tears. Poor little kid, he thought, with her thin dark hair so carefully screwed up into those tight curls at the back, and her awful dress, and her bright dark eyes. Her neck and arms were very thin. . . . There was a kind of childishness and innocence about her. . . . Only a very inexperienced girl would try to teach a fellow to dance at a Mayor's Ball, he thought.

'I was wondering,' he began in his most deferential tone, 'whether you would possibly have a dance of another kind with me, later? Lancers, you know, or a waltz—something I know and wouldn't be such a fool at? If you would forgive me, and let me have the first extra, I should be very grateful.'

'Oh, Captain Egmont!' breathed Lavinia, gazing at him adoringly. To be swept up out of the profound humiliation of a fearful social blunder to the heights of having two dances with Walter Egmont, was a transition from hell to heaven; she could have fallen in gratitude at his feet. The tears overflowed.

'Here, take this,' said Walter Egmont gruffly, proffering a large clean linen handkerchief.

Six months later they were married.

2

At first all went well. Walter seemed to enjoy tenderly and gravely instructing Lavinia in the ways of her new life; clearly his protective feelings must always have been very strong and were now finding full scope. On her side, Lavinia learned quickly; her nature was active and industrious and she became quite an efficient châtelaine of Mount Hall—perhaps just a little over-fussy at times when a full glass fell to the carpet or Walter was late for a meal, but no worse than many other wives of similar standing. She now dressed reasonably well in a dull way, knew the proper things to say, and altogether interfered with Walter's pursuits less than his friends had feared. Meanwhile the Annotsfield Corporation ran a new bus route along Irebridge Terrace, where Lavinia's dowry houses stood; the houses became shops and their rentable value rose considerably, which was pleasant—it was nice for Lavinia to have a little pocket-money of her own.

The first ill luck of the Walter Egmonts was in the matter of children. Lavinia experienced a terribly difficult confinement with her first child, and the little girl, christened Edith May after her two grandmothers, was born with a delicate constitution and a slight malformation of the left foot. Lavinia, who had really been very ill, rose up from bed before she was fit to do so in order to care for the child. Her devotion to little May was so intense and so tireless, with massage and medicaments whether internal or external she was so punctual and so exact, that the women of the Egmont circle began to feel a very considerable respect for her. That child owes Lavinia her life twice over, they said. Only Lavinia's absolute devotion has kept the poor little thing alive at all. But the Walter Egmonts had no more children, and—though May was a sweet, bright child—this must have been a great disappointment to them; whether it was due just to bad luck, or because Lavinia was not willing to try again on account of the bad time she'd had, or because the chivalrous Walter did not wish her to run the risk of another painful and dangerous confinement, was not of course publicly known, though the last alternative was regarded as most likely.

Presently Councillor Crabtree, during an outburst of fury at the General Strike of 1926, had a stroke and died. His affairs were found to be in some disorder. Walter of course tidied them up; it was rumoured that he found himself quite a bit out of pocket as a result. The widowed Mrs Crabtree was taken to live at Mount Hall. This could only be regarded as yet another piece of ill luck, for she was rather a disagreeable old woman, used to having her own way and horridly penetrating. Lavinia's care for her was really quite exemplary, and callers winced sympathetically for her beneath her mother's sarcasms.

The next piece of ill luck for Walter and Lavinia was that Councillor Crabtree's former partner, Lavinia's uncle Thomas Crabtree, quietly shot himself in order to avoid bankruptcy. It was now getting on towards the end of the nineteen-twenties, and the terrible shadow of business regression was creeping over England. Bankruptcy and suicide were not as unfamiliar now in the West Riding as they used to be, and nobody blamed Walter Egmont for allowing the Crabtree bankruptcy proceedings to take their course without any proffers of assistance on his part.

'No use throwing good money after bad,' said the West Riding textile trade sagely.

Walter Egmont did, however, take into his household Lavinia's youngest cousin Janet, a quiet, plain, good girl of seventeen or so, who made herself useful at Mount Hall—earned her keep, as it were—by helping to look after old Mrs Crabtree and little lame May.

So far, so good, one might say. Walter and Lavinia have had their troubles, but only such as the usual chances and changes of this mortal life might bring upon them. Walter has been the source, the well-spring, of all wealth and comfort; Lavinia has gladly received wealth and comfort from him for herself and her relations.

But now a change seemed to come over Walter. He became absent-minded and irritable. He looked haggard. He slept ill. He scolded the gardener over some twopenny-ha'penny bill for bulbs—he who had so often gently led Lavinia along the paths of open-handed liberality. He drove off in the morning to the Egmont mills with a look on his face as if he were a Christian entering a lion-filled arena; he returned at night pale, without appetite, exhausted. When Lavinia urged him to see a doctor, he positively shouted at her.

'Nonsense! Don't talk such nonsense, Vinny! I'm perfectly well!'

His uneasy, angry tone alarmed his wife and frightened May, who burst into tears.

'Don't cry, my darling. Don't mind Daddy,' said Walter, drawing the child to him and kissing her. Then he put her gently away, rose, pressed his wife's arm affectionately and left the room. Lavinia, May, and Janet were left staring at each other in dismay.

The truth was very simple. It was now 1931, and the fearful business slump had reached even the Egmont mills. There were few customers for the Egmont cloth, and those there were wished to buy it at the current low price, whereas it had been made from yarn bought from the spinner at a much higher price a month or two ago. One could either give in and cease to make cloth, in which case one was irretrievably bankrupt and ruined; or one could struggle on making cloth for stock, hoping for better days, and finding the money for the wages bill and the spinner's monthly account by throwing into the battle all one's other resources. The bank in Annotsfield, where once the Egmont credit was immense, impregnable, had now advanced an overdraft of many thousands of pounds to Walter, and held as security against it all the scrip of his other investments, together with the title deeds of the mills fabric and the Mount Hall estate. The date of the month when the just-mentioned incident occurred was the twenty-third. At that time—it is altered now—by long tradition the spinner's monthly account must inexorably be paid on the twenty-fifth. In spite of all his efforts, Walter was some three thousand pounds short of the necessary amount, and ruin, as the phrase goes, stared him in the face.

After a few moments he returned, looking white but composed, and said to his wife:

'I'd like to speak to you privately, Vinny.'

Lavinia rose and followed him to the room he called his study.

'Vinny,' said Walter quietly. 'My dear. I regret the necessity deeply, but I'm afraid I must ask you for some help.'

'Help? You're ill?' cried Lavinia.

'No. I am in financial difficulties,' said Walter.

Lavinia's eyes widened, and she gazed at him with incredulity.

'Everyone in the West Riding is more or less in financial difficulties today,' said Walter. 'I don't think I am more to blame than the next man. However, that's beside the point. The facts are——'

He explained his situation in simple terms, and concluded by asking her to lend him the title-deeds of her row of houses, so that he could deposit them at the bank and receive the necessary additional overdraft on their security.

'Will you do that for me, Vinny?'

'Of course, Walter,' said Lavinia smoothly.

She looked down at her hands and did not meet his grateful, loving gaze.

3

In Balzac's novel *La Cousine Bette* there is a superb passage where Bette, the old maid 'poor relation', hitherto meekly devoted to the interests of the family, suddenly discovers that the affections of the young Polish sculptor she loves and has befriended have been stolen from her by her pretty niece Hortense. Suddenly, says Balzac, her nature, like a branch hitherto pegged down to earth, was released from its ties and flew up with terrible force to its true line.

Something of this kind must have happened to Lavinia Egmont. Perhaps she had never really forgiven the Egmonts for that awful ballroom scene? Perhaps she had always at the bottom of her heart resented Walter's chivalry, his continual giving? (Who after all wants to be the everlasting object of chivalry, the continual recipient in the human exchange?) At any rate, in that moment Lavinia's whole aspect changed. Released from its obligations of gratitude, her nature flew up into its natural shape of domination.

Walter first became aware of this on the following morning when he took Lavinia to the manager of his bank in Annotsfield to deposit the title-deeds of Irebridge Terrace. He removed the deeds from his safe at Mount Hall, where they had reposed since Councillor Crabtree's death—in point of fact Walter had paid out as much to tidy up the Councillor's affairs as would have bought the whole Terrace outright, but this thought did not occur to him—and put them with a grave smile into Lavinia's hands, who took them firmly. Walter found himself a little surprised; he had somehow expected that his wife would return them to him. Of course Lavinia's signature would be necessary at the bank and the transaction of depositing the deeds must be officially hers, but somehow Walter did not quite like her attitude of possession meanwhile. It would have been more graceful if she had quickly and as it were warmly and sympathetically returned the deeds, pressing them urgently upon him. Lavinia, however, held them firmly in her lap throughout their drive to the bank. Still—this was just one of those failures in Lavinia, due to her faulty upbringing, which excited Walter's tenderest pity and love.

The interview was extremely painful to Walter; so painful indeed that sweat not only stood on his forehead but actually rolled down to his cheek. The thought that he, Walter Egmont, should positively have to borrow his wife's little property to extricate the great Egmont mills from a threat of bankruptcy, was terrible to him. He breathed quickly and felt choked in the manager's snug sanctum; he moved his big body about restlessly; he spoke with feverish haste; his great desire—the only one left in his life, he felt at that moment— was to get out of the bank into the air. Sign the papers, leave the deeds, get out. But the bank manager felt it his duty to explain to Lavinia exactly what the deposit of her title-deeds as security implied, and from that point, in some way which Walter did not quite understand, the man was led to embark on a résumé of the whole Egmont mills situation. The bank manager—who of course was in an agony himself, on the one hand continually pressed by his Head Office to tidy up the bank's quite frightful financial commitments in the West Riding and on the other seeing long-established businesses collapse at his mere word—concealed his trouble by an artificial smoothness, but his bland phrases dropped like some colourless but corrosive acid on Walter's skin, till he felt raw and bleeding from top to toe.

Lavinia on the other hand listened with keen attention. From the manager's admirably clear exposition she fully gasped the essential fact that she, Lavinia Crabtree, could save or ruin the great Egmonts by merely saying yes or no. She looked down at her hands to conceal the triumph which shone in her eyes.

'This is only a temporary measure—you'll soon have your deeds back, Lavinia, I promise you,' said Walter hoarsely.

'I shall be most happy to return them to Mrs Egmont as soon as this portion of the overdraft is cleared,' said the bank manager, bowing gravely to Lavinia.

At last the thing was done and they were outside.

'Thank you, Vinny my dear,' said Walter heavily. 'Now about the

car—we must get you home again—I'll get Brigg to drop me at
the mill and——'

He was about to make one of his usual courteous and generous
arrangements for his wife's comfort when Lavinia interrupted.

'I've some shopping to do in Resmond Street; Brigg can drive
me there,' she said.

Walter, though astonished and disconcerted, did not realize that
he was hearing Lavinia's first assertion of power. The power of
wealth. For all possession is wealth when others need it.

4

Lavinia's metamorphosis was physical as well as spiritual. She held
herself erect; her bust swelled; her dark eyes sharpened. Her thin
mouth now often wore a sophisticated, almost a quietly merry little
twist of triumph at its left corner—for example, when she was
winning a skirmish against old Mrs Crabtree, whom she defeated
with increasing frequency these days. Lavinia now chose her clothes
better and wore them with infinitely more assurance; she dressed
her hair in clearer lines. Her speech became more resonant, more
emphatic, more commanding; her vocabulary seemed to increase
and her accent improve.

Meanwhile, she 'stood by' Walter in his troubles in a most staunch
and wifely manner. She economized, she cut down staff, she undertook domestic duties herself and carried them out in a robustly
cheerful and efficient way. It was largely due to Lavinia, said elderly
Egmont aunts and young Egmont cousins, whose living all depended
upon the family business, that the mill pulled through the depression so well. Lavinia knew all its affairs, and questioned Walter every
day to keep her knowledge up to date. Her judgement was shrewd.
She harassed and harangued the easy-going Walter, she kept him up
to the mark and would not allow him to be generous and foolish.
If he showed a disposition to allow a merchant to cancel purchases
or to purchase at a lower price than he had contracted for, Lavinia
shut her mouth with a snap, gazed at Walter meaningly and was
silent. Walter then remembered the houses in Irebridge Terrace and
did as Lavinia wished.

Indeed, the real reason why the Egmont mills survived the slump
was probably because Walter gradually came to feel that Lavinia's
Irebridge Terrace houses must be retrieved if it was the last thing

he did—he couldn't even die till that damned terrace was redeemed. He stuck at the job, he declined to be defeated, he even learned to juggle bank accounts, and twice purposely missed the last post with cheques so as to give himself a few extra hours to ensure that they could be honoured. He rushed after business, he wrangled over details, he quite hounded his employees—who, terrified of being dismissed to join the ever-lengthening queue at the Labour Exchange, shared his anxiety to keep the mill afloat.

Walter did all this, and it saved the Egmont mills. But it was against his nature and he loathed it, and strange uneasy feelings increasingly troubled his hitherto uncomplicated heart.

England went off the gold standard. The slump slowly passed. The West Riding climbed painfully to its knees, and though trailing about its body like heavy weeds innumerable debts, overdrafts, mortgage payments and obligations, eventually stood up and raised its head. The Irebridge Terrace deeds had once or twice almost emerged from the bank's strong-room before but had been sucked back again by recurring emergencies. Now at last they could safely be released. Walter came home one evening with the long envelope in his hand and went into Lavinia's bedroom, where he could hear her talking on the telephone—he had been sleeping in his dressing-room lately, for he was suffering from obstinate insomnia and did not wish to disturb his wife.

Lavinia was laying down the law to the unfortunate secretary of some committee or other of which she was chairman, for she was chairman of many committees nowadays. In firm clear concise terms she informed the secretary of her duty and left her no alternative but to proceed with it promptly. As she nodded to her husband across the telephone, her eyes held that satisfied gleam which now so often brightened—and hardened—them. She finished the conversation and put the receiver down decisively.

'Yes, Walter?' she said.

'Here are the deeds of your Irebridge Terrace houses, Vinny,' said Walter, proffering the envelope. 'I'm glad I can put them safely in your hands again at last.'

He smiled, not without a touch of pride, and, simple loyal creature that he still was, expected a kiss, some thanks, a word of wifely praise. Instead he saw a strange expression cross his wife's face. She looked quite disconcerted and vexed, he thought. In fact, she looked disappointed. She *is* disappointed, thought Walter, amazed. She liked me to be in her debt. She liked me to be under an obligation to her. All the vague distaste and revolt he had felt recently suddenly rose up in him like a flood of nausea. He choked it down, but when it had gone he knew he no longer loved his wife.

'What shall we do about Janet?' said Lavinia crossly.

She was thinking aloud. As long as Walter was in her debt for the loan of the houses, she did not mind that he should have to support her cousin. But now Walter was out of her debt and she did not wish to return to the old humiliating situation of being in his debt—certainly not on Janet's account.

'Janet?' said Walter, perplexed by this to him inexplicable transition. (To Walter obligations were not measured in cash.) He worked it out on his own lines, slowly. 'You mean you think we ought to pay her, now that we can afford?'

'*Pay* her?'

'For looking after May, and being a kind of secretary to you, and so on.'

'Janet has too great a sense of her obligation to me to think of such a thing,' said Lavinia stiffly.

'What's the problem then?'

'Oh, never mind. You wouldn't understand,' said Lavinia.

'You say that rather too often to me nowadays, Vinny,' said Walter quietly.

Lavinia gave a brittle laugh. 'You used to say it to me.'

'I never said it to you.'

'Your mother did.'

'That's not the same thing, is it?'

'Oh, well—never mind. We must change or we shall be late,' said Lavinia dismissively.

She threw the packet of deeds carelessly down on the telephone table. They slipped off the edge and fell to the ground. Walter picked them up and replaced them on the table. He then without a word left his wife's bedroom, to which he never returned.

5

For several years after this incident the Egmonts maintained a decent façade of happy married life. Lavinia snapped at Walter more than was pleasant to hear, but then Lavinia nowadays snapped at everybody, so snapping at Walter meant nothing serious; it was clear she still regarded her husband with possessive conjugal affection. To Walter's friends it seemed that Walter's heart was not now in his married life, but he maintained his courtesy towards his wife so steadily that Lavinia did not perceive his alienation. Until one summer Sunday evening. In family life Sunday evening is often a dangerous time. The tedium of Sunday has accumulated, the problems of Monday loom; between boredom and apprehension the spirit tosses uneasily, vulnerable to offence.

Walter was sitting alone on the Mount Hall terrace, smoking a cigar. His large form overflowed the deck chair in which he lounged; one trouser leg, pulled up as he sat, revealed a cascading sock and an inch or two of ankle. Altogether he looked slack and dreamy and as if he were enjoying himself doing nothing, and this was irritating to the energetic Lavinia, who emerged from the french windows in a bad temper after a brush with her mother. The voices of May and Janet, who had been sent by Lavinia to water some prized antirrhinums at the side of the house, could be heard in the distance.

'Walter, have you written to your cousin?' said Lavinia sharply, referring to a letter of condolence she had urged Walter to despatch that night.

'No,' said Walter.

'Really, Walter!'

'I'm thinking what to say. I'll do it after supper.'

'Why not now?' said Lavinia with her infuriating smugness.

'The post's gone anyway.'

'Not in Annotsfield. Janet could easily run it down to the GPO.'

'I don't want to write it now, Lavinia,' said Walter quietly.

'No—you'd rather sit and do nothing. That's you all over, Walter. Nobody would ever do anything in this house if I didn't drive them to it.'

Walter still saying nothing and making no move, Lavinia's vexation mounted.

'If you knew how slack and stupid you look lounging there, Walter,' she said angrily in her quick vehement tones. 'You might be a young man in a dream of love.'

She laughed contemptuously.

Walter said nothing. Suddenly hot colour flooded Lavinia's face, she rushed forward to confront her husband and shouted:

'You are in love! You're in love with another woman!'

Walter slowly turned on her a strange deep look. Lavinia was used to seeing his brown eyes kind and attentive; tonight they appeared sardonic and cold.

'I'm certainly not in love with you, Lavinia,' he said.

Lavinia screamed abuse at him with all the fury of a woman quite unexpecting to be scorned.

'You vile beast! How dare you treat me so! And what about May?'

'Leave May out of this,' said Walter quickly.

'How can you leave her out?' shouted Lavinia, perceiving her advantage. 'If you don't give me your word of honour to give this up, I'll tell your daughter!'

'Tell her what, for heaven's sake?'

'About this—this affair of yours,' said Lavinia, trembling with fury.

'There's no affair. I've never spoken a word of love to any woman but you.'

'Give it up, or I'll tell your daughter—May shall know what kind of a man her father is, I promise you!'

'Lavinia, you're a wicked woman,' said Walter.

'Swear you'll give her up.'

'Give who up?'

'This woman of yours. Don't tell me you aren't in love with some woman or other, for I shan't believe you for a moment.'

'Very well. I won't tell you that. I will tell you that I've not the slightest intention of being unfaithful to my marriage vows—for May's sake.'

'You don't deny you're in love with someone?'

'What's the use, when you're determined not to believe me?'

'Did you call, mummy?' called May, limping round the side of the house.

'No, dear, no! Go on with your watering,' cried Lavinia, waving the child away imperiously. 'You had better keep your word, Walter,' she went on in a low savage tone, 'or I'll see to it that you never see May again. You're entirely in my power, you see. Just as you were over the house deeds.'

'Yes, I see that,' said Walter.

6

The Egmonts now gradually became known to their acquaintance as a typical example of the incompatible husband and wife who remain together only for the sake of their child. Walter's behaviour was courteous but cold and he avoided his wife's company whenever possible. Lavinia maintained the outward decencies, and did not attempt to discover the identity of the woman who had aroused those 'silly feelings' in Walter—she knew she could trust his word and unconsciously feared to rouse his anger by any such attempt, though to herself she said she could not 'condescend' to it. But she often wore her smile of triumph when she spoke to him; she was reflecting with satisfaction: 'Well, I nipped *that* in the bud.' People who first met Walter and Lavinia during this period could not believe that they had once been a mutually adoring couple. What had they ever had in common, enquired such new friends? Lavinia was widely detested for her intolerable bossiness, though almost as widely respected for her capacity to get public work done. Poor dear Walter was regarded as an absolute pet, but of course far too easy-going and slow. Where Lavinia's friends and her enemies concurred was in regarding her treatment of May as a mistake—though they differed as to its motive, her friends saying uneasily that Lavinia's devotion to the child led her astray, her enemies stating emphatically that Lavinia could not bear to let anyone in her power escape beyond its range.

Certainly Lavinia kept May at home all through her teens, allowing her to receive education only at a private day-school in Annotsfield, to and from which that nice Janet drove her every day. May's contemporaries, now that the slump was dissipating, went away to expensive boarding-schools—Roedean and Cheltenham and Wycombe or perhaps Harrogate; May would like to have followed their example and Walter was willing, but Lavinia scoffed the suggestion out of court. May, she said, was not strong enough yet to go away from home. May accepted this ruling dutifully, but listened to the school tales of returned cousins with such a wistful air that the hearts of mere friends quite ached for her, and even cross old Mrs Crabtree put in a plea on her behalf. This last interference excited Lavinia to fury. Having humiliated her mother into a palsied fury by reminding her that she was eating the bread of Walter's charity and had no right to a voice in any Egmont affairs, she swept off to the pleasant little room known as May's study, where she found May and Janet together, and demanded in ringing tones:

'Did you ask Grannie Crabtree to talk to me about going away to school, May?'

'No—yes—not exactly,' stammered May, her heart beating fast. 'She knew I wished to go—but I didn't ask her. That is——'

'I believe I mentioned it to Aunt Crabtree,' put in Janet quietly.

'Never *dare* to do such a thing again!' cried Lavinia at her most imperious. 'May is not fit to live a normal school life and the sooner she accepts that fact the better.'

She swept from the room. After a moment's pause, during which May sat white and trembling, her delicate mouth a-quiver, her large eyes full of tears, Janet sprang to the girl's side and took her in her arms. May buried her face on Janet's shoulder and the two wept together.

May was a clever, scholarly child, and another attempt was made to give full play to her undoubted ability when she reached university age. This time the attempt was supported by May's headmistress, whom most parents found formidable. But Lavinia easily defeated her.

'You are not a mother, Miss Pannell—you cannot quite enter into my feelings,' she said.

After this insulting thrust at Miss Pannell's spinsterhood she went on to hint at dark secrets in May's physiology; Miss Pannell withdrew her support from the university project and it fell to the ground.

So May stayed at home. Her life was not without its compensations, however. Lavinia indulged all her wishes save the one that really mattered, and May attended lectures and concerts and theatres, not only in Annotsfield but in Leeds and Bradford and even Manchester across the Pennines. It was observed that sometimes May was accompanied by her father, whom she loved dearly, sometimes by her mother, who loved her dearly, almost always by that nice Janet, her devoted companion, but never by Walter and Lavinia at the same time. There seemed to be a tacit understanding between husband and wife not to spoil each other's pleasure in their daughter's company. As the years went on it became generally recognized in Annotsfield that May Egmont—such beautiful eyes, my dear, and the sweetest disposition, musical too, such a shame about that foot—looked quite happy whenever her mother was not with her, and fortunately Lavinia was so busy nowadays with public Good Works (where bossiness had full scope) that she accompanied her daughter less frequently than of old.

Thus it happened that when one of the Armitages, a quiet, nice man in the thirties, a distant connection of the Egmonts with a university post in Oxford, began to pay 'attentions' to May, Lavinia was not there often enough to perceive their trend. She knew nothing of them, indeed, until one cold dark afternoon in the December of 1938. On sweeping into Mount Hall with her usual imperious step, smiling with triumphant glee over her chairmanship of the meeting that afternoon—she had got her own way by beating down a good deal of opposition—she learned from the maid that Miss Crabtree was upstairs reading the newspaper to old Mrs Crabtree, and Mr Egmont in the library having had tea.

'Where is May, Walter?' demanded Lavinia, sweeping in.

'She's gone to the Choral concert.'

'Oh—I'd forgotten it was tonight. But who's with her? And surely it's too early?' began Lavinia.

'Herbert Armitage has called and taken her off to the George for a bite before the show. I gave him my ticket,' drawled Walter.

'Herbert Armitage?' cried Lavinia in capital letters. 'You've let her go out alone with him?'

'Why not? I think he may possibly be attached to May, you know. A very nice fellow,' said Walter approvingly. 'No harm in being a little older. Suitable. Same tastes.'

'You don't mean to say he's thinking of *marrying* her?'

'He's hinted at it once or twice to me,' said Walter. 'In fact, I think he means to bring it to the point tonight.'

'She's much too young to think of such a thing.'

'She's eighteen.'

'It's preposterous! It's out of the question! You'll marry her off and then I suppose you think you'll be free to go off with *your* woman!' shouted Lavinia at the top of her voice.

Walter looked at her.

'Haven't you forgotten that yet, Lavinia?'

'No! And you haven't either,' said Lavinia brutally. 'Don't try to pretend to me that you have.'

'I've kept my word to you in the matter, however.'

'I'd soon have made you know it if you hadn't.'

Walter looked at her again.

'You were not like this when we married, Vinny,' he said.

'Whose fault is that?' cried Lavinia, rushing from the room.

She went straight out of the house by the side door to her car, which in spite of all her orders and instructions Brigg had not yet put away. Although this disobedience was at the moment convenient, it enraged Lavinia. The whole world seemed to conspire to thwart her, she thought as, panting slightly for she had put on weight the last few prosperous years, she climbed into the driving seat and slammed the door. Brigg delighted to misunderstand her instructions, Walter's whole heart was set on frustrating her, and now May! At the bottom of her heart Lavinia was deeply, painfully, unforgivably wounded by May's lack of confidence in her mother. That Walter should know about this Armitage man and not Lavinia! But Lavinia would show May! May should find out her mistake! May should learn she had a mother! Lavinia would confront the pair at the George. Of course, if May really wanted this Herbert Armitage ... But how could she? He was far too old, a dry old stick, not well-off—besides, May was not suited to the requirements of marriage, thought Lavinia, remembering with a pang compounded of jealousy, anger, and protective love, the misery of her own confinement. No! May must not marry! She must stay peacefully at home with her loving mother! It was important to catch them before the proposal was actually made, reflected Lavinia, swinging the car masterfully round into the front drive and pressing her foot on the accelerator.

7

The next moment, as it seemed, Lavinia opened her eyes to find herself gazing into the grave faces of Walter, May, Janet, old Mrs Crabtree, their family doctor and a starched white person who was presumably a nurse. It was daylight; the chill gloomy daylight of a winter dawn. The familiar furniture of her bedroom stood around her.

Lavinia had always been quick in the uptake, as the Yorkshire phrase goes, and she did not linger in comprehension now. She knew at once that in the dark she had driven full tilt into the left-hand pillar of the Mount Hall gateway, had smashed up herself and the car, and was now about to die.

She foresaw the consequences with her usual shrewdness. May would marry Herbert Armitage after her mother's death. Well, let her have him if she wants, thought Lavinia, feeling very virtuous at thus yielding to her daughter's wish, though in reality her motive was: 'If I can't be with May, neither shall Walter.' But Walter won't need May, she raced on; as soon as I'm dead Walter will of course rush after that woman of his, whoever she may be; he's only in his forties, he's still a good-looking man.

As she thought this, and gazed up into Walter's serious, pitying, but not grief-stricken face, a spasm of hatred convulsed Lavinia's heart.

'I'll stop it if it's the last thing I do,' she thought, grimly sardonic.

A smile of triumph curved her pale lips as in a flash she saw how the thing might be done.

'Walter,' she murmured. It was an effort to speak, but luckily, though her words came out in a hoarse croak, they were quite audible and distinct.

Walter gravely took her hand. For a moment his familiar clasp reminded her of the days when his touch had been an ecstasy, but this only strengthened her determination. He should not confer ecstasy on another woman.

'Walter,' she said: 'Look after May when I'm gone.'

'Yes, Vinny,' said Walter quietly.

'Walter, I want—I want—so as to be sure May is well looked after—I want you and Janet to marry and take care of her,' said Lavinia.

Walter's eyes widened and he gave her a strange look, while from the other side of the bed came a gasp. Lavinia decided not to make the effort needed to turn her head, but she knew that the gasp, of course, came from poor dear Janet. Oh, it was a wonderful stroke, wonderful! thought Lavinia with vindictive glee; killing two birds with one stone was nothing to it. A Crabtree cousin was handsomely provided for, a burden added to the Egmonts, and Walter kept for ever from his love. For he wouldn't dare to marry anybody but Janet after his wife had expressed a death-bed wish for the match. If he did everybody would talk, for of course the nurse would chatter; nurses always did. Lavinia smiled up at Walter in cruel triumph.

Just then a loud cackle came from old Mrs Crabtree, who was holding herself upright by clutching the foot of the bed in her gnarled hands. Lavinia looked at her. She read—correctly—what was in her mother's face. In horror she made a supreme effort, turned her eyes towards Janet and then towards Walter. Janet was softly radiant, Walter puzzled but content. Of course, of course! It was Janet whom Walter had been in love with all these last years! The good, quiet, nice Janet! Of course! They'd been too honourable to do anything about it, naturally, thought Lavinia with contempt, but Mrs Crabtree's basilisk eye could pierce the secrets of the most cunning hearts, let alone those so simple and straightforward as Janet's and Walter's. In a lurid flash of rage Lavinia perceived that her malice had overreached itself; her death-bed utterance had simply made it easy for Walter to marry his love. 'Well,' thought Lavinia angrily, 'at least I'll poison it for them; I'll——'

But it was too late now for Lavinia to do anything of any kind.

ALDOUS HUXLEY

Hubert and Minnie

FOR Hubert Lapell this first love affair was extremely important.
'Important' was the word he had used himself when he was writing about it in his diary. It was an event in his life, a real event for
a change. It marked, he felt, a genuine turning-point in his spiritual development.

'Voltaire,' he wrote in his diary—and he wrote it a second time
in one of his letters to Minnie—'Voltaire said that one died twice:
once with the death of the whole body and once before, with the
death of one's capacity to love. And in the same way one is born
twice, the second time being on the occasion when one first falls
in love. One is born, then, into a new world—a world of intenser
feelings, heightened values, more penetrating insights.' And so on.

In point of actual fact Hubert found this new world a little disappointing. The intenser feelings proved to be rather mild; not by
any means up to literary standards.

> I tell thee I am mad
> In Cressid's love. Thou answer'st: she is fair;
> Pour'st in the open ulcer of my heart
> Her eyes, her hair, her cheek, her gait, her voice. . . .

No, it certainly wasn't quite that. In his diary, in his letters to
Minnie, he painted, it is true, a series of brilliant and romantic
landscapes of the new world. But they were composite imaginary
landscapes in the manner of Salvator Rosa—richer, wilder, more
picturesquely clear-obscure than the real thing. Hubert would seize
with avidity on the least velleity of an unhappiness, a physical desire,
a spiritual yearning, to work it up in his letters and journals into
something substantially romantic. There were times, generally very
late at night, when he succeeded in persuading himself that he was
indeed the wildest, unhappiest, most passionate of lovers. But in the
daytime he went about his business nourishing something like a

grievance against love. The thing was a bit of a fraud; yes, really, he decided, rather a fraud. All the same, he supposed it was important.

For Minnie, however, love was no fraud at all. Almost from the first moment she had adored him. A common friend had brought him to one of her Wednesday evenings. 'This is Mr Lapell; but he's too young to be called anything but Hubert.' That was how he had been introduced. And, laughing, she had taken his hand and called him Hubert at once. He too had laughed, rather nervously. 'My name's Minnie,' she said. But he had been too shy to call her anything at all that evening. His brown hair was tufty and untidy, like a little boy's, and he had shy grey eyes that never looked at you for more than a glimpse at a time, but turned away almost at once, as though they were afraid. Quickly he glanced at you, eagerly—then away again; and his musical voice, with its sudden emphases, its quick modulations from high to low, seemed always to address itself to a ghost floating low down and a little to one side of the person to whom he was talking. Above the brows was a forehead beautifully domed, with a pensive wrinkle running up from between the eyes. In repose his full-lipped mouth pouted a little, as though he were expressing some chronic discontent with the world. And, of course, thought Minnie, the world wasn't beautiful enough for his idealism.

'But after all,' he had said earnestly that first evening, 'one has the world of thought to live in. That, at any rate, is simple and clear and beautiful. One can always live apart from the brutal scramble.'

And from the depths of the armchair in which, fragile, tired, and in these rather 'artistic' surroundings almost incongruously elegant, she was sitting, Helen Glamber laughed her clear little laugh. 'I think, on the contrary,' she said (Minnie remembered every incident of that first evening), 'I think one ought to rush about and know thousands of people, and eat and drink enormously, and make love incessantly, and shout and laugh and knock people over the head.' And having vented these Rabelaisian sentiments, Mrs Glamber dropped back with a sigh of fatigue, covering her eyes with a thin white hand; for she had a splitting headache, and the light hurt her.

'Really!' Minnie protested, laughing. She would have felt rather shocked if any one else had said that; but Helen Glamber was allowed to say anything.

Hubert reaffirmed his quietism. Elegant, weary, infinitely fragile, Mrs Glamber lay back in her armchair, listening. Or perhaps, under her covering hand, she was trying to go to sleep.

She had adored him at first sight. Now that she looked back she could see that it had been at first sight. Adored him protectively, maternally—for he was only twenty and very young, in spite of the wrinkle between his brows, and the long words, and the undergraduate's newly discovered knowledge; only twenty, and she was nearly twenty-nine. And she had fallen in love with his beauty, too. Ah, passionately.

Hubert, perceiving it later, was surprised and exceedingly flattered. This had never happened to him before. He enjoyed being worshipped, and since Minnie had fallen so violently in love with him, it seemed the most natural thing in the world for him to be in love with Minnie. True, if she had not started by adoring him, it would never have occurred to Hubert to fall in love with her. At their first meeting he had found her certainly very nice, but not particularly exciting. Afterwards, the manifest expression of her adoration had made him find her more interesting, and in the end he had fallen in love himself. But perhaps it was not to be wondered at if he found the process a little disappointing.

But still, he reflected on those secret occasions when he had to admit to himself that something was wrong with this passion, love without possession could never, surely, in the nature of things, be quite the genuine article. In his diary he recorded aptly those two quatrains of John Donne:

> So must pure lovers' souls descend
> To affections and to faculties,
> Which sense may reach and apprehend,
> Else a great prince in prison lies.
>
> To our bodies turn we then, that so
> Weak men on love revealed may look;
> Love's mysteries in souls do grow,
> But yet the body is his book.

At their next meeting he recited them to Minnie. The conversation which followed, compounded as it was of philosophy and personal confidences, was exquisite. It really, Hubert felt, came up to literary standards.

The next morning Minnie rang up her friend Helen Glamber and asked if she might come to tea that afternoon. She had several things to talk to her about. Mrs Glamber sighed as she hung up the receiver. 'Minnie's coming to tea,' she called, turning towards the open door.

From across the passage her husband's voice came back to her. 'Good Lord!' it said in a tone of far-away horror, of absent-minded resignation; for John Glamber was deep in his work and there was only a little of him left, so to speak, above the surface to react to the bad news.

Helen Glamber sighed again, and propping herself more comfortably against her pillows she reached for her book. She knew that far-away voice and what it meant. It meant that he wouldn't answer if she went on with the conversation; only say 'h'm' or 'm'yes'. And if she persisted after that, it meant that he'd say, plaintively, heart-breakingly, 'Darling, you *must* let me get on with my work.' And at that moment she would so much have liked to talk a little. Instead, she went on reading at the point where she had broken off to answer Minnie's telephone call.

'By this time the flames had enveloped the gynecaeum. Nineteen times did the heroic Patriarch of Alexandria venture into the blazing fabric, from which he succeeded in rescuing all but two of its lovely occupants, twenty-seven in number, all of whom he caused to be transported at once to his own private apartments. . . .'

It was one of those instructive books John liked her to read. History, mystery, lesson, and law. But at the moment she didn't feel much like history. She felt like talking. And that was out of the question; absolutely out of it.

She put down her book and began to file her nails and think of poor Minnie. Yes, poor Minnie. Why was it that one couldn't help saying Good Lord! heartfeltly, when one heard she was coming to tea? And why did one never have the heart to refuse to let her come to tea? She was pathetic, but pathetic in such a boring way. There are some people you like being kind to, people you want to help and befriend. People that look at you with the eyes of sick monkeys. Your heart breaks when you see them. But poor Minnie had none of the charms of a sick monkey. She was just a great big healthy young woman of twenty-eight who ought to have been married and the mother of children, and who wasn't. She would have made such a good wife, such an admirably solicitous and careful mother. But it just happened that none of the men she knew had ever wanted to marry her. And why should they want to? When

288 · *Aldous Huxley*

she came into a room, the light seemed to grow perceptibly dimmer, the electric tension slackened off. She brought no life with her; she absorbed what there was, she was like so much blotting-paper. No wonder nobody wanted to marry her. And yet, of course, it was the only thing. Particularly as she was always falling in love herself. The only thing.

'John!' Mrs Glamber suddenly called. 'Is it really true about ferrets?'

'Ferrets?' the voice from across the passage repeated with a remote irritation. 'Is what true about ferrets?'

'That the females die if they're not mated.'

'How on earth should I know?'

'But you generally know everything.'

'But, my darling, really . . .' The voice was plaintive, full of reproach. Mrs Glamber clapped her hand over her mouth and only took it off again to blow a kiss. 'All right,' she said very quickly. 'All right. Really. I'm sorry. I won't do it again. Really.' She blew another kiss towards the door.

'But ferrets . . .' repeated the voice.

'Sh—sh, sh—sh.'

'Why ferrets?'

'Darling,' said Mrs Glamber almost sternly, 'you really must go on with your work.'

Minnie came to tea. She put the case—hypothetically at first, as though it were the case of a third person; then, gaining courage, she put it personally. It was her own case. Out of the depths of her untroubled, pagan innocence, Helen Glamber brutally advised her. 'If you want to go to bed with the young man,' she said, 'go to bed with him. The thing has no importance in itself. At least not much. It's only important because it makes possible more secret confidences, because it strengthens affection, makes the man in a way dependent on you. And then, of course, it's the natural thing. I'm all for nature except when it comes to painting one's face. They say that ferrets . . .' But Minnie noticed that she never finished the sentence. Appalled and fascinated, shocked and yet convinced, she listened.

'My darling,' said Mrs Glamber that evening when her husband came home—for he hadn't been able to face Minnie; he had gone to the Club for tea—'who was it that invented religion, and sin, and all that? And why?'

John laughed. 'It was invented by Adam,' he said, 'for various little transcendental reasons which you would probably find it difficult to appreciate. But also for the very practical purpose of keeping Eve in order.'

'Well, if you call complicating people's lives keeping them in order, then I dare say you're right.' Mrs Glamber shook her head. 'I find it all too obscure. At sixteen, yes. But one really ought to have grown out of that sort of thing by twenty. And at thirty—the woman's nearly thirty, you know—well, really . . .'

In the end, Minnie wrote to Hubert telling him that she had made up her mind. Hubert was staying in Hertfordshire with his friend Watchett. It was a big house, the food was good, one was very comfortable; and old Mr Watchett, moreover, had a very sound library. In the impenetrable shade of the Wellingtonias Hubert and Ted Watchett played croquet and discussed the best methods of cultivating the Me. You could do a good deal, they decided, with art— books, you know, and pictures and music. 'Listen to Stravinsky's *Sacre*,' said Ted Watchett, 'and you're for ever excused from going to Tibet or the Gold Coast or any of those awful places. And then there's Dostoevsky instead of murder, and D. H. Lawrence as a substitute for sex.'

'All the same,' said Hubert, 'one must have a *certain* amount of actual non-imaginative experience.' He spoke earnestly, abstractedly; but Minnie's letter was in his pocket. '*Gnosce teipsum*. You can't really know yourself without coming into collision with events, can you?'

Next day, Ted's cousin, Phoebe, arrived. She had red hair and a milky skin, and was more or less on the musical comedy stage. 'One foot on and one foot off,' she explained. 'The splits.' And there and then she did them, the splits, on the drawing-room carpet. 'It's quite easy,' she said, laughing, and jumped up again with an easy grace that fairly took one's breath away. Ted didn't like her. 'Tiresome girl,' he said. 'So silly, too. Consciously silly, silly on purpose, which makes it worse.' And, it was true, she did like boasting about the amount of champagne she could put away without getting buffy, and the number of times she had exceeded the generous allowance and been 'blind to the world'. She liked talking about her admirers in terms which might make you suppose that they were all her accepted lovers. But then she had the justification of her vitality and her shining red hair.

'Vitality,' Hubert wrote in his diary (he contemplated a distant date, after, or preferably before, his death, when these confessions and aphorisms would be published), 'vitality can make claims on the world almost as imperiously as can beauty. Sometimes beauty and vitality meet in one person.'

It was Hubert who arranged that they should stay at the mill. One of his friends had once been there with a reading party, and found the place comfortable, secluded, and admirably quiet. Quiet, that is to say, with the special quietness peculiar to mills. For the silence there was not the silence of night on a mountain; it was a silence made of continuous thunder. At nine o'clock every morning the mill-wheel began to turn, and its roaring never stopped all day. For the first moments the noise was terrifying, was almost unbearable. Then, after a little, one grew accustomed to it. The thunder became, by reason of its very unintermittence, a perfect silence, wonderfully rich and profound.

At the back of the mill was a little garden hemmed in on three sides by the house, the outhouses, and a high brick wall, and open on the fourth towards the water. Looking over the parapet, Minnie watched it sliding past. It was like a brown snake with arrowy markings on its back; and it crawled, it glided, it slid along for ever. She sat there, waiting: her train, from London, had brought her here soon after lunch; Hubert, coming across country from the Watchetts, would hardly arrive before six. The water flowed beneath her eyes like time, like destiny, smoothly towards some new and violent event.

The immense noise that in this garden was silence enveloped her. Inured, her mind moved in it as though in its native element. From beyond the parapet came the coolness and the weedy smell of water. But if she turned back towards the garden, she breathed at once the hot perfume of sunlight beating on flowers and ripening fruit. In the afternoon sunlight all the world was ripe. The old red house lay there, ripe, like a dropped plum; the walls were riper than the fruits of the nectarine trees so tenderly and neatly crucified on their warm bricks. And that richer silence of unremitting thunder seemed, as it were, the powdery bloom on a day that had come to exquisite maturity and was hanging, round as a peach and juicy with life and happiness, waiting in the sunshine for the bite of eager teeth.

At the heart of this fruit-ripe world Minnie waited. The water flowed towards the wheel; smoothly, smoothly—then it fell, it broke itself to pieces on the turning wheel. And time was sliding onwards, quietly towards an event that would shatter all the smoothness of her life.

'If you really want to go to bed with the young man, go to bed with him.' She could hear Helen's clear, shrill voice saying impossible, brutal things. If any one else had said them, she would have run out of the room. But in Helen's mouth they seemed, somehow, so simple, so innocuous, and so true. And yet all that other people had said or implied—at home, at school, among the people she was used to meeting—seemed equally true.

But then, of course, there was love. Hubert had written a Shakespearean sonnet which began:

> Love hallows all whereon 'tis truly placed,
> Turns dross to gold with one touch of his dart,
> Makes matter mind, extremest passion chaste,
> And builds a temple in the lustful heart.

She thought that very beautiful. And very true. It seemed to throw a bridge between Helen and the other people. Love, true love, made all the difference. It justified. Love—how much, how much she loved!

Time passed and the light grew richer as the sun declined out of the height of the sky. The day grew more and more deliciously ripe, swelling with unheard-of sweetness. Over its sun-flushed cheeks the thundery silence of the mill-wheel spread the softest, peachiest of blooms. Minnie sat on the parapet, waiting. Sometimes she looked down at the sliding water, sometimes she turned her eyes towards the garden. Time flowed, but she was now no more afraid of that shattering event that thundered there, in the future. The ripe sweetness of the afternoon seemed to enter into her spirit, filling it to the brim. There was no more room for doubts, or fearful anticipations, or regrets. She was happy. Tenderly, with a tenderness she could not have expressed in words, only with the gentlest of light kisses, with fingers caressingly drawn through the ruffled hair, she thought of Hubert, her Hubert.

Hubert, Hubert. . . . And suddenly, startlingly, he was standing there at her side.

'Oh,' she said, and for a moment she stared at him with round brown eyes, in which there was nothing but astonishment. Then the expression changed. 'Hubert,' she said softly.

Hubert took her hand and dropped it again; looked at her for an instant, then turned away. Leaning on the parapet, he stared down into the sliding water; his face was unsmiling. For a long time both were silent. Minnie remained where she was, sitting quite still, her eyes fixed on the young man's averted face. She was happy, happy, happy. The long day ripened and ripened, perfection after perfection.

'Minnie,' said the young man suddenly, and with a loud abruptness, as though he had been a long time deciding himself to speak and had at last succeeded in bringing out the prepared and pent-up words, 'I feel I've behaved very badly towards you. I never ought to have asked you to come here. It was wrong. I'm sorry.'

'But I came because I wanted to,' Minnie exclaimed.

Hubert glanced at her, then turned away his eyes and went on addressing a ghost that floated, it seemed, just above the face of the sliding water. 'It was too much to ask. I shouldn't have done it. For a man it's different. But for a woman . . .'

'But, I tell you, I wanted to.'

'It's too much.'

'It's nothing,' said Minnie, 'because I love you.' And leaning forward, she ran her fingers through his hair. Ah, tenderness that no words could express! 'You silly boy,' she whispered. 'Did you think I didn't love you enough for that?'

Hubert did not look up. The water slid and slid away before his eyes; Minnie's fingers played in his hair, ran caressingly over the nape of his neck. He felt suddenly a positive hatred for this woman. Idiot! Why couldn't she take a hint? He didn't want her. And why on earth had he ever imagined that he did? All the way in the train he had been asking himself that question. Why? Why? And the question had asked itself still more urgently just now as, standing at the garden door, he had looked out between the apple tree and watched her, unobserved, through a long minute—watched her sitting there on the parapet, turning her vague brown eyes now at the water, now towards the garden, and smiling to herself with an expression that had seemed to him so dim and vacuous that he could almost have fancied her an imbecile.

And with Phoebe yesterday he had stood on the crest of the bare chalk down. Like a sea at their feet stretched the plain, and above the dim horizon towered heroic clouds. Fingers of the wind lifted the red locks of her hair. She stood as though poised, ready to leap off into the boisterous air. 'How I should like to fly!' she said. 'There's something particularly attractive about airmen, I always think.' And she had gone running down the hill.

But Minnie, with her dull hair, her apple-red cheeks, and big, slow body, was like a peasant girl. How had he ever persuaded himself that he wanted her? And what made it much worse, of course, was that she adored him, embarrassingly, tiresomely, like a too affectionate spaniel that insists on tumbling about at your feet and licking your hand just when you want to sit quietly and concentrate on serious things.

Hubert moved away, out of reach of her caressing hand. He lifted towards her for a moment a pair of eyes that had become, as it were, opaque with a cold anger; then dropped them again.

'The sacrifice is too great,' he said in a voice that sounded to him like somebody else's voice. He found it very difficult to say this sort of thing convincingly. 'I can't ask it of you,' the actor pursued. 'I won't.'

'But it isn't a sacrifice,' Minnie protested. 'It's a joy, it's happiness. Oh, can't you understand?'

Hubert did not answer. Motionless, his elbows on the parapet, he stared down into the water. Minnie looked at him, perplexed only, at first; but all at once she was seized with a nameless agonizing doubt that grew and grew within her, as the silence prolonged itself, like some dreadful cancer of the spirit, until it had eaten away all her happiness, until there was nothing left in her mind but doubt and apprehension.

'What is it?' she said at last. 'Why are you so strange? What is it, Hubert? What is it?'

Leaning anxiously forward, she laid her two hands on either side of his averted face and turned it towards her. Blank and opaque with anger were the eyes. 'What is it?' she repeated. 'Hubert, what is it?'

Hubert disengaged himself. 'It's no good,' he said in a smothered voice. 'No good at all. It was a mistake. I'm sorry. I think I'd better go away. The trap's still at the door.'

And without waiting for her to say anything, without explaining himself any further, he turned and walked quickly away, almost ran, towards the house. Well, thank goodness, he said to himself, he was out of that. He hadn't done it very well, or handsomely, or courageously; but, at any rate, he was out of it. Poor Minnie! He felt sorry for her; but after all, what could he do about it? Poor Minnie! Still, it rather flattered his vanity to think that she would be mourning over him. And in any case, he reassured his conscience, she couldn't really mind very much. But on the other hand, his vanity reminded him, she did adore him. Oh, she absolutely worshipped . . .

The door closed behind him. Minnie was alone again in the garden. Ripe, ripe it lay there in the late sunshine. Half of it was in shadow now; but the rest of it, in the coloured evening light, seemed to have come to the final and absolute perfection of maturity. Bloomy with thundery silence, the choicest fruit of all time hung there, deliciously sweet, sweet to the core; hung flushed and beautiful on the brink of darkness.

Minnie sat there quite still, wondering what had happened. Had he gone, had he really gone? The door closed behind him with a bang, and almost as though the sound were a signal prearranged, a man walked out from the mill on to the dam and closed the sluice. And all at once the wheel was still. Apocalyptically there was silence; the silence of soundlessness took the place of that other silence that was uninterrupted sound. Gulfs opened endlessly out around her; she was alone. Across the void of soundlessness a belated bee trailed its thin buzzing; the sparrows chirped, and from across the water came the sound of voices and far-away laughter. And as though woken from a sleep, Minnie looked up and listened, fearfully, turning her head from side to side.

ELIZABETH BOWEN

A Love Story
1939

MIST lay over the estuary, over the terrace, over the hollows of the gummy, subtropical garden of the hotel. Now and then a soft, sucking sigh came from the water, as though someone were turning over in his sleep. At the head of the steps down to the boat-house, a patch of hydrangeas still flowered and rotted, though it was December. It was now six o'clock, dark—chinks of light from the hotel lay yellow and blurred on the density. The mist's muffling silence could be everywhere felt. Light from the double glass doors fell down the damp steps. At the head of the steps the cast-iron standard lamps were unlit.

Inside the double glass doors, the lounge with its high curtained bow windows was empty. Brilliantly hotly lit by electric light, it looked like a stage on which there has been a hitch. Light blared on the *vieux rose* curtains and on the ocean of carpet with its jazz design. The armchairs and settees with their taut stuffing had an air of brutal, resilient strength. Brass ashtrays without a segment of ash stood on small tables dotted over the lounge. A glass screen kept the lounge from any draughts from the door; a glass screen protected the lounge from the stairs. But there was nothing to dread: the heating was on, only a smell of tinder-dry turkey carpet, ivory paint, polish, and radiators came downstairs from the empty floors above. In the immense tiled fireplace a fire burned with a visible, silent roar.

From a cabinet came a voice announcing the six o'clock news. In the middle of this, three berries fell from a vase of holly and pattered noisily into a brass tray. The temperate voice of the announcer paused for a moment, half-way through a disaster, as though disturbed by the noise. A spurt of gas from a coal sent a whicker up through the fire. The unheard news came to an end.

Two women came up the steps and pushed in at the glass doors. Their hair was sticky from the damp of the mist. The girl steered her mother round the screen to the fire, then went across and turned off the wireless. The mother unbuttoned her leather coat and threw it back from her handsome, full chest. Keyed up by the sudden electric light, her manner was swaggering and excitable. She looked with contempt at the wireless cabinet and said: 'I don't care what I hear—now!'

'Do shut up, mother. Do sit down.'

'Do stop being so nervous of me, Teresa. Whatever do you think I'm going to do?'

Teresa took off her trenchcoat and slung it over a chair, then crossed the lounge with her loose, cross walk, in her slacks. 'I know what you want,' she said flatly, ringing the bell. She sat down in an armchair by the fire and stuck her young slender jaw out and crossed her legs. Her mother stayed standing up, with her shoulders braced back; she kept pushing her hair back from her forehead with her long, plump, fine-wristed ringed hand. 'I daresay you're right to be so nervous,' she said. 'I don't know myself what I'll do, from minute to minute. Why did I have to come here—can you tell me that? Why was this the only thing I could do? Do you know when I was last here—who I was with?'

'I suppose I know,' said Teresa, defensively. 'You know you don't want me to understand you, mother, so I'm not trying to.'

'It's a terrible thing to say,' said Mrs Massey, 'but it would be better if this had happened to you. I'd rather see you suffer than have no feelings. You're not like a woman, Teresa. And he was your age, not my age.'

'Is that so?' Teresa said, in a voice too lifeless for irony.

Mrs Massey looked angrily round the lounge and said: 'They've changed the chairs round, since.' She pointed to an empty space on the carpet and said: '*That* was where he sat . . . There isn't even his chair.'

Teresa looked pointedly off down the corridor. 'Michael's coming,' she said. A boy in a white cotton coat, with a dark, vivid, Kerry face, beamed at them through the glass screen, then came round the screen for orders. 'Good evening, Michael,' said Teresa.

'Good evening, miss. Good evening to you, ma'am.'

'It's not a good evening for me, I'm afraid, Michael.'

Michael lowered his eyes. 'I'm sorry to hear that,' he said, in a trembling and feeling voice. 'It's a long time since we saw you.'

'Does it seem so——?' Mrs Massey began wildly. But Teresa put up her hand and in a curt, raised voice ordered her mother's drink . . . 'But I wanted a double,' objected Mrs Massey, when Michael had gone.

'You know you had that at home,' said Teresa, 'and more than once.' More coldly, she added: 'And how fed up Teddy used to get.'

Frank and Linda, their fingers loosely linked, came downstairs on their way to their private sitting-room. They glanced vacantly through the screen and turned left down the corridor. 'We missed the news again,' she said, as he shut the door. 'We always seem to run late.' 'We can't help that, darling,' he said. Their fire had been made up while they were upstairs. She gave it an unnecessary kick with her heel, and said: 'Did you see those two making a scene in the lounge?'

'I sort of did see the girl,' Frank said. 'Which was the other?'

'I thought they looked like locals in for a drink. Or I daresay they came round here to make a scene. I do think the Irish are exhibitionists.'

'Well, we can't help that, darling, can we?' said Frank, ringing the bell. He sat down in a chair and said: 'Oh, my God . . .' Linda dropping into the chair opposite. 'Well, really . . .' Frank said. 'However, I feel fine. I don't care what time it is.'

Up in a sitting-room on the first floor, the Perry-Duntons' two dogs slept in front of the fire, bellies taut to the heat. Legs rigid, they lay in running attitudes, like stuffed dogs knocked over on to their sides. On the sofa pulled up opposite the fire was Clifford— feet braced against one end, backbone against the other, knees up, typewriter in the pit of his stomach, chin tucked down into his chest. With elbows in to his ribs in a trussed position, he now and then made a cramped dash at the keys. When the keys stopped, he stayed frowning at them. Sheet after sheet, completed without conviction, fluttered on to the hearthrug between the dogs.

Polly Perry-Dunton's armchair was pushed up so that one arm made telepathic contact with Clifford's sofa. Curled up childishly in the cushions, she held a Penguin volume a little above her face. She kept the stiff Penguin open by means of an anxious pressure from her thumb. She read like someone told to pose with a book, and seemed unable to read without holding her breath.

Crackles came now and then from the *Daily Sketch* that Clifford had folded under his feet. Light blazed on their two heads from a marble bowl near the ceiling. The top of the mantelpiece was stacked with Penguins; the other armchair was stacked with American magazines. Polly's portable wireless in its shagreen cover stood silent on the floor by her chair. An art photograph of Clifford and Polly, profiles just overlapping like heads on a coin, was propped on the whatnot and kept from slipping by Polly's toy panda from Fortnum's.

Clifford reached out his right hand, apparently vaguely: Polly uncoiled like a spring from the armchair, knelt on the hearthrug and lit him a cigarette. Cigarette pressed tightly between his lips, Clifford turned back to frown at the keys again. She sat back on her heels to adore his frown, his curls, his fresh skin—then she locked her arms tightly around his neck. The impulsive, light little-girlishness of the movement let him still say nothing, not even turn his head.

She said into his cheek: 'May Polly say one thing?'

'Mm-mm.'

'I've left my pussy gloves in the car.'

'Mm-mm . . . You don't want them, do you?'

'No, not indoors. I wouldn't want gloves indoors. But let's remember tomorrow . . . Look, you crumpled one sheet right up. Did you mean to?'

'I meant to.'

Polly reverently uncrumpled the sheet. 'Pity,' she said. 'It's beautifully typed. Do you mean you're *not* going to say all that?'

'No. I'm trying to think of something else.'

'I should think most people could never think of so much that they were even not going to say.'

Clifford waited a minute, then he unfastened Polly's arms from his neck with as little emotion as a woman undoing a boa. He then typed five or six lines in a sort of rush. She returned with a glutted sigh to her chair, thumbed her book, held her breath, and thought of her pussy gloves.

Clifford's voice to Polly was always the same: resignation or irony kept it on one note. The two of them had been over here on honeymoon when the war began; here they still were, because of the war. Some days he went out with his gun along the foot of the

mountain, some days they ran the motor-boat in and out of white
inlets or to an island, some days they went out in Polly's big car.
When they had run the car back into the lock-up they would walk
back, her hand creeping inside his, down the tarmac curve to the
hotel between walls of evergreen. At this hour, the tarmac gleamed
wet-white in the lasting, luminous Irish dusk. From this hour, claus-
trophobia resumed its sway. Polly hardly reached up to Clifford's
shoulders; she walked beside him with her little skip-and-jump. She
felt that his being so tall, she so little, cancelled out their adverse
difference in age. She was thirty-two, he twenty-four. Her trim
little sexless figure, her kilted skirts, socks, and little-girl snooded
hair that flopped forward so softly could make her look fourteen.
Without the ring of technicians who got her up she could have
easily looked faded and sluttish, like a little girl in Woolworth's wilt-
ing behind the goods. But she had a childish hard will, and by day
she never looked old.

She grew up when she was asleep. Then, a map of unwilling
adult awareness—lines, tensions, and hollows—appeared in her exposed
face. Harsh sleep froze her liquidity; her features assembled themselves and became austere. An expression of watching wrote itself
on the lids of her shut eyes. The dread she denied all day came out
while she slept and stood in the door. The flittering of a palm tree,
the bump of a moored boat as the tide rose, the collapse of a last
coal in their grate went straight to the nerves upright under her
sleep. She slept tenaciously, late into the daylight—but Clifford never
looked at her long.

Her rape of Clifford—with his animal muteness, nonchalance,
mystery, and the charm of the obstination of his wish to write—
had been the climax of Polly's first real wish. Her will had detected
the flaw in his will that made the bid possible. Her father had
bought him for her. Till they met, her wealth and her years of
styleless, backgroundless dullness had atrophied Polly. The impulse
with which she first put her arms round Clifford's neck and told
him never to leave her had been, however, unforced and pure.
Rain—a little rain, not much—fell on her small parched nature
at Clifford's tentative kiss. There had seemed no threat to Polly
in Clifford's nature till the war came, with its masculine threat.
Their sequestration now, here, remained outwardly simple: Clifford
handled no money, Polly drew all the cheques.

They stayed on here where they were hidden and easy—any move might end in some fatal way. The Perry-Duntons knew almost nothing of the hotel. They had meals served in their suite, and only went down or upstairs or through the lounge on their way outdoors or in. During such appearances, Polly's service-flat temperament sheathed her in passive, moronic unseeingness. Her blindness made everything negative—Clifford saw nothing, either. He walked out or in through the public rooms beside her, tense, persecuted by the idea of notice, with his baited, defensive frown. The hotel had come to return the Perry-Duntons' indifference. The out-of-season skeleton staff of servants served them without interest, acting the automata Polly took them to be. Servants love love and money, but the Perry-Duntons bored the servants, by now. By now even Mrs Coughlan, the manageress, thought and spoke of them with apathy. The Perry-Duntons deadened the air round them with their static, depleting intimacy.

Now, Clifford twitched one more sheet off the machine. Leaning sideways over from the sofa, he, with absorption, began to tickle a dog's belly with an edge of the sheet. The dog bent itself further backward, into a bow. Watchful, Polly judged that this meant a break. She got up and began to tug like a bird at the *Daily Sketch* under Clifford's feet. 'What's that there for?' she said. 'I don't think I've looked at it yet.'

'Sorry,' said Clifford, raising his feet.

'But what's it *there* for, Clifford?'

'I was taught not to put my boots up on things—not straight up on things, that is.'

'How funny, because you generally do. I wonder what made you just think of that?'

Clifford could not tell her. He swung his feet off the sofa on to the hearthrug between the dogs. Sitting forward on the edge of the sofa, elbows on his wide-apart knees, he dug his heels slowly, without passion, into the rug. He looked slowly down from his hands with their hanging bunches of fingers to the oriental pattern under them. Polly picked up a sheet of type-writing and began to read. 'Goodness,' she said, after an interval, 'I hope you're not going to *throw* this one away! . . . What's the matter?'

'I'm going out for your gloves.'

'Oh, but I don't want them.'

'I'd like to go out for them, rather. I'd like a stretch.'

'*Alone,* Clifford?'

'There's a mist.'

'You might get lost. You might walk into the water. Do you really *want* to go out?'

At this, the dogs got up and looked eager. He pushed at them with his feet. 'No, stay with Polly,' he said. 'I won't be long.'

'You do promise?' She folded herself away from him in an abandon of puzzled sadness. Clifford kicked the dogs back again and went quietly round the door.

Frank stepped across the corridor to the office to get a stamp for Linda. The plate-glass and mahogany front of the office was framed in tariffs of summer trips, sets of view postcards printed in dark blue, and a bill of the working-hours of the Protestant church. The glass hatch was down: Frank put his face against it and looked flirtatiously into the back recess. On an inside ledge, the register was just out of view. Mrs Coughlan put up the glass hatch, like a lady playing at keeping shop. She received the full blast of Frank's full-blooded charm. 'Stamp?' she said. 'Oh dear, now Miss Heally knows where they are. To tell you the truth, I'm afraid I don't, and Miss Heally's just upstairs having a little rest. We're very quiet just now. Don't you find it terribly quiet—Major Mull?'

'Mr Mull,' said Frank. 'Oh, we love it,' he said.

'Still, it's not like the season, is it? Will you be back with us then?'

'Will I not!' said Frank, using his eyes.

'Is the stamp for yourself?'

'Well, it's not: it's for my cousin.'

'Ah yes,' said Mrs Coughlan, not batting an eyelid. 'The post went, you know; it went about five minutes. But I tell you what— Were you never in the last war?'—'I was,' said Frank. 'But I'm not in this one, thank God.'—'Now Miss Heally thought you had some military rank—I tell you what I could do, I could let you have a stamp I have, if I could trouble you to step this way.'

She pressed with her corsets against the door of the counter, and Frank let her out. She preceded him down the warm, half-lit, spongey-carpeted corridor to the door of her sitting-room: from this, she recoiled on to Frank's toe, at the same time blowing a whisper in at his right ear. 'I won't ask you in here,' she said, 'if you don't mind. I've a lady in here who is a little upset.' As she spoke, the door of the sitting-room opened, and the, to Frank's eye, snappy form of Teresa appeared, outlined in electric light. Teresa glowered at Frank, then said: 'We'll be going now, Mrs Coughlan. I think my mother would really rather be home.'

'I would not rather!' exclaimed unseen Mrs Massey. 'For God's sake, Teresa, let me alone.'

'No, don't let me barge in,' said Frank, standing firmly just where he was. Mrs Coughlan flashed at him the recognition that *he* would be always the gentleman. 'Well, if you'll excuse me,' she said, 'for just a jiffy, I'll bring the stamp along to your sitting-room.'

Frank went back to Linda. He left their door an inch open and, while they were waiting, rang for a glass of port. 'What's that for?' said Linda. 'I wanted a stamp.'

'That's for Mrs Coughlan. You'll get your stamp to play with. But of course you know that the post's gone?' 'Then hell, what is the good of a stamp?' 'You said you wanted a stamp, so I'm getting a stamp for you. I love getting you anything that you want.' 'Then what's the point of me having written this letter?' 'None, darling; I told you that. Writing letters is just fidgets. Never mind, it will come in some time when you want a letter to post.'

Disengaging herself from Frank's kiss, Linda propped the letter up on the mantelpiece, on a carton of cigarettes. While he kissed her again, she looked at it out of one eye. This made Frank look too. 'Oh, *that's* who it's to,' he said. He made faces at it, while Linda, still held pressed to his chest, giggled contentedly. 'I sort of had to,' she said, 'or he wouldn't know where I am.'

Mrs Coughlan came in with the stamp. The port was brought in by Michael and put on the mantelpiece. She started at it, but after a certain amount of fuss was induced to lift her glass daintily. 'Well, here's to you,' she said. 'And to you too,' she said to Linda. 'But isn't this really dreadful, at this hour.'

'Good for the heart,' said Frank. 'Not that your heart needs it, I'm sure. But your caller sounded to me a bit off.'

'Oh, Mrs Massey's had bad news. She came round here with her daughter, then didn't feel well.'

'Was she in the lounge?' said Linda.

'She was first, but it didn't seem fit for her, so Miss Teresa made her come in to me. You don't know who might come into a public room. So I said, to come in to me for a little rest, while I kept an eye on the office while Miss Heally was up. We are all devoted to Mrs Massey,' said Mrs Coughlan, meeting the eye of Linda just a shade stonily. 'I was saying to Miss Heally only this morning, wasn't it too long since we'd seen Teresa or her. They're in and out, as a rule, with the friends Mrs Massey has staying. They're quite near to here, through the woods, though it's longer if you take the two avenues. They've a sweet place, there, but it's lonely; they've nothing there but the sea.'

'Through the woods?' said Linda. 'Then, do you mean that pink house?—That's that house *we* want,' she said to Frank. Mrs Coughlan glanced primly midway between the two of them. 'Yes, it's a sweet place, Palmlawn,' said Mrs Coughlan. 'We often say, she seems quite wedded to it.'

Frank said: 'Is Teresa the tiger cat?'

Far too much won by Frank's eye and manner, Mrs Coughlan had to pause to prop up her loyalties. 'Well, her manner's just a weeshy bit short,' she said. 'And this evening, of course, *she's* upset, too.'

'She sounded more fed up.'

Mrs Coughlan, replacing her glass on the mantelpiece, dabbed her mouth with an *eau de nil* handkerchief charged with *Muguet de Coty*. Reassembling herself as manageress, she threw an inventorial glance round their sitting-room. 'I hope,' she said, 'you have everything? Everything comfy? Ring if it isn't, won't you?' 'Yes, thanks,' said Linda, 'we're very cosy in here.' Mrs Coughlan, whose business it was to know how to take everything, knew perfectly well how to take this. 'Well, I must be running along. Thank you very much, Major Mull—Mr Mull—I hope you'll join *me* for a minute or two this evening, unless, of course, you're engaged . . . Isn't this war shocking?'

'Shocking,' said Frank. 'I sell cars.'

'Very,' said Linda. 'Why?'

'I can't help thinking,' said Mrs Coughlan, 'of poor Mrs Massey's friend. A flying man. He was often in here, you know.'

Fumbling with the slimy lock in the mist, Clifford unlocked the lock-up. He reached into the Alvis, switched the dashboard lights on and got in and sat in the car to look for Polly's gloves. Mist came curdling into the lock-up after him. He put the wrist-length, fluffy gloves in one pocket. Then he checked up on the petrol: there were six gallons still. Then he plunged his hand slowly into another of his pockets, touched the pennies, thumbed the two half-crowns. In the dark his body recorded, not for the first time, yet another shock of the recurrent idea. The shock, as always, dulled out. He switched the lights off, folded his arms, slid forward and sat in the dark deflated—completely deflated, a dying pig that has died.

Frank and Linda, intently, silently cosy in front of their sitting-room fire in the dark, heard people break into the passage from Mrs Coughlan's room. At this Frank, with pussy-cat stealth and quickness, raised his face from the top of Linda's head. His clean ears, close to his head, might have been said to prick up. 'Damn,' said Linda, missing Frank, 'something is always happening.' The concourse passed their door. 'That's Mrs Massey, that was.' Frank at once pressed his hands on Linda's shoulders. But he said: 'Should I just have a look-see?' He got up, padded across the room, opened the door an inch and put one eye to the inch.

Mrs Coughlan had not gone far. She immediately came back and put her mouth into the inch of door. 'Mr Mull, could I trouble you just a minute?' she said. Frank edged round the door and Linda was left alone.

Mrs Massey was not equal to the walk back. This—only felt by herself as an additional rush of sorrow—was clear to Teresa, and also to Mrs Coughlan, as a predicament. There had been talk, before they left Mrs Coughlan's parlour, of telephoning to the village for a car. Mrs Massey would not brook the idea. 'I won't give trouble,' she said. 'There's trouble enough already.' Magnificent with protest, she now stood trembling and talking loudly and sweeping her hair back at the foot of the stairs. 'I should never have come,' she said. 'But how could I stay where I was? We'll go home now; we'll just go quietly home—Are you gummed there, Teresa? Come home: we've been here quite long enough.' She gave Frank a haunted look as Mrs Coughlan brought him up. 'This is Mr Mull, Mrs Massey,' said Mrs Coughlan. 'Mr Mull says he'll just get his car out and run you home.'

Mrs Massey said: 'I don't know what you all think.'

Teresa, taking no notice, put on her trenchcoat and tightly buckled the belt. 'That is good of you,' she said to Frank slightingly. 'Aren't you busy?' 'Not in the world,' said Frank. 'Hold on while I get the car round.'

'You needn't do that, thank you: Mother and I can walk as far as the car.'

Teresa and Frank, with Mrs Massey between them, started off down the aisle of carpet to the glass doors. 'Aren't the steps dreadfully dark for her!' helped Miss Heally, who was there with the rest—she shot ahead to switch on the outdoor lamps. The three passed down the steps in the blur of a blaze of lights, as though leaving a ball. 'Good night now. Safe home, Mrs Massey dear!' called Miss Heally and Mrs Coughlan from the top of the steps. Linda, hearing the noise, hearing Frank's step on the gravel, threw a window up and leaned into the mist. She called: 'Frank?' He replied if at all, with a gesture that she could not see: he was busy steering the party. 'Left turn,' he said, patting at Mrs Massey's elbow. The mother and daughter wheeled docilely.

'Do you know where we are, at all?'

'Oh, I'm used to all this.'

'Do you come from London, then?' Teresa said.

'I've come back from London.'

'On leave?' said Teresa quickly.

'No, thank God. I sell cars.'

'You won't sell many just now.' Teresa's trenchcoat brushed on the evergreens. Majestic and dazed between her escort, Mrs Massey stumbled along in a shackled way. In the yard, the open doors of the lock-up beside Frank's stuck out clammy into the mist: they almost walked into them. 'That lunatic's taken that Alvis out,' said Frank. Teresa, in her not encouraging way, said: 'Well, you'll be another lunatic, in a minute.' Mrs Massey, ignoring the dialogue, detached herself quietly from Teresa. While Frank and his torch and key were busy over a padlock, Mrs Massey passed quietly into the open lock-up next door. She bumped her knee on the Alvis and started to climb round it. 'It's all right, Teresa, the car's in here,' she called back, with quite an approach to her usual gaiety.

Clifford's reflex to the bump on the car was to blaze all his lights on. Inside, his lock-up became one curdled glare; his tail light spread a ruby stain on the mist. He turned his head sharply and stayed with his coinlike profile immobilized against the glaring end wall. Mrs Massey came scrambling into view. Clifford put down one window. 'I beg your pardon?' he said.

'Better back out a little,' said Mrs Massey. 'I can't get in this side while you're in here.' Clifford started his engine and backed out. But then he pulled up, got up, and got half out of the car. 'I'm afraid this is not your car,' he said.

'How could it be my car,' said Mrs Massey, 'when my car's at home? This is so kind of you—I don't know what you must think. Let me in now, though.' Clifford shrank back; she got in and settled herself by him contentedly. 'There's my daughter to come,' she said, 'and a man from the hotel. Just wait, now, and they'll show you the way.'

Frank had only just got his lock-up open when Teresa was at his elbow again. 'We'll hang on a minute,' he said, 'and let this other chap out. I'll start up. Be getting your mother in at the back.'

'My mother's got into the other car.'

'Which car?'

'I don't know. Don't dawdle there—are you mad? Mother might be off anywhere!'

Frank went out to blink. The Alvis, almost silently turning, swept a choked glare through the mist. 'Oh, *that* chap,' Frank said. 'That chap won't eat anyone. Cut along, Teresa—look, he's waiting for you.'

'I don't know him.'

'Mother knows him by now.'

'You're well out of us,' said Teresa, standing still bitterly.

'If that's what you think,' Frank said, 'I'll come along too.'

Linda was told of Frank's kindness in volunteering to drive the Masseys home. Mrs Coughlan was very much pleased and could not praise him enough. He should be back at the hotel in twenty minutes—but Linda knew he would not be. Frank's superabundance of good feeling made Linda pretty cross—his gusto, his sociability, his human fun, and his conquering bossiness. He liked life, and wherever he was things happened. This evening, first Mrs Coughlan, now Mrs Massey . . . Except in bed, one was seldom alone with Frank. Having interfered once more, and got one more kind act

in, he would come back like a cat full of rabbit again. Linda felt
quite suspended. She wished there were pin tables in this high-class
hotel. She rang for a drink, and two packs of cards and sat down
and laid out a complex patience on the octagonal table below the
sitting-room light. She thanked God she was not as young as she
had been and no longer fell into desperations or piques. It was not
that Frank did not concentrate, but he did not concentrate con-
secutively. She looked up once from her patience at her stamped
letter, and half thought of tearing it up and writing a warmer one.

Mrs Coughlan and Miss Heally returned to their sitting-room:
opening the piano they began to play a duet.

Polly Perry-Dunton, as well as Linda, heard the piano. Every
three minutes Polly looked at her watch. After ten minutes, Polly
left her sitting-room and went and lay on her bed in a sort of
rigour. She pulled Clifford's pyjamas out from under the pillow and
buried her face in them.

The Alvis, dip lights squinting along the row of sticky trees on the
left, nosed its way through the mist down the avenue. Mrs Massey,
in absolute quiescence, leaned back by Clifford's shoulder: he drove
in silence. Frank, in the back of the car beside Teresa, had non-
committally drawn her arm through his. Teresa did not take her
eyes from the back of her mother's head. When the open white
gates loomed up, Teresa leaned forward and told Clifford which way
to turn. About a mile down the main road Teresa again spoke up.
Clifford turned through more gates, and the four of them passed
with well-sprung smoothness over the bumps of a peaty wet avenue.
An uneasy smell of the sea came up the mist. Rhododendrons lolled
and brushed the sides of the car. The left wheels mounted an edge
of lawn. Clifford took a sweep and undipped his lights on veranda-
posts and the pallid walls of a house.

'Teresa,' said Mrs Massey, 'tell them to come in.'

Teresa lit the two oil lamps under their dark pink shades. Mrs Massey,
one hand on her drawing-room mantelpiece, swayed with the noble
naturalness of a tree. Her form, above a smoulder of peat fire, was
reflected in a mirror between the two dark windows—a mirror that
ran from ceiling to floor. The room with its possessions, its air of
bravura and slipshod moodiness, its low, smoked ceiling, armchairs

with sunk seats, cabinets of dull glass began to be seen in the dark light. Clifford's scraggy Nordic figure, and Frank's thick-set springy figure, firmly poised on its heels, were also seen in the mirror, making a crowd.

'Sit down,' said Mrs Massey, 'I feel more like standing. I'm afraid I'm restless—I had bad news, you know.'

'That is frightfully tough,' said Frank.

'I feel bad,' said Mrs Massey, 'at not knowing your names. Yes, it's tough to be dead isn't it? He was about your age,' she said to Clifford. '—Teresa dear, are you gummed there? Go and look for the drinks.'

Through the shadows in which they were all still standing up, Clifford threw a quick, begging look at Frank. Frank had to defer to Clifford's panic, and to Clifford's being unable to speak. 'Look, we must be pushing along,' Frank reluctantly, firmly said. Clifford bowed his heroic head sharply and took two steps to the door: the nightmare of being wanted was beginning, in this room, to close in round him again.

Mrs Massey only removed her eyes from Clifford to attend to a cigarette she was lighting over a lamp. Obliterated in shadows round the unglowing fire, Teresa, crouching, puffed at peat with a bellows. 'Teresa,' said her mother, 'do *you* see who he's so like——?'

'—There's no drink left, as you know,' said Teresa quickly. 'I could make some tea, but they're just off.'

Clifford said: 'I'm afraid we *are* just off!'

In reply, Mrs Massey lifted the lamp from its low table to hold it, unsteadily, on a level with Clifford's face. She took a step or two forward, with the lamp. 'It's extraordinary,' she said, 'though you don't know it, that you should be in this house *tonight*. You mustn't mind what I say or do: I'm upset—you're English, too, aren't you? He looks like a hero, doesn't he?' she said appealingly to Frank.

'Now we've all had a look at each other,' said Frank firmly, 'let me take this out of your way.' Taking the wobbling lamp from Mrs Massey, he put it safely back on its table again.

'I wish I were proud of my country,' said Mrs Massey. 'But I'm ashamed of this country to tell you the truth.'

'Oh, come,' said Frank. 'We have much to be thankful for.'

Teresa crashed the bellows into the grate and went out of the room through the open door. Outside, she pulled up a chair and stood on it to light the lamp in the hall. Frank strolled after her and leaned in the door to watch. He said: 'Are you very fed up?' The hanging lamp spun round, and Teresa's eyes, fixed on the burner, glittered. 'Is it bad?' Frank said. 'You don't tell me anything. Did *you* love the poor chap?'

'Did I get a chance?'

The chair she stood on wobbled on the uneven flagstones: Frank came and stood close up to steady the chair. 'Come down off that,' he said, 'like a good girl.' Teresa stepped down off the chair into Frank's arms—but she stood inside them like steel. He let her go, and watched her pick up her trenchcoat and walk off down a stone passage to hang it up. There she stayed, as though she were falling and could fall no further, with her breast and face thrust into the hanging coats. Her shoulder-blades showed through her sweater, and Frank, coming up gently, put his two hands on them. 'She'd rather him dead,' said Teresa into the coats, 'she'd rather him dead than gone from her.' She kept moving her shoulders under Frank's hands.

'Could you cry? Could you have a cry if I took you off now in that car?'

Teresa, into the coats, said something he could not hear. 'And leave those two?' she said in a louder voice.

Frank had to agree: he looked back at the drawing-room door.

Mrs Massey and Clifford, waiting for Frank, now sat in two armchairs opposite the fire. 'I don't understand,' she said. 'How did we come in your car?'

'You got in . . .' he said tentatively.

'And where had you been going?'

'Nowhere; I was looking for my wife's gloves.' He pulled the pussy gloves out of his pocket and showed them, to show he spoke the truth. Looking intently at the pussy gloves, Mrs Massey's eyes for the first time filled with tears. The access of some new feeling, a feeling with no context, resculptured her face. In the musty dark of her drawing-room, the dark round the dull fire, her new face looked alabaster and pure. The outline of her mist-clotted fair hair shook, as though shaken by the unconscious silent force of her tears.

'Aren't they small!' she said. 'Is your wife quite a little thing? Are you two very happy, then?'

'Very.'

'Take her gloves back safe . . . How English you are.'

Frank came in and said they must be pushing along. Teresa did not come in; she was opening the hall door. Out there on the sweep above the lawn and the sea, Clifford's lights were still blazing into the mist. Teresa went out and examined, as much by touch as anything, the wonderful car. An idea of going away for ever lifted and moved her heart, like a tide coming in. A whiteness up in the mist showed where there should have been the moon; the sleep-locked sea of the bay sighed. A smell of fern-rot and sea-water and gravel passed by Teresa into the house. Frank came to the hall door and saw her in the mist close to the car. He thought, calmly, of Linda wondering where he was, and wanted to go, and wanted to stay, and conceived how foolish it was, in love, to have to differentiate between women. In love there is no right and wrong, only the wish. However, he left Teresa alone and, going back into the drawing-room, said something further to Clifford about dinner.

Mrs Massey was just detaching her arms from Clifford's neck. 'I had to kiss him,' she said. 'He'll never understand why.' She went slowly ahead of the two men out to the car. 'Dinner?' she said. 'Is that really what time it is? . . . Teresa?'

But there was no reply.

Up the mist between the formless rhododendrons the Alvis, with Frank and Clifford, crawled back to the main road. 'If you thought of turning this car in before leaving this country,' Frank said, 'you might let me know first? My name's Mull—Mull, Cork always finds me.'

'My name is Perry-Dunton,' said Clifford, after a pause.

'Yes, I thought it might be.'

'Why?' said Clifford, alarmed.

'Caught my eye on the register. You two seem to like it here. And how right you are. Staying on?'

'Well, we're not quite sure of our plans.'

'I wish I wasn't—we've only got the weekend. Look, why don't you two drop down for a drink with us after dinner? My cousin would be delighted.'

'It is most awfully nice of you, but I don't think——'

'Right-o,' said Frank, nodding his head.

V. S. PRITCHETT

Blind Love

'I'M beginning to be worried about Mr "Wolverhampton" Smith,'
said Mr Armitage to Mrs Johnson, who was sitting in his study with
her notebook on her knee and glancing from time to time at the
window. She was watching the gardener's dog rooting in a flower
bed. 'Would you read his letter again: the second paragraph about
the question of a partnership?'

Since Mr Armitage was blind it was one of Mrs Johnson's duties
to read his correspondence.

'He had the money—that is certain; but I can't make out on
what conditions,' he said.

'I'd say he helped himself. He didn't put it into the business at
Ealing—he used it to pay off the arrears on the place at Wolverhampton,' she said in her cheerful manner.

'I'm afraid you're right. It's his character I'm worried about,' said
Mr Armitage.

'There isn't a single full stop in his letter—a full page on both
sides. None. And all his words are joined together. It's like one
word two pages long,' said Mrs Johnson.

'Is that so?' said Mr Armitage. 'I'm afraid he has an unpunctuated moral sense.'

Coming from a blind man whose open eyes and face had the
fixed gleam of expression you might have seen on a piece of rock,
the word 'unpunctuated' had a sarcasm unlike an ordinary sarcasm.
It seemed, quite delusively, to come from a clearer knowledge than
any available to the sighted.

'I think I'll go and smell out what he's like. Where is Leverton
Grove? Isn't it on the way to the station? I'll drop in when I go
up to London tomorrow morning,' said Mr Armitage.

The next morning he was driven in his Rolls-Royce to Mr
Smith's house, one of two or three little villas that were part of a

building speculation that had come to nothing fifty years before. The yellow-brick place was darkened by the firs that were thick in this district. Mrs Johnson, who had been brought up in London houses like this, winced at the sight of them. (Afterwards she said to Mr Armitage, 'It brings it back.' They were talking about her earlier life.) The chauffeur opened the car door, Mrs Johnson got out, saying 'No kerb,' but Armitage waving her aside, stepped out unhelped and stood stiff with the sainted upward gaze of the blind; then, like an Army detail, the party made a sharp right turn, walked two paces, then a sharp left to the wooden gate, which the chauffeur opened, and went forward in step.

'Daffodils,' said Mrs Johnson, noting a flower bed. She was wearing blue to match her bold, practical eyes, and led the way up the short path to the door. It was opened before she rang by an elderly, sick-looking woman with swollen knuckles who half hid behind the door as she held it, to expose Smith standing with his grey jacket open, his hands in his pockets—the whole man an arrangement of soft smiles from his snowball head to his waistcoat, from his fly to his knees, sixteen stone of modest welcome with nothing to hide.

'It is good of you to come,' he said. He had a reverent voice.

'On my way to the station,' said Armitage.

Smith was not quite so welcoming to Mrs Johnson. He gave her a dismissive frown and glanced peremptorily at his wife.

'In here?' said Mrs Johnson, briskly taking Armitage's arm in the narrow hall.

'Yes,' he said.

They all stood just inside the doorway of the front room. A fir tree darkened it. It had, Mrs Johnson recorded at once, two fenders in the fireplace, and two sets of fire-irons; then she saw two of everything—two clocks on the fireplace, two small sofas, a dining table folded up, even two carpets on the floor, for underneath the red one, there was the fringe of a worn yellow one.

Mr Smith saw that she noted this and, raising a grand chin and now unsmiling, said, 'We're sharing the 'ouse, the house, until we get into something bigger.'

And at this, Mrs Smith looked with the searching look of an agony in her eyes, begging Mrs Johnson for a word.

'Bigger,' echoed Mrs Smith and watched to see the word sink

in. And then, putting her fingers over her face, she said, 'Much bigger,' and laughed.

'Perhaps,' said Mr Smith, who did not care for his wife's laugh, 'while we talk—er . . .'

'I'll wait outside in the car,' said the decisive Mrs Johnson, and when she was in the car she saw Mrs Smith's gaze of appeal from the step.

A half an hour later, the door opened and Mrs Johnson went to fetch Mr Armitage.

'At this time of the year the daffodils are wonderful round here,' said Armitage as he shook hands with Smith, to show that if he could not see there were a lot of things he knew. Mr Smith took the point and replaced his smiling voice with one of sportive yet friendly rebuke, putting Mr Armitage in his place.

'There is only one eye,' he stated as if reading aloud. 'The eye of God.'

Softly the Rolls drove off, with Mrs Smith looking at it fearfully from the edge of the window curtain.

'Very rum fellow,' said Armitage in the car. 'I'm afraid he's in a mess. The Inland Revenue are after him as well. He's quite happy because there's nothing to be got out of him. Remarkable. I'm afraid his friends have lost their money.'

Mrs Johnson was indignant.

'What's he going to do down here? He can't open up again.'

'He's come here,' Armitage said, 'because of the chalk in London water. The chalk, he says, gets into the system with the result that the whole of London is riddled with arthritis and nervous diseases. Or rather the whole of London is riddled with arthritis and nervous diseases because it believes in the reality of chalk. Now, chalk has no reality. We are not living on chalk or even on gravel: we dwell in God. Mr Smith explains that God led him to manage a chemist's shop in Wolverhampton, and to open one of his own in Ealing without capital. He now realizes that he was following his own will, not the will of God. He is now doing God's work. Yesterday he had a cable from California. He showed it to me. "Mary's cancer cured gratitude cheque follows." He's a faith healer.'

'He ought to be in jail,' said Mrs Johnson.

'Oh, no. He's in heaven,' said Armitage. 'I'm glad I went to see him. I didn't know about his religion, but it's perfect: you get witnesses like him in court every day, always moving on to higher things.'

The Rolls arrived at the station and Mr Armitage picked up his white stick.

'Cancer today. Why not blindness tomorrow? Eh?' he said. Armitage gave one low laugh from a wide mouth. And though she enjoyed his dryness, his rare laugh gave a dangerous animal expression to a face that was usually closed. He got out of the car and she watched him walk into the booking hall and saw knots of people divide to make way for him on the platform.

In the damp town at the bottom of the hills, in the shops, at the railway station where twice a week the Rolls waited for him to come back from London, it was agreed that Armitage was a wonder. A gentleman, of course, they said; he's well-off, that helps. And there is that secretary-housekeeper, Mrs Johnson. That's how he can keep up his legal business. He takes his stick to London, but down here he never uses it. In London he has his lunch in his office or in his club, and can manage the club stairs which worry some of the members when they come out of the bar. He knows what's in the papers—ever had an argument with him?—of course Mrs Johnson reads them to him.

All true. His house stood, with a sudden flash of Edwardian prosperity, between two larch coppices on a hill five miles out and he could walk out on to the brick terrace and smell the lavender in its season and the grass of the lawns that went steeply down to his rose garden and the blue tiles of his swimming pool boxed in by yew.

'Fabian Tudor. Bernard Shaw used to come here—before our time, of course,' he would say, disparaging the high, panelled hall. He was really referring to his wife, who had left him when he was going blind twenty-two years ago. She had chosen and furnished the house. She liked leaded windows, brass, plain velvet curtains, Persian carpets, brick fireplaces and the expensive smell of wood smoke.

'All fake,' he would say, 'like me.'

You could see that pride made him like to embarrass. He seemed to know the effect of jokes from a dead face. But, in fact, if he had no animation—Mrs Johnson had soon perceived in her commonsensical way—this was because he was not affected, as people are, by the movements on other faces. Our faces, she had learned from Armitage, threw their lives away every minute. He stored his. She knew this because she stored hers. She did not put it like this, in fact what she said appeared to contradict it. She liked a joke.

'It's no good brooding. As Mother used to say, as long as you've got your legs you can give yourself an airing.'

Mrs Johnson had done this. She had fair hair, a good figure, and active legs, but usually turned her head aside when she was talking, as if to an imaginary friend. Mrs Johnson had needed an airing very badly when she came to work for Mr Armitage.

At their first interview—he met her in the panelled hall: 'You do realize, don't you, that I am totally blind. I have been blind for more than twenty years,' he said.

'Yes,' she said. 'I was told by Dr James.' She had been working for a doctor in London.

He held out his hand and she did not take it at once. It was not her habit to shake hands with people; now, as always, when she gave in she turned her head away. He held her hand for a long time and she knew he was feeling the bones. She had heard that the blind do this, and she took a breath as if to prevent her bones or her skin passing any knowledge of herself to him. But she could feel her dry hand coming to life and she drew it away. She was surprised that, at the touch, her nervousness had gone.

To her, Armitage's house was a wonderful place. The space, the light made friendly by the small panes of the tall leaded windows, charmed her.

'Not a bit like Peckham,' she said cheerfully.

Mr Armitage took her through the long sitting-room, where there were yellow roses in a bowl, into his study. He had been playing a record and put it off.

'Do you like music?' he said. 'That was Mozart.'

'I like a bit of a singsong,' she said. 'I can't honestly say I like the classical stuff.'

He took her round the house, stopped to point to a picture or two and, once more down in the long room, took her to a window and said, 'This is a bad day for it. The haze hasn't lifted. On a clear day you can see Sevenham Cathedral. It's twelve miles away. Do you like the country?'

'Frankly I've never tried it.'

'Are you a widow, Mrs Johnson?'

'No. I changed my name from Thompson to Johnson and not for the better. I divorced my husband,' said Mrs Johnson crisply.

'Will you read something to me—out of the paper?' he said. 'A court case.'

She read and read.

'Go on,' he said. 'Pick out something livelier.'

'Lonely monkeys at the zoo?'

'That will do.'

She read again and she laughed.

'Good,' he said.

'As Father used to say, "Speak up . . ."' she began, but stopped. Mr Armitage did not want to hear what Father said.

'Will you allow me,' Armitage said, getting up from his desk, 'would you allow me to touch your face?'

Mrs Johnson had forgotten that the blind sometimes asked this.

She did not answer at once. She had been piqued from the beginning because he could not see her. She had been to the hairdresser's. She had bought a blouse with a high frilled neck which was meant to set off the look of boyish impudence and frankness of her face. She had forgotten about touch. She feared he would have a pleading look, but she saw that the wish was part of an exercise for him. He clearly expected her to make no difficulty about it.

'All right,' she said, but she meant him to notice the pause, 'if you want to.'

She faced him and did not flinch as his hand lightly touched her brow and cheek and chin. He was, she thought, 'after her bones' not her skin, and that, though she stiffened with resistance, was 'OK by her.' But when, for a second, the hand seemed about to rest on her jaw, she turned her head.

'I weigh eight stone,' she said in her bright way.

'I would have thought less,' he said. That was the nearest he came to a compliment. 'It was the first time,' she said afterwards to her friend Marge in the town, 'that I ever heard of a secretary being bought by weight.'

She had been his secretary and housekeeper for a long time now. She had understood him at once. The saintly look was nonsense. He was neither a saint nor a martyr. He was very vain; especially

he was vain of never being deceived, though in fact his earlier secretaries had not been a success. There had been three or four before
her. One of them—the cook told her—imagined him to be a martyr because she had a taste for martyrdom and drank to gratify it;
another yearned to offer the compassion he hated, and muddled
everything. One reckoning widow lasted only a month. Blatantly
she had added up his property and wanted to marry him. The last,
a 'lady', helped herself to the household money, behind a screen of
wheezing grandeur and name-dropping.

Remembering the widow, the people who came to visit Mr
Armitage when he gave a party were relieved after their meeting
with Mrs Johnson.

'A good honest-to-God Cockney' or 'Such a cheery soul.' 'Down
to earth,' they said. She said she had 'knocked about a bit'. 'Yes,
sounds as if she had': they supposed they were denigrating. She was
obviously not the kind of woman who would have any dangerous
appeal to an injured man. And she, for her part, would go to the
pictures when she had time off or simply flop down in a chair at
the house of her friend Marge and say, 'Whew, Marge. His nibs has
gone to London. Give me a strong cuppa. Let's relax.'

'You're too conscientious.'

'Oh, I don't mind the work. I like it. It occupies your mind. He
has interesting cases. But sometimes I get keyed up.'

Mrs Johnson could not herself describe what 'keyed her up'—
perhaps being on the watch? Her mind was stretched. She found
herself translating the world to him and it took her time to realize
that it did not matter that she was not 'educated up to it'. He obviously liked her version of the world, but it was a strain having versions. In the mornings she had to read his letters. This bothered
her. She was very moral about privacy. She had to invent an imper-
sonal, uninterested voice. His lack of privacy irked her; she liked
gossip and news as much as any woman, but here it lacked the salt
of the secret, the whispered, the found out. It was all information
and statement. Armitage's life was an abstraction for him. He had
to know what he could not see. What she liked best was reading
legal documents to him.

He dressed very well and it was her duty to see that his clothes
were right. For an orderly, practical mind like hers, the order in
which he lived was a new pleasure. They lived under fixed laws:

no chair or table, even no ashtray must be moved. Everything must be in its place. There must be no hazards. This was understandable: the ease with which he moved without accident in the house or garden depended on it. She did not believe when he said, 'I can hear things before I get to them. A wall can shout, you know.' When visitors came she noticed he stood in a fixed spot: he did not turn his head when people spoke to him and among all the head-turning and gesturing he was the still figure, the lawgiver. But he was very cunning. If someone described a film they had seen, he was soon talking as if he had been there. Mrs Johnson, who had duties when he had visitors, would smile to herself, at the surprise on the faces of people who had not noticed the quickness with which he collected every image or scene or character described. Sometimes, a lady would say to her, 'I do think he's absolutely marvellous,' and, if he overheard this—and his hearing was acute—Mrs Johnson would notice a look of ugly boredom on his face. He was, she noted, particularly vain of his care of money and accounts. This pleased Mrs Johnson because she was quick to understand that here a blind man who had servants might be swindled. She was indignant about the delinquency of her predecessor. He must have known he was being swindled.

Once a month Mrs Johnson would go through the accounts with him. She would make out the cheques and take them to his study and put them on his desk.

The scene that followed always impressed her. She really admired him for this. How efficient and devious he was! He placed the cheque at a known point on his blotter. The blunt fingers of his hairless hands had the art of gliding and never groping, knowing the inches of distance; and then, as accurately as a geometrician, he signed. There might be a pause as the fingers secretly measured, a pause alarming to her in the early days, but now no longer alarming; sometimes she detected a shade of cruelty in this pause. He was listening for a small gasp of anxiety as she watched.

There was one experience which was decisive for her. It occurred in the first month of her employment and had the lasting stamp of a revelation. (Later on, she thought he had staged the incident in order to show her what his life was like and to fix in her mind the nature of his peculiar authority.) She came into the sitting-room one evening in the winter to find a newspaper and heard sharp, unbelievable sounds coming from his study. The door was open and the room was in darkness. She went to it, switched on the light, and saw he was sitting there typing in the darkness. Well, she could have done that if she had been put to it—but now she *saw* that for him there was no difference between darkness and light.

'Overtime, I see,' she said, careful not to show surprise.

This was when she saw that his mind was a store of maps and measured things; a store of sounds and touches and smells that became an enormous translated paraphernalia.

'You'd feel sorry for a man like that,' her friend Marge said.

'He'd half kill you if you showed you were sorry,' Mrs Johnson said. 'I don't feel sorry. I really don't.'

'Does he ever talk about his wife?'

'No.'

'A terrible thing to do to leave a man because he's blind.'

'She had a right to her life, hadn't she?' said Mrs Johnson flatly. 'Who would want to marry a blind man?'

'You are hard,' Marge said.

'It's not my business,' said Mrs Johnson. 'If you start pitying people you end up by hating them. I've seen it. I've been married, don't forget.'

'I just wish you had a more normal life, dear.'

'It suits me,' said Mrs Johnson.

'He ought to be very grateful to you.'

'Why should he be? I do my job. Gratitude doesn't come into it. Let's go and play tennis.'

The two women went out and played tennis in the park and Mrs Johnson kept her friend running from court to court.

'I smell tennis balls and grass,' said Mr Armitage when she returned.

In the March of her third year a bad thing happened. The winter was late. There was a long spell of hard frost and you could see the cathedral tower clearly over the low-lying woods on most days. The frost coppered the lawns and scarcely faded in the middle of the day. The hedges were spiked and white. She had moved her typing table into the sitting-room close to the window to be near a radiator and when she changed a page she would glance out at the garden. Mr Armitage was out there somewhere and she had got into the habit of being on the watch. Now she saw him walk down the three lawns and find the brick steps that led to the swimming pool. It was enclosed by a yew hedge and was frozen over. She could see Armitage at the far side of it pulling at a small fallen branch that had been caught by the ice. His foot had struck it. On the other side of the hedge, the gardener was cutting cabbage in the kitchen garden and his dog was snuffling about. Suddenly a rabbit ran out, ears down, and the dog was yelping after it. The rabbit ran through the hedge and almost over Armitage's feet with the dog nearly on it. The gardener shouted. The next moment Armitage, who was squatting, had the dog under his legs, lost his balance, and fell full length through the ice into the pool. Mrs Johnson saw this. She saw the gardener drop his knife and run to the gap in the hedge to help Armitage out. He was clambering over the side. She saw him wave the gardener's hand away and shout at him and the gardener step away as Armitage got out. He stood clawing weed off his face, out of his hair, wringing his sleeves and brushing ice off his shirt as he marched back fast up the garden. He banged the garden door in a rage as he came in.

'That bloody man. I'll have that dog shot,' shouted Armitage. She hurried to meet him. He had pulled off his jacket and thrown it on a chair. Water ran off his trousers and sucked in his shoes. Mrs Johnson was appalled.

'Go and change your things quickly,' she said. And she easily raced him to the stairs to the landing and to his room. By the time he got there she had opened several drawers, looking for underclothes, and had pulled out a suit from his cupboard. Which suit? She pulled out another. He came squelching after her into the room.

'Towel,' she cried. 'Get it all off. You'll get pneumonia.'

'Get out. Leave me alone,' shouted Armitage, who had been tugging his shirt over his head as he came upstairs.

She saw then that she had done a terrible thing. By opening drawers and putting clothes on the bed, she had destroyed one of his systems. She saw him grope. She had never seen him do this before. His bare white arms stretched out in a helpless way and his brown hands pitiably closed on air. The action was slow and his fingers frightened her.

'I told you to leave me alone,' he shouted.

She saw she had humiliated him. She had broken one of the laws. For the first time she had been incompetent.

Mrs Johnson went out and quietly shut the door. She walked across the landing to the passage in the wing where her own room was, looking at the wet marks of his muddy shoes on the carpet, each one accusing her. She sat down on the edge of her bed. How could she have been such a fool! How could she have forgotten his rule? Half naked to the waist, hairy on the chest and arms, he shocked because the rage seemed to be not in his mind but in his body like an animal's. The rage had the pathos of an animal's. Perhaps when he was alone he often groped; perhaps the drilled man she was used to, who came out of his bedroom or his study, was the expert survival of a dozen concealed disasters?

Mrs Johnson sat on her bed listening. She had never known Armitage to be angry; he was a monotonously considerate man. The shout abashed her and there was a strange pleasure in being abashed; but her mistake was not a mere mistake. She saw that it struck at the foundation of his life and was so gross that the surface of her own confidence was cracked. She was a woman who could reckon on herself, but now her mind was scattered. Useless to say to herself, 'What a fuss about nothing,' or 'Keep calm'. Or, about him, 'Nasty temper'. His shout, 'Get out. I told you to leave me alone,' had, without reason (except that a trivial shame is a spark that sets fire to a long string of greater shames), burned out all the security of her present life.

She had heard those words, almost exactly those words, before. Her husband had said them. A week after their wedding.

Well, *he* had had something to shout about, poor devil. She admitted it. Something a lot more serious than falling into a pool and having someone commit the crime of being kind to you and hurting your silly little pride.

She got up from the bed and turned on the tap of the washbasin to cool down her hot face and wash her hands of the dirt of the jacket she had brought upstairs. She took off her blouse and as she sluiced her face she looked through the water at herself in the mirror. There was a small birthmark the size of a red leaf which many people noticed and which, as it showed over the neck of the high blouses she usually wore, had the enticement of some signal or fancy of the blood; but under it, and invisible to them, were two smaller ones and then a great spreading ragged liver-coloured island of skin which spread under the tape of her slip and crossed her breast and seemed to end in a curdle of skin below it. She was stamped with an ineradicable bloody insult. It might have been an attempt to impose another woman on her. She was used to seeing it, but she carried it about with her under her clothes, hiding it and yet vaunting.

Now she was reaching for a towel and inside the towel, as she dried herself, she was talking to Armitage.

'If you want to know what shame and pride are, what about marrying a man who goes plain sick at the sight of your body and who says "You deceived me. You didn't tell me."'

She finished drying her face and put the towel on the warm rail and went to her dressing table. The hairbrush she picked up had been a wedding present and at each hard stroke of the brush on her lively fair hair, her face put up a fight, but it exhausted her. She brushed the image of Armitage away and she was left staring at the half-forgotten but never-forgotten self she had been.

How could she have been such a fool as to deceive her husband? It was not through wickedness. She had been blinded too—blinded by love; in a way, love had made her so full of herself that perhaps she had never seen *him*. And her deceptions: she could not stop herself smiling at them, but they were really pitiable because she was so afraid of losing him and to lose him would be to lose this new beautifully deluded self. She ought to have told him. There were chances. For example, in his flat with the grey sofa with the spring that bit your bottom going clang, clang at every kiss, when he used to carry on about her wearing dresses that a man couldn't get a hand into. He knew very well she had had affairs with men, but why, when they were both 'worked up', wouldn't she undress and go to the bedroom? The sofa was too short. She remembered how shocked his face looked when she pulled up her skirts and lay on the floor. She said she believed in sex before marriage, but she thought some things ought to wait: it would be wrong for him to see her naked before their wedding day. And to show him she was no prude—there was that time they pretended to be looking out of the window at a cricket match; or Fridays in his office when the staff was gone and the cleaners were only at the end of the passage.

'You've got a mole on your neck,' he said one day.

'Mother went mad with wanting plums when she was carrying me. It's a birthmark.'

'It's pretty,' he said and kissed it.

He kissed it. He kissed it. She clung to that when after the wedding they got to the hotel and she hid her face in his shoulder and let him pull down the zip of her dress. She stepped away, and pretending to be shy, she undressed under her slip. At last the slip came off over her head. They both looked at each other, she with brazen fear and he—she couldn't forget the shocked blank disgust on his face. From the neck over the left shoulder down to the breast and below, and spreading like a red tongue to the back was this ugly blob—dark as blood, like a ragged liver on a butcher's window, or some obscene island with ragged edges. It was as if a bucket of paint had been thrown over her.

'You didn't tell me,' he said. If only she had told him, but how could she have done? She knew she had been cursed.

'That's why you wouldn't undress, you little hypocrite.'

He himself was in his underpants with his trousers on the bed and with his cuff links in his hand, which made his words absurd and awful. His ridiculous look made him tragic and his hatred frightening. It was terrible that for two hours while they talked he did not undress and worse that he gave her a dressing gown to cover herself. She heard him going through the catalogue of her tricks.

'When . . .' he began in a pathetic voice. And then she screamed at him.

'What do you think? Do you think I got it done, that I got myself tattooed in the Waterloo Road? I was born like it.'

'Ssh,' he said. 'You'll wake the people in the next room.'

'Let them hear. I'll go and show them,' she screamed. It was kind of him to put his arm round her. When she had recovered, she put on her fatal, sporty manner. 'Some men like it,' she said.

He hit her across the face. It was not then but in the following weeks when pity followed and pity turned to cruelty he had said, 'Get out. Leave me alone.'

Mrs Johnson went to her drawer and got out a clean blouse.

Her bedroom in Armitage's house was a pretty one, far prettier than any she had ever had. Up till now she had been used to bed-sitters since her marriage. But was it really the luxury of the house and the power she would have in it that had weighed with her when she had decided to take on this strange job? She understood now something else had moved her in the low state she had been in when she came. As a punished and self-hating person she was drawn to work with a punished man. It was a return to her girlhood: injury had led her to injury.

She looked out of the window at the garden. The diamond panes chopped up the sight of the frozen lawns and the firs that were frost-whiskered. She was used to the view. It was a view of the real world; that, after all, was her world, not his. She saw that gradually in three years she had drifted out of it and had taken to living in Armitage's filed memory. If he said, for example, 'That rambler is getting wild. It must be cut back,' because a thorn caught his jacket, or if he made his famous remark about seeing the cathedral on a clear day, the landscape limited itself to these things and in general reduced itself to the imposed topographical sketch in his mind. She had allowed him, as a matter of abnegation and duty, to impose his world on hers. Now this shock brought back a lost sense of the right to her own landscape; and then to the protest that this country was not hers at all. The country bored her. The fir trees bored her. The lanes bored her. The view from this window or the tame protected view of the country from the Rolls-Royce window bored her. She wanted to go back to London, to the streets, the buses, and the crowds, to crowds of people with eyes in their heads. And—her spirits rising—'To hell with it, I want people who can *see* me.'

She went downstairs to give orders for the carpet to be brushed.

In the sitting-room she saw the top of Armitage's dark head. She had not heard him go down. He was sitting in what she called the cathedral chair facing the window and she was forced to smile when she saw a bit of green weed sticking to his hair. She also saw a heavy glass ashtray had fallen off the table beside him. 'Clumsy,' she said. She picked it up and lightly pulled off the piece of weed from his hair. He did not notice this.

'Mr Armitage,' she said in her decisive manner, 'I lost my head. I'm sorry.'

He was silent.

'I understand how you feel,' she said. For this (she had decided in her room) was the time for honesty and for having things out. The impersonality could not go on, as it had done for three years.

'I want to go back to London,' she said.

'Don't be a damn fool,' he said.

Well, she was not going to be sworn at. 'I'm not a damn fool,' she said. 'I understand your situation.' And then, before she could stop herself, her voice shaking and loud, she broke out with: 'I know what humiliation is.'

'Who is humiliated?' said Armitage. 'Sit down.'

'I am not speaking about you,' she said stiffly.

That surprised him, she saw, for he turned his head.

'I'm sorry, I lost my temper,' he said. 'But that stupid fellow and his dog . . .'

'I am speaking about myself,' she said. 'We have our pride, too.'

'Who is *we*?' he said, without curiosity.

'Women,' she said.

He got up from his chair, and she stepped back. He did not move and she saw that he really had not recovered from the fall in the pool, for he was uncertain. He was not sure where the table was.

'Here,' he said roughly, putting out a hand. 'Give me a hand out of this.'

She obediently took him by the arm and stood him clear of the table.

'Listen to me. You couldn't help what happened and neither could I. There's nothing to apologize for. You're not leaving. We get on very well. Take my advice. Don't be hard on yourself.'

'It is better to be hard,' she said. 'Where would you have been if you had not been hard? I'm not a girl, I'm thirty-nine.' He moved towards her and put his hand on her right shoulder and she quickly turned her head. He laughed and said, 'You've brushed your hair back'. He knew. He always knew.

She watched him make for his study and saw him take the wrong course, brush against the sofa by the fireplace, and then a yard or two further, he shouldered the wall.

'Damn,' he said.

At dinner, conversation was difficult. He offered her a glass of wine which she refused. He poured himself a second glass and as he sat down he grimaced with pain.

'Did you hurt your back this afternoon?' she asked.

'No,' he said. 'I was thinking about my wife.'

Mrs Johnson blushed. He had scarcely ever mentioned his wife.

She knew only what Marge Brook had told her of the town gossip: how his wife could not stand his blindness and had gone off with someone and that he had given her a lot of money. Someone said, ten thousand pounds. What madness! In the dining-room Mrs Johnson often thought of all those notes flying about over the table and out of the window. He was too rich. Ten thousand pounds of hatred and rage, or love, or madness. In the first place, she wouldn't have touched it.

'She made me build the pool,' he said.

'A good idea,' she said.

'I don't know why. I never thought of throwing her into it,' he said.

Mrs Johnson said, 'Shall I read the paper?' She did not want to hear more about his wife.

Mrs Johnson went off to bed early. Switching on the radio in her room and then switching it off because it was playing classical music, she said to herself, 'Well, funny things bring things back. What a day!' and stepped yawning out of her skirt. Soon she was in bed and asleep.

An hour later she woke up, hearing her name.

'Mrs Johnson. The water got into my watch, would you set it for me?' He was standing there in his dressing gown.

'Yes,' she said. She was a woman who woke up alert and clear-headed.

'I'm sorry. I thought you were listening to a programme. I didn't know you were in bed,' he said. He was holding the watch to his ear.

'Would you set it for me and put my alarm right?' He had the habit of giving orders. They were orders spoken into space—and she was the space, nonexistent. He gave her the watch and went off. She put on her dressing gown and followed him to his room. He had switched on the light for her. She went to the bedside table and bent down to wind the clock. Suddenly she felt his arms round her, pulling her upright, and he was kissing her head. The alarm went off suddenly and she dropped the clock. It went on screeching on the floor at her feet.

'Mr Armitage,' she said in a low angry voice, but not struggling. He turned her round and he was trying to kiss her on the lips. At this she did struggle. She twisted her head this way and that to stop him, so that it was her head rather than her body that was resisting him. Her blue eyes fought with all their light, but his eyes were dead as stone.

'Really, Mr Armitage. Stop it,' she managed to mutter. 'The door is open. Cook will hear.'

She was angry at being kissed by a man who could not see her face, but she felt the shamed insulted woman in her, that blotched inhabitant, blaze up in her skin.

The bell of the alarm clock was weakening and then choked to a stop and in her pettish struggle she stepped on it; her slipper had come off.

'I've hurt my foot.' Distracted by the pain she stopped struggling, and Armitage took his opportunity and kissed her on the lips. She looked with pain into his sightless eyes. There was no help there. She was terrified of being drawn into the dark where he lived. And then the kiss seemed to go down her throat and spread into her shoulders, into her breasts and branch into all the veins and arteries of her body and it was the tongue of the shamed woman who had sprung up in her that touched his.

'What are you doing?' she was trying to say, but could only groan the words. When he touched the stained breast she struck back violently, saying, 'No, no'.

'Come to bed with me,' he said.

'Please let me go. I've hurt my foot.'

The surprising thing was that he did let her go, and as she sat panting and white in the face on the bed to look at her foot, she looked mockingly at him. She forgot that he could not see her mockery. He sat beside her but did not touch her and he was silent. There was no scratch on her foot. She picked up the clock and put it back on the table.

Mrs Johnson was proud of the adroitness with which she had kept men away from her since her marriage. It was a war with the inhabitant of the ragged island on her body. That creature craved for the furtive, for the hand that slipped under a skirt, for the scuffle in the back seat of a car, for a five-minute disappearance into a locked office.

But the other Mrs Johnson, the cheerful one, was virtuous. She took advantage of his silence and got quickly up to get away; she

dodged past him, but he was quick too. He was at the closed door.
For a moment she was wily. It would be easy for her to dodge him
in the room. And then she saw once more the sight she could not
bear that melted her more certainly than the kisses which had filled
her mouth and throat: she saw his hands begin to open and search
and grope in the air as he came towards the sound of her breathing. She could not move. His hand caught her. The woman inside
her seemed to shout, 'Why not? You're all right. He cannot see.'
In her struggle she had not thought of that. In three years he had
made her forget that blindness meant not seeing.

'All right,' she said, and the virtue in Mrs Johnson pouted. She
gently tapped his chest with her fingers and said with the sullenness of desire, 'I'll be back in a minute'.

It was a revenge: that was the pleasure.

'Dick,' she called to her husband, 'look at this,' when the man
was on top of her. Revenge was the only pleasure and his excitement was soon over. To please him she patted him on the head as
he lay beside her and said, 'You've got long legs'. And she nearly
said, 'You are a naughty boy' and 'Do you feel better?' but she
stopped herself and her mind went off on to what she had to do
in the morning; she listened and wondered how long it would be
before he would fall asleep and she could stealthily get away. Revenge
astonished by its quickness.

She slyly moved. He knew at once and held her. She waited.
She wondered where Dick was now. She wished she could tell him.
But presently this blind man in the bed leaned up and put both his
hands on her face and head and carefully followed the round of her
forehead, the line of her brow, her nose and lips and chin, to the
line of her throat, and then to her nape and shoulders. She trembled, for after his hands had passed, what had been touched seemed
to be new. She winced as his hand passed over the stained shoulder and breast and he paused, knowing that she winced, and she
gave a groan of pleasure to deceive him; but he went on, as if he
were modelling her, feeling the pit under the arms, the space of
ribs and belly and the waist of which she was proud, measuring
them, feeling their depth, the roundness of her legs, the bone in
her knees until, throwing all clothes back, he was holding her ankle,
the arch of her foot, and her toes. Her skin and her bones became

alive. His hands knew her body as she had never known it. In her brief love affairs, which had excited her because of the risk of being caught, the first touch of a man stirred her at once and afterwards left her looking demurely at him; but she had let no one know her with a pedantry like his. She suddenly sat up and put her arms round him, and now she went wild. It was not a revenge now; it was a triumph. She lifted the sad breast to his lips. And when they lay back she kissed his chest and then—with daring—she kissed his eyes.

It was six o'clock before she left him, and when she got to her room the stained woman seemed to bloom like a flower. It was only after she had slept and saw her room in daylight again that she realized that once more she had deceived a man.

It was late. She looked out of the window and saw Armitage in his city clothes talking to the chauffeur in the garden. She watched them walk to the garage.

'OK,' she said dryly to defend herself. 'It was a rape.' During the day there would be moments when she could feel his hands moving over her skin. Her legs tingled. She posed as if she were a new-made statue. But as the day went on she hardened and instead of waiting for him to return she went into the town to see Marge.

'You've put your hair up,' Marge said.

'Do you like it?'

'I don't know. It's different. It makes you look severe. No, not severe. Something. Restless.'

'I am not going back to dinner this evening,' she said. 'I want a change. Leonard's gone to London.'

'Leonard!' said Marge.

Mrs Johnson wanted to confide in Marge, but Marge bored her. They ate a meal together and she ate fast. To Marge's astonishment she said, 'I must fly'.

'You *are* in a mood,' Marge said.

Mrs Johnson was unable to control a longing to see Armitage. When she got back to the house and saw him sitting by the fire she wanted him to get up and at least put his arms round her; but he did not move, he was listening to music. It was always the signal that he wanted to be alone.

'It is just ending,' said Armitage.

The music ended in a roll of drums.

'Do you want something, Helen?' he said.

She tried to be mocking, but her voice could not mock and she said seriously, 'About last night. It must not happen again. I don't want to be in a false position. I could not go on living in the house.'

She did not intend to say this; her voice, between rebuke and tenderness, betrayed this.

'Sit down.'

She did not move.

'I have been very happy here,' she said. 'I don't want to spoil it.'

'You are angry,' he said.

'No, I'm not,' she said.

'Yes, you are; that is why you were not here when I got back,' he said.

'You did not wait for me this morning,' she said. 'I was glad you didn't. I don't want it to go on.'

He came nearer to her and put his hand on her hair.

'I like the way your hair shows your ears,' he said. And he kissed them.

'Now, please,' she said.

'I love you,' he said and kissed her on the forehead and she did not turn her head.

'Do you? I'm glad you said that. I don't think you do. When something has been good, don't spoil it. I don't like love affairs,' she said.

And then she changed. 'It was a party. Good night.'

'You made me happy,' he said, holding on to her hand.

'Were you thinking about it a long time?' she said in another voice, lingering for one more word.

'Yes,' he said.

'It is very nice of you to say that. It is what you ought to say. But I mean what I said. Now, really, good night. And,' giving a pat to his arm, she said, 'keep your watch wound up.'

Two nights later he called to her loudly and curtly from the stairs: 'Mrs Johnson, where are you?' and when she came into the hall he said quietly, 'Helen.'

She liked that. They slept together again. They did not talk.

Their life went on as if nothing had happened. She began to be vain of the stain on her body and could not resist silently displaying, almost taunting him, when she undressed, with what he could not see. She liked the play of deceiving him like this; she was paying him out for not being able to see her; and when she was ashamed of doing this the shame itself would rouse her desire: two women uniting in her. And fear roused her too; she was afraid of his blindness. Sometimes the fear was that the blind can see into the mind. It often terrified her at the height of her pleasure that she was being carried into the dark where he lived. She knew she was not but she could not resist the excitement of imagining it. Afterwards she would turn her back to him, ashamed of her fancies, and as his finger followed the bow of her spine she would drive away the cynical thought that he was just filing this affair away in one of the systems of his memory.

Yet she liked these doubts. How dead her life had been in its practical certainties. She liked the tenderness and violence of sexual love, the simple kindness of the skin. She once said to him, 'My skin is your skin'. But she stuck to it that she did not love him and that he did not love her. She wanted to be simply a body: a woman like Marge who was always talking about love seemed to her a fool. She liked it that she and Armitage were linked to each other only by signs. And she became vain of her disfigurement, and looking at it, even thought of it as the lure.

I know what would happen to me if I got drunk, she thought at one of Armitage's cocktail parties, I'm the sort of woman who would start taking her clothes off. When she was a young woman she had once started doing so, and someone, thank God, stopped her.

But these fancies were bravado.

They were intended to stop her from telling him.

On Sundays Mrs Johnson went to church in the village near the house. She had made a habit of it from the beginning, because she thought it the proper thing to do: to go to church had made her feel she need not reproach herself for impropriety in living in the same house as a man. It was a practical matter: before her love affair the tragic words of the service had spoken to her evil. If God had done this to her, He must put up with the sight of her in His house. She was not a religious woman; going to church was an assertion that she had as much right to fair play as anyone else. It also stopped her from being 'such a fool' as to fall to the temptation of destroying her new wholeness by telling him. It was normal to go to church and normality had been her craving ever since her girlhood. She had always taken her body, not her mind, to church.

Armitage teased her about her churchgoing when she first came to work for him; but lately his teasing became sharper: 'Going to listen to Dearly Beloved Brethren?' he would say.

'Oh, leave him alone,' she said.

He had made up a tale about her being in love with the vicar; at first it was a joke, but now there was a sharp edge to it. 'A very respectable man,' he said.

When the church bells rang on Sunday evening he said, 'He's calling to you.' She began to see that this joke had the grit of jealousy in it; not of the vicar, of course, but a jealousy of many things in her life.

'Why do you go there? I'd like to understand, seriously,' he said.

'I like to get out,' she said.

She saw pain on his face. There was never much movement in it beyond the deepening of two lines at the corners of his mouth; but when his face went really dead, it was as sullen as earth in the garden. In her sense, she knew, he never went out. He lived in a system of tunnels. She had to admit that when she saw the grey church she was glad, because it was not his house. She knew from gossip that neither he nor his wife had ever been to it.

There was something else in this new life; now he had freed her they were both more watchful of each other. One Sunday in April she saw his jealousy in the open. She had come in from church and she was telling him about the people who were there. She was sitting on the sofa beside him.

'How many lovers have you had?' he said. 'That doctor you worked for, now?'

'Indeed not,' she said. 'I was married.'

'I know you were married. But when you were working for those people in Manchester? And in Canada after the war?'

'No one else. That was just a trip.'

'I don't believe you.'

'Honestly, it's true.'

'In court I never believe a witness who says "Honestly".'

She blushed, for she had had three or four lovers, but she was defending herself. They were no business of his.

The subject became darker.

'Your husband,' he said. 'He saw you. They all saw you.'

She knew what he meant, and this scared her.

'My husband. Of course he saw me. Only my husband.'

'Ah, so there were others.'

'Only my husband saw me,' she said. 'I told you about it. How he walked out of the hotel after a week.'

This was a moment when she could have told him, but to see his jealousy destroy the happiness he had restored to her made her indignant.

'He couldn't bear the sight of me. He had wanted,' she invented, 'to marry another woman. He told me on the first night of our marriage. In the hotel. Please don't talk about it.'

'Which hotel was this?' he said.

The triviality of the question confused her. 'In Kensington.'

'What was the name?'

'Oh, I forget, the something Royal . . .'

'You don't forget.'

'I do honestly . . .'

'Honestly!' he said.

He was in a rage of jealousy. He kept questioning her about the hotel, the length of their marriage. He pestered for addresses, for dates, and tried to confuse her by putting his questions again and again.

'So he didn't leave you at the hotel!' he said.

'Look,' she said. 'I can't stand jealous men and I'm not going to be questioned like one of your clients.'

He did not move or shout. Her husband had shouted and paced up and down, waving his arms. This man sat bolt upright and still, and spoke in a dry, exacting voice.

'I'm sorry,' he said.

She took his hand, the hand that groped like a helpless tentacle and that had modelled her; it was the most disturbing and living thing about him.

'Are you still in love with your husband?'

'Certainly not.'

'He saw you and I have never seen you.' He circled again to his obsession.

'It is just as well. I'm not a beautiful woman,' she laughed. 'My legs are too short, my bottom is too big. You be grateful—my husband couldn't stand the sight of me.'

'You have a skin like an apple,' he said.

She pushed his hand away and said, 'Your hands know too much'.

'*He* had hands. And he had eyes,' he said in a voice grinding with violence.

'I'm very tired. I am going to bed,' she said. 'Good night.'

'You see,' he said. 'There is no answer.'

He picked up a braille book and his hand moved fast over the sheets.

She went to her room and kicked off her shoes and stepped out of her dress.

I've been living in a dream, she thought. Just like Marge, who always thinks her husband's coming back every time the gate goes. It is a mistake, she thought, living in the same house.

The jealous fit seemed to pass. It was a fire, she understood, that flared up just as her shame used to flare, but two Sundays later the fit came on again. He must hate God, she thought, and pitied him. Perhaps the music that usually consoled him had tormented him. At any rate, he stopped it when she came in and put her prayer book on the table. There was a red begonia, which came from the greenhouse, on the table beside the sofa where he was sitting very upright, as if he had been waiting impatiently for her to come back.

'Come and sit down,' he said and began kindly enough. 'What was church like? Did they tell you what to do?'

'I was nearly asleep,' she said. 'After last night. Do you know what time it was?' She took his hand and laughed.

He thought about this for a while. Then he said, 'Give me your hands. No. Both of them. That's right. Now spit on them.'

'Spit!'

'Yes, that is what the church tells you.'

'What *are* you talking about?' she said, trying to get her hands away.

'Spit on them.' And he forced her hands, though not roughly, to her lips.

'What are you doing?' She laughed nervously and spat on her fingers.

'Now—rub the spittle on my eyes.'

'Oh, no,' she said.

He let go of her wrist.

'Do as I tell you. It's what your Jesus Christ did when he cured the blind man.'

He sat there waiting and she waited.

'He put dust or earth or something on them,' he said. 'Get some.'

'No,' she said.

'There's some here. Put your fingers in it,' he said shortly. She was frightened of him.

'In the pot,' he insisted as he held one of her wrists so that she could not get away. She dabbed her wet fingers in the earth of the begonia pot.

'Put it on my eyes.'

'I can't do that. I really can't,' she said.

'Put it on my eyes,' he said.

'It will hurt them.'

'They are hurt already,' he said. 'Do as I tell you.' She bent to him and, with disgust, she put her dirty fingers on the wet eyeballs. The sensation was horrible, and when she saw the dirty patches on his eyes, like two filthy smudges, she thought he looked like an ape.

'That is what you are supposed to do,' he said. Jealousy had made him mad.

I can't stay with a mad man, she thought. He's malicious. She did not know what to do, but he solved that for her. He reached for his braille book. She got up and left him there. The next day he went to London.

His habits changed. He went several times into the nearby town on his own and she was relieved that he came back in a silent mood which seemed happy. The horrible scene went out of her mind. She had gone so far as to lock her bedroom door for several nights after that scene, but now she unlocked it. He had brought her a bracelet from London; she drifted into unguarded happiness. She knew so well how torment comes and goes.

It was full undreaming June, the leaves in the garden still undarkened, and for several days people were surprised when day after day the sun was up and hot and unclouded. Mrs Johnson went down to the pool. Armitage and his guests often tried to persuade her to go in but she always refused.

'They once tried to get me to go down to Peckham Baths when I was a kid, but I screamed,' she said.

The guests left her alone. They were snobbish about Peckham Baths.

But Mrs Johnson decided to become a secret bather. One afternoon when Armitage was in London and the cook and gardener had their day off, she went down with the gardener's dog. She wore a black bathing suit that covered her body and lowered herself by the steps into the water. Then she splashed at the shallow end of the pool and hung on to the rail while the dog barked at her. He stopped barking when she got out and sniffed round the hedge where she pulled down her bathing dress to her waist and lay down to get sun-drunk on her towel.

She was displaying herself to the sun, the sky and the trees. The air was like hands that played on her as Armitage did and she lay listening to the snuffles of the dog and the humming of the bees in the yew hedge. She had been there an hour when the dog barked at the hedge. She quickly picked up a towel and covered herself and called to the dog: 'What is it?'

He went on barking and then gave up and came to her. She sat down. Suddenly the dog barked again. Mrs Johnson stood up and tried to look through one of the thinner places in the hedge. A man who must have been close to the pool and who must have passed along the footpath from the lane, a path used only by the gardener, was walking up the lawns towards the house carrying a trilby hat in his hand. He was not the gardener. He stopped twice to get his breath and turned to look at the view. She recognized the smiling grey suit, the wide figure and snowball head: it was 'Wolverhampton' Smith. She waited and saw him go on to the house and ring a bell. Then he disappeared round the corner and went to the front of the house. Mrs Johnson quickly dressed. Presently he came back to look into the windows of the sitting-room. He found the door and for a minute or two went into the house and then came out.

'The cheek,' she said. She finished dressing and went up the lawn to him.

'Ah, there you are,' he said. 'What a sweet place this is. I was looking for Mr Armitage.'

'He's in London.'

'I thought he might be in the pool,' he said. Mr Smith looked rich with arch, smiling insinuation.

'When will he be back?'

'About six. Is there anything I can do?'

'No, no, no,' said Mr Smith in a variety of genial notes, waving a hand. 'I was out for a walk.'

'A long walk—seven miles.'

'I came,' said Mr Smith, modestly lowering his eyes in financial confession, 'by bus.'

'The best way. Can I give you a drink?'

'I never touch it,' Mr Smith said, putting up an austere hand. 'Well, a glass of water perhaps. As the Americans say, "I'm mighty thirsty". My wife and I came down here for the water, you know. London water is chalky. It was very bad for my wife's arthritis. It's bad for everyone, really. There's a significant increase in neuralgia, neuritis, arthritis in a city like London. The chalky water does it. People don't realize it'—and here Mr Smith stopped smiling and put on a stern excommunicating air—'If you believe that man's life is ruled by water. I personally don't.'

'Not by water only, anyway,' said Mrs Johnson.

'I mean,' said Mr Smith gravely, 'if you believe that the material body exists.' And when he said this, the whole sixteen stone of him looked scornfully at the landscape which, no doubt, concealed thousands of people who believed they had bodies. He expanded: he seemed to threaten to vanish.

Mrs Johnson fetched a glass of water. 'I'm glad to see you're still there,' she laughed when she came back.

Mr Smith was resting on the garden seat. 'I was just thinking— thank you—there's a lot of upkeep in a place like this,' he said.

'There is.'

'And yet—what is upkeep? Money—so it seems. And if we believe in the body, we believe in money, we believe in upkeep, and so it goes on,' said Mr Smith sunnily, waving his glass at the garden. And then sharply and loftily, free of this evil: 'It gives employment.' Firmly telling her she was employed. 'But,' he added, in warm contemplation, putting down his glass and opening his arms, gathering in the landscape, 'but there is only one employer.'

'There are a hell of a lot of employers.'

Mr Smith raised an eyebrow at the word 'hell' and said, 'Let me correct you there. I happen to believe that God is the only employer.'

'I'm employed by Mr Armitage,' she said. 'Mr Armitage loves this place. You don't have to see to love a garden.'

'It's a sweet place,' said Mr Smith. He got up and took a deep breath. 'Pine trees. Wonderful. The smell! My wife doesn't like pine trees. She is depressed by them. It's all in the mind,' said Mr Smith. 'As Shakespeare says. By the way, I suppose the water's warming up in the pool? June—it would be. That's what I should like—a swim.'

He *did* see me! thought Mrs Johnson.

'You should ask Mr Armitage,' she said coldly.

'Oh, no, no,' said Mr Smith. 'I just *feel* that to swim and have a sunbathe would be the right idea. I should like a place with a swimming pool. And a view like this. I feel it would suit me. And, by the way,' he became stern again, 'don't let me hear you say again that Mr Armitage enjoys this place although he doesn't see it. Don't tie his blindness on him. You'll hold him back. He *does* see it. He reflects all-seeing God. I told him so on Wednesday.'

'On Wednesday?'

'Yes,' he said. 'When he came for treatment. I managed to fit him in. Good godfathers, look at the time! I've to get the bus back. I'm sorry to miss Mr Armitage. Just tell him I called. I just had a thought to give him, that's all. He'll appreciate it.'

'And now,' Mr Smith said sportively, 'I must try and avoid taking a dive into that pool as I go by, mustn't I?'

She watched his stout marching figure go off down the path.

For treatment! What on earth did Mr Smith mean? She knew the rest when Armitage came home.

'He came for his cheque,' he said. 'Would you make out a cheque for a hundred and twenty pounds—'

'A hundred and twenty pounds!' she exclaimed.

'For Mr Smith,' he repeated. 'He is treating my eyes.'

'Your eyes! He's not an ophthalmic surgeon.'

'No,' said Armitage coldly. 'I have tried those.'

'You're not going to a faith healer!'

'I am.'

And so they moved into their second quarrel. It was baffling to quarrel with Armitage. He could hear the firm ring of your voice but he could not see your eyes blooming wider and bluer with obstinacy; for her, her eyes were herself. If was like quarrelling with a man who had no self, or perhaps with one that was always hidden.

'Your church goes in for it,' he said.

'Proper faith healing,' she said.

'What is proper?' he said.

She had a strong belief in propriety.

'A hundred and twenty pounds! You told me yourself Smith is a fraud. I mean, you refused his case. How can you go to a fraud?'

'I don't think I said fraud,' he said.

'You didn't like the way he got five thousand pounds out of that silly young man.'

'Two thousand,' he said.

'He's after your money,' she said. 'He's a swindler.'

In her heart, having been brought up poor, she thought it was a scandal that Armitage was well-off; it was even more scandalous to throw money away.

'Probably. At the end of his tether,' he said. He was conveying, she knew, that he was at the end of his tether too.

'And you fall for that? You can't possibly believe the nonsense he talks.'

'Don't you think God was a crook? When you think of what He's done?'

'No, I don't.' (But in fact the stained woman thought He was.)

'What did Smith talk about?'

'I was in the pool. I think he was spying on me. I forget what he was talking about—water, chalky water, was it?'

'He's odd about chalk!' Armitage laughed. Then he became grim again: 'You see—even Smith can see *you*. You see people, you see Smith, everyone sees everything, and so they can afford to throw away what they see and forget. But I have to remember everything. You know what it is like trying to remember a dream. Smith is right, I'm dreaming a dream,' Armitage added sardonically. 'He says that I'm only dreaming I cannot see.'

She could not make out whether Armitage was serious.

'All right. I don't understand, but all right. What happens next?'

'You can wake up.'

Mr Armitage gave one of his cruel smiles. 'I told you. When I used to go to the courts I often listened to witnesses like Smith. They were always bringing "God is my witness" into it. I never knew a more religious lot of men than dishonest witnesses. They were always bringing in a higher power. Perhaps they were in contact with it.'

'You don't mean that. You are making fun of me,' she said. And then vehemently: 'I hate to see you going to an ignorant man like that. I thought you were too proud. What has happened to you?'

She had never spoken her mind so forcibly to him before.

'If a man can't see,' he said, 'if *you* couldn't see, humiliation is what you'd fear most. I thought I ought to accept it.'

He had never been so open with her.

'You couldn't go lower than Mr Smith,' she said.

'We're proud. That is our vice,' he said. 'Proud in the dark. Everyone else has to put up with humiliation. You said you knew what it was—I always remember that. Millions of people are humiliated: perhaps it makes them stronger because they forget it. I want to join them.'

'No, you don't,' she said.

They were lying in bed and leaning over him she put her breast to his lips, but he lay lifeless. She could not bear it that he had changed her and that she had stirred this profound wretchedness in him. She hated confession: to her it was the male weakness—self-love. She got out of bed.

'Come to that,' she said. 'It's you who are humiliating me. You are going to this quack man because we've slept together. I don't like the compliment.'

'And you say you don't love me,' he said.

'I admire you,' she said. She dreaded the word 'love'. She picked up her clothes and left the room. She hadn't the courage to say she hadn't the courage. She stuck to what she had felt since she was a child: that she was a body. He had healed it with his body.

Once more she thought, I shall have to go. I ought to have stuck to it and gone before. If I'd been living in the town and just been coming up for the day it would have been OK. Living in the house was your mistake, my girl. You'll have to go and get another job. But of course when she calmed down, she realized that all this was self-deception: she was afraid to tell him. She brusquely drove off the thought, and her mind went to the practical.

That hundred and twenty pounds! She was determined not to see him swindled. She went with him to Mr Smith's next time. The roof of the Rolls-Royce gleamed over the shrubbery of the uncut hedge of Mr Smith's house. A cat was sitting on the window sill. Waiting on the doorstep was the little man, wide-waisted and with his hands in his optimistic pockets, and changing his smile of welcome to a reminder of secret knowledge when he saw her. Behind the undressing smile of Mr Smith stood the kind, cringing figure of his wife, looking as they all walked into the narrow hall.

'Straight through?' said Mrs Johnson in her managing voice. 'And leave them to themselves, I suppose?'

'The back gets the sun. At the front it's all these trees,' said Mrs Smith, encouraged by Mrs Johnson's presence to speak out in a weak voice, as if it was all she did get. 'I was a London girl.'

'So am I,' said Mrs Johnson.

'But you've got a beautiful place up there. Have you got these pine trees too?'

'A few.'

'They give me the pip,' said Mrs Smith. 'Coffee? Shall I take your coat? My husband said you'd got pines.'

'No, thank you, I'll keep it,' said Mrs Johnson. 'Yes, we've got pines. I can't say they're my favourite trees. I like to see leaves come off. And I like a bit of traffic myself. I like to see a shop.'

'Oh, you would,' said Mrs Smith.

The two women looked with the shrewd London look at each other.

'I'm so busy up there I couldn't come before. I don't like Mr Armitage coming alone. I like to keep an eye on him,' said Mrs Johnson, set for attack.

'Oh, yes, an eye.'

'Frankly, I didn't know he was coming to see Mr Smith.'

But Mrs Johnson got nothing out of Mrs Smith. They were both half listening to the rumble of men's voices next door. Then the meeting was over and they went out to meet the men. In his jolly way Mr Smith said to Mrs Johnson as they left, 'Don't forget about that swim!'

Ostentatiously to show her command and to annoy Armitage, she armed him down the path.

'I hope you haven't invited that man to swim in the pool,' said Mrs Johnson to Mr Armitage on the way home.

'You've made an impression on Smith,' said Armitage.

'No, I haven't.'

'Poor Mrs Smith,' said Mrs Johnson.
Otherwise they were silent.

She went a second, then a third time to the Smiths' house. She sat each time in the kitchen talking and listening to the men's voices in the next room. Sometimes there were long silences.
'Is Mr Smith praying?' Mrs Johnson asked.
'I expect so,' said Mrs Smith. 'Or reading.'
'Because it *is* prayer, isn't it?' said Mrs Johnson.
Mrs Smith was afraid of this healthy downright woman and it was an effort for her to make a stand on what evidently for most of her married life had been poor ground.
'I suppose it is. Prayer, yes, that is what it would be. Dad . . .' — she changed her mind—'my husband has always had faith.' And with this, Mrs Smith looked nervously at being able loyally to put forward the incomprehensible.
'But what does he actually *do*? I thought he had a chemist's shop,' pursued Mrs Johnson.
Mrs Smith was a timid woman who wavered now between the relics of dignity and a secretive craving to impart.
'He has retired,' said Mrs Smith. 'When we closed the shop he took this up.' She said this, hoping to clutch a certainty.
Mrs Johnson gave a bustling laugh. 'No, you misunderstand me. What I mean is, what does he actually *do*? What is the treatment?'
Mrs Smith was lost. She nodded, as it were, to nothingness several times.
'Yes,' she said. 'I suppose you'd call it prayer. I don't really understand it.'
'Nor do I,' said Mrs Johnson. 'I expect you've got enough to do keeping house. I have my work cut out too.'
They still heard the men talking. Mrs Johnson nodded to the wall.
'Still at it,' said Mrs Johnson. 'I'll be frank with you, Mrs Smith. I am sure your husband does whatever he does do for the best . . .'
'Oh, yes, for the best,' nodded Mrs Smith. 'It's saved us. He had a writ out against him when Mr Armitage's cheque came in. I know he's grateful.'
'But I believe in being open . . .'
'Open,' nodded Mrs Smith.

'I've told him and I've told Mr Armitage that I just don't believe a man who has been blind for twenty-two years—'

'Terrible,' said Mrs Smith.

'—can be cured. Certainly not by—whatever this is. Do you believe it, Mrs Smith?'

Mrs Smith was cornered.

'Our Lord did it,' she said desperately. 'That is what my husband says . . .'

'I was a nurse during the war and I have worked for doctors,' said Mrs Johnson. 'I am sure it is impossible. I've knocked about a lot. You're a sensible woman, Mrs Smith. I don't want to offend you, but you don't believe it yourself, do you?'

Mrs Johnson's eyes grew larger and Mrs Smith's older eyes were helpless and small. She longed for a friend. She was hypnotized by Mrs Johnson, whose face and pretty neck grew firmly out of her frilled and high-necked blouse.

'I try to have faith . . .' said Mrs Smith, rallying to her husband. 'He says I hold him back. I don't know.'

'Some men need to be held back,' said Mrs Johnson, and she gave a fighting shake to her healthy head. All Mrs Smith could do in her panic was to watch every move of Mrs Johnson's, study her expensive shoes and stockings, her capable skirt, her painted nails. Now, at the shake of Mrs Johnson's head, she saw on the right side of the neck the small petal of the birthmark just above the frill of the collar.

'None of us are perfect,' said Mrs Smith slyly.

'I have been with Mr Armitage four years,' Mrs Johnson said.

'It is a lovely place up there,' said Mrs Smith, eager to change the subject. 'It must be terrible to live in such a lovely place and never see it . . .'

'Don't you believe it,' said Mrs Johnson. 'He knows that place better than any of us, better than me.'

'No,' groaned Mrs Smith. 'We had a blind dog when I was a girl. It used to nip hold of my dress to hold me back if it heard a car coming when I was going to cross the road. It belonged to my aunt and she said "That dog can see. It's a miracle." '

'He heard the car coming,' said Mrs Johnson. 'It's common sense.'

The words struck Mrs Smith.

'Yes, it is, really,' she said. 'If you come to think of it.'

She got up and went to the gas stove to make more coffee and new courage came to her. We know why she doesn't want Mr Armitage to see again! She was thinking: the frightening Mrs Johnson was really weak. Housekeeper and secretary to a rich man, sitting very pretty up there, the best of everything. Plenty of money, staff, cook, gardener, chauffeur, Rolls-Royce—if he was cured where would her job be? Oh, she looks full of herself now, but she is afraid. I expect she's got round him to leave her a bit.

The coffee began to bubble up in the pot and that urgent noise put excitement into her and her old skin blushed.

'Up there with a man alone. As I said to Dad, a woman can tell! Where would she get another man with that spot spreading all over? She's artful. She's picked the right one.' She was telling the tale to herself.

The coffee boiled over and hissed on the stove and a sudden forgotten jealousy hissed up in Mrs Smith's uncertain mind. She took the pot to the table and poured out a boiling-hot cup and, as the steam clouded up from it, screening her daring stare at the figure of Mrs Johnson, Mrs Smith wanted to say: 'Lying there stark naked by that swimming pool right in the face of my husband. What was he doing up there anyway?'

She could not say it. There was not much pleasure in Mrs Smith's life; jealousy was the only one that enlivened her years with Mr Smith. She had flown at him when he came home and had told her that God had guided him, that prayer always uncovered evil and brought it to the surface; it had revealed to him that the Devil had put his mark on Mrs Johnson, and that he wouldn't be surprised if that was what was holding up the healing of Mr Armitage.

'What were you doing,' she screamed at him, 'looking at a woman?'

The steam cleared and Mrs Smith's nervousness returned as she saw that composed face. She was frightened now of her own imagination and of her husband's. She knew him. He was always up to something.

'Don't you dare say anything to Mr Armitage about this!' she had shouted at him.

But now she fell back on admiring Mrs Johnson again.

Settled for life, she sighed. She's young. She is only fighting for her own. She's a woman.

And Mrs Smith's pride was stirred. Her courage was fitful and weakened by what she had lived through. She had heard Mrs Johnson was divorced and it gave Mrs Smith strength as a woman who had 'stuck to her husband'. She had not gone round taking up with men as she guessed Mrs Johnson might have done. She was a respectable married woman.

Her voice trembled at first but became stronger.

'Dad wanted to be a doctor when he was a boy,' Mrs Smith was saying, 'but there wasn't the money so he worked in a chemist's but it was always church on Sundays. I wasn't much of a one for church myself. But you must have capital and being just behind the counter doesn't lead anywhere. Of course I tried to egg him on to get his diploma and he got the papers—but I used to watch him. He'd start his studying and then he'd get impatient. He's a very impatient man and he'd say "Amy, I'll try the ministry"—he's got a good voice—"church people have money." '

'And did he?'

'No, he always wanted to, but he couldn't seem to settle to a church—I mean a religion. I'll say this for him, he's a fighter. Nixon, his first guv'nor, thought the world of him: quick with the sales. Nixon's Cough Mixture—well, he didn't invent it, but he changed the bottles and the labels, made it look—fashionable, dear—you know? A lot of Wesleyans took it.'

Mrs Smith spread her hands over her face and laughed through her fingers.

'When Nixon died someone in the church put up some money, a very religious, good man. One day Dad said to me—I always remember it—"It's not medicine. It's faith does it." He's got faith. Faith is—well, faith.'

'In himself?' suggested Mrs Johnson.

'That's it! That's it!' cried Mrs Smith with excitement. Then she quietened and dabbed a tear from her cheek. 'I begged him not to come down here. But this Mrs Rogers, the lady who owns the house, she's deaf and on her own, he knew her. She believes in him. She calls him Daniel. He's treating her for deafness, she can't hear a word, so we brought our things down after we closed up in Ealing, that's why it's so crowded, two of everything, I have to laugh.'

'So you don't own the house?'

'Oh, no, dear—oh, no,' Mrs Smith said, frightened of the idea. 'He wants something bigger. He wants space for his work.'

Mrs Smith hesitated and looked at the wall through which the sound of Mr Smith's voice was coming. And then, fearing she had been disloyal, she said, 'She's much better. She's very funny. She came down yesterday calling him. "Daniel. Daniel. I hear the cuckoo." Of course I didn't say anything: it was the man calling out "Coal". But she is better. She wouldn't have heard him at all when we came here.'

They were both silent.

'You can't live your life from A to Z,' Mrs Smith said, waking up. 'We all make mistakes. We've been married for forty-two years. I expect you have your troubles too, even in that lovely place.'

After the hour Mr Smith came into the kitchen to get Mrs Johnson.

'What a chatter!' he said to her. 'I never heard such a tittle-tattle in my life.'

'Yes, we had a fine chat, didn't we?'

'Oh, yes,' said Mrs Smith boldly.

'How is it going on?' said Mrs Johnson.

'Now, now,' Mr Smith corrected her. 'These cases seemingly take time. You have to get to the bottom of it. We don't intend to, but we keep people back by the thoughts we hold over them.'

And then, in direct attack on her—'I don't want you to hold no wrong thoughts over me. You have no power over divine love.' And he turned to his wife to silence her.

'And how would I do that?' said Mrs Johnson.

'Cast the mote out of thine own eye,' said Smith. 'Heal yourself. We all have to.' He smiled broadly at her.

'I don't know what all this talk about divine love is,' said Mrs Johnson. 'But I love Mr Armitage as he is.'

Smith did not answer.

Armitage had found his way to the door of the kitchen. He listened and said, 'Good-bye, Mrs Smith.' And to Mr Smith: 'Send me your bill. I'm having the footpath closed.'

They drove away.

'I love Mr Armitage as he is.' The words had been forced out of her by the detestable man. She hated that she had said to him what she could not say to Armitage. They surprised her. She hoped Armitage had not heard them.

He was silent in the car. He did not answer any of her questions. 'I'm having that path closed,' he repeated.

I know! she thought. Smith has said something about me. Surely not about 'it'!

When they got out of the car at the house he said to the chauffeur, 'Did you see Mr Smith when he came up here three weeks ago? It was a Thursday. Were you down at the pool?'

'It's my afternoon off, sir.'

'I know that. I asked whether you were anywhere near the pool. Or in the garden?'

'No, sir.'

Oh, God, Mrs Johnson groaned. Now he's turned on Jim.

'Jim went off on his motorbike. I saw him,' said Mrs Johnson.

They went into the house.

'You don't know who you can trust,' Armitage said and went across to the stairs and started up. But instead of putting his hand to the rail which was on the right, he put it out to the left, and not finding it, stood bewildered. Mrs Johnson quietly went to that side of him and nudged him in the right direction.

When he came down to lunch he sat in silence before the cutlets on his plate.

'After all these years! I know the rail is on the right and I put out my left hand.'

'You just forgot,' she said. 'Why don't you try forgetting a few more things?'

She was cross about the questioning of the chauffeur.

'Say, one thing a day,' she said.

He listened and this was one of those days when he cruelly paused a long time before replying. A minute went by and she started to eat.

'Like this?' he said, and he deliberately knocked his glass of water over. The water spread over the cloth towards her plate.

'What's this silly temper?' she said, and lifting her plate away, she lifted the cloth and started mopping with her table napkin and picked up the glass.

'I'm fed up with you blind people,' she said angrily. 'All jealousy and malice, just childish. You're so clever, aren't you? What happened? Didn't that good Mr Smith do the magic trick? I don't wonder your wife walked out on you. Pity the poor blind! What about other people? I've had enough. You have an easy life; you sail down in your Rolls and think you can buy God from Mr Smith just because—I don't know why—but if he's a fraud you're a fraud.' Suddenly the wronged inhabitant inside her started to shout: 'I'll tell you something about that Peeping Jesus: he saw the lot. Oh, yes, I hadn't a stitch on. The lot!' she was shouting. And then she started to unzip her dress and pull it down over her shoulder and drag her arm out of it. 'You can't see it, you silly fool. The whole bloody Hebrides, the whole plate of liver.'

And she went to his place, got him by the shoulder and rubbed her stained shoulder and breast against his face.

'Do you want to see more?' she shouted. 'It made my husband sick. That's what you've been sleeping with. And'—she got away as he tried to grip her and laughed—'you didn't know! *He* did.'

She sat down and cried hysterically with her head and arms on the table.

Armitage stumbled in the direction of her crying and put his hand on her bare shoulder.

'Don't touch me! I hate your hands.' And she got up, dodged round him to the door and ran out sobbing; slower than she was, he was too late to hear her steps. He found his way back to the serving hatch and called to the cook.

'Go up to Mrs Johnson. She's in her room. She's ill,' he said.

He stood in the hall waiting; the cook came downstairs and went into the sitting-room.

'She's not there. She must have gone into the garden.' And then she said at the window, 'She's down by the pool.'

'Go and talk to her,' he said.

The cook went out of the garden door and on to the terrace. She was a thin round-shouldered woman. She saw Mrs Johnson move back to the near side of the pool; she seemed to be staring at something in the water. Then the cook stopped and came shouting back to the house.

'She's fallen in. With all her clothes on. She can't swim. I know she can't swim.' And then the cook called out, 'Jim! Jim!' and ran down the lawns.

Armitage stood helpless.

'Where's the door?' he called. There was no one there.

Armitage made an effort to recover his system, but it was lost.

He found himself blocked by a chair, but he had forgotten which chair. He waited to sense the movement of air in order to detect where the door was, but a window was half open and he found himself against glass. He made his way feeling along the wall, but he was travelling away from the door. He stood still again, and smelling a kitchen smell he made his way back across the centre of the long room and at last found the first door and then the door to the garden. He stepped out, but he was exhausted and his will had gone. He could only stand in the breeze, the disorderly scent of the flowers and the grass mocking him. A jeering bird flew up. He heard the gardener's dog barking below and a voice, the gardener's voice, shouting 'Quiet!' Then he heard voices coming slowly nearer up the lawn.

'Helen,' called Armitage, but they pushed past him. He felt her wet dress brush his hand and her foot struck his leg; the gardener was carrying her.

'Marge,' Armitage heard her voice as she choked and was sick.

'Upstairs. I'll get her clothes off,' said the cook.

'No,' said Armitage.

'Be quiet,' said the cook.

'In my room,' said Armitage.

'What an idea!' said the cook. 'Stay where you are. Mind you don't slip on all this wet.'

He stood, left behind in the hall, listening, helpless. Only when the doctor came did he go up.

She was sitting up in bed and Armitage held her hand.

'I'm sorry,' she said. 'You'd better fill that pool up. It hasn't brought you any luck.'

Armitage and Mrs Johnson are in Italy now; for how long it is hard to say. They themselves don't know. Some people call her Mrs Armitage, some call her Mrs Johnson; this uncertainty pleases her. She has always had a secret and she is too old, she says, to give up the habit now. It still pleases Armitage to baffle people. It is impossible for her to deny that she loves Armitage, because he heard what she said to Smith; she has had to give in about that. And she does love him because his system has broken down completely in Italy. 'You are my eyes,' he says. 'Everything sounds different here.' 'I like a bit of noise,' she says.

Pictures in churches and galleries he is mad about and he likes listening to her descriptions of them and often laughs at some of her remarks, and she is beginning, she says, to get 'a kick out of the classical stuff' herself.

There was an awkward moment before they set off for Italy when he made her write out a cheque for Smith and she tried to stop him.

'No,' he said. 'He got it out of you. I owe you to him.'

She was fighting the humiliating suspicion that in his nasty prying way Smith had told Armitage about her before *she* had told him. But Armitage said, 'I knew all the time. From the beginning. I knew everything about you.'

She still does not know whether to believe him or not. When she does believe, she is more awed than shamed; when she does not believe she feels carelessly happy. He depends on her entirely here. One afternoon, standing at the window of their room and looking at the people walking in the lemonish light across the square, she suddenly said, 'I love you. I feel gaudy!' She notices that the only thing he doesn't like is to hear a man talk to her.

GRAHAM GREENE

The Blue Film

'OTHER people enjoy themselves,' Mrs Carter said.

'Well,' her husband replied, 'we've seen . . .'

'The reclining Buddha, the emerald Buddha, the floating markets,' Mrs Carter said. 'We have dinner and then go home to bed.'

'Last night we went to Chez Eve . . .'

'If you weren't with *me*,' Mrs Carter said, 'you'd find . . . you know what I mean, Spots.'

It was true, Carter thought, eyeing his wife over the coffee-cups: her slave bangles chinked in time with her coffee-spoon: she had reached an age when the satisfied woman is at her most beautiful, but the lines of discontent had formed. When he looked at her neck he was reminded of how difficult it was to unstring a turkey. Is it my fault, he wondered, or hers—or was it the fault of her birth, some glandular deficiency, some inherited characteristic? It was sad how when one was young, one so often mistook the signs of frigidity for a kind of distinction.

'You promised we'd smoke opium,' Mrs Carter said.

'Not here, darling. In Saigon. Here it's "not done" to smoke.'

'How conventional you are.'

'There'd be only the dirtiest of coolie places. You'd be conspicuous. They'd stare at you.' He played his winning card. 'There'd be cockroaches.'

'I should be taken to plenty of Spots if I wasn't with a husband.'

He tried hopefully, 'The Japanese strip-teasers . . .' but she had heard all about them. 'Ugly women in bras,' she said. His irritation rose. He thought of the money he had spent to take his wife with him and to ease his conscience—he had been away too often without her, but there is no company more cheerless than that of a woman who is not desired. He tried to drink his coffee calmly: he wanted to bite the edge of the cup.

'You've spilt your coffee,' Mrs Carter said.

'I'm sorry.' He got up abruptly and said, 'All right. I'll fix something. Stay here.' He leant across the table. 'You'd better not be shocked,' he said. 'You've asked for it.'

'I don't think I'm usually the one who is shocked,' Mrs Carter said with a thin smile.

Carter left the hotel and walked up towards the New Road. A boy hung at his side and said, 'Young girl?'

'I've got a woman of my own,' Carter said gloomily.

'Boy?'

'No thanks.'

'French films?'

Carter paused. 'How much?'

They stood and haggled awhile at the corner of the drab street. What with the taxi, the guide, the films, it was going to cost the best part of eight pounds, but it was worth it, Carter thought, if it closed her mouth for ever from demanding 'Spots'. He went back to fetch Mrs Carter.

They drove a long way and came to a halt by a bridge over a canal, a dingy lane overcast with indeterminate smells. The guide said, 'Follow me'.

Mrs Carter put a hand on Carter's arm. 'Is it safe?' she asked.

'How would I know?' he replied, stiffening under her hand.

They walked about fifty unlighted yards and halted by a bamboo fence. The guide knocked several times. When they were admitted it was to a tiny earth-floored yard and a wooden hut. Something— presumably human—was humped in the dark under a mosquito-net. The owner showed them into a tiny stuffy room with two chairs and a portrait of the King. The screen was about the size of a folio volume.

The first film was peculiarly unattractive and showed the rejuvenation of an elderly man at the hands of two blonde masseuses. From the style of the women's hairdressing the film must have been made in the late twenties. Carter and his wife sat in mutual embarrassment as the film whirled and clicked to a stop.

'Not a very good one,' Carter said, as though he were a connoisseur.

'So that's what they call a blue film,' Mrs Carter said. 'Ugly and not exciting.'

A second film started.

There was very little story in this. A young man—one couldn't see his face because of the period soft hat—picked up a girl in the street (her cloche hat extinguished her like a meat-cover) and accompanied her to her room. The actors were young: there was some charm and excitement in the picture. Carter thought, when the girl took off her hat, I know that face, and a memory which had been buried for more than a quarter of a century moved. A doll over a telephone, a pin-up girl of the period over the double bed. The girl undressed, folding her clothes very neatly: she leant over to adjust the bed, exposing herself to the camera's eye and to the young man: he kept his head turned from the camera. Afterwards, she helped him in turn to take off his clothes. It was only then he remembered—that particular playfulness confirmed by the birthmark on the man's shoulder.

Mrs Carter shifted on her chair. 'I wonder how they find the actors,' she said hoarsely.

'A prostitute,' he said. 'It's a bit raw, isn't it? Wouldn't you like to leave?' he urged her, waiting for the man to turn his head. The girl knelt on the bed and held the youth around the waist—she couldn't have been more than twenty. No, he made a calculation, twenty-one.

'We'll stay,' Mrs Carter said, 'we've paid.' She laid a dry hot hand on his knee.

'I'm sure we could find a better place than this.'

'No.'

The young man lay on his back and the girl for a moment left him. Briefly, as though by accident, he looked at the camera. Mrs Carter's hand shook on his knee. 'Good God,' she said, 'it's you.'

'It *was* me,' Carter said, 'thirty years ago.' The girl was climbing back on to the bed.

'It's revolting,' Mrs Carter said.

'I don't remember it as revolting,' Carter replied.

'I suppose you went and gloated, both of you.'

'No, I never saw it.'

'Why did you do it? I can't look at you. It's shameful.'

'I asked you to come away.'

'Did they pay you?'

'They paid her. Fifty pounds. She needed the money badly.'

'And you had your fun for nothing?'

'Yes.'

'I'd never have married you if I'd known. Never.'

'That was a long time afterwards.'

'You still haven't said why. Haven't you any excuse?' She stopped. He knew she was watching, leaning forward, caught up herself in the heat of that climax more than a quarter of a century old.

Carter said, 'It was the only way I could help her. She'd never acted in one before. She wanted a friend.'

'A friend,' Mrs Carter said.

'I loved her.'

'You couldn't love a tart.'

'Oh yes, you can. Make no mistake about that.'

'You queued for her, I suppose.'

'You put it too crudely,' Carter said.

'What happened to her?'

'She disappeared. They always disappear.'

The girl leant over the young man's body and put out the light. It was the end of the film. 'I have new ones coming next week,' the Siamese said, bowing deeply. They followed their guide back down the dark lane to the taxi.

In the taxi Mrs Carter said, 'What was her name?'

'I don't remember.' A lie was easiest.

As they turned into the New Road she broke her bitter silence again. 'How could you have brought yourself . . . ? It's so degrading. Suppose someone you knew—in business—recognized you.'

'People don't talk about seeing things like that. Anyway, I wasn't in business in those days.'

'Did it never worry you?'

'I don't believe I have thought of it once in thirty years.'

'How long did you know her?'

'Twelve months perhaps.'

'She must look pretty awful by now if she's alive. After all she was common even then.'

'I thought she looked lovely,' Carter said.

They went upstairs in silence. He went straight to the bathroom and locked the door. The mosquitoes gathered around the lamp and the great jar of water. As he undressed he caught glimpses of himself in the small mirror: thirty years had not been kind: he felt his thickness and his middle age. He thought: I hope to God she's dead. Please, God, he said, let her be dead. When I go back in there, the insults will start again.

But when he returned Mrs Carter was standing by the mirror. She had partly undressed. Her thin bare legs reminded him of a heron waiting for fish. She came and put her arms round him: a slave bangle joggled against his shoulder. She said, 'I'd forgotten how nice you looked.'

'I'm sorry. One changes.'

'I didn't mean that. I like you as you are.'

She was dry and hot and implacable in her desire. 'Go on,' she said, 'go on,' and then she screamed like an angry and hurt bird. Afterwards she said, 'It's years since that happened,' and continued to talk for what seemed a long half hour excitedly at his side. Carter lay in the dark silent, with a feeling of loneliness and guilt. It seemed to him that he had betrayed that night the only woman he loved.

Stone Boy with Dolphin

BECAUSE Bamber banged into her bike in Market Hill, spilling oranges, figs, and a paper packet of pink-frosted cakes, and gave her the invitation to make up for it all, Dody Ventura decided to go to the party. Under the striped canvas awnings of the fruit stall she balanced her rust-encrusted Raleigh and let Bamber scramble for the oranges. He wore his monkish red beard barbed and scraggy. Summer sandals buckled over his cotton socks although the February air burned blue and cold.

'You're coming, aren't you?' Albino eyes fixed hers. Pale, bony hands rolled the bright tang-skinned oranges into her wicker bike-basket. 'Unfortunately,' Bamber restored the packet of cakes, 'a bit mashed.'

Dody glanced, evasive, down Great St Mary's Passage, lined with its parked bikes, wheels upon wheels. The stone façade of King's and the pinnacles of the chapel stood elaborate, frosty, against a thin watercolour-blue sky. On such hinges fate turned.

'Who'll be there?' Dody parried. She felt her fingers crisped, empty in the cold. Fallen into disuse, into desuetude, I freeze.

Bamber spread his big hands into chalk webs covering the people universe. 'Everybody. All the literary boys. You know them?'

'No.' But Dody read them. Mick. Leonard. Especially Leonard. She didn't know him, but she knew him by heart. With him, when he was up from London, with Larson and the boys, Adele lunched. Only two American girls at Cambridge and Adele would have to nip Leonard in the bud. Hardly bud: bloom it was, full-bloom and mid-career. Not room for the two of us, Dody told Adele the day Adele returned the books she had borrowed, all newly underlined and noted in the margins. 'But *you* underline,' Adele justified sweetly, her face guileless in its cup of sheened blonde hair. 'I beat my own brats,' Dody said, 'you wipe your handmarks off.' For some reason,

at the game of queening, Adele won: adorably, all innocent surprise. Dody retreated with a taste of lemons into her green sanctum at Arden with her stone facsimile of Verrocchio's boy. To dust,
to worship: vocation enough.

'I'll come,' Dody suddenly said.

'With whom?'

'Send Hamish along.'

Bamber sighed. 'He'll be there.'

Dody pedalled off toward Benet Street, red plaid scarf and black
gown whipping back in the wind. Hamish: safe, slow. Like travelling by mule, minus mule-kicks. Dody chose with care, with care
and a curtsey to the stone figure in her garden. As long as it was
someone who didn't matter, it didn't matter. Ever since the start of
Lent term she had taken to brushing snow from the face of the
winged, dolphin-carrying boy centred in the snow-filled college garden. Leaving the long tables of black-gowned girls chattering and
clinking glasses of water over the sodden dinners of spaghetti, turnips,
and slick fried egg, with purple raspberry fool for dessert, Dody
would push back her chair, gliding, eyes lowered, obsequious, a false
demure face on, past high table where Victorian-vintage dons dined
on apples, chunks of cheese, and dietetic biscuits. Out of the scrolled
white painted hall with its gilt-framed portraits of Principals in high-
necked gowns leaning altruistic and radiant from the walls, far from
the drawn, wan blue-and-gold ferned draperies, she walked. Bare
halls echoed to her heels.

In the vacant college garden, dark-needled pines made their sharp
assaults of scent on her nostrils and the stone boy poised on one
foot, wings of stone balancing like feathered fans on the wind, holding his waterless dolphin through the rude, clamorous weathers of
an alien climate. Nightly after snows, with bare fingers, Dody scraped
the caked snow from his stone-lidded eyes, and from his plump
stone cherub foot. If not I, who then?

Tracking across the snow-sheeted tennis courts back to Arden,
the foreign students' house with its small, elect group of South
Africans, Indians, and Americans, she begged, wordless, of the orange
bonfire-glow of the town showing faint over the bare treetops, and
of the distant jewel-pricks of the stars: let something happen. Let
something happen. Something terrible, something bloody. Something
to end this endless flaking snowdrift of airmail letters, of blank pages

turning in library books. How we go waste, how we go squandering ourselves on air. Let me walk into *Phèdre* and put on that red cloak of doom. Let me leave my mark.

But the days dawned and set, neatly, nicely, toward an Honours BA, and Mrs Guinea came round, regular as clockwork, every Saturday night, arms laden with freshly laundered sheets and pillowcases, a testimony to the resolute and eternally renewable whiteness of the world. Mrs Guinea, the Scottish housekeeper, for whom beer and men were ugly words. When Mr Guinea died his memory had been folded up for ever like a scrap-book newspaper, labelled, and stored, and Mrs Guinea bloomed scentless, virgin again after all these years, resurrected somehow in miraculous maidenhood.

This Friday night, waiting for Hamish, Dody wore a black jersey and a black-and-white checked wool skirt, clipped to her waist by a wide red belt. I will bear pain, she testified to the air, painting her fingernails Applecart Red. A paper on the imagery in *Phèdre*, half-done, stuck up its seventh white sheet in her typewriter. Through suffering, wisdom. In her third-floor attic room she listened, catching the pitch of last shrieks; listened: to witches on the rack, to Joan of Arc crackling at the stake, to anonymous ladies flaring like torches in the rending metal of Riviera roadsters, to Zelda enlightened, burning behind the bars of her madness. What visions were to be had came under thumbscrews, not in the mortal comfort of a hot-water-bottle-cosy cot. Unwincing, in her mind's eye, she bared her flesh. Here, strike home.

A knock beat on the blank white door. Dody finished lacquering the nail of her left little finger, capped the bottle of blood-bright enamel, holding Hamish off. And then, waving her hand to dry the polish, gingerly she opened the door.

Bland pink face and thin lips set ready for a wiseguy smile, Hamish wore the immaculate navy blue blazer with brass buttons which made him resemble a prep school boy, or an off-duty yachtsman.

'Hello,' Dody said.

'How', Hamish walked in without her asking him, 'are you?'

'I've got sinus.' She sniffed thickly. Her throat clotted, obliging, with an ugly frogging sound.

'Look,' Hamish laved her with waterblue eyes, 'I figure you and I should quit giving each other such a hard time.'

'Sure.' Dody handed him her red wool coat and bunched up her academic gown into a black, funereal bundle. 'Sure thing.' She slipped her arms into the red coat as Hamish held it flared. 'Carry my gown, will you?'

She flicked off the light as they left the room and closed the door behind them. Ahead of Hamish down the two flights of stairs, step by step, she descended. The lower hall stood empty, walled with numbered doors and dark wainscotting. No sound, except for the hollow ticking of the grandfather clock in the stair-well.

'I'll just sign out.'

'No you won't,' said Hamish. 'You'll be late tonight. And you've got a key.'

'How do you know?'

'All the girls in this house have keys.'

'But', Dody whispered in protest as he swung the front door open, 'Miss Minchell has such sharp ears.'

'Minchell?'

'Our college secretary. She sleeps with us, she keeps us.' Miss Minchell presided, tight-lipped and grim, over the Arden breakfast table. She'd stopped speaking, it was rumoured, when the American girls started wearing pyjamas to breakfast under their bathrobes. All British girls in the college came down fully dressed and starched for their morning hot tea, kippers, and white bread. The Americans at Arden were fortunate beyond thought, Miss Minchell sniffed pointedly, in having a toaster. Ample quarter pounds of butter were allotted each girl on Sunday morning to last through the week. Only gluttons bought extra butter at the Home and Colonial Stores and slathered it double-thick on toast while Miss Minchell dipped her dry toast with disapproval into her second cup of tea, indulging her nerves.

A black taxicab loomed in the ring of light from the porch lamp where moths beat their wings to powder on spring nights. No moths now, only the winter air like the great pinions of an arctic bird, fanning shivers up Dody's spine. The rear door of the cab, open on its black hinges, showed a bare interior, a roomy cracked-leather seat. Hamish handed her in and followed her up. He slammed the door shut, and, as at a signal, the taxi spun off down the drive, gravel spurting away under the wheels.

Sodium vapour lights from the Fen Causeway wove their weird

orange glare among the leafless poplars on Sheep's Green and the houses and storefronts of Newnham Village reflected the sallow glow as the cab bounced along the narrow pot-holed road, turning with a lurch up Silver Street.

Hamish hadn't said a word to the driver. Dody laughed. 'You've got it all set, haven't you?'

'I always do.' In the sulphur light from the street lamps Hamish's features assumed an oddly oriental cast, his pale eyes like vacant slits above high cheekbones. Dody knew him for dead, a beer-sodden Canadian, his wax-mask escorting her, for her own convenience, to the party of tea-time poets and petty university D. H. Lawrences. Only Leonard's words cut through the witty rot. She didn't know him, but that she knew, that shaped her sword. Let what come, come.

'I always plan ahead,' Hamish said. 'Like I've planned for us to drink for an hour. And then the party. Nobody'll be there this early. Later they might even have a few dons.'

'Will Mick and Leonard be there?'

'You know them?'

'No. Just read them.'

'Oh, they'll be there. If anybody is. But keep away from them.'

'Why? Why should I?' Worth keeping from is worth going to. Did she will such meetings, or did the stars dictate her days, Orion dragging her, shackled, at his spurred heel?

'Because they're phonies. They are also the biggest seducers in Cambridge.'

'I can take care of myself.' Because when I give, I never really give at all. Always some shrewd miser Dody sits back, hugging the last, the most valuable crown jewel. Always safe, nun-tending her statue. Her winged stone statue with nobody's face.

'Sure,' said Hamish. 'Sure.'

The cab pulled up opposite the pinnacled stone façade of King's, starched lace in the lamplight, masquerading as stone. Black-gowned boys strode in twos and threes out of the gate by the porter's lodge.

'Don't worry.' Hamish handed her down to the sidewalk, stopping to count his coppers into the palm of the featureless cabdriver. 'It's all arranged.'

From the polished wooden bar of Miller's, Dody looked to the far end of the carpeted room at the couples going up and down the plush-covered stair to the diningroom: hungry going up, stuffed coming down. Greasy lip-prints on the goblet edge, partridge fat congealing, ruby-set with semiprecious chunks of currant jelly. The whisky was starting to burn her sinus trouble away, but her voice was going along with it, as it always did. Very low and sawdusty.

'Hamish.' She tried it.

'Where have you been?' His warm hand under her elbow felt good as anybody's warm hand. People swam past, undulant, with no feet, no faces. Outside the window, bordered with green-leaved rubber plants, face-shapes bloomed toward the glass from the dark outside sea and drifted away again, wan underwater plantlets at the fringe of vision.

'Ready?'

'Ready. Have you got my gown?' Hamish showed the black patch of cloth draped over his arm, and started to shoulder a path through the crowds around the bar toward the swinging glass door. Dody walked after him with fastidious care, focusing her eyes on his broad navy blue back, and, as he opened the door, ushering her ahead of him onto the sidewalk, she took his arm. Steady as he was, she felt safe, tethered like a balloon, giddy, dangerously buoyant, but still quite safe in the boisterous air. Step on a crack, break your mother's back. With care, she square-walked.

'You'd better put your gown on,' Hamish said after they'd been walking a bit. 'I don't want any proctors to nab us. Especially tonight.'

'Why especially?'

'They'll be looking for me tonight. Bulldogs and all.'

So at Peas Hill, under the green-lit marquee of the Arts theatre, Hamish helped her to slip her arms into the two holes of the black gown. 'It's ripped here on the shoulder.'

'I know. It always makes me feel as if I'm in a straitjacket. Keeps slipping down and pinning my arms to my sides.'

'They're throwing gowns away now, if they catch you in a ripped one. They just come over and ask for it and tear it up on the spot.'

'I'd sew it up,' Dody said. Mend. Mend the torn, the tattered. Salvage the ravelled sleeve. 'With black embroidery thread. So it wouldn't show.'

'They'd love that.'

Through the cobbled open square of Market Hill they walked

hand in hand. Stars showed faint above the blackened flank of Great St Mary's Church which had housed, last week, penitent hordes hearing Billy Graham. Past the wooden posts of the empty market stalls. Then up Petty Cury, past the wine merchant's with his windows of Chilean burgundy and South African sherry, past the shuttered butcher shops, and the leaded panes of Heffer's where the books on display spoke their words over and over in a silent litany on the eyeless air. The street stretched bare to the baroque turrets of Lloyd's, deserted except for a few students hurrying to late dinners or theatre parties, black gowns flapping out behind them like rooks' wings on the chill wind.

Dody gulped cold air. A last benison. In the dark, crooked alleyway of Falcon Yard, light spilled out of upper-storey windows, bursts of laughter came, dovetailing with the low, syncopated, strut of a piano. A doorway opened its slat of light to them. Halfway up the glaring steepness of the stair, Dody felt the building waver, rocking under the railing her hand held, her hand slimed chill with sweat. Snail-tracks, fever-tracks. But the fever would make everything flow right, burning its brand into her cheeks, blotting out the brown scar on her left cheek in a rose of red. Like the time she went to the circus when she was nine, with a fever, after putting ice under her tongue so the thermometer wouldn't register, and her cold had vanished when the sword-swallower sauntered into the ring and she fell for him on the spot.

Leonard would be upstairs. In the room at the top of the stairs she and Hamish were now ascending, according to the clocked stations of the stars.

'You're doing fine.' Hamish, just behind her shoulder, his hand firm under her elbow, lifted her upward. Step. And then, step.

'I'm not drunk.'

'Of course not.'

The doorframe hung suspended in a maze of stairs, walls lowering, rising, shutting off all the other rooms, all the other exits but this one. Obedient angels in pink gauze trolleyed away on invisible wires the surplus scenery. In the middle of the doorway Dody poised. Life is a tree with many limbs. Choosing this limb, I crawl out for my bunch of apples. I gather unto me my winesaps, my coxes, my bramleys, my jonathans. Such as I choose. Or do I choose?

'Dody's here.'

'Where?' Larson, beaming, his open American face hearty, faintly shiny, as always, with an unsquelchable easy pride, came up, glass in hand. Hamish did away with Dody's coat and gown and she laid her scarred brown leather pocketbook on the nearest windowsill. Mark that.

'I've drunk a lot,' Larson observed, amiable, shining with that ridiculous pride, as if he had just successfully delivered quadruplets in a nearby maternity ward. 'So don't mind what I say.' He, waiting for Adele, stored niceness spilled honey-prodigal, with Adele's lily head in mind. Dody knew him only by hellos and goodbyes, with Adele ever in attendance. 'Mick's gone already.' Larson jutted his thumb into the seethe and flux of dancers, sweat smells, and the Friday night stew of pungent warring perfumes.

Through the loose twining rhythms of the piano, through the blue heron-hover of smoke, Dody picked out the boy who was Mick, sideburns dark and hair rumpled, he doing a slow wide brand of British jive with a girl in sweater and skirt of hunter's green close-cleaving as frog-skin.

'His hair's standing up like devil's horns,' Dody said. They would all be girled then, Larson, Leonard. Leonard up from London to celebrate the launching of the new magazine. Straight-faced, she had taken in Adele's rumours, questioning, casual, spying from her battlement until Leonard loomed like the one statue-breaker in her mind's eye, knowing no statues of his own. 'Is that Mick's artist girl?'

Larson beamed. 'That's the ballet dancer. We're taking ballet now.' A deep knee-bend, sloshing his glass, spilled half. 'You know, Mick is Satanic. Like you say. You know what he did when we were kids in Tennessee?'

'No.' Dody's eyes scanned the peopled room, flicking over faces, checking accounts for the unknown plus. 'What did he do?'

There. In the far corner, by the wooden table, bare of glasses now, the punch bowl holding only a slush of lemonpeel and orangerind, a tall one. Back to her, shoulders hunched in a thick black sweater with a rolled-up collar, elbows of his green twill shirt stuck through the sweater-holes. His hands shot up, out, and scissored air to shape his unheard talk. The girl. Of course, the girl. Pale, freckled, with no mouth but a pink dim distant rosebud, willowed reedy, wide-eyed to the streaming of his words. It would be what's-her-name. Dolores. Or Cheryl. Or Iris. Wordless and pallid companion of Dody's classical tragedy hours. She. Silent, fawn-eyed. Clever. Sending her corpse for a stand-in at supervisions. To read about the problem of Prometheus in a rustling, dust-under-the-bed voice. While shut miles away, sanctuaried safe, she knelt in her sheet before the pedestalled marble. A statue-worshipper. She, too. So.

'Who', Dody asked, sure now, 'is that?'

But nobody answered.

'About wild dogs,' Larson said. 'And Mick was king of the wild dogs and made us fetch and carry. . . .'

'Drink?' Hamish emerged at her elbow with two glasses. The music stopped. Applause spattered. Ragged scum on the surge of voices. Mick came, finning the crowd apart with his elbows.

'Dance?'

'Sure.' Mick held Leonard's hours in his navyman's hand. Dody lifted her glass and the drink rose up to meet her mouth. The ceiling wavered and walls buckled. Windows melted, belling inward.

'Oh, Dody,' Larson grinned. 'You've spilled.'

Wet drops watered the back of Dody's hand, a dark stain extended, spreading on her skirt. Marked already. 'I want to meet some of these writers.'

Larson craned his thick neck. 'Here's Brian. The editor himself. Will he do?'

'Hello.' Dody looked down at Brian who looked up at her, dark-haired, impeccable, a dandy little package of a man. Her limbs began to mammoth, arm up the chimney, leg through the window. All because of those revolting little cakes. So she grew, crowding the room. 'You wrote that one about the jewels. The emerald's lettuce-light. The diamond's eye. I thought it was. . . .'

Beside the polished black hearse of the piano Milton Chubb lifted his saxophone, his great body sweating dark crescents under the arms. Dilys, shy, fuzzy chick of a thing that she was, nestled under his arm, blinking her lashless lids. He would crush her. He must be four times her size. Already, at college, a private fund had been raised among the girls to send Dilys to London to rid herself and her small rounding belly of Milton's burgeoning and unwanted heir. A whine. A thump thump.

Mick's fingers gripped for Dody's. His hand, lean, rope-hard, palm calloused, swung her off the hook of her thought and she kept going out, out of gravity's clutch. Planets sparked in the far reaches of her head. M. Vem. Jaysun Pa. Mercury. Venus. Earth. Mars. I'll get there. Jupiter. Saturn. Turning strange. Uranus? Neptune, tridented, green-haired. Far. Mongoloid-lidded Pluto, then. And asteroids innumerable, a buzz of gilded bees. Out, out. Bumping against someone, rebounding gently, and moving back to Mick again. To the here, to the now.

'I can't dance at all.'

But Mick turned a deaf ear, whorls waxed against siren-calls. Grinning at her from far, from farther away, he receded. Over the river and into the woods. His Cheshire cat grin hung luminous. Couldn't hear a word in his canary-feathered heaven.

'You wrote those poems,' Dody shouted over the roar of the music which swelled loud, louder, like the continuous roar of airplanes taking off from the runway across Boston Harbour. She taxied in for a close-up, the room blinking one, seen through the wrong end of a telescope. A red-haired boy bent over the piano, fingers cake-walking invisible. Chubb, sweating and flushed, lifted the horn and wailed, and Bamber, there too, flicked his bony chalk hand over and over the guitar.

'Those words. You made them.' But Mick, wrinkled and gone in his baggy checked pants, swung her out, and back, and caught her up again with Leonard nowhere. Nowhere at all. All the hours wasting. She, squandering hours like salt-shaker grains on the salt sea in her hunt. That one hunt.

Hamish's face kindled before her like a sudden candle from the ring of faces that spun away, features blurred and smeared as warming wax. Hamish, watchful, guardian angeling, waited in attendance, coming no nearer. But the man in the black sweater had come near. His shoulders, hunching, closed out the room piece by piece by piece. Pink, luminous and ineffectual, the face of Hamish winked out behind the blackness of the worn, torn sweater.

'Hello.' His square chin was green and rough. 'I'm out at the elbows.' It was a beard of moss on his chin. Room and voices hushed in the first faint twirl of a rising wind. Air sallowed, the storm to come. Air sultry now. Leaves turning up white-bellied sides in the queer sulphur light. Flags of havoc. His poem said.

'Patch the havoc.' But the four winds rose, unbuckled, from the stone cave of the revolving world. Come thou, North. Come thou, South. East. West. And blow.

'Not all their ceremony can patch the havoc.'

'You like that?'

Wind smacked and bellowed in the steel girders of the world's house. Perilous scaffold. If she walked very carefully. Knees gone jelly-weak. The room of the party hung in her eye like a death's-door camera-shot; Mick beginning again to dance with the girl in green, Larson's smile widening great as the grin on Humpty's head. Knitting up the sleeve of circumstance. She moved. And moved into the small new room.

A door banged shut. People's coats slumped in piles on the tables, cast-off sheaths and shells. Ghosts gone gallivanting. I chose this limb, this room.

'Leonard.'

'Brandy?' Leonard plucked a fogged glass from the yellowing sink. Raw reddish liquid sloshed out of the bottle into the glass. Dody reached. Her hands came away drenched. Full of nothing.

'Try again.'

Again. The glass rose and flew, executing first a perfect arc, an exquisite death-leap, onto the flat umber-ugly wall. A flower of winking sparks made sudden music, unpetalling then in a crystalline glissade. Leonard pushed back the wall with his left arm and set her in the space between his left arm and his face. Dody pitched her voice above the rising of the winds, but they rose higher in her ears. Then, bridging the gap, she stamped. Shut those four winds up in their goat-skin bags. Stamp. The floor resounded.

'You're all there,' Leonard said. 'Aren't you.'

'Listen. I've got this statue.' Stone-lidded eyes crinkled above a smile. The smile millstoned around her neck. 'I've got this statue to break.'

'So?'

'So there's this stone angel. Only I'm not sure it's an angel. This stone gargoyle maybe. A nasty thing with its tongue stuck out.' Under floorboards tornadoes rumbled and muttered. 'I'm crazy maybe.' They stopped their circus to listen. 'Can you do it?'

For answer, Leonard stamped. Stamped out the floor. Stamp, the walls went. Stamp, the ceiling flew to kingdom come. Stripping her red hairband off, he put it in his pocket. Green shadow, moss shadow, raked her mouth. And in the centre of the maze, in the sanctum of the garden, a stone boy cracked, splintered, million-pieced.

'When can I see you again?' Fever-cured, she stood, foot set victorious on a dimpled stone arm. Mark that, my fallen gargoyle, my prince of pebbles.

'I work in London.'

'When?'

'I've got obligations.' The walls closed in, wood grains, glass grains, all in place. 'In the next room.' The four winds sounded retreat, defeat, hooing off down their tunnel in the world's sea-girdled girth. O hollow, hollow. Hollow in the chambered stone.

Leonard bent to his last supper. She waited. Waited, sighting the whiteness of his cheek with its verdigris stain, moving by her mouth.

Teeth gouged. And held. Salt, warm salt, laving the tastebuds of her tongue. Teeth dug to meet. An ache started far off at their bone-root. Mark that, mark that. But he shook. Shook her bang against the solid-grained substance of the wall. Teeth shut on thin air. No word, but a black back turned, diminished, diminishing, through a sudden sprung-up doorway. Grains of wood moulding, level floorboard grains, righted the world. The wrong world. Air flowed, filling the hollow his shape left. But nothing at all filled the hollow in her eye.

The half-open door thronged with snickers, with whispers. On the smokeburdened air of the party that fissured through the crack Hamish came, intent, behind a glistening pink rubber mask.

'Are you all right?'

'Of course I'm all right.'

'I'll get your coat. We're going now.' Hamish went away again. A small boy wearing glasses and a drab mustard-coloured suit scuttled from a hole in the wall on his way to the lavatory. He ogled her, propped against the wall as she was, and she felt her hand, held to her mouth, jerking suddenly like a spastic's.

'Can I get you anything?' A queer light flickered in his eye, the light people have when the blood of a street accident gathers, puddling prodigal on the pavement. How they came to stare. Curious arenas of eyes.

'My pocketbook,' Dody steadily said. 'I left it behind the curtain on the first windowsill.'

The boy went out. Hamish appeared with her red coat, black gown dangling its rag of crepe. She shoved her arms in, obedient. But her face burned, unskinned, undone.

'Is there a mirror?'

Hamish pointed. A blurred, cracked oblong of glass hung over the once-white sink that was yellowed with a hundred years of vomit and liquor stains. She leaned to the mirror and a worn, known face with vacant brown eyes and a seamed brown scar on the left cheek came swimming at her through the mist. There was no mouth on the face: the mouth-place was the same sallow colour as the rest of the skin, defining its shape as a badly-botched piece of sculpture defines its shape, by shadows under the raised and swollen parts.

The boy stood beside her holding up a pocketbook of scratched brown leather. Dody took it. With a cartridge of red lipstick she followed the mouth-shape and made the colour come back. Thank you, she smiled at the boy with her bright new red mouth.

'Take care of me now,' she told Hamish. 'I have been rather lousy.'

'You're all right.' But that was not what the others would say.

Hamish pushed the door open. Out into the room. No one stared: a ring of turned backs, averted faces. The piano notes still sauntered underneath the talk. The people were laughing very much now. Beside the piano Leonard hunched, holding a white hand-kerchief to his left cheek. Tall, pale, Dolores-Cheryl-Iris with the tiger-lily freckles willowed up to help him blot the blood. I did that, Dody informed the deaf air. But the obligation got in the way, smirking. Obligations. Soap-and-water would not wash off that ring of holes for a good week. Dody Ventura. Mark me, mark that.

Because of Hamish, protecting, not angry at all, she got to the doorway of the room with no stone thrown, not wanting to go, but going. Starting down the narrow angled stair, with Adele's face, cupped by the shining blonde hair, coming up at her, open and frank and inviolable as a waterlily, that white-blondness, all pure, all folding purely within itself. Multi-manned, yet virginal, her mere appearance shaped a reprimand like the hushed presence of a nun. Oswald backed her up, and behind him marched the tall, gawky, and depressive Atherton. Oswald, his receding Neanderthal head brushed straight across with slicked hair to hide the shiny retreating slope, peered at Dody through his tortoise-shell glasses.

'Tell us something about bone-structure, Dody.' She saw, clear in the yet unbreached light of minutes to come, the three of them, together, walking into the room brimming with her act, with versions and variations on the theme of her act which would have marked her by tomorrow like the browned scar on her cheek among all the colleges and all the town. Mothers would stop in Market Hill, pointing to their children: 'There's the girl who bit the boy. He died a day after.' Hark, hark, the dogs do bark.

'That was last week.' Dody's voice rasped hollow, as from the bottom of a weed-grown well. Adele kept smiling her sublime, altruistic smile. Because she knew already what she would find in the room; no grab-bag of star-sent circumstance, but her chosen friends, and Larson, her special friend. Who would tell her everything, and keep the story on the tongues, changing, switching its colours, like a chameleon over smeared and lurid territory.

Back to the wall, Dody let Adele, Oswald and Atherton move past her up the stair to the room she was leaving and to the red circle of teethmarks and Leonard's obligation. Cold air struck, scything her shins. But no faces came to recognize Dody, nor fingers, censorious, to point her out. Blind storefronts and eyeless alley walls said: comfort ye, comfort ye. Black sky spaces spoke of the hugeness, the indifference of the universe. Greaning pricks of stars told her how little they cared.

Every time Dody wanted to say Leonard to a lamppost she would say Hamish, because Hamish was taking the lead, leading her away, safely, though damaged and with interior lesions, but safe, now, through the nameless streets. Somewhere, from the dark sanctuarial belly of Great St Mary's, or from deep, deeper within the town, a clock bonged out. Bong.

Black streets, except for the thin string of lights at the main corners. Townfolks all abed. A game began, a game of hide-and-go-seek with nobody. Nobody. Hamish stationed her behind a car, advancing, alone, peering around corners, then returning to lead her after him. Then, before the next corner, Dody ducking again behind a car, feeling the metal fender like dry ice, magnet-gripping her skin. Hamish leaving her, again, walking off to look again, and then coming back and saying it was safe so far.

'The proctors', he said, 'will be out after me.'

A damp mist rose and spired about their knees, blurring patches of the buildings and the bare trees, a mist blued to phosphor by the high, clear moon, dropping over a maple tree, a garden shed, here, there, its theatrical scrim of furred blue haze. After back alleys, after crossing the corner of Trumpington Street under the blackened scabrous walls of Pembroke College, a graveyard on the right, askew with stones, snow drifted white in patches and patches of dark where ground showed, they came to Silver Street. Boldly now they walked past the woodwork frame of the butcher shop with its surgical white venetian blind drawn on all the hanging heel-hooked pigs and the counters full of freckled pork sausages and red-purpled kidneys. At the gate of Queens', locked for the night, five boys in black gowns were milling under the moon. One began to sing:

A-las my love you do me wrong

'Wait.' Hamish placed Dody in a corner outside the spiked gates. 'Wait, and I'll find out a good place to get you over.'

To cast me off dis-courteously

The five boys surrounded Dody. They had no features at all, only pale, translucent moons for face-shapes, so she would never know them again. And her face, too, felt to be a featureless moon. They could never recognize her in the light of day.

'What are you doing here?'

'Are you all right?'

The voices whispered, batlike, about her face, her hands.

'My, you smell nice.'

'That perfume.'

'May we kiss you.'

Their voices, gentle and light as paper streamers, fell, gentle, touching her, like leaves, like wings. Voices webwinged.

'What are you doing here?'

Backed up against the barbed fence, staring at the white snow-field beyond the crescent of dark Queens' buildings, and at the blued fen fog floating waist-high over the snow, Dody stood her ground. And the boys dropped back, because Hamish had come up. The boys began to climb, one by one, over the spiked fence. Dody counted. Three. Four. Five. Sheep-counting sleepward. Holding onto the metal railing, they went swinging themselves over the pointed black spikes into the grounds of Queens', eft and drunken, reeling pussyfooted on the crusted snow.

'Who are they?'

'Just some late guys going into the court.' The boys were all over now, and they went away across the arched wooden bridge over the narrow green river, the bridge that Newton had once put together without bolts.

'We're going over the wall,' Hamish said. 'They've found a good place. Only you mustn't talk until we're in.'

'I can't go over. Not with this tight skirt. I'll get spikes through my hands.'

'I'll help you.'

'But I'll fall.' Still, Dody pulled her tweed skirt up to her thighs, to the top of her nylon stockings, and put one foot up on the wall. Game, oh, game. She lifted her left leg over the spikes where they were lowest, but the black tips caught and pierced through her skirt. Hamish was helping, but she stuck there, one leg over the spikes, teetering. Would it hurt? Would she bleed at all? Because the spikes were going through her hands, and her hands were so cold she couldn't feel them. And then Hamish was all at once on the inside of the fence, cupping his hands into a stirrup for her to step in, and without arguing it out or thinking, she simply stepped, pivoting herself over with her hands, and the spikes looked to be going right through them.

'My hands,' she began, 'they'll bleed . . .'

'Shh!' Hamish put his hand over her mouth. He was looking around the inside of the crescent toward a dark doorway. The night stood still and the moon, far off and cold in its coat of borrowed light, made a round O mouth at her, Dody Ventura, coming into Queens' court at three in the morning because there was nowhere else to go, because it was a station on the way. A place to get warm in, for she felt very cold. Wasted, wasting, her blood gone to redden the circle of teethmarks on Leonard's cheek, and she, a bloodless husk, left drifting in limbo. Here with Hamish.

Dody followed Hamish down the side of the building, tracing her fingers along the rough-textured brick until they were at the doorway, with Hamish being furtive and quiet for no reason because there was no sound, only the great snow silence and the silence of the moon and the hundreds of Queens' men breathing silent in their deep early morning sleep before the dawn. The first stair on the landing creaked, even though they had taken their shoes off. The next was quiet. And so the next.

A room all by itself. Hamish shut the ponderous oaken door behind them, and then the thin inner door, and lit a match. The big room jumped into Dody's view, with its dark, shiny cracked-leather couch and thick rugs and a wallful of books.

'Made it. I'm in a good entry.'

From behind the panelled wainscotting, a bed creaked. There sounded a stifled sigh.

'What's that? Rats?'

'No rats. My roommate. He's all right. . . .' Hamish vanished, and the room with him. Another match scritched, and the room came back. Hamish, squatting, turned on the gas jet for the fire. The hissing sound lighted with a soft whoosh, a blue flare, and the gas flames in their neat row behind the white asbestos lattice started shadows flickering behind the great couch and the heavy chairs.

'I'm so cold.' Dody sat on the rug, before the fire which made Hamish's face yellowish, instead of pink, and his pale eyes dark. She rubbed her feet, putting her red shoes, which looked black, into the grate before the fire. The shoes were all wet inside, she could feel the dampness with her finger, but she could not feel the cold, only the numb hurt of her toes as she rubbed them, rubbing the blood back into them.

Then Hamish pushed her back on the rug, so her hair fell away from her face and wound among the tufts of the rug, for it was a deep rug, thick-piled, with the smell of shoeleather about it, and ancient tobacco. What I do, I do not do. In limbo one does not really burn. Hamish began kissing her mouth, and she felt him kiss her. Nothing stirred. Inert, she lay staring toward the high ceiling crossed by the dark wood beams, hearing the worms of the ages moving in them, riddling them with countless passages and little worm-size labyrinths, and Hamish let his weight down on top of her, so it was warm. Fallen into disuse, into desuetude, I shall not be. (It is simple, if not heroic, to endure.)

And then at last Hamish just lay there with his face in her neck, and she could feel his breathing quieten.

'Please scold me.' Dody heard her voice, strange and constricted in her chest, from lying on her back on the floor, from the sinus, from the whisky. I am sick of labelled statues. In a grey world no fires burn. Faces wear no names. No Leonards can be for no Leonards live: Leonard is no name.

'What for?' Hamish's mouth moved against her neck, and she felt now again how unnaturally long her neck was, so that her head nodded far from her body, on a long stem, like the picture of Alice after eating the mushroom, with her head on its serpent neck above the leaves of the treetops. A pigeon flew up, scolding. Serpents, serpents. How to keep the eggs safe?

'I am a bitch,' Dody heard her voice announce from out of the doll-box in her chest, and she listened to it, wondering what absurd thing it would say next. 'I am a slut,' it said with no conviction.

'No you're not.' Hamish made a kiss-shape with his mouth on her neck. 'But you should have learned your lesson. I told you about them, and you should have learned your lesson.'

'I've learned it,' the small voice lied. But Dody hadn't learned her lesson, unless it was the lesson of this limbo where no one got hurt because no one took a name to tie the hurt to like a battered can. Nameless I rise. Nameless and undefiled.

One more lap of her journey loomed ahead: the safe getting in the door at Arden, and then up to her room with no stairs creaking. With no simmering Miss Minchell bursting out of her room on the landing between the first and second stair, raging in her red flannel bathrobe, her hair undone for the night from the bun and hanging in a straight black braid down her back, with the grey strands braided into it, down to her buttocks, and no one to see. No one to know that Miss Minchell's hair, when undone, reached her buttocks. Some day, some year hence, it would be a braid of battleship grey, probably, by that time, reaching down to her knees. And by the time it grew to touch the floor, it would be turned pure white. White, and wasting its whiteness on the blank air.

'I am going now.'

Hamish heaved himself up, and Dody lay indifferent, feeling the warm place where he had been, and the warm sweat drying and cooling on the cool air through her sweater. 'You do just what I tell you,' Hamish said. 'Or we'll never get out.'

Dody put on her ribboned shoes, grown so hot from the fire that they seared her footsoles.

'Do you want to climb over the spikes again? Or try the brook?'

'The brook?' Dody looked up at Hamish, standing over her, solid and warm, like a horse, breathing hay in its stable. 'Is it deep?' It might have been Larson, or Oswald, or even Atherton, standing there, standing in with the pleasant warmth common to horses. Immortal horse, for one replaced another. And so all was well in an eternity of horses.

'Deep? It's frozen over. I'd test it first, anyway.'

'The brook, then.'

Hamish stationed Dody by the doorway. First he opened the inside door, and then, after peering out the crack, the outside door. 'You wait here.' He wedged her against the doorjamb.

'When I signal, come.'

Stairs chirked faintly under his weight, and then, after a pause, a match flared, lighting the entrance, showing the grains of wood, worn to a satin patina by the hands of ghosts. Dody began to descend. How we pass and repass ourselves, never fusing, never solidifying into the perfect stances of our dreams. Tiptoeing down, her right hand sliding along the rail, Dody felt all Queens' crescent list and recover, and list again, a ship rolling on heavy seas. Then a splinter entered her index finger, but she kept her hand sliding down along the rail, right on into it. Unwincing. Here. Strike home. The splinter broke off, imbedded in her finger with a small nagging twinge. Hamish stationed her in the dark niche of the entry, a dressmaker's dummy.

'Wait,' he whispered, and the whisper ran up the stairs, twining around the banisters, and there might be someone on the next landing, wary, listening, with flashlights and an official badge. 'I'll beckon if it's all clear, and you run like hell. Even if anyone starts coming after, you run, and we'll get over the brook and across the road before they can catch us up.'

'What if they arrest you?'

'They won't do any more than send me down.' Hamish dropped the match to the ground. He crushed it under his foot. The small yellow world went out and the courtyard flowered, large, luminous, blue in the light of the moon. Hamish stepped out into the courtyard, his dark shape cut itself clear against the snow, a pasteboard silhouette, moving, diminishing, blending into the darkness of the bushes bordering the brook.

Dody watched, hearing her own breathing, a cardboard stranger's, until a dark figure detached itself from the shrubbery. It made a motion. She ran out. Her shoes crunched loud, breaking through the crust of the snow, each step crackling, as if someone were crumpling up newspapers, one after the other. Her heart beat, and the blood beat up in her face, and still the snow crusts broke and broke under her feet. She could feel the soft snow dropping like powder into her shoes, in the space between the arch of her foot and the instep of the shoe, dry, and then melting cold. No sudden search-light, no shouts.

Hamish reached for her as she stumbled up and they stood for a moment by the hedge. Then Hamish began shouldering through the rough-thicketed bush, making a path for her, and she followed him, setting her feet down, tramping the lower branches, scratching and scraping her legs on the brittle twigs. They were through, at the bank of the brook, and the hedge closed behind them its gate of briars, dark, unbroken.

Hamish slid down the bank, ankle-deep in snow, and held out his hand, so Dody would not fall coming down. Snow-covered ice bore them up, but before they had reached the other shore, the ice began to boom and crack in its depths. They jumped clear onto the opposite bank and started to crawl up the steep, slippery side, losing their footing, reaching for the top of the bank with their hands, their hands full of snow, their fingers stinging.

Crossing the snow-field toward the bare expanse of Queen's Road, stilled now, muted and relieved of the daily thunder of lorries and market vans, they walked hand in hand, not saying a word. A clock struck clear out of the dead quiet. Bong. Bong. And bong. Newnham Village slumbered behind glazed windows, a toy town constructed of pale orange taffy. They met no one.

Porch light and all the house lights out, Arden stood dark in the weak blue wash of the setting moon. Wordless, Dody put her key in the lock, turned it, and pressed the door handle down. The door clicked open on the black hall, thick with the ticking of the coffin-shaped clock and hushed with the unheard breathing of sleeping girls. Hamish leaned and put his mouth to her mouth. A kiss that savoured of stale hay through the imperfect clothwork of their faces.

The door shut him away. A mule that didn't kick. She went to the pantry closet just outside Mrs Guinea's quarters and opened the door. The smell of bread and cold bacon rose to meet her nostrils, but she was not hungry. She reached down until her hand met the cool glass shape of a milk bottle. Taking off her shoes again, and her black gown and her coat, she started up the back stairs with the milk bottle, weary, yet preparing, from a great distance, the lies what would say, if necessary, how she had been in Adele's room, talking with Adele until late, and had just come up. But she remembered with lucid calm that she had not looked in the signing-out book to see if Adele had checked herself back yet. Probably Adele had not signed out either, so there was no knowing, unless she tried Adele's door, whether Adele really was back. But Adele's room was on the first floor, and it was too late now. And then she remembered why she did not want to see Adele at all anyway.

When Dody flicked on the light switch, her room leapt to greet her, bright, welcoming, with its grass-green carpet and the two great book-cases full of books she had bought on her book-allowance and might never read, not until she had a year of nothing to do but sit, with a locked door, and food hoisted up by pulleys, and then she might read through them. Nothing, the room affirmed, has happened at all. I, Dody Ventura, am the same coming in as I was going out. Dody dropped her coat on the floor, and her torn gown. The gown lay in a black patch, like a hole, a black doorway into nowhere.

Carefully Dody put her shoes on the armchair so she would not wake Miss Minchell who slept directly below, coiled up for the night in her braid of hair. The gas ring on the hearth, black and greasy, was stuck with combings of hair, speckled with face powder fallen from past makeup jobs in front of the mirror on the mantel over the fireplace. Taking a kleenex, she wiped the gas ring clean and threw the stained tissue into the wicker waste-paper basket. The room always got musty over the weekend and only really cleared on Tuesdays when Mrs Guinea came in with the vacuum cleaner and her bouquet of brushes and feather dusters.

Dody took one match from the box with the swan on it which she kept on the floor by the grey gas-meter with all its myriad round dial-faces and numbers stencilled black on white. She lit the gas fire and then the gas ring, its circle of flames flaring up blue to her retreating hand, leaping to scorch. For a minute she squatted there, absorbed, to remove the splinter from her right hand where it had dug itself into a little pocket of flesh, showing dark under the transparent covering of skin. With thumb and forefinger of her left hand she pinched the skin together and the head of the splinter came out, black, and she took the thin sliver between her fingernails, slowly drawing it out until it came clear. Then she put the small battered aluminum pot on the gas ring, poured the pint of milk into it, and sat on the floor, cross-legged. But her stockings cut tight into her thighs, so she got up and ripped down her girdle like the peel of a fruit, and pulled the stockings off, still gartered to it, because they were shredded past saving from the twigs of the bushes outside Queens'. And she sat down again in her slip, rocking back and forth gently, her mind blank and still, her arms around her knees and her knees hugged against her breasts, until the milk began to show bubbles around the brim of the pan. She sat then in the green-covered chair, sipping the milk from the Dutch pottery cup she had picked up in New Compton Street that first week in London.

The milk seared her tongue, but she drank it down. And knew that tomorrow the milk would not pass, all of it, out of her system, extricable as a splinter, but that it would stay to become part of herself, inextricable, Dody. Dody Ventura. And then, slowly, upon this thought, all the linked causes and consequences of her words and acts began to gather in her mind, slowly, like slow-running sores. The circle of teethmarks hung out its ring of bloodied roses for Dody Ventura to claim. And the invariable minutes with Hamish would not be spat out like thistles, but clung, clung fast. No limbo's nameless lamb, she. But stained, deep-grained with all the words and acts of all the Dodys from birth-cry on. Dody Ventura. She saw. Who to tell it to? Dody Ventura I am.

The top floor of Arden did not respond, but remained dead still in the black dawn. Nothing outside hurt enough to equal the inside mark, a Siamese-twin circle of teethmarks, fit emblem of loss. I lived: that once. And must shoulder the bundle, the burden of my dead selves until I, again, live.

Barefoot, Dody stripped off her white nylon slip, and her bra and pants. Electricity crackled as the warmed silk tore clear of her skin. She flicked out the light and moved from the wall of flame, and from the ring of flame, toward the black oblong of the window. Rubbing a clear porthole in the misted pane, she peered out at the morning, caught now in a queer no-man's-land light between moonset and sunrise. Noplace. Noplace yet. But someplace, someplace in Falcon Yard, the panes of the diamond-paned windows were falling in jagged shards to the street below, catching the light from the single lamp as they fell. Crash. Bang. Jing-jangle. Booted feet kicked the venerable panes through before dawning.

Dody undid the catch on the window and flung it open. The frame screaked on its hinges, banging back to thud against the gable.

Kneeling naked on the two-seated couch in the window-niche, she leaned out far over the dead dried garden. Over the marrowless stems marking iris roots, bulb of narcissus and daffodil. Over the bud-nubbed branches of the cherry tree and the intricate arbour of laburnum boughs. Over the great waste of earth roof under the greater waste of sky. Orion stood above the peaked end of Arden, his gold imperishable joints polished in the cold air, speaking, the way he always spoke, his bright-minted words out of the vast wastage of space: space where, his testified, space where the Miss Minchells, the Hamishes, all the extra Athertons and the unwanted Oswalds of the world went round and round, like rockets, squandering the smoky fuse of their lives in the limbo of unlove. Patching the great gap in the cosmos with four o'clock teas and crumpets and a sticky-sweet paste of lemon curd and marzipan.

The cold took her body like a death. No fist through glass, no torn hair, strewn ash and bloody fingers. Only the lone, lame gesture for the unbreakable stone boy in the garden, ironic, with Leonard's look, poised on that sculpted foot, holding fast to his dolphin, stone-lidded eyes fixed on a world beyond the clipped privet hedge, beyond the box borders and the raked gravel of the cramped and formal garden paths. A world of no waste, but of savings and cherishings: a world love-kindled, love-championed. As Orion went treading riveted on his track toward the rim of that unseen country, his glitter paling in the blue undersea light, the first cock crew.

Stars doused their burning wicks against the coming of the sun. Dody slept the sleep of the drowned.

Nor saw yet, or fathomed how now, downstairs in the back kitchen, Mrs Guinea began another day. Saver, cherisher. No waster, she. Splitting the bony kippers into the black iron frying pan, crisping the fat-soaked toast in the oven, she creakily hummed. Grease jumped and spat. Sun bloomed virginal in the steel-rimmed rounds of her eyeglasses and clear light fountained from her widowed bosom, giving back the day its purity.

To her potted hyacinths, budding on the window-sill in their rare ethereal soil of mother-of-pearl shells, Mrs Guinea affirmed, and would forever affirm, winter aside, what a fine, lovely day it was after all.

PAUL THEROUX

An English Unofficial Rose

THE fashion in London that year was rags—expensive ones, but rags all the same. Women wore torn blouses and patched jeans, and their shoes were painted to make them look scuffed and wrongly paired. Their hair was cut in a raggedy way—front hanks of it dyed pink and green and bright orange and blue. They wore plastic badges and safety pins, and they called themselves punks. The idea was for them to seem threadbare. It was a popular look, but it was not easy to achieve. It took imagination, and time, and a great deal of money for these spoiled wealthy girls to appear down and out.

But Sophie Graveney wore a smooth blouse of light silk the texture of skin and a close-fitting skirt slit all the way to her hip, and steeply pitched spike-heeled shoes. The weather was uncertain, but most days were warm enough for a jacket. Sophie's was bottle green velvet, with two gold clasps where there might have been buttons. She said she could not bear to be mistaken for someone poor, and was willing to risk being called unfashionable for her rich clothes. Styles change, but beauty is never out of fashion—I told her that. And no one expected this rag business and coloured hair to last very long. People stared at Sophie. She was no punk. Horton, my boss at the London embassy, had called her 'an English rose'.

I find it impossible to see a well-dressed woman without thinking that she is calling attention to her charms. Isn't that lady with the plunging neckline and that coin-slot between her squeezed breasts—isn't she declaring an interest? Certainly that attractive woman in the tight skirt is making a general promise. At the same time, such women are betraying a certain self-love. Narcissism is necessary to that kind of beauty. It is the aspect that maddens lovers, because it is unreachable. Sophie's self-possession was a kind of inaccessible narcissism. In her beauty there was both effort and ease. Her hair had been softly curled, her eyes and mouth delicately painted, but beneath her make-up and under her lovely clothes was a tall strong girl in the full bloom of thirty, who jogged four miles before breakfast. She was healthy, she was reliable, she dressed as if she was trying to please me. I was flattered, and grateful. So far, I had no friends in London who weren't connected with the embassy. I liked the promises of her clothes. I needed someone like Sophie.

After month here I had a routine. It was a bachelor's consolation—my job, my office, my hotel-room—and I hated it. It made everything serious and purposeful, and I suppose I began to look like one of those super-solemn diplomats, all shadows and monosyllables, who carry out secret missions against treacherous patriots in the (believe me) laughably false plots of political thrillers. It seemed pointless, this austerity, and I did not believe in my own efficiency. I wanted to break free of it, to prove to myself that my job did not matter that much. I hated the implied timidity, the repetition, the lack of surprise in this routine. In a poor country—a Hardship Post—I could have justified these dull days by telling myself that I was making a necessary sacrifice. It is some comfort, when one is braving tedium, to know that one is setting a good example. But in London? I wanted to live a little. I knew I was missing something.

No longer: Sophie and I were dining at 'Le Gavroche', having just seen a spirited *Hamlet* at the Royal Court. She smiled at me from across the table. There was a flicker of light in her eyes, a willingness to agree, good humour, a scent of jasmine on her shoulders, and a certain pressure of her fingers on my hand that offered hope and a promise of mildly rowdy sex. I was happy.

She talked the whole time, which was fine with me. By habit and inclination I never discussed my work with anyone outside the embassy. I listened gladly to everything she said; I was grateful that I did not have to ask my ignorant questions about London. And yet, though she talked mostly about herself, she revealed very little. She told me her plans—she wanted to travel, to see Brazil ('again')—she had friends in Hong Kong and New York. She was vague about what she was doing at the moment. She seemed surprised and a little annoyed that I should ask.

'"What do you do for a living?"' Her accent was the adenoids-and-chewing-gum American drawl that the British put on when they are feeling particularly skittish, which, thank God, is seldom. She went on, 'It's not a question people ask in England.'

'It wasn't my question. I didn't say, "What do you do for a living?" I said, What are you doing at the moment?'

'I know what you meant, and you shouldn't have asked.'

'I wonder why.'

'Because it's bloody rude, that's why,' she said softly, and seemed pleased with herself. 'Anyway, why should one do anything? I know plenty of people who don't do anything at all—absolutely nothing.'

'You like that, do you?'

'Yes, I think there's something really fantastic about pure idleness.'

'"Consider the lilies of the field", etcetera, etcetera.'

'Not only that. If a person doesn't really do anything, you have to take him for what he is rather than what he does. Your asking me what I'm doing is just a cheap way of finding out what sort of person I am. That's cheating.'

I said, 'I don't see why.'

She shrugged and said, 'Daddy didn't do much, but Daddy was a gentleman. You probably think I'm a frivolous empty-headed girl who sits around the house all day varnishing her nails, waiting for parties to begin.' She worked her tongue against her teeth and said, 'Well, I am!'

'It's been the ruin of many a Foreign Service marriage—I mean, the wife with nothing to do but advance her husband's career. All that stage-managing, all those tea parties, all that insincerity.'

'I'd love it. I wouldn't complain. My headmistress used to say, "Find a husband who'll give you a beautiful kitchen, and lovely flowers to pick, and lots of expensive silver to polish." That sort of thing's not fashionable now, is it? But I don't care. I like luxury.'

And although this was only the second time I had seen her, I began seriously to calculate the chances of my marrying her. She was glamorous and intelligent; she was good company. Men stared at her. She had taste, and she was confident enough in her taste so that she would never be a slave to fashion.

I was turning these things over in my mind when she said, 'What do I do? A bit of modelling, a little television, some lunchtime theatre. You probably think it's all a waste of time.'

'You're an actress,' I said.

'No,' Sophie said, 'I just do a little acting. It's not what you'd call a career. Everyone criticizes me for not being ambitious. Crikey, of course I spend time, but I don't waste time—are you wasting time if you're enjoying yourself?' She did not wait for my reply. She said, 'I'm enjoying myself right now.'

'Shall we do this again some time?'

'Again and again,' she said slowly in a kind of heated contentment. 'Would you like that?'

'Yes,' I said, 'I really would.'

She reached over and touched my face, brushed the aroma of jasmine on my cheek—it was the most intimate, the most disarming gesture—and said, 'It's getting late—'

I kissed her in the taxi going back to her house. She did not push me away. But after a few minutes she lifted her head.

'What's wrong?'

'This is Prince of Wales Drive,' she said. 'Aren't those mansion blocks fantastic?' She kissed me again, then she took my arm and said, 'Wouldn't you like to live there?'

They were not my idea of mansions, but I found myself agreeing with her: yes, I said, and looked through the taxi window at the balconies. It was as if we were choosing a location for a lovenest. Sophie squeezed my arm and said, 'That one's fun.'

I saw dark windows.

'Wouldn't it be super to live here?' she said. And it seemed as if she was speaking for both of us.

I said, 'It sure would.'

'Are you looking for a place to rent? Your hotel must be rather cramped.'

'I'm moving the first chance I get. I'm going to buy a place—renting is pointless, and anyway I've got two years' accumulated hardship allowance to spend.'

She kissed me then, and we were still kissing as the taxi sped on, turned into a side street, and came to rest on Albert Bridge Road in front of a tall terrace of narrow houses. I paid for the taxi, then walked with her to the front gate.

She said, 'Your taxi's driving away.'

'I've paid him. I told him to go.'

'That was silly. You'll never get another one around here—and the buses have stopped running.'

I said, 'Then I'll walk,' and clung to her hand, 'although I don't want to.'

'It's not far to your hotel.'

'I didn't mean that. I just meant I'd rather stay here with you.'

'I know,' she said. 'You're sweet.'

The English are frugal. They can even economize on words. Sophie gave nothing away. She planted a rather perfunctory kiss on my cheek, and when I tried to embrace her she eased out of my grasp and said comically, 'Do you *mind*?' and took out her door-key.

'You're beautiful,' I said.

'I'm tired,' she said. 'I must get some sleep. I have a big day tomorrow—a screening—and I have to be up at the crack of dawn.' She gave me another brisk kiss and said lightly, 'Otherwise I'd invite you in.'

I said, 'I want to scc you again soon.'

'I'd like that,' she said.

I was half in love with her by then and in that mood—half-true, half-false—I strolled home whistling, congratulating myself on my good luck. London is kind to lovers—it offers them privacy and quiet nights and spectacles. Albert Bridge was alight. In the day-time it is a classic bridge, but at night all its thousands of yellow lightbulbs and its freshly painted curves give it the look of a circus midway suspended in the sky. The lights on its great sweeps are very cheering at midnight over the empty river.

The next day I wanted to call her, but a long meeting with Scaduto held me up. It was eight o'clock before I left the office. Scaduto furiously preened himself in the elevator mirror as we descended to Grosvenor Square. He said he had called his wife to tell her he'd be late. She had screamed at him.

'Get this,' he said. 'She says to me, "You never listen." That's interesting, isn't it? What does it mean, "You never listen"? Isn't it a paradox, or some kind of contradiction? Tell me something—has anyone ever said that to you? "You never listen"?'

I said no.

'Right. Because you're not married,' Scaduto said. 'You've got to be married to hear things like that. Isn't that terrible?' He began to laugh, and said, 'You wouldn't believe the things married people say to each other. You can't imagine the hostility. "You never listen" is nothing. The rest is murder.'

'Awful things?'

'Horrendous things,' he said. 'What are you smiling for?'

'What does it matter what people say, if you never listen?'

Steam came out of Scaduto's nose—the sound of steam, at any rate. Then he said, 'I've seen guys like you—nice, happy, single guys. They get married. They get ruined. Unhappy? You have no idea.'

I was indignant at this because I took everything he said to be a criticism of Sophie. His conceited and miserable presumption belittled her. I thought: *How dare you*—because his cynicism was about life in general, the hell of marriage, the tyranny of women. He was cheating me out of my pleasant mood, the afterglow of having met someone I genuinely liked and wanted to be with. I hated his sullen egotism: his marriage was all marriages, his wife was all women, he and I were brothers. *Ain't it awful* was the slogan of this fatuous freemasonry of male victims.

I said, 'I pity you.'

'Keep your pity,' Scaduto said. 'You'll need it for yourself.'

His voice was full of fatigue and experience—and ham. The married man so often tries to sound like a war veteran, and the divorced one like a man discharged because of being wounded in action.

I met Spohie for a drink a few days later. We went out to eat again the following week. On our first date I had wanted to go to bed with her. That desire had not passed, and yet another feeling, a deeper one, like loyalty and trust, asserted itself. It was compatible with lechery—in fact, it gave lechery and honourable glow.

And now she called me occasionally at work. She had a touching telephone habit of saying, 'It's only me—' What could be easier or more intimate? She liked to talk on the phone. It was fun, she said, whispering into my ear.

About two weeks after *Hamlet* she called and said, 'Are you free this evening?'

'Yes,' I said, and thought of an excuse to dispose of the appointment I had—a journalist that Jeeps had urged me to meet. I could meet him anytime, but Sophie—

'It's a flat,' she said.

What was she talking about?

'Just what you've been looking for,' she said. 'Bang on Prince of Wales Drive. Overstrand Mansions. It's at the front with that lovely view.'

'That's wonderful—shall we meet there?'

'I'm afraid I can't make it. I've got a screening on. But you should go. I'll give you the owner's number. It's a friend of a friend.'

'I was hoping to see you,' I said, interrupting her as she told me the price. 'What about going with me tomorrow?'

'This flat might not be available tomorrow,' she said.

'I'll look at it this evening then.'

'Super.'

'Will you be available tomorrow?' I said.

'Quite available.' She said that in what I thought of as her actress's voice. Whenever she said anything very serious or very definite, she used this voice, and sometimes an American accent.

I went to see the flat. Its balcony was the brow of this red brick mansion block, and from it I could see, my own hotel beyond the park and the river. This pleased me—my own landmark, in this enormous city, among the slate roofs and steeples and treetops.

The flat was larger than I wanted, but I thought of Sophie and began to covet it for its extra rooms. The owner, a friendly German, offered me a drink.

He said, 'As you probably gathered, my wife and I decided to split up.'

I told him I had gathered no such thing, that it was none of my business, but the longer I sat there trying to stop him telling me about his divorce (it seemed to cast a blight on the place), the more I felt I was sitting in my own room, enclosed by my own walls, the crisp shadow spikes of my balcony's grille-work printed on my own floor.

'She is now back in Germany,' he said. 'She is an extremely attractive woman.'

Because I felt it was already mine, and because I knew it was a sure way of getting him off the subject of his wife, I said, 'I want it—let's make a deal.'

Later I gave him the name of the embassy lawyer and said I wanted to move quickly. By noon the next day my deposit was down and a surveyor was on his way to Overstrand Mansions. Within a week papers were examined and contracts exchanged. It was the fastest financial transaction I had ever made, but I was paying cash—my accumulated hardship allowance from my Malaysian post, and the rest of my savings. It was my first property deal, but I felt in my heart that I was not in it alone and not acting solely for myself.

I had called Sophie the day after visiting the flat. I was, I realize, intent upon impressing her. Would she want me if she saw I was powerful and decisive? When I finally found her, she was pleased but said she couldn't meet me. 'Quite available' meant busy. She had a 'sitting' or perhaps a 'shooting' or a 'screening' or a 'viewing' or an 'opening' or a 'session'. What did she mean? I had never come across these obscure urgencies before. Language is deceptive; and though English is subtle it also allows a clever person—one alert to the ambiguities of English—to play tricks with mock precision and to combine vagueness with politeness. English is perfect for diplomats and lovers.

Some days later I was making Sophie a drink in my hotel room—a whisky. I had the bottle in my hand.

'It should be champagne,' I said. 'We're celebrating—I've exchanged contracts.'

'Whisky's warmer than champagne,' she said, and sat down to watch me.

'How do you like it?'

'Straight,' she said. She was not looking at the glass. 'As it comes.'

'How much?'

'Filled,' she said, and showed me her teeth.

'How many inches is that?'

'Right up,' she said, and sighed and smiled. She had said that in her actress's voice.

There was no hitch, the survey encouraged me, and Horton—as if praising my on-the-job initiative—said that London property was a great investment. I was more than hopeful; I had, mentally, already begun to live at Overstrand Mansions. In this imagining Sophie was often standing at the balcony with a drink in her hand, or in her tracksuit, damp with dew and effort (running raised her sexual odours, the mingled aroma of fish and flowers), and she was laughing, saying 'Do you *mind*?' as I tried to hold her, and driving me wild.

I had to be reassured that she needed me as much. We had not so far used the word love. We pretended we had an easy-going, trusting friendship. I think I joked with her too much, but I was very eager—foolishly so. Instead of simply saying that I wanted to see her and making a date with her, I said, 'Sophie, you're avoiding me.'

It was facetious. I could not blame her for missing the feeble joke. But, unexpectedly, it made her defensive. She took it as an accusation, and explained carefully that she had very much wanted to see me but that she was busy with—what?—a 'shooting' or a 'viewing'. Then I was sorry for what I'd said.

The arrival of my sea-freight a day later gave me an excuse to call her. She was excited. She said, 'You've got the key!'

'Not yet.'

She made a sympathetic noise. She sounded genuinely sorry I hadn't moved in. And then, 'What if something goes wrong with the deal?'

'I'll find something else.'

'No, no,' she said. 'Nothing will go wrong. Actually, I can quite see you there in Overstrand Mansions—'

She didn't say *us*, she excluded herself; but this talk of me and my flat bored me. And I was a little disappointed. I listened dimly, then hung up having forgotten to tell her my real reason for calling—that my sea-freight had passed through customs and was at the warehouse.

It was furniture, my Malaysian treasures, my *nat* from Burma, a temple painting from Vietnam, Balinese masks, *wayang* puppets and my Buddha and the assortment of cutthroat swords and knives (a *kris* from the Sultan, a *kukri* from the DC) I had been given as going-away presents. I had bought the furniture in Malacca. It was Chinese—an opium-smoker's couch, and a carved settee with lion's head legs. The bed had carved and gilded panels and four uprights for a mosquito-net canopy. And I had teak chests with carved drawers, and polished rosewood chairs, and brassware and pewter. These and my books. I had nothing else—no plates or dinnerware, no glasses, no cooking pots, nothing practical.

I wanted Sophie to see my collection of Asian things. I knew she would be impressed. She would marvel at them, she would want me more. I longed to leave my small hotel room on Chelsea embankment and spread out in Overstrand Mansions. I yearned to be with her.

She had picked out the flat, and in buying it I had never acted so quickly, so decisively. I was glad. She had made me bold. But I tried not to think that I had bought it for us, because it was too early—she was not mine yet. I hoped she knew how badly I wanted her. I could not imagine that a desire as strong as mine could be thwarted. At times it seemed simple: I would have her because I wanted her.

I thought: If only she could see these treasures from Asia! And I tried to imagine our life together. It was a wonderful combination of bliss and purpose, and it made my bachelor solitude seem selfish. What was the point in living alone? Secretly, I believed we were the perfect couple.

All this happened in the space of three weeks—the exchanged contracts, the arrival of my furniture, the numerous phone calls. I did not see Sophie in the third week, and it was frustrating because now it was Sunday. The German had given me the key yesterday; I was moving in tomorrow.

I moved in. She had led me here. I was grateful to her that morning as the men carried my tea-chests of Asian treasures upstairs (and they called their moving van a 'pantechnicon'—I had never heard the word before and it pleased me). There was space for everything. This was the apartment I needed. She had known that, somehow, or guessed—another indication that she understood me. I was delighted because Sophie had made this her concern. But where was she?

I called her but got no answer. I tried again and managed, by speaking slowly, to leave a message with her charlady who was exasperated at having to write it down. She read the message back to me with uncertainty and resentment.

That night I woke up and was so excited to be in a place of my own I got out of bed and walked up and down, and through all the rooms and finally onto the balcony. I was so pleased at this outcome I vowed that I would send Sophie a case of champagne. I lingered on the balcony—I liked everyone out there in the dark.

My roaming in the night made me oversleep. I did not get to the embassy until after eleven, and my desk was stacked with pink *While You Were Out* . . . message slips. Scaduto had called and so had Horton's secretary, and there was still some paperwork to do on my apartment—insurance and some estimates for painting it. But most of the messages were from Sophie. Five slips of paper—she had been ringing at twenty-minute intervals.

My happiness was complete. It was what I wanted most, and it seemed to me as if I had everything I wanted and was in danger of being overwhelmed by it. The phone-calls were the proof that she wanted me. I would send her the case of champagne, of course; but that was a detail. She could move in with me anytime. We would do what people did these days—live together, see how we got along. It was a wonderful tolerant world that made such arrangements possible. I would have a routine security check done on Sophie, but if Horton questioned the wisdom of our living together I could always reply that I had met her at his house and that he had a share in creating this romance.

The phone rang. Sophie's voice was eager. 'You've moved in—that's super.'

'You've been a great help,' I said. 'When can you come over to look around?'

'My life's a bit fraught at the moment,' she said. Her voice became cautious and a bit detached. But she had rung me five times this morning! Then all the eagerness was out of her voice and with composure she said, 'I expect I'll be able to manage it one of these days. I'm not far away.'

'We could have a drink on the balcony. The way you like it. Right up.'

'Yes,' she said, with uncertainty. She had forgotten.

Then I felt awkward and over-intimate. Had I said too much?

'It's a very nice flat,' I said.

'I'm so glad for you. I knew you'd like it.'

I wanted to say, *Come and live with me! There's enough room for both of us! I won't crowd you—I'll make you happy in my Chinese bed!*

We worked at the London embassy with the doors open. I could see Vic Scaduto just outside my office, talking to my secretary. He was impatient and held a file in his hand that he clearly wanted to show me. He made all the motions of wanting to interrupt me; he made his impatience look like patience. At times like this Scaduto tap-danced.

I said, 'Sophie, I have to go.'

'There was something else,' she said.

'I'll call you back.'

'I've rung you half a dozen times this morning. Please. I've got so much else to do.'

She sounded irritated, and I could see Scaduto's feet—shuffle-tap, shuffle-tap—and the flap of the file as he juggled it.

I said to Sophie, 'What is it?'

'You've moved in—you've got the flat. So it's all settled.'

'I'm going to buy you a case of champagne,' I said. 'I'll help you drink it. I know a place—'

'That's very sweet of you,' she said. 'But two per cent is the usual commission.'

I waited for her to say more. There was no more.

I said, 'Are you joking?'

'No.' She sounded more than irritated now. She was angry: I was being wilfully stupid.

'Is that why you've been ringing me this morning—for your commission?'

'I found you a flat. You had an exclusive viewing. You bought it for a reasonable price—'

I said, 'Did you fix the price?'

But she was still talking.

'—and now you seem to be jibbing at paying me my commission.'

Scaduto put his head into my office and said, 'Have you got a minute?'

'Write me a letter,' I said, and still heard her voice protesting in the little arc the receiver made, the distance between my ear and the desk.

Scaduto smiled. He said, 'For a minute there you looked married.'

Because Sophie's letter was delivered by hand and arrived at the front door of the embassy it was treated as if it contained a bomb or a threat or an explosive device. It was x-rayed, it was passed through a metal detector, it was sniffed by a trained dog. I complained to the Security Guard about the delay, but in the event I wished that the letter had never come.

It could not have been more businesslike or broken my spirit more. It was one chilly paragraph telling me that I had moved in, that she had been instrumental in finding me the flat—'following your instructions'—and that in such a situation two per cent was the usual commission.

It was not a great deal of money, the equivalent of a few thousand dollars—not enough to be really useful, only enough to ruin a friendship. I could have paid her immediately, but I didn't want her to be my agent—I wanted her love.

Instead of writing what I felt, I wrote logically: I had not given her an order to find me a flat; she had not negotiated the price; she had not been present when I reached agreement with the owner; she had played no part in the contract or any subsequent negotiations. Hers had been an informal, friendly function. If I had known that the fee was going to be two per cent I would have taken it into account and adjusted my offer. She was, I said, presuming.

Then I contemplated tearing up the letter. I had either to destroy it or send it—I didn't want it around.

Sophie rang me two days later. She said, 'How dare you! Don't write me letters like that. What do you take me for?'

I said, 'I thought you were an actress.'

She turned abusive. She swore at me. Until that moment I had marvelled at how different her English was from mine. And then, with a few blunt swears, she lost her nationality and became any loud, crude, bad-tempered bitch spitting thorns at me.

I sent her the champagne. She did not acknowledge it. And she dropped out of my life.

I learned one thing more. One day I found an earring in the kitchen. I called the German, who now lived in a smaller place in Pimlico. He came over and had a drink. He was grateful—it had belonged not to his wife but to his mother. He showed no signs of wanting to leave. My whisky made him sentimental. He said that we were both foreigners here in London. We had a lot in common. We ought to be friends.

To get him off the subject, I asked him about Sophie.

'She brought us together, you and me,' the German said.

'She charged me two per cent. But it was worth it. Here we are, drinking together as friends.' He glanced around the flat. He said, 'These English girls—especially the ones with money—can be very businesslike. And did you notice? She is very pretty. She lives with an Iranian chap. They all want Iranians these days.' The German laughed out loud. 'Even if you call them Persians they still seem boring!'

And then, to my relief, he began telling me about his ex-wife.

The Loveliness of the Long-Distance Runner

I SIT at my desk and make a list of all the things I am not going to think about for the next four and a half hours. Although it is still early the day is conducive to laziness—hot and golden. I am determined that I will not be lazy. The list reads:

1. My lover is running in an organized marathon race. I hate it.

2. Pheidippides, the Greek who ran the first Marathon, dropped dead at the end of it. And his marathon was four miles shorter than hers is going to be. There is also heat stroke, torn achilles tendons, shin splints, and cramp. Any and all of which, including the first option, will serve her right. And will also break my heart.

3. The women who are going to support her, love her, pour water down her back and drinks down her throat are not me. I am jealous of them.

4. Marathon running is a goddam competitive, sexist, lousy thing to do.

5. My lover has the most beautiful body in the world. Because she runs. I fell in love with her because she had the most beautiful body I had ever seen. What, when it comes down to it, is the difference between my devouring of her as a sex-object and her competitive running? Anyway she says that she does not run competitively. Anyway I say that I do not any longer love her just because she has the most beautiful body.

Now she will be doing her warm-up exercises. I know these well, as she does them every day. She was doing them the first time I saw her. I had gone to the country to stay the weekend with her sister, who's a lawyer colleague of mine and a good friend. We were doing some work together. We were sitting in her living room and she was feeding her baby and Jane came in, in running shorts, T-shirt, and yards and yards of leg. Katy had often joked about her sister who was a games mistress in an all-girls' school, and I assumed that this was she. Standing by the front door, with the sun on her hair, she started these amazing exercises. She stretched herself from the waist and put her hands flat on the floor; she took her slender foot in her hand and bent over backwards. The blue shorts strained slightly; there was nothing spare on her, just miles and miles of tight, hard, thin muscle. And as she exhibited all this peerless flesh she chatted casually of this and that—how's the baby, and where she was going to run. She disappeared through the door. I said to Katy,

'Does she know I'm gay?'

Katy grinned and said, 'Oh, yes.'

'I feel set up.'

'That's what they're called—setting-up exercises.'

I felt very angry. Katy laughed and said, 'She is too.'

'Is what?' I asked.

'Gay.' I melted into a pool of desire.

It's better to have started. The pre-race excitement makes me feel a little sick. Tension. But also . . . people punching the air and shouting 'Let's go, let's go.' Psyching themselves up. Casing each other out. Who's better than who? Don't like it. Don't want to do it. Wish I hadn't worn this T-shirt. It has 'I am a feminist jogger' on it. Beth and Emma gave it to me. Turns people on though. Men. Not on to me but on to beating me. I won't care. There's a high on starting though, crossing the line. Good to be going, good to have got here. Doesn't feel different because someone has called it a marathon, rather than a good long run. Keep it that way. But I would like to break three and a half hours. Step by step. Feel good. Fitter than I've ever been in my life, and I like it. Don't care what Sally says. Mad to despise body when she loves it so. Dualist. I like running. Like me running. Space and good feeling. Want to run clear of this crowd—too many people, too many paces. Want to find someone to run my own pace with. Have to wait. Pace; endurance; deferment of pleasure; patience; power. Sally ought to like it—likes the benefits alright. Bloke nearby wearing a T-shirt that reads, 'Runners make the best lovers'. He grins at me. Bastard. I'll show him: run for the Women's Movement. A trick. Keep the rules. My number one rule is 'run for yourself'. But I bet I can run faster than him.

Hurt myself running once, because of that. Ran a ten-mile race, years ago, with Annie, meant to be a fun-run and no sweat. There was this jock; a real pig; he kept passing us, dawdling, letting us pass him, passing again.

And every time these remarks—the vaseline stains from our nipples, or women getting him too turned on to run. Stuff like that; and finally he runs off, all sprightly and tough, patronizing. We ran on. Came into the last mile or so and there he was in front of us, tiring. I could see he was tired. 'Shall we?' I said to Annie, but she was tired too. 'Go on then,' she was laughing at me, and I did. Hitched up a gear or two, felt great, zoomed down the hill after him, cruised alongside, made it look easy, said, 'Hello, sweetheart, you look tired' and sailed on. Grinned back over my shoulder, he had to know who it was, and pulled a muscle in my neck. Didn't care—he was really pissed off. Glided over the finishing line and felt great for twenty minutes. Then I felt bad; should have known better— my neck hurt like hell, my legs cramped from over-running. But it wasn't just physical. Felt bad mentally. Playing those games.

Not today. Just run and feel good. Run into your own body and feel it. Feel road meeting foot, one by one, a good feeling. Wish Sally knew why I do it. Pray she'll come and see me finish. She won't. Stubborn bitch. Won't think about that. Just check leg muscles and pace and watch your ankles. Run.

If she likes to run that much of course I don't mind. It's nice some evenings when she goes out, and comes back and lies in the bath. A good salty woman. A flavour that I like. But I can't accept this marathon business: who wants to run 26 miles and 385 yards, in a competitive race? Jane does. For the last three months at least our lives have been taken over by those 26 miles, what we eat, what we do, where we go, and I have learned to hate every one of them. I've tried, 'why' I've asked over and over again; but she just says things like, 'because it's there, the ultimate'. Or 'Just once Sally, I'll never do it again.' I *bet*, I think viciously. Sometimes she rationalizes: women have to do it. Or, it's important to the women she teaches. Or, it has to be a race because nowhere else is set up for it: you need the other runners, the solidarity, the motivation. 'Call it sisterhood. You can't do it alone. You need . . .' And I interrupt and say, 'You need the competition; you need people to beat. Can't you see?' And she says, 'You're wrong. You're also talking about something you know nothing about. So shut up. You'll just have to believe me: you need the other runners and mostly they need you and want you to finish. And the crowd wants you to finish, they say. I want to experience that solidarity, of other people wanting you to do what you want to do.' Which is a slap in the face for me, because I don't want her to do what she wants to do.

And yet—I love the leanness of her, which is a gift to me from marathon training. I love what her body is and what it can do, and go on doing and not be tired by doing. She has the most beautiful legs, hard, stripped down, with no wastage and her Achilles' tendons are like flexible rock. Running does that for her. And then I think, damn, damn, damn. I will not love her for those reasons; but I will love her because she is tough and enduring and wryly ironic. Because she is clear about what she wants and prepared to go through great pain to get it; and because her mind is clear, careful, and still open to complexity. She wants to stop being a Phys. Ed. teacher because now that women are getting as much money for athletic programmes the authorities suddenly demand that they should get into competition, winning trips. Whereas when she started it was fun for her and for women being together as women, doing the things they had been laughed at for, as children.

She says I'm a dualist and she laughs at me. She says I want to separate body and soul while she runs them together. When she runs she thinks: not ABC like I think with my tidy well-trained mind, but in flashes—she'll trot out with some problem and run twelve or fifteen miles and come home with the kinks smoothed out. She says that after eight or ten miles she hits a euphoric high— grows free—like meditation or something, but better. She tells me that I get steamed up through a combination of tension and inactivity. She can run out that stress and be perfectly relaxed while perfectly active. She comes clean. Ten or twelve miles at about eight minutes per mile: about where she'll be getting to now.

I have spent another half hour thinking about the things I was not going to think about. Tension and inactivity. I cannot concentrate the mind.

When I bend my head forward and Emma squeezes the sponge onto my neck, I can feel each separate drop of water flow down my back or over my shoulders and down between my breasts. I listen to my heart beat and it seems strong and sturdy. As I turn Emma's wrist to see her watch her blue veins seem translucent and fine. Mine seem like strong wires conducting energy. I don't want to drink and have it lying there in my stomach, but I know I should. Obedient, giving over to Emma, I suck the bottle. Tell myself I owe it to her. Her parents did not want her to spend a hot Saturday afternoon nursing her games teacher. When I'm back in rhythm I feel the benefits of the drink. Emma is a good kid. Her parents' unnamed suspicions are correct. I was in love with a games teacher once. She was a big strong woman, full of energy. I pretended to share what the others thought and mocked her. We called her Tarzan and how I loved her. In secret dreams I wanted to be with her. 'You Tarzan, me Jane,' I would mutter, contemplating her badly-shaved underarms, and would fly with her through green trees, swing on lianas of delight. She was my first love; she helped make me a strong woman. The beauty, the immensity of her. When we swam she would hover over the side of the pool and as I looked up through the broken, sparkly water there she would be hauling me through with her strength.

Like Sally hauls me through bad dreams, looming over me in the night as I breathe up through the broken darkness. She hauls me through muddle with her sparkly mind. Her mind floats, green with sequinned points of fire. Sally's mind. Lovely. My mind wears Nike running shoes with the neat white flash curling back on itself. It fits well and leaves room for my toes to flex. If I weren't a games teacher I could be a feminist chiropodist—or a midwife. Teach other women the contours of their own bodies—show them the new places where their bodies can take them. Sally doesn't want to be taken—only in the head. Sex of course is hardly in her head. In the heart? My heart beats nearly 20 pulses a minute slower than hers: we test them together lying in the darkness, together. 'You'll die, you shit,' I want to yell at her. 'You'll die and leave me. Your heart isn't strong enough.' I never say it. Nice if your hearts matched. The Zulu warrior women could run fifty miles a day and fight at the end of it. Fifty miles together, perfectly in step, so the veldt drummed with it. Did their hearts beat as one? My heart can beat with theirs, slow and strong and efficient—pumping energy.

Jane de Chantal, after whom I was named, must have been a jogger. She first saw the Sacred Heart—how else could she have known that slow, rich stroke which is at the heart of everything? Especially back then when the idea of heart meant only emotions. But she was right. The body, the heart at the heart of it all: no brain, no clitoris without that strong slow heart. Thesis: was a seventeenth-century nun the first jogger? Come on; this is rubbish. Think about footstrike and stride length. Not this garbage. Only one Swedish garbage-collector, in the whole history of Swedish municipal rubbish collection, has ever worked through to retirement age—what perseverance, endurance. What a man. Person. Say garbage person. Sally says so. Love her. Damn her. She is my princess. I'm the younger son (say person) in the fairy story. But running is my wise animal. If I'm nice to my running it will give me good advice on how to win the princess. Float with it. Love it. Love her. There has to be a clue.

Emma is here again. Car? Bicycle? She can't have run it. She and Beth come out and give me another drink, wipe my face. Lovely hands. I come down and look around. After twenty miles they say there are two sorts of smiles among runners—the smiles of those who are suffering and the smiles of those who aren't. 'You're running too fast,' says Beth, 'You're too high. Pace yourself, you silly twit. You're going to hurt.' 'No,' I say. 'I'm feeling good.' But I know she's right. Discipline counts. Self-discipline, but Beth will help with that. 'We need you to finish,' says Emma. 'Of course she'll finish,' says Beth. I love them and I run away from them, my mouth feeling good with orange juice and soda water. Ought to have been Sally though. Source of sweetness. How could she do this to me? How could she leave me? Desert me in the desert. Make a desert. This is my quest—my princess should be here. Princess: she'd hate that. I hate that. Running is disgusting; makes you think those thoughts. I hurt. I hurt and I am tired. They have lots of advice for this point in a marathon. They say think of all the months that are wasted if you stop now. But not wasted because I enjoyed them. They say, whoever wanted it to be easy? I did. They say, think of that man who runs marathons with only one leg. And that's meant to be inspirational. He's mad. We're all mad. There's no reason but pride. Well, pride then. Pride and the thought of Sally suppressing her gloating if I go home and say it hurt too much. I need a good reason to run into and through this tiredness.

Something stabs my eyes with orange. Nothing really hurt before but now it hurts. Takes me all of three paces to locate the hurt: cramp in the upper thighs. Sally's fault; I think of her and tense up. Ridiculous. But I'll be damned if I quit now. Run into the pain; I know it will go away and I don't believe it. Keep breathing steadily. It hurts. I know it hurts, shut up, shut up, shut up. Who cares if it hurts? I do. Don't do this. Seek out a shirt in front of you and look at the number. Keep looking at the number. 297. Do some sums with that. Can't think of any. Not divisible by 2, or 3, or 5. Nor 7.9? 9 into 29 goes 3.3 and carry 2. 9 into 27. Always works. If you can divide by something the cramp goes away. Is that where women go in childbirth—into the place of charms? All gay women should run marathons—gives them solidarity with their labouring sisters. I feel sick instead. I look ahead and there is nothing but the long hill. Heartbreaking. I cannot.

Shirt 297 belongs to a woman, a little older than me perhaps. I run beside her, she is tired too. I feel better and we run together. We exchange a smile. Ignore the fact that catching up with her gives me a lift. We exchange another smile. She is slowing. She grins and deliberately reduces her pace so that I can go ahead without feeling bad. That's love. I love her. I want to turn round, jog back and say, 'I will leave my lover for you.' 'Dear Sally,' I will write, 'I am leaving you for a lady who' (and Sally's mental red pencil will correct to 'whom') 'I met during the marathon and unlike you she was nice and generous to me.' Alternative letter, 'Dear Sally, I have quit because long distance running brings you up against difficulties and cramps and I cannot take the pain.' Perseverance, endurance, patience, and accepting love are part of running a marathon. She won't see it. Damn her.

Must be getting near now because there's a crowd watching. They'll laugh at me. 'Use the crowd,' say those who've been here before. 'They want you to finish. Use that.' Lies. Sally doesn't want me to finish. What sort of princess doesn't want the quest finished? Wants things cool and easy? Well pardon me, your Royal Highness. Royal Highness: the marathon is 26 miles and 385 yards long because some princess wanted to see the start of the 1908 Olympic Marathon from Windsor Palace and the finish from her box in the White City Stadium. Two miles longer than before. Now standardized. By appointment. Damn the Royal Princess. Damn Sally.

Finally I accept that I'm not going to do any work today. It takes me several more minutes to accept what that means—that I'm involved in that bloody race. People tend, I notice, to equate accepting with liking—but it's not that simple. I don't like it. But, accepting, I get the car out and drive to the shops and buy the most expensive bath oil I can find. It's so expensive that the box is perfectly modest—no advertising, no half-naked women. I like half-naked women as a matter of fact, but there are such things as principles. Impulsively I also buy some matching lotion, thinking that I will rub it on her feet tonight. Jane's long slender feet are one part of her body that owe nothing to running. This fact alone is enough to turn me into a foot fetishist.

After I have bought the stuff and slavered a bit over the thought of rubbing it into her poor battered feet (I worked it out once.

Each foot hits the ground about 800 times per mile. The force of the impact is three times her weight. 122 pounds times 800 times 26 miles. It does not bear thinking about). I realize the implications of rubbing sweet ointment into the tired feet of the beloved person. At first I am embarrassed and then I think, well Mary Magdalen is one way through the sex–object, true love dichotomy. Endurance, perseverance, love. She must have thought the crucifixion a bit mad too. Having got this far in acceptance I think that I might as well go down to the finish and make her happy. We've come a long way together. So I get back into the car and do just that.

It is true, actually. In the last few miles the crowd holds you together. This is not the noble hero against the world. Did I want that? But this is better. A little kid ducked under the rope and gave me a half-eaten ice-lolly— raspberry flavour. Didn't want it. Couldn't refuse such an act of love. Took it. Felt fine. Smiled. She smiled back. It was a joy. Thank you sister. The people roar for you, hold you through the sweat and the tears. They have no faces. The finishing line just is. Is there. You are meant to raise your arms and shout, 'Rejoice, we conquer' as you cross it. Like Pheidippides did when he entered Athens and history. And death. But all I think is 'Christ, I've let my anti-gravity muscles get tight.' They hurt. Sally is here. I don't believe it. Beth drapes a towel over my shoulders without making me stop moving. Emma appears, squeaking, 'Three hours, twenty-six and a half. That's great. That's bloody great.' I don't care. Sally has cool soft arms. I look for them. They hold me. 'This is a sentimental ending', I try to say. I'm dry. Beth gives me a beer. I cannot pour it properly. It flows over my chin, soft and cold, blissfully cold. I manage a grin and it spreads all over me. I feel great. I lean against Sally again. I say, 'Never, never again.' She grins back and, not without irony, says, 'Rejoice, we conquer'.

ADAM MARS-JONES

A Small Spade

BERNARD adjusted quickly and well, so well in fact that he began to think it said something rather odd about him. Or perhaps it was something to be proud of. After he had met Neil a couple of times, he told friends that he was willing to act as a support group for this sweet-seeming stranger, this so young stranger, so far from home. He also said that if you were going to offer support, it might as well be to someone you fancied. Then he started to cut down on the self-mocking pronouncements altogether, partly because he was seeing less of his friends, and more of Neil.

The circumstances of their meeting smoothed the adjustment. The place was a pub in Nine Elms which hosted an evening, every two weeks, for people who had been exposed to a virus. The great advantage, of course, was that the subject of illness, or potential illness, could be taken for granted and need never be mentioned, except where the context demanded. It could also be taken for granted, human nature permitting, that no further risks would be taken by the people who gathered there.

Consequently it was Bernard who needed to do the explaining. When it came up in conversation that he was negative in the matter of antibodies, he felt almost exposed as a fraud, as if he had been caught stretching his legs after sitting in a wheelchair, explaining feebly that there had been nowhere else to sit. In theory, those evenings were for anyone who put a high priority on healthy sexual living, but Bernard thought he could detect a whiff of disapproval —not from Neil—for the relatively assured future which branded him as not a serious person.

Neil was from New Zealand, very tall and young enough to make Bernard uneasy, twenty-four as against Bernard's thirty-two. He had been told of his antibody-positive status two months before his projected trip to London, and had not let it upset his plans. He wrote home more regularly than he would have otherwise, that was all, or that was what he said was all. He made sure that he didn't look any skinnier, in the photos he sent back to his parents, than his naturally skinny self.

Bernard found Neil's calm eerie, and guessed that Neil found his awkward animation wearing. But he took the trouble to write his phone number on the back of a raffle ticket—raffles for relevant charities were a big feature of those evenings—and to tuck it into the back pocket of Neil's jeans as he left. An absurdly elevated pocket. Neil laughed and went on talking, to a softer, furry-edged person whom Bernard thought was probably much more his type.

He was right in this assessment, or at any rate he learned later that Neil had gone home with this other person; any fidelity in their relationship was likely to be approximate, and that was all very grown-up and reassuring. But Neil had phoned the next week.

At close quarters, once he got to know him, Bernard could see that Neil made more concessions to his doubtful health than frequent letters home; but they were concessions that somehow suited Bernard. If Neil was tired, he lay down and made no apology for it. If he was hungry, he ate right away. Bernard enjoyed this programme of snacks and siestas during the time they spent together. It was never an effort to take a nap, or at least a lie-down. It was odd, but not unpleasant, to be the older man and have the junior energy. He ate whenever Neil ate, and if he didn't imitate Neil's moderation that wasn't really an issue. Long before this illness had shown up, love affairs had been divided for him into the ones that made you fat and smug, and the ones that made you skinny and neurotic. He was quite content, for a change, to put on a few pounds.

He found Neil's profession harder to adjust to than his compromised health. Neil worked as a hairdresser, and hairdressers in Bernard's mind were necessarily fatuous people, whose fatuousness extended to their choice of lovers. Never mind that he himself had regular haircuts at an establishment which, if not exactly up-market—it stopped short of consultations, conditioner, and cups of coffee—charged at least enough money to command respect for those who had earned it. Bernard's prejudice remained. To compensate for it, he announced Neil's profession in conversation far more often than was necessary, as if unless he kept mentioning it he might be suspected of a liaison with a royal duke. This went on until a friend asked, without malice, 'Which hairdresser do you mean, the one who cuts your hair or the one who messes it up?' Bernard found himself blushing almost to the point of haemorrhage, and promised himself to do better in future.

Neil did yoga every Wednesday, with a group of similarly affected people, and swam several times a week. Bernard joined him in the swimming when he could fit it in. Neil had a relaxed antipodean style of crawl, but his stamina was only moderate, so Bernard could outswim him, though not by the same generous margin that he outate him.

Neil's shortness of breath was also noticeable in bed, where it had, again, a reassuring aspect. Hearing his lover's breathing return to normal after climax so much more slowly than his own, Bernard was at least free of fears that he was being sexually humoured. On a purely cardiovascular level, Neil's experience was the more intense.

He worried about Neil, of course, seeing him only two or three times a week, but then worrying had always been the great romantic privilege, and it was a pleasure not to have it resented. He thought that perhaps romance always had a basis in fear; it was just that this time the fear was clearly defined, and external.

Bernard's worry for himself took the form of an increased superficial cherishing of the body. He had begun by shaving more carefully than usual on days when he would be seeing Neil, and put plasters on any cuts he incurred even if the results were unsightly, until Neil confessed to a labour-saving preference for at least a hint of stubble. Now Bernard stayed unshaven on the days of their meetings. His growth of beard was modest, so he could skip a day without particular comment from his colleagues. He was spared the routine questions of whether he was growing a beard, as if that was a matter of educational policy and might be controversial.

Bernard kept his worry within bounds when, as now, Neil was late for a meeting. Neil wore no watch; his character had been shaped to some extent by a late strain of New Zealand hippyism, based round sunshine, cheap dope, and free rock festivals in remote areas. Giving up Smoking, with the capital S, when he found that the habit was immunosuppressive, was the hardest sacrifice his new status had yet required of him.

Bernard had bought tickets for the train, and spent the time while he waited for Neil trying to identify gay couples engaged on the same ritual as himself: the weekend in Brighton. He hadn't himself visited Brighton since he was a schoolboy, and hadn't made an expedition with Neil any further than the cinema. It seemed to him, as he spotted couples mustering for their expeditions, that he could spot at least as many fun-hungry types stepping out of trains from Brighton, intent on the opposite ritual, of getting back in the sexual swim.

At last he saw Neil moving towards him, at a pace too slow to be described even as an amble. At first he had found this exaggerated leisure of pace irritating; there seemed to him little point in being an agile man of six foot four if you moved more slowly than someone plump and four foot tall, in a hobble skirt. But gradually he had retarded his own speed of walking, and Neil had slightly accelerated, not so much to meet him half-way as because the cooling air made sauntering less and less rewarding a style of motion. Already in early November there had been days, apparently, as cold as New Zealand ever got, and Neil had a respect edged with panic for the colder months to come.

He was carrying, all the same, only a small nylon holdall. Neil had a flair for travelling light, and had much to teach Bernard, who was ballasted by any number of magazines and library books, in that department. Neil was proposing to tour Europe late in the coming spring with very little more luggage than he was carrying now, and Bernard was persuaded he would manage it. He might even still be carrying the same book, *Grandchildren of Dune*, which he wasn't actually reading but carried as emergency rations, a sort of literary pemmican. His home library was equally basic: *Budget Europe*, *On Death and Dying*, and a grainy-paged paperback of pornography entitled *Black Punk Hustler*.

Any discussion of Neil's European trip, or the possibility of Bernard's changing jobs, or—as they started to trust each other's interest—a party a few weeks off, required the formal closure, originated by Neil but now spoken by either one of them, of the phrase: 'Oh, we'll be well over by then.'

Neil carried his liking for paring things down, for travelling light, to the point of naturism. He had found, after a couple of months in London, a couple of swimming pools, one in Stockwell, one in Hornsey, which held weekly naturist swims, for men only. At one of these sessions, Neil had met someone who had subsequently become his landlord, in the upper reaches of the Bakerloo Line.

Bernard and Neil had agreed to meet at midday, without reference to the times of trains; Neil's strong preference was for relaxation over efficiency. By the time that Neil arrived, a few minutes late, they had in fact missed the first train of the afternoon; they would have to wait half an hour for the next one. Bernard was a little irritated, in a way that gave him fresh evidence of the satisfying disparity of their temperaments, and looked around for one of the expresso-and-croissant stalls that nowadays brightened some of London's main line stations. Victoria seemed to have escaped such brightening, and offered only hamburger-joints, without the distorted grins and hair-trigger service, honed against their competitors, which made similar places in high streets entertaining.

Neil took it in his slow, unhurried stride. He ordered a fish sandwich and a cup of hot chocolate, while Bernard settled for coffee. As Neil raised his cup to his lips he said, 'Nice to have two days free, eh, before it all starts again. It's been flat stick all week.' Bernard had a mild romantic fetish for that mid-sentence *eh*, which for all he knew was a mannerism Neil shared even with the sheep in New Zealand, but was unique in his experience.

Neil singled out the idea of the weekend for praise and appreciation because it was a characteristic of his new job; he had been fired from his old one—where he had worked on Saturdays but had Wednesdays off—for being antibody-positive. He hadn't announced the fact, but a colleague had spotted a badge with the phrase Body Positive on it, when Neil had unzipped his holdall to retrieve a pot of yoghurt for his lunch. Neil's colleague seemed enlightened, and mentioned several friends of his as being in the same condition. He promised discretion. Then one Thursday, after Neil had dealt with a couple of clients, he was summoned to the basement by the manager. Did Neil have something to tell him? Neil was mystified and asked what this was all about. Then the manager said that three juniors had left work in tears the day before, and had phoned in to say they weren't willing to work with him any more (their mothers seemed to have played a part in this decision). He asked if Neil denied being a 'carrier'. The money that Neil was owed, plus a week's wages, was ready in an envelope, so he didn't even bother to argue. He had to leave on the spot, walking out through colleagues who seemed to be focusing on their clients rather more narrowly than usual. He took with him a fleshy-fingered little cactus that Bernard had bought him, and entrusted it to a friend who worked in the salon of Dickins and Jones.

Again, Neil reacted to this disturbance with relative calm. He was angry for about an hour, depressed for about a day; he swam a little more than usual, slept a little more than usual, ate a little less. The sentence that took the longest to break down into inoffensiveness was the manager's last word: 'It was very foolish of you, you know, to pretend you didn't know what I was talking about.' But it was Bernard who worked the incident up into a party-piece, and into an indictment of hairdressers. He couldn't help feeling that Neil was overdoing the British phlegm, or perhaps it was yogic indifference. There was such a thing, he knew, as burying toxic waste so deep you poisoned the water table. It was a possibility he sometimes mentioned to his current affairs class.

Neil seemed utterly free of poison. Closely examined though, he looked a little different today, in a way that would prompt Bernard, with anyone else, to ask if he had had a haircut. But life for Neil was one continuous haircut; he and his co-workers were forever giving each other trims in the quiet times between busy times. Over the months Bernard had known him, his hair—black with a haze of grey at the crown—had followed a general trend from crew cut to a fuller look, but with countless adjustments and accents. His beard went from stubbled to almost full, before being trimmed recurrently back.

Bernard had to admit, though, that Neil was by some way the least narcissistic person in the salon. It seemed to him that the other employees, male and female, straight and gay, would have done any work that involved their being surrounded by mirrors. If being a butcher had met that condition, most of them would be wearing blood-stained aprons by now, pleased to have themselves to themselves in the mirrors, without human competition.

Bernard checked his watch all the more because Neil did without. He started to get restless when they had fifteen minutes in hand before the train, exaggerating the effect on their progress of Neil's slow pace. Neil consented to set off at last, using his tongue to press the last of the hot chocolate from his whiskers. Then it turned out that of the two trains to Brighton every hour, one was departing from Croydon, so that repairs could be carried out on the line. This was the one they were now set on catching; they would have to take a suburban train to Croydon to meet it. Bernard shepherded Neil on to the platform, where Neil found himself a baggage wagon to sit on.

Almost immediately an abraded voice on the Tannoy announced a change of platform. Bernard couldn't make out the message itself, but could reconstruct it from its instantaneous effect on their fellow travellers, who picked up their bags and ran. By the time he had convinced Neil that this was more than a piece of random British eccentricity, and that, yes, you had to play hide-and-seek with the trains in this country if you wanted to get anywhere, they were at the rear of a long queue, backed up outside the entrance to the platform proper.

There were few free seats left on the train when they reached it. The nearest they could get to sitting together was to be in sight of each other, occupying aisle seats, with two rows of passengers intervening. Bernard could see a newspaper sticking out of Neil's holdall, but was too far away to identify it. Neil bought a different paper every day, and was never satisfied, since he had to confront the highest concentration of distressing nonsense about the illness that threatened him, if he was also to find a reasonable minimum of the stories he liked (royalty features, pop gossip). Whatever his particular choice this Saturday, he wasn't reading it. His eyes were almost closed. He might very well be meditating, or practising autogenic training. Or just falling asleep in the normal manner of people on trains. Bernard had a book with him, which a strange isotope of loyalty would have prevented him from reading if Neil had been sitting next to him, so he turned their separation to good account.

At Croydon there was the same co-ordinated rush to the waiting train. Neil trailed behind without embarrassment, and Bernard forced himself to accept the idea of standing for the rest of the journey. In fact, this new train was much longer than the suburban one, and they were able to find seats in the buffet car, which was deserted. After about ten minutes, Bernard walked down the car and found to his joy and amazement that the buffet was staffed. The steward was standing in the shadows rather, and doing nothing to advertise his presence; perhaps he had eased up the grille of the buffet inch by inch in its groove of grease so as not to attract attention. But he was certainly there, and even on duty. When his bluff was called, he was willing to dispense refreshment.

Bernard knew he had no prospect of explaining to Neil his sense of the extraordinariness of this coincidence of serving-counter and steward, but his heart was wholly lifted by it. For the first time he had the sense that this outing would be a success, and he almost pranced back along the buffet car, carrying another coffee for himself and another hot chocolate for Neil.

'It's made with soya milk,' he said as he put Neil's cup down.

'Really?'

'British Rail have always used soya milk. And the bread for their sandwiches is made from bulgar wheat. That's why people are always complaining about the catering. People just aren't ready for progress.' As he spoke, Bernard adopted a patently ironic tone so that Neil could know he was being teased.

The tease was undermined by the fact that Neil was no doctrinaire vegetarian, as the fish sandwich at Victoria rather tended to prove. He ate meat when it was prepared for him, and his avoidance of it when he could choose had more to do with being poor, and disliking cheap cuts smothered with sauces, than with any moral stand. He no longer bothered to explain the distinction, and acknowledged Bernard's teasing only with a broad smile. As Bernard noticed a little guiltily, he did remarkably little teasing himself.

Bernard had no idea why he teased Neil, or anybody else. Perhaps it was some evolutionary leftover, like an appendix, and he should only worry if it filled up with poison.

As the train approached Brighton, Neil became more and more perky, though he was too accustomed to ocean from New Zealand—and blue ocean at that—to be more than moderately pleased when the sea hove into sight. At the station he vetoed Bernard's suggestion that they buy a map, but this turned out to be less hippyish a gesture than Bernard first thought. He had looked at a friend's map the day before and thought he had a reasonable idea of the general layout of the town.

They set off in the direction that Neil indicated, at his preferred pace. The day was bright but with a chill to it. Neil was wearing gloves, but fingerless ones which emphasized his long, beautiful fingers, and the jacket of a suit inherited from his grandfather, long enough for him and actually a bit broad in the shoulder. It was rather too thin for the weather. Neil's grandfather, by dying when Neil was six, had given him his only example of a dead person, with the result that death seemed to have acquired the status of an optional event, almost a distinction. After a few minutes Neil fished out a knitted woollen watch-cap from his holdall and put it on. Bernard was wearing an identical cap, bought for £1.80 from Laurence Corner at the same time as Neil's, and he found growing in him the urge to take it off. He was content to be part of a couple, but he strongly resisted being part of a matching pair.

Since Neil rolled his cap down to cover his ears, while Bernard rolled his up into the smallest practicable shape, so that it clung to the back of his head only be fibrous tension, they were already taking steps to differentiate themselves. There was very little chance of their being mistaken for each other. Still Bernard unzipped his jacket and wore it open, as if the effort of sustained walking had warmed him up, and under cover of that pretext took off his cap a few minutes later. He took long refreshed breaths of sea air. He scrabbled at his hair with both hands to restore it to a roughly human contour, so that it looked at least like a loved haystack rather than a despised one.

They had only penetrated a few yards into Brighton before they were offered their first second-hand clothes shop. In theory Neil's needs were the greater, since his wardrobe was scanty and his fear of winter real, but it was Bernard who dived in and started riffling through the racks. Neil had set aside the coming Saturday, rather than this one, for buying The Winter Coat, an item for which he had drawn up almost arctic specifications. Half-heartedly he tried a couple of coats on, but each time asked Bernard to feel their weave and weight. Would this one be an adequate defence? How about this one? Bernard didn't want to swear to it, not being in a hurry to shoulder blame at a later date. Neil had shopped impulsively for The Winter Boots and was regretting it. Neil's feet were size twelves, and The Winter Boots were size elevens; their waterproof days were over already. But size twelves never showed· up in sales, and even size elevens—or so Bernard gathered—weren't common enough to pass up.

Bernard bought a string vest of sea island cotton after trying it on in a changing-room so small—a dirty curtain held a little away from the wall—that it reminded him of the dressing-rooms for the school play now in rehearsal (*Twelfth Night*, with Viola and Sebastian played by a pair of Pakistani twins, their resemblance not yet botched by puberty). This was not a welcome thought, since he was supposed to be devising the costumes for it—*designing* was too grand a word for what he had in mind, which would include found objects and black plastic bin-liners as important elements. But however modest his responsibilities, today would have been a logical day to devote to them.

A little further into town, the moment Brighton made any sort of impersonation of a resort, Neil started taking photographs. He didn't waste film on views, but took a couple of photographs of Bernard. More important was for Bernard to take the camera from him and to take photographs suitable for sending home. He gave Neil plenty of warning, so that he could blow out his cheeks a little, and push out his tummy. He was holding weight well, as far as Bernard could see, but from Neil's parents' point of view there was no such thing as overdoing it.

For the first photograph Neil puffed out his cheeks almost to bursting point, until laughter broke his lips open. But he was undoubtedly happier when the camera contained a good stockpile of fat photos. He could put the camera away and start enjoying himself on his own account, and not for the benefit of a mantelpiece in suburban Auckland.

Neil liked to look in the window of every hairdressers they passed, which in a town as dedicated to grooming as Brighton seemed to mean crossing from side to side of the street more or less non-stop. He got satisfaction of some sort from what he saw through these windows, but made no comment. Bernard tried to decide whether he was simply gloating over these people who had to be cutting hair when he was free, or checking the tariffs to reassure himself that his Brighton equivalents earned even less than he did. The only certain thing was that he wasn't engaged in industrial espionage. He wasn't serious about hairdressing, and Bernard took comfort from that. It enabled him to construct two categories of hairdresser, the casual and the committed, with all the stigma attaching to the committed.

Neil was casual about his job, but well short of slapdash. Bernard had seen him more than once cutting a little girl's hair, kneeling on a towel by the chair—a chair made in Japan, for no known reason—

although there were stylists much less tall, whom Bernard thought would find the job less awkward. Patiently, he cut the merest centimetre from her hair, combing her soothingly, so that she seemed not to realize she was no longer crying, though her posture was still sulky and she still held her doll in the combined crook of her elbows.

But he certainly had no great respect for his profession. The only hairdresser he admired was a friend called Joel, now working freelance, and that was because of what he managed to get away with. Joel still used the pair of scissors he had had at hairdressing school, the cheapest pair of Ice Gottas on the market, and turned up for magazine shoots—he did make-up as well as hair—with an old plastic bag bearing the motto 'That's the Wonder of Woolies', full of Outdoor Girl cosmetics. The magazine put different names for the cosmetics next to the pictures they printed, but then they did that anyway. But Joel's great achievement, so far as Neil was concerned, was to give ordinary cuts at enormous speed and inflated prices to a few selected clients in his own home, a small, shabby and disorderly flat. It was one thing to do a bad job in a pretentious salon, quite another to do a bad job—and get away with it—where the client could see his old tea-bags and underpants. Once, Neil and Joel had been about to go out for lunch when a client arrived whom Joel had forgotten. She wanted highlights, and Joel obliged in ten minutes, rather than the usual three hours, simply combing the lotion on to the hair. The results, according to Neil, were high-lumps rather than highlights, and Joel charged £55 for his labour, but the client was highly delighted.

Among the hairdressers of Brighton were health-food shops and whole-food cafés. Bernard and Neil chose one that looked quiet, The Pantry, for a sit-down and a snack. It was narrow, with chunky tables of rough wood, and crammed with selfconsciously tacky 1950s artefacts, some free-standing, some stuck on the walls, and some even hung on utility coat-racks: advertisements, sculptures, jokey ashtrays given a different status from the working ashtrays on the tables. In a tiny alcove there was even a mobile disco, twin turntables with a microphone attached, though it was hard to imagine anyone dancing there. Queuing for food was quite awkward enough in the cramped space, and a lot of apologizing went on even with relatively few people ordering and collecting food. Perhaps the disco was only kept there off duty, and was set up somewhere else; but it was difficult to imagine any of the helpers—three women of different generations and perhaps actually a whole-food dynasty, a matrilineal succession of carers—acting as DJ. The youngest, an early teenager, seemed to have her duties confined to clearing up and, to judge by the frequency with which she dropped things, would not be trusted with the boxes of scuffed singles sitting next to the disco.

When Neil had finished his salad and Bernard his wholemeal lasagne, they carried on towards what Neil's homing instinct or memory for maps told him was the historic city centre. Neil had picked up the word 'historic', which he used with deliberate lack of discrimination, from his least favourite client, an American woman who would smoke a cigarette and put on make-up while being blow-dried. Neil's boss had followed his usual practice of overcharging tourists, but this tourist was not to be deterred from returning, and always asked for Neil. He punished her by taking on this particularly hated element of her vocabulary.

Brighton showed no great increase in historical interest as they walked on, but to judge by the air of escalating chichi they were on the right track. Finally they came in sight of the Pavilion, which they had agreed on as their obligatory piece of sightseeing. It had for the time being a complex façade of boards and scaffolding, but was still open for business. By taking the tour they would be treating Brighton as a city in its own right, not just as a collection of gay-oriented businesses with a reasonably pleasant climate.

There was no tour of the Pavilion as such. If there had been, or if they had invested in one of the expensive guide books from the gift shop, they would have been given a definite idea of the Pavilion to accept or reject. As it was, they had to come to their own conclusions. It dawned on Bernard, as they entered a ballroom containing a grand organ, that he was now in one of the most piss-elegant environments in the world. 'This is certainly historic,' said Neil.

'Worse than that. In its own way it's actually Otaran.' Otara, as he had gathered from Neil, was some sort of Maori heartland, and therefore a sort of New Zealand shorthand for tackiness. Neil himself, of Yugoslav blood and unpronounceable surname, had been the only white person in his class at school. All the Maori boys were called Rangi, or so he claimed, and all the girls were Debra. He had ended up saying things like, 'J'wanta come down the Spice Inviders in my Veliant?' Thereafter, he had fallen in eagerly with his friends in their dismissal of anything Maori, though he had also had one or two affairs with Maoris not called Rangi.

Neil seemed thrown by Bernard's borrowing of a Kiwi expression, as he was on the rare occasions when Bernard said *obliverated* to mean drunk, *rapt* for pleased, *crack a horn* for acquire an erection. Neil's own accent, if his family were telling the truth on their occasional phone calls, was now pure Oxbridge. 'Well, I don't know, that place we had lunch was Otaran. This place is a bit different.'

'What then?' asked Bernard.

'This place is . . . Papatoetoan.'

'What's that?'

'Papatoetoe. It's not as far as Otara.'

Bernard laughed, and they moved through the preposterous rooms in a rare daze of unanimity. It turned out that there was an alarm system installed in the Pavilion, which gave off a series of electronic yelps if anyone infringed on the velvet rope, or even approached the edges of the aisle permitted to visitors. Each time the yelping sounded, the guard in whatever room it happened to be would intone, 'Please don't touch. Keep your distance.'

In one room the guard, who wore a stylized moustache, was young and busy with his eyes. Bernard nudged the rope, so as to make him deliver his recorded message. Then he couldn't help murmuring to Neil, 'What are the odds he turns up to a bar we're in tonight? Except he won't be saying *keep your distance* then, I'll bet.'

'Keep your distance, please don't touch,' said the guard again, as someone else triggered the alarm. Neil was normally resistant to Bernard's line of banter, but this time they were on a wavelength, and he laughed, in one little burst and then another.

The passed through to the kitchens, where Bernard saw the first things he actually admired, the endless rows of copper pots, all the way up to Moby Dick fish-kettles; the lids were sensibly provided with their own handles, raised above the rest of the lids for coolness' sake. Neil found further fuel for his laughing jag in a stuffed rat caught in a trap, and displayed under one of the kitchen tables. It was almost absurdly unlifelike, perhaps to avoid frightening schoolchildren, and the plastic fruit and veg on the broad pale-scrubbed tables would be a suitable diet for it.

Once the Pavilion had loosed its historic hold on them, they started to think about finding their hotel. There Neil's memory for maps, however impressive, couldn't be expected to help them. Bernard remembered the address as Derbishire Place, and they asked passers-by where that was. No one knew. Bernard didn't check the advertisements in *Capital Gay*, from which he had got the phone number. One reason for his reluctance was the name of the hotel, which was called Rogues. He had phoned another hotel first, advertised in the same journal but with a nudge-free name. It was full. He had asked the receptionist to recommend another establishment, relying on impartiality now that distortions of rivalry could be discounted, and it was then that Rogues was suggested. With a heavy heart he made the call, and would have put the phone down if he had been offered the Scallywag Suite, or been told about the cheap cocktails during Naughty Hour in the Vagabond Room. He wanted to stay in a hotel called Rogues every bit as much as he wanted to have a lover who was a hairdresser, though he hoped for similar compensations once the sacrifice was made.

Another reason for wanting to leave *Capital Gay* in his bag was the sheer depressingness of the paper itself. This was hardly the paper's fault; the journalists did their best to make up jaunty head-lines. But every week there were more obituaries, and the obituaries became more flippant. The conventions of obituary-writing, either that death had set the seal on a long and useful life, or that death had cut off young promise in its prime, began to break down now that untimeliness was becoming the rule. Many of the casualties were too young even to be promising. The boss of a gay business wrote of a dead employee, in the issue that Bernard was keeping in his bag, 'He told us he did not expect to live after Friday. Punctuality was never his *forte* and it came as no surprise to us that he was $2\frac{3}{4}$ hours late.' The dead men weren't ready to die. The obituarists weren't ready to write obituaries.

Derbishire Place continued to ring no bells with the people he asked about it. When people asked what exactly he was looking for, hoping that would give them a clue, Bernard became very tight-lipped, while Neil gave him what was not a look of forgiving superiority, but which if fed and watered would grow up to be one. Finally they gave in and bought a local map from a stationers, but Derbishire Place was missing from it, along with all other places beginning with Derbishire. He went back to the stationers to check other maps of greater price and detail, but Derbishire Place was missing from them all.

At last Bernard fished out *Capital Gay* for the lowdown on Rogues. The address turned out to be Devonshire Place, which was not only marked on every map, however rudimentary, but which they had passed a few streets back.

Devonshire Place was a steep little street, and Bernard felt quite tired as they reached its upper end. To his relief, the frontage of Rogues was plain, its name appearing only on a small brass plaque. He had been bracing himself for black balloons and pink neon. The man who opened the door was a further relief. He was wearing socks and sheepskin slippers, and underneath his green polo-shirt could be traced in relief the outline of a thermal vest. Not for the first time in Bernard's experience, but much to his reassurance, gay life promised the depraved and delivered the cosy.

Their host led them into a lounge with a television, which was showing the omnibus edition of a soap opera which Neil followed, without fanaticism. It seemed to be one of the few British pro-grammes which wasn't exported to New Zealand, and that gave it, in Neil's eyes, a slight extra kick. Their host left them at the mercy of the television, and promised them a cup of tea in a couple of shakes. They sprawled on the sofa, and Neil gave Bernard one of his trademark kisses, an amorous stubbled plosive full on the ear. In a world where bodies had unrestricted access to each other, this would come near the bottom of Bernard's list of favourite gestures. He braced himself for the detonation. In essence, he thought it was about as erotic a gesture as dropping a firework through someone's letter-box. But he could not now afford to despise any permissible act, and he had worked on his reactions until the symbolic sensa-tion gave him pleasure. Now, on the sofa, he welcomed it.

'Who's that?' he asked, pointing at the television screen. 'Is that what's-his-face's boyfriend?'

'Don't know.'

'Didn't you see it on Tuesday?'

'Yes.'

'Well, who is it then?'

'I don't know.' Seeing Bernard's expression he tightened his hug a notch or two. 'Don't worry, 'I'm not going gaga before my time,

I'm not getting the dementia. If I am I've always had it. I've always had a short attention span.'

'You have?'

'Yup. I think I've had a little snooze in every film we've been to, and you didn't notice, eh?'

'Can't say I did.'

'Maybe your attention's not so hot yourself. And if you work out who these people are, don't bother to tell me. I'm not that interested.'

'Do you think we can turn it off?' The lounge might in theory be the guests' terrain, but it was full of the landlord's presence, not to mention his cigarettes and two planks of a KitKat, half-unwrapped from their foil.

Before they could decide, the landlord came back with the promised tray of tea, a register, and some leaflets. He needed some details for the register, and offered in exchange a map of Brighton with its gay attractions marked in. A number of venues had been deleted; it was, after all, off-season. There were, though, still places to go, and the hotelier made out little passes for them, vouching for their status as bona-fide visitors, with which they could get in free at a number of key nightspots. Then he left them to their tea and the television.

A little later he returned with two bulky keys, and showed them to their room. Rogues was a modest private house lightly disguised as a hotel; Neil's and Bernard's room, at the rear of the first floor, corresponded to the master bedroom of most terraced houses. There couldn't, Bernard thought, be more than three other rooms.

The underside of the door scraped on the thick carpet, almost to the point of sticking, as it opened. Inside were posters of exhibitions at the British Museum, and a colour scheme of striated greens hinting at leafy bamboo and derived from the Brighton Pavilion. It occurred to Bernard that there must be easily one or two hotel rooms in Brighton untouched by the Pavilion in decorative scheme, but he accepted that they would cost rather more than the others, and would need to be booked some months in advance.

The hotel owner padded out and left them alone, and they tried out the bed. Neil was unswervingly loyal to his futon, but Bernard had no great love for it. This was a little squashy, squashier than his own at home, but it would do. Neil seemed to think so too, whatever his stated position: he fell asleep almost immediately. Bernard tried as a general rule not to bombard him with concern, and had managed not to ask him, earlier in the day, if he was tired. Now he began to feel, from the avidness and depth of Neil's sleep, that he should have been more tender.

Bernard wondered if perhaps at some stage he and Neil would have to decide whether 'antibody-positive' was not now an understatement of Neil's condition. Perhaps that was a secret they were keeping from each other.

Neil was curled sweetly against him in sleep. Neil's sexuality seemed to Bernard altogether caressive rather than penetrational; that was certainly the role he played with Bernard, and the role Bernard played with him. Neil had called him 'cuddly' on one occasion, meaning fond of hugging, until Bernard broke it to him that in Britain cuddly was just a friend's word for fat, so would he please retract it. Neil had even given Bernard a teddy bear for his birthday. Bernard had slept with it one night, so as to atone for his embarrassment when it was handed over, and so that he could mention its usefulness without lying. He was rather appalled to wake up freezing in the middle of the night, still clutching the bear, in a shipwreck of bedclothes. The bear's stitched smile had a vindicated smugness about it.

At an earlier stage, of course, Neil's persona had been a little different. About five years previously, while still in his teens, he had gone through a phase of anal shenanigans; that must have been the time of his exposure to infection. He still had a sharp nostalgia for oral sex, which was not these days categorized as particularly risky; but Bernard hesitated, and seeing his hesitation Neil changed the sexual subject.

Bernard rolled quietly off the bed and went for a walk. He would have liked to find a café where he could have a cup of coffee and read, but the only café that was at all promising seemed to be mutating in some mysterious way into a wine bar. It had been open until a little while before, it would be open in a little while to come, and even now it was not exactly closed; but when he suggested to the waitress that he might sit in a quiet corner with a book and a cup of coffee, she wouldn't hear of it.

Thwarted of his civilized interlude, Bernard walked down to the sea front, then headed back to the hotel, not wanting to experience anything too distinctively Brighton without the partner that the whole weekend was arranged around.

Neil was stirring when he returned to the hotel room. He rolled slowly off the bed and started doing yoga exercises, hardly even opening his eyes. Bernard took his turn at lying on the bed, but after a moment he couldn't resist peering over the edge at Neil's slow smooth complex movements, and the quickened roughened breathing that went with them. He felt like an Indian scout creeping to the edge of a cliff to spy on the war games of a rival tribe.

There was one exercise that particularly appealed to him. Neil lay on his front and stretched back his head, arms and legs, giving his body a bowed shape and a resemblance to a parachutist in free fall. Bernard had an impulse to lean over and tickle one of the elongated feet, themselves sharply bowed, outstretched below him, an action which would have shattered Neil's calm—he was extremely ticklish—beyond the power of any mantra to reinstate. It was only a distantly mischievous impulse and he was able to rise above it with a small flexing of willpower.

Neil finished the tempting exercise, and moved on to the next. Yoga was known to benefit the immune system. It was agreed between Neil and Bernard, without any basis in evidence, that Neil was unlikely to have been exposed, as long ago as 1981 and as far from the centre of the gay world as New Zealand, to the full grown-up horror of the virus. It was much more likely, surely, that he had encountered some nasty intermediate form, some mid-mutation that was no fun to have aboard but bore no real grudge against him.

There were factors that worked against this theory. Neil had had affairs, in that distant period, with not one but two airline stewards. He was some way from the capital of danger, but he wasn't exactly in the provinces. Bernard had an image of airline stewards (flight attendants, whatever euphemism you cared to choose) as sheer vectors of sexual transmission, their buttocks a blur all the time they weren't actually handing out soft drinks and headphones. He reacted with relative sanity to press coverage of the illness, screening out the idiocies and focusing on the few scraps of undistorted information, but he had a little obsession of his own. If any political party had included in its platform the compulsory fitting of chastity belts to airline stewards, he would have thrown his full electoral weight behind it.

Neil finished his exercises, and lay back on the floor in feigned collapse. He was hoping for a hug to revive him, but Bernard thought he could offer him something better. The advert in *Capital Gay* had mentioned a shower in every room. It was simply a matter of locating the fitted cupboard that contained it. He strode towards the cupboard nearest the window and flipped the door open. Inside were the dark green tiles and gleaming fitments he had been hoping for.

Neil was pleased, and only took a moment to take his clothes off as he walked across the carpet to the shower. Bernard noticed again his furry thighs and the dark skin tone (Yugoslav blood) that he had at first assumed was a tan, and would fade. His preferred colour for his own skin was slug-white, and he still felt the same spasm of involuntary sympathy for tanned flesh—artificial or the real thing—that he could feel for the flayed tissue of a crocodile handbag.

Neil used soap only once a week, and washed his hair only about as often, in marked contrast to his colleagues at the salon. This was down-under hippie simplicity, to be sure, but it was also mild superstition. In his teens he had suffered so terribly from acne that he had become little short of a hermit, dropping out of school and shunning company. He had once been beaten by his Physical Education teacher for refusing to take his shirt off. Now that he was clear of acne, except for the high-water mark it had left on his shoulders, he left his outside alone as far as possible. Acne had affected him profoundly, or to put it another way, on the surface; the virus in his bloodstream seemed to have changed him less. He seemed surprised, even now, to be a survivor of acne. He had suffered nothing worse at the hands of the virus, so far, than the loss of a margin for error, once the defining privilege of youth. He remained calm when possible treatments of the virus came up in conversation, but his voice took on a glow when he mentioned Roacutane, the desperate drug that had finally seen off his acne. He said he would be willing to endorse Roacutane on television, make a pilgrimage, carry a placard in the street, testifying to its healing powers. At the time it had made his bones ache, turned his lips yellow and given him bleeding from the nose and the rectum, but he regarded that as the smallest of payments. Roacutane had made his skin dry where once it had been extremely oily, but he was grateful to have working skin back, of whatever description.

A fan had switched itself on when Neil pressed the light switch to the shower, but steam was still drifting into the room. Bernard remembered, then put it out of his mind, that Neil had had one anomalous outbreak of acne after Roacutane, which suggested that his skin was having its ability to police itself undermined in some way.

Neil emerged from the shower with a small towel round his waist, dripping shamelessly on the carpet. He lay down on the bed after the briefest period of towelling, enjoying the hotel guest's privilege of treating the facilities to mild abuse. He beckoned Bernard towards him.

Bernard hung back a little. He had brought no finery for the weekend, but he had no intention of getting what he was wearing wet, just as they were going out to dinner.

Neil tried a different nuance of flirtation. 'Do you want a fashion show now or later?'

Bernard thought for a moment. 'Later.' Neil had promised to show him the costumes he had devised for the gay naturists' fancy-dress party, to be worn by his landlord and himself. The theme was Rude. Bernard was proud that he had kept his curiosity within bounds, so that Neil would satisfy it without making him wait too long. In fact his mind was ablaze with the need to know what Rude Naturist Fancy Dress could actually look like.

Neil didn't seem displeased by the prospect of a few more hours' mystery-making. 'Get dressed and go to dinner, eh?' he crooned up from the bed.

Bernard entrusted the choice of a place for dinner to Neil; it turned out to be a lengthy business. There were plenty of restaurants to choose from, but it seemed silly to walk into the first one that offered. Bernard had spotted on his walk a place that offered Genghis Khan barbecues, served by waitresses who seemed—from a peer through bottled glass—to be dressed in rags of Mongolian cut, but once that option was discarded, it was a matter of choosing from the competitive clamour of good taste, and deciphering a plausible menu from pages of scrawled French. Most of the restaurants, which after a few minutes seemed almost continuous, had permanent menus in their windows and blackboards with the daily specials out in the street, so a certain amount of cross-indexing was called for.

Finally Neil plumped for a place that seemed spacious. They were immediately shown up a narrow staircase to an upper room full of little tables; it turned out that the main dining-room had been booked by a large party. One beneficial side-effect of the cramped conditions was that they had to sit with their legs meshed together, in a way that would have got them thrown out of the main dining-room.

Neil ordered a rare steak, mildly to Bernard's irritation, since he had vetoed a number of places that had appealed to him personally, on the unstated grounds that they offered nothing to vegetarians, beyond salads that might just as well have had stencilled on their drooping leaves No Fun But Good For You. Bernard ordered mussels. He had a weakness for meals that needed to be processed as much as eaten, for spare ribs and artichokes, for foods that needed to be eaten with your hands, for dishes that left a satisfying pile of debris. It gave him a sense of occasion to be engaging in an almost adversarial relationship with food, instead of simply placing it inside him.

As he levered open the savoury hinges of the mussels, taking an almost philistine pleasure in the destruction, he became aware that another hinge, Neil's knee, was pressing against his trouser-fork with a force that went beyond affection. Bernard looked up, startled. Neil laid his knife and fork down neatly and leaned forward, putting a hand on each side of the table. His voice was dark with anger, angrier than Bernard had ever heard it. 'Do you hear what those people are saying?'

'No. Which people?'

'Behind us.'

Behind Neil were two ordinary-seeming middle-aged couples. The only fragments of conversation he had heard from that quarter had concerned schools and horse riding.

'What are they saying?'

'Listen.'

Bernard did his best to screen out the sounds of crockery and actual eating, the thick soundtrack of conversation. He thought he was able to focus on the offending quadrant of chat. The sentence he thought he heard was: 'And then of course that starts off a chain.'

'I think they're talking about moving house,' he explained, 'you know, someone makes an offer for a house, but they can only come through with the money if someone else buys their house, and *they're* in the same position. So it's called a chain, and sometimes people can get snagged up for ages.'

Neil was still gripping the table, and his voice had not lost rage. 'That's not what they're talking about.' Bernard couldn't help dropping his eyes to Neil's plate, wondering if this aggressiveness was what happened when a habitual vegetarian dabbled in rare meat. The idea, as he could see as soon as it was fully formulated, was ridiculous, and in any case Neil had made only minor inroads into his steak.

'So what are they talking about? Why are you so angry?'

'They're talking about a certain . . . infection and its—what do you call it—methods of transmission.' He relaxed the grip of his fingers on the table. 'They're full of ideas. Ignorant fuckers.' He rested his hands on his lap for a moment, then took up his knife and fork again.

Bernard, finally, was in touch with his anger. 'That's outrageous. That's the last thing we need to hear.' Now that he had started to feel anger, he felt the need to work it up into action. He couldn't stop the virus itself from playing gooseberry, but there was a limit to what he had to put up with. There was no reason why he should sit back while these people broadcasted their idiotic editorials. 'Do you want me to talk to them?'

Neil gave a small smile, his mouth full of his steak's unaccustomed juiciness. 'Don't bother.' Bernard was forced to realize that if he made any protest, the people he ticked off would feel only that their rights were being violated: their right to make no distinction between public and private, their right to have the world remain as it was advertised to be. He returned reluctantly to his mussels, which had cooled off almost as quickly as Neil had, and were nowhere near as appetizing as they had been when he had last looked at them. They were no longer sending up steam to signal their deliciousness.

Neil's burst of temper hadn't lasted long, but it was still out of character. His personality held very little of the aggressive. Only in one family story that he had passed on to Bernard was there a trace of hostility mixed in with the warmth, and even there the aggressiveness was sweetened and made palatable. As a boy he had dreamed that New Zealand was stricken by a famine. At a family conference it was decided that they should eat Neil's elder brother Robin— who had been weeping quietly throughout—since he was made of trifle. Neil and the others took small spoonfuls from the place they felt would be least painful, just above the hips.

Bernard pushed away the graveyard plate of mussels. 'I'm stuffed,' he said. 'How about you?'

Neil looked startled. 'I'm not too stuffed, I've still got some inergy left,' he said. He used the same pinched vowel that made the word 'sex' on his lips sound like the number after five. Bernard didn't grasp for a moment the reason for Neil talking about energy, when he himself was asking about food. Then he remembered that 'stuffed', in the Kiwi lexicon, meant tired rather than full.

'I'm not stuffed either. What I meant to say was full up. Could you manage something else? I saw trifle on the menu.'

Neil seemed indifferent to trifle, in a way that suggested he was still upset about their fellow diners, who were now greeting the sweet course with a round of hushed exclamations, gasps of complicity in sugar and resolutions to take exercise. One of them was saying, 'As long as I ride enough, I don't have to worry. It just shakes off.'

For form's sake, Bernard enquired about the composition of the trifle. Neil would touch only teetotal trifle, since for some reason possibly to do with the virus, alcohol and sugar collaborated to make his teeth sing at the time, and screech the next day. The message came back from the cook by way of the waitress, who gave a proud grin, that the trifle was full of good things. 'You could wring the sponge out and fill a liqueur glass with it,' she said. 'A real Saturday night treat.' Bernard asked for the bill, and they left.

The nearest gay pub marked on the map that their host at Rogues had given them was called The Waterman. As they entered, their novelty ensured them the equivalent of a ticker-tape welcome. The Waterman had the usual amenities of a gay bar that had evolved stage by stage from a straight one, that is, no chairs, so that turning round to stare involved no violence to furniture. The pub was too crowded for conversation actually to stop, but everyone there gave them an aggressively searching look in their first ten seconds in the pub. Bernard knew the commercial gay scene well enough to realize that interest and approval were often signalled with a coldly accusing stare, but it still seemed strange to him. You would have thought that The Waterman was playing host to a convention of bounty hunters, he thought, who couldn't help comparing any unfamiliar faces with the Wanted posters in their minds. Neil and Bernard felt Wanted all right. It wasn't particularly pleasant.

When they had been served Neil took a single sip from his orange juice, narrowed his eyes and said, 'This should give you some idea of gay life in New Zealand. Imagine this being the only bar in Auckland. Those boys over there, eh, the cream of the local talent.' He nodded his head towards a group of bleached-blonds in multi-coloured tracksuits, drinking gin and tonics. 'About the same number of punch-and-pricks.'

'What are punch-and-pricks?' asked Bernard, wondering if this was a word from the Kiwi lexicon or a term of gay argot that he was too old to be familiar with. It turned out to to be professional slang.

'Punch-and-pricks? You know,' he lowered his voice significantly as a man passed between them on his way to the lavatory, 'hair transplants.'

'How do you rate that one?'

'Five out of ten.' He leaned forward against Bernard's ear, so that he expected a public version of Neil's trademark kiss. Instead he murmured, with the same moist intimacy, 'Yip yip yip.'

'What's that mean?'

'Don't look now.' He nudged Bernard's head into the appropriate alignment. '*Keep your distance*, remember? *Please don't touch?*'

Neil was right. The attendant from the Pavilion, now wearing jeans and a check shirt, was standing guard, with the same paranoid glint, over a pint of lager. 'Sharp eyes,' said Bernard. 'You must have been pretty good in Ye Olde Kiwi Gay Bar.'

Neil didn't deny it. 'Well, you don't want to drag home anyone too soft or tragic. Not with your friends watching. And they didn't have anywhere else to go either.'

The man who had been identified by Neil as a punch-and-prick paused on his way back from the lavatory. He was short enough for Bernard to be able to see his head from above; for Neil this was presumably the normal angle of vision, since he was so tall and spent his professional time hovering about people's heads with scissors. The punch-and-prick gave a broad smile. 'When you've had enough of these tired provincial queens,' he said, 'come over and talk. I'm with friends. You'll like them.'

There wasn't a lot Bernard could think of to say to that. Neil nodded amiably. When they left the pub, a little later, on their way to a nightspot marked on the map from Rogues, they could only hope not to be too visibly passing up this invitation. Given Neil's height and the pub's single exit, which meant passing near where the punch-and-prick and his party must have set up their rampart of masculinity, there was not much chance of their going un-noticed. At least they could hope that the punch-and-prick wouldn't turn out to be the owner of the club they were heading to now, or the little free admission vouchers from Rogues might not be enough to smooth their passage.

Vouchers or no, they had to wait quite a while on the steps head-ing up to the club. Bernard spent the time inveighing against the name of the club, Stompers. Why did every place that offered even the mildest pleasure after dark need to call itself by some idiotic plural: Stompers, Bumpers, Bangs, Rogues, Spats? Why did pleasant pubs called the Churchill Arms install a few spotlights and reopen as Churchills? Did it bother Neil as it bothered him?

Neil said, 'I can live with it.' Bernard was about to back up his objections when he realized he was only inches away from one of his classroom tirades, against crimes like Grocer's Apostrophe (Apple's and Pear's). He shut himself up.

The vouchers from Rogues, which Bernard had been nervously locating in his pockets at intervals throughout the evening, turned out to entitle them only to half-price admission. This would have taken the gilt off the gingerbread, except that no one waiting on those narrow stairs, after being buzzed through the street door, could have been expecting gilt or even gingerbread. There was something eerily familiar, Bernard thought as he explored with a drink, about the layout of the club, its chain of undersized rooms. Then he real-ized that like Rogues, the night-club was the smallest possible con-version from a terraced house. He had been briefly fooled by the staircase, which caused them to enter where the top landing would have been.

The upper bar had taken the place of a back bedroom; the lower one was substituting for the front parlour. Eventually Bernard and Neil found their way to the disco dance-floor, which had once—

perhaps even recently—been a kitchen. Bernard was pleased to see that the oldest man in the club was dancing with the best of them, was dancing in fact even when he was the only one on the little dance-floor, though he seemed to need little twists of tissue paper stuffed in his ears to make the experience bearable. From time to time he adjusted the paper-twists to block out more of the music that gave the dancing its excuse, before going back to his interpretative movement.

Bernard kept examining Neil for signs of fatigue. The whole visit to Stompers was something of a token gesture, to prove to themselves that they had gone to Brighton and done the whole bit, and he didn't want Neil tiring himself out for a gesture's sake. He asked Neil to dance as a preliminary to suggesting that they might as well think of going home, but neither of them was particularly light on his feet. Neil, when he danced, betrayed the awkwardness he must have had in school photographs—assuming they had such things as school photographs in New Zealand––towering year after year above the massed Rangis and Debras. Bernard for his part was kept well below his normal modest level of competence by thoughts of the primal kitchen which the disco had supplanted. The kitchen lurked reproachfully under the thin crust of night-life. He tried to make up his mind about what exactly the DJ was replacing. Would it be the fridge or the draining board?

When they had finished dancing and were sweating lightly in the kitchen passage, Bernard suggested they go back to the hotel. 'Do you want to?' asked Neil.

'Yes, why not?' Bernard was moved partly by consideration for Neil. Neil suffered from social strangury, though the word he used was *piss-shy*. He was unable to urinate in public; even taking turns in the bathroom with Bernard after sex, he couldn't perform at the bowl with Bernard there. He needed a couple of minutes to himself before his inhibited duct opened up again.

Bernard was pleased by this foible in such a sturdy naturist, Neil's bladder living by a more reticent code than his pelt's. But by now it must be several hours since he had been to the lavatory, several hours of taking in liquid without any alcohol to drive it off. He had been for the last time in the hotel before dinner, using the shared facility with a little difficulty.

Back at Rogues, Neil made no obvious dash for the bathroom;

in fact he insisted on putting on his fashion-show at last. Bernard obediently faced the window while Neil undressed, and then made intricate adjustments. Bernard thought he could hear a snapping noise, either of elastic or some sort of fastening, as well as the faint dry swish of material on skin. Then Neil announced, 'You can turn round now.' His costume was worth waiting for. Rude, naturist, fancy dress; it fulfilled all the requirements. Neil was wearing a jock-strap with the pouch cut out, so that his genitals dangled freely; the jock-strap was held up—though this was purely a visual touch, the elastic waistband being perfectly adequate—by a pair of braces. Hanging diagonally across his chest, in the manner of a beauty-pageant sash, was a strip of towelling that Bernard recognized as being a strip cut from a corporation swimming towel, bearing the woven legend BOROUGH OF CAMDEN 1986. Neil advanced towards him to be embraced. 'It's wonderful. Really,' Bernard said. 'And is your landlord's just the same?'

'Yes. Except he's Mr Borough of Islington.' Neil's embrace became more rhythmic; he rocked their combined bodies from side to side. Bernard needed to do some marking, and broke the embrace to say so. 'I should have done it earlier on,' he said, 'I know. But I can't work on trains.'

Neil made no protest. He took another shower, calling from the misty cubicle that it wasn't a cold one, not by a long stretch, while Bernard did some perfunctory, guilt-appeasing marking. Then Neil brushed his teeth with his usual thoroughness. Bernard had conscientiously left his toothbrush at home, so as not to do the same through force of habit. Neil's gums had a tendency to bleed, and even when they weren't affected Bernard had been led more than once to the ultimate inverted-Judas gesture of withholding a kiss. Sometimes his tongue stood aside from a kiss even when he wanted to involve it. Neil, it had to be said, even at his most passionate, was not a great one for tongue-stabbing, and his reticence increased, understandably enough, when thrush made his saliva soupy.

Bernard's fear of going to the dentist had not long survived the onset of the health crisis. It had been quite a big fear until then, and he sometimes wondered where it had gone. It seemed likely that he had the same total quantity of fear in him, only now it was salted away in little packets rather than gathered in a single large consignment.

The dentist had become tolerable once Bernard had realized that kissing was the only possibly dangerous thing he intended to go on doing. The safety of kissing seemed to be assumed and disavowed almost by turns in the publications he consulted, but either way it was only sensible to have his mouth's defences regularly seen to. He had confessed to his dentist that he avoided brushing when he was going to be kissing soon after, expecting to be told not to be so silly. He had been disconcerted when the dentist had said that of course there was only a possible risk when his partner was 'shedding virus' (whatever that meant), but yes, brushing the teeth could abrade the gums and lead to bleeding. Brushing was a necessity in the long term but did involve a tiny risk, a really tiny risk, in the short. Not brushing before, er, intimate contact might be a realistic precaution.

So it was that Bernard smelled mintiness and freshness on Neil's breath, and Neil smelled whatever Bernard had been eating. This hardly seemed a fair exchange, except that the smell of toothpaste had come to seem definitely sinister to Bernard, even when he was brushing his teeth in the morning, in total security.

Bernard was still hanging over his marking, but had not been taking it in for quite a time. Neil, meanwhile, was already asleep. Bernard packed away the pile of exercise books, turned out the light and went to join him. He approached the bed from the near side, but as he lifted the duvet and prepared to slide in he encountered a large, heat-filled leg. He went round to the other side, but Neil was there too. He had the habit, when he went to bed before Bernard, of stretching out like a starfish, or at least of occupying the diagonal, so that Bernard would be certain to wake him.

When Neil reached a deeper level of sleep, Bernard knew, his personality would change, would lose this responsiveness. He would turn into a warm elongated bobbin and gradually wind the bedclothes around him, winding the warmth off Bernard. He was the last person on earth Bernard would have suspected of being a blanket-fascist, but there it was, you could never tell.

Bernard nudged his way into the bed, triggering Neil's reflexes of welcome. Neil shared his hoarded heat. His body offered a wide variety of textures, not just the ghosts of acne on his shoulders and the back of his neck, but the little fleshy pebbles seeded across his face and forehead which he said the doctors called *molluscum*—a term which Bernard refrained, as an act of love, from looking up in the medical encyclopaedia. On Neil's back were the extraordinary parallel scars he had acquired as a schoolboy athlete, his speciality inevitably the highjump since it involved a modified fall from his embarrassing height to the enviable equality of the sandpit. Once he had practised a Fosbury Flop over a barbed-wire fence, and the long striations of scar tissue on his back were the result.

Neil's scars had a sentimental value for Bernard. Neil had mentioned them in an early conversation in a way that Bernard had found inexplicable. Then he realized that Neil was disposing of embarrassment in advance, and was anticipating, consciously or unconsciously, a conversation in which the subject would necessarily arise if it hadn't been dealt with already: a conversation in which both of them would be naked.

Lower down on Neil, the textural variety continued. He invariably wore bedsocks; night for him was always a cold country no matter what the temperature of day. Since mid-October he had taken to wearing two pairs, and no amount of central heating could coax his feet out of their coverings.

Neil's embrace was semi-conscious now, but Bernard couldn't resist asking, 'Neil, is there anywhere you've been in the world where you haven't worn bedsocks?'

Neil grunted faintly into the pillow but admitted it. 'Yeah.'

'Where?'

'Hawaii.'

Something else struck Bernard as odd. Neil hadn't actually been to the bathroom since they had got back from the disco. 'Neil . . . have you had a piss since we got back?'

Neil grunted again. 'No.'

'I thought you'd be dying for one.'

Neil thought for a moment, still muffled against the pillow. 'Is that why we left so early?' He struggled to the edge of the bed. 'I need a piss now anyway.'

When he had come back and settled back under the duvet, Neil said, with a deliberateness that was almost the same as sleepiness, but not quite, 'You really piss me off when you decide things for me like that.' His voice slowed down and lost definition. 'That really makes me . . .' on the edge of sleep, he found the appropriate Kiwi word, '. . . ropable.'

'Now you know that's not the way it works,' Bernard said. 'It's not me that pisses you off, it's you that pisses you off. Remember Re-birthing? You told me that was the whole principle of the thing. Taking responsibility.' There was no answer. 'So what you mean is, you really piss yourself off when you let me decide things for you like that. Isn't that right?' Even while he was saying all this he was wondering why he was fighting so dirty, using heavy ammunition— and more to the point, irreplaceable ammunition—in the smallest little squabble. He could only hope that Neil was fully asleep. He waited a few moments for a reply. Then he stretched out next to Neil, turning his back so their buttocks touched lightly.

He still wasn't satisfied that Neil was really asleep. There was only one way of telling for sure. Thanks to some aberration of the New Zealand educational system, Neil spoke good German, while Bernard was only now studying the language at an elementary level with an evening class. Neil didn't waste his academic advantage. So now Bernard breathed a simple sentence, knowing that if Neil was less than deeply asleep he would inevitably surface to correct Bernard's pronunciation, which he found laughable in its exaggeration. '*Der Friseur liegt hinter dem Lehrer,*' he murmured, but making the consonants clash like sabres in a duel. There was no answer, and this time Bernard was satisfied. That made it official.

Bernard himself slept well, except for a dream which had no characteristics until he diagnosed it as a dream, and decided to leave it. Then it became intensely confining. He tried twisting his arms and legs to be free of it, but they were dream arms and legs, and powerless. He started to cry out instead, and was so afraid they would be cries only inside the dream that he kept on making them. He produced, in reality, four low shouts. Neil put his arms round him and said, 'I'm here.' Bernard was now fully awake, while Neil had surfaced only long enough to give out that single breath of assurance.

Bernard lay awake for a while, thinking that in Neil's place he would have wanted to give reassurance too, but the phrases he would have used for the job were 'Neil . . . Neil . . . Neil' and 'You're having a nightmare.' Not very helpful. It would never have occurred to him that it would bring comfort to say, 'I'm here'. But Neil's sleeping self seemed to include, as well as the blanket-fascist, a sweetly competent disperser of nightmares that Bernard could only admire and find mysterious.

He was woken in the morning by what he thought was rain,

until it turned out to be the sound of Neil getting his money's worth out of the shower. The time was 10.15. He stretched under the duvet, remembering what the hotel-owner had said about breakfast. Breakfast lasted from nine to eleven. 'So I'll turn the toaster on at five to,' he said.

'Oh, Neil and I were thinking of having an early breakfast and going for a walk.'

The hotel-owner nodded. 'Yes, people do say that.'

Bernard protested feebly. He didn't know whether the implication was lechery or laziness. He remembered a friend telling him about a weekend in Brighton with a new boyfriend, when they had broken a bed on their first night. The landlord had been very understanding. The next night they broke the other bed. Bernard wondered if perhaps he should reassure this hotel-owner that his furnishings and fittings were likely to survive the weekend. He settled for simple repetition. 'Oh, I think we'll have breakfast early and go for a walk.'

'See you then, then,' said the landlord politely.

Neil had dried himself by now, and returned to the bed. Bernard hugged him. 'When I heard you in the shower, I thought it must be rain.'

'Rain, eh? In England? At a weekend?'

'It was a wild idea and I bitterly regret it.'

'Have you looked out of the window?'

'No.'

'Raining. Just thought you'd like to know.'

Bernard took his turn in the shower. By the time they reached the dining-room, it was a little before eleven. Their host made no reference, even with a smile, to the planned walk, didn't for instance produce plates of shrivelled food, vintage nine o'clock. It was some consolation that the other breakfasters—there were only four of them—were just being served their test-tubes of orange-juice, and so couldn't have been down much before them.

After breakfast, Bernard settled the bill. They could still take their walk, but now they would have to take their bags with them. It seemed a good idea, all the same, and when Neil had wrapped around his neck his collection of Oxfam-shop scarves they set off down the hill to the seafront.

They took a turn along the promenade. One bus shelter in two

seemed to be open to the sky, asserting in the teeth of the evidence that a resort once favoured by royalty could never run out of
sunshine. Looking out to sea from the promenade, they could see
the weather being formed some way offshore. Beyond a certain
distance, the sky was an undifferentiated grey. On the near side
of an invisible barrier, clouds appeared and were driven towards
land. It was bad weather, but at least it was new weather, and there
was some status in that. At least they had got to it before anyone
else.

Bernard wanted to get down to the gravel beach, not because he
wanted a paddle or a chance to make gravel-castles, but because
somehow there was no point in going to Brighton and doing anything else. Neil hung back, either because the sea shore didn't meet
his spoiled southern-hemisphere definition of beach, or because the
going underfoot would prove too tough for what was left of The
Winter Boots. 'We could have a swim, though,' he suggested. Bernard
stared. 'In a pool,' Neil added.

'On a Sunday?'

'Why not?' Neil was optimistic.

'We'll have to break in.'

'I don't think so.' Neil held up the map. 'We can try, eh?'

It took them a few wrong turns, all the same, to find the swim-
ming pool, but when they got there it was open. It was also called
The Prince Regent Swimming Centre. 'Isn't that just as piss-
elegant as you'd expect,' said Bernard as they queued for tickets.
'Other people have pools. The Prince Regent has a Swimming
Centre.'

'I think it looks stunning. There's a water slide.'

The changing rooms were certainly well equipped. Because of
their bags, Neil and Bernard had to use a relay of lockers, locking
each key in the next compartment along to avoid pincushioning
their trunks with safety pins.

Besides the water slide, the swimming centre had a separate div-
ing pool, and a supervised lane for serious swimmers. Neil and
Bernard included themselves in this category, and had the goggles—
guaranteed against misting and leakage—to prove it.

Bernard admired Neil's efficient unflustered crawl, his progress
through the water in a series of easy windmilling shrugs. Once, as
they passed each other in opposite directions, Neil slid his hand

between Bernard's legs, breaching lane discipline for a moment in order to do so.

Afterwards, when they had dried and dressed themselves, Bernard said, 'I enjoyed that.'

'Yes, there's nothing like a good swim.'

'I don't mean that, quite. I mean when you touched me.'

Neil smiled. His face had a badger's-mask look to it, from where his goggles had left their shape on his skin. 'I couldn't be sure it was you. So I had to touch up everybody in the pool.'

When Bernard regained his bearings after leaving the pool, he realized that they were only some little way from The Pantry, where they had had such a pleasant snack the day before. Why not go there again, or try it anyway? If they were now in a town where swimming-pools were open on the Sabbath, perhaps they had been transplanted bodily to a universe where—in spite of its resemblance to Britain—anything you wanted might be had when you wanted it. Neil fell in with the suggestion, and Bernard obliged him by falling in with his lazy pace.

The Pantry was indeed open, though almost empty. The only addition since the previous day was a lavish spread of Sunday papers; the only subtraction was the middle generation of the staff. Today the old lady served, and the young girl once again cleared up.

Neil had a small salad and an orange juice—he always asked simply for 'juice', since he was now in a country where no one would think of looking for juice in anything but an orange, or rather a can of orange juice. Bernard ordered a coffee and some garlic bread, which took a little time to arrive. When it did, it repeated, he felt, the triumph that the mussels had had the day before, until they were obscurely sabotaged by the people at the next table: the bread was thick, the way Bernard liked it (and Neil didn't) and so saturated with garlic butter it might have been injected with it, like a Chicken Kiev.

Neil had already nearly finished by the time the garlic bread arrived, but Bernard felt no need to hurry. 'I should have had this before we had our swim.'

'And got cramp, eh?'

'Maybe, but at least I would have had a lane to myself. *Headlamps* of garlic.'

Neil leaned sideways and down, then sat up again with a yelp.

Bernard said, 'What's the matter?' Neil said, 'Splinter'. Bernard gave a smiling wince of fellow-feeling and returned to his colour supplement, slightly smeared as it was with garlic butter. He licked the last of the butter off his fingers, enjoying his last tastes of it. When he looked up, there was still pain on Neil's face, and he was still inspecting his hand. 'Is it a bad one?'

'It's in a bad place, anyway.' The splinter had run under the nail of his left index finger. Neil held the hand out to him. The splinter seemed to have gone all the way to the back of the nail. Most splinters are like small spears; this one was like a small spade, as Bernard could see through the pale shield of Neil's fingernail before blood obscured it.

Bernard said, 'What were you doing, exactly?'

'Looking in my bag for the map. To see how far we are from the station. Only I didn't get as far as my bag. I must have got caught on the bottom of the table.'

Gingerly, Bernard patted the underside of the table, which was rougher even than the unpolished top. He thought for a moment. 'We need a pin.'

'Well, I haven't got one.' Neil was pressing down on the tip of his nail, to prevent any issue of blood, in a way that looked particularly painful.

Blood in general, and blood like Neil's in particular, had acquired a demonic status over the few previous years. Before that time, blood seemed largely a symbolic substance, and people's attitudes towards it signs of something else. Being a blood donor involved only a symbolic courage, and squeamishness about blood was an odd though perhaps significant little cowardice. Now blood had taken back its seriousness as a stuff. Bernard spent needless thought worrying about what would happen if a drop of blood landed on the table, as if the customers had the habit of running their tongues along the lacerating wood. They would indeed need to be pretty quick off the mark anyway, to have any hope of putting themselves at risk.

'Could have been worse, eh?' Neil said. 'I could have had a nosebleed.'

'I'll see if there's someone here with a pin,' Bernard said. The grandmother of the establishment was in a kitchen full of steam and the smell of burnt toast. Bernard tried to explain his need for a pin, but succeeded only in flustering her. He glimpsed, meanwhile, a bottle of bleach on a shelf by the sink, which a sense of responsibility to the public would oblige him to use if Neil shed his blood at all widely.

The young girl slipped in through the swing door and watched with a neutral interest. Bernard found himself missing that intermediate generation of staff, the competent mother-daughter who would make everything all right.

The grandmother produced at first some tiny forks with wooden handles, designed for the convenient handling of corn on the cob, and then a safety pin, which Bernard carried in sombre triumph back to Neil in the eating area.

Neil was still pressing his nail down, and had managed to prevent any real leakage. 'We'd better not do it here,' Bernard said. 'Put people off their food.' In fact the few people in the café were stubbornly focused on their plates and Sunday papers, but Neil followed Bernard obediently back to the kitchen.

Now for a change Neil pulled up the end of the nail, with a shiver of pain, and Bernard used the safety-pin, trying to skewer the splinter and draw it out. The field hospital established in her kitchen seemed to distress the grandmother more, if anything, than impromptu surgery would have upset her customers. She kept fluttering up to them from the stove, and saying, 'Are you sure you shouldn't go to the hospital?'

'We'll get the splinter out first,' said Bernard, speaking with false confidence, 'then we might get the hospital to take a look.'

He tried to peer under the rim of the nail, hoping to see the contour of the splinter again. By working the safety-pin gingerly from side to side, he was able to snag the thin stem of the splinter. Neil's hand gave a little jerk as the pin started to pull on the embedded fragment. Bernard tried to move his hand as slowly and smoothly as possible. Neil gave another involuntary pull, and the narrow part of the splinter broke off, leaving the rest of it lodged in the quick.

Bernard pulled out a chair for Neil to sit down, and told the grandmother what she had been telling him for some time. 'I think we'd better go to the hospital. Is it near? Walking distance? Do you have a car?' He thought driving them to hospital was the least she could do to atone for the dangerous roughness of her table, but she shook her head in answer to the question about a car. He was surprised when she took her coat from the back of the kitchen door and put it on. 'We're not on the phone here,' she explained. 'I'll ring from my daughter's.'

'Does she live in Brighton?' Bernard asked, aiming at a joke.

She didn't smile. 'Just round the corner. I'll be back in a minute.' She murmured something to the girl, before she left, about being in charge.

The girl, all the same, chose to stay in the kitchen rather than attend to her customers. By and large they were patient Sunday customers, but every now and then a little self-righteous queue built up, and she would have to venture out to serve them.

Bernard's worries had transferred from spilled blood, no longer a risk now that Neil's clotting agents had started to work, to the safety-pin. He shouldn't leave it without some attempt at disinfection. He could pour a little bleach over it, before the girl came back in. Or might Neil be offended? Then again, if he had been a smoker, he could have lit up, and held the match flame under the safety-pin just for a few seconds, before blowing it out.

The girl came back in, and Bernard abandoned any plan of eliminating contamination on the premises. Her grandmother—if they were in fact more than professionally connected—came back the next minute. She hung up her coat and offered to make tea, on the house. Bernard only regretted that they had paid when they had ordered, and so had no opportunity of expressing emotion by withholding payment. Neil wanted to be ready for the taxi when it arrived, so they sat in the eating area, at the table next to the door.

There was no sign of the taxi. 'If this was America,' Bernard said, 'they'd be so afraid of being sued they'd treat us a lot better than this. We'd have a chauffeur to the hospital, I dare say.'

'If this was New Zealand,' Neil said, 'they'd polish the tables in the first place.' He had wrapped a paper napkin round the finger.

Again Bernard tried for the light note. 'Not much point in going to a veggie restaurant, eh, if the furniture goes and bites you.'

His impatience got the better of him and he stepped out on to the pavement to greet the taxi when it arrived. There were infuriating numbers of taxis rushing past already, but none of them so much as slowed down. They all seemed to have their signs illuminated, and Bernard tried frantically to flag them down, feeling that this emergency justified the breaking of his promise to the taxi that was on its way.

The taxis ignored him anyway, but not from solidarity. It became clear that Brighton was not a town where taxis could be hailed. They had to be ordered, and if they had an illuminated sign on top, that was to say 'I am a taxi,' not 'I will take you where you want to go.'

After several frustrating minutes, Bernard went back into The Pantry. He swept into the kitchen and announced that it was now twenty-five minutes since the taxi was called, not consulting his watch in case the true figure was less impressive. He bullied the grandmother until she offered to phone again, reaching once more for her coat on the back of the door. Bernard caught sight of the safety-pin on the table and picked it up, murmuring hollowly that he'd better take it along in case there was more he could do on the way to the hospital. As the grandmother left, he took a seat next to Neil near the door.

'How's it feel?'

'Not bad.'

'Hurt a lot?'

'Not much.'

Bernard hadn't seen him often enough in situations of ordinary adversity to know whether the stiff upper lip was a reflex or a performance. Then the grandmother knocked on the window next to them, and pointed at a cab that had drawn up at the kerb.

The taxi-driver needed some convincing that he was picking up the right party. Bernard began to feel that a telephone call was not enough to secure a taxi in Brighton; you needed a letter from the mayor. But once the driver was satisfied that he had got hold of the right people, he drove them rapidly and without conversation to the hospital, which was a little out of town to the east. As they passed, Bernard recognized the street that Rogues was in.

The hospital was shabby and far from new. An old lady was having difficulty in opening the door as she left; automatic doors were clearly a thing of the future in this part of the world. The casualty department was full of glum waiting people. Bernard pressed a button at the reception counter, which was unmanned, and a receptionist appeared after a few moments. Neil advanced his finger towards her, and she said, 'That looks nasty.' She took his details and told them to take a seat.

After a while, a nurse came timidly down the line of seats, calling a version of Neil's awkward Yugoslav name. Her despairing intonation suggested she spent most of the day calling out names that their
owners regarded as parodies of the real thing. She took a look at
Neil's hand, and said it looked nasty. Bernard was impressed by this
prompt response into thinking that the health service was not quite
as clapped-out as it seemed, until the nurse told them it would be
at least an hour and a half before they were seen to.

Neil smoothly settled down to writing a letter to his parents in
New Zealand. He expressed to Bernard his relief that it wasn't his
writing hand that was affected. Bernard tried to settle with a book
(there wasn't the desk-space necessary for marking) but found himself unable. He looked round at the rows of silent, passive people
waiting to be attended to. After the hotel and the disco, both trying hard to pretend not to be bourgeois homes, it should have been
refreshing that the hospital made no attempt to be anything but
what it was.

He stood up, and asked the receptionist where he could find a
toilet. Across the corridor, she told him, with a slightly furtive intonation that was explained when Bernard realized they were staff toi-
lets, not in theory open to the laity. On his way back from using
them—they seemed no more sophisticated than the usual ones, and
demanded no extra skills—he spotted a hot-drinks dispenser. This
too was labelled Staff Use Only. One of the items it offered was
hot chocolate, so Bernard searched through his pockets for change.
A pair of shoes strode through the corridor, and stopped behind
him in a way he felt was intended to pass a message. They had the
acoustic properties unique to white lace-ups worn by a trained person. For an absurd moment he thought he was going to burst into
tears. He straightened up, and stopped the search in his pockets,
which had so far yielded only copper coins and the safety-pin—in
the closed position, mercifully—that he had planned to dispose of
so responsibly. He trailed defeated back to the seat next to Neil's.

Neil's letter was reaching its closing stages, with the phrase 'Bernard
says hello'. Neil passed the biro across to him and he wrote, embarrassed, 'hello', wishing either that he could embellish this message
a fraction with something more personal, or that he could be excused
from contributing at all. Out of the corner of his eye he could see
that Neil was writing *Bernard says hello* in brackets after his word of
greeting. It seemed like a schoolboy's letter home, but he had to

admit that Neil currently held the monopoly on adult calm. It was Bernard who had the schoolboy restlessness.

He had intended to wait at least until Neil had finished his letter, but found himself asking prematurely 'Are you going to tell them?'

Neil didn't need the meaning of the question clarified. 'I don't know,' he said. Normally he was scrupulous about disclosing his antibody status, with the result that he was still waiting, after four months, for a dentist's appointment. If when Neil's appointment arrived—and it was still likely to be several months off—any work was necessary, Bernard knew that the dentist would use a low-speed drill to make sure he didn't volatilize any saliva, which might then be inhaled. Perhaps that was why, Bernard thought, it was taking so long for Neil's turn to come round. He could imagine the dentist spending hours on every filling with his hammer and chisel, murmuring behind his mask that people got these things out of proportion, when a few simple procedures were enough to eliminate any risk.

Bernard said, 'It shouldn't make any difference, should it, whether you tell them or not?'

'But Brighton is a provincial town, eh?'

'A provincial town full of gay men, mind you. You're going to have to make up your own mind.' He hoped it didn't sound as if he were washing his hands of the matter. His private preference was for telling them—whoever 'they' turned out to be—but he didn't want to make Neil feel like a danger to health, quietly being quarantined.

'I doubt if it matters anyway.'

Towards the end of the stated time, another nurse, who turned out to be a doctor, paid a visit. She kept her hands in the pockets of her white coat, while Neil dutifully held out the finger. She peered through her glasses at it, then looked over the top of them and said, 'Come with me, please.' Neil followed her, and Bernard included himself in the expedition. They went to a room full of little cubicles.

The doctor, though only about Bernard's age, had a feathery growth of hair on her upper lip, which looked oddly touching in spite of its incongruousness. It was like an adolescent's moustache, a shy fanfare of hormones. She kept her hands in her pockets so long that Bernard expected them to be warty, or at least covered in hair, but when she did at last bring them into the open, and touched Neil's finger, they were sightly and even shapely. She put them back in her pockets immediately, in what was clearly the defining posture of her profession. Then she said, 'It's fairly clean, but I may have to cut the nail.' This at least made a change from calling it nasty. 'How long since you had a tetanus injection?'

'Years.'

'Two years?'

'Ten years.'

'You'll be needing one of them, then,' she said. Neil looked uncomfortable. 'And I have to move you again, I'm afraid, to where I keep the long-nosed tweezers. Don't worry,' she said, perhaps seeing Neil's expression. 'I'll give you an anaesthetic. Follow me, please. Your friend can come too.'

They followed her along the corridor to Minor Surgery, where Neil and Bernard had to take their shoes off. As he took off the ragged Winter Boots, Neil said, 'Perhaps someone will steal them, eh? With any luck.' Then he turned to the doctor, and said 'I'm antibody-positive, you know.' Bernard assumed that Neil was urged to frankness by the doctor's willingness to have Bernard along. A relaxed worldliness could be deduced from that. 'I see. That's unfortunate,' the doctor said, frowning as she washed her hands.

'In what way?' said Bernard truculently, assuming that she would now make difficulties about operating on Neil.

'My dear man, you hardly need me to tell you that. It's unfortunate because it makes life so very difficult.' She coaxed Neil on to the operating table.

Bernard's anger still had some momentum to it. 'I think anybody who doesn't work with people who are antibody-positive should be sacked on the spot, not because they're prejudiced but because they must be incompetent to be taking any risks.' He paused for breath.

'Funny you should say that,' said the doctor, and then when Bernard was preparing to ask, 'Why so?', 'That's just what I think myself.'

She helped Neil to push his finger through a sort of stiff cowl of material, so that it was singled out for surgery. Deprived of its fellows it looked almost amputated, even before the doctor had unpacked the case where she kept her long-nosed tweezers.

Sheepishly, Bernard fished the safety-pin out of his pocket and strolled over to a vivid yellow box labelled Contaminated Sharps. He dropped it into the hole in the top, feeling a bit ridiculous but reminding himself that it was, after all, contaminated and it was, after all, sharp. The doctor was unwrapping instruments, individually wrapped in gauze, from a sterilized tin box. Bernard noticed that although she was already wearing surgical gloves, she put on another pair from inside the box. 'Is that necessary?' he asked, with a slight turn of his earlier truculence.

'It's routine,' she said. 'Rubber gloves don't stay sterile for ever, you know. I could have taken the first pair off, but this seemed more sensible. Now shut up,' she said, without heat. 'But you can hold the patient's hand if you like.'

She began to unpack her long-nosed tweezers. Neil turned his head resolutely away, and Bernard locked glances with him. They stayed like that for a little while, like people trying competitively not to blink, then Bernard started flicking sideways glances at the fingernail. The doctor said, 'I'm putting the local in now.' Bernard could see her sliding two needles, one after the other, into the top of the finger. Neil blinked a few times rapidly in succession, and Bernard could feel his hand-grip tightening in spite of itself.

After some probing, the doctor said, 'No, this won't work, I'm going to have to cut the nail.'

'Cut as little as possible, eh?' said Neil, 'I've got a full-head bleach to do tomorrow morning at 10.30.'

The doctor gave a little laugh. She seemed to find this ambition amusing. 'We'll sort something out with the nurse, see if we can't get you a lightweight dressing of some sort.'

Bernard stopped taking his sideways glances, having no wish to see Neil's nail being cut. The two locked glances again, like pieces of heroic statuary. In a moment, the doctor said, 'All done.'

Bernard did the talking. 'How much have you cut?'

'The tiniest sliver. Take a look.'

Bernard kept his eyes where they were. 'Will you be able to reach the splinter?'

'I already have. All done, I told you. Take a look.' She was holding out the stub of the splinter in the mouth of her long-nosed tweezers.

Bernard could feel Neil relaxing against him. He tensed up again when the doctor said, 'Nurse will give you a tetanus injection.' She took off all her rubber gloves, scrubbed up, shook hands pleasantly and left.

Before doing any injections, the nurse fitted Neil with a lightweight dressing, as promised, and told him to go to a casualty department in London in a few days if he needed another. Bernard put his arms round Neil's neck while the injection was done. It occurred to him how stupid he was not to have done it earlier. A local anaesthetic involved having a needle stuck in you just as much as an inoculation did, but somehow the word 'local' made it sound trivial, something you shouldn't need to be helped through. A tetanus jab gave cowardice a wider scope, and Bernard took advantage of it.

Down the corridor there was a telephone which did not, for a wonder, bear the message Staff Use Only. Bernard used it to call a taxi, while Neil climbed awkwardly into his jacket.

It was already fully dark, although not as late by his watch as Bernard had expected. Neither of them knew the times of trains, but they went straight to the station, prepared to take their chances.

'How's it feel now?' Bernard asked.

'Not too bad. Throbs a bit. They say it'll be worse tonight when the local wears off. I may need a sleeping tablet, but we got off pretty lightly, eh?'

Bernard had to agree. They had got off lightly. He had underestimated the amount of practice the hospital would have had with this whole new world of risk and stigma. But he still felt damaged, and found it hard to be cheerful for Neil's benefit.

There was a London-bound train waiting in the station, already very full. There were only isolated seats free, so once again Neil and Bernard sat apart, though visible to each other.

Bernard was grateful for their separation. He needed time to recover independently, always assuming the damage was reversible. The train filled up still more before it pulled out of the station, so that there were people standing, who intermittently broke his view of Neil. From what he could see, Neil had his eyes closed, was asleep or meditating.

The train was a slow one, and stopped at every station it saw. Work on the track diverted it, and at least once it stopped—to judge by the absence of lights—in open country. Near Bernard there stood a woman dressed for a party, complete with bunch of flowers, and a harried mother, come to that, but Bernard felt no inclination to give up his seat. He felt he had a claim on it that outranked theirs. He was still in shock, apparently, though nothing had happened directly to him.

Something had happened to him all the same. He knew that love starts off inspired and ends up merely competent. He didn't resent that. That was bargained for. But he hadn't foreseen, in all his mental preparation, that the passage could be so drastically foreshortened. A tiled corridor filled with doctors and nurses opened off every room he would ever share with Neil. He had always known it was there, but today the door to it had briefly been opened.

He thought with nostalgia of the time when people had got so exercised about who loved who, and how much. Now it was simply a question of what character of love would be demanded of him, and how soon. It was as if he had been pierced in a tender place which he had thought adequately defended, by a second splinter, not visible. The word *sick*, even the word *death*, had no power to match the fact of hospital. As with the first splinter, he had managed to break off the protruding part, but not to remove it. It gnawed at the nail-bed.

BIOGRAPHICAL NOTES

In putting the following notes together I have drawn on: *The Oxford Companion to English Literature*, 5th edn., ed. Margaret Drabble (Oxford: Oxford University Press, 1985); *The Cambridge Guide to Literature in English*, ed. Ian Ousby (Cambridge: Cambridge University Press and Hamlyn Publishing Group, 1988); *The Feminist Companion to Literature in English*, eds. Virginia Blain, Patricia Clements, Isobel Grundy (London: Yale University Press, 1990); *The Reader's Companion to the Twentieth-Century Novel*, ed. Peter Parker (London: Fourth Estate and Helicon, 1994).

APHRA BEHN (*née* Johnson?, *c.*1640–89). Cited in *The Feminist Companion to Literature in English* as 'the first professionally-writing English woman'. The daughter of an innkeeper, she travelled to Surinam with her family in 1663–4 (see her novel, *Oroonoko*, 1688). She evidently married a Dutch merchant called Behn, in 1664. The marriage seems to have lasted only two years. Behn began writing plays in 1670, and thereafter her output in drama and fiction was massive. As the *Feminist Companion* records, 'She had more than one lover; some poems hint at love between women'.

WILLIAM HAZLITT (1778–1830). Born at Maidstone, the son of a Unitarian minister. Moved to London as a young man, where he was helped by Charles Lamb to embark on his career as a massively productive man of letters. In 1819 he fell violently in love with Sarah Walker, his landlord's daughter. Three years later he divorced his wife, and in 1823 published the record of his love for Walker, *Liber Amoris*—a production which his friend De Quincey called 'an explosion of frenzy' and which his enemies saw as proof of his madness. His best known collection of essays, *The Spirit of the Age*, was published in 1825.

MARY WOLLSTONECRAFT SHELLEY (*née* Godwin, 1797–1851). Daughter of William Godwin and Mary Wollstonecraft, who died giving birth to her. She was educated by her philosopher father. In 1814, aged just 17, she left England with her lover, Percy Bysshe Shelley. They married in 1817. Only one of their children survived infancy. Her best-known novel, *Frankenstein*, was published in 1818. Shelley was drowned in 1822. Thereafter, Mary supported herself in England as a woman of letters.

ELIZABETH CLEGHORN GASKELL ('Mrs Gaskell', *née* Stevenson, 1810–65). Elizabeth Stevenson was born in London, the daughter of an ex-Unitarian minister, and civil servant. Her mother died in 1811, which led to her being brought up in Knutsford, Cheshire (subsequently immortalized as 'Cranford'). In 1822 she married a Unitarian minister, William Gaskell. As the *Feminist Companion* records, 'Her marriage was essentially happy, and she accepted the primacy of wifehood and motherhood'. There were four surviving daughters to the marriage. She began writing seriously in the mid-1840s, partly as therapy for her son William's premature death. Her first hit was with the 'social problem novel', *Mary Barton* (1848). A string of successful works of fiction followed. Her most successful longer love story is *Cousin Phillis* (1864).

WILLIAM MAKEPEACE THACKERAY (1811–63). Thackeray was born in India, and educated at Charterhouse public school and Cambridge University. After several false starts in art, law, and having lost his patrimony gambling, he became a professional writer for the London magazines in the early 1830s. In 1836 he married for love Isabella Shawe, an Irishwoman. The couple had two surviving daughters, but Isabella fell into incurable madness in the early 1840s. It is to this dark period that 'Dennis Haggarty's Wife' belongs. Thackeray's fortunes mended with the huge success of *Vanity Fair* in 1848, after which he was one of the most revered and prosperous writers of the age. He had an unfortunate love affair with his best friend's wife, Jane Brookfield, which is reflected in his sombre historical novel, *Henry Esmond* (1852).

ANTHONY TROLLOPE (1815–82). The son of an unsuccessful and hypochondriacal barrister and a novel-writing mother (Frances Milton Trollope) Anthony Trollope was educated at Harrow. On leaving school in 1834, he entered the Post Office. After a very inauspicious start, his fortunes improved after being posted to Ireland in 1841. He married Rose Heseltine, whom he met in Ireland, in 1844. The marriage was very happy, and produced two sons. Trollope began publishing novels in 1847, and had racked up forty-seven by the time of his death. He retired from the Post Office in 1867, but kept up the fox-hunting which he loved until well into his fifties. In later life he had what seems to have been a platonic affair with a young American, Kate Field, which has been seen to influence the romantic plots of his fiction.

ANNE ISABELLA RITCHIE (*née* Thackeray, later Lady Ritchie, 1837–1919). A daughter of W. M. Thackeray. Her early childhood was disturbed by her mother's insanity, but she and her sister were united with their father in London in the mid-1840s, at which point his career as a novelist was secure. She served as her father's amanuensis until his death in 1863. Her first novel, *The Story of Elizabeth*, was published in 1863. After her father's death she wrote other novels, biographies, and much magazine journalism. In 1877 she married a cousin, Richmond Ritchie, who was much younger than herself.

THOMAS HARDY (1840–1928). Hardy was born in Dorset, the son of a stonemason. At the age of 16, he was apprenticed as an architect. In 1862 he moved to London. In early manhood, Hardy seems to have had an unhappy love affair with Tryphena Sparks, a young woman who was supposed to be his cousin but may have been his niece. His first published novel was *Desperate Remedies* (1871). It was followed up by the more popular Wessex regional works, on which his fame rests. Unhappy love is the staple theme of Hardy's fiction and much of his poetry. In 1874 he married Emma Gifford. The marriage was passionate, but the couple found themselves ill assorted. On Emma's death, in 1912, Hardy wrote his most famous love poems. In 1914 he married Florence Dugdale, later his biographer.

C. C. K. GONNER. This is clearly a *nom de plume*. Apart from the one story published in the *Cornhill Magazine*, August 1887, there is nothing else listed by this pseudonymous author, either in the *Wellesley Index to Victorian Periodicals* or in the British Library Catalogue.

RUDYARD KIPLING (1865–1936). Kipling was born in Bombay, the son of an art teacher, illustrator, and later Director of the Lahore Museum. Rudyard came to England at the age of 6, and spent the next seven years in a boarding school at Southsea. He went on to the United Services College, 1878–82 (see *Stalky & Co.*, 1899). On leaving he worked for seven years as a journalist in India, where he began writing poems and stories. He returned to England in 1889, and in 1892 married Caroline Balestier, the sister of his American agent. The couple lived for some years in America, eventually settling in Sussex in 1902. In 1907 he was the first English writer to win the Nobel Prize for Literature.

HERBERT GEORGE WELLS ('H. G. Wells', 1866–1946). Wells was born in Bromley, Kent, where his father was an unsuccessful tradesman and former professional cricketer. Herbert was briefly apprenticed as a draper (see *Kipps*, 1905). He worked for a period subsequently as a schoolteacher, before winning a scholarship in 1884 to the Normal School of Science in London, where he came under the charismatic influence of 'Darwin's Bulldog', T. H. Huxley. Huxley's influence can be strongly felt in the 'scientific romances' which began with *The Time Machine* (1895). Wells's love-life was tangled and promiscuous throughout his long career. He made an unhappy marriage in 1891 to his cousin Isabel and ran away with a student, Jane Robbins, whom he married in in 1895. Among his many affairs was one with Rebecca West, by whom he had a son. Wells was also a force in the formation of English socialism in the early twentieth century.

JOHN GALSWORTHY (1867–1933). Galsworthy was born in Surrey and educated at Harrow and Oxford. After a false start in law, and influenced by Conrad, he took to writing. He was strongly encouraged in his new career by his future wife, and the literary editor David Garnett. His first volume of stories was published in 1897. The first of the 'Forsyte Saga' novels appeared in 1906 and the whole cycle was published in 1922. Galsworthy received the Nobel Prize for Literature in 1932.

ENOCH ARNOLD BENNETT ('Arnold Bennett', 1867–1931). Bennett was born at Hanley, in the Staffordshire Potteries, a region he was later to make famous in his fiction centred on the 'Five Towns'. The son of a solicitor, Bennett gave up a career in the same line for literature. His first novel, *A Man from the North*, was published in 1898. In 1902 he moved to Paris. His first marriage in 1907 to a French wife, Marguerite Soulie, collapsed and he returned to England in 1912. He separated from Marguerite in 1921 and for the rest of his life lived with Dorothy Cheston, by whom he had a daughter.

WILLIAM SOMERSET MAUGHAM ('Somerset Maugham', 1874–1965). Maugham was born in Paris, where his father was a lawyer attached to the British Embassy. Orphaned by the age of 10, he was brought up by relatives. After progressing from the King's School Canterbury to Heidelberg, he trained as a doctor in London. His first novel, *Liza of Lambeth* (1897) set him on an immensely successful career in fiction and drama. A love affair with Syrie Wellcome produced a daughter, Liza, in 1915. Maugham married Syrie in 1917, but the couple lived apart. Maugham's companion for most of his life was his secretary, Gerald Haxton. From 1926 Maugham lived on the French Riviera.

ALFRED EDGAR COPPARD ('A. E. Coppard', 1878–1957). The son of a tailor, Coppard was educated in Sussex, before leaving school, aged 9, to work as an apprentice tailor in London. He had miscellaneous menial occupations in London and Oxford, until becoming a full-time writer in 1919. His first volume of stories, *Adam and Eve and Pinch Me*, was published in 1921.

ADELINE VIRGINIA WOOLF ('Virginia Woolf', *née* Stephen, 1882–1941). Woolf was born in London, the daughter of the man of letters Leslie Stephen and Julia Duckworth. After her father's death in 1904, the family moved to Bloomsbury, which later gave its name to the group with which she was to be primarily associated as a writer. She began writing literary journalism in 1905 and her first novel, *The Voyage Out*, appeared in 1915. In 1912 she married Leonard Woolf, and together they founded the Hogarth Press in 1917. As the *Feminist Companion* notes, 'severe breakdowns and suicide attempts' followed her decision to marry Leonard. Woolf's novels established her as the leading modernist writer of fiction in England. Woolf drowned herself in 1941.

DAVID HERBERT LAWRENCE ('D. H. Lawrence', 1885–1930). The son of a Nottinghamshire miner and a schoolteacher (see *Sons and Lovers*, 1913), Lawrence's childhood was troubled by illness (in later life, it would develop into the tuberculosis that killed him prematurely). As a scholarship boy he spent three years at Nottingham High School, before leaving to work in a surgical appliance factory. He subsequently trained as a schoolteacher. Lawrence had an early and formative love affair with a farmer's daughter, Jessie Chambers ('Miriam' in *Sons and Lovers*). His first novel, *The White Peacock*, was published in 1911. In 1912 he met Mrs Frieda Weekley (*née* von Richthofen), the wife of a professor at Nottingham. Frieda and Lawrence ran away, and married after her divorce in 1914. The marriage was turbulent. After the First World War the Lawrences travelled widely in Europe and America. He died in France.

ARTHUR JOYCE LUNEL CARY ('Joyce Cary', 1888–1957). Cary was born in Londonderry and educated at Clifton College and Oxford. After a false start in art, and service in the Balkan War (1912–13) he joined the Nigerian political service as a district magistrate. In 1920 after wartime service with the Nigerian regiment, he returned to England where he took up writing full time. His first novel, *Aissa Saved* (1932), was, like much of his early fiction, set in Africa. His most popular African novel was *Mister Johnson* (1939), and his most popular novel with a British setting *The Horse's Mouth* (1944), the study of an amiable bohemian artist, Gulley Jimson.

KATHERINE MANSFIELD (pseud. of Kathleen Mansfield Beauchamp, 1888–1923). Mansfield was born in Wellington, the daughter of the chairman of the Bank of New Zealand. After school in Wellington, she studied at Queen's College London (1903–6), before returning to her home country where she attended Wellington Technical College. In 1908 she returned to London. Carrying another man's child (later still-born) she made a brief and disastrous marriage. Mansfield began publishing stories in 1910. At the same period she began living with John Middleton Murry, whom she married in 1918. By this period the tuberculosis which eventually killed her was acute.

PHYLLIS ELEANOR BENTLEY ('Phyllis Bentley', 1894–1977). The daughter of a textile manufacturer, Bentley was born and brought up in Halifax. In 1914 she graduated with a BA from London University. After war work, she took up work as a teacher then as a librarian. Her long sequence of 'West Riding' novels began with *Environment* (1922). Bentley did much to promote the work of her co-regionalists, the Brontës, and she had a long friendship with the Yorkshire writer Winifred Holtby. Bentley's most successful novel was, probably, the regional saga *Inheritance* (1932), a work which contains autobiographical material.

ALDOUS LEONARD HUXLEY ('Aldous Huxley', 1894–1963). A grandson of T. H. Huxley, brother of Julian Huxley, and nephew of Mrs Humphry Ward (by whom he was connected to the Arnolds), Huxley was educated at Eton and Oxford. Precociously brilliant, he achieved huge success with his first novel, *Crome Yellow* (1921). Thereafter he travelled widely with his wife Maria, spending long periods in France and— latterly—America. In 1937 he settled in California, partly because of failing eyesight, partly because of disillusionment with Europe. A leading novelist of ideas, Huxley's most reprinted work is the dystopian vision of the future, *Brave New World* (1932). His experiments with mysticism and mind-altering drugs (see *The Doors of Perception*, 1954) were influential in the 1960s.

ELIZABETH DOROTHEA COLE BOWEN ('Elizabeth Bowen', 1899–1973). The daughter of a Dublin barrister, she was brought up in County Cork. During her school years her father was declared insane and her mother died in 1912. On leaving school in 1917, she worked for a time as a wartime nurse, and subsequently studied art. She married Alan Cameron in 1923, and began publishing stories at the same period. Thereafter, she lived in England and Ireland. Her first novel, *The Hotel*, was published in 1927. During the Second World War she worked in London for the government, a period during which she wrote many of her most effective short stories.

VICTOR SAWDON PRITCHETT ('V. S. Pritchett', later 'Sir Victor', b. 1900). Pritchett was born in Suffolk, the son of a travelling salesman, and went to school in south London. He left aged 15 to work in the leather trade (see *Nothing like Leather*, 1935). He moved to Paris six years later, and eventually turned to journalism. His first novel, *Clare Drummer*, was published in 1929. Pritchett made the following short declaration about his career: 'my chief interests have been: travel, specially Spanish; short stories, which I value most; literary criticism over the years for the *New Statesman*' (of which paper he was for many years a director). Pritchett was knighted in 1975.

HENRY GRAHAM GREENE ('Graham Greene', 1904–91). Greene was educated at Berkhamsted School, Hertfordshire, where his father was headmaster. After Oxford, he worked on *The Times* (1926–30). Greene converted to Catholicism in 1926 and married in 1927. During the 1930s and thereafter Greene travelled widely. His first novel, *The Man Within*, was published in 1929, but it was not until *Brighton Rock* in 1938 that he achieved an international readership.

SYLVIA PLATH (1932–63). Plath was born in Boston, Massachusetts to an American-Austrian mother and a German father. Her father, a professor of entomology, died in 1940. Plath attended Smith College and subsequently went as a Fulbright scholar to Cambridge, where she met Ted Hughes, whom she married in 1957. They returned for two years to America, before taking up residence in England in 1960. By this period, Plath had made a reputation for herself as a poet, drawing on the innovations of her teacher, Robert Lowell. Her last years were tragic. As the *Feminist Companion* records, 'Living in an old house in Devon, often alone, and having discovered her husband was having an affair, Plath made a bonfire of manuscripts, hers and his. She took her children to London, where, at a time of intense cold and furious creativity, she gassed herself.'

PAUL THEROUX (b. 1941). Theroux was born in Medford, Massachusetts and took his first degree (BA in English) at Amherst. He married in 1967, and taught for some years in Africa. His first novel, *Waldo*, was published in 1967. Since the 1970s he has lived largely in England. His travel books (notably *The Great Railway Bazaar*, 1975) have been very successful as have novels such as *Saint Jack* (1973) and *The Mosquito Coast* (1981) which have been adapted into films.

SARA MAITLAND (b. 1950). Sara Maitland was born in London, moving shortly thereafter with her family to south-west Scotland, where her father had inherited property. She took a degree in English at Oxford in 1971, where she discovered 'femininism, socialism, friendship and Christianity'. She married Donald Lee (now a clergyman) in 1972.

ADAM MARS-JONES (b. 1954). The son of a judge father and a barrister mother, Mars-Jones was born in London and attended Westminster School. He took a BA in English from Cambridge in 1976. *Lantern Lecture* (1981) won the Somerset Maugham Award. Since 1986, he has been a film reviewer on the *Independent* newspaper, and has published numerous short stories. Among his other collections, *Monopolies of Loss* (1992), whose general theme is love, has been highly commended by critics.